THE
SECOND
SISTER

Also by Claire Kendal

The Book of You

THE SECOND SISTER

A Novel

CLAIRE KENDAL

HARPER

An Imprint of HarperCollins*Publishers*

Originally published in the United Kingdom in 2017 by HarperCollins UK.

THE SECOND SISTER. Copyright © 2017 by Claire Kendal. All rights reserved.
Printed in the United States of America. No part of this book may be used or
reproduced in any manner whatsoever without written permission except in the
case of brief quotations embodied in critical articles and reviews. For information,
address HarperCollins Publishers, 195 Broadway, New York, NY 10007.

HarperCollins books may be purchased for educational, business,
or sales promotional use. For information, please email the
Special Markets Department at SPsales@harpercollins.com.

FIRST U.S. EDITION

Library of Congress Cataloging-in-Publication Data has been applied for.

ISBN 978-0-06-229764-8 (pbk.)
ISBN 978-0-06-279867-1 (library edition)

17 18 19 20 21 LSC 10 9 8 7 6 5 4 3 2 1

For my Sister.
And for my Daughters.

She had no rest or peace until she set out secretly, and went forth into the wide world to trace out her brothers and set them free, let it cost what it might.

The Brothers Grimm, 'The Seven Ravens'

Contents

THE
SECOND
SISTER

Late November

Eyes Like Yours

Somebody said recently that I have eyes like yours. Not just literally. Not just because they are blue. They said that I see like you too.

When I glimpse myself in the looking glass, your face looks out at me like a once-beautiful witch who is sickening under a curse. Those jewel eyes, losing their brightness. That pale skin and long black hair. It's only the little pit by your left brow that isn't there.

I see you everywhere.

If I really had eyes like yours, I wouldn't be about to ask a question that you are going to hate. I would already know the answer. But here it is. What would you do if the police wanted to talk to you? Because I need to follow where you lead.

Just forming these words makes me see what to do. The police ask their questions and I am supposed to give them the answers they are hoping to hear. I am almost sorry for them, with their innocent faith that they can capture you on an official form, kept to a page or at most a few.

We wish to seek the whole truth, they say. *You are a key witness*, they say. *We are concerned for your welfare*, they say. *We need to obtain the best evidence*, they say. *We will deal appropriately with the information you provide*, they say. *You can trust us*, they say. *The success of any subsequent prosecution will depend on accuracy and detail*, they say. *Other lives may be at stake*, they say.

Am I supposed to be impressed? Flattered? Grateful? Scared? Intimidated? All of the above is my guess. So I will allow them to think that they have had their desired effect, as they take their careful notes and talk their tick-box talk in the calm and reassuring style that they have obviously rehearsed.

I will *read the notes over to confirm their accuracy*. I will appear to *cooperate*. I will *sign the witness statement* they prepare for me. I will *date it* too, with their help, because I have lost track of time a little, lately. Still, these motions are easy to go through. They do not matter.

What matters is that I am quietly writing my own witness statement, my own way, day after day. Compelled not by them but by you. That is what this is, and I am pretending that you are asking the questions and I am telling it all to you. I am writing down the things you want to know. The real things.

I will say this, though, Miranda, in my one concession to police speak. *What follows comes from my personal knowledge of what I saw, heard and felt. I, Ella Allegra Brooke, believe that the facts in this witness statement are true.* This is your story, but it is mine too, and I am our best witness. Maybe I do have eyes like yours, after all.

There is one more important thing I must tell you

before I begin and it is this. It is that you mustn't worry. Because I haven't forgotten the confidentiality clause and I never will. You have taught me too well. What goes in this statement stays in this statement. It is for you alone. I am the sister of the sister and you are part of me. Wherever you are, I always will be. All my love, Melanie.

Saturday, 29 October

The Two Sisters

There is no visible sign that anything is out of place. But there is something wrong in the air, a mist of scent so faint I may be imagining it.

'I was wondering,' Luke says.

'Wondering what?' I am scanning every inch of our little clearing in the woods.

'Why are so many fairy tales about sisters saving their brothers? All the ones you told me last week were.'

He is right. 'Hansel and Gretel'. 'The Seven Ravens'. 'The Twelve Brothers'. Our mother seemed to know hundreds of them.

'We should write a different story,' I say.

'I want one with a sister who saves her sister.'

I touch his cheek. 'So do I.'

He marches straight into the centre of our clearing, dispersing any scent that might have lingered here.

This is where you and I used to make our own private house, playing together inside of walls made of tree trunks. We would eat the picnic lunches that Mum would bring out to us. We would plait each other's hair and tickle each other's backs.

When I think of your back, I see the milky skin beneath the tips of my fingers, my touch as light as a butterfly kiss. But this snapshot from our childhood disappears. Instead, I imagine your shoulder blade, and a flower drawn in blood. I hear you screaming. You are in a room below ground and I cannot get to you.

I blink several times in this weak autumn sun and remind myself of where I am and who I am with and that I cannot know that this is what happened.

I hear your voice. Even after ten years your words are with me. *Find a different picture*, you say. *Remember the things that are real.* This is what you used to tell me when I was scared that there was a monster underneath my bed.

I look around our clearing. This, I tell myself, is real. This is where Ted and I used to lie on a carpet of grass on summer days when we were children, holding hands and looking up through the gaps in the treetop roof. There would be snippets of blue sky and white cloud, and a pink snow of cherry blossom.

Your son is the most real thing of all. He bends down to scoop up a handful of papery leaves. 'Hold your hands out,' he says. When I do, he showers my palms with deep red. 'Fire leaves,' he says.

I shut out the flower made of blood. I manage to smile.

He cups a light orange pile. 'Sun leaves,' he says, throwing them high into the air and letting them rain upon us.

He finds green leaves, too. 'Spring leaves,' he says.

I lean over to choose some yellow leaves from our cherry tree, then offer them to Luke. 'What do you call these?'

'Summer leaves.' This is when he blurts it out. 'I want to live with you, Auntie Ella.'

I stare into Luke's clear blue eyes, which are exactly like yours. When I zero in on them I can almost fool myself that you are here. And it hits me again. I imagine your eyes, wide open in pain and fear, your lashes wet with tears.

For the last few years, my waking nightmares about you have mostly been dormant. It took me so long to be able to control them. But a spate of fresh headlines last week shattered the defences I'd built.

Unsolved Case – New Link Discovered Between Evil Jason Thorne and Missing Miranda.

Eight years ago, when Thorne was arrested for torturing and killing three women, there was speculation that you were one of his victims. We begged the police for information. They would neither confirm nor deny the rumours, just as they refused to comment on the stories about what he did to the women. Perhaps we were too eager to interpret this as a signal that the stories were empty tabloid air. We were desperate to know what happened, but we didn't want it to be Jason Thorne.

Dad spoke to the police again a few days ago, prompted by the fresh headlines. Once more they would neither confirm nor deny. Once more, Mum and Dad grabbed at anything which would let them believe that there was never any connection between you and Thorne. But I think they are only pretending to believe this to keep me calm, and their strategy isn't working.

The possibility that Thorne took you seems much more real this time round. Journalists are now claiming that there is telephone evidence of contact between the two of you. They are also saying that Thorne communicated with his victims before stalking and snatching them. If these things are true, the police must have known all along, but they have never admitted any of it.

'Don't you want me?' Luke says.

Thoughts of Jason Thorne have no business anywhere near your son.

'Luke,' I start to say.

He hears that something is wrong, though I reassure myself that he cannot guess what it really is. He walks in circles, kicking more leaves. They have dried in the lull we have had since yesterday's lunchtime rain. 'You don't,' he says.

Luke, you say. *Focus on Luke.*

I swallow hard. 'Of course I do. I have always wanted you.'

Don't think about my eyes, you say.

But everything is a trigger. I study Luke's dark hair, so like ours, and imagine yours in Thorne's hands, a tangle of black silk twining around his fingers.

How many times do I need to tell you to change the picture?

I try again to change the picture, but there is little in Luke that doesn't visually evoke you. I search his face, and I am struck by the honey tint of his skin. Luke can actually tan, while you and Mum and Dad and I burn crimson and then peel.

He must have got this from The Mystery Man. I once teased you by referring to Luke's father in this way, hoping it would provoke you into slipping out something about him. But all it provoked was a glare that I thought would vaporise me on the spot.

'Granny and Grandpa and I have always been happy that we share you,' I say. 'It's what your mummy wanted. You know that. She even made a will to make sure you'd be safe with us. She thought of that while you were still in her tummy.'

Luke wrinkles his nose to exaggerate his disdain. 'In her tummy? I'm ten, not two, Auntie Ella.'

'Sorry. When she was pregnant.'

But why? It is not the first time this question has nagged me. *What made you make that will then?* Were you simply being responsible? Do lots of people finally make a will when they are expecting a child? Or was it something more? Did you have a fear of dying while giving birth, however low pregnancy-related mortality may be in this country? If you did, you would have told me. I think you must have had other reasons for an increased sense of vulnerability. Jason Thorne is not the only possible solution to the puzzle of what happened to you.

Luke is waving a hand in front of my face. He is snapping his fingers. 'Hello. Hello hello. Anyone in there?'

Whatever questions I may have, I tell him what I absolutely know to be true. 'That was one of the many ways she showed how much she loved you, how much she considered you. But it's complicated, the question of where you live. It isn't the kind of decision you and I can make on our own.'

I don't tell him how much our parents would miss him if he weren't with them. *Too much information*, I hear you say.

He smiles in a way that makes me certain he knows the match is his, and he is amused that I am about to discover this. 'If you share me then it shouldn't make a difference if I live with you instead of them.'

'True.' There is nothing else I can say to that one, especially when I am enchanted by this new vision of having him with me all the time. I cannot help but smile and add, 'You will be a barrister someday.'

'No way. Policeman. Like Ted.' He kicks the leaves harder. Fire and sun and spring and summer fly in all directions. But nothing derails your son. 'I told Granny and Grandpa it's what I want. They said they'd talk about it with you. They said it might be possible. They're getting old, you know. And Grandpa could get sick again . . . '

'Your grandpa is setting a record for the longest remission in human history.'

'Okay.'

'And Granny sat there calmly while you said all this?'

'She cried a little, maybe.'

'Maybe?'

'Okay. Definitely. She tried not to let me see. But Grandpa said it might be better for me to be raised by someone younger.'

I'm sure our mother loved his saying that. No doubt Dad would have had several hours of silent treatment afterwards. Our mother is incapable of being straight-forward at the best of times, and this is certainly not a topic she would want to pursue. She would have hoped it would go away if she didn't mention it to me.

'Then we will,' I say. 'Of course we'll talk about it.' He is not looking at me. 'Can you stay still for a minute please, Luke?'

There is a rustling in the trees at the edge of the woods, followed by a breeze that lifts my hair from my face, then gently drops it.

Luke doesn't notice, which makes me question my instinct that somebody is spying on us. Ever since we lost you I have imagined a man, hiding in the shadows, watching me, watching Luke. At least it cannot be Jason Thorne. He is locked away in a high-security psychiatric hospital.

I walk close to Luke, in case somebody really is ready to spring out at us. When the rustling grows nearer, he turns his head towards it. I am no longer in any doubt that I heard something. I put a hand on his shoulder and stand more squarely on both feet.

A doe pokes out her head, straightening her white throat and pricking up her ears to inspect us. She seems to be considering whether to turn back. All at once, she makes up her mind, crossing in front of us in two bounds, hardly seeming to touch the ground before she flees through the trees.

'Wow,' Luke says.

'She was beautiful. Granny would say that seeing her was a blessing. A moment of grace is what she would call it.'

'I can't wait to tell Grandpa,' Luke says.

I smooth Luke's hair. 'Happier now?' He nods. 'Are you going to tell me what brought on these new feelings about where you live?'

'I want to go to that secondary school in Bath next year. Why would Granny take me to the open day and then not let me go? She said my preference mattered. But I won't get in if she doesn't use your address.'

'Isn't the application due on Monday?'

'Yeah. But Granny keeps saying she's still thinking about it. It should be my choice.'

'With our guidance, Luke. It wouldn't be fair to you otherwise – it's too much of a responsibility for you to make this kind of decision by yourself. Granny never leaves things until the last minute, so she must still be weighing it all up very carefully. I'll raise it with her and Grandpa after breakfast – I can see it's urgent.'

'It's my life.'

'Is that why you wanted this private walk before Granny and Grandpa are up? To talk about this?'

'Yeah.' He kicks again. 'And before you say it, I don't mind that none of my friends are going there. As Granny keeps reminding me.'

The school is perfect for Luke. It is seriously academic, and sits beside the circular park I've been taking him to since he was five. It's also within reach of one of our favourite walks, along the clifftop overlooking the city. These are places he loves. Touchstones matter to Luke.

'I want to be in Bath with you,' he says. 'Everything's too far away from here.'

'Stinky little lost village,' I say.

He looks at me in surprise.

'That's what your mummy used to say.'

Would you be pleased by how hard I try to keep you present for him? How we all do?

I take his hand. 'The school's not as far away as it seems to you. It's only a twenty-five-minute journey from Granny and Grandpa's. Maybe you can live with me for half the week and Granny and Grandpa for the other half. I know we can work something out that everyone's happy with.'

I promised Luke when I finally got a mortgage and moved out of our parents' house that he would always have a room of his own with me. He was five then, and I nearly didn't go, but our mother made me. 'You need your own life,' she said, squaring those ballerina shoulders of hers. 'Your sister would want you to have a life. Miranda does not believe in self-sacrifice.'

I thought, then, that our mother was right. Because you certainly weren't – aren't – one for self-sacrifice.

Now, standing in our clearing with your son, I imagine you teasing me. *Yeah. Because it suits you to believe it. So you can do what you want. Since when do you think our mother is right?* Though the words are barbed, the voice is affectionate. The insight is there only because you apply the same filter to our mother that I use.

Luke turns back towards the woods. 'Did you hear that, Auntie Ella? Like somebody coughed but tried to muffle it? It didn't sound like our deer.'

I think of the interview I did a few months ago. Mum and Dad and I had always refused until then. But this was for a local newspaper, to publicise the charity. It seemed important to us, as the ten-year anniversary of your disappearance drew near. I talked about everything I do. The personal safety classes, the support group for family members of victims, the home safety visits, the risk assessment clinics.

There was no mention of you, but Mum and Dad were still worried by the caption that appeared beneath the photograph they snapped of me. *Ella Brooke – Making a Real Difference for Victims.* My arms are crossed and there is no smile on my face. My head is tilted to the side but my eyes are boring straight into the man behind the camera. I look like you, except for the severe ponytail and ready-for-action black T-shirt and leggings.

Could that photograph have set something off? Set someone off? Perhaps I hoped it would, and that was why I agreed to let them take it.

I catch Luke's hand and pull him back to me. 'Probably a rambler. It's morning. It's broad daylight. We are perfectly safe.'

'So you don't think it's an axe murderer.' He says this with relish, ever-hopeful.

'Not today, I'm afraid.'

'Well if it is, you'd kick their ass.'

'Don't let Granny hear you talk like that.' The sun stabs me in the head – warmth and pain together – and I squeeze my eyes shut on it for a few seconds, trying at the same time to squeeze out the worry that somebody is watching us. I am also trying – and failing yet again – to lock out the images of what you would have suffered if Thorne really did take you.

'Do you have a headache, Auntie Ella?'

Luke doesn't know he pronounces it 'head egg'. I find this charming, but I worry that he may be teased.

Should I correct him? I didn't imagine I'd be buying up parenting books when I was only twenty, and that they would become my bedtime reading for the next decade. They don't usually have the answers I need, but I know that you would.

'No headache. Thank you for asking.' I smile to show Luke that I mean it.

'I think Mummy would like me to live with you.'

I love how he calls you Mummy. That's how Mum and Dad and I speak of you to him. I wonder if we got stuck on Mummy because you never had time to outgrow it. Mummy is the name that people tend to use during the baby stage. You were never allowed to become Mum. Or mother, perhaps, though that always sounds slightly angry and over-formal.

'If I live with you part of the time, can we get more of her things in my room?'

'What things do you have in mind?'

'Granny put her doll's house up in the attic.'

'It's my doll's house too.' As soon as the words are out of my mouth, I realise that I sound like a little girl, fighting with you over a toy.

Luke smiles when he mimics our father's reasoned tone. 'Don't you share it?'

'Yes.' I lift an eyebrow. 'So you'd like a doll's house?'

'No. Of course not. I'm a boy. I don't like doll's houses.'

'There's nothing wrong with a boy liking doll's houses.'

'Well I don't. But why would Granny put it out of the way like that?'

'It hurt her to see it, Luke.'

He scowls. 'It shouldn't be hidden away in the attic. Get it back from her.' He sounds like you, issuing a command that must be obeyed.

Three crows lift from a tree, squawking. Luke and I snap our heads to watch them fly off, so glossy and black they appear to have brushed their feathers with oil.

'Do you think something startled them?' He takes a fire leaf from his pocket.

'Probably an animal.'

He is studying the leaf, tracing a finger over its veins. He doesn't look at me when he says, super casually, 'Can you make Granny give you that new box of Mummy's things?'

There's a funny little clutch in my stomach. I am not sure I heard him right. 'What things?'

'Don't know. Stuff the police returned to Granny a couple weeks ago.'

'Granny didn't tell me that. How do you know?'

'I'm a good spy. Like you. I heard her talking about them with Grandpa.'

'Did Granny open it? Did she look in it?'

'Not that she mentioned when I was listening.'

'Did she say anything about why the police finally returned Mummy's things?'

'Nope. Get the box too. Make Granny give it to you.'

Getting that box is exactly what I want to do. Very, very much. 'Okay,' I say, though I mumble secretly to myself about the challenge of making our mother do anything. Our mother gives orders. She does not take them.

'Auntie Ella?'

'Yes.'

'She would have come back for me if she could have, wouldn't she?'

I think of one of the headlines that appeared soon after you vanished, claiming you'd run away. I put my arms around him tightly. We have always tried to protect him from such stories. Since last week's spate of new headlines about Thorne, we have been monitoring Luke's Internet use even more carefully. But we can't know what he might have stumbled on, and I am nervous that a school friend has said something.

I kiss the top of his head and inhale. We have only been out for forty minutes but already he smells like a puppy who has run all the way back from a damp walk. 'She would have come back for you.' It is not raining but my cheeks are wet.

Luke wriggles out of my arms. He wipes at his cheeks too. 'Are you sure?'

'One hundred per cent. Nothing would have kept her from you if she had a choice.'

He bites his lower lip and looks down, scrunching his fists over his eyes.

Was I right to tell him these two true things, one beautiful and one too terrible to bear? That you were driven by your love for him, and that something unimaginably horrible happened to you?

Another thought creeps in, a guilty one. Is it easier for me to imagine you suffering a terrible death than to contemplate the possibility that you made a new life for yourself somewhere, as the police have sometimes suggested? I think of Thorne and shudder, absolutely clear that the answer is no.

'She wanted you so much.' It is extremely difficult to get these words out, but somehow I do, in a kind of croak.

'It's okay, Auntie Ella.' He has so much courage, this boy, as he takes his fists from his eyes and comforts me when I should be comforting him. He waits for me to catch my breath. 'I found a picture of her holding me,' he says. 'It's one I hadn't seen before. At first I thought it was you. You look like her.'

'I think maybe that's more true now than it used to be.'

'Because you're thirty now.'

'Thanks for reminding me.'

'I know. It's really old.'

I stifle a mock-sob.

'Sorry,' he says.

'You look stricken with remorse.'

'I'm just saying it because now you're her age. That's why you're looking so much more like her. You can see it in that newspaper picture of you too.' He clears his throat. 'Did you really try everything you could to find her?'

Did I? At first we barely functioned. Mum didn't leave her bed. Dad stumbled around trying to make sure we had what we needed, cooking and cleaning and shopping, trying to get Mum to eat. I lurched through the house, trying to care for a two-and-a-half-month-old baby. Mostly we were reactive, answering the police questions, giving them access to your things. But we got in touch with everyone we could think of, did the appeals.

I stuck pictures of your face to lampposts, between

the posters of missing cats and dogs. One of them stayed up for a year, fading as rain and wind and snow hit it, flapping at a bottom corner where the tape came off, dissolving at the edges but miraculously holding on.

I tell Luke as much of this as I can, as gently as I can, but he shakes his head.

'I need you to try again,' he says. 'I need you to. I need to know. Even if it's the worst thing, I need to.' His voice rises with each sentence.

I grab a bottle of water from my jacket pocket and pass it to him. He gulps down half.

'Is this why you want me to get her things from Granny?'

'Yes.' He wipes his mouth with the back of his hand. 'You have to. Tell me you will. You have to look at everything.'

'The police already did.'

'No they didn't. I hear much more than you think after I've gone to bed. I've heard all of you say how useless they are. Except Ted.'

I inhale slowly, then blow out air. 'Okay.'

'You'll do it?'

I nod. 'I will.' My stomach drops as if I am running and an abyss has suddenly opened in front of me. Because there *is* something I can do that we haven't tried before. I can request a visit with Jason Thorne. I reach for Luke's hand. 'But only on one condition.'

'What?'

'You will have to trust my judgement about what I can share with you.'

'If you mean you might have to wait a little while,

yeah. Like, until I'm a bit older. But you can't not ever tell me.'

Thinking about Jason Thorne makes it hard to breathe. The possibility of Luke knowing about him makes it even harder. But I manage to keep the pictures out of my head.

'I need to do what I think is best for you, Luke. It's going to depend on what I find out. And you need to be prepared for the possibility that this might be nothing at all – that's what's most likely.'

'I guess that's the best agreement I can get.'

'You guess right.'

His forehead creases. 'There's something else that bothers me,' he says.

I am beginning to think I may actually be sick. 'Tell me.' I realise I'm holding my breath.

'Granny says you didn't do well enough on your exams because you didn't go back to University afterwards.'

Afterwards. He never says 'after Mummy disappeared' or 'after Mummy vanished'. There is before. There is after. The thing in between is too big for him to name.

But at least he isn't worrying about Jason Thorne. This is easy, compared to that. 'I did go back,' I say. 'But they made special arrangements for me to do it from a distance so I could help Granny and Grandpa take care of you.'

'But Granny says you should have done better. She says you wanted to be a scientist, but I heard her telling Grandpa that Ted was distracting you even before you moved back home. It's not really Ted's fault, is it?'

'It's nobody's fault, and I wanted to be a biology teacher, not a scientist. But I don't any more. The charity work is important – it means so much to me.' I smooth his hair again, silky like yours, silky like mine. This time, I am not ambushed by an image of Thorne grabbing you by it.

'It was my fault,' Luke says. 'You wouldn't have messed up your degree if it weren't for me.'

'Luke,' I say. 'Look at me.' I tip up his face. 'Being your aunt is the best thing that has ever happened to me. That is definitely your fault.'

'And Mummy's,' he says.

'Yes. And Mummy's. I miss her so much and you are the only thing that makes it hurt less. Looking after you taught me more than those lecturers ever could. I wouldn't have wanted to do anything else. It's what I chose.'

His head whips round. 'There's that coughing noise again.' We both listen. 'And that's a different sound. Like somebody tripped in the leaves.'

'Probably someone on their morning walk. Someone clumsy with a cold.'

'Should we look?'

'They'll be gone before we get there.' I take his hand. 'If it's really a spy, he's not very good, is he?'

'Not as good as me. Plus he won't know what he's up against with you.'

'Let's go in. Granny promised to make pancakes for breakfast.'

'I'd better tell Granny and Grandpa about what we heard.'

'We can tell them together. And you know that if anybody comes near the house, one of the cameras will pick him up. I'll check the footage before I leave. You don't have to worry.'

He nods sagely. 'Can you stay for the afternoon and take me to my karate lesson?'

'I'd love to. I'll have to rush off as soon as you finish though. I promised Sadie I'd go to her party.'

'Is it her birthday?'

'It's to celebrate moving in with her new boyfriend.'

Luke wrinkles his nose. 'Ted says Mummy never liked Sadie.'

She thinks everyone is out to get her – she's the most bitter person ever born.

She talks behind everyone's back and it's just a matter of time before she turns on you.

She's always telling herself she's a victim but she's actually the aggressor.

These were your favourite warnings to me about Sadie. You made your assessment when she was four and never saw any reason to change it.

My friendship with Sadie has certainly lasted beyond its natural life. I try to explain why. 'I've known her since my first day at school.'

'Like Ted.'

'Yes. But she doesn't have many friends. She gets mad at people and drives them away.'

'So you feel sorry for her?'

'Kind of. I guess I always have.'

'What if she gets mad at you?'

'It's probably only a matter of time before she does. I'm too busy to see her much – I suppose that reduces the opportunities for her to find fault with me.'

'Don't go. Stay here with me and Granny and Grandpa.'

'That is tempting. But she's really nervous about the

party. She has hardly anyone of her own to invite and she's scared Brian will think that's weird. It'll be all his doctor friends.'

'Fun,' he says. 'Not.'

'Definitely not as fun as your karate lesson.'

'They'll let you watch me. I'm getting better. You'll be proud.'

'I'm already proud. Can I join in?'

He shakes his head no solemnly, partly not wanting to hurt my feelings, partly amazed by my silliness. 'It's for kids, Auntie Ella. Plus I'd have to pretend not to know you because you'd show off. You'd execute a flying spin and kick my teacher in the face with a knockout blow.'

'Never.'

'I don't believe you.'

'Well, maybe a little knifehand strike to the ribs.'

The Costume Party

Sadie is passionately kissing Brian. She is pressing her breasts against his chest. I am standing in front of the two of them in Brian's crowded kitchen, trying not to appear disconcerted – only a few seconds ago the three of us were politely talking.

'Autumn in New York' is playing, telling me about how new love mixes with pain, making me think of you as Sadie cups Brian's cheek with one hand and traces his lips with the index finger of the other. She stares into his handsome-in-a-geeky-way face and strokes his dark hair. 'You obsess me.' Her whisper is deadly serious.

'And you obsess me.' His whisper is a tease. She frowns, wondering where his eyes are darting to. The frown gets bigger when she sees they are darting to me.

I've never met anyone as sickly sweet on the outside and full of poison on the inside.

Your pronouncements on Sadie were endless.

Sadie is six feet tall, so perhaps one of the things she

likes about Brian is his great height. I am only five feet five. You always said that the thing Sadie likes best about me is that she can literally look down, though you pretended not to hear when I said she could do that with most people.

Sadie adjusts the rectangular frames of Brian's nerdy-cool spectacles, which have slipped down his nose. Brian is a dermatologist and I cannot help but imagine those spectacles falling off as he bends over a patient's head, smacking them on the forehead and leaving a bad blemish or maybe even interfering with the performance of some vital instrument.

She turns from Brian to examine me, though she curves his arm around her waist and holds it there in a way that makes my heart twinge for her. 'You're actually wearing a dress!' she says. 'I didn't think you owned any.'

'It was Miranda's.'

She motions me to turn around. I catch Brian watching me and I hope – though I am not quite sure – that he manages to tear his eyes away by the time Sadie glances at him to check.

Sadie has spent the last five years trying and failing to be in a serious relationship. She desperately wants Brian to be The One. She is sneakily buying wedding magazines already.

'Is that DVF?' She peeks at the label of your dress, scratching the back of my neck with a nail. 'Christ, Ella,' she says. 'These are £500 a pop in silk.'

How could you have afforded this kind of thing on your nurse's salary? This is a recurring question for me.

The police wondered about it too. Like so much else, it remains unanswered.

'Miranda had one in red as well,' I say. 'But red isn't really my colour.'

I imagine how furious you would be at my letting out one of your shopping secrets to Sadie. It was bad enough that I told the police. *But you signed the confidentiality clause, Melanie. The confidentiality clause never expires.*

Only you were allowed to call me Melanie, as if you wanted to make me yours alone. To name somebody is a powerful act, and you like powerful acts. You extracted Ella from the middle of my name, adding an extra L. You commanded everyone else to use it. Even Mum and Dad obeyed you. They still obey you. Was it out of guilt that they'd been careless and spoiled your decade as an only child by saddling you with an accidental baby sister?

'I'm not sure you're right about red,' Brian says.

My stomach tightens, but Sadie lets the comment pass. 'Those wrap dresses don't date,' she says. 'They're classic.'

'This one is a consolation prize, awarded by my mother.'

'For what?' Sadie asks.

For the box, I silently think.

Our mother actually grabbed me when I started towards the attic this afternoon to retrieve it. I was drawing strange men after me and Luke, she said. I was stirring up danger in my refusal to leave things alone, she said, especially after the newspaper article.

'Ignoring things, hiding them from each other, that's the real danger,' I said.

She didn't answer.

'The difficult things aren't going to go away because you pretend not to see them,' I said.

Stalemate is the rose-tinted view of where the two of us were when we parted, the box still up in the roof space beneath the eaves. But our mother took this midnight-blue dress from her shrine of your things and pressed it into my hands, along with a pair of strappy sandals you never even wore. She was horrified by the prospect of my going to a party in the jeans and sweat-shirt I'd been wearing all day.

Your dress flowed and swirled as I walked out their door in it. I even swished my hips like you used to, to try to jolt our mother into reacting, to try to shock her into giving me my way and handing over the box when she saw how like you I look.

Yeah, right. I imagine you rolling your eyes at the impossibility. *Like that's really going to work.*

I shrug away Sadie's question as if I am bewildered by it. I put a hand up to my neck, an unconscious reflex, near the place she scratched when she searched for the label. I'm startled when my finger pad comes away with blood. There is no doubt that she is being even spikier than usual, and that this heightening of her default state of resentment has something to do with Brian.

'Don't be such a baby, Ella – I was fixing your neckline.'

You follow me through this party like a sardonic ghost,

whispering in my ear. *Sadie's perfect at the can't-do-enough-for-you act. Every good deed is a little stab.*

'I have some extremely expensive overnight cream from a new line Brian recommends.' Sadie runs a beauty clinic. She first met Brian a few months ago, to discuss the possibility of his doing some treatments on her clients, the kinds of procedures she needs a proper dermatologist for. 'Would your mother like to try it?'

'That's nice of you. I'm sure she would,' I say.

'Evening, everyone.' The voice is talk-show host smooth and charming, and vaguely familiar. When I turn to its owner and realise who he is I want to sink into the floor because I had the misfortune of being assigned to Dr Blossom when our mother dragged me for tests to investigate why my periods vanished at the same time as you.

Sadie does not know this, so she feels the need to introduce me and Dr Blossom feels the need to pretend he has never seen me before in his life and certainly has never peered at my reproductive organs and pored over countless tests of my hormone levels only to diagnose the fact that my ovaries are in a decade-long and extremely mysterious coma. Something I could have told him myself.

Sadie is more agitated than usual, at this party full of doctors she barely knows. She is making lots of self-mocking jokes, which is what she always does when she is ill at ease. She glances under each of her arms and says, 'God, this room is hot. Good thing this dress is sleeveless.'

Dr Blossom says, 'Get Brian to inject you with some

Botox.' He points under Sadie's arms, in case there is any confusion about where the injections need to go. 'That'll stop the perspiration.' He touches the top of his absurdly flaxen head, as if to check that his hair has not flattened. 'Not sure it's available on the NHS, though. You'll probably need to do it privately.' He thinks he is being very funny.

But Sadie is funnier. 'Brian already injects me privately. Twice a day, morning and night.'

A laugh shoots out of me so fast I practically snort, and I am glad to be reminded of how quick and funny Sadie can be. But Brian flashes red, so I decide that this would be a good time to look for Ted.

I excuse myself and Dr Blossom nods understanding, making his shimmery curls bob.

Ted is not in the fake-gentleman's club of a living room. Barely any time has passed before Brian follows me in with Sadie close behind him. She cuts in front of him and sits next to me, wafting jasmine.

'Brian thinks you're pretty.' Sadie pulls him onto the sofa, keeping herself in the middle. 'He said so after lunch last month.'

I am at a complete loss about how to react, because Sadie sounds as if she is reporting a murder confession and Brian looks as if he has been sentenced to hang by the neck until dead. But at least I have more insight into why Sadie is out for blood.

'Does that please you, Ella?' Sadie says. 'Because you certainly looked pleased.'

'I'm sure you were being kind, Brian,' I say to Brian. 'Your dress is beautiful, Sadie,' I say to Sadie. It is jade satin, cut low without being too low, fitted at the bodice and slightly flared in the skirt.

'Thank you,' she says. 'Please don't change the subject.'

'I wasn't. I've been wanting to tell you since I got here how elegant you look.' I scan again for Ted, hoping against all reason for rescue, but his dark blond head and green eyes are nowhere to be seen.

Sadie notices me searching the room. 'Ted's not here,' she says. 'In case you were wondering.'

'I was a bit.'

'Have you and Brian ever met on your own?' Her eyes flick between the two of us.

'No,' we both say at once.

Sadie bites her bottom lip. 'Are you sure?' she says.

'Yes,' we both say at once.

I decide to reduce the amount of time before my getaway. 'Perhaps Ted is working?' I say, hoping very hard that there is no risk of his turning up only to find me gone – for him to be on his own at this party would not be a happy thing.

'He said he wasn't,' Sadie says. 'But he was cagey when I asked why he couldn't make it.'

Ted holding my hand in the playground when we were six, not caring that the other boys teased him.

She goes on. 'I think he's seeing someone. When exactly did he and his wife divorce?'

I inhale quickly, as if I have been kicked in the stomach. 'A year ago.' My voice is dull in my own dull head.

'Didn't last long on his own, did he?'

Stealing a kiss from me in the wooden playhouse on top of the climbing frame in the park when we were eight.

'How do you know that?'

Weeping in your arms when I was ten because Ted had appendicitis and I'd been terrified to see him so ill.

'From how he was when I asked him to the party,' she says. 'Definitely evasive. I wouldn't have invited him if you hadn't made me, Ella.'

Ted once told me that the antipathy between him and Sadie goes all the way back to reception class, when Sadie had a crush on him and couldn't forgive him for his complete lack of interest in her and his extremely big interest in me.

'Maybe he likes his privacy,' Brian says.

'Marrying one woman to get over another is never a good plan,' Sadie says. 'But you can't expect him to wait for you forever.'

Falling asleep on the phone with him when I was twelve and waking the next morning to hear his breath through the handset.

'I don't expect that.' This is a lie. I have expected exactly that. In recent months, since renewing what we both shyly call our 'friendship', I have thought that at last our time together would properly begin. I thought he felt this too.

Making love for the first time when we were sixteen.

We'd worried about pregnancy, then, like most teenagers. Not a worry I've needed to have for the last ten years.

As Dr Blossom knows. He is wearing his intelligent

face as he studies me, posing by the chimney piece with every one of his gilded hairs in place, stroking his perfectly square chin. He looks as if he expects several cameras to go off. Is he following me from room to room?

There is the ping of a text on Brian's phone. Sadie looks on as he reads. 'A kiss?' she says. 'That bitch. I want to kill her.'

Every once in a while Sadie loses control and has a social media meltdown. She is shrewd enough to cover it up quickly or delete madly, but she is perpetually in agony about who might have glimpsed or even filed away a screenshot of one of her public outbursts.

She turns to me, scowling. 'Did you put kisses on letters to Ted when he was still married?'

'We didn't have any contact while he was married.'

Brian plays with Sadie's honey-coloured hair, but he is looking at me.

'Right,' says Sadie, clearly meaning the opposite.

This insinuation that I am a marriage wrecker makes me recall one of the tabloid headlines from soon after your disappearance. It enraged our father, a man who is not given to rages.

Missing Nurse Spotted on Caribbean Yacht with Married Drug Lord Lover.

It seems a good idea to say, 'I would never go near a married man, or a man who has a girlfriend.'

Sadie tells Brian, 'Ella and Ted had a big fight because Ted was frustrated just being Ella's friend. So he started seeing this other woman, some police photographer. Then he married her. Ella cried for months.' She tears her attention from Brian and shoots it at me. 'But spare me the little fairy tale that you had nothing to do with him while he was with his wife.'

Ted and I saw each other or spoke every day from the time we were four years old until we were twenty-seven. Then nothing until we were thirty.

'There were three full years of absolute radio silence,' I say.

'Sadie tells me you're talking to him again now,' Brian says.

'Only recently. Ted came to my dad's seventieth birthday party this summer.'

'What made that happen?' Is it natural that this man should be so curious? Perhaps Sadie has reason to distrust him.

'My nephew invited him. I didn't know Ted was coming until he walked through the door.'

Ted and his wife were apart by then, but Ted never stopped checking up on Luke, even during his marriage. Luke has always idolised him.

Sadie cannot decide where to aim her surveillance. Her eyes dart to Brian's phone, then to me, then to Brian, then back to the phone, which seems to be pulsing with the contraband text. 'Who is she?' Sadie asks him.

'Someone I work with. A nurse. It's nothing, Sadie.' He kisses the tip of her nose. 'X is a letter of the alphabet. It doesn't mean anything.'

Sadie's hands are in fists. 'That's really unprofessional. To put a kiss on a message to anyone other than your true love is a betrayal.'

This makes me fantasise about emailing Brian with a string of kisses. xxxxxxxxx. It's the kind of thing you would do. But of course I won't.

'You are not going to answer her,' Sadie says. 'That is the only message she deserves.' Sadie puts out a hand. 'No secrets,' Sadie says.

Brian hesitates, then silently hands over his phone. The first thing Sadie does is to check his contacts and his call log. 'You're not there,' she says to me.

'Of course I'm not.'

Brian shakes his head. 'Sadie. Can you stop.'

Sadie holds his phone out and makes a show of deleting the text. Her passion-induced craziness evokes another of the many headlines you inspired.

'She was in love with love.' Missing Miranda's Romantic Obsessions.

'I need some water,' I say.

'What are you doing, Ella? Seriously. What is with you?'

'Nothing.' I sound clipped and cool.

'Literally digging out your sister's dress?'

'Really, Sadie. I am just thirsty.' I sound dangerous.

'The crap you are. Are you opening up that stuff with Miranda again? After all this time? Why would you do that?'

'It doesn't affect you.' I sound like you practising icy dismissal. And like Mum.

'Is it the attention? Are you missing it? Is that what this is about, now that the fuss about her has properly died down? Is that why you gave that stupid interview about the charity, and let them run your photograph?'

'That doesn't deserve a response.' The sofa squelches embarrassingly when I stand up. Luke would make a joke about this.

'Don't you dare leave.' Sadie catches my wrist. 'You're always doing that when you don't like my questions.'

'She needs a drink.' Brian peels her fingers from my skin. 'Let her go.'

The Three Suitors

I head straight for the front door. I get as far as the entry hall when a man approaches me, standing too close. The alcohol fumes are coming off his skin so thickly I can practically see them, mixing with his sweat.

I step back and he steps forward. I step back again and stick my arm out, visibly warding him off.

His hair is silver, to the middle of his neck, and slick. 'Let me get you a drink,' he says.

I cannot believe this surreal nightmare of a party is actually getting worse. 'No thank you.'

'You sure, sweetheart?' Indiana Jones would get away with calling me sweetheart. This man cannot. His shirt is silk and purple and has way too many buttons undone.

'Completely certain.'

He doesn't even try to disguise the fact that his eyes are moving up and down my body, from the top of my head to the tips of my toes, lingering at my breasts. 'I'll go get us some mineral water. We need to keep hydrated. Trust me. I'm a doctor.'

I am all too aware of the verbal manoeuvre – this attempt to encroach upon me by speaking as if he and I are a team, followed by his bad joke. I begin to walk away but the man puts a hand on my waist.

'Take your hand off me now.' Anyone who knows me would hear the dead seriousness of my voice.

But this man does not know me. When he tightens his grip on my waist and starts to move the front of his body towards mine I unbalance him with exactly enough force to leave him two choices. Let go of me, or fall over. He takes option one.

'What the fuck is wrong with you?' The man shakes his head and squeezes his eyes and moves his mouth from side to side. Then he lurches upstairs.

I brush off my hands. Once. Twice. Firmly and completely done.

But there are two consequences of these mild physical exertions. The first is that a lock of hair has escaped the low knot at the nape of my neck. The second is that your stupid dress flew open without my noticing because when I look down I see that my skimpy black underwear is showing and I remember why I hate this wrap style that you love.

This is when I realise that another man has come into the hall. He has been watching the entire show, so unmoving in the shadow cast by the stairway I haven't noticed him. He must have seen the spectacle of the gaping dress before I readjusted it.

The man's black eyes are creased at the corners, I

think in amusement. Beyond that, his expression is neutral. My guess is that he is ten years older than I am. The age you would be. Maybe, just maybe, the age you are. Though his face is young, his hair is grey. It's peppered a little with black. He is one of those model-beautiful grey-haired men.

'I'd like to offer you a drink,' he says, 'but I can see that might be dangerous.'

'Well you would be correct,' I say. I double-check that there isn't even the slightest visible tremble in my fingers. There is not.

'I'm Adam,' he says.

I manage to incline my head slightly in response. It is not that I am trying to be rude to him, even though that is probably what he will think. It is that I need a few more seconds to collect myself before I can speak properly.

'And you, clearly, are the woman with no name. I'll call you the Kickboxer.'

'That wasn't remotely like kickboxing. That was gentle dissuasion.'

He actually smiles. 'And you've gently avoided telling me your name.'

'Ella.'

He repeats the word as if it were a question, as if he has decided he likes it.

I squint at him. 'Have I seen you somewhere before?'

'If I'd seen you before, I'd remember,' he says.

'Good one.' I start to walk away, only to be stopped by Brian, who has somehow extricated himself from Sadie to come in search of me.

'I wanted to check you're okay,' he says.

'Fine. Thank you.'

Brian looks uncertain, but he nods. 'Glad to see you've met Adam.' His frown is at odds with his words. 'I'll leave you two to talk.' He looks over his shoulder, then disappears upstairs, taking them two at a time.

'Brian seems . . . ' Adam falters.

'Throwing a party can be stressful,' I say.

'You're right. And I owe you an apology.'

'For what?'

'That line about how I'd remember you if I'd seen you before. It was cheesy.' He waits a beat. 'But true.'

For so long, I haven't properly grasped why you adored male attention. Your need for it bordered on mental illness. But this man's admiration makes me warm, which isn't something that happens to me very often.

'Let me guess,' I say. 'You're a doctor?'

He smiles again. 'You have the gift of mind reading.'

'My sister used to say that.' There really is something familiar about him. All at once, I see what it is. It is that he is a type. He is your type. The tall, dark and handsome type. This man is commanding, but he is restraining his power, a tension you always found irresistible. I am discovering that I like it too.

'I need to be somewhere,' I say. Somewhere as in, *not* this new love nest of Sadie and Brian's. Somewhere as in home, where there are no doctors to interrogate me. And where there is no supposed-friend to shoot barbs at me.

'Somewhere interesting, I hope,' he says.

Is he like this with patients, too? Does he make anybody he talks to feel as if they are the most fascinating person he has ever met? A lot of men couldn't do this without being sleazy, but this man is gentlemanly, urbane-seeming. The type of man Ted would hate and you would adore. But Ted, as I am all too aware, is not here.

'Lovely to meet you,' I say.

'Can I see you again? I have a fondness for the martial arts.'

'I am not in the habit of seeing strange men. Especially not strange men who tease me.'

'I'm not strange. But yes, I couldn't stop myself from teasing you. I'm sorry about that.'

'That was not a sincere apology.'

'Perhaps not.' He takes out a business card and offers it to me. I don't take the card and he lets his arm fall back to his side. 'We can meet at my place of work. Between clinics, so you wouldn't have to put up with me for too long if I bore you.' He raises his arm to offer the card again. 'It's not often that I invite women there.'

'How often is not often?'

'Not often as in never before. You'll see why if you look.'

Fuck you, Ted, I think. *Fuck your games and fuck your remoteness and fuck your impatience.*

I squint at Adam for a few seconds. To my surprise, my own arm rises and somehow the card is in my hand. I glance at it. *Dr Adam Holderness, Consultant Psychiatrist.*

He is based in the secure mental hospital outside of town, where Jason Thorne is indefinitely confined. He probably thinks I ought to be an inmate. I suppose it's inevitable that in a house stuffed with doctors, at least one of them would work there.

'It's a great place to meet for coffee,' he says.

I am making silent fun of myself in a bad bleak way. I decided in the woods this morning that I would write a letter to one of the most horrifying serial killers in recent decades, asking if I can visit him. What normal woman thinks it is good news that she may have improved her chances of getting access to such a man?

I don't need Adam Holderness for that access, but having him behind me might help. It occurs to me that he probably knows who I am, but is being too polite to say. It is all too likely that Brian or Sadie told him. If so, he must guess that I will be drawn to his hospital by a more powerful force than a love of caffeine or a wish to date him.

I say, 'Do you find that your acquaintance with Jason Thorne is much of an inducement?'

'Only to an extremely select crowd. I tend to keep that one quiet.'

I fantasise a picture of Luke, proud of me, and happy, finding you at last, running into your arms, smiling at me over your shoulder. But I cannot stop a vision of what his response will be if the truth I discover is a dark one. And I cannot help but consider that if by some miracle we do find you alive, you will take Luke away from me.

The unexpected thing, though, since I made my promise to Luke this morning, is that the terrible visions of what Thorne might have done to you have stopped. Before that promise, nothing I tried would block them – last week's headlines brought them on with a relentlessness that I couldn't figure out how to fight.

'You know what I do,' Adam says. 'How about you? Or is your job classified?'

'Hardly mysterious. I'm a personal safety advisor and trainer. Mostly I work with victims, but also sometimes with family members of victims.'

'Oh yes,' he says. 'I remember Brian mentioning that. For a private charity your family founded?'

'Yes.'

'Sounds like important work. And difficult.'

'I get a lot of support from my mother. She does most of the admin, usually the helpline messages.'

'She must be very organised.'

'She has on occasion been described that way.' You would say, *If organised means control freak bossy, then yes.* But I have already confided more to this man than I do to most. 'Please excuse me. I need to go, Dr Holderness.' I use his title and surname to impose formality and distance, but it comes out like a flirtatious tease.

'What about that coffee?'

'I like coffee,' I say. This seems flirtatious too. It is a register I didn't know I had. It is not the register I was trying for. Again I sound like you.

'So do I. Goodbye for now, Ella.' With these words he steps away and disappears into the kitchen so I don't have to do any more work at extracting myself. It occurs to me that Adam Holderness has an instinct for doing many of the things that I like men to do. Most of them involve not invading my space bubble.

The Fight

Sadie makes her presence felt in the hallway, though I have been aware of her hovering at the edge of the kitchen, arms crossed and glaring at me, during the last minute of my talk with Adam Holderness.

I say, 'Why are you so angry? I'm trying to be understanding, but you're pushing it.'

'It is no longer possible to trust anything you say.' She swallows hard. 'You're so impulsive.'

'Sadie—'

She cuts me off. 'I never know what you're going to do next. When you're around I'm constantly on edge. Do you think it's normal to beat up my guests?'

'He deserved it.'

'My boyfriend's brother deserved for you to knock him over?'

'I didn't knock him over. I adjusted things to get him to take his hand off my ass. I didn't know who he was but it wouldn't have made a difference if I had.'

'It was embarrassing. So was watching you crawl all

over Adam Holderness. At least he got you to leave Brian alone.'

In a flash, Sadie has moved from ambivalent affection to naked hatred. I have seen her do this to other people. At last, after a period of grace that has lasted longer than I ever expected it to, Brian's wandering eye has triggered her rage at me.

'How much have you drunk tonight?' I say.

'Two glasses of wine. I don't need alcohol to see you clearly for what you are.'

'Are you ill?'

'Brian belongs to me. I should know by now how little such things mean to you. You never stopped running after Ted while he was married.'

'That was cruel. You know it's not true.'

'How dare you flirt with my boyfriend under my nose? How dare you meet up with him behind my back?' She steps towards me.

I step away, trying to keep space between us, repeating the manoeuvre I used a few minutes earlier with her would-be brother-in-law. 'You can't seriously believe that.'

'If it's not about your sister it's about making sure every man in the room is watching you. You'll do anything for attention.'

I am starting to shake, but with anger more than hurt. 'Get out of my way so I can leave.'

'Are you actually ashamed of the things you do? Do you know how sick you are? You're sick. Sick sick sick.'

'I told you to get out of my way,' I say. 'Don't make me make you.'

'Going to practise your self-defence on me? Or do you

only beat up boys?' She shoves me so hard I crash backwards into the door. I look up to see her towering over me. 'Get out of my face, you sick fraud.'

A tiny, disinterested part of me is fascinated by the question of whether I only beat up boys, because it is something I have never considered before. I have no doubt that I could send Sadie flying, despite her big advantage over me in height and weight. But could I push back at a woman? Everything about me centres on protecting women, but if my life depended on it, yes. Certainly if Luke's did.

Sadie does not deserve to know any of this. I choose not to shove back, but I close over, giving her nothing more than the silence she is now earning.

'You're so fake,' she says. 'Even what you have people call you is fake. You're not Ella. You're Melanie. Melanie, Melanie, Melanie.'

'You have no right to use that name.' I stand up smoothly. Our mother taught us to rise from the floor the way she used to when she was in the *corps de ballet*, before she got pregnant with you and gave up her dream of being principal ballerina. I face up to Sadie, taking command of the stage.

You have your mother's strength and single-mindedness. Dad has always said this to both of us. *That's why your love is so powerful. It's also why your arguments are so fierce.*

Sadie steps back. She actually looks afraid. Her voice trembles, despite her words. 'I know things about you. I know everything about you. Stay the fuck away from my boyfriend. Get the hell out of our house.'

And that is what I do. I get the hell out, not letting myself look back. I can hear the door slam behind me, followed by a kick and a scream of rage so loud they echo through the thick wood. But already I see the truth of Sadie. Not a new Sadie but the one who has been there all along, hiding from me in plain sight.

Another of your Sadie pronouncements is hurtling around in my head. *She's pathological in her concern for what people think of her. She must lie awake at night worrying about who knows the truth of what she's really like.*

Within ten seconds she will turn around and smile sweetly and remark on how violent and noisy the wind and rain are. And if any of her guests suspect the true source of the fury and noise, they will be too well mannered to say.

Monday, 31 October

The Scented Garden

The park keeper is waiting for us at the black iron gates of the scented garden. Already a *Closed to the Public* sign is dangling from them. I hang a second sign beside it – *Self-Defence Class Taking Place* – because I don't want passers-by to be alarmed by the noises we make. He ushers us in. All the while, I am looking over my shoulder, wondering where Ted is and triple-checking my phone in case I have missed a text from him.

Maybe he isn't going to turn up. Maybe he is busy with the new woman Sadie thinks he is seeing, though I have been wondering since Saturday if Sadie was lying.

Wishful thinking, you say.

While I clear away beer cans and cigarette butts and decide that this place ought to be renamed the Alcopop Garden, the women mill about in the late autumn sunshine, which has burnt away most of the wetness from the grass since Saturday night's rain. One woman crouches at the edge of the pond, watching the water lilies and goldfish as if they are the most fascinating things she has ever seen. Another has her nose buried in the climbing roses, her eyes closed as she inhales. The other two sit and whisper together on a wooden bench beneath a wisteria-covered bower.

As I slip my phone into my bag, it buzzes with a text from Ted, who tells me he is waiting at the gate.

Your voice is in my ear. *You are too forgiving. Too desperate. Don't make the same mistakes as me.*

'Do you want to gather over there on the grass?' I say to the women, gesturing towards the circle of towels I have set up at the far edge of the garden, off to the side and out of the sightline of anyone standing at the gate. 'I'm going to go and meet Ted so he and I can talk through what we'll be doing. We'll start in ten minutes.'

Ted is dressed like a football player this morning and it suits him, with his navy T-shirt untucked over the elastic waistband of his black shorts. I like the way this looks, like a little boy. He is not hiding or covering up, though – his stomach is as flat as it was when we were teenagers.

I say, 'I missed you Saturday night.'

He blows out air. 'Sadie's party. That can't have been fun.'

'She broke up with me.'

'More fun than I would have thought, then. Can't say I'm sorry. Or surprised.'

'She said you're seeing someone. She said that that's why you didn't come.'

He exaggerates a backwards stagger, as if I have thrown too much at him. 'Sadie's jumping to the wrong conclusions as usual and wanting to fuck things up for us.' He almost smiles. 'But did you dislike the idea?'

'Yes.' I say this softly. He gives me that melting look of his, so I feel a qualm at breaking the mood. My promise to Luke has taken me over and I am not going to have Ted alone for long – I need to ask him quickly, while I have a chance. 'You know your friend Mike, who you brought to Dad's birthday party?'

The melting look goes in an instant. He is as guarded as he would be talking to a drug dealer on the street. He has guessed what is coming. 'Obviously I know him. Since I brought him.'

'He was telling me how sorry he was for our family. You know how people get nervous about what to say. He seemed genuinely nice, though, Ted.'

'He's a good guy.'

'I think he really cared, that he was sad for us, sad that we still don't have answers. Maybe it's especially uncomfortable for a police officer when he's off duty and trying to be social.'

'Christ. That's why he's best kept in a room with machines and not let loose on actual human beings.'

'You're the one who took him out.'

'And I am kicking myself for that.'

'I asked him how he knew about her. He said he was in High Tech Crime when she disappeared. He still is.'

Ted crosses his arms. 'Making polite conversation, were you?'

'It got me thinking. He would have worked on her laptop. The police finally returned some of Miranda's things. My mother swears she hasn't opened the box yet.'

Ted makes a harrumph of scepticism at this. 'I know,' I say. 'She got Dad to put the box in the attic. He says from the weight and feel of it he doesn't think the laptop is inside. I wonder if you had any thoughts about why they might have kept it.'

'None. I'm Serious Crime, Ella, not High Tech, as you well know. Jesus – Luke had to teach me to work my smart phone. You know I've never had anything to do with Miranda's case because of my personal involvement with your family.'

'I know officially you know nothing, but I also know how all of you talk to each other.' He almost lets himself smirk but manages to hold it in. 'I thought maybe Mike said something.'

'No.'

'He did. I know you, Ted. I can read your expressions.'

'You can't ever let us have a moment, can you?'

'Yes I can.'

'You might think you can read my expressions but you can't read yourself.'

'I don't have a moment. Not for this. I need to know yesterday. I won't have peace until I do. Luke won't either.'

He shakes his head so vigorously I think of a puppy emerging from the sea. 'I wish I hadn't brought Mike to that party.'

'But you did.' My hand is on the bare skin of his wrist and I'm not even sure how it got there. The hairs are soft and feathery and dark gold.

'I saw you talking to him. I knew it would come back to bite me. You should work in Interrogation.'

'Despite your tone, I will take that as a compliment.'

'I was nervous going to that party, seeing you after so long. That's why I brought Mike.' His face flushes but I don't take my hand away. 'You can't let us be peaceful. You can't let things calm down enough for us to have a chance.'

My fingers slide up his arm, wrap around hard muscle. 'What is it they say? You had me at hello – that's it, isn't it? The minute you walked into Dad's party you had me. But the best way to create that kind of chance for us – for Luke – would be to find out what happened to her, to put all this behind us, finally.'

'That's more likely to destroy us than help.'

'Not knowing hasn't exactly done us wonders, has it?'

'I can't go through all of this with you again. I had enough of these arguments – I thought you'd finished with all that.'

'I never led you to believe that.'

'Luke is ten years old, Ella. He is a child. He has no understanding.'

'You know him better than that. How can you look me in the eye if you're withholding something crucial? That would always be between us.'

'Mike shouldn't have opened his mouth. It'll be a disciplinary for sure. He'd be lucky to escape with just a formal verbal warning.'

'I won't let anything come back to Mike.' My hand makes a broken circle around his bicep, with a very big gap between the end of my thumb and the tips of my other fingers.

'Don't.' He peels my fingers from his arm as if they were leeches. 'You don't give a damn about the havoc you leave behind.' He has never broken physical contact with me before. It's normally me who breaks it first.

You always warned me about my temper. My bad EKGs, you called them, as if you could see the spikes in my emotions plotted on a graph. Yours are the same, though more frequent.

My EKG must be off the scale right now, fired by the adrenaline that makes me counter-attack. 'So where were you actually, then, on Saturday night?'

Ted glares at me, refusing to answer, and I have to stop myself from visibly doubling over as an old headline unexpectedly jabs me in the stomach.

Master Joiner Thorne Detained Indefinitely in High-Security Psychiatric Hospital.

I hit Ted from another direction. 'Since you're already angry at me, it's a perfect time to tell you that I am going to try to see Jason Thorne. I wrote to him. Now it's wait-and-see as to whether he accepts my request to visit, puts me on his list.'

Local Carpenter in Bodies-in-Basement Horror.

'Have fun with that.'

I cross my arms. 'He's a patient, not a prisoner.'

Thorne in Our Side. Families' Outrage as Suspect Deemed Unfit to Stand Trial.

Ted mirrors me and crosses his arms too. 'So they say of all the scumbags in that place. You're not up to seeing Thorne. You never will be.'

I think of the worst of the headlines from eight years ago, when Thorne was first captured.

Evil Sadist Thorne's Grisly Decorations: Flowers and Vines Carved onto Victims' Bodies.

That headline made me hyperventilate. It took hours for Dad to calm me down. Mum had to hurry Luke out of the house so he wouldn't witness my hysteria.

'There's no connection between her and Thorne, Ella,' Dad said. 'The police would tell us if there was. This story about the carvings is tabloid sensationalism – I'm not sure it's even physically possible to do that. And they've only just arrested him – no real details of what he did have been released by the investigators.'

'Are you listening to me, Ella?' Ted is saying. 'Try to remember what all of this did to you when they first got Thorne. You nearly had a breakdown.'

'That was eight years ago,' I say. 'I'm stronger now.'

Whatever happened to you, I will not turn from it. Whatever you faced, I will face. I brace myself for the pictures. For the sound of your screams. For tangled hair and frightened eyes. But the pictures do not come. I have now gone forty-eight hours without any.

'You were falling apart more recently than eight years ago.'

'I won't let fear and horror stop me, Ted. I owe her more than that.'

'Thorne has been compliant as a teddy bear since his arrest. He is a model of good behaviour but you will still be the object of his fantasies. You wouldn't want to imagine what they are.'

'I can live with that.'

'He has refused all visitor requests so far, but I am betting he will accept you.'

'I hope you're right.'

'I hope I'm wrong. You will be entertainment. He will consider you a toy.'

'I don't care how he considers me.'

'There's no point in letting yourself be Thorne's wet dream. There was a huge amount of evidence tying Thorne to those three women. There's nothing physical to connect him to your sister.'

'Really? Nothing? Those news stories last week saying there'd been phone calls between them are nothing? Those journalists were pretty specific. Phone calls are evidence.'

'Since when do you believe that tabloid shit?'

'There were reports that they were looking at Thorne for Miranda when he was first arrested. You know it. We asked the police back then but they wouldn't admit anything. Now the idea is surfacing again, and with much more detail.'

'It's a slow news month.'

'They're saying—'

'Journalists are saying, Ella. The police aren't saying.'

'Too right the police aren't saying. The police never say anything. We learn more from tabloid newspapers than we do from them.'

'There's a big difference in those sources. You know that.'

'The police have probably known all along that she talked to Thorne – we asked them eight years ago and they wouldn't comment.'

'You were a basket case eight years ago. Maybe they did confirm it and your dad didn't tell you. Your parents were trying to protect you then. So was I.'

'No way. My dad would never lie to me.'

He considers this. 'Probably true. Your mum would, not your dad.'

'Anyway, Dad asked them again a few days ago and again he got silence from them. They won't ever be straight with us.'

'You're not being fair.'

'Do you think I want it to be true?'

'Of course I don't.'

'The tabloids are saying she phoned Thorne from her landline a month before she vanished. That's more precise than eight years ago. Eight years ago there were just general rumours. If she talked to Thorne, would the police know for sure?' He doesn't answer. 'They have the phone records, don't they?' Again nothing. 'Do *you* know if she spoke to him?'

'How many times do I have to tell you? I have no information. I can tell you though that whatever those journalists are saying, the police aren't behaving as if they think it's a new breakthrough. They wouldn't have returned your sister's things if they thought the case was about to crack open. If there actually is evidence that she talked to Thorne, my guess is they've always known and decided it was irrelevant.'

'Then why wouldn't they admit it to us, if they knew? What would be the harm in telling us? Why is this new information coming out now?' I tug his wrist in exasperation. 'Ted! Can you please answer my questions?'

'Not if I don't know the answers.'

'Do you think a journalist got hold of the phone records?'

'Not possible.'

'Well someone told a journalist something. Who else if not the police?'

'Why now, Ella? Why this moment for this new story?'

'Shouldn't you and your buddies be figuring that out?'

'Not me.'

'So you keep saying. Whatever the reason, it made me remember something else. A little while before she disappeared she told me she was looking for a carpenter to build bookshelves for her living room. It makes sense that she called Thorne.' My voice is calmer than my pulse.

'Then why wasn't her body in his basement with the others?'

'Even if Thorne didn't take her, he may know something. Somebody may have bragged to him. These kinds of people do that.'

'In movies, maybe. He's clever. He doesn't reveal anything he doesn't want to.'

'Not that clever. They still found the women.'

'Okay. Let's say for argument's sake that she did talk to Thorne. That doesn't mean he's responsible for taking her. You accept that, don't you? Never assume. If you really want to think about what happened to her, you need to be open-minded.'

'You're right. I need to remember that more. I might sleep better if I do.'

'Good.' He pulls me into his arms. 'Don't go. Don't visit Thorne.'

'I still need to try to talk to him, Ted.'

'I don't want you near him.' I can feel him gulp into the top of my head. 'I want to protect you. Why won't you let me?'

My anger has blown away. I disentangle myself from Ted as gently as I can. I touch his cheek lightly. 'I need to be able to protect myself. You know that.' Despite my speaking with what I thought was tenderness, he looks as if I have struck him.

'It's all I have ever wanted to do, protect you. Since the first time I saw you.'

His words take me back twenty-six years, to the day we met.

We were four years old and it was our first day of school. I fell in love with Ted during playtime for punching a boy who'd been teasing me about the birthmark on the underside of my chin.

I stood beneath the climbing frame beside my brand-new friend Sadie, but she was slowly moving away to watch the excitement from a safe distance. I was covering my face with my hand, blinking back tears as the boy jeered at me, laughing with some of the others. 'Look at the baby crying. Bet she still wears nappies.'

'Leave her alone,' Ted said. That was the first time I ever heard his voice. Even then it was calm but forceful, the policeman's tone already there.

But the bully boy didn't leave me alone. 'She's a witch,'

the boy said. 'It's a witch's mark.' Looking back now, it was rather poetic for a child's taunt. I later learned his father was some sort of writer, so maybe they talked like that all the time at home. But I didn't think it was very poetic then. 'Let's see it again.' The boy made a lunge towards me and I jumped back. 'Take your hand away, witch.'

The boy moved again, reaching towards me. That was a mistake. His fingers only managed to brush my wrist before Ted grabbed the boy's arm and hit at his face. I don't know if Ted's childlike blows really sent the boy to the ground, or if the boy threw himself there to try to get Ted in trouble. But there was no mistaking the blood and tears and snot smeared over the boy's nose and mouth.

Ted ignored the boy's screams and sobs, coming from somewhere near our feet. He touched my hand and said, 'Don't cover it up.'

It was only a few seconds before a teacher was at Ted's side to scrape the mean boy up and drag him and Ted off to the headmaster. Ted looked over his shoulder as he moved, and I only vaguely noticed that Sadie had returned to my side to put her arm around me. All I could think about was Ted, and how glad I was that he could see me take my hand away from my chin.

That night, when you asked about my first day of school, I told you about Ted and the boy and my birthmark. 'Your magic is in it,' you said, kissing it.

The birthmark has faded now. It is almost invisible. A mottled pink shadow the size and shape of a small strawberry.

When it first started to diminish, not long after Ted's fight with the boy, I worried that my magic would dwindle away too.

'The magic goes more deeply inside you,' you said. 'It grows more powerful because it's hidden so nobody knows it's there. It's your secret weapon.'

Remembering this, it strikes me that Ted has now been in my life for longer than you. So has Sadie.

I try to reassure him. 'There are guards everywhere in that hospital, Ted. Nurses. Syringes full of tranquillisers. Thorne must be drugged up to his eyeballs anyway as part of his daily routine, to keep him sluggish and slow and harmless.'

'Nothing can make Jason Thorne harmless. You know better.'

'They wouldn't let him have a visitor if they didn't think it was safe. They are constantly assessing him.'

'There's a gulf between what counts as safe behaviour for Thorne and safe behaviour for ordinary people.'

'He will need a long record of good behaviour before they let anyone near him. Not a few hours or days. I'm talking years of observing and treating him – they'll be confident that he's capable of civilised interaction. They know what they are doing.'

'Nice to see you put your faith in authority figures when it suits you.' He slings his bag over a shoulder. 'Luke will be hurt if you get his hopes up.' He starts to walk away but then he halts and turns. 'Have you thought about what it would do to him if something happened to you? There are real dangers.' He squeezes his eyes shut, then opens them with a jerk of his head, as if he does not really want to. 'The women are waiting. This conversation is over.'

'This conversation has only just begun.'

'You need to stop stirring things.'

'Stirring things is exactly what I want to do. It's what I should have done long ago. The ten-year timer is about to go off.' I push past him, determined to have the last word. If he has anything further to say, it will have to be to my retreating back.

Trick or Treat

The women shift around to make the circle wider and create an empty space for Ted on the grass beside my towel. Ted nods thanks and drops into place, saying hello.

This is the second time he has come to help the group – the first time was last month. The police think it is a good thing for officers to do volunteer work in the community, and I made sure that the women were all happy for him to join us.

'I want to thank Ted for being here. He has come on his day off to let us kick and punch him, which is extremely kind.' To my relief, everyone laughs, including Ted, who is doing a good job of pretending that we are not furious with each other.

I always worry about making jokes, even though the women and I agree that we must. Telling jokes is a way of defying the things that were done to them. They are all here because they have been victims of sexual assaults and they are determined not to lock themselves away forever in the aftermath of what happened to them.

'Ella's been beating me up since we were four,' Ted says, and they all laugh again, though my laugh is a half-hearted mask for sadness and guilt, as well as fury and distrust. He and I both hear the complex history behind this comment, including our recent argument, though thankfully they cannot.

Ted leans over to unzip his duffle bag, then pulls out what looks like a puffy astronaut suit. His predator costume. It is navy blue, a poor mimicry of a man's jeans and T-shirt. Only his forearms and hands remain bare – he will need to use those hands. He stands up, talking as he steps into the suit, and the others stand up too.

'Here's the thing,' Ted says. 'It's not about size. Ella's barely eight stone but she can floor a man more than twice her weight.

'Slap an assailant's jaw, he will smile. Punch his stomach, he will laugh.

'But jab his throat, he's going to clutch it with both hands and his eyes will water. Hook your thumb into his nose or mouth, he won't move for fear of your tearing his flesh.

'So you don't hesitate. You fight as hard as you can. You give me everything Ella taught you. You can't hurt me in this suit and I'm wearing protective shoes as well as the helmet over my head and face. So kick – I can see you all obeyed Ella's instructions to wear trainers and they can't do me any damage. Punch. Push. Scream. Stomp. Keep it going. Make noise. I am not going to hold back when I attack, so you are going to need to work hard. If your moves work on me, you can bet they are going to work on an assailant.

'The idea is muscle memory. If you can go through the motions physically, really fighting, then you are going to have the confidence you can do it. Your body is going to remember what to do.

'I want you awake,' Ted says. 'Not afraid. Awake. That is the point of all this.

'The thing about policemen is we know how scumbags think. Today I am the scumbag. Ella will talk you through the scenarios. But first, she and I are going to enact a new threat and response, so you can see what she wants you to work towards.'

I say his name in surprise. We had not agreed we would do this. We didn't when he came last month. But he only shoots me his hard villain look, which actually makes a shot of fear go through me.

He continues to talk to the women without pause, clearly not prepared to allow any interruption. 'You need to promise not to laugh once I've got this zipped up. I know it's Halloween but this is not my costume.'

And of course they do laugh as soon as he says this, because Ted has disappeared into the suit. But his head – that serious mouth, those green eyes, that ruffled hair – are all still visible as he cradles the giant silver helmet in his huge hands. He is a stuffed man, a creature made of dough. When he moves, he makes me think of a life-sized toy space explorer making his way through a gravity-free atmosphere.

'I'm going to be a bad guy,' he says. 'And I am going to approach you in lots of different ways, giving each of you a turn to fight me off. The best thing you can do is to avoid being in a dangerous situation. Avoid being in a position where you need to fight. I want you to deal with me with that in mind. But everyone here knows that avoidance is not always possible. Ready, Ella?'

I move towards Ted, not wanting to look reluctant in front of the women, but it feels like I am dragging myself through mud.

'You're in your bedroom asleep,' Ted says. 'It's the middle of the night and you're woken by an intruder.'

One of the women gives a little gasp in the background.

'I haven't gone through this kind of situation yet.' My whisper is a low hiss that I am pretty sure the women cannot hear. 'You know how fragile some of them are. We normally do the role play and talk it all through before a session so they're prepared. I – they – don't like surprises.'

'Better for them to see how it works while you've got me here.' Ted pulls me by the hand into the centre of the circle as they watch. 'I hate wasted opportunities.' There is an edge to his voice but the others cannot hear it. They must be thinking that this is what we have rehearsed and planned. 'Practice is always better than theory alone.' He points down at the grass.

'Fine.' I lie down and curl up on my left side.

'Close your eyes,' he says. 'I'm putting the helmet on now. Don't make me wear it any longer than I have to.'

'Don't tempt me.' The grass is tickling my left cheek and I am trying hard not to scratch it. There is a small pebble beneath my hip and I am not sure how much longer I can ignore it.

Ted puts on the giant silver helmet, which is lined with shock-absorbing material. He zips himself the rest of the way into the suit. His eyes are not the jewelled green of emeralds. They are the earthy green of moss, one of my favourite colours, and I wish I could see them but I can't. They are hidden beneath two squares of reinforced plastic that look black from outside.

A hand slams onto the ground only inches from my head. Ted is screaming, 'Wake up.' His voice is as muffled and scary as anyone's can be. He is grabbing my right shoulder and rolling me onto my back, pinning both of my arms down and pressing me onto the grass with the full weight of his body. Everything is in slow motion and my ears are buzzing and the sun is dazzling. One of the women cries out.

I have been turned to stone. Every trained reflex I have is paralysed. All that I have practised is dead. Is this what he really wants to do? How he really wants it to be?

I disappear from the park. I am somewhere else, in a city by the sea, and it is almost ten years ago, the last time Ted and I were lying in this position. And I want him on top of me, in this narrow single bed in this rambling old house that seems to come out of a dream and is full of twisting corridors and hidden bathrooms and seemingly vanishing loos as well as multiple other inhabitants I hardly ever see. Whenever he is able to visit, we spend all the time we can in this basement room, pressed against each other, the ocean in our ears. He is so beautiful as we kiss, his expression so soft and blurred, as if our kissing is all there is in the world, and he is lost in it, lost to himself. His eyes are closed but mine are open, wanting to see, unable to look away from his face, which I have loved since I first saw him in the playground sixteen years ago. He seems half asleep and half in a trance. All the time we make love I look at him, not knowing that this is the last time we ever will. Not knowing that as we kiss and I watch him, at this exact moment, you are vanishing.

There is a hissing in my ear, bringing me back. There is grass beneath me and sky above me and the scent of honeysuckle all around me though I am not sure how that can be possible and all I can think is that you loved honeysuckle.

There is a voice spitting questions and commands. *Are you scared? Spread your legs.* Were these the last ugly words you ever heard? There is a man squirming his feet between mine and using his knees to try to force my legs apart. There is a pebble bruising the small of my back, reminding me where I am.

But still I cannot move. There are women's voices and they are saying my name over and over again, as if urging me to do something, but I cannot understand what it is. I cannot think who they are.

There is a horror-film face above mine and I do not know who it belongs to. I hear my name. It is not a question, and even though it is still in that same strange voice, it is not said with hatred. Even beneath its static fizz there is a note of concern that brings me back and I remember that the face is behind a mask and it is Ted's face and I am glad I cannot see his expression. I am glad his murky green eyes are hidden beneath the tinted visor, and his hair is beneath the helmet so that I cannot be reminded of what it felt like ten years ago when I last cupped his head in my hands and pulled it towards me.

He is inching my knees farther apart and I am trying to keep my legs as fixed as marble but it isn't working. My name is getting louder but Ted isn't saying it. My name is a screamed chorus of female voices and it isn't coming from me but it goes through my bones like an electric shock and jolts me and jolts me and jolts me awake.

I let out a grunt and roll onto my left side, taking Ted with me, taking him by surprise and in one continuous motion kneeing his upper thigh once, twice, three times in quick succession. He is crouching now, coming at me again, and I am sitting up with my legs bent in front of me. I raise a leg and kick him hard in the face again and again, until he falls onto his back. I scoot closer to him and bring my heel down on the helmet-shaped cage that covers his mouth and nose. Again it is once, twice, three times. Always the magic number three. My movements are controlled and exact. The impact is precisely as I wish it to be.

He is completely still. Everything is silent. Slowly I stand up, knees bent, looking all around me, holding my hands in front of my face for protection in case he pops back up.

'Ted?' I say.

He sits, pulls off the helmet, gives his head a shake. When he speaks this time, there is no hint of the muzzled villain. 'Each and every one of you is going to be that good by the time she finishes with you,' he says to the women.

I offer a hand and he takes it to pull himself up. 'Then reward me,' I say, so quietly that only Ted can hear. 'Tell me what was on her laptop.'

'What you need to emulate in Ella,' he says to the women, 'is that she never gives up.'

I pick up my towel and thrust it at him to mop up the sweat. 'Too right.'

That snaps him back. He is beside me again. His mouth is near the side of my face so that his whisper whistles right down my eardrum. 'If you meet Thorne you're going to need to practise every move there is. And not just the physical ones. He's an expert at the mind fuck.' He turns to the women, restored to his usual relaxed and friendly stance. 'So. Who wants to beat me up next?'

Friday, 4 November

Small Explosions

I am driving away from Bath, where I now live and you used to live. I am driving away from the city that you and I love, to the house in the countryside that our parents brought both of us home to as babies. They will never leave it. They want you to be able to find them. We all want this.

It is only midday, but the dense branches of the trees on either side of this rural lane meet and tangle overhead, plunging me into near darkness for what seems to be an endless stretch. For many miles, I do not pass another car. There are still no cameras along this winding lane. There are still no mobile phone masts. This is the road you made your last known journey on, and it would be all too easy to intercept somebody along it.

He could have moved you under cover of woods, or over one of the many tracks, or through fields on some sort of farm vehicle. He could have got you into a building and hidden you. He could have wound along this narrow lane, then accessed the large road that circles this land before speeding you into another county.

I am working so hard to imagine the different possibilities I nearly overshoot the turning to our parents' village. It is a turning you and I have made countless times, and one I normally navigate on autopilot. I force myself to look around me more carefully, though I know this landscape so well it is the place I must always go to in my dreams. The old church and graveyard. The pub. The closed-down schoolhouse Dad converted several decades ago, now occupied by our parents' closest neighbours.

Five minutes after the nearly missed turn, I am sitting with Dad at the same scrubbed kitchen table you and I used to do our homework on. Your son uses it the same way these days, though not right now, because he is in school eating the sandwiches Mum packed for him. She and Dad and I are about to have some private bonding time over the lunch she has cooked for us, and is currently putting the finishing touches to.

I start with the easier thing. 'Luke wants me to take the doll's house,' I say. 'He wants to have something Miranda loved when he's with me.'

'I'm not sure Miranda loved it as much as you did,' our father says. 'Though she knew how much it meant to you.'

'Really?' I am seriously surprised.

'*Miranda loves it.*' It is our mother's usual correction of tense. '*She knows how much it meant* . . . But your father is right.' She puts a bowl of broccoli on the table. 'Cancer cells hate broccoli,' she says.

'They do,' I say. 'Can I take the doll's house, then?' I say. 'Seeing as you both agree that I love it most.'

'I suppose so.' She touches our father's bristly orange head, flitting away from the subject as she does. 'Only your father has a full head of hair at his age. And not a speck of grey. Look at him and then at his friends. Your father is still handsome. It's because I take such good care of him.'

Dad laughs. 'You certainly take good care of me, Rosamund.'

Our father's head still looks as if it is topped by a scouring pad that has rusted to dull copper. When Luke was six he drew a picture of Dad as one of the creatures from *Where the Wild Things Are*, snaggle-toothed and goggle-eyed. He drew another picture around that time, of you and me, in imitation of *Outside Over There*. How can I have forgotten this? I file the memory away, so I can remind Luke that there is a story of a sister searching for her lost sister. And finding her. He made me read him those exquisite books so many times I still know them both by heart.

'I'm with Mum,' I say.

'It's your mother who hasn't changed a bit since the very first time I saw her.'

'Yeah. Dancing that poor man to death during the *Giselle* rehearsal. Don't say you weren't warned, Dad.'

'Very funny, Ella.' But she is smiling. 'Your sister tells the same joke.'

'I was supposed to be working,' Dad says. 'Building something last-minute for the set. But the only thing I could see was your mother. She stood out from all those other *Wilis*. I nearly fell off my ladder, twisting around to watch her.'

How many times has our father told us this romantic tale? One of his tricks for pleasing Mum, who never tires of it. You used to circle your throat with your thumb and index finger and pretend to mock-choke yourself whenever he did.

'I love this story,' I say. 'And ten months later, Miranda was here.'

'Yes,' Mum says. 'Yes she was.' She closes her eyes and reaches out a hand. Dad grabs it.

'Your mother was an enchantress, Ella, from the first time I saw her,' Dad says.

Mum brushes the compliment away. 'Your father was the real enchanter,' she says. 'The three of us lived among the dust and rubble as he turned a crumbling old wreck of a house into the beautiful thing it is now.' She gestures her arms slowly out, a ballerina on the stage showing us the world. 'He made all of this for his family.'

'You are both magical,' I say, imagining you closing your eyes, yawning widely, and fainting your head sideways into your cupped hand with a slapping noise.

'What could the police have been doing with Miranda's things for the best part of a decade?' I try to sound casual, despite my abrupt change of subject. I pick up my water glass and lift it towards my lips before realising it is empty.

'Letting them gather dust in a store cupboard somewhere,' our mother says. She gives me her sharp look as she sits down. She knows where I am headed. She scoops fish pie from the casserole dish and onto our plates with studied grace and care. 'Eat your lunch,' she says.

'But why finally give them back now?' I say.

Dad fills my glass from the jug Mum has already put on the table.

'They probably wanted the space for more recent cases.' Mum can't stifle a laugh when Dad signals with a wordless frown that she hasn't given him enough fish pie, though he has four-times the bird-like quantity she took for herself.

'They made a big show of victim's rights when they returned the box, saying it was important that families had their loved ones' belongings returned as soon as was practicable,' Dad says.

'A decade is hardly soon,' I say. 'Do you think the timing means anything? So close to the ten-year anniversary, and the new stories about Jason Thorne?'

'I don't want you thinking about Thorne, Ella. It simply means that they'd forgotten about Miranda's things until now.' Our mother puts more food on Dad's plate. 'It's a mistake to credit them with any plan. It's all coincidence.'

Dad's eyes bulge. 'It's a confirmation that she no longer matters to them. They put the data into their fancy predictive analytics and the computer tells them where to focus their energy and funds, where the future dangers and risks are. Finding Miranda at this point in time isn't likely to save someone else. She will be at the bottom of their list.'

'Where did you get that term, Dad? Predictive analytics?'

'Ted. He doesn't like it much either.'

'It's just that – I wondered if one of you asked for her things?' I am searching for any flicker of a reaction from either of them. 'Maybe if one of you wrote to the police? I can't make sense of what else would have prompted this.'

'I certainly didn't,' our mother says. She pops out of her chair and turns her back on us to root around in a cupboard.

Dad stares down at the table, moves his glass an inch. His cheeks flush. He looks up and catches my eye before hastily shovelling food into his mouth.

Mum is still facing away, mumbling. 'Where is it? – Nobody in this family ever puts anything in the right place.'

I mouth the word, 'Why?' but Dad shakes his head in warning, a single slow movement to one side and back. When I get him alone I will find out.

Although bonfire night isn't until tomorrow, somebody in the village is already playing with fireworks. The first burst makes our mother whirl away from the cupboard clutching a grinder filled with black peppercorns. She huffs in irritation as she sits down. 'Probably some truanting kids.'

'Yes. Probably.' Dad watches me lift my glass in the silent toast to absent loved ones that he and I always make. I am looking at your empty chair as I do this. Only Luke ever sits in your chair. Mum and Dad and I always take the places we have occupied for as long as I can remember.

'You can't have the box, Ella,' our mother says. 'How many times do I need to repeat myself?'

'Why can't she have it?' Our father reaches out a hand but she leans out of reach. 'Rosamund?' He stretches farther, until his fingers brush hers.

'It's not the box,' she says. 'Ella is losing sight of her priorities.'

'Excuse me, but I am in the room. You don't need to talk about me in the third person. And I don't need predictive analytics to see where our priorities lie.'

'Reviving all of this will lead nowhere.' She gives our father's hand a brief squeeze before she slowly rises, her lunch barely touched.

'Can you say what you mean please, for once, Mum, in plain English? It's obvious that something's bothering you but it's not fair if you don't tell me what it is.'

'This isn't good for Luke.'

'What isn't?'

'Talking about his mother stirs up his feelings. Don't forget that he's only ten years old. I realise he is mature for his age, but don't treat him like a grown-up.'

'Maybe you shouldn't treat him like a baby.'

'How dare you speak to me like that, young lady?'

'I dare because I'm not young and I'm certainly no lady, that's how.'

There is another explosion. A plate slips from her hand and lands in the dishwasher with a clatter, but doesn't break. 'Damn,' she says. Your mouth would fall open, to hear her swear. If you were here, the two of us would cackle and mockingly scold her and threaten to wash her mouth out with soap as she used to threaten us, though she never actually went through with it.

Dad holds his hands out to both of us. 'Can we please

start the afternoon over? I don't usually get my two best girls on their own.'

Our mother looks like she is about to slap him. Or cry. 'Three best girls. You have three.'

'Of course,' he says. 'I'm sorry. That was careless but you know I never forget.'

She wipes her eyes. 'I do, Jacob. Of course I do.'

'We're all on the same side here,' he says.

I nod in agreement and say, 'Yes.' Then I say, 'I'm very sorry, Mum. I shouldn't have talked to you like that. I need to be more understanding and careful.'

'Be careful of yourself and be careful of my grandson.'

'I'm always careful of your grandson.' I try to hand her Dad's empty plate but she snatches it from me. 'I thought we promised each other to be open. Always. To share worries and information. We agreed that would be safest. We agreed that sticking our heads in the sand was the dangerous thing. That it was emotionally dangerous to do that and very possibly physically dangerous too.'

'Every new development needs to be evaluated. There is no single rule that can apply to all of it, Ella,' she says.

'I thought it was just a box of stuff that the police think is irrelevant.'

There is another explosion outside, which earns the window a death glare. 'Why can't they wait until tomorrow night?' She is still terrified of fireworks. You and I were never allowed near them, and she finds reasons to keep Luke away too. I know this would make you furious. I know I need to change this. *Don't let her coddle him, Melanie. Don't let her ruin him.* That is what you would say.

I catch Dad's eye. 'Are you afraid of what I might find in the box, Mum?'

'No. Because there's nothing there. What I am afraid of is raising Luke's expectations. Of churning up his feelings about all of this. Of frightening him.'

'Your mother makes a good point.'

'He's ten now. The impetus is coming from him. We can't ignore it.'

'You make a good point, too,' he says. Our father is still the family peacemaker.

'Always the diplomat,' I say.

'I do my best. You and your mother don't always make it easy.' But he is smiling, as if this is how he likes it.

Our mother stands behind her empty chair. 'It is not good for your soul, Ella. You're already too churned up. Remember how you were when it first happened. I don't want you falling apart again.'

'I'm not going to. I haven't come close to that for over seven years.'

'More like six,' she says.

'I'm much, much tougher. I am not the person I was then.'

'I liked that person,' she says.

'People need to change.'

'Not as much as you have,' she says.

'I'll tell you anything I uncover. We promised each other we'd do that and I will. I'll share anything and everything. Even if it's dangerous.'

'Especially if it's dangerous,' Dad says.

'What about Saturday morning?' She picks up my plate, slots it into the dishwasher. 'Do you really think someone was watching the two of you?'

'Possibly. But do you see how I really do tell you everything? Even the stuff I know will come back and bite me? Most likely it was some random walker out early. It's doubtful they could even see us through the trees.'

'Whatever you said to Luke that morning obviously disturbed him.'

'I don't think that's true. Or fair. And he was so happy about the doe. He keeps going on about it being magical.'

Dad looks solemn, which is not a look he readily does. 'Ella checked the footage from the outside cameras before she left for Sadie's party. There was nothing, Rosamund. But I did report it to the police.'

'I'm sure that pushed us right to the top of their predictive analytics list,' she says.

'I think we've talked enough about this,' Dad says. Mum glowers. It isn't often he shuts her down. 'Luke and I will bring the doll's house and the box tomorrow night,' he says. 'His consolation prize for missing another bonfire night.' I didn't think anything could make Mum's glower deepen, but this last comment does.

I am frightened of our father trying to move the doll's house with only Luke to help. It is far too large and heavy. I think of the tiny satellite of malignancy in his spine, shrunk down and kept dormant by the injections they give him each month to suppress the male hormones that the prostate cancer cells love. Our father's bones have weak points, but he refuses to act as if this is the case.

'Leave the doll's house for now,' I say. 'I'll come for it another time. Just bring Luke and the box.'

'No need,' he says. 'Luke and I can manage a doll's house.'

Our mother shoots me a sharp shrewd look that our father cannot see.

'Thanks but no.' I manage something more concrete. 'I need to clear some space for it first.'

What our mother says next is at odds with the small thumbs up she gives me behind Dad's back. 'I won't be coming with your father and Luke tomorrow.'

'I wish you would. We can order in pizza. Luke would like that. It would be fun.'

'I'll eat pizza.' Our father quickly turns to her. 'If your mother doesn't mind.'

'You do what you like, Jacob.' It is her martyred voice, the one that used to make you scream. She turns to me. 'You're not going to sneak Luke off to a fireworks display?'

'I wouldn't do something like that behind your back.'

'I let you take him out for Halloween on Monday even though it was a school night.' She makes it sound like this was the most extraordinary concession. 'Luke says you made a wonderful Catwoman. He was proud.'

'My everyday clothes,' I say.

'True.' She can't suppress a small smile. Then she gives me The Look. 'He mentioned that Ted came along. Dressed as the Joker.'

'He makes a great super-villain,' I say.

Ted and I were still furious with each other that night. The morning's self-defence class was still too fresh for both of us. All of our communication was to Luke, who was dressed as a policeman and too happy in his trick-or-treating to notice the stiffness between the two of us as we followed him from house to house.

'I promised Luke I'd take him to a fireworks display next year.' I'm shaking my left foot up and down in nervousness. 'Halloween and bonfire night aren't the same thing. He wants both.'

'Absolutely not. I've told you before. Bonfire night is dangerous.'

'He is a boy, Mum. He's not made of porcelain. He's going to be angry if you don't let him try things.'

'He's going to get hurt if you let him try too much. Your father and I may need to reconsider how much time he spends with you.'

'That's a bit hasty, Rosamund,' our father says.

Our father is the recipient of yet more glowering. 'Don't keep pushing, Ella,' our mother says. 'You're getting the box and the doll's house.'

My eyes are prickly with tears, but I know myself well enough to realise they are made of anger as much as sadness. 'Why are you being so mean? You still have me, you know. I'm still here.'

'And I want to make sure that doesn't change. Do you think about what it would do to us if we lost you too? Do you consider how terrified I am?' Her voice cracks. 'Imagine how you would feel if something happened to Luke.'

I wave for her to stop. I shake my head for her not to say another word. I cover my ears like a small superstitious child. Because to hear these words about Luke is too much for me.

'Yes. Exactly. And that is the best analogy I can give

you.' She takes the dessert from the oven. 'I worry about how far you will go to find out. I don't think you'll stop at anything.' She closes the door with a loud bang. 'You're like your sister.'

'I'm not.' I know you would agree.

She places a bowl in front of me with heightened care and precision, even for her. 'You have her determination.'

'She was the beautiful one.' I want to deflect our mother from a point that is too true and too frightening for me to contemplate.

'You look like her twin. You are equally beautiful.' Our father is still caught in his own loop of paternal fairness to daughters.

'Well I don't want to be.'

'That is where the real difference is,' our father says. 'Miranda turned the dazzle on. She sparkled because she wanted all eyes on her.'

'Jacob.' Our mother's voice is a warning and a command. It means, *Stop and go no farther*. It means, *Do not ever say anything that is critical of Miranda*.

He makes an attempt at appeasement. 'You both take after your mother. You have her beauty. But you keep the dimmer switch on, Ella. If you flicked it, those eyes would stick to you too.'

'I am more comfortable in poor lighting.'

'I know you are,' he says. 'But still you shine. The two of you were so alike, but so different.'

'Not *were*.' Our mother sits down and begins to scoop out apple-and-blackberry crumble. 'Are.' She manages a weak smile and leans closer to kiss my cheek, a serving spoon full of crumble still in her hand, dripping purple syrup. Our mother never drips anything, normally. She is not a woman who spills. The kiss makes me blink away tears. I kiss her back.

'Right,' my father says. 'The two of you are.'

'It's sweetened with apple juice concentrate,' our mother says. 'You know your father can't have sugar. Cancer cells love sugar.'

'You mentioned it once or twice before, Mum.'

'I am keeping your father alive, Ella.'

'I know you are.'

'You can't tell the difference,' she says.

Our father sneaks a tremor of disagreement and winks at me.

'I saw that, Jacob,' our mother says. She wanders to the side of the room, and turns her back on us to stare at a photograph hanging on the wall. It is the last one of you and Mum and me together. Dad snapped it. Mum and I are sitting side by side at a wedding. You are standing behind us, upright and elegant, the front section of your hair pulled back in a jewelled clasp.

The photograph is washed out despite Mum's care to hang it where the sunlight doesn't reach. Your dress is a perfect-fitting organza bleached into cream, its sprinkling of bright blue painted flowers drained into pale grey. Your made-up face is faded, the deep maroon lipstick now the lightest pink. Is all of this blanching a trick of the light? I do not want to see it as a sign.

Mum puts my thoughts into words. 'I look at that, and she is somehow already ghostly.' She cups the side of her face in her hand, her head tilted to the side. 'I think she is standing behind us, watching over us.' She clamps that hand to her mouth and straightens her head, realising that even though she is using the present tense, she has broken her own rule and spoken as if you are dead.

The Photograph

The email is anonymous and already I am betting it won't be easy to trace. It landed in the charity's inbox five minutes ago. The sender's name is 'An Interested Party'. The subject heading says, 'Lovers at a Café'. Attached is a single photograph, probably taken with a smartphone and certainly with the location services and time stamp turned on because it was snapped six minutes ago and the name of the café appears on it too.

I do not want our mother to see this, so I sit in my car in front of our parents' house and forward the email to my personal account. Then I wipe all traces of it from the charity's. As I am about to drop the phone into my bag, it rings, making me jump a little. It is a blocked number. Normally I don't answer blocked numbers, but this time I do.

'Hello?' My voice is weak. 'Hello,' I say again, forcing a strength I do not feel into the word. But there is only silence at the other end of the line, and it is a silence that is so perfect they must have muted the call. 'Sadie?'

Still there is nothing. I cannot shake the idea that it is her, but I will not give her the satisfaction of hearing a single syllable more of my uncertainty. I tap the red circle to make her go away. Immediately it rings again – once more from a blocked number – and I hit ignore before turning the phone to silent.

I force myself to study the photograph. I need to see in person. I need to know that this is no trick. I throw the phone into my bag with a kind of violence and reverse quickly out of our parents' driveway. I speed along the winding lane faster than I ever have before, dangerously fast, my wipers on full power but still not quick enough to clear the windscreen in the heavy rain.

Half an hour later, I run my nearside tyres over double yellow lines and stop the car on the corner, not caring if I get a ticket, indifferent even to the possibility of being towed through this Georgian Square that Jane Austen's characters sniffed at but I have always thought beautiful.

I am not sneaking. If he is still here, I don't care if he sees me seeing him. Seeing them. This is the only thought I am aware of as I push through the glass door of a café that he knows I have always hated. Is this why he chose it? Because he knows there is little risk of my running into him here?

This place gets rapturous praise for its artisan coffee. My taste buds seem to be the only ones on the planet to find it bitter. It is even more crowded than usual, because so many have rushed in to escape the rain.

Despite my initial bravado about whether he catches me here, I am glad to hide in the thick queue.

What has changed his feelings towards me so drastically? Has he finally decided that a decade is long enough to be patient? Is it work ambition? Some top secret new knowledge about you that he doesn't trust himself not to share? His pure fury that I won't take his advice and give up the idea of visiting Thorne?

A split second before I see him, a trickle of sweat runs down my back and my skin prickles and I think I am going to panic. Something in me, some sense somewhere, knows before I really know. A change in the air carried by his voice or scent. A glimpse in my peripheral vision. Simply his material presence in the building. My heart freezes. My stomach goes hollow.

Liar. I want to scream the word at him. But I don't. I swallow it back and feel as if it will choke me.

Ted is sitting at a small corner table with a woman whose face I cannot see, though the back of her head – her dark silky hair – is visible. That hair is so like my own my stomach seems to lurch up to my throat and there is a flame at the top of my head that rushes down my spine to my toes.

Is it you? I grab the arm of the stranger standing next to me to steady myself before he looks down and asks if I am okay, which shakes away my crazy split-second thought that you are actually here. I mumble that I am fine, I stumbled, I am so sorry.

The two of them haven't changed position since the photograph was taken. Ted is facing the room with his back to the wall of draughty glass, so he can keep watch.

But he isn't watching. He doesn't notice me, and not because of all the bodies between us. He doesn't notice me because he is looking at her with such deep interest.

I think of Sadie a year ago, when she and I ran into her latest ex-boyfriend. He was holding hands in a restaurant with his new girlfriend. Sadie marched right up to them. Her performance was received in stunned silence. There is no doubt it was memorable. I certainly have not forgotten it, and I doubt her audience ever will.

Hi. I'm the ex-girlfriend. Has he moved his mother in yet to give you lessons on how to clean and cook for him? You know, until I met Donald I thought it was a myth that all men wanted anal. If you haven't yet, you're about to learn from him that it's no myth. Do you enjoy it when that nasty brat of his wipes his snot all over you and screams until he gets his way? I hope the two of you get all the happiness you deserve.

I am not Sadie. I do not want to be anything like her. I do not want to go anywhere near Ted and this woman. I can taste bile, coming up from my stomach and into my throat. Did Sadie take the photo and send the anonymous email, following it up with her silent phone call to gloat? Who else could have done it?

I consider Ted's ex-wife. I have never properly met her. I haven't searched for her on the internet. I feared that even a glimpse of her face would be like staring down Medusa and I would be turned to stone. More than anything, I feared that once I started to look at her I wouldn't be able to stop.

Maybe his ex-wife suspects me of luring Ted away from her, of sleeping with him while they were still together. Maybe she blames me for their failed marriage. She is a photographer. It is perfectly possible to imagine her sending me a carefully selected image.

I am faint and jumbled to the core as I continue to watch the woman sitting across from Ted. Her shoulders are slim and her back is straight. The fabric of whatever dress or blouse she is wearing is navy blue with black stripes, a kind of zebra print. I cannot help but be certain that her face is as lovely and interesting as her waterfall hair, and this is why Ted is staring at her so closely. This is why I am doubly and triply safe from him noticing me as I peek through the gaps between these coffee addicts' arms, over their damp handbags. Their closed umbrellas drip onto my boots and rub against my jumper so that the wet seeps through and into my skin – I hadn't bothered to grab my coat when I rushed from my illegally parked car.

Ted isn't on duty. He is wearing a Christmas jumper of all things. I bought it for him five years ago. Fair Isle, with small reindeer parading across its variously toned charcoal stripes. Why would Ted wear something I gave him if he were on a date? This thought makes my stomach unclench a tiny bit.

In that way I have of letting my mind open up to find out what it knows before I am conscious of it, I think of Ruby, from my personal safety class. She didn't come to class on Monday and hasn't returned the concerned message I left her the next day. In a rush of certainty, I know who the woman is, and my jealousy is complicated by worry. The worry grows bigger when she turns her head to look off to the side and I see that there are tears on her cheek. Has Ted made her cry? Or is he supporting her while she cries about something else? Six months ago, she was raped by a fake meter-reading man who tricked his way into her house. Ted reaches out and touches her hand, lightly and quickly, but doesn't keep it on top of hers. He frowns.

What is he doing with her? Could he have known her before last month's self-defence class? Could he be meeting her as part of the investigation into her assault? No – he wouldn't do that in a café.

Whatever the reason, what should disturb me most? That Ted is here with a woman when he swore to me he wasn't seeing anyone? That Ruby is vulnerable and he may hurt her? Or that somebody cared enough to clock their meeting and photograph them?

Whoever that somebody is, they know who I am, and who Ted is. They know what Ted and I are to each other. And they knew how to find me through the charity's website. Whether they are for me or against me remains to be seen, though if it is Sadie or Ted's ex-wife it is all too clear which group she is a member of.

Whoever sent it, whatever their reason, I am actually glad they did it. They gave me a gift even if they didn't mean to. I would rather know than not know. Always. My stance on everything. Because the information – the fact that Ted is in this café with Ruby – is louder than everything else. It is so loud it is drowning out the context. Even if my brain is asking the right questions about the circumstances which got that photograph to me, my emotions are engaged only by what it shows.

Saturday, 5 November

Bonfire Night

It is after seven by the time I have finished my daily run, followed by my usual sit-ups and presses and pull-ups and stretches. I have barely stepped out of the shower before I hear Luke's keys in the locks, then the front door of my little Victorian house crashing open and his shout, 'Stay out of the way, Auntie Ella. Back in a minute.'

I shrug off the oversized towelling bathrobe that Ted left with me shortly before you disappeared. It is navy blue. It is so big I used to wrap me and Luke in it together when he was a baby and I wandered through the house late at night, trying to lull him out of crying and into sleep. There are holes and loose threads from uncountable washes, but this old thing of Ted's is an object of comfort to me still.

I shimmy into a jumper and jeans, tie my wet hair into a ponytail, and fly down the stairs to the sight of Luke and our father, lurching sideways into the hall. They are each clutching one side of the doll's house, which is shaped like a medium-sized chest of drawers.

Ted is rear and centre, taking most of the weight. Above Ted's head, in the clear black night that followed the afternoon storm, there is an explosion of silver stars. They fall from the sky as if to announce him.

Luke cranes his neck to watch. 'Awesome,' he says.

'Luke asked me to help.' Ted says this like an apology. He looks at Luke, not me, when he speaks, and a wave of sickness moves through my body.

Somebody on my street has lit a bonfire. The air is thick with smoke. Ash floats into the house. My eyes are burning. I blink and rub them. I think of the disappointed embarrassment that coloured my parting from Ted on Monday night, after trick-or-treating and dinner, which I see now he only went through for Luke.

'Ted came out to Granny and Grandpa's tonight,' Luke says. 'He helped us get the doll's house down from the attic and into Grandpa's van. He followed us here.'

'That was kind.' I am moving backwards, up the stairs again, out of their way.

'Luke and I could have managed,' our father says. I wink at Luke without our father seeing.

Once the doll's house is in Luke's room, there is a great deal of whooping and high-fiving between our father and your son and my furtive ex-boyfriend.

'So what have you and your aunt got planned for tomorrow?' It is infinitely easier for Ted to talk to Luke than to me.

'How about the zoo?' I say.

'Yessssss,' Luke says. He puts out a hand for some more high-fiving with Ted.

'Luke and I will run to the van to get the box.' Our

father is trying to channel our mother's matchmaking impulses but not managing her social smoothness. Ted and I stand awkwardly in Luke's room after they are gone, looking at our own feet.

My heart is squeezing as if I were a teenaged girl about to ask a boy to a dance. But what I have to say is not at all romantic, and it hardly matters anyway because it doesn't seem possible to piss Ted off any more than I already have. Besides, it's not like I will lose him – I have been there and done that several times over – and it looks as if I am about to repeat the experience. Once that happens my chance of learning what I need to will vanish forever.

'Tell me about her laptop,' I say. 'Tell me what they found on it.'

He actually sighs. 'You will never stop.'

'No. But I am willing to say please if it helps.'

'I wouldn't want you to do something so unnatural.' He shakes his head slowly. 'You won't believe me.'

'Try me.'

'They found nothing. The laptop's empty.'

'Then why are they holding on to it? Why does it still matter to them?'

'I said you wouldn't believe me. It's lose-lose with you, no matter what I do.'

'I am not the one making it lose-lose for us.' My fingers are fidgety and nervous, brushing hair from my eyes that isn't there because it is already pulled into a ponytail.

'What the hell is that supposed to mean?'

'You know exactly what.'

'Is there something you want to get off your chest, Ella?'

'No.' For now, I want the power of having knowledge without his knowing that I do. 'So why did you make such a big deal of refusing to tell me about the laptop if there's nothing to tell? Was it some kind of power game for you?'

'Low blow. That was beneath you. When I say there was nothing, I mean that whatever is there is hidden. Tech have kept the laptop in the hope that some future tool might uncover something.'

'You're saying she used the laptop, but everything she ever did on it is invisible?'

'So far as I can understand, yes. One of the things they think she did was to use an onion router to mask all of her online activity.'

My amazement actually drives the photograph and the café and Ruby from my head. 'But that's impossible. She wouldn't know what an onion router is.' My head snaps up. 'What is an onion router?'

'You're talking deep web. That internet world where nothing leaves a trace anywhere. None of the search engines you'd recognise.'

'But she was seriously useless at technology.'

'Evidently not.'

'But she can't have done that. If MI5 gave her a spying device she wouldn't know how to turn it on.'

'Well she did. And it wasn't the kind of technology ordinary people have access to.'

'Then someone else set it up and taught her. We need to know who. And why.'

I spend my days warning women of the importance of guarding their privacy to keep safe. But your skill at doing this – your talent for secrets – might have been the very thing that put you in jeopardy. Did you continue your conversation with Jason Thorne that way, after the phone calls the tabloids said you made to him?

Ted is frowning. 'You're going dangerously quiet.'

'Just thinking. Thank you for telling me. I mean it.'

'Don't drop me or Mike in it.'

'I won't. I never would. You know that.'

'I know you wouldn't want to, but you might not be able to help yourself.'

'I'll be careful for you. I'd always be careful for you.' And of you, I silently add.

He doesn't look convinced. 'That's the end of it. Don't ask me for more.'

This is not a promise I can make, so I change the subject in the crudest way possible, mostly for Luke's sake, but partly for my own. 'Will you stay for pizza?'

'I'd like to but I have to be somewhere.' He glances at his watch and I imagine Ruby waiting for him in a French restaurant, or in her little house, where she has cooked him dinner and lit candles. 'Half an hour ago, actually.' Ted is wearing black jeans and a black shirt and something that smells of woods. Even yesterday, I might have secretly hoped these things were for me, but today I know they are not.

'Next time,' I say.

'Yeah,' Ted says.

'My dad . . . Thank you . . . '

'I know, Ella. You don't need to say.'

Pandora's Box

Dad leaves with his phone to his ear, talking to Mum in a hushed voice. Luke wants to get straight to the box, but he is still sweaty from his afternoon karate lesson so I make him take a shower first.

'Fastest shower ever,' I say, when I walk into his room to find him waiting for me. He is wearing the football club pyjamas I bought for him a few weeks ago, and they make him look achingly sweet and young. He is sitting in front of the giant oak wardrobe that used to be yours, cross-legged on carpet that was also yours. I had these moved here from your flat three years ago when our parents were finally able to sell it and close your bank accounts and put the money safely away for Luke.

The carpet is pale beige, with a white trellis pattern, and beautiful, like everything you choose. Luke loves the fact that it was in the Georgian flat where the two of you lived together for such a short time.

I sit across from Luke and lift the lid of the cardboard box between us. 'Should we start?'

'Have I told you lately that you're brilliant, Auntie Ella?'

I raise my arms and tilt my head to the side, an upper-body-only curtain call, careful at the same time not to spill any of the Mexican beer I'm holding in my right hand. I take a sip.

'I've heard Granny tell you that ladies should never drink from bottles.'

Even wet from the shower, Luke's funny cowlick is as unruly as ever, a tight swirl above his left temple. I poke a finger into its centre and twizzle it around until he laughs. 'I'm not a lady.'

'Granny told Grandpa before we left that he wasn't allowed to drink.'

'She worries about his health, Luke. And she knew he was driving.'

'*Beer is made of sugar. Cancer cells love sugar.*' Your son's imitation of our mother is terrifyingly good. I try not to laugh but I can't stop myself. I nearly spray Luke with a mouthful of liquid death.

'Can I have a sip?' he says.

'No! But nice try. Smoothly done.'

He pauses to watch a dazzling waterfall of blue pouring into the night, followed by a streak of red fire zinging upwards like a reverse comet and screaming all the way. 'Please will you take me next year?' He is still staring out the window.

'I hope so. I'll keep talking to Granny.'

Luke rolls his eyes and turns back to the box. The cardboard has thinned in places, where sticky tape ripped off layers. 'Do you think Granny's looked through it?'

'No – I asked – she said she didn't.' But I'm sure she has. I wouldn't be surprised if she's actually taken something out. I have already snuck a phone call to her to ask this very thing, but she will not depart from her little charade that she never even looked inside.

I am not sure what we are expecting. Some obvious clue the police missed? Presumably they have already combed it all for DNA.

'What's this?' Luke is holding a scrap of soft white wool, edged in silk and fraying.

I reach out a finger to touch it, smiling. 'The sole surviving piece of Mummy's baby blanket. She used to tuck it into your cot with you.'

He buries his face in it, then jumps up and sticks it beneath his pillow. 'Please know that I will have to kill you if you tell anyone.'

'Never.' I glance at the doll's house, half-expecting to see a spectral glow behind the paned windows. 'Will you mind having this if you bring friends back here? You won't be embarrassed?'

'Nah. I'll say it's yours and you insist on keeping it in my room.'

'Well that's true.'

'Part of the truth. Not all.' He gives me a look. 'I learned that from you. And Granny. Probably not from Grandpa, though.'

I think of our father's secret request for the police to return your things. Luke and I wouldn't have this box at all, if it weren't for him. 'Your grandpa is a man of many wonders. I think your grandpa is a visionary.'

'He's the master puppeteer.'

I look at him in surprise. 'He is, yes. Though few people guess. Which is why he is so effective.'

Luke picks up a pink plastic compact. 'What's this?'

'Some kind of travel mirror? Face powder or blush, maybe?' All of your make-up had designer labels on the containers, but this doesn't. 'Shall we see?'

'Yep.' He finds the clasp and it opens like a clam shell. Inside is a circle of pills, faded in colour. Each pill is numbered, to keep track of the days of a lunar month. Numbers 1 through 21 are pale yellow. Numbers 22 through 28 are light blue. The two of us squint at them. 'Same question, again, Auntie Ella. What is this?'

I gulp so much beer the bottle depletes by two inches. 'They're birth control pills. Women use them so they can have sex without getting pregnant.'

He makes a face and thrusts the container at me as if we were playing hot potato. 'Do you think Mummy used them?'

'Probably, but she must have taken a break from them. Which is an extremely lucky thing for all of us. Because she wanted to have you.'

All at once, he flushes. His nose begins to run. He looks down.

My heart begins to beat faster. 'What's wrong, Luke?'

But he can't speak. I scoot close to him and he climbs onto my lap and I cradle him as if he were a baby, though he is bony and gangly. He sniffles onto my shoulder while I hold him tighter and rock back and forth, kissing the top of his head. His hair smells like the shower gel Ted uses – he must have persuaded Ted to get some for him.

Luke pulls away to catch my eye. His own are red. 'You won't stop looking at things again because I got upset?' He wipes his nose on a pyjama sleeve.

'No. I won't do that.'

He climbs off my lap and sits opposite me, with the box between us again. He swallows hard. 'Maybe she wanted me but my father didn't. What I'm most scared of is that I'm the reason he hurt her.' He shakes his head. 'You wouldn't admit it if you thought so, though, would you?'

What should I do? What would you do with this tearful boy, asking such direct questions? My instinct is to be as straight with him as I can be, but I am worried about misjudging it. Am I treating him too much like a grown-up, as our mother says? I think again about the possibility that you were in contact with Jason Thorne. There is no etiquette book for talking to a child about such horrors.

I say, 'I'll always try to be honest with you about what I think, Luke.'

'I wish I could remember her.'

'I wish you could, too.' I take a deep breath. 'When she's in a room, you can't look anywhere else. She's the most charismatic person ever born.'

'I know,' he says.

'Why don't you go wash your face, sweet boy? I think we need a break. We can do some more of this another time.'

'I don't want to stop. I won't be able to sleep. I've been waiting too long.'

I know my stomach is lined with nerves. They must be the source of the punch in the gut that makes me take a deep breath. 'Okay then.' I reach into the box for a plastic file pocket. Specially chosen by me, it is corn-flower blue and covered in ditsy flowers. When my fingertips brush it there is a small electric shock. I lift it out and hold it before me like a sacred document. I sit back on my heels and place it on my lap. 'I think this will help us.'

My hand floats to my belly. There is a piercing ache low down, on the left side. When I last touched this folder I was twenty and you were thirty and right next to me with Luke inside you.

'It's a bit girly, whatever it is,' Luke says.

'I didn't know you were a boy when I bought it. You were born a couple of days after that.' I manage a smile. 'Mummy always gave me the fun jobs.'

'So what's in it?'

'Her antenatal notes. She got me to photocopy them after her last midwife appointment. It took forever, standing at the machine in the library, feeding it coins.'

'Why did she make you do that?'

'For the memories. She knew the hospital would keep hold of her notes once she was admitted to the labour ward. She wanted duplicates.' I trail a finger around the neck of the beer bottle thoughtfully, then pick it up and take several sips. 'Give me a few minutes to check some-thing.'

He shuffles next to me so he can read too. Your hospital number is top and centre on the first page. For *Next of Kin* you put Mum and Dad's names – of course you wouldn't be lured into telling us who Luke's father is that easily.

I begin to flip through the notes. There is your blood group. AB+, the same as mine. We liked to smile at our rareness. Luke is AB+ too, so his father could be type A, type B, or type AB. Those three types account for about 55 per cent of the population. When it comes to narrowing things down, Luke's blood group doesn't help much.

'What does this mean?' He touches the word Chlamydia, which has always struck me as a pretty word for an ugly thing. It is the first word in a box that includes other ugly things. Gonorrhoea. Herpes. HIV.

'There are certain diseases that can hurt a baby when it's inside the womb or while it's being born. They test all pregnant women for these. This shows that Mummy didn't have any of them.'

He touches my hand. 'What exactly are we looking for?'

I hastily skim through the list of every appointment you attended, each with a date, the number of weeks gestation, the height of your fundus, your blood pressure, repeated affirmations that there was no protein in your urine.

'I want to confirm something that isn't here. It will make you feel better.'

I already know more than I wish to about intimate partner violence and homicide. But there is conflicting evidence as to whether a woman's risk increases during pregnancy and when she is newly post-partum.

'It's as I thought.' I look up at Luke. 'There is nothing here to suggest that the people who cared for Mummy while she was pregnant thought she was at risk of violence or abuse.'

'But they wouldn't write it here. They'd worry that the person who was hurting her would snoop in her notes and see they were onto him.'

'God you're smart.'

'You're always saying that.'

'Because you are. And you're right again. They wouldn't have stated any worries explicitly, but they would have found excuses to keep a closer eye on her. They didn't do that. See how the medical staff filled it in after each appointment? There is nothing extra anywhere. Routine pregnancy. Routine visits. No additional scans or specialist treatments or bloodwork.'

I leaf through the pages some more. It is so quick. Only in my line of vision for a few seconds. A single note popping out after several blank boxes in a row. I have already turned the page before it registers. I see the brief entry through a kind of replay.

Amniocentesis. The word. The date. The gestation you were at that time – sixteen weeks – which I remember from my second-year Genetics class is the absolute earliest they would do such a test. So you must have been desperately eager to have it, and to know the result as soon as possible.

Some women want to make sure the baby is okay before they tell anyone, but you went well beyond the customary three-month cut-off. You announced your pregnancy at twenty weeks. You had the amniocentesis one month before that. I am in no doubt that you needed to know the findings before deciding to share the news.

Twenty weeks pregnant and taken by surprise, you said, laughing and claiming that you'd only just realised it. I remember looking at you in suspicion – you are so aware of your menstrual cycles you stick a tampon in an hour before you even start bleeding. You didn't meet my eye. Did the entry in this fat stack of papers slip past your notice? It must have. Because clearly you didn't want us to know.

My degree in Human Biology taught me so much about experiences I will never have. The irony isn't lost on me that my favourite module was the one I took on Human Reproduction during my third year – I did most of the work for it while looking after Luke.

I know amniocentesis is not routine. I know it is a test women opt for, either in response to medical advice or for reasons of their own. So why on earth did you have it? You were only thirty years old. Hardly the advanced maternal age that would make them want to screen you for genetic abnormalities. Twenty weeks is the usual time for an amnio. You must have pushed hard to have yours early. Few people can say no to you. Not even medical professionals.

Luke touches my arm. 'What are you thinking?'

'I'm thinking that I hope Mummy's hospital notes reassure you.'

'A bit. But I wish they said who my father is.'

I realise I am biting my lip. I make myself stop. 'So do I.'

'I thought maybe you knew.'

'Oh, Luke. Do you think I could keep something like that from you?' I pick a piece of fluff from his pyjama top. 'I know your mummy so well. I think he must have been a good man, and she must have loved him very much, and he would never hurt her.'

'Maybe he died or went away before she could tell him about me.'

'That's possible. I've wondered about that.' I close the box. 'Go blow your nose?'

'Okay.' He pops up and goes next door to the bathroom.

It seems only a few seconds before he is back, but he pauses to grab the bar I installed in his door frame. He knocks out two pull-ups. Three months ago he couldn't do a single one. I am in serious danger of crying with pride and happiness, but I manage to restrain myself. 'You make those look easy,' I say.

He hangs for a few seconds before he drops down casually to emphasise that it was nothing. He sits back down and opens the box again, giving me your just *you try to stop me* look. He peers inside, excitement and surprise moving across his face. 'We missed something.' He reaches in and pulls out a book.

The quilted cloth cover is dusty and faded. The fabric is an Art Nouveau design. The black background is sprinkled with drooping cream snowdrops and little cream dots. The spine is worn, the fabric coming away from its top and bottom.

'Oh,' I say, and I shiver.

Luke puts it in my hands. 'What is it?'

'Mummy's old address book.' I turn it over, then over again. A precious thing. 'Grandpa gave her this for her sixteenth birthday. She loved it. She never used anything else.'

The headlines seem to play themselves out in my head in an endless loop. I argue with almost every one of them, but that doesn't make them stop.

Runaway Theory in Nurse Disappearance.

You didn't run away. None of your clothes were missing. Your passport was still in your desk. And you'd left your address book, which was a kind of bible to you. You would never have gone anywhere without it.

Luke presses a finger onto the cover, testing the sponginess of the quilting. He does this several times, seeming to enjoy its texture. 'Do you think you'll find a clue in here?'

There is another explosion. The sky is erupting with giant dandelions in emerald and fuchsia and violet and sapphire. 'Maybe.' Each flower pops, then vaporises. 'I think though that you and I need a break from all of this. Okay?'

He looks disappointed, but nods. 'Yeah. Okay. But you can't forget your promise. You have to try to find her.'

'I'm going to try.'

'Why are you smiling, Auntie Ella?'

'I think I may say that a lot.'

'That you're going to try?'

'Sometimes when Ted catches me at it, he says, "Yes, you're very trying."'

'He's messing with you.'

I tap a finger beneath his chin, forcing a laugh from him that he doesn't want to release and making him protest that it tickles. 'Well he's good at that,' I say.

'So are you with him,' my nephew says wisely.

Monday, 7 November

The Doll's House

On Luke's bedside table is a photograph of you and me. We are sitting on a patchwork quilt in our garden. You are eleven and I am one. In every childhood photograph of the two of us, you are looking at the camera, smiling your closed-mouth secret smile, and I am looking at you, a flower following my sun. Your hands rest serenely in your lap. My chubby fingers grip your arm. Your posture is straight, your dress immaculate, while I lean into you with all of my baby weight, chewing a pink plastic plate.

I barely take my eyes from the photo as I sit on Luke's bed and dial our mother to ask if she knew about your amniocentesis.

'I'm sure you're wrong, Ella,' she says. 'Miranda would have told me if she was having one. What makes you think she did?'

'It's in her hospital notes. I don't know if you remember? I made copies for her. They were in the box.' *As if you didn't know.*

'I need to go. Your father's back from the school with Luke.'

'So you don't have any thoughts about why she might have had that test?'

'None.' She is happy to end the call and let the question of your amniocentesis blow away. For an instant, I find her incuriosity surprising. Then I remember that our mother's need to be the world expert on you is strong. She does not like to linger over mere details that might put this expertise in doubt.

But our mother is not the only potential source of information about the test. I grab my laptop from Luke's floor and fire off an email to the hospital, asking for a copy of all reports and data relating to your amniocentesis. I explain that I am allowed access because you were declared dead three years ago and I am one of the executors of your estate. I attach the paperwork to prove it.

At last, I turn to the doll's house. The outside walls are a honey-coloured wash of Bath stone. The front swings open in two parts, like a cupboard, for access to the rooms. The doll's house belonged to our grandmother when she was a little girl.

I feel like a giant peeping into an ordinary human house, squinting between the glazing bars and below the festoon blinds of a twelve-paned window.

The children's bedrooms are on the second floor, separated by the central staircase. In one of them, a teenaged Miranda doll and a little girl Melanie doll are sleeping on the same feather mattress, holding hands. I told Luke that you and I used to do this. I would sneak out of my room and into yours and you would grumble but never send me away. He must have set it all up early on Sunday morning.

Your doll's house bedroom is papered in an offcut from your childhood bedroom. Flowers in different shapes and colours entwine with berries on a cream background. I'd always wanted wallpaper like yours. I'd always wanted everything of yours.

In the living room, sitting on a greeny-blue sofa patterned with small gilt medallions, are the doll versions of our parents. The nursery's perfect replica of a rosewood cot now has a tiny baby Luke sleeping beneath its lace coverlet. I sit cross-legged on the carpet and open up this house that Luke has never known in real life, with all of us happily together in it.

I slip the tips of my fingers beneath the feather mattress that the doll versions of me and you sleep upon. I slide my hand from the top of the bed towards the bottom, waiting for the small bump. There it is. A dried green pea. Luke must have put it there for me, like you used to. I'd told him how I used to pretend that my doll self was too sensitive to sleep with a pea under the bed.

My fingers reach towards the Miranda doll, hover above her, and finally drop to her shiny black hair. My fingers remember when I pulled that hair in real life and wouldn't let go. You had to walk around for a full minute with me gripping on in a temper. What made me release it was your whispered promise to cut off my hair while I slept. I was terrified for weeks afterwards that you would do this anyway.

'Talk to me, Miranda.' I startle myself that I have spoken

these words out loud, casting a magic spell I don't believe in. 'Tell me where you are.' The miniaturised Miranda's eyes are closed in sleep. 'Tell me what happened.' If I were to stand the doll up, her eyes would fly open, but I don't do this because those painted doll eyes will tell me nothing. 'I'm sorry I pulled your hair,' I say. 'I'm sorry I lied to you,' I say.

It isn't just the news headlines that still waylay me. Phrases from the advice leaflets I pored over ten years ago do this too.

When someone goes missing, do not give up.

Our parents still say that with no proof of death, there must be life. I mumble my dissent but do not elaborate on the fallacious reasoning here. How can they say this when you have been declared dead? When they themselves pushed for this declaration, against all of my protests?

This is the double think of those of us who love the missing. We cannot help but cling to hope when there is no body. Yet this hope is in tension with demands to access property and dissolve estates and meet the needs of those left behind.

My last five words are a whisper. 'I miss you every day.' They are the truest and most obvious words I can say.

I don't quite know why what happens next happens. One doll's house disaster follows the other, domino-like and near-comic, if it weren't so deadly serious.

My fingers have messed up the Miranda doll's hair. When I try to smooth it back I only make it worse. I pluck her out of the bed, a monster grasping a fairy, but my hand is shaking so I drop her. When I pick her up my fist knocks into the bed and that shoves out of place too, making the doll version of me fall out of it to roll along the embroidered rug before halting on the polished floor. I put the mini-Miranda back. I put the mini-me beside her.

My hand wraps around the bed, my thumb on top of the fringed counterpane, which is the colour of weak tea because that is what you dipped it in to help me make it look antique. My finger pads grip the bedframe's wooden underside and find a bump that shouldn't be here. I turn the bed over, letting the miniaturised versions of you and me tumble once more to the floor, along with the satin coverlet.

The paper is a familiar faded gold. It is folded into a tiny square and held in place by tape that was once clear but is now yellowing.

I continue to speak aloud, as if you were in the room. 'I said, "Talk to me." Are you actually doing it? Since when do you follow my commands?'

You will not know that Mum and Dad and I check the post every day. We catch each other at it. Half-expecting a letter from the person who snatched you away. Living in hope of a clue. Perhaps even a card from you. But I wasn't looking for anything here, in this private postal system of your invention.

The tape has been applied exactly, with your nurse's skill, along each of the four sides. Carefully, carefully, my heart thumping so loudly it seems to be between my ears, I peel away a corner. The paper has been here so long the tape has lost most of its stickiness, so it comes away cleanly.

I imagine your voice. *What took you so long, Melanie?*

There is a hint of teasing laughter. *I was counting on you, Melanie.*

There is hurt and disappointment, too. *Really? Suicide? Running away? Me? You know I'm full of tricks and schemes, but running away has never been one of them. And my self-preservation instincts are strong.*

I unfold the tiny square you made. The blue forget-me-nots are no longer vivid but I recognise the paper, which is from a small notepad I bought when you were pregnant. I am moved that you used it, my cheap little gift on a student budget – you had to work hard to pretend to like it, and you weren't entirely convincing. The stuff you normally favoured was thick and handmade and pressed from fabric pulp.

It is as if your ghost has led me here. The thought is poetic more than supernatural. I do not believe in ghosts. I do believe our mother though, who says again and again, to me, to Luke, to our father, 'Love never dies.'

That's convenient, you say.

But this is what I say. You didn't want to be invisible. You didn't want every trace to disappear. Even if you were mostly willing to let that happen at the behest of someone else, you still wanted something material to remain.

I study your dear handwriting, made by your dear hand. It is perfect and delicate and considered. It is strangely like my own. My breath is coming very, very fast as I read.

M + N + ??

That is all you wrote, surrounded by a heart.

What did I expect? A warning that if anything ever happened to you I should suspect that Professor Plum did it with a candlestick in the drawing room?

Don't be so lazy, you say. *Get going on decoding. You're good at that.*

The likelihood is that M is for Miranda. It could be for Melanie but I don't think so. The question marks narrow the time frame of when you wrote it. It had to have been while you were pregnant but before Luke was born. In any note or card during that period you always designated the baby's signature with two question marks. *Lots of love from Miranda and ??* That is what you would always write, so happily and proudly.

But if my deductions are right, then who was N? Luke's father? The man who took his mother? Even if N were either or both of these things, there are countless male names that start with that letter.

For you to put this little love token under the bed of our doll's house must have had the force of a charm for you. A blessing or a wish. Maybe both. Certainly some kind of power you were trying to invoke.

Such an act is in keeping with your superstitious tendencies. There were mugs that you shunned, perhaps because a person you disliked had drunk from one, or it was a souvenir from an unhappy trip. You would tip steaming liquid into the sink if someone – never me – mistakenly forgot and made you a cup of tea in a forbidden vessel. You would not take a single sip.

Should I share this message with our parents? With the police? My first impulse, born of the sisterly habits of hushed confidences between me and you, is that the note is mine and mine alone, left in a place you knew I would eventually find.

I remember what Dad said about the doll's house. *She knew how much it meant to you.*

I jump up before I change my mind. I snap several shots of the note with my camera phone, then slip it into zippered plastic before stowing it in the side compartment of my handbag. I will take it to Mum and Dad and discuss it with them on Friday after Luke goes to bed. They can pass it on to the police if they want to. Assuming they think the police will care.

M + N + ?? Even with the note out of my sight, I keep seeing it. *Who was N? Who was N? Who was N?* This is a question I know I will ask again.

Tuesday, 8 November

The Address Book

As soon as I see the sender's name in my inbox, I know that something is wrong. Justice Administrator. They have written only one sentence. *You will pay for what you have done.* I think simply, *Sadie*, and imagine Ted saying, *Never assume.*

Whatever Ted may say, Sadie's mad new hatred ought to make me sick with distress and shock. But it hardly registers against the hurt of being without you. It is nothing compared to the tightening in my belly at the prospect of losing Ted all over again. Some loves matter much more than others.

Sadie was always jealous of you, you say. *I never trusted her*, you say.

So what made her turn on me so violently, so suddenly? What could have made her think that I was sneaking around with her boyfriend, who I had only met once, at her behest and with her in the room, before that nightmare party?

I know that for an offence of Harassment to be

committed, there must be a 'course of conduct'. This means I need at least two messages like the one from Justice Administrator before the police can do anything. Even then, they may not judge that a reasonable person would feel a sufficiently pressing sense of alarm, distress or torment for them to act. Still, I find myself wishing for a second message. That I should have such a wish makes me want to scream.

I do three things. One, I take a screenshot. Two, I send the letter to my printer. Three, I forward it to the special address my email provider lists for documenting abuse, though I know they get countless messages a day and are highly unlikely to reply.

It occurs to me that this message could also come under the offence of Malicious Communications. That offence only requires one piece of evidence. For the hell of it, I do a fourth thing, and send the details to the police using their online Report a Crime or Incident form. I am not holding my breath for a response – they are hardly likely to see me as being in imminent danger – but at least I now have it on file with them.

I want to scream when I consider how much of my morning this email has wasted. I close it down, determined not to let it sour my day, and glance at Luke's karate-pose wall clock. I am working out how much time I have before I need to leave for my day of individual home safety assessments. I actually have a full hour to explore a little more of what Ted bitterly refers to as the Museum of Miranda.

I pick my way through an assortment of Luke's wiggle

worms and glow slime and safari animals, all from Ted. To avoid crushing the wing of a model aeroplane Luke is building, I bring the side of my boot down onto some joke putty. There is an obscene squelching noise that Ted would find gratifying and I cannot help but laugh.

The wardrobe has three doors, each with a drawer beneath it. Until late Saturday night, the middle drawer was empty. But after Luke fell asleep, the room lit only by the landing light outside, I filled it with the things from your box. On the floor is another of Ted's presents for Luke, a secret message kit.

Again I hear your teasing voice, in your most over-dramatically comical tone, *It's a sign*, and I am struck by the thought that, as I grow older, you grow with me. Even without you here, my closeness to you hasn't stopped and our relationship hasn't frozen. In some weird way I can't yet understand, it is continuing to develop and change. This constellation of ideas makes me smile as I open your drawer.

The address book is at the top. Dust puffs from the fabric when I pick it up. Once more, your funny, sweet voice rings so clearly in my head I can almost fool myself into thinking you are really here. *I always wanted to talk to you. You weren't ready to listen properly until now.*

I find a puddle of carpet that isn't strewn with Luke's toys and curl my legs beneath me in your best mermaid pose. But instead of combing my hair and studying my looking glass, I open the book and flick through the pages in order.

The first entry to make me pause is under H. All I can see is heavy black marker. You have filled in every square millimetre of the box with the person's name, address and number. I am not sure even a forensic X-ray machine could uncover what was once beneath this. Did the police attempt it?

You would have used a trick our mother taught us. You would have written arbitrary words over the original, many different times, building layer upon layer of letters. It's unlikely that the police could have deciphered this even before you added the extra protection of the thick marker.

You must have felt this person's importance the first time you wrote their name. So why did you go to so much trouble to cover it up? Did you change your mind about them, perhaps coming to loathe them and not wanting to be reminded of their existence? Perhaps you were hiding them from somebody else?

Did the man who took you scrawl over his entry himself? Almost immediately I dismiss the idea. The cross-out is too Miranda-like. It is your technique all the way. Plus, any serious criminal who knew of the book's existence and managed to get his hands on it would have burnt it or dissolved it in acid or buried it in a very deep and intolerably smelly dungheap. He would not have simply overwritten his details and risked the book falling into the hands of a forensics expert.

You, on the other hand, loved this present from Dad too much to dispose of it. That is why you obliterated the entry rather than the entire book.

I study the other names under H. Your usual habit was to write in pencil, so you could easily erase an entry if you eradicated the person from your life. What draws my attention to *N. Henrickson* is your rare use of ink – this was someone you knew you wanted to keep. The other odd thing is that you put only an initial rather than the full first name. You didn't do this in any of the earlier entries.

I flip quickly through the rest of the book. Ted's name rushes past me, and Sadie's too, despite your dislike of her, but that is no surprise and they are not what I am looking for. What I want to see is if you've used a first initial for any of the later entries. You haven't.

M + N + ??

Is this the same N? Is this entry some kind of code? A record you wanted to preserve but in a form that nobody else would notice, or even if they did, not be able to identify?

It makes me remember a trick you and Mum used to play. Whenever the two of you couldn't help but talk in front of me, but wanted to disguise who you were talking about, you would make up a silly name. The fake name would always sound ridiculous, have the same number of syllables as the real one, and start with the same letter as the actual person. They would live in a preposterous place extremely far away. And they would be a long-lost distant relative I had never heard of.

I am four years old and I am sitting high up in my booster seat in the rear of the car. Our mother is driving. You are fourteen and sitting next to her and I am extremely cross that I cannot sit in the front so I press my feet into the back of your seat.

'Stop kicking, Melanie,' you say.

'Sorry.' I kick again.

'Stop it now,' you say, 'or I'll make you stop.' You twist around to try to grab my ankle but I dodge out of your reach, laughing as you strain in your seatbelt. 'God you're a brat,' you say.

I squish a shoe into what I think is your bottom.

You look straight at me. Your eyes are moody blue. 'Fine. Have it your way, Brat. No baking this afternoon.'

I picture the ingredients for chocolate-chip cookies that you arranged on the kitchen table before we left, promising what we would do if I behaved well on the shopping expedition for the many things you and I still need before starting school.

I don't know that tomorrow I will meet Ted for the first time. I don't know that I have only sixteen years left of a life that has you in it.

'Please, Miranda,' I say. 'Please make cookies with me. I'm really sorry.'

'No way. Too late. You don't deserve baking.'

'I promise I'll be good.'

You ignore me. Mum's knuckles are going white from squeezing the wheel.

'Please change your mind,' I say. 'I've stopped. Please.'

'No.'

'Please. Please, please, please.'

'If you promise not to talk for the next five minutes. Not even a whisper. Five absolutely perfect minutes of peace from you. That's the price you have to pay. Open your mouth once and no cookies.'

I nod my head, worried that this is a trick and even to say a word of agreement with you will mean no baking. I silently count pairs of magpies and pretend not to see any of the single ones. All the while, I am lulled by your voice and Mum's. You are both laughing, so I tune in. You are talking about somebody who has awful hair.

'Who has awful hair?' I say.

'It hasn't been five minutes,' you say.

'Yes it has. I was watching the clock. It changed one second before I talked.'

'I should have made it ten minutes,' you say. 'Or better yet, forever.'

I hate it when you leave me out. 'Tell me,' I say. 'Who?'

'Cousin Petunia from Cucamonga.' I can hear that you are trying not to laugh. 'That's who we were talking about. Her hair is really, really bad.'

Mum is pressing her lips together.

'Do we really have a cousin called Petunia? And is there really a place called Cucamonga and does our cousin really have awful hair?'

'Yes, yes and yes,' you say. But I can tell there is at least one lie in those three yeses of yours.

'Your friend Pamela has awful hair like Cousin Petunia, Mummy. Is Pamela really Petunia?'

'Of course not.' Mum purses her lips, as if trying to stop her face from doing what it really wants to do by distracting it with weird moves.

You snort and then complain that the snort made you get water up your nose.

'Why does Pamela make her hair so frizzled? Is it supposed to be like that? Does she mean for it to be green? It's not pretty green like a sea princess's.'

You are choking with laughter. 'We need to change the game,' you say.

I laugh too, to show I'm in on the joke, even though I am not. I say, 'Can I meet Cousin Petunia? I would like to go to Cucamonga.'

Is *N. Henrickson* a version of that trick you and Mum used to try to play, to reveal your secrets right in front of me in the hope that I wouldn't understand them?

It occurs to me that Henrickson fits neatly with the surname of the psychiatrist I met at Sadie's nightmare party. Holderness and Henrickson. Both have ten letters and begin with 'H'. Is it a variation of that silly name trick, but switched from first name to last? I quickly decide it cannot be a secret reference to Adam Holderness, because the first name of this entry begins with N, not A.

I use my phone to snap a picture of the double-page spread of H entries, so I will have N. Henrickson's details to hand as well as an image of the blocked-out box.

I dial our mother, who puts me on speakerphone so that she can go on clattering saucepans and dishes in the kitchen.

'Are you alone in there?' I ask.

'Your nephew's about to leave for school. He's sitting at the table doing some last-minute homework – he got behind after last weekend. You should have got him back to us earlier on Sunday.'

'That's not true, Granny,' Luke says. 'She made sure I did all of it. This is from yesterday.'

I smile at his defence of me but say nothing. He goes on. 'Granny says you need to bring crisps on Friday, Auntie Ella.'

'I said no such thing.'

'Sorry, Mum,' I say. 'I already bought them – your grandson got to me first. Luke, I need Granny on her own for a minute.'

'I'm so hurt.' He pretends to weep.

'Go tell Grandpa it's time to leave or you'll be late,' she says.

I wait until I hear a door slam. 'Take me off speaker-phone, please, Mum.' I get right to the point. 'You know Miranda's address book?'

She thinks for a few seconds. 'The fabric-covered one?'

'The one Dad gave her. It was in the box with the stuff from the police.'

'Was it?'

'Yes.' The charade of absent-minded casualness suits our mother less than anyone I can imagine. 'Did the police ever ask you any questions about it?'

'Only to double-check a couple of the names. That was soon after she disappeared.'

'I've been looking at it. Did she ever mention someone called N. Henrickson?'

'She put just the initial?'

'Yes.'

'I remember the police asked about that. It's not some-one I knew of.'

'There's another weird entry under H. One that's completely crossed out so you can't see what she origi-nally wrote. Did the police mention that?'

'Not that I remember.'

'Can you think of anyone she might have wanted to obliterate any record of?'

'Lots of people. When Miranda is finished with you, she is finished. A switch flips and she turns off. That is how she is.'

You are like one of those terribly sweet and seemingly gentle little dinosaurs I once saw in a film. They are oh-so-pretty, making their squeaky cute noises to lure their victim close and hypnotise him with their charm and beauty before they tear him to pieces. Few people can survive getting close to you. I am not sure if I have.

'But not with you,' Mum says. 'Never with you.'

'Mostly not.'

'That's how you are, too. Someone can push and push, but then they push that final inch and you shut down forever on them.'

I think of Sadie, and know our mother is right, though Ted seems to have indefinite immunity. 'Maybe,' I say.

'Is that the best you can give me?'

'Definitely.'

Our mother misses nothing. 'Definitely the best you can give me, or definitely I'm right?'

'Definitely you're right, Mum.'

'Good. Now I need to go.' In her usual fashion, our mother clicks off on a last word that pleases her. She is more like you than she knows. And so am I.

Wednesday, 9 November

The Catalyst

The rational part of me is whispering that the police probably did this ten years ago. But the doubting part of me is louder. And the part of me that wants to stir things, to nudge anyone that may lead me to you, to find anything that isn't Jason Thorne, is practically screaming.

I think of what Mum said. *I worry about how far you will go.*

How far is that? Would I risk my life? Probably not. Have sex? Just possibly. Risk Luke? Never ever. It is unlikely I will ever be tested in any of these ways.

By the time I have driven the five minutes from my little house on the outskirts of Bath to the Georgian terraces in its centre, the night is about to close in. The arrangement of this street and its buildings makes me think of a gigantic bicycle wheel. The eighteenth-century houses are laid out as if on top of the rubber tyre, with parking places radiating from the outer parts of the spokes and a fountain at the hub.

Your old flat was on a side street that branches off

this road. It would take only a few minutes to walk to it from here. Was the proximity deliberate? You lived in it for two and a half years before you vanished.

I loop around the fountain, hoping a parking space will become vacant. The fountain is overflowing with bubbles. Students are always pouring liquid soap into it. They must have used something extra-powerful this time, because the bubbles are churning into a dense white foam. The breeze detaches small balls of the foam from the main body, then floats them through the air. I seem to be inside a snow globe.

I get lucky. Somebody jumps into a car and drives away. The space is right in front of the address you wrote down for N. Henrickson. As I walk towards the building, a cloud of jackdaws wheel and shriek slowly beneath a creeping grey sky. So many of them, teeming above the rooftops.

Four marble steps lead up to an outside landing and the green double doors that mark the entrance. There is a gold plaque to the right of the doors. *Henrietta Mansions*. To the left of the doors is a metal square with a camera, intercom, and numbered metal buttons for the flats. The occupants are clearly security savvy, because there are no names. I push the button for 'Flat 7' and wait. Nothing happens. I press it again, wondering if the occupant of Flat 7 is watching me. Still nothing.

I lean against the wall, my head against the gold plaque. A foam ball drops from the air and rolls around in front of my feet. I take out my phone. I dial the number listed by N. Henrickson's name and get through to an automated recording from a mobile network provider I have never heard of. The computerised voice invites me to leave a message.

I think of a scientific word I have always loved. Catalyst. That is what I hope to be. The spark to make things happen. But can I really remain unchanged?

I leave my message, an uncharacteristic one in which I reveal concrete information about myself. 'Hello. My name is Ella Brooke. My sister is Miranda Brooke. I think Miranda knows you. Can you please ring me? Hopefully my number will be on your phone, but just in case . . . '

I always turn my phone off at night. As I press end on the call I notice that I forgot to switch the sound back on this morning. When I look in the log of missed calls, I see that the most recent one is from Mum, from ten minutes ago, along with a message commanding me not to be late on Friday. There is a missed call and voicemail from Ted, too, left half an hour ago, asking me to phone him, and this makes my heart race as if I were a teenaged girl whose big crush has unexpectedly rung.

Four missed calls came in the middle of the night, all from a withheld number. The rational explanation is that these are from someone trying to sell me something. But my instinct tells me that this is personal. I think again of Sadie and the muted voice from five days ago. For now, though, I have more important things to worry about than Sadie.

I punch the bell for Flat 7 again. I use my phone to do some quick internet searches while I wait. First I try the unfamiliar mobile network provider, but there are no hits. Is it defunct? Or deliberately hidden? I try another search engine, but still nothing. I plug in the word Henrickson. Though several possibilities come up, none of them have first names beginning with N and they are not even based in the UK.

The sky is darkening rapidly. I do yet another search, this time for the marketing history of Flat 7. I don't expect to find anything, but I quickly learn that it hasn't changed hands for twenty-one years, when it was bought by a company called E.B. Property Services. I search for that too, but the results are more dead ends. Was the company dissolved? Why is there no trace of it, beyond the initial purchase?

There is an email address below N. Henrickson's number in the address book, with a provider I have never heard of. I search for the provider on the internet, only to discover it charges a high fee because it uses end-to-end encryption so that no third party can monitor it. Its servers are in Switzerland, so no government can shut it down or demand the data be handed over.

What kind of person chooses an email provider like this, and how did you know them? The answer is all too obvious – a person who is expert at staying invisible, and wanted you that way too, at least in relation to him. And you must have known this and not minded. It is in keeping with your seemingly empty laptop drive.

I type an email along the same lines as the telephone message and expect it to bounce back, but when I check my inbox there is nothing there to tell me it failed to deliver.

As I consider what else I might do, a woman approaches the building, probably in her late eighties. She is wearing shell-pink trousers, a shell-pink blouse and a shell-pink tailored jacket, all in the same fabric and visible beneath her lavender tweed coat. She is pulling a navy-blue shopping bag on wheels. Practically every old lady I have ever seen tugs one of these bags, but our mother swears I must kill her before allowing her to own one. I hurry down to ask this woman if I can carry it up the steps for her.

When she looks at me she startles and blinks several times, as if to clear her vision. 'I'm afraid the bag is heavy.' Her skin is blanched but her voice is calm.

I lift it and see she is right. When we are both standing before the building's entrance, she takes a key card from a side pocket of the bag and waves it over an electronic pad. A light flashes green and the right-hand door pops open with a click.

'Would you like me to take your bag up to your flat for you?' I am not being a good Samaritan. I want to get into the building. But the personal safety expert part of me hopes she is smart enough to refuse.

She hesitates. For an instant, I think she really is going to invite me in. Instead she says, 'I am afraid we need to be careful not to let even charming strangers into the building. Resident Association rules.'

'That's wise.' I push the door open wider and look inside as I hold it for her.

There is an elegant carpeted foyer with a chandelier, several mock-eighteenth-century chairs, and a dark wood coffee table stacked with the sort of magazines read by people who own both town flats and country houses. The building you lived in was similarly grand.

The smell of furniture polish wafts towards me. 'Can I ask you a quick question or two?' I say.

She moves past me and stands in the doorway, blocking any further view of the interior but smiling permission.

'Have you lived here a long time?'

She is studying me as intently as I am studying her building. 'Twenty-one years. Since my husband died.'

She is lonely, this woman. She is steely and careful, but her need for talk and companionship is working against this. How hard will it be to get her to let me in?

I decide to be blunt, imagining Ted laughing at my doing so crudely what he does so smoothly. 'I'm trying to find Mr Henrickson in Flat 7. Do you know him?'

There is a flash of surprise, then calculation, that she tries to mask. 'I need to respect my neighbours' privacy.'

'I only want to know if you've seen him here lately.'

She waves a hand and shakes her head, a helpless non-committal gesture.

I write my name and number on a scrap of paper and hand it to her. 'If he comes back, will you call me? I can ring the bell to his flat and he can choose whether or not to let me in. Surely that would be okay?'

'No. It would not.' She presses the paper back into my palm.

I decide to tell her what I don't readily tell. 'My sister went missing ten years ago. This is her.' I write your name below my own, on the paper scrap, and underline it with my finger.

'I'm very sorry.'

I take out a framed photograph of you that the press never got hold of. We are sitting on our parents' living room sofa a few months before you got pregnant with

Luke. We are both holding glasses and cracking up, clinging to each other and in real danger of spilling red wine. Our faces are creased in the hysterical, unstoppable laugh that was almost always at our mother's expense, which she says she never minded from the two of us. She says she misses our conspiracies against her.

The woman looks carefully at me, then the photograph. 'She's beautiful. How very like you she is.'

I study the photograph along with her, wondering what secret plans were in your head, and already in play, even then.

She touches my arm. 'Tissue?'

'Thank you.' I take the tissue and blow my nose with an extremely unpretty noise. 'We're approaching the anniversary of her disappearance. It's always a difficult time for my family.' The near-welling with tears is not fake, but I know I could control it if I chose to. I know I am letting it happen to manipulate this woman.

And it works. 'Come inside for a few minutes.' I follow her into the foyer, sit beside her on an ivory sofa with my boots resting on the thick gold rug arranged before it. She pats my knee. 'Better?'

'Yes. You didn't tell me your name,' I say.

'I'm Mrs Buenrostro.'

'That's lovely.'

'My husband was Spanish. It means good face. Handsome face.' She smiles. 'It suited him.'

'Do you have any children?'

She spends too long considering the answer to a question that ought to be straightforward.

'No.' She gathers herself as if that word has hurt her and I wonder at the untold story here. A long period of trying for a child but never managing it? A child who died? There is something, but I do not dare press it. At last, she takes a breath. 'I don't know much about the man in Flat 7.' She fidgets with her hair, a long grey plait coiled and pinned low, just above her neck.

'Has the flat been occupied by anyone else since you've lived here?'

'No.'

'Can you describe Mr Henrickson?'

'I would say tall, dark hair. You'd probably call him handsome.' She sounds proud when she says this. She speaks of this man as if she cannot help herself, as if she knows she should not but is impelled to partake of a guilty pleasure.

'Does he ever have visitors?'

She weighs up whether to say more, but then does, again in the manner of someone who is visibly saying something she shouldn't, but cannot stop herself. 'I once saw a woman and a baby go in.'

When did this encounter turn round, so that she is the one probing for information, rather than me? When did she start watching my reactions as carefully as I have been watching hers? Has it been from the start?

'How long ago?' My voice is sharper than I mean it to be.

She shakes her head, as if perplexed.

'Could it have been ten years ago?'

'I can't be sure.' Once more she is stroking that grey coil. 'You must understand, these flats are owned by the very rich. Many of them are investment properties. People are happy to leave them empty for long periods.'

'Can you remember if the baby was a boy or a girl?'

'It was swaddled. Nothing memorably pink or blue. I approve of that. I don't hold with all that gendering by colour. Don't you agree?'

I imagine Luke's horror if I were to buy him something pink. But I say, 'I do.'

'The woman rushed past me. I do remember that, because I'd hoped to look at the baby but she clearly didn't want me to. I like babies. Do you like babies?'

'Very much.'

'Do you have one?'

'I have a nephew. My sister's son.'

'Do you have a photo of him?'

The question makes the top of my scalp tingle. 'Not with me.' My phone is filled with pictures of Luke, but I am not about to show one of them to this stranger. Am I right in my instinct that her interest in Luke goes beyond the simply polite? I say, 'Can you remember anything else about the baby? How old it was, maybe?'

'It was very small. No more than a few weeks.'

'What about the time of year? The month or season?'

'Late summer. Maybe early autumn? I remember worrying that the baby might be too hot for the weather. It was so wrapped up.'

'And the woman? Can you remember what she looked like?'

'It was barely a glimpse. I remember though that she had long dark hair, your sort of colour, but a bit longer.' She places a hand on top of mine. 'You've gone pale.'

'Can you remember what she was wearing?'

'Just that it was pretty. Like her. Something floaty, I think. Let me see your sister's photograph again.'

I hold it out. Unlike Luke's image, yours is all over the internet. 'Are you thinking that she was the woman you saw go into Flat 7?'

She peers at it, more carefully this time. She turns it to a different angle and looks some more. 'Possibly.'

I tuck the picture safely back into my bag and again offer her the paper scrap. Your name flashes at me, below my own. 'Please ring me if the man in Flat 7 comes back. Or the woman. They might help me find my sister.'

'Shouldn't the police be doing that?'

I hesitate before what I say next. 'Did they ever talk to you?'

'No.'

'Were you aware of them talking to anyone here about Mr Henrickson? Or maybe talking to him?'

'Not that I know of. But that doesn't mean they didn't. Don't you have – what is it they're called – a family liaison officer? Don't you have one of those to update you on what they've done, what they're doing?'

'The police never got anywhere and we were never assigned a family liaison officer. Not everyone is. But did you not hear of the case?'

Her mouth dips before she speaks, as if she is getting ready to tell a lie. 'No. I'm sorry.' I am still holding out the paper scrap. She takes it from me. 'I will phone you if anybody returns to Flat 7.'

'Thank you.' I have another thought. 'Is there CCTV in the building?'

'I'm afraid there isn't.'

'What about when someone rings your doorbell? I know you get a live visual of the outside landing so you can see who it is. I don't suppose those images are recorded?'

'Again no. The majority of residents value privacy over security.'

'I see.' I stand up. 'You have been so kind, Mrs Buenrostro, and generous with your time. I must leave you in peace.'

She watches me make my way to the door. I can see her through its slit of stained glass. She checks that the wood swings shut and locks before she turns away.

Thursday, 10 November

The Woman in the Chair

The first person at my morning risk assessment clinic is sitting in a cracked vinyl chair and sobbing so hard she can barely speak. Her eye is red and swollen – it will be purple in a day or two – with another large bruise below it. There is an open cut where the skin above her cheekbone split like ripe fruit upon impact.

I am holding her baby, who is screaming as I walk up and down the room to try to soothe him while his mother gets a chance to calm down. This woman makes me puzzle even harder over the things that your medical notes could not tell me. Did I miss the physical signs that someone was hurting you?

You were always lifting your dress or top to show me the progress of your bump, pressing my hand against your tummy to feel him kick, pulling my ear to your belly in the hope that I would hear his heart. You would make me inspect every inch of your body and swear under oath that you were not gaining weight anywhere besides your bump. I know I was right to lie when I said

again and again that you weren't. Your skin was unblem-
ished but for the small blossom of stretch marks that
appeared at the top of your left thigh at thirty-seven
weeks, making you swear against cruel fate.

I need to shake you away and concentrate on the
screaming baby. I bounce him gently on my shoulder,
managing at the same time to grab my unopened bottle
of water and set it down near his mother. I scoot the
box of tissues closer to her too. The movement makes
her visibly startle.

On the floor is the woman's massive tote bag. When
I cross the room to retrieve my first aid kit, my shoe
bumps the bag, making the blue plastic crackle. Baby
clothes and nappies spill onto the grubby carpet, which
is ugly beige to match the ugly chairs and ugly walls of
this furnished office whose only virtue is the cheap rent
and the fact that they are willing to let me have it for
just one day a week.

At last, the baby is quiet. His mother is finally quiet
too. I hand him to her and when she flinches I see that
her wrist is swollen.

Eye, cheek, wrist – and these are the injuries I can see.
I want to photograph them. If I can't get her to go to the
police herself, at least I will be able to provide them with
the medical evidence for an assault investigation and
potential Actual Bodily Harm charge.

She consents to the photographs in a flat voice,
adjusting her body as I snap away with my camera phone,
wincing in a way that makes me suspect she has been
kicked or punched in the ribs. Her shallow breaths go
with this, so I ask if she can concentrate on trying to

breathe more evenly. The two of us inhale and exhale together for a few minutes, until she is calmer. Afterwards, she lets me clean the cut on her cheek with saline and apply wound glue to hold it together and protect it from infection.

'You're good at that,' the woman says.

'My sister was a nurse.'

Was. As ever, I hear our mother's quiet fury.

I activate an ice pack with a snap, wrap it in a cloth, and ask the woman to hold it against her eye, which she does with a zombie's indifference.

Were you in this kind of trouble? Was I too young then to see, not yet doing the work that your vanishing turned me to? Wouldn't Mum and Dad have noticed? As an orthopaedic nurse, you knew too much about the signs of abuse. You had seen too many bones broken accidentally-on-purpose.

I decide to confide something personal, in the hope she will be more comfortable with me. And because talking about you is something I like to do. 'Our father had prostate cancer,' I say. 'That's why my sister wanted to be a nurse.'

This is your official story of why you came to do what you did, and one that I have always, at least partly, been puzzled by. For the first time, I envision other motives for your choice of a life as Florence Nightingale. Not just because you wanted to help people like Dad. But because it was part of your disguise. Part of what made people trust you. Made them let you in.

More than anything, it brought you into contact with all kinds of different men. Rich doctors you could assist in their heroic orthopaedic efforts. Male patients with manly sports injuries for whom you could perform your beautiful angel routine. You knew what you were doing when you chose a job in the private sector – where there is plenty of money and the work is not quite so punishing.

'Is she still a nurse?' The woman is more alert than I first thought.

'Not any more, no.' This is where any talk of you must stop. 'Do you feel able to tell me what happened?' My voice is very soft.

As I expect, she is at last fleeing from domestic abuse – a story I have heard more times than I would wish. This is why I have a lone worker safety device built into my wristwatch, with GPS tracking and an SOS button wired straight to the provider's emergency centre. I always activate and wear it when I'm working. If her husband follows her here, there are measures I can take to protect us both.

With her consent, I begin making phone calls and arrangements. 'There are so many of us out here, wanting to help you. Wanting to make sure you don't slip through the net. There are so many places you can turn. You only have to ask.'

'I said no police.'

'The police are starting to make domestic violence a priority. They have had a lot of criticism, so they are really trying to respond to that.' Ted would faint if he heard me saying this.

'He'll take my baby away if I leave him. He says I'm not a fit mother. The police will see that. They'll see I'm mentally unstable and depressed – I've had pills before. They'll see I can't support a child by myself.'

'Depression can be situational.' My voice is so calm I am amazed to hear it, as if it belongs to somebody else. 'Depression doesn't make you an unfit parent.' I need to be neutral, but I worry that you will make me mess this up badly. Because neutral is the last thing I am. 'Have you considered that if the police have his violence on record, then it will help your legal position?'

'They already have a voicemail. I went to my mum's last year and he said he knew where I was and he was going to do me in. But I withdrew my statement that it was his voice and number on the recording. I think the police were angry, because it meant they couldn't prosecute him. And because I went back to him.'

'Why?'

'I still loved him. He was drunk when he left that voicemail. He didn't mean it.' She veers to another thought. 'The house is in his name. He said if I leave again he'll take the house and take the baby.'

'You have rights too. There are some excellent helplines where you can get free legal advice. I've written a couple of them down for you.' I put my hand on top of hers and squeeze, then wrap her fingers round the paper. 'I'll book a taxi for you. I'll arrange for the driver to take you to the doctor's. You need more medical attention than I can give. When you're finished there, the taxi will get you to the shelter.'

She looks at the baby, asleep at last across her lap. Tears roll down her cheeks and plop onto his tummy. When the paper slips from her hand I pick it up and reach over and drop it into her big crinkly bag. She watches me do this. I hope this is a symptom of canny self-preservation, the hidden resilience of the secret street fighter in all of us. She shifts her eyes to her feet. 'You must think I'm pathetic.'

'What I think is that you are amazingly brave and strong to come here. You were clever to get out as soon as he left for work this morning, in the biggest window you had. Your son is lucky to have a mother who loves him so much.'

She shakes her head in denial that this could be true. 'I don't have any money for the taxi. He doesn't let me have money of my own.'

'The charity will pay for that. I'll give the driver cash in advance.'

I type a text to order the taxi. She grabs my hand just after I hit Send.

'No,' she says. 'Cancel it.'

'Why?'

'I can't. I can't do this to him. It's not all his fault.'

'Sitting where I am, it's difficult to see that.'

'But I provoke him.'

I can't stop pushing her. 'What was different about what he did to you this morning? There must have been something to make you take action.'

There is a clicking noise, deep in her throat. 'It was in front of the baby. That's never happened before.'

My face is hot. 'You came to me for my assessment of your risk. My assessment is that you are at considerable risk and you need to get safe. Now. Your baby is at risk too.'

'He has so much on his mind, trying to make a living for us. I make too many demands.'

My heart is beating faster.

'What about the injury to your wrist? And your eye and your cheek? There is no possible way to justify those. If he was happy to leave visible evidence of violence on your face I think it's highly likely there are bruises beneath your clothes. He punched you in the upper body, too, didn't he? Am I right?'

'He might kill himself if he comes home and finds us gone. I can't leave.'

The heat on my skin and the speed of my heart are signs that I should keep quiet. Signs that you have finally blown away my ability to do the job you carved for me. But I cannot stop myself. I am looking at her baby and thinking of your son.

Thinking of what it means for a baby to lose his mother. Remembering what it means in the flesh.

Walking up and down with Luke. Bouncing him. Singing to him. Trying to get him to drink from the new bottle he hated. Buying up teats in every size and shape and material ever made. Taking him into bed with me. Hours and hours of being useless as he screamed all night and every night after you were gone. Driving around at three a.m. to try to lull him to sleep. So tired myself I wasn't safe behind the wheel.

A friend of Ted's pulled me over for careless driving during one of those aimless journeys. Who was crying louder, then? Me or Luke?

'I promise if you don't write that ticket I will go straight home and never do this again. I swear it. I'll take an advanced driving course, too.' How did I manage to get those words out? How did he even understand me through the sobs?

He didn't write the ticket. He followed me back to our parents' house and watched me carry your baby inside. All Luke wanted was your smell, your milk, your voice. Your way of holding him. The two of us fell into an exhausted sleep, Luke on my chest, both of us hot and flushed and sticky, our cheeks stained with tears.

Ted's policeman friend reported it all to him, and Ted was there early the next morning to check on us. What room could there have been for Ted in all of that? Always understanding. Always agreeing that Luke was what mattered most.

'You're doing what she would want. You're doing everything you can.' That is what Ted said, again and again. At least at first. Before the fights started. Over you. Always over you. Still over you. No wonder he is moving on to Ruby. My message to him hasn't changed. You and Luke are first, last and always.

Even as the words shoot out at this woman I know they are the wrong ones and I shouldn't say them. 'That's fine. You go home. Next time I come across your name it will be because you've been murdered or you've gone missing.'

Her mouth drops open into a perfect O, then shuts again like a fish's.

I am about to say I'm sorry. I am about to say I shouldn't have said what I did.

But she speaks first. 'You're right,' she says. 'I actually hate him. Hate him.'

So I remain silent and decide to forgive myself for saying the wrong things and not being perfect. You used to tell me that it was okay not to be perfect. You used to say that perfection was terrible. You used to say that you were not perfect and I must always forgive you for it.

My phone buzzes with a text announcing the arrival of the taxi. I look out of the grimy window and see the driver next to his car.

When the woman and I stand up I take in the sack-like floral dress she is wearing. There are holes in the thin fabric and it is faded from being laundered too many times. She is shivering with cold – she doesn't have a coat. I drape my own over her back, the two of us juggling the baby as I help her to fit each arm into a sleeve. I heave up her huge bag, which contains only baby things. 'They'll provide you with what you need at the shelter,' I say before I open the door and lead her into the corridor. She is limping. He must have done something to her leg or hip, too.

Most of the people who come to my risk assessment clinic are women. But this morning there is a familiar-looking man sitting outside the office, on one of the stained, cloth-covered chairs. He has the discretion to look intently at his telephone screen when the battered woman passes him.

I guide her into the grey rain and the grey air beneath the grey sky and settle her in the back of the grey taxi with her son in her arms. She holds out a hand. For a split second I imagine that her hand is grey too. I squeeze the hand, which is not grey after all, but is reddened and coarse and flaky with dry skin. I lean into the taxi and put my arms around her, then kiss the top of the baby's head, a mix of silk and cradle cap.

I press banknotes into the driver's hand – he and I have been through this routine many times before – and let him shut her in. I stand on the pavement, not caring that I am getting soaked as I watch the woman bend her face over her baby. I do not move until the car turns the corner and glides out of my sight.

The Man in the Corridor

When I re-enter the building, the man in the corridor stands and says hello, greeting me by name and putting out his hand.

Other than his hair, there is nothing grey about Adam Holderness. His jumper is black and his jeans are black. His eyes are black too. His skin is pale, like mine, but there is a shadow of dark stubble wanting to break through.

You used to call me Snow White. Though I could have said the same of you. *As white as snow, and as red as blood, and her hair was as black as ebony.*

This man could be Snow White's male counterpart. Though it strikes me that gentleman vampire is a better description. While Ted is sturdy and muscled from weightlifting in the police gym and weekend rugby whenever he can, Adam Holderness is an inch taller and a stone lighter but looks equally strong beneath his expensive clothes. I wonder if there will ever be a man I don't compare to Ted.

I am struck again by the thought that Adam Holderness really is the kind of man you liked. I feel a clutch low in my stomach and I cannot decide if it is excitement or fear. Perhaps it is both.

I am still holding the main door open. 'It's nice to see you again,' I say. I manage to stick out an awkward hand to shake his briefly. The rain is growing so heavy it is slanting in and hitting me. 'I'm running my walk-in clinic this morning.' I look outside, as if to suggest that that is where he should go.

But he doesn't. 'That's why I'm here.'

I remind myself that anybody can be a victim, or love somebody who has been one, or feel that they are at risk. So I say, as carefully as I can, 'Do you need my help?'

'Not personally. I'm here for professional reasons. Can I come into your office to talk to you?' He moves his head slightly, taking in the empty corridor. 'If there were anyone else here, I'd let them go first. I won't take much of your time.' It is a bedside manner. Friendly courtesy but with confident firmness behind it. 'You're getting wet, Ella.' He sounds sincerely concerned. More of that extremely practised courtesy.

I let the main door fall closed and motion him to follow me into the office, gesturing for him to take the chair so recently vacated by the mother and her baby.

He says, 'I'd like to support the work you're doing.'

'How did you know I'd be here this morning, Mr Holderness?' Again I fail in my attempt to impose formality with his title and surname. I end up sounding like a woman whispering to her lover in bed, playing at a distance that is patently not there.

'You talked about the charity.' He says this mildly and I begin to see that he is imperturbable. I must look puzzled, because he adds, 'At Brian's party.'

'Oh yes – I'd forgotten.'

'I rang the number on the website a couple of times but it kept going to voicemail.'

I don't explain that we almost never answer that number. Our mother picks up the messages as soon as she can, though she occasionally diverts them to my phone.

He goes on. 'I thought coming here would be easier than leaving a message.'

'Isn't coming here a lot more trouble than speaking for a few seconds into a recording?'

'I wanted to see you.' He pauses. 'Sadie and Brian told me about your sister.'

He says this with such neutrality I cannot infer what tone Sadie used to speak about me, and what defamation of my character she almost certainly unleashed. She has moved so irrevocably from friend to enemy. Our mother was right – when I am done I am done. Just like you.

'As soon as they mentioned your sister's case, I realised I'd heard of it.'

'Most people have.' I had guessed that Sadie and Brian told him, but I still have to adjust to knowing that he knows, something that gets easier but never feels normal. I sit back and cross my legs. 'When did you last talk to Sadie?'

'I dropped by on Sunday to see Brian.' He is squinting at me. A slight squint, but a squint nonetheless, as if he thinks he will be able to see inside my head and into my brain if he only looks hard enough. 'He wasn't there but Sadie was.'

'Oh,' I say.

'You don't know, do you?'

I lift my shoulders, puzzled.

'He'd put her things outside and changed the locks. He tried to end it gently, but it seems that gentle doesn't work with Sadie. He thinks she's crazy – his word, not mine – and she managed to hide it until she moved in with him. She was packing her car when I turned up.'

I realise that I now have even more reason to look out for a Sadie hurricane blowing my way.

'Is that why you came here? To warn me about her?' I think of the email from 'Justice Administrator'. It seems likely that Brian's rejection has pushed her over the edge.

'Her rage is . . . How to put it politely? Disturbing. You seem to be the target.'

'Did she mention where she was going?'

'To her mother's, she said.'

'Then that's a neighbourhood I will avoid.'

'I was concerned. But I can see that you have enough expertise to manage someone like Sadie.' He thinks for a few seconds. 'Why do you do what you do?'

Your disappearance changed everything. Our mother and Ted are right to say it changed me. But I give Adam Holderness the public script. The one he will already have read on the website. 'There are lots of support services in London. But there's nothing hands-on in smaller cities like Bath for people who need help. Not unless they can pay huge sums of money for advice and protection.'

'It says on the website that you run a support group for families of victims. I'd like to come along to help.' He pulls out his wallet and extracts a laminated card, a photo ID with his name and title. 'In case you're worried that I'm not who I say I am.'

It is an expressionless photograph, mouth straight, eyes serious, hair shorter and even more extremely military than it is now. I know from the internet searches I did after Sadie's party that he is ex-army. I found a photo online, taken fifteen years ago, during his final few months as a medical officer in Iraq. It is certainly him, but different. His pale, pale skin is actually tanned. And his hair is still pure black.

Did something happen, some stress event, to change it overnight? I know he left the army to become a civilian doctor after his minimum four-year commitment. I know he worked in the psychiatric unit of the same private hospital you worked at, though you were over in Orthopaedics.

I decide I have nothing to lose by asking blunt questions. 'Did you know my sister?' I want to catch him off guard, though my voice is casual.

But he is as smooth as ever. 'I can see you have good reason to be wary of everyone you meet.' He looks right into my eyes. 'Even when you actually like them.'

'True,' I say, not making it clear which of the two points I am ratifying.

'Do you suspect every man you meet of your sister's disappearance?'

'Pretty much.'

'If I had anything to do with that, do you think I'd come here and make myself known to you?'

'That's the sort of thing people like that do. You should know that in your line of work.'

'Only in films and novels. Not in real life.'

I remember Ted saying something like that to me about Thorne. 'I think you and my sister worked at the same hospital.'

'Not in the same area of medicine.' He speaks as if he is disappointed that he cannot provide me with stronger evidence of a connection between the two of you. 'There are scores of people who work in the same place but don't know each other.'

'I wondered if there was anywhere else she could have run into you?'

'Not unless she spent time in Iraqi field hospitals.'

I consider the types of things this man would have learned in officer training. Leadership. Weapons handling. Knots. Survival. And much more than this in conflict zones. All transferable skills. He would know how to hide, how to spy, how not to leave traces. Probably even how to make someone vanish.

'Where do you live?' I am thinking of the countryside that surrounds the winding lane where you made your last known journey.

My questions and changes of tack don't ruffle him. 'Near Brian,' he says. 'A lot of doctors own houses in those villages.' Is he over-explaining? He says, 'I think I saw you talking to Jonathan Blossom, didn't I?'

'Yes,' I say.

'John lives around there too. So does Brian's brother.' There is a glint in his eye with this last one. 'You'd be welcome to visit me.'

The photograph of Ted and Ruby was emailed via the charity's contact page, and Adam has just told me that he used the charity website to find me. 'Can you remember what you were doing on Friday of last week?'

He gives me a confused but tolerant smile. 'Only because I was in the hospital so much I barely saw any natural light. Why do you ask?'

If this is the truth, he could not have taken that picture. I tell a calculated fib. 'I thought perhaps I glimpsed you in a café that day.'

'That wouldn't have been possible,' he says, 'but I'd have liked bumping into you.' There is no tell. There is no sign. There is nothing to signal that he is lying.

I consider Ted's contempt for psychiatrists. He thinks they thwart justice when they advise judges that murderers and predators are not fit to stand trial. He is disgusted by their hospitals for criminals, which he regards as hotels. Ted would not love Adam Holderness.

I realise I am still holding his identification card. I hand it back to him, then try to say the passionate words I am about to utter in the most dispassionate tone I can. 'Given the fact that you spend most of your time trying to help the men who hurt their loved ones, why would my support group want anything to do with you?'

'Insight.'

'Are you willing to give me any insight into Jason Thorne?'

His voice is very gentle when he says, 'I think you know I can't discuss patients with you. At least let me help where I can. Let me help with your group.'

'Perhaps.'

'If a single one of them reaches a new level of under-standing, isn't that worth it? What you do and what I do are on a continuum. We're closer than you allow. I already made an online donation.' He looks almost tired after he finishes this speech, and a little embarrassed that he isn't above telling me he has given money. But it is the kind of abashed demeanour that extremely well-bred people deploy when they have been complimented for an exceptional achievement.

It occurs to me that he is used to people trying to persuade him. Trying to convince him they are not dangerous. Trying to explain that their actions were justifiable. Trying to persuade him not to medicate them, not to take away their privileges. Trying above all to argue that he should let them out. Perhaps it is even the reverse sometimes, and they try to persuade him to keep them in, seeing the locked ward as preferable to a real prison.

Whatever the case, it is not supposed to be this way round, with him trying to sell himself. This powerful man who works hard to appear gentle and kind but also strong and reasonable. He is in charge of some of the most dangerous human beings alive. Thorne is only one of many.

There is the creak of the outer door to the building opening and shutting, then a sigh and a rustle in the corridor. He stands. 'Full disclosure. If you're wondering whether I came here because I'm interested in you or in your charity, the answer is both.'

My face is warm. It has been ten years, I tell myself. Ten years since Ted and I were together. Ten years since you were taken. Ten years since I have been to bed with anybody, which is a mortifying thing to admit even if it is just to myself. I am thirty years old and I have only ever slept with my childhood sweetheart. And now Ted is moving on and will probably cut me off and I am not sure I can endure it again. It isn't criminal to be pleased that this handsome, intelligent man likes me. Is it?

The kind of man you liked likes me. And I like him too. This silent admission pinches my chest.

'Incidentally,' he says, 'there's something on your shoulder.'

I look down at a splodge of what appears to be congealed cream. I know from my experience with Luke that it is baby sick. He passes me the box of tissues and I do my best to wipe it off. Then I cross the room to the door and open it wide. Neither of us says another word.

I wait until he exits the building, then turn to the two people who arrived while he and I were speaking. There is a slim woman in a professional navy skirt and white blouse in one of the chairs. Beside her is a man, but his face is entirely hidden by the open newspaper he holds in front of it. Only his long, suited legs and expensive leather shoes are visible.

I ask if they can please bear with me for a few minutes. The woman gives me a stiff nod. The man does not lower the paper.

'Sir?' I say. 'Is that okay?'

He puts the paper on his lap. Dark hair slicked back. Serious mouth. A nose that looks as if it was broken sometime in his past, and stops his face from being perfect, which is a good thing. Designer stubble that would actually be a beard if it were a millimetre or two longer. Black shirt beneath his jacket. No tie.

'No problem,' he says. His brown eyes hold mine.

I vanish into the office to check the charity bank account. Adam Holderness's donation is at the top of the transaction list: £100. Generous but not excessive. Like him, somehow.

I return to the corridor to beckon in the waiting woman, only to find that two more have appeared in the chairs either side of her. But the man with the newspaper is gone.

As the woman settles herself where Adam Holderness was sitting only five minutes ago, I glance once more out of the smudged window and I am surprised by what I see. A thing that somehow doesn't belong in this room, in this month. It is only a tiny ray, but it is really there. Sun.

The Letters

I am in Luke's room, at the end of a long and challenging day. What draws me here is you. Tomorrow, the people who most love you will gather together to comfort each other and think of you. You'd never have deliberately left us to this. Would you?

I sit at the edge of Luke's bed and stare at our doll's house, puzzling over hidden messages. You and I never tired of playing with the doll's house together, despite the ten-year age gap. Or at least that is what I thought until recently, when Mum admitted that she used to bribe you with 'babysitting' money to entertain me.

My phone is on the bed, sinking into Luke's blue-striped quilt. It pings to alert me that a voicemail has been left on the charity helpline. I think of Sadie, whipped into a fury that she will want to blame me for, and feel a sick pang that it may be her, trying to trick herself through to me by using the charity number instead of my own.

But the message is not from Sadie. It is from a journalist, who wonders if this charity is indeed run by

Miranda Brooke's family, and if the Ella Brooke from the recent newspaper article is actually Miranda's sister, and if so, would she like to meet with him for an interview to mark the decade since Miranda's disappearance.

It occurs to me that this man may not be a journalist at all. He may be someone connected with you, trying to get hold of me but not wanting to disclose his real identity. Maybe in response to the messages I have been firing off, or my visit to Mrs Buenrostro. I wanted to be a catalyst. Perhaps I really have become one.

I close the voicemail screen and open my personal email. I am so distracted by my murderous thoughts towards the journalist that I have to look once, twice, three times, before I properly take in the two messages sitting at the top of my inbox.

Like most longed-for letters, these arrived when I stopped checking for them. What confuses me at first is that both of them are from hospitals. It takes me a few seconds to grasp that they are two different institutions. One email is a response from the hospital where you had your amniocentesis and gave birth to Luke. The other is from the psychiatric hospital where Jason Thorne is imprisoned.

It is easy to choose which one to read first. The letter about Thorne will be a yes or no to my request to visit him. It will require no complex analysis from me. So this is where I begin. My heart beats faster as the message pops open and I squeeze my eyes shut for a few seconds, too nervous to look at it.

I am not certain if I am more frightened of the prospect of coming face-to-face with Thorne, or the possibility that I will not be allowed to. The latter is more likely, given what Ted said about Thorne's refusal to grant the wishes of those who want to come and gawp at a human monster.

I make myself look. The letter is short and to the point. Jason Thorne has accepted my request to see him. I inhale, several jagged breaths.

There is an attachment that I need to print off and bring with me. They have scheduled an appointment for the afternoon of Tuesday, 15 November, in just five days. Seven hours have passed since Adam Holderness's visit this morning. The timing of this message is unlikely to be an accident. He couldn't discuss Thorne, but he must have at least done this for me.

I do a quick reconnaissance of the other attachment Thorne's keepers have tagged to the email. Pages and pages of rules and regulations and instructions. I close the message and open the one from the hospital where you had your obstetric care.

The body of the email contains only one sentence. *Please see attached letter.* I immediately tap on the small grey box and watch it bloom into a document. I read it over and over again, squinting at the tiny type, as if by doing so I will somehow discover a coded secret hidden inside these clinical words.

Dear Miss Brooke,
Thank you for your request for access to the medical records pertaining to your sister MIRANDA CHARLOTTE BROOKE. Your application to view the results of her amniocentesis test was considered by the undersigned.

There are a number of grounds upon which information should not be disclosed. Your request is being denied in accordance with the following exemption[s]:

- *the information you have asked for relates to a third party who has not given consent to disclosure (where that third party is not a health professional who has cared for the patient).*

We take our duty to safeguard the confidentiality and security of personal information extremely seriously. We regret that we are unable to assist you on this occasion.

Yours sincerely,

Miss M. J. Atworth

Medical Records Officer and Data Controller

I put the phone on Luke's bedside table, my heart beating faster.

There is a message here and Miss M. J. Atworth has not made any attempt to hide it. Miss M. J. Atworth's regret is not appropriate, because she has, in fact, *assisted me on this occasion.*

The information you have asked for relates to a third party who has not given consent to disclosure.

First, I make myself run through an obvious point. The third party cannot be Luke. Luke's identity is already known. And in legal terms, sixteen weeks into the pregnancy, he was regarded as part of you. He was not a third party.

Even without seeing your medical records, I now understand. You must have been desperate, given how paranoid you were about anything that could cause miscarriage. You would have been terrified of the risk to the foetus from that needle. But there was no other way to do a paternity test.

The hospital would have required the DNA of one of the two possible fathers so they could compare it with your unborn baby's. Whoever's DNA it was, he would have needed to consent to their testing it, though not to their revealing his identity. This means at least one of those men knew about the test, and the result.

I am guessing it was the man you didn't want. You would have been horrified by the prospect of the man you loved discovering you'd slept with someone else. You would not have wanted him to know that the paternity could be in doubt. Either of these men could have hurt you in the wake of his jealousy and anger.

How did you hide all of this from me? I am imagining your panic, feeling in my own bones what it must have been like to live with this secret for so many months. I see now why you didn't tell us about the pregnancy until you were twenty weeks, once the genetic tests gave you the answer you'd been praying for.

If the answer had been otherwise, I think you would have ended the pregnancy. You'd had months to steel yourself to do this. You would have been prepared to add another secret to your collection.

It occurs to me that you could have had an early abortion, then tried again with the man whose baby you wanted, in circumstances where there would be no doubt. But you didn't. Was this because the opportunities to become pregnant by him were limited? $M + N + ??$ I think you couldn't bear to lose the child if there was even a slim chance of his belonging to the man you loved. And you wanted to give the baby every chance.

You talked so often about finding your true love, and that is what Luke's father must have been to you. So why did you sleep with someone else? This question makes my stomach drop – perhaps you didn't want to and he made you.

There is another question, too, a more obvious one. Why on earth didn't you let us meet the man who must have been your life's great passion? Surely you were bursting to introduce him to your family? But every question I answer only breeds countless more that I cannot.

Friday, 11 November

The Anniversary

I stand at my bedroom window, squinting out at the sodden graveyard as the light fades. I replay what I was doing the day you vanished, trying to map my every minute against yours. Will I notice something new, something important that I have forgotten, if I continue to go over it? Does the man who took you do this too?

Exactly ten years ago, when I was twenty and in the final year of my undergraduate degree in Biology, you dropped your ten-week-old son off with our mother. It was a Friday morning. It was 8.30 a.m. It was *that morning*.

You and Luke should have been visiting me, making a long weekend of it. You were going to stay in an extremely grand seafront hotel near my student room. It was to be your first real trip with Luke. But a few days earlier, I'd phoned to put you off. All because Ted discovered he could be with me that weekend.

. . .

'So your boyfriend's more important than your sister and nephew?' you said.

And I lied. I said it wasn't Ted, that I was behind with coursework, that I had to work day and night to catch up or they would kick me out of university.

'So Ted won't be coming to stay with you in Brighton then?'

'No.'

'Don't kid a kidder, Melanie. Lie to anybody but never to me. I am the one person who will always know.'

I hardly ever lie. I don't know why I did then. 'I'm not lying,' I said, which was a big lie.

'Just tell the truth. It's me you're talking to.'

'I know that.'

'I know what it's like to love someone and not be able to see them anything like as much as you want to. I'll understand. But fess up now. I hate you lying to me.'

I learned then what you already knew well. That once you lie, it is hard to admit you have done it and even harder to dig your way out. Instead, I used a Miranda technique right back at you. 'I can't believe you don't believe me.'

'Good one. Taught by a master. But remember this. Whatever mistakes I make, I never choose *anybody* over my family. And I never choose *anybody* over you.'

'Really?'

'When the coin drops, it always comes up with your face on top.'

'Miranda—'

'Don't lie about men. Don't ever do that. I promise it's not worth it.'

I thought of something our mother once said. *If you lie, make it simple or you will catch yourself out. You will forget what you said.* But I deteriorated, in the grip of my lie. 'I'm not—'

'Ted's not worth it. You're way too good for him and I haven't got time for this crap, Melanie.'

'Please—'

'The baby's crying.'

'Let me explain—'

'I can't do this.' And the phone slammed down on the last thing you ever said to me. Our last conversation and one of the worst we ever had.

Never say goodbye in anger. Our mother cautioned us about this over and over again. My last memory of you is that you were furious with me. And I will never stop being furious with myself. I chose Ted over you and Luke. If I hadn't done that, everything would have been different.

That morning – the two words creep in again and again – you parked your metallic black BMW in our parents' driveway and carried Luke into the house.

A-List Tastes of Missing Nurse.

This is one of the few headlines that actually had a ring of truth. How did you afford that shiny new BMW on your nurse's salary? We asked you this. Of course we did. But I never believed anything you ever said on the subject of money and even Dad used to joke that you were never to be given the keys to the family vault.

You just said the car was 'baby friendly' and they'd

offered you an 'amazing deal' because they could see that someone like you would bring them extra customers because anyone who saw you driving that car would have to have one too.

Nobody could argue with you when you talked like this, especially when your lies were at their most preposterous. Our mother didn't dare. Was it because she feared your huffing away forever if the charade was exposed? Or that you would fall apart? Then again, there is a chance you were actually telling the truth. If anybody could charm a salesman into giving them a luxury car at a preposterously huge discount, it is you. But whenever our father uttered even the tiniest sceptical question our mother would shut him up and you would happily pretend he hadn't spoken.

Is this why he went behind Mum's back to ask the police to return your things? Knowing that I wouldn't let it rest? That I would do the work for him, so he could have a peaceful time with Mum?

The police asked about your finances, after learning you paid cash for the car, but we didn't have a reasonable answer. The new practices to stamp out money laundering were not in place ten years ago. It was easier to spend large amounts of cash, then, and to deposit them, completely without trace. The police were intensely curious about your money at first. But all at once, they seemed to lose interest. I wonder now if they did discover something, but deliberately let it go.

That morning, our mother held Luke up to the living room window and waved his little baby hand as you walked back to your shiny car. Your leaving Luke with Mum was a last-minute thing. You rang her the night before to arrange it. You didn't, of course, tell her where you were going. And she, of course, did not dare to ask.

As I stare out at the graveyard and try to reconstruct your last known movements, I think again of the advice leaflets I read when you vanished.

When someone goes missing, make a note of the clothing they were wearing when they were last seen.

You were wearing a smoky blue shirt dress that fell to just above your knees.

'Was she wearing a poppy?' the police asked.

'No.' Our mother was anxious that they disapproved of your lack of patriotism, fearing that they wouldn't try as hard to find you if they didn't like you.

The dress was silky, bought with cash the afternoon before you vanished. The salesgirl remembers that you took the dress in both the colours it came in without even trying it on.

I picture the covered buttons, torn from the front of the dress as the man who stole you ripped it away. I imagine the tie. Around your wrists instead of your waist. Around your throat. I try not to give credence to the rumours about what Jason Thorne did. I fail at this.

The second dress was brown, a colour you seldom wear, and still hanging with its tags dangling in your wardrobe. Above it was a shelf on which you stored a handful of designer bags, costing tens of thousands of pounds. Below it were several pairs of film-star worthy shoes. There is no record of your ever having bought these things. It seems likely they were gifts from Luke's father.

You left these glitzy objects to me. Three years ago, when you were declared dead, I had the bags auctioned and donated the funds to the charity. The Birkin bag was made of teal-coloured crocodile skin and I could hardly bear to touch it, though I made myself examine it as I did with each and every thing, in case you'd hidden a note in a pocket or sewn a secret into a lining.

'Where did you get that?' I would occasionally ask you, which also meant *How* did you get that. The answer would always begin with the words 'You wouldn't believe what happened . . . ' and a laugh, then the phrase 'Long story short . . . ' though the story would always be the complete opposite of short. You would invariably recount a series of events so complex and strange I could barely remember the beginning by the time you reached the end.

'You're making that silly smirk face,' I'd say. 'It's your lying face. I know you're lying. You always make that ridiculous fish mouth when you lie.'

You would laugh, and give it away even more. 'You need to teach me to lie, Melanie,' you'd say. 'You're the best liar I ever met. To everybody but me.' Then you'd say, 'You'd never bust me, would you? You'd never tell if you caught me in a lie?'

That morning, you were wearing a platinum locket on a platinum chain around your neck. You always wore that locket, with my photograph on one side and Luke's on the other. You gave me one exactly like it. Even our mother frowned to consider what they must have cost. In mine, it is your photograph that accompanies Luke's. I never take it off. The locket's existence is something the police withheld from the public.

Because there is no physical evidence that someone took you, the police have told us that we need to allow for the possibility that you chose to die on your own somewhere or that you ran off with a rich lover.

When someone goes missing, follow your intuition.

My intuition is that there is no way you were depressed. You didn't do depression. You would never have killed yourself. You never would have left Luke. Not even for a fortune. He is the only thing you would have passed over a fortune for.

But I hear Ted's voice again, which seems to be on a loop these days. *Are you sure about that? Are you sure you really knew her?*

My answer to both questions, the single word a hiss, is *Yes.*

I fear that whoever stole you kept you for a time. Jason Thorne did that to the women he took.

What must it have been like for you as your breasts filled, reminding you how badly Luke needed you? You might have got a fever, unable to release the milk. You'd already had a course of antibiotics for mastitis, only finishing it a few days before you disappeared. The mastitis could have recurred. Your disappearance meant you missed a doctor's appointment you'd set up for late that afternoon.

. . .

Is it any wonder the blood froze in my body? I can hear Dr Blossom, giving me my diagnosis as if he were reading poetry. *Temporary alteration of the function of the hypothalamus. Stress-induced Amenorrhea.*

Although 'temporary' has stretched to ten years, Dr Blossom tells me cheerfully that it is not premature menopause. He says that my ovarian reserve is normal for my age, and not diminished. However many eggs I may have, they sit there, undeveloped and going nowhere. Month after month after month.

Ted wants children. He wants lots of children to make up for the loneliness of growing up with just his mother, a woman he always seemed to want to keep as far away from me as he could. I used to tease him that he only loved me for my father, but I was right to perceive how much Dad means to him.

Ted used to say we would have at least a dozen children because we wouldn't be able to keep our hands off each other. How could I have tied him to me, when his great wish was for a huge family?

That is probably why he has given up on me so quickly, so readily falling back into our old fighting ways. Despite a brief renewal of his fantasies about me, he wants a woman he can have a child of his own with. It is all too easy for him to repeat the same old grievance that I am too obsessed with finding you.

Stop living with the dead, he once said. And like our mother I shot back, *Don't you call her dead.*

How can the life-making part of you not turn to ice

when you are imagining the worst possible things happening to someone you love?

Whatever diagnosis Dr Blossom makes, I think something inside my body froze in the face of the pictures I was living with during the first few years of your absence. The pictures were like a slideshow. It made no difference whether my eyes were open or closed, however hard I tried to turn from them.

When Ted and I woke up late on your last morning, we took a bath together in a huge old iron tub, soaping each other's bodies, laughing. Afterwards, Ted planted tiny kisses all over my chest. He trailed a finger over my shoulder and down my arm.

When someone goes missing, do not delay in searching.

By 2 p.m. you were an hour late to collect Luke. You were not famous for punctuality but where Luke was concerned you were uncharacteristically dependable. Especially when your breasts were filling with milk for his next feed.

When someone goes missing, contact friends and family to see if they are aware of the person's whereabouts.

The calls to you and me that our parents started making at 3 p.m. went nowhere. Your battery was already out of charge and my phone was off.

Our parents had a major crisis on their hands – you were missing. And a minor crisis too – your son was starving. The emergency breast milk you'd stored in their freezer defrosted perfectly but there was a flaw in the plan. After three hours of nonstop crying, they couldn't persuade Luke to drink it from a bottle.

At 5 p.m. there was a knock on the door of my basement room. I later learned it was someone from the housing office. They were trying to find me at the request of our parents, who were hoping that I knew where you were.

As the knocking continued, Ted and I pulled the covers over our heads and ignored whoever it was until they went away.

When someone goes missing, it is never too soon to tell the police, especially if the disappearance is out of character.

At 6 p.m. our parents alerted the police.

When someone goes missing, do not panic.

At 8 p.m. your car was found.

When someone goes missing, do not blame yourself.

At 10 p.m. there were more knocks on the door. Ted put his hand over my mouth to stop the noise of my laughing as he tickled me. Then there was my name, repeated several times in the kind of stern male voice Ted uses when he is working and has to deliver bad news, and an announcement that this was the police, and the knock became an incessant pounding that wouldn't stop, and Ted and I pulled apart and everything went into slow motion as he wrapped a towel around his hips and went to answer the door and we learned that we were living *that day*.

I was sure – I am still sure – that an evil magician made you disappear. I spend my life imagining the tricks he used, and trying to stop other people falling for them, and figuring out how I can fight them, if my own time ever comes.

. . .

The light is almost gone. I must leave soon if I am not to be late for the dinnertime start of my weekend with Mum and Dad and Luke, but I can't make myself move. I am playing shadow tricks with myself as I peer out of my bedroom window.

If I am quick enough, I will catch sight of you in the graveyard, raven-haired and pale-faced as Giselle's ghost, flitting between the broken stones. You are searching for me, as you did when I was a little girl. You seeking me. It seems an impossibility that that was how it used to be.

Something makes me freeze. A man, dressed all in black, presses himself against a small tomb the size and shape of a gingerbread house, then disappears behind it.

I consider rushing outside to search. Your cries are ringing in my ears. *Don't you dare.* What stops me, though, is the futility of the chase, rather than the danger. He would be gone before I could get there. And it is already too dark to see.

I imagine what Ted would say. *Just someone on a walk. Nothing to do with you.* But I cannot shake the feeling that that man was everything to do with me, and he deliberately positioned himself with a perfect view of my bedroom window.

Never ignore your instincts. This is one of the precepts that I drum into the women who come to my self-defence class. I am not about to discount my own advice. There is no need to catch him now. If my instincts are right, he will be back.

Saturday, 12 November

Yellow Roses

I am traipsing after Luke through the woods, chattering and smiling, though my head is pounding from all the wine I got through last night.

After Luke went to bed, I sat in your little wooden chair by the side of the fireplace as if I were keeping it warm for you. I fiddled with the yellow roses I'd brought for Mum because they are your favourite. They were arranged within my reach, on a low table.

I tried not to see it as a curse when I pricked my finger. I tried not to regard it as a bad omen that the roses were drying out so quickly and browning at the edges of the petals. I so wished they would stop dropping off. But despite the sachet of liquid nutrients I'd tipped into the vase, the petals seemed to be falling even faster. And though I tinkered and tinkered, I couldn't get the roses to stay in a pleasing shape. One would always tilt away, leaving a gap.

You didn't know when you fell in love with yellow

roses that yellow is the colour of the missing. You didn't imagine that yellow was to become your colour. Most families of the missing tie yellow ribbons to trees or fences. We do that too, but we also fill the house with yellow roses.

So I played with your roses and sucked on my bleeding finger and poured glass after glass of wine, trying to drive out all thoughts of Jason Thorne and the roses he supposedly prefers. But all I could do was count down the hours to my seeing him. Mum frowned at the drinking and the obvious cause. Her frown deepened when I handed over your hidden forget-me-not note and told them about Mrs Buenrostro.

Dad left early this morning to deliver the note to the police. He will probably have to wait there for hours while they decide what to do with it. Lose it accidentally-on-purpose, most likely.

As ever, Luke is drawn to the split oak that you always loved. He keeps a photograph by his bed of you sitting in it a few days after he was born, holding him in the late summer sun of the brand-new September. You are so completely beautiful, smiling at the swaddled lump in your arms.

As Luke and I approach your tree, I put a hand on his shoulder and pull him closer. In the soft earth at the base of the trunk is a man's partial shoeprint. Only the front of the shoe, but there is no doubting what it is.

I think of the man in the graveyard yesterday and continue to study the landscape, trying to work out what it is that is bothering me so much about this print. That is when I realise. It is because there is just the one and it is incomplete. Whoever left it made an effort not to leave any others. Nothing leads to or from it.

How did he do this? Maybe by placing something on the ground with each step? But he got careless with the one he did leave. Was he interrupted? Startled into a lapse from habitual carefulness? I keep my hand on Luke's shoulder, lightly and casually, as I check and double-check until I am absolutely certain that whoever left that print is now gone.

All the while, I am watching the sky. Smoky black clouds are rushing towards us. A damp, old-newspaper smell is rising from the earth. Any minute and the sun will disappear. Soon after, the rain will start and the shoeprint will melt away. The police are hardly likely to send out a crack team of crime scene investigators for this, let alone order them to race here ahead of the clouds.

I let my hand drop away. 'Can you run into the house for my phone, Luke?'

'Sure sure.'

I love the way he always doubles this word. As he moves off I think of something else. 'Wait a sec.'

I have a vision of me and Luke when he was much smaller, filling moulds with plaster of Paris and then painting them. Entire seas of fantastical creatures. Enough animals to fill a miniature zoo. 'Can you also bring me your school ruler? And Granny's hairspray? It's the matt-gold aerosol on her dressing table.'

He raises an eyebrow. 'Do you wear hairspray? I didn't think you did that kind of stuff.'

'I thought we could embark on some consumer testing. How strong a hold does Brand A have on soil . . . '

'Intriguing.' He says this like the master spy he wants to be and makes me laugh. 'Don't worry. I'm super-fast.' I like that he still defaults to ten-year-old-boy mode, mixed in with all that maturity. Right now he is too excited about having an adventure with me to consider being frightened. He is already moving and I see that I don't need to worry about scaring him. At least for the moment.

I watch him run, a clumsy run that I love, his arms waving. Not a natural athlete's run. Until he started primary school, whenever Luke ran, he'd do what I called his happy laugh. It came out of him like breath. But the teasing he got for it in the playground made the happy laugh disappear. I am not sure when I first noticed its absence. I am still hoping he will let it out again someday.

I return to your tree and crouch on the other side of it, away from the shoeprint. I am looking at the stones that Luke and I arranged in an M after his birthday party on the last day of August. M for Miranda. M for Mummy. M for me.

Luke and I collected the stones from the beach at Norfolk when I took him there for a little holiday earlier that month. The stones are not as we left them. The left side of the M is shorter than the right, though we had taken great care to make them both the same length, using Luke's arm as a measuring stick. The pink-shaded stones are gone. We had started at the lower left tip of the M with the earth-stained pinks, then used purples, then blues, then greys, until we got to the lower right tip.

They are too heavy to have blown away. The earth, though moist, is too solid to have swallowed them. I do not see any strewn pebbles to indicate that an animal disturbed them, and an animal would not carry them away. The pinks have been removed neatly, without any of the rest of the M being affected. Only a human being could have done this so systematically, but there are no footsteps anywhere close.

I study the next oak tree over. The nearby weeds are bent. Did he pause there too, after circling through the woods and around the house? After deciding that the cameras I put on each of its four sides would not penetrate the thick trees he hid in?

Did he watch us as if we were human-sized dolls in their house of green sandstone? Did he hear our mother at the piano and our father at the double bass as Luke and I whooped and laughed and trumpeted? Did he see our silhouettes through the gauzy curtains as the two of us lunged in and out of view, huge then small, dancing a wild rumpus that could only be elephants?

It seems hardly any time has passed, but already Luke is back. 'You're so muddy, Auntie Ella. Granny's gonna kill you.'

I look down at my jeans and see that he is right. Even the bottom of my jumper is sticky and smeared. 'I'm about to get muddier. So are you.'

'Cool.'

I take the things from Luke. 'Can you run back in and get one of your old plaster of Paris kits?'

Luke rolls his eyes exactly as he did after our mother last gave him one.

'I know. We all sometimes forget how grown-up you're getting. But trust me – you're going to like this – you'll thank Granny. Go stir up the powder and water – you're better at that than I am.'

'It never sets when you do it. It stays gooey or it cracks as soon as you take it out of the mould.'

'I know. I'm a disgrace of a builder's daughter. Use Granny's glass jug.'

'She'll go crazy if we put plaster in it.'

'I'll wash it, after – bring the mixture out as soon as it's ready.'

Again he is already running his special Luke run. 'On it.'

A drop of water hits me splat on the nose and I crouch by the shoeprint, crossing fingers and toes that it won't soon be splashed away. I aim the aerosol towards the depression and pump one dose of spray at it. I hold my breath and pump again. The theory I am going on is that it will firm things up and help to hold the print in place in the damp earth for a little longer, despite the rain.

I lay the ruler along the sides and top and bottom of the print and snap pictures with my phone. I get up and repeat the process with the damaged M. It's while I'm aiming the phone at the subtle disturbances on the forest floor that I hear Luke, rustling through leaves, his steps uncharacteristically slow and careful. When I look up, he is only a few feet away, holding a jug of grey gloop.

'Yummy,' I say. 'I'm hungry.'

He laughs.

'Over here.' I motion for him to join me near the shoeprint. Another drop of rain hits me, this time in the eye. 'Crap.'

'Granny said ladies don't swear.'

'It's the usual problem with that little piece of etiquette.'

'You're not a lady?' He grins, never tiring of this old joke between us.

'Exactly.' I point at the small depression in the ground. 'Here. This is what we're going to cast.' Luke drops to his knees beside me and we pour the mixture in.

After we set the jug aside, he hands me his waterproof coat, school regulation navy. 'I thought this might help,' he says.

The two of us lie on our stomachs with the cold damp of the earth seeping into our clothes and beneath our skin. We are propped on our elbows with the shoeprint between us, holding the coat over it together, shielding it from the rain, which is now coming down properly from a sky the colour of pewter.

'I can hold the coat myself if you're tired,' he says, heroic as ever. 'Give you a rest.'

'I like doing it as a team.'

'So do I.' He smudges his nose with a muddy finger. 'I forgot to tell you, the directions say it dries in half an hour, but it won't be properly strong for two days.'

'That's really helpful.'

He looks hard at me. 'Is this to do with your promise about Mum?'

Mum. The word punches the air out of my stomach. He has never called you that before. It is a progression from the babyish Mummy that we have all clung to for him, probably for too long. Does he know he has done this, to signal to himself and to me that he is growing up? I remember him crying in my arms on Bonfire Night, thinking that whatever happened to you happened because of his very existence. So many declarations of his loss of innocence.

How should I answer his extremely direct question? He is way too smart for evasiveness or lies. As he reminded me only two weeks ago, he is ten, not two. *But ten*, I hear you say, *is still a child*. Something you forgot too readily with me.

'Remember that show you watched about police investigators?' I say. 'They were talking about the transience of crime scenes?'

'Yeah. How you can't count on evidence being preserved, especially outside. The elements can get to it.'

'Exactly. And you want to be a policeman. So I thought it would be fun to try to document this footprint.' Because, I silently add, I'm pretty sure the police will not be inclined to spend time and money doing it themselves. And even if they were, it will be gone before they get here.

'Cool,' he says.

'Yep.'

He laughs at my imitation of him and I laugh too, though my thoughts are dark as I consider what this anniversary may mean. So much has changed. There is the fresh and sickening possibility of Jason Thorne, but that isn't the only potential source of information. Someone new could come forward. Perhaps a friend of the man who took you. Maybe they were loyal to him then but hate him now.

People fall out. That's what you used to say about Sadie, ever-hopeful that the end of my friendship with her was imminent.

'Can you help me with my maths when we go in?' Luke says. 'I want to do really well on my test on Monday. Mum used to help you, didn't she?'

Mum. That new word again. It is your son's right to decide how to name you. It is natural for me to follow his lead. I say, 'Do you think Granny will pay me? She used to pay Mum.'

'Very funny.'

'I'm not joking.'

'Auntie Ella.' He sounds genuinely exasperated.

'Of course I'll help.'

He moves his arms, to try to get more comfortable holding the coat over the shoeprint. 'What are you going to do with the cast?'

'If it doesn't break, I'll put it in the living room as a souvenir of time with you.' I am already plotting to tell Luke a tragic tale of a fate like Humpty Dumpty's for the cast. In reality, I will be giving it to Ted, even though I have a mild fear that he will take it to the dump rather than risk the scorn of the property clerk.

'Will you stay tonight, too?'

'I'll stay for lunch and help you with your maths, but I have stuff I need to do at home after.' He doesn't need to know that I want to have a look at the graveyard before nightfall.

'I like Saturday mornings with you, Auntie Ella.'

'I like them with you too, Luke.'

Sunday, 13 November

Hide and Seek

The graveyard is filled with mist. The sun is only just beginning to rise. There has been no frost but it is so cold Ted is wearing his black knitted hat and I have on that old one of yours, made of cream-coloured wool and pulled over my ears.

Ted checks his watch. The white numbers and dials on the illuminated face are huge and clear even from where I am standing: 6.05. He needs to be at work at 7.00.

The moss is spongy beneath my wellington boots and Ted's solid black shoes. I look more closely at his trousers, then notice the white shirt and epaulettes beneath his civilian coat. 'You're in half blues off-duty,' I say. 'That's not safe.'

'Wouldn't have had time to meet you otherwise.'

I imagine Ted taking his turn in the succession of images of the recently fallen on the police roll of honour. Ted's picture would be the snapshot I took of him after a rugby match eleven years ago, and I feel sick and guilty at how vividly I see it.

'I want you to be safe,' I say. A cross looms above us, seeming to materialise out of the fog. It sits on top of multiple squares of granite that are stacked like a child's super-sized building blocks. I halt a few inches short of crashing into them.

My abrupt stop causes Ted to bump into me. His arms go round my waist to stop me falling over. A row of winged angels tower over us in their flowing gowns, hands clasped over their hearts, clutching passion lilies and seeming to watch us through their lowered eyes.

We look at each other for an instant. Ted's face is so close to mine I can smell the coffee on his breath. It makes me wish I could drink some coffee. It makes me wish I could kiss the coffee from his lips.

But I don't. We quickly break the contact, and I think – I am not sure, but I think – that he moves away a split second before I do.

I tuck a strand of hair behind my ear and pull your hat back down over it. 'Do you know, Luke still has that knitted doll you gave him when he was a baby, the little police constable? He sneaks it into bed every night. We all pretend not to see.'

Ted smiles, the first whole-hearted smile I have seen this morning. 'He's a great kid.' The smile fades as he considers. 'How did he do on Friday?'

'He did great,' I say. 'He keeps the rest of us strong.'

There's a cut on Ted's cheek from shaving. A drop of blood blooms out and I pull a tissue from my jacket pocket to clean it away. I kiss my middle three fingers and lightly, briefly, touch them to his cheek, smiling faintly.

Ted's face softens. His eyes seem to cloud. 'Thank you.'

'I'm always happy to tend your wounds.'

'You know exactly where they are – you made most of them.'

I scrunch the tissue up and hide it away. 'Luke's with me part of next weekend. Do you want to come for Sunday lunch? Maybe kick a ball around with him?'

He pauses before answering. It is slight, but definitely a pause. 'I'm away.'

I picture him and Ruby in that café. I feel weak and sick, as if my blood sugar has dropped. But I know it hasn't.

'Another time, then.' I try to sound casual, but I don't think I do.

'Where will you be at eleven?' he says.

'The Remembrance Day service. Luke tried to stow-away in my car when I was leaving yesterday. He made me promise to meet them in church.'

He doesn't laugh in fond commiseration as I expect him to. 'She wasn't perfect, you know.'

'Sorry?'

'Your sister wasn't perfect. Stop idealising her.'

'She didn't need to be perfect. You can still love imperfect things.'

'I should know better than anybody how true that is.' He is looking hard at me.

'You can make mistakes and have all sorts of faults and still deserve to be loved, deserve to be missed.' His face tightens as I say this.

'We need to be careful of Luke, Ella. He's at an age where we can mix him up.'

'You've lost interest in me and you're using Luke as an excuse. Sadie warned me you'd do this.'

'Sadie's—' He stops himself. 'Why would you listen to her? She hates you. Always has. Her greatest wish is to fuck up your life.'

'That doesn't mean every word she ever said is untrue.'

'I haven't lost interest in you. That appears to be a biological impossibility.'

'I thought you were seeing Ruby.'

'From your self-defence class? Why would you think that?'

I shrug. 'Why do you think I might think that?'

'Stop playing games, Ella.'

'So you're saying you haven't seen her at all? Except for the class?'

He pauses for a beat too long. 'Yes. That's what I'm saying. Can we move on now, please? Why am I here?'

'You'll see.' When I pass a tomb topped with a bird, I jolt and halt in my steps. Am I really seeing a vulture? I blink, and the stone shapes itself into an eagle. Even my vision is distorted.

A minute later, we reach the tomb where I saw the man. It is the size and shape of a playhouse with its triangular roof. I point in front of me and upwards. 'The mist is in the way, but this is a perfect vantage point for my bedroom window.'

Ted frowns. 'You checked all of your video footage? House and dash cam?'

'There's nothing. But there are blind spots – he could be exploiting them deliberately.' I turn back to the vault and drop to my knees. 'Look.'

He doesn't look. He crosses his arms. He says nothing.

'I actually saw a man here, Ted.'

'When?'

'Friday. As the sun was going down. I'm pretty sure he was watching me.'

'Pretty sure? Listen to yourself, Ella. You saw a man in a graveyard. Men walk in graveyards. All the time. You found a shoeprint in the woods. People walk in those too – there's a public footpath through them.'

I whirl at him. 'Why are you dismissing me? Why have you always tried to stop me looking at all of this?' His face flushes. 'Is there something you don't want me to know, Ted?' The thought has never crossed my mind before, but now it blocks out everything else. 'Something about you I might uncover if I look at all of this afresh?'

His flush deepens. However controlled a man Ted is, he is not in command of his blood supply. 'Do I need to remind you where I was when she disappeared, Ella? Don't you see how all of this damages your ability to think and act rationally?'

'No. I don't. Plus there's something else. There's this man I met. Adam Holderness. He works in the hospital where they've locked up Jason Thorne—'

'Are you trying to make me jealous?' His face is twisted in rage. 'Trying to make me see that another man is clearly interested in you?'

I am so shocked, and so ashamed he could think this, and so outraged by his hypocrisy, that my mouth opens and closes with nothing coming out.

He is practically growling at me. 'In case you were in

any doubt, it wouldn't be hard for you to do that. Does that make you happy?'

'You should know me better than that.' I think of his blatant falsehood about Ruby. You and I were uniquely schooled in our mother's principles for lying and not getting caught. Ted clearly was not. 'How could you be so self-righteous?'

'This has been ruining your life for ten years. It nearly ruined mine. It's ruined us. I thought I'd escaped it when I got married but even that got fucked up by it.'

'Are you actually blaming me for your fucked-up marriage?' My heart is pounding. My blood is thrumming in my ears. 'Given what you've done?'

His face completely drains of colour. 'What do you mean?'

'You're a liar, Ted. You lied to my face. I saw you and Ruby.' I say each of these five words with deadly quiet clarity but somehow hear them as a scream.

A tremor passes through his mouth and jaw. 'You what?'

'You heard me. I saw you in that café.'

'What the hell were you doing there?' He is clearly furious that he has been the object of surveillance. He can do that to others but nobody can do it to him.

I glare and shake my head in disgust and say that I needed coffee.

He grabs both of my arms. 'Were you following me?'

I knock him away. 'Somebody sent me a photo of you. It was location and time-stamped.' I take out my phone and flash the email and photograph at him.

'The fucking bastard. Forward it to me. Tell me if you get another one.'

'Fine.'

'It's not what you think, Ella, with Ruby. It's work.'

'How convenient. Is that supposed to excuse your lying?' The leaves of an old cedar tree lift gently in the still air as if moved by a ghost. 'I don't trust you, Ted.'

'That's a mistake. I hope you'll change your mind.' His voice is measured again, even if his circulation is not.

'Can I ask you something?'

'What.' It's not a question.

'If I disappeared off the face of the earth, would you ever stop looking for me?'

His voice is choked. 'You know I wouldn't. I'd never stop.'

'Well I can't stop looking for her. I won't let her go. She wouldn't if it was me. Ten years and absolutely nothing. Then all of these things start happening.'

'Ten years doesn't mean it's time to go back, Ella. It means it's time to move on. To take stock. I have and you should too. The police did everything they should.'

Can I love a man who keeps secrets from me? Who lies? What kind of a life would that be? I suspect that you could offer some expert advice on this one.

'You talk all the time about the police family.' I am startled by the bitterness in my voice. 'They're your family, not mine. Our loyalties aren't the same.'

'That's why I need to stay out of it. Why I need to stay objective and talk you down.' His murky green eyes are fixed on the grass.

'See how the twigs just there are broken, as if somebody's stepped on them?' I say.

'That could have been anybody. And even if some creep is watching you, it doesn't mean he had anything to do with Miranda.'

I startle when Ted says your name, realising for the first time that he rarely does. For now, I file the observation away.

'Look how the dust is a little thinner here.' I point to the side of the vault's ornate double doors, beneath the roof's overhang. 'Like somebody's shoulders and head rubbed against it. He sat here for some time and leaned back.' I squat down. 'The moss is compressed in front of it, too. See? From his weight while he was sitting.'

'Why do you assume it was a man? It could have been Sadie. The photo too.'

'The person was all in black, but they were tall.' I point to where their heels dug in. 'If it wasn't a man it was a big woman. So yes – it could have been Sadie.'

He gets onto his knees beside me. 'You came here on your own?'

'I did. It's my neighbourhood, Ted. It's hardly a war zone.'

'The gravestones are all falling over. None of these structures are safe.'

'They've been here hundreds of years. I doubt they're going to crumble to powder today.' I stand up. 'I want to look inside.'

Ted stands too. He crosses his arms. 'Why did you ask me to come here if you don't want to listen to anything I say?'

'Because I want to know the counterarguments.' I look straight at him. 'And because I wanted to see you.' I have really messed with his blood flow this morning, but whether this new flush is in gladness or alarm, I cannot tell. I push open one of the iron doors with a horror-movie creak. 'I'm going in with or without you. I doubt the roof is about to fall in.' And with that I squash myself through the opening.

It is difficult to see much, with only the crack of misted daylight from outside. But then Ted is beside me, crouched low so his head doesn't hit the roof. 'Here,' he says, scanning the little chamber with a torch that he must have had in his coat pocket. 'I hope we don't get buried alive.'

I fumble for his hand, let my fingers brush his skin, notice the usual shiver. Even though I fear that he no longer feels this too, I can't resist the impulse to send him little reminders, in case they ping something in him. 'Thank you,' I say. He lets his fingers entwine in mine, making me think of Hansel and Gretel clutching on to each other in the gingerbread cottage. But his touch is fleeting.

There are two gigantic rectangular boxes. They sit on either side of the room and rise to half its height. He is systematic, moving the torch's beam over every inch of the stone slabs beneath our feet. He guides it over the top of the boxes too.

There is no disturbance that I can see. There is nothing in this little house. No clue. It is damp and dusty and earthy smelling, but there is nothing in the air to suggest anyone was in here for any length of time. No residue of smoke from a portable stove. No smell of urine or faeces. This place hasn't been used to camp in.

'Wait a minute. Just inside the doorway, Ted. You didn't shine it here.'

He groans but aims the torch where I have commanded. That is when I see it. Something black. A button. So small and flat and average a button, lying in these shadows, it is a miracle we spotted it at all. I fall onto my knees to peer more closely.

Ted sees too, and guesses what I am thinking in his quickness to dismantle it. 'That could have come from anyone who's passed through this place.'

'Yes, but most of them don't go into the tombs.'

'We have no way of knowing how long it's been here. Plastic doesn't weather quickly. It doesn't rust or tarnish.'

'Maybe.' I snap a few quick pics of the button in situ, using the flash. 'Hand me an evidence bag.' I know he always carries one.

'Did you hear what I said, Ella? It's not something we need to call in the crime scene team for.'

'I heard you. But he could have left DNA on it. Or maybe, if we can finally identify a suspect, he'll have the shirt it came from. It will show he was here.'

'There's no way Jason Thorne left that button. You do admit that?' He speaks as if he is trying to establish whether I was the vandal who spray-painted graffiti on a church.

'Yes.' I stick out a hand. 'Evidence bag, please.'

'I'm not supposed to get involved.'

'If you don't then you're neglecting your duty in serving the public. I am a member of the public and I need you to serve me.'

He says something about how he's been serving me

for as long as he can remember but he still pulls a plastic bag from one of the huge pockets at the bottom of his jacket. He ignores my outstretched hand. Instead, he swoops the bag down and swallows the button up with it himself, avoiding any contact between the button and his own skin. Then he squeezes himself out of the building and I follow.

'Let me have it for a minute,' I say, once we are fully out in the light. 'I'll give it back.'

He drapes it over my palm, making sure that the transparent side faces up, and the side with the opaque white box and blue writing faces down. I snap a few more pictures with my phone, so I can have a record of the button to scale. Then I give the bag back to Ted and stand up. 'You'll write up all the information on it later?'

'Yep.'

Yep. I see now why Luke always says that, imitating the idol otherwise known as Ted. 'You're going to drop it in a bin as soon as I'm out of sight, aren't you?'

'Nope.'

'You're worrying about what the property clerk will say, aren't you?'

'You want to know what he's going to say? He's going to say, "I'm booking in a fucking button? You're asking me to book in a fucking button?" I'll pass this one on, then I'm done. Anything else, deliver it to the station yourself or get your dad to.'

He walks away, not looking back, not caring whether I stay or follow him out. He moves steadily through the fog towards the archway through which all the dead bodies in this graveyard passed, then he melts out of my view.

It actually hurts to breathe and I feel like I might throw up – as if I have somehow ingested his disgust with me and need to expel it. I stand near this mockery of a playhouse, hoping he will call something to me over his shoulder. In all of the countless fights since you vanished, he has never before walked away so angrily, at least not without relenting within minutes. But if he does call back, the words are lost in the mist.

Monday, 14 November

Never Climb Down

I am wandering through the cobbled lanes in search of something to wear for my meeting with Jason Thorne tomorrow. I forwarded the hospital's official advice about suitable dress to our mother, deciding that including her in the preparations would be the best way to manage her.

As ever, though, she is managing me. She has hijacked this excursion to make sure I do it right. She is walking beside me, reading bits of the leaflet aloud from her phone. 'The rules are there for a reason, Ella,' she says. She looks up, seduced by the windows of one of the small but extremely expensive boutiques the two of you love.

I, by contrast, cannot tear my eyes from the gigantic plane tree in the middle of the square. 'Remember when I made all four of us reach round the trunk to hold hands?' I say.

'You must have been about four.' Mum smiles. 'We had to strain, but we did it. It's a good thing we had Dad with us that day or we wouldn't have made it.'

'Miranda only did it under sufferance,' I say.

'You used to imagine when the tree was a baby. You once drew a picture of a tiny girl from the eighteenth century. You put her in a perfect miniature Georgian dress so she was the same height as the tree, all those centuries ago.'

'I've always loved this tree.' I pull Mum beneath it.

'Come on,' Mum says, and drags me away and around a corner to another cobbled street. Each time Mum points to a shop I shake my head no, grab her arm, and keep walking.

'I passed Sadie's clinic on my way to meet you,' Mum says. 'It was closed. Isn't that odd at this time of year? No lights. No sign. But it's the season when women want manicures and facials and hair removal.'

'I suppose,' I say. 'All of the parties.'

'Exactly. I peeked through the letter box. There was a pile of post on the floor. Perhaps she's gone away with her new boyfriend? But wouldn't it be a busy period for him right now too?'

'Probably,' I say.

'It makes me see how thoughtful she is,' Mum says.

I look up sharply. 'What does?'

'Well, she's gone away, but she still took the trouble to send chocolates and a card before she went.'

My cheeks are burning and the tips of my fingers are tingling, little spears circling the nail beds. 'When exactly did she send them?'

Mum thinks. 'Thursday, I think. Because of the anniversary. She said she wanted us to know she was thinking of us. It was kind.'

'Tell me exactly what she said.'

'It was just a card. *Thinking of you* was printed on the front, with red chrysanthemums. She signed her name inside.'

'So a condolence card?'

'I suppose it was, yes.'

I picture Sadie, furious and distraught after losing Brian. All the while, she is blaming me for everything that has gone wrong for her. But she takes the time and trouble to send our mother a card and some chocolates. There is a big big problem with this picture. Sadie and kind are not two words that should ever be used together. *Thinking of you*, on a card chosen by Sadie, is a threat, not an act of love.

'You can't keep those things, Mum.'

'What?'

'Sadie is . . . ' I don't know what Sadie is, or why. A functional psychopath? Adam could probably give her a diagnosis. 'Miranda always said she's full of poison. She's not our friend. She didn't send those things to be kind.'

'You need to be specific, Ella.'

'I don't want to upset you with the details, but I don't want her anywhere near you or Luke or Dad.'

'You're acting as if you think she put cyanide in those chocolates.'

'Probably not, but there is a small risk.'

'The box is sealed in plastic.' Mum sighs. You know that sigh. I seem to push the button for it a lot. 'Do you think you're being paranoid? That going over and over what happened to your sister is winding you up?'

'No.' I try not to make the word sound like a hiss.

'Fine.' There is another sigh. 'I'll get rid of the chocolates and recycle the card.'

'Sorry. I wasn't clear. I don't mean for you to throw
them away. I want them, in case I need to go to the police.
I'll collect them when I see you on Thursday.'

'Is that really necessary?'

'Hopefully not, but I want to be prepared.' I take her
hand in mine. 'If you hear from her again, please tell
me. And keep anything she sends. You will, won't you?'

'Yes,' she says.

I suspect she only agrees because I have reminded her
that you never liked Sadie. She wouldn't listen to me,
but we both still listen to you. She also agrees because
she wants to shut me up. But that will never happen.

'Good,' I say. 'No more Sadie. Shall we walk on? Find
some more shops?' The last sentence is calculated to
please Mum.

I cannot tear my eyes from the arches of twinkling
Christmas decorations. It is only the middle of November
and already they are up.

Mum has her phone out again. She has returned to
the hospital leaflet. She is reading something about
'modest dress'.

'They actually wrote that?' I say. '"Modest"?'

'Modest isn't a dirty word.' She peers at me. 'Your
father and I are really not happy about this business of
visiting Thorne.'

'I'm hardly happy about it myself. But we said we'd
try not to argue, didn't we? We promised each other.'

'Yes. Yes, we did.' She points up, at the strands of
waterfall lights. 'They are like shooting stars.'

'Why do the bells and snowflakes look like they're made of frosted barbed wire?'

'I give up,' she says. 'Perhaps they are.' And then she shocks me, which is something she loves to do. Just like you. 'There are a few things we need to talk about. The first is that I have made a discovery about Mr Henrickson.'

I halt so abruptly another pedestrian has to swerve to avoid me. 'You what?'

'I believe I spoke clearly, Ella.' She looks like a snowdrop in her white coat and hat, which she makes careful adjustments to, using a shop window as her looking glass. Only you and Mum could wear these colours without worrying about getting them dirty.

'But you keep saying you don't want me doing any of this.'

'I don't. But I must confess that I was curious.'

'"Must confess" isn't usually part of your vocabulary.'

'Do you want me to share or not?'

'I want you to share.' I steer her out of the lanes and into the courtyard on the side of the Abbey, searching for an empty bench. There is already a scattering of temporary wooden chalets trimmed with greenery, selling Christmas things. I notice one with a display of gingerbread-house kits, another with sachets of mulled wine.

'Please tell me what you found out.' I try to pull her beside me, onto a bench, but she won't let me until she has taken out a packet of tissues and wiped it.

'You have your sister's patience.' She shakes her head as if I am exhausting her beyond endurance. 'I phoned up Henrietta Mansions Management Company, who run the building. I said, "Hello, this is Mrs Buenrostro from Flat 6."'

'You what?!'

'Please do not interrupt. The woman on the line said, "Hello, Mrs Buenrostro." I hung up without saying anything else. But there is no question of the flat number Mrs Buenrostro lives in. The woman confirmed my guess about that, because 6 is definitely next door to 7 – I checked a building plan I found online.'

'Impressive,' I say.

'Isn't it?' Our mother looks deservedly proud of herself. 'So Mrs Buenrostro and N. Henrickson are close neighbours. One wall between them.'

'You withheld your telephone number?'

'Of course. But here is the really significant thing. When E.B. Property Services bought Flat 7 twenty-one years ago, they also bought Flat 6.'

My excitement and perplexity at this intelligence is competing with my admiration for her sneaky cleverness. 'You searched the Land Registry?'

'Yes.' She pauses. 'The likelihood is that both flats are investment properties owned by the same company.'

'Mrs Buenrostro said she bought her flat.' I am thinking aloud. 'Perhaps she's behind E.B. Property Services? The B could be for Buenrostro. But it's odd that she didn't admit any connection with the flat next door. I asked her again and again about its occupier.'

'There's one more thing, still. It's the thing that seems most important.'

'You're better at this than I am, Mum.'

'Of course.' We both smile.

'When did you do all this?'

'Friday morning. But I didn't want to talk about it on the anniversary. You had enough of your own to say – it made me wish I hadn't opened all of this up. I thought of not telling you at all.'

'You were right to tell me. And it's only fair. I'm telling you everything. What's the other thing you found?'

'It's to do with Miranda's flat.' She touches my fingers lightly, giving me an electric shock. 'Something made me look through the old paperwork. She bought it from E.B. Property Services. They owned it before she did.'

We had assumed you rented your flat. You were happy to let us think that. Only after you disappeared did we discover you owned it. You wouldn't have been able to come up with an explanation for that one – even Mum wouldn't have been able to sit quietly and pretend to believe you'd managed it on your nurse's salary. No mortgage for a first-floor Georgian flat. Nobody normal does that. There was no payment trail but all of the papers were in your name.

Now we have a likely explanation. 'Oh,' I say. 'Wow,' I say. 'There's no question, then, of a link between Miranda and Henrickson that she kept off our radar. It's as if E.B. Property Services made it over to her.'

'Why would they do that?'

I look hard at her. 'As payment for something. Or out of love. A love gift. Maybe from Luke's father.'

'No.' She shakes her head, too, for emphasis. 'No. I don't want anything to bring him out of the woodwork.'

'Did you really not consider the possibility, when you found all of this out?'

'No. I did not. Don't you dare open that up, Ella.'

'I'm not sure I'm the one who did.'

'No more.'

'Okay.'

She touches my cheek with the back of her freezing hand and I turn my head to kiss it. 'Shall we walk on?' she says. 'It's starting to drizzle. It may turn heavy.'

'Good plan,' I say, and we step onto grey paving stones that are already spattered with dark spots. 'Why did you help, Mum? It can't have been mere curiosity.'

'Once you know you can't un-know. You can't not act. You can't not share. But I am feeling more and more that this is going to pull you down, Ella. Especially after last night.' Uncharacteristically, our ballerina mother slips a little and I steady her.

'What happened last night?'

'That's what I need to discuss with you.' She bites her lip in that way she has when she is about to deliver bad news. She did it when she told us Grandma died.

'Should I be scared?'

She doesn't answer.

'Let's get some lunch,' I say. 'It's later than I realised and you were right – it's getting wetter – we should be inside.'

'I'm not hungry. Just a cup of tea, please.'

The Abbey's stones usually look like honey, but today they are grey. We skirt the side of the building, beneath Gothic rows of arched stained-glass windows. I steer her into another cobbled lane, where there is a cosy, old-fashioned café that Mum likes. I open the door for her and she glides in like the queen.

The furniture is dark wood and draped in white cloths. Reproduction prints of eighteenth-century portraits hang on walls papered in blue damask. There are displays of sweet things on lace doilies that you would scorn. Coffee walnut and chocolate fudge and lemon drizzle cakes. Scones and Florentines and treacle tarts.

We sit in a corner and Mum delays whatever it is that she really wants to tell me with chatter about the little girls in the ballet class she teaches once a week. At last she says, 'Things aren't right with you, Ella. You're looking tired. Is it Ted?'

This is the big thing she wants to talk about? 'No.'

The waitress puts peppermint tea in front of Mum and black coffee in front of me. I take a sip and feel physically sick.

She looks shrewdly at me. 'I knew you'd make things hard on yourself, with all of this. Whatever is going on between you and Ted, you should trust him.'

'I didn't think you were a great fan of his.'

'People change, Ella. Things aren't always as they appear. You have to forgive them their mistakes.'

I reach across the table to give her arm a little squeeze. 'I'm in a plain old bad mood. It'll pass. I'll try not to be so bah humbug.'

'You will be careful with Thorne, won't you?'

'Of course. And I'll call you as soon as I'm safely home. But can you tell me what happened last night? You've worried me.'

She considers for a few seconds. 'Perhaps now isn't the time.'

'Maybe if I go first with a tricky subject, you can feel better about going next?'

She inclines her head slightly but says nothing.

'You have always said how twirly and happy Miranda was on that last morning. But she seemed' – I fumble for the right words – 'more of a mix of moods, around then. So I wondered – were there maybe other things you noticed?'

She frowns. 'Of course not. How can you ask me that?'

Our mother would never want to climb down from the evidence she gave the police as the last known person to see you. She would never want to be found out. Especially not by our father, who would not understand, perhaps would not even forgive, if she'd kept something important back that might have helped us to find you. Her pride would be involved too. She cares about what she looks like to others. Whatever our mother really saw in you that morning, she will take it to her grave.

But I still have to press her, however futile it may be. 'Memory is difficult. Sometimes things come to us over time. We were all in such shock and distress, then. It's understandable if some detail slipped your mind. But maybe it's resurfaced?'

'There is nothing to resurface. You're the one who should be asking yourself about what you may be failing to notice.'

Something about her tone makes my heart start to beat faster.

She goes on. 'Your father didn't want me to say anything to you but Luke had a nightmare last night. I think you may be sharing too much with him.'

I take a sip of coffee and it goes down like a hard lump. When cornered, our mother can counter-attack very quickly. 'Did he say what the nightmare was about?'

'Just that you were being hurt. Your father went to him.'

'I'll be more careful.'

'It's too late, Ella. I warned you but you didn't listen. Your father and I are going to have to consider whether it's still appropriate for him to visit you.'

I try to speak lightly, though I feel as if there's a boulder in my stomach. 'Isn't that a bit of an overreaction to a bad dream?'

'He doesn't normally have them. Your father and I have no choice.'

'You can't be serious. You can't do that.'

'I am and I can.'

'He's living with me at least half the week from next year. We agreed he would go to school in Bath.'

'School choices can be changed.' Her voice is brisk no-nonsense.

'You're fucking joking. Is this some kind of revenge because I got too close to something you don't want to admit about the morning she disappeared? Too close to the truth about how and why she got her flat?'

'Don't you speak to me that way.'

'This is what Miranda hated about you. You can't change these decisions on a whim. Not for next year and not for now. He's spending Saturday night with me – it's all arranged. And I said I'd come to his football match on Thursday afternoon.'

'I don't think it's wise for you to be near his school

right now. My priority is what's best for Luke. You never appreciate how much it means to me to keep him safe.' She is blinking those grey eyes of hers so fast I think of hummingbird wings, as if she is in the REM stage of sleep, though she is as awake as she has ever been. 'I have no power to do that for you any more, but I do for him.'

'I would never put him in danger. I don't understand how finding out what happened to her isn't the most powerful force there is for you.'

She seems not to hear me. 'And your father. You don't see when he gets a twinge and thinks his cancer has woken up. He doesn't let you see. You're not the one who has to calm him down.'

'I know that. I know how hard that must be for you.' I clasp her hand in mine. When she bats it away I feel a small stab in my heart.

'And you never support me over making sure he eats right.'

'Oh my Lord. So the real reason you're punishing me is because I think you're a control freak about Dad's diet? Have you been listening to a word I say?'

'Of course I have. Of course I want to know about your sister, Ella. But I can't lose the rest of you. The fear of that is stronger than anything else.'

'I understand that. I'm sorry if I'm not sensitive enough about that. But I think if you knew what happened to Miranda it would release you. It would release all of us.'

'I don't want you to find Luke's father. I don't want some strange man coming into our lives and trying to take him from us.'

'It's not fair to Luke to keep him in the dark. What

would he feel if he knew it was in our power to find his father but we chose not to?'

'He's not going to know.'

'There's little risk of us losing him. No judge is going to remove a ten-year-old boy from the only family he has ever known and give him to some stranger.'

'Even if they share the same DNA?'

'Even then. Not at this stage of his life. We'd have to face the fact that the courts would want to consider if contact is appropriate. But they would put Luke first. As we do. And we share his DNA too.'

'The best compromise I can offer is that when you see Luke, Dad or I will need to be there too. And only at home. You can't take him out or go near his school.'

I try again to put my hand over hers, as if touching her will stop this war between us, but I half-wonder if I am holding a monster's claw. 'Luke needs time on his own with me as well as with you and Dad.'

She pulls her hand from mine. 'There's no alternative. What you're doing is affecting his well-being.'

'No. What I'm doing is good for him. And I'm not involving him in any way that puts him at risk. You can't put people in prison to keep them safe.'

'Well I don't agree.'

'Whether you agree or not doesn't matter. You aren't the God of Luke. I'm thirty now. I'm not a child. I'm a responsible consenting adult.'

'I'm not sure about responsible.'

'Then it's a good thing you have no official status as judge and jury. Dad won't tolerate you doing this.'

'You're wrong. Your father's with me.'

'No way. Did you know that Dad asked the police for her things? That that's why they finally returned them? He's sick of you shutting all of us up about her.'

'Do you really think you could possibly tell me something about your father that I don't already know?'

'I think I just did, but you're too self-obsessed and controlling to admit it.'

Her eyes fill with tears but they don't leak out and I can't help but wonder if it is some old theatrical trick from her ballet days to get herself in character. 'It isn't easy for me to say these things to you,' she says.

'Well you make it look effortless. Do you realise that, if it came to it, the court would ask Luke what he felt, at his age? They wouldn't let you take him for yourself.' How can I get through to her? Appeasement and anger have failed. Perhaps I need to try harder with reason. With facts. 'You're overestimating your legal power. You seem to have forgotten that I have shared custody.'

'Yes, but he still mostly lives with your father and me. No judge will want to upset that. And as you pointed out, the courts will always look again at child custody if circumstances change. What you are doing is changing the circumstances, so your rights with Luke may no longer be appropriate in the court's eyes.'

I want to shake her but I literally sit on my hands. 'Are you saying I'm unfit?' She doesn't answer. Her silence is her answer. 'Have you stopped to think about the moral rights and wrongs of this? Not just legal – clearly you've been busy with that.'

'Of course I have,' she says.

'Miranda would hate what you are suggesting.'

'Don't you presume to know my daughter better than I do.'

'Don't you presume to know my sister better than I do.' I croak out something that sounds like an evil cackle. 'And you wonder why she never told you anything? Why she was so secretive?'

'Your sister confided more to me than you could ever imagine.' She clamps her mouth shut as if I have provoked her into saying more than she intended.

'Easy for you to say that now. If you weren't the way you are, she wouldn't have made herself vulnerable by keeping everything hidden.' I stand up so fast the table rocks and my coffee sloshes from its china cup. Our mother's tea spills onto her fingers and when she winces I actually feel pleasure.

'Please calm down, Ella.'

'What do you expect?' I blink hard, refusing to cry. 'I've tried to reason with you but you are impossible. I can't talk to you. I can't even look at you. If you try to do this you will fail and your grandson will hate you and I will hate you and you will lose the only child you have left.'

'Don't talk about her as if she's dead.'

'That's all you have to say? That's your first thought? For the child who isn't here, rather than the one who actually is? Save your breath, Mother.'

I have never called her Mother before. If Luke can change the word for the woman who gave birth to him, so can I. The word is cold on my tongue. It makes me stand straighter.

I have one more point I must make. 'Do you think it's

good for Luke to have the three people he loves and depends on most fighting over him?'

'Sit down and lower your voice. People are looking.'

'Do you think I care?' I shake my head. 'When Luke said he wanted to live with me I told him the three of us shared him. I didn't for an instant exploit that, even though I'd love to have him with me all the time. I talked to you and Dad about it with total honesty and fairness and we negotiated. If you weren't such a monster I'd be sorry for you. You're not keeping anybody safe. You can't control the whole fucking world.'

I can hear our mother sob out a little gasp, but I don't look at her. I grab my coat and stomp from the café without turning back, slamming the door so hard I am surprised that the paned glass doesn't break.

The Masquerade Ball

I am so filled with rage and desolation and fear I hardly notice where I am going. I have deactivated my usual scanning of everything and everyone around me. It is only three in the afternoon, but already the dark is setting in as I stumble over the bridge, then the little side street that borders the scented garden where Ted helped with the self-defence class only two weeks ago.

I'm not sure how long I have been walking before a policeman materialises out of the shadows, like a ghost who has been waiting for me in a nightmare. 'Sorry to startle you.' He moves away from the wrought-iron gate that is meant to stop pedestrians falling off the pavement and smashing onto the mildewed grey slabs of the basement garden below. He positions himself between me and my little charcoal hatchback. All thoughts of our mother fly away.

He gestures towards the number plate. 'Is this your car?' He has the kind of bulky arms that men get when they work out too much and take steroids. He looks like a nightclub bouncer. He has a mole the size of a blueberry below his left eye, high on his cheek.

I don't answer. I stand more squarely on my feet. It is a stance. It is readiness.

'I'm PC Finn,' he says. PC Finn is not wearing a hat. Not a flat cap. Not a helmet. His dark brown hair is curly and close to his scalp. It is cold outside. Heads are vulnerable. Why is PC Finn not protecting his?

'Are you Miss Ella Brooke?' His hair continues into small, distinct sideburns, impeccably shaped to end above his earlobes in a point.

'How do you know my name?'

'Came up from your number plate when I called it in.'

Shouldn't he have asked if I was Melanie? I'm pretty sure my car is registered in the full version of my name.

His radio is stuck to his black vest above the breast, like a big ugly brooch. It looks authentic. So why do I keep thinking something is wrong about that radio?

'Someone was trying to break into your car. We want to make sure you're okay.'

I can't see any obvious evidence that anyone has tampered with my car. I think some more about the radio. PC Finn's radio is absolutely silent but Ted's is always on a mumbling low when he is interacting with the public, so he can listen out for a potentially urgent call. He never turns that radio off when he is on duty.

'Why is your radio off?' I say.

He looks up and down the road. 'I'm supposed to ask the questions.'

'Only of suspects and criminals. I'd appreciate it if you would answer my question.'

What he says is, 'So I can hear you properly.' What I hear is, *All the better to hear you with, my dear.*

'Are you a real policeman?' I say.

'Never been asked that one before. But we appreciate members of the public taking care. Can you please accompany me to the station in your car?'

He reaches for my arm and I pull away before he can touch it. 'I will not. And I know that I am under no obligation to do so.'

'I need to accompany you to the station, where we are holding the man who did this.'

The uniform looks real. Standard black trousers. A white shirt and dark tie peeking out from the high-visibility jacket. 'If the man who did this is at the station, then I'm quite safe on my own. I'll get myself there and meet you.'

Something is bothering me about the epaulettes. There's no collar number, but that's not necessarily a sign that anything is wrong. I say, 'I'd like to see your warrant card, please.'

'I can't let you touch my warrant card. No officer will allow a member of the public to do that.'

'I don't need to touch it. Hold it out for me. Then I can phone the station and check that you are who you say you are.'

I am looking at the scene as if from outside my own body. All of my practised responses are kicking in. I keep enough distance between us to move quickly. I open my bag and root around, so that my high-powered LED torch is towards the top and easily grasped. I am feeling more and more like Little Red Riding Hood trying to outsmart the wolf.

He puts a hand in a jacket pocket to search for the card. As he moves, one of the epaulettes glints into closer focus and I realise what the problem is. He has pinned two silvery Order of the Bath stars to one of the epaulettes but not the other. The man said he was a PC, but he is wearing the rank insignia of an inspector and only on one shoulder. Inspectors do not go on foot patrol. The uniform isn't fake but I'm certain it isn't his. And he has only been able to lay hands on some of it, hence the missing headwear and the single, wrong epaulette.

I take my phone out to wait for his warrant number, wondering how he is going to play this one. Using the buttons on the side of my phone, I snap pictures of his face, the birthmark high on his cheek, the pointy side-burns, his uniform, the epaulettes, all without his knowing it.

'I can't seem to find my warrant card.'

My adrenaline levels must be as high as when Ted buttonholed me into playing out the intruder-in-the-night scenario with him just a few metres away in the park. 'Tell me your collar number, then. I can phone the station and read it to them.'

'I really do need to talk to you. It's very important.'

'So you keep saying.'

He steps forward and as I move away I snatch the torch and engage the strobe function, temporarily blinding him. He gasps and sways. The hand he slaps over his eyes to shield them won't make the big white spots he is seeing disappear any time soon. I go from stillness to motion in a split second, imagining sparks flying from my heels as I speed back towards the town end of the street, plotting to bash him on the forehead with the torch if he catches me, though I doubt very much that he can.

I don't hear him behind me so I risk a quick glance over my shoulder. At last, the fake PC has recovered enough to run, veering off into the park. Does he have the faintest idea that I have his photograph? Whether or not he does, I know where I need to take it.

Despite my long history with Ted, I haven't spent much time in the police station. Wherever possible, our father has mediated between our family and the police. The insect-like buzz of the reception area's strip lights and its half-full vending machines are as strange and depressing to me as they would be to anyone.

I have needed to pee for the last half hour so I brave the small public loo. The walls and ceiling are snot green. I know from Ted that this is to stop drug addicts from using this murky little room as a place to inject – the colour stops them from being able to see their veins. As I pee – crouching rather than sitting, and thinking of our mother, who brainwashed us both to do this in public loos to avoid germs – I look around in dread for a camera. I can't see one but it isn't easy to see much in this sickly fluorescent glow. I wash my hands, examining my skin in the cloudy shatterproof mirror. Your face, tinted green, looks out at me.

Cold metal chairs are bolted to the waiting room floor. I don't sit for long before a real police constable calls my name and shows me through a steel door that leads directly from the reception area into a small consultation room with a green light on the outside to signal availability. Inside, there is a computer for digital capture of interviews, which he fiddles with before we begin.

I sit on yet another bolted chair, watched by yet more cameras. But I am startled by the seriousness of this man's interest in my story and the photographs I took of the fake policeman, by the care with which he writes down everything I tell him, despite the recording device. His primary concern seems to be to listen and talk openly to me.

I slide my telephone over to him. 'You don't recognise him, do you?' I ask.

'No. Not known to me. You were sharp to pick up on his using the wrong form of your name, and to see that the uniform doesn't add up.' I have liked this real policeman until now. But when he puts a thumb beneath his chin and glides his fingers back and forth over his mouth, I am no longer sure I trust him. All the while he peers at me, as if wanting an explanation for my insight. When I do not give it, he continues. 'It's high-order fakery. Most members of the public wouldn't clock it. It wouldn't have been easy to get hold of these items. I'd like to know how he did.'

'That thought occurred to me too.'

He intensifies his professional manner. 'We'll feed the images through our systems to see if we can get a hit on who he is.' He pushes a paper towards me with an email address. 'Can you please email them to our technical support unit?'

I do this instantly, then check my sent box. 'They seem to have got through.'

'Good. We'll post your images on our website and social media before the day is out. Let's hope someone can identify him.'

'You'll let me know if you discover anything?'

'If it is in our power to do so.' He is talking with his hand over his mouth again. 'We can't risk compromising any further investigation or charges.'

I have to strain not to roll my eyes at how many times I have heard this before, usually ventriloquised by our father. 'Do you have any ideas about what he was after?' I ask.

He only throws the question back at me. 'I wondered if you had a pulse on that.'

I shake my head. 'My first thought was that he was a predator, trying to lure a woman into getting in her car with him. I wanted as much information about him as I could get, so he wouldn't do it to anyone else. Another thought I had was that he's a journalist, and he wanted some sort of story about my reactions.' I pause to explain briefly about you, glad he doesn't know who I am until I do. I also tell him about my work with victims of violence.

'So you're saying it may have been some sort of test, and he could then write about the encounter?'

'I can see you think that sounds silly. I'm not confident about either of those explanations, but the ten-year anniversary of my sister's disappearance was on Friday. That could explain the interest, if he really is a journalist.'

'Was there any publicity?'

'No. But a journalist did leave a voicemail. I didn't call him back. Here. Listen.'

I play the message on speakerphone and he makes notes.

'Listening to that again, it could be the man I met today. I'm not sure.' I'm kicking myself that I didn't record as well as photograph him.

'I'd like you to share the voicemail with us. Use the same address you sent the photos to.'

A few taps on my phone and it is done.

'I apologise for what I'm about to ask,' he says, 'but do you have any enemies?'

I tell him about Sadie, followed by the anonymous silent phone calls as well as the email from Justice Administrator that I already logged with the police. I even mention the chocolates and the card to my parents, though I realise I'm probably unique in regarding the phrase *Thinking of You* as a threat, and that these won't count because they weren't sent to me.

'There isn't enough for us to do anything at this stage, but forward everything to us to log – we'll see if the sender can be identified. And if anything else happens, we'll pay her a visit,' he says.

I open my mouth to tell him about the photo of Ted and Ruby, but nothing comes out. Do I really want to risk getting Ted in trouble at work? Or at the very least embarrassing him? In any case, I forwarded the email and its attachment to Ted already, which is as good as logging it with the police. I am not about to suggest to this man that I don't trust Ted to do the right thing with it. My habits of protectiveness towards him cannot be broken.

So instead I say, 'It's just as well if you hold off on visiting her for now. It could make her angrier. Make her escalate things, if it actually is her behind those communications. She may calm down, now that she's let off steam.'

'And if she doesn't, you'll come straight back to us.'

'Yes.'

'Let's return to the man from earlier today. You will know that impersonating a police officer is an extremely serious offence.'

'I do know that,' I say. And then, 'I'm sure I wasn't a random target. He knew who I was and he planned that ambush. What I deeply want to know is why.'

The real police constable nods. His hand is not covering his mouth when he next speaks. 'I'd like to know that too,' he says. And to my great surprise, I actually believe him.

Tuesday, 15 November

The Tour

I have seen this place from the road many times before, driving along what locals still call Lucifer's Lane,
though it has never officially been given that name. In
the road atlas, it is just a numbered road skirting atop
a sunken valley. Inside this valley sits the hospital for
the criminally insane that Jason Thorne is unlikely ever
to leave.

The hospital itself is an imposing Victorian building,
typically beautiful and terrifying from the elevated road.
It looks like something from a Gothic nightmare, despite
the propaganda in the information leaflet. *Patients, not
prisoners.* How many different ways did they manage to
stress this?

There is a last glimpse of the whole complex before
I follow the narrow slip-road down the hill and wind my
way to the car park. When I emerge from my car, I can
hear no screams from inside the building. At least
nothing piercing enough to escape its thick red bricks
and the high walls circling the entire grounds.

Hospital, not prison. Really? The walls are topped with razor wire.

I find my way to the main reception building and murmur my name into an intercom. The door clicks and swings open, and I step over the threshold and towards the barrier of safety glass that encloses the receptionist.

'I'm Ella Brooke.' I slide my passport into the shallow metal tunnel that runs beneath the safety window. My hands are visibly trembling and I hope she doesn't notice. 'I have an appointment with Jason Thorne, but I'm meeting Adam Holderness first.'

She shoots me a tight professional smile before extracting the passport from her side and examining it. 'It says your name is Melanie.'

'Melanie is on my birth certificate but I go by Ella.'

Do you see how much trouble you cause me?

Really? What about when I saved your ass yesterday because I changed your name?

The woman scrutinises the passport again, flicking her eyes between my face and the photograph. She puts the passport onto a photocopy bed, then returns it to the tunnel without comment, leaving me wondering if she will let me in.

'Is everything okay?' I ask.

'I suppose the image matches your face.' Her hair is so over bleached and over straightened and over long it seems to exemplify every warning you ever gave me about the things that cause hair to look and feel like straw.

'That's a relief.' She doesn't laugh. 'Here's my letter of invitation, to see Mr Thorne.' I slide it through.

She stretches her nose and purses her lips in the manner of a banker regarding a forged £10,000 note. But she seems to decide that I am not an imposter with a master plan to free all the inmates. She gives me a name badge and points me towards the search area, which is full of guards with guns on their belts.

Patients not prisoners. Did the people who wrote this really not mean it to become one of those ironic refrains you cannot get out of your head?

The guards X-ray my bag, then direct me to stow it in a locker. I shove my coat in too. A female guard takes my fingerprints and an image of my eye before snapping my photograph. She conducts a body search by patting my arms and legs and even my torso. She makes double sure by waving a wand over every inch of me. More security guards signal me to go through the body scan's archway. I pass through it and practically bump into Adam, who is waiting for me on the other side.

His pupils are so big in his black eyes that I cannot see where they begin and end. It occurs to me that he has watched the body search. I have walked into all of this in full knowledge of the fact that this man is pursuing me – it has happened before, but I have never had reason to play on it until now, sickeningly faithful to my lost true love for too many years.

Is our mother right to worry that whatever it takes, I will do? You would know the answer to this question. I do not. Do you remember that little note you once wrote me? I still have it, taped to the mirror over my dressing table.

I told you so.
Love, Your Intuition.

I'd never heard it before. Until last year, when I saw somebody wearing that slogan on a T-shirt, I thought you had invented it yourself.

I had planned to raid my wardrobe for my best approximation of the tasteful clothes I failed to buy during the disastrous expedition with our mother. But I went for a last-minute change of plan. My smoky blue shirt dress and block heel boots match the ones you were last seen in, though I have had to leave the fabric tie off the dress's waist because it is a potential weapon.

The space between my breasts is empty. I put a panicked hand to my chest, thinking I have lost my locket, only to remember that I left it at home in deference to their long list of proscribed items. Like the tie, a chain of precious metal could be used to strangle somebody.

I am not used to heels like these. How did you walk in them? I take a wobbly step and nearly fall on my face, only just catching myself. The preposterous entrance makes me blush.

Adam has the grace to pretend it never happened. 'I can show you some of the grounds if you'd like, before your appointment.' His well-mannered professionalism is exactly what I need, but there is warmth mixed in too.

I manage a half-smile. 'That would be good.' He knows how deeply curious I am about this place and its inhabitants.

He motions me to follow him through another door

into an airlocked, metal-lined room that reminds me of a space-capsule and makes me feel as if I can't breathe. He opens a second door, which spills us onto the other side of the perimeter wall, facing an elaborate arrangement of squat outbuildings around the towering main hospital. To access this complex, we walk through a corridor of grim steel fences with lock after lock that he opens so we can pass through barrier after barrier.

He sees me squinting at the wall-mounted cameras. 'You get used to them,' he says.

I have never seen so many, so ostentatiously close together, so obviously moving to survey us, either adjusted remotely by an army of unseen observers in a control room somewhere or triggered automatically by motion.

'I'm glad you came.' His voice is casual-friendly but his eyes are not.

I remind myself of his expertise. Figuring out people's thoughts, the way their minds work, so he can try to manipulate them. 'It was kind of you to invite me.'

He allows himself an ironic raised eyebrow. 'You're the first woman who has ever subjected herself to a full body search and biometrics to have coffee with me.'

'I find that difficult to believe.' *See Ted*, I think. *I can do flirting.*

His black eyes don't waver from mine. 'I'd like to think that Thorne wasn't your only inducement.'

'I have a general interest in criminal rehabilitation. And in talking to you.'

'Glad to hear it.' He frowns. 'And Sadie? Have you heard from her?'

'Not directly.' Literally truthful but also evasive. One of your best tricks.

Though I must not be as good at it as you. I can see from the seriousness of his expression that he hears something in my tone, but doesn't press it.

'This way,' he says, and leads me through an extremely well-manicured garden, though it is dull and unadorned. He motions around him. 'The patients do this. Cut the grass. Trim the hedges. We have kitchen gardens, where they plant vegetables. It's all part of their occupational therapy.'

'You're actually proud of them, aren't you?'

'Yes. I am.' He points to a large, single-storey outbuilding, built of more grey stucco with a flat black iron roof. 'They do woodwork in here. Primarily it's patients who've come a long way in their treatment. Want to see?'

'Very much.' We both know it is no accident that he is suggesting this particular workshop.

I am hugging myself, getting goosebumps out here, beneath a dark grey sky that seems to reflect the security fencing. All I have on is this filmy Miranda dress. Were you always freezing, skipping about in such things?

'You're cold,' he says.

'Not at all.' I lead him towards the woodwork studio as if this were my world rather than his. He unlocks the door by holding his identification card to a small scanner that flashes green. That is it. The only security there is for this building.

The studio is one large room. It is so light in here, with the walls made mostly of windows and the rows of rectangular fluorescent bulbs on the ceiling. There are large wooden workbenches and pieces of heavy metal equipment. Table saws and planers and vices and sanders, all of them potentially lethal weapons. Considering the warnings that visitors can't even bring in plastic cutlery due to the risk of it being turned into an instrument of death, I cannot help but appear surprised.

'These are human beings, Ella. They have talents. We need to help them develop those talents. The hospital is remedial in every way it can be. As I said, they only get access to this particular workshop when they're doing well.'

This man really does seem to read my mind, which isn't something many people can do. I give him an *I'm not convinced* look, feeling my face echo yours. 'Not well enough not to be in a secure mental hospital. They are confined here because they've done unspeakable things.'

'As you'll see shortly, there's heavy supervision. Patients need to develop their skills. They need stimulation. They have to feel the things they do are meaningful. That their lives have value.'

I think of Thorne's indefinite detention order. 'Even the ones who will never leave?'

He knows who I am talking about. 'Even those,' he says.

'All it takes is a blip in his good behaviour and you can end up with your wrist shoved between those blades,' I say.

'You're one of those people who is funny without meaning to be, aren't you?'

'Hilarious. Or your neck. Maybe get the skin of your arm sanded off with the planer or your fingers in the vice.'

'It's controlled. We train them in computer technology too, though everything they do is monitored and recorded.'

I am fixated on a rocking horse that is so exquisite it could be a gift for a baby prince. To be faced with evidence of Thorne's considerable carving skills makes me want to cry. I replay what Adam has said and look up from its intricate face. 'Do the patients know they are being spied on?'

He doesn't answer, but I persist. 'Do you ever learn anything useful?'

Again he doesn't answer.

'They must reveal things,' I say. 'When they've let their guard down. When they are immersed. Is that the real incentive for all of this skills development?'

'The education team report to us on how they're doing.'

'Not exactly what I was asking. I mean, do you discover more about the people they have hurt, the things they've done?'

'Occasionally.'

I am thinking of the onion router that made your laptop seem as clean and shiny as a brand-new machine. I am thinking also of the recent headlines linking you to Thorne, as well as the interview I did a few months before they appeared. Could Thorne have seen my interview, then somehow instigated those news stories himself?

'I bet some of them are clever enough to circumvent your computer spyware. Maybe visit websites or communicate in ways you don't know about.'

'No.'

'I wouldn't be so confident – they must be finding back doors.'

He moves his head to acknowledge the possibility, but only as a matter of politeness.

I run my hand over the smooth top rail of a perfectly carved chair.

Killer's Woodwork Fetches High Price at Auction.

'Whoever made that rocking horse is talented. And this chair.'

Murderer Donates Auction Proceeds to Hospital for Sick Children.

Thorne never hurt children. Just the three women whose frozen bodies were found in the room he'd dug and fitted beneath his house.

Adam touches the chair too. When his fingers bump into mine I let the contact stay for a few seconds before I pull them away to brush hair from my face.

Thorne Too Disturbed to Be Interviewed by Detectives.

I pick up a jewellery box. Its top and sides have been carved with tiny daisies and vines. Did he use this pattern on skin too? I turn it over, looking for his initials – he was rumoured to have engraved them on the women he tortured.

The two letters seem to blaze at me. *JT.* A man who was capable of the most terrible acts of ugliness made this breathtaking thing.

I cannot tear my eyes from the box as I say to Adam, 'I'd like your expertise.'

'I already offered you that.'

'Not for the people I help.' I'm still studying the box as if looking away from it would be the most impossible thing in the world. 'I want it for myself.'

'As a patient?' He takes the box from my hands as

if it were a deadly weapon. 'Because you must know that's not how it works.' He walks towards the door and I follow him.

I touch his hand, briefly, as he moves to open it. 'Of course not as a patient.'

He pauses to look at me. 'It doesn't take an expert to see that you're still traumatised by your sister's disappearance. That it was a deep stress event for you and you can't let her go. I have never seen anyone hold on as tightly as you do. Do you talk to her?'

I push past him to open the door and walk out but he quickly catches up.

'Please stop for a minute, Ella,' he says.

His emotional ambush makes me reel almost as violently as our mother's. My hand finds its way to the building and I lean on it, as if that will stop me from falling.

'Does she talk back to you?' he says. 'Do you hear her?'

I blink at him.

'Are there ever other voices than hers? I suspect yes, but that it's predominantly her. Am I right?'

I swallow and try to move my mouth to speak but nothing comes out.

'There isn't any treatment I would want to give you for these symptoms. They are situational. They arise from a specific trauma. They are not co-morbid. I'm inclined to think this private communication works for you, keeps you functioning and actually keeps you well. That these are your tools rather than any sort of pathology.'

I cannot speak at all. How does he know this? Nobody has ever guessed it.

'I'm sorry,' he says. 'I've upset you. I said too much. I want to know you as a person, not a patient, Ella. So let's close this subject.' His phone rings. He answers and talks in monosyllables before ringing off. 'I need to go,' he says. 'I'll take you back to Reception. You can wait there until your appointment with Jason Thorne.'

'I can find my way back.' My voice comes out as a croak.

He shakes his head. 'Visitors need to be escorted at all times.' He reaches over to brush my shoulder.

Despite the electric shock he gives me, and my small jump backwards into a flower border, his fingers seem to pause to test the silk of your dress between them.

'What are you doing?' My voice is shrill.

'Baby spider.' His voice is calm and unworried, a parent to a toddler who is in the grip of irrational fear. He holds out his hand and I can see the tiny creature dangling there by its fine strand. 'What did you think I was doing?'

'Nothing.' I sound like a child telling a ridiculous lie.

He continues with that chivalrous patience of his. He is concentrating. Gently, he moves his hand, floating the wisp of spider silk to a rose bush, letting it catch on a branch. The spider baby wafts into the green leaves and disappears.

The Door at the End

I stumble along in your clunky-heeled boots, following a beefy security man who probably moonlights as a nightclub bouncer. Soon, I am back at the glassed-in reception counter. Another encounter with the grumpy frazzle-haired woman is enough to shake away the near-paralysis induced by Adam's unasked-for diagnosis.

'I have an appointment with Jason Thorne at 2 p.m.,' I say.

She looks at me blankly.

'I gave you my letter of invitation when I first arrived,' I say.

Has Ted done something to stop the visit? Maybe he wanted to keep me away not just from Thorne but Adam too. I hear our mother's voice. *Paranoid.* Then I remember the intensity of Ted's eyes on Ruby, and the contempt of those same eyes when they were turned on me. I should not fool myself that Ted would care at all.

The woman starts click-clacking on her keyboard.

'I made the request two weeks ago and it was approved last Thursday,' I say. 'Mr Thorne consented to the visit and put me on his list. Dr Holderness knows about it.'

She is reading a series of notes on her computer screen, continuing to act as if I am a ghost she cannot see or hear. She sucks in air, grimacing as if she has come across something extremely disturbing, and I can see plum lipstick on her teeth.

'I was led to understand that there are no clinical grounds to deny my visit,' I say. 'Is there a problem?'

'No problem.' She pushes her spectacles down her nose so that she can give me a sharp look over the frames. 'Please be patient.'

Some people don't have much power, Melanie. So they exercise the little they do in the smallest, nastiest ways they can.

Were you thinking of someone in particular? I remember you coming home from the hospital in an especially bad mood when you made this pronouncement.

At last, the woman says, 'Dr Holderness will not be personally escorting you this time. That is not what he usually does.'

Maybe she has a crush on Adam and that is why she detests me. 'Of course,' I say. 'I don't mind who escorts me.' I smile sweetly and she pretends not to notice.

Jason Thorne lives in the main hospital building, in a ward for patients with dangerous and severe personality disorders. I am sitting on a red upholstered chair, part of a row of six that are linked together like the snap-apart pieces of a cereal box prize. I was deposited in this secure area by a security guard after retracing the route through the tunnel of locked gates, then yet another silvery airlock.

A door swings open and Adam walks through it, despite the grumpy woman's assertion that he would not be escorting me again. He looks confident and elegant in his dark suit. I cannot help but like him for the pink shirt he is wearing beneath it.

'I'm sorry I was called away,' he says. 'Emergency with another patient. I owe you a coffee.'

'It's fine. I understand.'

'I'll take you in,' he says. 'He's under my care.'

My knees are shaking so much I am pressing on them to try to keep them still. I say, 'Are you sure it's safe to expose him to someone you diagnosed with multiple personality disorder?'

'I haven't diagnosed you with anything. I said you are functioning well.'

I am not going to stop talking to you, even if this man has guessed that I do. If there is a name for it, even if it is a disease, I do not care.

He clears his throat, as if that will draw a line beneath the subject.

'Did you approve my request to see Jason Thorne?'

'I may have acted a bit more quickly when I saw your name. Sped the paperwork through – I wanted to do something to help.' He catches my eye. 'It would have still happened without me, just a bit slower.'

I stand to follow him. 'Thank you, Adam.'

He startles at my use of his Christian name for the first time. But this is no occasion for him to smile. 'He's taking his meds. He's stable. His behaviour has been satisfactory for several years now.'

'Will he be in restraints?' My voice is trembling, though I am trying to steady it.

'He's deemed to be low risk – he's made good progress since he first came here and the visit will be carefully supervised. There are security measures in place, but if he needed restraints you wouldn't be seeing him.'

I give up on trying to hide my anxiety. 'Will there be a barrier between us?'

He shakes his head. 'This isn't a prison, Ella. We want patients to have the most natural interactions possible with their guests. The Visitors' Centre is like a living room. It is as un-medical as it can be. But there will be staff quite close. They will be watching carefully. They are in a position to act quickly, if necessary. Does that make you feel better?'

'A little.'

'He has a legal and humanitarian right to visitors, but his ability to exercise that right is subject to quite stringent medical criteria. That approval is appropriate in his case, on clinical grounds, and has been for some time.'

Adam flashes a card at an electronic reader, punches in an access code, and opens the door. 'It was his choice to see you. If he had refused your request, I couldn't and wouldn't have done anything.'

The sight of the long corridor lined with locked metal doors makes my stomach drop.

'Ready?' Adam says.

I try to say yes but the word stops in my throat. I swallow. I manage a nod.

'Good. It's the door at the end. He's waiting.'

Jewels

It is more like a Victorian drawing room than a hospital visitors' area. It is big, but Jason Thorne is so huge he seems to be the only thing in it. He is also the only thing I can hear. A thunderous bellow erupts from his belly and I understand why the smell of cabbage and faeces is mixed with the lemony disinfectant they must use on every surface and spray into the air to try to disguise the scent of male sweat that is inescapable in this place.

All I see in the room is him. He is spilling over the single cushion of a sofa that is upholstered in gold fabric traced with vines and flowers in a deeper shade of the same colour. I know Adam said they'd designed the Visitors' Centre to be homey and unclinical, but it still seems an absurd piece of furniture for a secure mental hospital.

Thorne was tall and thin in the newspaper photographs published after they caught him. Now he is obese. The sofa is shaped into a perfect half-circle and reminds me of a piece of doll's house furniture. He is a giant atop a dainty toy that seems about to collapse beneath his enormous weight.

He stands to greet me, all six foot four of him, and it is clear that he wouldn't need to jump high or hard for his bald head to crash into the ceiling.

'Lovely to meet you.' He speaks like a politician greeting his guest of honour but his voice is such a bellow I have to resist the urge to slap a hand over my ear. The voice alone could knock me over. A few minutes of this and I will need to go into a decompression chamber to recover. His movement sets off another roar and an intensification of the smell that is so horrible it is a struggle not to bury my nose in my hair so that I can inhale my soapy-fresh shampoo to try to mask him. It is the same shampoo you used, and I like it because the scent reminds me of you. It occurs to me that this may be the case for Jason Thorne too.

He beams at me and puts out his huge paws, waiting to take mine between them. They look like normal hands, but for their giant size. How can a pair of hands have done what these did but not have a mark or a sign? I stare at them, as if searching for one. But there is nothing, of course.

My inability to move or speak or breathe goes on for an uncomfortably long time and I keep my own hands firmly at my sides. My feet are frozen on the ludicrously thick green carpet. My heart is thumping so loud I think he can hear it. All the while, he smiles understandingly, slightly amused, as if he is a movie star patronising an awestruck fan. His stomach does something that sounds exactly like a wolf's howl.

He shrugs and slowly lowers his arms. 'Thank you for bringing her,' he says to Adam, dismissing a servant. 'You can leave now. My visitor and I would like to speak privately.'

My normal inclination to correct a strange man for teaming himself with me is paralysed. Above all else I do not want to be left alone with Jason Thorne. I am groping for the right words to say so but Adam saves me from needing to.

'You know the rules, Jason. Ward staff need to be present. Today I'm one of them.'

'Interesting step down from your usual activities, Dr Doom.'

'If you're not happy with the arrangement, Miss Brooke will need to leave now.'

I still haven't moved or spoken. The room is starting to spin and there is a serious danger that my legs will buckle.

Two hulking male nurses who look more like body-guards than medical professionals are sitting at a shiny wood-veneered table, positioned five feet from Thorne's side of the sofa. Is their close-by table close enough? They appear to be working their way through papers, but I am certain they are listening to every word. I am certain they have perfected the art of seeming to read when in fact they are watching us, ready to punch tran-quilliser needles into Jason Thorne's tree-trunk arms if he moves too quickly. I am certain that I am not deluding myself with this impression. Adam said that there would be carefully trained staff nearby. He said there were security measures in place, but I wish they were more obvious.

They must need to special order Thorne's jeans. The hospital kitchen probably tries to control his weight, but he has to be carrying an extra two hundred pounds at least. Why has this happened to him? Is it the medication? Comfort eating? They will be wheeling him out of this place some day in an industrial crate. Rolls of fat are visible beneath his red lumberjack shirt, but his sheer bulk makes him dangerously strong.

Thorne pats the thin sliver of sofa beside him. He really does love to play the genial host. 'Please sit here and make yourself comfortable, Melanie.'

My head whips up at my full name. Did he hear you use it?

I remind myself it is on the passport I showed the frazzle-haired woman. It has probably been transmitted all over the hospital since I arrived, perhaps repeated to Thorne. I imagine a ward nurse approaching him. 'Melanie Brooke has arrived for you, Jason,' the nurse would say.

Thorne reads my mind. His eyes flick to my chest. I look down and see the sticker the receptionist gave me, above my left breast. Melanie Brooke is written on it in permanent ink. I had forgotten about it.

At last, I speak. 'I'd be more comfortable in a chair, thank you.' I grab one, a small-scale version of the sofa that is clearly part of a set, and drag it across the room. I place the chair opposite Thorne, glad of the low coffee table between us, made of more of that unidentifiable blonde wood veneer they have used all over the room to make it look like a pseudo drawing room.

The cushion is slippery. It squeaks when I move but

I am relieved to be sitting down. It means I am no longer in danger of falling over. Already I am beginning to feel less faint. Adam takes a chair that matches mine and places it beside me.

'Good to know you can talk,' Thorne says.

How would I fight a man like Thorne? How quickly could he get to me? Could he grab me before one of the bouncer nurses got to him with knockout drugs and restraints? A big part of the strategy would involve making sure he couldn't possibly pin me down with his body, because once that happened the options would be limited. Small things would work best. Eye gouges. Breaking his pinky finger. Using his weight against him as he crashed down. The most important thing would be stunning him and getting out of his reach.

There are cameras everywhere. I suspect there are hidden microphones too. I am certain that Adam is listening intently, though he looks as if he is about to have a beer with an old friend in his living room. His legs are far out and he is slouching in his chair over his clipboard with unbelievable casualness. I have never seen him slouch before. Is he trying to be less visible? Less threatening to Thorne?

The only way to get through this, I realise, is to try to pretend that Thorne is normal. To speak to him as if this were an ordinary encounter. As far as possible, anyway. Because the alternative to tricking myself in this way is total shutdown.

'I saw some of the things you made, Mr Thorne,' I say. 'The rocking horse is beautiful.' My voice is steadier than I thought it would be.

He ignores the compliment with studied well-manneredness but his face lights up. 'I like to make things for children,' he says. 'I like children. Do you?'

'Yes.'

'I don't like people who hurt children,' he says.

'Nor do I.'

'Call me Jason.' He says this as if he is giving me a gift.

I move my head in acknowledgement but I do not call him Jason. It would be difficult to breathe, if you were too near him. There is a cloud of sour sweat in the air around him. Was this the last thing you ever smelled, obliterating your memories of fresh air and rain, making you forget your baby's milky-sweet skin? Bile is rising in my throat and I have to work hard to swallow it down.

'I thought you'd come.' His face is so fleshy, when he smiles. I do not like this politician's smile of his. 'I always thought you would. I've been waiting for you.'

Adam barely looks up from his clipboard. 'How long is always?' Thorne ignores him and Adam asks another question. 'What made you think that?'

'This is my party. You get to be a silent guest, if you insist on crashing it.' Thorne speaks as if he is in charge and Adam is the one locked in the mental ward for criminal psychopaths. Is this really 'satisfactory behaviour', as Adam called it? The standards of measurement are clearly different here.

Adam simply continues in his sleepy pose, while Thorne turns back to me, his face full of concern, enjoying the obvious difference in the way he is treating me and Adam. 'I'm deeply sorry about the disruption, dear Melanie.'

'How and when did you become aware of my existence, Mr Thorne?'

'It is too early in our relationship for us to be so personal.'

'Do you know something of interest to me, that made you think I would seek you?'

'Again, we are not yet ready for such confidences. You will need to be patient. Why don't we begin with your telling me why you wanted to come here.'

'I think you know why.'

He nods, as if proud of me for living up to his expectations. 'Do I repulse you?'

I don't answer this. I won't answer this. My refusal to answer is an answer.

He holds out his hands, shrugs, and looks down at his body. The series of theatrical gestures verges on comical, because they are so overdramatic. 'I mean this corporeal shell, lest there be any doubt.'

Corporeal shell. Where did he learn to talk? What does he read?

I don't acknowledge the words or the movement. He studies my face and I force myself not to squirm, not to move. Just to meet his gaze evenly.

'You're not a liar,' he says.

Little the fuck do you know, I think.

'I didn't take your sister,' he says. 'Have you been having bad dreams, Melanie, thinking that I did?'

I am not about to tell this man anything about my dreams. Or my nightmares.

'Was she much like you?' he says.

'A lot of people seem to think so.'

'Tea, Melanie. Allow me to make you a cup.' The offer isn't a question.

I can't help my surprise. 'They let you near boiling water?'

'You're funny. I like a sense of humour. But you don't have to worry. There is a maximum temperature. Never hot enough to injure. Everything is toddler-proof. I am afraid that the tea will not be as I would wish it for you.'

'No thank you.' He must guess that I will not drink anything he has touched.

'Then squash. I insist.' He pours orange liquid from a clear jug that looks like glass but is actually made of something shatterproof. Those sausage fingers of his are remarkably adroit and precise. When he places a blue tumbler in front of me something flakes from his wrist and into the drink.

That is when I notice his bracelet. It is a short string threaded with dead bluebottles. The centrepiece is a desiccated moth, shedding dust, with the corpse of a wasp on each side.

He holds out his wrist, smiling. 'Do you like it?'

'Were they already dead or did you make them dead?'

He looks at Adam, whose eyes flick up to watch his answer. 'Of course they were already dead.' He is practically laughing with the lie. 'If I killed living things I'd lose my privileges. I'd like to try a necklace but I am only allowed frustratingly short pieces of string.'

Yet they let you near saws and planers. I point to a dried slug, marbled black and curled through one of his buttonholes. 'That too?'

'More found art.' He opens his eyes wide in fake regret.

'Convenient that it died in that position. It's a perfect fit.'

'Before my repentance, I got excellent results by putting them in an oven alive and cooking them slowly.' He moves his expression into shocked innocence. 'One patient, far less well than I, has been known to trap them beneath a cup on his windowsill, when the sun is hot.

'Not to your taste, alas,' he says. 'You're very controlled, Melanie, but not perfectly – I can still see.' He points to the drink that he has seasoned with his most recent victims. 'You must be thirsty.'

'Not at the moment.' I can feel Adam trying to suppress a smile. 'Why should I believe you when you say you didn't take her?'

'Biscuit, Melanie?' I shake my head no. 'Please take one.' He picks up a plate of sugar cookies and offers it across the low table, set for a toddler's tea party—but for the small murdered guests. A wasp's wing falls onto snowy icing. 'The patients make them. Part of that occupational therapy our doctor friend thinks is so important. What a good man he is, our Dr Holderness.'

I choose a wasp-free biscuit in the shape of a star, so that Thorne smiles that hateful smile again. 'Perhaps I will be hungry later,' I say, accepting the napkin he graciously hands me. I put the biscuit on the napkin, beside the tumbler. Every move this man makes, every word out of his mouth, is a power game. 'You didn't answer my question, Mr Thorne.'

He shrugs, sighs, shakes his head in bewilderment as if he and I are unfairly persecuted victims together. 'I would like to help you,' he says.

'Why? Is Dr Holderness's treatment working so well that you have become selfless?'

He laughs. 'No compliments for the do-gooding doctor. Do you find do-gooders tedious? And pious? And exhausting? Because I do. But I am bored, Melanie. I seek amusement where I can.'

'I find it difficult to see how you can help me.'

'Insight, at least at first. Do you ever think about what he did with her body?'

I say nothing.

'I think you do think about this,' he says. 'I think you lose sleep thinking about it. But I can see it is painful to you. Do you like pigs?'

Again I say nothing.

'Ah. You must be vegetarian – you have already made it clear that you don't like violence. Good to know, in case I am ever able to entertain you.'

'One more remark like that and Miss Brooke will leave,' Adam says.

'An innocent comment, Dr Dire. Please accept my apologies, Melanie. I meant no offence. Quite the opposite.' He eats me up with his eyes and I refuse to shrink. 'I am a deeply creative person, you know,' he says. 'Everything I do, I do for art. I think I may have found my new muse in you.'

'You were talking about pigs, Mr Thorne?'

He makes a show of his patience with me. 'They'll eat anything. They'll make anything vanish.'

'I read a novel recently where the villain does that.' I shake my head in contempt. 'That's always happening in books and I always think it is silly. Are you trying to say you think that's what happened to my sister?' My anger is helping me. It is too big to let me properly imagine such a desecration. 'Can't you do better than that? Tell me the truth about why you want to help me, but don't waste my time.'

'I like company. I especially like your company. I like beautiful things, beautiful women. I used to like for them to become part of my vision, so I could make them even more beautiful. But they didn't want to. It was very sad. Not unless I persuaded them. Of course, this is not what I want any more.' The last sentence is uttered with such ironic insincerity it would be laughable if it were not so sickening.

'How did you persuade them?'

'Free carpentry. Wooden gifts. A visit to my workshop. In here, the only lure I have is information. Understanding.'

'And you have this information and understanding because of the things you yourself have done?'

'Not to your sister. But yes.' He glances at Adam and adds a quick, ostentatiously phoney, 'I am very sad to say.'

'Did you meet her?'

'Not in person. I spoke to her. She phoned me.' His eyes narrow. 'You didn't know, did you? Tell me the truth, Melanie.'

'I suspected recently.'

His face flushes. 'The tabloids, a few weeks ago?' he says.

'Yes.'

'Surely the police told you before then?'

'No.'

'It was on her phone records,' he says. 'The police checked them soon after they caught me. Went on and on about it in my interviews. Did you ask them about me?'

'My family did, but they wouldn't confirm any contact between you. Not when you were first arrested and not when we asked again last month.'

He nods and sighs. 'I can assure you the police have known all along. They are bastards, aren't they? Excuse my language. The journalists tell you more than they do. We see eye-to-eye on so many things, you and I, Melanie.'

'How many times did you speak to my sister?'

'Just one long telephone conversation. She started with a view to saying yes but ended with no.' He laughs. 'So often the case for me.'

'What exactly did she say no to?'

'My doing a carpentry job for her.'

'The telephone was your only means of communication?'

'Interesting question.'

'That isn't an answer.'

'Her only means of communication with me, yes.'

'What other means might there be, Mr Thorne? And with whom?'

'Good questions. I'd like to give you answers, Melanie. If I weren't trapped in this place, I'd find more of them for you – I'd do anything for you. Unfortunately, in the circumstances, you will need to do this yourself.' He shrugs tragically, and goes on. 'Something else for you to consider. She dealt in cash, your sister, didn't she?'

'Sometimes. But you're not telling me anything the

police don't already know. If you want my company you're going to need to do better. You said you'd find more answers. More implies you already have some.'

I can't decide if those amber eyes of his are actually small or if they appear that way because the rest of him is so big. There is a glint in one of them and he gives me a *Who Me?* shrug that looks absurd and obscene at once. 'I kept my business aboveboard. Everything recorded. Taxes paid. You get it, don't you?'

'You didn't want anyone looking at you carefully, uncovering the more serious dangers you posed.'

'Exactly. But your sister didn't want a paper trail of her payment to me. That's why she changed her mind. Got me wondering, after she disappeared, who was really paying for the work she wanted done?' He smiles. 'You've thought about that too. Your face is guarded, Melanie, but there are cracks in your armour.'

This is the second time he has said this. He has been right both times.

'By the way,' he says, 'do you like field hedges?'

'What?'

'Old English field hedges. Do you like them?'

I think of the countless family walks of my childhood, the earlier ones with you there too, and blackberry picking in September, and the quests for the dwindling nightingales that I still make with Luke in late spring. 'I do.'

'Are you any good at geometry?'

'I'm okay at it.'

'Forty-five-degree angles. I want you to visualise a forty-five-degree angle.'

'Sorry?' Immediately I am angry at myself for using this word to him.

'Please don't apologise.' He laughs at his own wit. He lowers his voice to a bedroom voice that I really, really do not want to hear. 'I never want you to be sorry with me.' Thorne picks up the biscuit with the wasp wing on it, licks the edge, takes a large bite, chews slowly.

Adam sits forward a little but his neutral expression doesn't change and he continues to scribble on his clipboard in writing that is so small and cramped I have to struggle to read even one word from where I'm sitting. I squint harder and my own name pops out.

Thorne downs a tumbler of orange squash in one gulp. 'I am ready to continue with your geometry lesson.

'Step 1. Dig a sloping hole that goes into the ground at a forty-five-degree angle, so that the hole finishes directly beneath the hedge. You want the hole to be the length of the body you need to bury.

'Step 2. Roll the body down. No detector is going to find that body. Not with that hedge above it. My bet is those hedges thrive because of the fertiliser. Some of them are hundreds of years old. Some of them are protected.'

He licks his lips. His tongue is fat too. He sighs. 'I miss the great outdoors. There is such a wonderful variety of plant life. Brambles, of course. Hawthorne. Ivy. All tangled together. All complex. Better yet, a hedge in a private field in the grounds of a private house, probably on private farmland, so he can keep her close.'

'Theory or experience, Mr Thorne?'

'Theory, of course, Melanie. But in my view it is the

strongest explanation there is as to your sister's where-abouts. I lived in a small house with no private hedges. The police searched it so thoroughly they practically demolished it. I promise you won't find her there.'

'So why should this matter to me?'

'Your sister was not the sort he would want to be entirely rid of. He would want to know where she is, to see that place whenever he wants. I can't tell you if she was his first, but whether or not she was, she won't be his last. She won't be enough. He will want another like her.'

'Why do you speak as if you are certain that she is dead?'

'It's difficult to imagine anything else, isn't it? You don't lie to others. Why do you lie to yourself?'

'What am I not seeing, Mr Thorne? What have the police missed?'

'You are thinking too much about type. About who *he* would choose. Which, yes, is you. And your sister. You would certainly be my choice. In many ways, though, you two were quite different, weren't you? You, I would want to keep. For a long time. I would want us to enjoy our time together.'

Adam shifts in his chair and begins to make another noise of protest, but Thorne brushes him away.

'You should be thinking about the type *she* would choose. That's a better starting point for you than the needle in the haystack of who would choose her.'

'Any ideas?'

'Yes, as a matter of fact.' He turns those tawny eyes on Adam. 'Someone like the good doctor.'

Adam doesn't react. He simply makes another note.

'Educated. Gentlemanly. Strong. The sort whose words are carefully chosen. And he would like her too. He certainly likes you.' Thorne glances at Adam and laughs. 'I've made the gooseberry blush. The only problem is that I don't think even Dr Dimwit would have been able to keep her in the style to which she wanted to grow accustomed.'

'Why are you so interested in my sister?'

'Missing women are my hobby. They are yours too. We have a lot in common, you and I. Everyone needs something to live for.'

'How do you know so much about her?'

'There's a lot in the newspapers. I have an eye for what might be true and what might not. I can find the real story hidden in the margins of what they don't say. I am like you, Melanie. I am good at interpretation. You find a small clue and you understand its significance while most would stick it in a file and let it moulder away. We should have been psychiatrists, you and I. Or detectives.'

'Has someone in here told you something specific?'

He shoos the question away with a hand, then swoops down on the biscuits, catching another and gulping it down in one bite. 'She liked nice things, didn't she? Expensive things. I could tell from talking to her. I never told the police what she wanted. Shall I tell you?'

'Yes.'

'You are very cold, Melanie. What would warm you up?'

Adam's eyes flick over me, quickly, as if he wonders about this too.

Thorne moves on, knowing there is no way I will

dignify that question with a response. 'Shelves in her living room. She wanted roses carved into them. That is all. I thought she had a beautiful vision, if a bit limited. I also thought she was the sort of woman who knew what she wanted and would accept nothing less.'

'Did you visit her flat?'

'I told you I did not.' He sits up, shakes crumbs from his hands, catches sight of his bracelet when one of the flies falls off and onto his lap. 'It is ephemeral art, regrettably. Most of my creations are.' He smiles a terrible smile at Adam, the rictus smile of a snarling corpse in a horror film, and flicks the fly into the air with a finger, making me visibly startle, so that he fails to suppress a smile. The fly thuds onto Adam's clipboard with surprising weight. Adam's only reaction is to tip it onto the floor, calmly.

'I am afraid we need to say goodbye for now, Melanie. Time for my afternoon nap. The drugs they insist on giving me. When I refuse, well, they have ways of incentivising me to accept them, don't you, Doctor? Isn't incentivising the ugly word you sometimes use? *Comply with your treatment and you will be rewarded with a visit to the workshop, Jason.* I hope you will come and see me again, Melanie. I really enjoyed our little talk.'

I stand. My knees are wobbly. I grab the back of the chair to steady myself. 'Thank you for your time, Mr Thorne.'

'My true pleasure. I will consider you, Melanie. I will consider your sister. Shall I let you know if anything further occurs? Is that the only way I will see you again?'

'Yes,' I say, in answer to both questions.

'In that case, I will tell you that I have at least one fact at my disposal which will certainly interest you.' He sees me freeze. 'There will be a price to pay, for this little fact. Would you like to hear it?'

'You know I would.'

'You will need to play a game with me, then. A little game. A perfectly safe little game that Dr Dreamboat cannot possibly object to. Your wish to know will incentivise you – Ah, but it gives me pleasure to use that word to somebody else. Are you willing to play with me, Melanie? Are you sufficiently incentivised?'

I turn away, with Adam beside me and the nurse-guards watching.

As I am about to step through the door, Thorne calls out his parting shot. 'Lovely dress, Melanie.'

I inhale. My back arches. I stop short and the silky fabric gives a final swish against my legs before fluttering still. I do not know how long it is until I move again. I remind myself he could have seen the reconstruction. He did not necessarily see that dress on you. I do not look back. I do not answer him. For now, I have nothing more to say.

Wednesday, 16 November

The Cuckoo in the Nest

This is not a club that anyone would choose to be a member of. *Support Group for Family Members of Victims.* Christmas is still over a month away. The fact that it is already visible everywhere makes this gathering in the library meeting room especially challenging and important.

If you drew a line through the centre of this children's alphabet rug, Adam and I would be at opposite ends of it. I introduce him to the others, explaining that he is a consultant psychiatrist who works at the nearby secure mental hospital, and that he hopes to provide us with some alternative insights.

'Thank you for letting me come,' he says.

He is wearing black jeans and a dark grey jumper with a sliver of charcoal T-shirt at the neckline. There is a glimpse of orange socks. His model-handsome face is bristly with dark stubble. Perhaps he wasn't at work today? I find myself wondering what it would feel like to press my lips against his cheek. You better than anyone would understand these derailments. You would applaud them.

Concentrate, Ella, I tell myself.

Helen offers Adam a small nod of acknowledgement. She suffers from a neurological condition that causes any pain she feels, even a tiny twinge, to be amplified. The kindness of Helen's nod reminds me of where I am and why I am here and what I need to do, something I do not normally allow myself to forget.

Like a good teacher, Adam mirrors Helen and nods back. 'Would you like to tell me why you're here?' he asks her.

'My son was stabbed outside a nightclub,' she says. 'Early this year.'

Adam is regarding Helen with sympathetic calm. Thorne got nothing but a level stare, and only when looking at him could not be avoided. Yesterday's slouchy posture was clearly Adam's strategy for managing him.

'I'm not really in a talking mood,' Helen says. 'But thank you for asking.'

We sit for a minute, all of us sending our care to Helen. Then the door to the room opens and the man who sat in the corridor outside my risk assessment clinic steps inside.

'Hello,' I say. 'Are you here to join us?'

'If that's okay. I'm sorry I couldn't wait to see you last week. Something came up.' There is a tension around his eyes.

I rise to get another plastic folding chair. Two of the others, Betty and Patrick, move away from each other to make room, and the man with the once-broken nose squeezes the chair between them and sits down.

I pause to explain about the confidentiality of the group, and our guidelines and purpose. Then I ask if he would like to tell us about what brought him here.

He hesitates. 'My partner went missing.' He stretches out his long legs and crosses them at the ankles, as he did when I first saw him. He is dressed more casually today, in dark denim jeans and an aqua paisley shirt, which is untucked. His jaw stiffens. 'Perhaps I can say more later? Introduce myself properly then? I'm conscious of the fact that I've disrupted things.'

There are murmurs of 'Not at all' and 'We're very sorry about your partner'.

Helen turns to Adam. 'You asked why I'm here,' she says. 'It's important to be around people who understand. My friends find me depressing. They get tired of my going on about it all the time. Even Martin gets bored of it. But none of you do.'

Martin is Helen's husband. He rarely speaks at meetings, but he says, 'I don't get bored of it.'

I look at the newest member of the group, but he shakes his head to say, Not me, not yet, so I look instead at the man between him and Adam. 'Patrick?'

Patrick leans back and crosses his arms over his chest. He is chewing gum. Is it possible for cheeks to move aggressively? Because his seem to. His red hair sticks up as if he has put his finger into a socket.

Patrick is Ruby's father. His struggle to cope with the aftermath of her assault is heartbreaking. Ruby herself pressed him to join the group.

'How are you doing today?' I ask him.

I always ask about just one day. Never a general *How are you?* What is anybody in this room supposed to say to that one?

Patrick grunts and shoots a foul glance at Adam. 'Don't think you can swagger in here and expect all of us to start finding forgiveness.'

The new man has been looking sleepy, his chin so low his designer stubble is scratching his collar. His head shoots up to study Adam.

'I didn't say anything about forgiveness,' Adam says quietly. 'I am a psychiatrist, not a vicar.'

Patrick leans forward, slams a hand on each thigh, bends his knees so his feet are flat on the floor, and lifts one heel, then the other, in turn. 'Treating those men as if they were patients and not criminals. You make me sick.'

'I understand why you feel that,' Adam says.

'Don't fucking patronise me. You look after the evil cunt who took Ella's sister.' He turns to me. 'Why do you give this bastard the time of day, Ella?'

It flashes at me that I must visit Thorne again – a realisation that makes my breath so tight I feel as though I have been laced into a corset and sprayed with dead bugs.

'You're hurting Ella, spewing that tabloid rubbish.' Martin is glaring at Patrick. 'Look at her face. Look at what you've done.'

My voice is calm but my heart is beating too fast. 'This isn't supposed to be about me.'

Adam turns from Patrick, locking those black eyes of

his on mine. I am aware of the new man's eyes on me too. Everyone strains to listen above the small children singing outside the door. 'Why can't it be about you?' Adam says.

'I'm the leader of this group,' I say. 'I'm here to help others.'

'You do this because you're one of us.' Helen puts a light hand on my arm. 'You couldn't do what you do if you weren't. You deserve attention too.'

'She gets too much attention from the doctor,' Patrick says.

Martin throws his words at Patrick, seeming to throw a knife out of nowhere. 'At least your child isn't dead.'

Helen gasps and wraps her crooked fingers around Martin's elbow, as if by grabbing her husband she can undo what he has said. Her movement is too fast and hard, and she cries out in pain.

Patrick jumps out of his seat so violently it falls backwards with a crash. He makes a show of stepping over Adam's feet, stomps to the door, wrenches it open, and waits there as if deciding what to say before exiting. 'Silent Night' floats in, carried by sweet toddler voices.

But my attention is caught by something else. Or rather, someone else, standing by a rack of magazines she is clearly not interested in. She is ten feet away from the door. She sees me seeing her. She meets my gaze deliberately and holds it for a few seconds. Then she walks away as quickly as an elderly lady can. Mrs Buenrostro. I nearly pop out of my own chair to rush after her but the tornado I seem to be in the centre of is whirling too fiercely around me.

Helen tries to heave herself up to go to Patrick, but her body doesn't move quickly and before she can rise completely he holds out a traffic policeman's arm and she sinks back down, refusing Martin's attempts to help.

'Please don't leave us, Patrick,' she says. 'You belong here too. Martin didn't mean it.'

Something trickles down my cheek. I brush away a tear. 'This group is for anyone whose loved one has been the victim of a violent crime. It doesn't matter what type.' The Christmas carol has halted. I can hear a woman's voice, hushing a child. 'It isn't limited to families of murder victims. We all belong here.'

'Too fucking right, Ella. Except him.' Patrick jerks a thumb towards Adam. The partition walls of the little meeting room shake with his final slam of the door.

'Are you going to go after him?' The anger and distress of people she cares for have forced Betty out of the quiet invisibility that she wanted today. Her delicate hands are in such tight fists I am certain her nails will leave gouges in her flesh.

I reach out my right hand to touch the sleeve of her silky silver dress, then brush a speck of dust from her hair, which is silky and silver too. She slowly releases her fingers and gives me an almost-smile. I say, 'He is free to go, Betty. We all are. And he is free to come back if and when he wants to. I hope he will soon.'

The new man stands. He walks past Patrick's empty chair and somehow evades Adam's long legs without any theatricality or clumsiness. In seconds, he has the door open again. 'I find – I must go too. I hope to return sometime very soon. Thank you for making me welcome.'

I am only halfway through objecting that we do not even know his name before he is gone. I want to scream in frustration. This man has twice approached me, and twice bailed out. It takes courage, coming to a support group like this, or to the risk assessment clinic. He and I are both haunted by somebody who is missing. This makes me want to help him all the more.

'He obviously found us irresistible,' Betty says.

'It would be good to have a break,' I say. My cheeks are flaming. 'A few minutes for some water, and to catch our breath.' Already I am rising and moving towards the fake beech units at the back of the room, slipping five bright cups from the stack of child-safe drinkware on the draining board.

Adam is standing beside me, close enough for me to notice his soap, which smells of ginseng and citrus and black pepper. He takes the cups from me one at a time, filling them from the swan's-neck tap. My fingers are shaking. Visible evidence of my dissolving composure. Behind me, Adam is serving Helen, Martin and Betty their water as if they are his guests, as if he is not the visitor.

When I sit down again they all smile and I say, 'Well, that was interesting,' and everyone laughs, and Helen says, 'It's not a bad thing to change things, you know, Ella. Don't go home and regret asking Adam to come.'

Did I ask him? I am not sure which of us proposed the arrangement as we said goodbye at the hospital yesterday. I was still too dazed by my encounter with Thorne.

Helen looks directly in front of her. She says, 'I'd like to know how the last month has been for you, Betty.'

Betty gazes at her own feet, which are encased in silver ballet flats decorated with tiny crystal beads. Her toes must be freezing. 'My sister isn't talking to me,' Betty says.

'Why?' Adam doesn't move when he lets the word out.

'I said I couldn't go to my niece's wedding. The last time I went to a wedding I had to leave. Christenings too. I hate them. I hate celebrating these things. These young women having their lives, having the things Alice never got a chance to have.'

'I feel that way too,' says Helen.

'Of course you do,' Betty says. Her voice is even, gentle, as if talking to a small child to reassure them.

I rarely say anything about our family, but something in the last few minutes has torn down my usual rules and defences. I hear our mother's voice on Friday night. *I think of all the things she is missing.* And my anger towards her melts a little.

'My mother feels like that,' I say, and another tear leaks out.

Betty squeezes my hand. 'I wish my sister would understand. She says, "It's been two years." As if I should be over it.' Betty's words are not defensive. They are not edgy or angry. They are a little tired, though her voice is still lilting.

'No,' I say. 'Two years is not enough.' Ten years is not enough either. Is there ever a number of years that are enough?

'The man who did that to your daughter is a monster.'
Martin's eyes are bulging.

Betty is so calm, so quiet and soft. 'You won't understand him if you call him a monster. Your only chance is to find his humanness. To find the ways that the two of you are alike. That is the only way to predict and stop him. The only way to find your own peace.'

I think of the grotesque monster I faced yesterday. Will I get more out of Thorne if I try to see his humanness? Try to understand him better? How dangerous would it be to show him more kindness? What if I had lied and told him I didn't find him repulsive, when he pointed to his own body and asked me directly if I did? I remember that flash of joy when I praised his rocking horse. A blaze of pity for him rips through me at the thought, taking me by surprise.

'There are no ways in which we are alike.' Martin crosses his arms.

'When you were a child,' Adam says, 'did you ever pop out at someone and say boo?'

Martin makes a barely visible 'of course' gesture.

'What you were doing then was taking pleasure in someone else's fear. In feeling excited by scaring them. My guess is that you enjoyed it as a child when your friends, or maybe your sister or brother, booed out at you in return. Don't you think it's evidence of the human capacity to enjoy fear?' Alice and Betty are moving their heads up and down in empathic we-agree-with-you-and-are-listening gestures. 'It's a spectrum,' Adam says. 'We are all on it.'

Adam goes on. 'Has anyone in this room ever found

out someone's email address or telephone number without asking them if they were happy for you to have it? How about you, Ella? Have you ever driven by the house of somebody you're interested in to see if their car is there? If their lights are on?'

I know this isn't a case of his turning to the teacher for help. He really wants to know if I have ever done this. And I have. I did exactly this to Ted last week. His lights were off. How is it that this man guesses so much about my secret ways of thinking and behaving? He even guessed that I talk to you. And that you talk back.

'No,' I say. 'I have never done anything like that.' My face must be giving me away with its change of colour.

He sits back in his chair. 'Ever phoned anyone to see who answered, then hung up without speaking?'

'No,' I say. This is another lie. I know what Ted's ex-wife sounds like. It was just once – I knew if I didn't stop immediately I never would.

I consider my indignation towards Sadie for making those blocked calls and feel a twinge of shame, though the thought of her coming anywhere near me or my family quickly makes it vanish.

'Who would do such a thing?' Helen asks.

Hanging above our heads is a green ribbon strung with holiday bunting, each triangle decorated by a child. I cannot take my eyes from a picture of a stick figure man chopping off the head of a stick figure woman. Why did they put that one up there, amongst the elves ringed in hearts and the smiling snowmen and red-nosed reindeer and fat Father Christmases and sparkly stars?

Was it a small act of librarian sabotage, the failure not to dispose of this piece of toddler art made by a future psychopath?

'Anyone.' Adam's eyes seem to burn into my own. 'Anyone can do such a thing.'

Warning Signs

Adam lingers in his chair, looking at emails on his phone while I hug Betty goodbye, brush my lips against Helen's cheek so lightly they barely touch her, and beam the warmest smile I can manage at Martin.

As soon as the door closes behind them, Adam switches his phone off. 'Time for that coffee? We were cheated yesterday.'

I think of the text that came from Ted at lunchtime, still unanswered. *We should talk.* The sentence seems to be pulsing away through my blood, so that it moves through my veins faster, knowing what I am about to do, and gets faster still when I say, 'I'd love that, yes,' and watch Adam's eyes light up. They brighten more when I say, 'But can we make it something stronger?'

It comes to me in a rush that he was nervous to ask, anxious that I would say no. He smiles. Not his usual careful smile, but such a big smile that his face is not his usual careful face, but a shining face with crinkles around his eyes and mouth that I hadn't imagined were possible. I am not sure if my heart is hurting for Ted, or for the way I am using Adam's attraction to me. I think it is hurting for both.

That smile of his evaporates as we pass through the library's electronic security gates and a voice calls out your name.

I halt but don't say anything. At first, all I can see are warning signs. *No trespassing* in red. *CCTV in Operation* in yellow. Then I see a woman, standing before the glass of the semicircular window, lit by the street lamps below. She clearly belongs to the child who is bobbing up and down in the toy postal van, screaming that she wants another go.

'Miranda?' she says again.

I am not quite sure how, but my feet are slowly moving across a landing that is bigger than my entire upstairs, my fingers absently trailing the gilded bannister as I walk towards her, barely noticing that Adam is by my side.

She is shaking her head, as if in amazement. 'You look exactly the same.' She fumbles in her purse as the child's screams grow louder. She holds out some change. 'You don't happen to have a pound coin for this, do you?'

Adam passes over a coin and she drops several into his palm, then puts the pound in the slot of the toy van, which starts to jiggle and play a theme tune.

'You must have a painting in your attic,' she says.

'I'm not—'

She turns to Adam. 'And you're Miranda's partner?' She laughs and gives me a conspiratorial wink. 'You haven't changed your taste in men.' She looks at Adam and his frozen lack of response unnerves her.

Somehow, finally, I get the words out. 'I'm not Miranda. I'm her sister.'

The woman is hardly quick, especially with the child distracting her while she tries to recover her social self, but at last she is beginning to see that something is wrong and it isn't simply that she has mistaken my identity. 'But you look exactly like her.' She falters. 'Is she well?'

I am so used to the horror of everybody knowing. Of that being the only thing there is, the most important thing to know about me. That you are lost.

'You don't know?' Adam says.

She swallows several times. 'I've said something wrong. I can see that I have.'

'Miranda's been missing for the last ten years,' I say. 'We don't know what happened to her. It's been in the news. Everyone knows. People I don't know know.'

The ride is over again. 'Excuse me.' The woman tries to pluck the toddler out. The little girl clings to the wheel, but the mother manages to extract her and plop her onto a hip. The child clings on like a koala bear and this woman who knew you before you were snatched away strokes her child's golden hair, which matches hers.

'I can't imagine what you must be feeling.' Her face is blotchy.

Adam strokes his scalp. This isn't something I have ever seen him do. I think he is somehow taking the words out of my head and into his own, so he can form them for me. 'How is it that you didn't know?'

'My husband is South African. We moved there eleven years ago – the news didn't reach me. We've only recently returned to England.'

'And you know Miranda how?' I say.

'We worked together.'

'You're a nurse, too? Were you on the orthopaedic ward with her?' My shock is competing with my reflex impulse to gather intelligence.

She hushes the child. 'I was, yes. Your sister was a real heartbreaker, you know.'

Of course I know. But I don't confirm it to this stranger.

'And you are?' Adam is coldly polite.

'Veronica Skelton.' Veronica turns back to me. 'She was so beautiful,' she says. 'Like you,' she says.

It certainly wasn't an accident that Mrs Buenrostro came tonight. Is it really a coincidence that this woman who knew you is standing outside the library where I am running a publicly advertised group, in a position where I cannot fail to pass her on my way out? But if she has deliberately run into me, why go through the pretence of not knowing about you? Of striking up a conversation with me in this strange way?

And of bringing her child with her? The last factor is what makes me think her presence here probably is a fluke. Our mother would say that my wondering about this at all is yet more evidence that I am losing my mind, that I am a danger to everyone around me. Ted would agree that I am a paranoid conspiracy theorist.

'You say my sister was a heartbreaker. Did you notice any particular man whose heart she broke?'

She thinks for a few seconds. 'She didn't confide in me. I'm not sure she confided in anyone.'

This sounds like you.

'I wonder if there was a doctor, perhaps?' I look at

Adam, who returns my gaze steadily. 'Perhaps you knew Adam?' I say, presenting him to her with a gesture. 'He worked at the hospital, then.'

I know I am not being fair to him. Most of the consultants in Bath worked at that hospital at some point, including Brian, his brother, and Dr Blossom.

'Yes,' Adam says. 'In Psychiatry.' His face remains calm. He doesn't flush or twitch. There is no flicker of an eye upwards or to the left or right. There is no tell.

She pulls a biscuit from her bag and hands it to the little girl, a series of movements so quick and automatic she barely looks as she makes them.

She gives Adam an apologetic look. 'Sorry not to remember you.' There is no tell with her either as she says this. 'Did we meet?'

'Not that I can recall. You can't know everyone,' Adam says.

'Was there really nobody?' I am startled by the near-hysteria in my voice. 'No acquaintance ever that you noticed Miranda with?'

'Absolutely there was. But you were asking me about doctors and the man who comes to mind wasn't a doctor. He was a patient.'

'When? When was he a patient?'

'Maybe three years before I left.' She pauses to calculate. 'So about fourteen years ago.' She appears to be replaying a film reel inside her own head. 'He was really taken with her. I remember that. We all noticed.'

'Why was he in hospital? Do you remember that sort of thing with patients?'

'Not usually from so long ago, but this man was pretty

unforgettable. Incredibly charismatic and handsome, quite smooth and polished. He'd ruptured his Achilles' tendon. I don't recall how he did it, exactly. Only that he went to theatre for a surgical repair.'

I close my eyes and see the imprint of the boot in the woods, with the outsole worn so heavily. Could that be because its wearer was compensating for an old injury?

'Can you remember his name?'

'Not his surname. But I remember the first. Noah.' She looks dreamy, thinking of it. 'It's because I always loved the name. I'd always fantasised about having a little boy and naming him that.' She strokes her daughter's hair. 'But I got my lovely girl instead. Maybe next time.'

M + N + ?? My heart is hammering with excitement. 'Can you remember what he looked like?'

'Dark hair and eyes. Close-cut beard and moustache. Like that Spanish actor? God. Really famous. So frustrating . . . I can't think of his name . . . '

'That's more than fine. Thank you,' I say.

'I'm so sorry,' she says again, 'for the mix-up. That must have freaked you out.'

'I like it that seeing me brings her alive for someone else.' I look at Adam as I say this.

'You really do look like her, you know,' she says again.

I don't know what makes me say what I do next. 'Was it really an accident that you were here?'

Her face flushes red but I cannot be sure if it is because I have mortified her by making such an offensive suggestion or because I have confronted her with the truth.

'Do you want to tell me why you sought me out?' I

know as soon as the words are out of my mouth that I should have swallowed them back.

She shakes her head violently. 'I didn't seek you out.' Her phone rings. One ring, then nothing more. 'I have to go,' she says. 'That'll be my taxi.'

As she hurries away I rush after her. 'Can you give me your number so I can reach you again? I'd like to talk some more. Please.'

She shakes her head no. She clutches the child to her, fleeing from a baby-eating monster. I am following her down the stairs, though I glance briefly behind to see Adam staring after us in his measured way.

She halts in front of the glass double doors to the street. 'I've told you everything I can.' She pushes through the doors. There really is a taxi and she quickly gets in. Before it speeds away, I snap a picture of the beacon on top of it, with the company name and the car number. I know that data protection means I'll never get the taxi company to tell me where their car went. But it is possible there will come a time when I will need her as a witness, and if I give these details to the police they should be able to trace where the taxi took her.

I watch the taxi's rear lights until the small red dots are swallowed by darkness. Adam is beside me, his hand on my arm, lightly. 'You get home,' he says. 'We'll have that drink another time. It's been quite a night.'

'Just the usual.' I stand on my toes a little so that I can kiss his cheek, and watch him light up like a Christmas tree.

Thursday, 17 November

Guessing Games

There are at least a dozen empty parking spaces when I arrive at the circle of Georgian houses where Mrs Buenrostro lives. The sun has only just come up but I have a lot to do before Luke's football match this afternoon. It will not surprise you to know that I will be there. I have never broken a promise to Luke and I do not intend to start now.

For the hell of it, because I cannot resist an opportunity to try, I press the button for Flat 7, the Henrickson flat. There is no answer. Of course there is not. So I move my finger pad up an inch and plunge it onto Flat 6.

It isn't long before I hear white noise, then her voice. 'Who is it?'

She knows the answer to this already. She and I discussed the camera that is wrapped into the building's intercom system – she will be watching my grainy face on a small black-and-white screen inside her entry hall.

'It's Ella Brooke, Mrs Buenrostro. Are you going to let

me in, or do you prefer to lurk near the places where I'm working?'

'I wasn't lurking. I'd only arrived a minute before that man burst out. I'd thought to catch you afterwards, until I saw how things were.' She pauses for breath. 'How did you know my flat number?'

I lie easily, leaving our mother's detective work out of it. 'I planned to try them all but I got lucky with my first guess.'

She begins to give me elaborate directions for navigating the corridors of Henrietta Mansions and finding Flat 6.

I cut her off. 'I know the way.' I do not explain that this is because I have already looked at the floor plans using the land registry website. There is a buzz and the click of the lock releasing. With that, I am free to roam the building I could barely penetrate only a week ago.

When I reach the door to Flat 6, it is already open. Mrs Buenrostro stands inside. She is wearing another matchy-matchy trouser suit, this time powder blue. She has applied lipstick. Like our mother, this woman does not like to be seen in anything other than her best face. I do not bother to hide the fact that I am studying the L-shaped bend farther along the corridor that I know leads to Flat 7.

'Won't you come in?' she says.

I am practised at not looking at my watch, at not alerting anyone to the functions that circle my wrist. I have left a pre-alert voice message on my lone worker safety device, as well as an old-fashioned scrawled note on my own kitchen counter, detailing my plan to visit her. I am not expecting to disappear, but if I do, those who look for me will have a starting point. As long as I stay attached to the watch they will have real-time tracking too. I will throw the note away when I am safely home, and delete the message.

'Why did you seek me out last night, Mrs Buenrostro?'

'I needed to talk to you.'

'You have my telephone number.'

'In person.'

'Is Mrs Buenrostro your real name? Nothing comes up when I search for you on the internet.'

She looks behind me. She lowers her voice. 'It is a family name, my husband's great-grandmother's name. It is not carried in any written record that would lead to me.'

'That's why you chose it?'

She is actually whispering. 'Yes. To avoid leaving my footprint. I have had good advice in that regard.'

I think of you and your invisible internet life. I am fairly certain that you and Mrs Buenrostro had the same tutor.

'Please. Let's talk inside.' She motions for me to follow her, leads me into her beautifully proportioned living room. There are cornices and mouldings. There is a ceiling rose, high in the centre.

I choose a stiff-backed gold chair covered in fabric buttons, which poke into my spine. 'What do you want from me?'

What she says next is not the turn I expect the conversation to take. 'Do you know anything about undercover policing, Ella?'

'A little. I know about stealing the identities of dead

children. Sleeping with targets, deceiving them. Even having babies with them.'

She turns to look at a photograph on the chimney piece. She'd said she had no children. As far as I can judge from three metres away, the photograph is of a young boy. She wipes away a tear.

'Is that your son?' I say, as gently as I can. 'Did he die, Mrs Buenrostro? Did they take his identity? I'm very sorry for you.'

'You misunderstand.'

'Then help me to understand.'

'Not all undercover policemen do the terrible things you speak of. Do you know the term "deep swimmer"?'

I shake my head no.

'It's somebody who goes undercover for a long time, sometimes many years. Sometimes they can't go near their real life at all. Or only very occasionally.'

'I still don't understand.' But I am beginning to.

'We thought it would be easiest if we stayed as close to the truth as possible.'

She sounds like our mother. She sounds like you. And like me. She sounds like someone who has been coached in the methods and principles of covert policing.

I look again at the photo. Just the one. That is all. I am in no doubt that it is to remind her of who she is, what she is for, who she loves.

It is almost a physical pain not to inspect that photo. I do not want her to stop talking but I do want a closer look.

'You see, I must live discreetly. Someone close to me is working undercover. Very deeply and long term. He doesn't tell me much detail. I hardly see him and when I do, only secretly. It's never predictable.' Her voice catches. 'Family members make them vulnerable. They can expose them.'

'Why are you telling me? Isn't that dangerous for him? For you?'

'Only if you decide to speak of it. I think I know enough about you to feel confident that you would not put me at risk by doing so. It is your vocation to protect the vulnerable, Ella. Anyone can see that.'

'You don't know me at all. I'd throw you under a bus for my family, Mrs Buenrostro. I hope it never comes to that, but please consider yourself warned.'

She deliberately looks towards the photograph. I stand, but need to grab the back of the chair for a second to get my balance. My legs seem to have lost their very bones. Somehow, I walk with apparent steadiness to the chimney piece. She joins me. I stare at the picture while she stares at me, watching for a reaction that I am determined not to give.

The boy is sitting in the crook of an olive tree's trunk, the branches twisting off behind him and to both sides, so he seems to be cupped by them. He is grinning at his own daring, at being so high. It is a close-up, so there isn't enough landscape for me to be confident of my guess that he is in Spain or Greece. I can tell by the light that it is early summer, and by the sweet green of the leaves and olives. The picture was taken on the kind of instant camera that was popular several decades ago.

The boy is eight or nine. Not quite as old as Luke but not far behind him. His hair is the same near-black as

Luke's. His eyes are brown as opposed to the bright blue that I see when I look in the mirror or at Luke or our father or you. But what really strikes me is the familiar shape of the chin and the dimples I love so much on another face, as well as the honey tint of his skin from the sun, which he didn't get from you. There is the cowlick too, twirling itself into a little coil above the left temple.

I press my arms against my sides to stop them from visibly shaking. I keep my face unreactive. I make myself look at Mrs Buenrostro, brace myself to meet her gaze calmly.

She picks up the photograph, trails a finger over the smooth wood of the simple frame, which is overlaid with gold paint. 'Don't you imagine the other reason why I feel safe talking to you? Why I trust you not to throw me under a bus, as you so charmingly put it? Shall we sit, Ella? I get tired.'

'Let me get you a glass of water.' The offer is more for myself than for her. I need to be out of her sight for a minute.

She sinks onto a squishy sofa that is covered in country roses. She keeps the photograph on her lap. 'That would be kind,' she says. 'I suspect you know where the kitchen is.' She sounds faintly amused, as if it has occurred to her that I researched her floor plans.

Her flat is a square, with the kitchen in one corner, the living room in another, and bedrooms in the other two. The entry hall slices through the square's centre, with doors to the four rooms branching off and the bathroom at its end. The bedroom doors are closed. Mrs Buenrostro cannot see them from where she sits.

As quietly as I can, hoping there won't be a squeak, I open the first door. What do I expect? A man to be crouched behind it, waiting to spring out? And what kind of man? Criminal or undercover policeman? Do such people themselves forget which they are? There is nothing but a bed, prettily made with an ivory counterpane. There is a beautiful old wooden closet. My heart seems to stop when I pull the door open, but it is full of winter coats and makes me think of the *Narnia* books I read to Luke.

I try the second door. This must be where Mrs Buenrostro sleeps. It is furnished identically, but for the addition of a dressing table with her carefully arranged face creams and scents and an old-fashioned comb and brush set, made of engraved silver. Nobody is hiding in here either. The door squeaks when I shut it but I am beyond caring. She can probably feel where I am in the flat, anyway.

There is nothing remarkable in the kitchen. The walls are white porcelain, the floor is black slate, and it is filled with shiny expensive gadgets that appear never to be used. It is scrupulously neat and clean, like everything else about Mrs Buenrostro. She keeps nothing that might give her away, as if she herself were engaged in covert policing, too. Only the boy on the chimney piece.

She calls my name, so I hurriedly get the water and return to the living room. I put the glass in her hand, then sit once more in the uncomfortable chair.

'It wasn't true,' she says, 'when I said I had no child.'

I glance at the photograph on her lap. 'That much is clear now.'

'He was a much-wanted late-in-life baby. I was forty-two when he was born. We had given up hope.' She pauses at my quick inhalation of breath, but goes on. 'He works abroad. He is useful to them, because he speaks so many languages. Since I moved here I have hardly seen him. I don't know where he is, at any given time. He does visit, but very rarely. He never gives me advance notice. He has – ways – of letting me know.'

I look around this impersonal but expensive space in the centre of Bath. I think of your car and flat, your designer clothes, your cash-filled savings accounts. 'Are most covert policemen as rich as your son?'

'There is family money. My son does what he does because he thinks it's important. Like you, Ella.'

'So you were talking about your son, when you spoke of the man in Flat 7? When you spoke of Mr Henrickson?'

'Nobody has ever turned up asking about him. I can't tell you what a fright it gave me.' She almost smiles. 'But you don't look like an assassin or spy.'

'You'd be surprised,' I say.

'I remembered the woman who visited him as soon as I saw you.'

My back becomes clammy. My fingers start to tingle.

But she goes on, oblivious, caught up in her own story. 'That's the other reason I let you in. I thought at first you actually were her. You look so like her.'

'It didn't occur to you to go to the police when she disappeared shortly after you saw her with your son?'

'I didn't know who the woman was until you told me your sister's name and showed me her picture. As soon as you left I searched the internet. It left no doubt in my mind that your sister was the woman who visited Flat 7.'

I can't keep the sarcasm from my voice. 'Did you never pick up a paper or watch the news?'

'Somehow, I missed it.'

'You might have saved her. If you had come forward with this information, the police might have found something.'

'I am telling you the truth. I didn't know, then.'

Is she like our mother? Unable to climb down from a position once she takes it?

'And your son didn't tell you who she was? He didn't talk about the fact that this woman you saw him with had gone missing?'

She shakes her head. 'He made it clear he didn't want to talk about her or the baby when he left later that same day. That it wasn't safe to, for their sakes, and he didn't want me to raise the subject again.'

'Did he lie to my sister? Did she know who he really was? What he does?'

'He'd never have told her anything operational, but he'd never have let her involve herself with him unless she knew the bare bones of the truth. My son has integrity.'

'Did it occur to you that whoever took my sister might have done so because of her relationship with your son? That they were using her to get at him?'

She shakes her head more violently than a woman her age ought. 'It's not possible. He's far too careful. He would never let them find the people from his real life.'

'How could he even think of exposing someone else

to those dangers? How could he ask her to give up so much for him? To give up any chance of a normal life?'

'He had a rule not to let himself get involved. For exactly those reasons. He broke that rule for your sister.'

'It must have been unimaginably hard for her.'

'It would have been, yes. It wouldn't have been easy for her to trust him when he could say so little. He'd never be able to predict the times he could see her. Their contact would have been infrequent.'

'How often does he visit you?'

'I haven't seen him since the day he was here with your sister.'

'You don't think it's suspicious that he disappeared from view when she did?'

'It means he was deeply enmeshed in an operation. It doesn't mean he hurt her.'

'You really haven't seen your son for over ten years?'

'You don't ask questions of someone who does what my son does.'

'My sister would have.'

'I don't know how he even manages to remember who he actually is. You've no idea what he needs to see and do to keep other people safe. What a long-term prize he is after. You've no idea how much the families lose.'

'Poor you. Poor him.' I sound like our mother, with these bitter words. 'Do you think that someone, some-where stopped them looking properly at what happened to my sister to protect him from exposure? To make sure whatever he's doing isn't spoiled?'

'He wouldn't allow that.'

'I'm not sure it would be up to him.'

Tears fill her eyes, drip down her cheeks. 'Do you understand now why I had to see you again? Why I had to talk to you?'

'No,' I say. And I move my head from side to side too. But I do know why.

'I think your nephew is my grandson,' she says. 'I suspected it when your sister came that day with the baby.'

'Did you meet her? Did your son introduce you to her?'

'Everything I told you about what happened that day was true. She didn't look up, didn't acknowledge me, didn't want to see me. I don't think she had any idea who I was. I'm sure he didn't tell her. He wouldn't have risked telling anyone. He would have told her what she needed to know about him. But not about me. He would have been scrupulous about what he did and didn't say.'

'Why are you confessing all of this now?' My voice is icy icy cold, so cold it makes our mother seem warm when at her most brittle. I am her daughter. I am your sister. I have a vision of this woman and her son turning up on our doorstep and running away with Luke in the night. For the first time, our mother's terror is in my own bones.

'I don't know,' she says. 'I don't know what I want. Not anything that could hurt Luke.'

Don't say his name. I don't say this. As powerfully as I feel it, I can't strike her like that. But I can't stop myself from thinking, *Don't say his name again or I won't be able to stand it.*

'I wish – I long to see him. Please, you must have a photograph.'

'No.' The word seems to make a visible cut through the air.

'I know I asked last time and I didn't blame you for saying no then, before you knew – I thought you were right not to show his picture to strangers – but I know everyone has photographs on their phones these days. Please.'

'However strongly you believe in your son, the last time you saw him was a few weeks before my sister disappeared. Undercover policemen are as capable of murder as civilians. If that woman really was my sister – and you said the baby was very new, maybe a month or two old, so I can't discount the possibility – then your son is probably connected to what happened to her. Either because of what he does, or because he hurt her.'

'He wouldn't. He would never hurt a woman.'

'I don't want you near my nephew. I don't want your son sneaking back into the country and going anywhere near him.'

'Don't you see? Don't you see how much my son must have loved your sister? He put himself at unimaginable risk to see her, to have a child with her.'

'He put her at unimaginable risk,' I say.

'If harm came to her, it wasn't because of him. Think how much care he has taken. How much restraint and self-control he shows. Think of Luke. Noah left him with you and your parents, knowing that was the best thing for him.'

'Noah?' I say the word as if I am tasting it. *M + N + ??* Veronica Skelton remembered the name she loved. She witnessed an infatuation so strong between you and a patient she couldn't help but recall it.

'Yes.'

'Is that his real name?'

'Yes. Most undercover policemen use their given Christian names. It's safer that way. I don't know what surname he uses in his work. Lots of different ones, I should guess.'

'Presumably he goes by Henrickson in his personal life?'

'Yes. Noah chose it. His father was Enrique. You probably know that's Spanish for Henry? So son of Henry.'

I had wondered if Henrickson was a trick like the one you and Mum used to play with names, so that it would evoke the real person but at the same time disguise them. This man's trick had the same purpose as yours and Mum's, but it was his own invention.

'That way,' Mrs Buenrostro says, 'when Noah slips into England, there is a safe identity for him to wear.'

'How easy is it for him to slip in?'

There is contempt in her shrug. 'Think how easily the UK borders can be penetrated. It isn't hard if you know what you're doing. If you have money and help. Noah has both.'

I jump up. I walk to the window and look out of her filmy curtains. The fountain is bubbling as usual. My car's nose is inches away from the trunk of a hornbeam tree. Everything looks as it did yesterday and the day before and the day before that. But everything is different. 'How old is your son, Mrs Buenrostro?'

'Forty-six.'

Six years older than you would be. The kind of age difference you liked.

'And he has been – how do you put it – a deep swimmer the whole time?'

'For the last fifteen years. My husband died twenty-one years ago. Noah started covert policing soon after that, but only occasional jobs at first.'

She pauses. 'Noah loves football. Like his father. Does your nephew?'

'I understand that you want to believe your son is some kind of hero, and that you think you are doing the right thing.' She visibly flinches at my refusal to talk about Luke. 'You have spent many years doing that. But I have spent the last decade with a big fat hole in my life that is shaped exactly like my sister. I want you to go to the police and tell them everything you told me.'

'There's no point. There won't even be any evidence that Noah was in the country ten years ago. There won't be records of him. The ordinary police will hit a wall with any kind of enquiry about him.'

'Even undercover policemen aren't allowed to commit crimes. I can see they may be allowed to break the law when it involves drug lords or mafia leaders, when they're in character. But not in their real lives, not against innocent civilians. Your son may well have committed what for my family is the worst crime there has ever been.'

'I have told you the kind of man my son is. There is no way he did that.'

'Go to the police yourself or I'll do it for you. They might treat you more sympathetically that way, if you explain you didn't realise who she was until now.' I can't bring myself to speak your name to her. 'Maybe they won't be as sceptical as I am. I will give you until the end of the weekend.'

'You won't let me see your nephew's picture?'

I squint. 'I don't want to hurt you but I feel duty-bound to tell you that if you go anywhere near my nephew I will call the police. The *ordinary* police,' I say with bitter emphasis. 'And I will be instructing my parents to do the same.'

I feel a stab in my stomach, almost a physical blow. Our mother is right – it isn't safe for me to go near Luke until I have figured out every bit of this.

She actually smiles. 'I'm disappointed, but I'm glad too. That boy is lucky. You may not be his mother, but you act as if you are. You're as fierce as a lioness.'

Tell that to my mother, I think. I am astonished that Mrs Buenrostro has said one of the most beautiful things I have ever heard.

'Perhaps you really haven't seen your son in a decade. But I don't believe that the two of you didn't set up some emergency way you could get hold of him.'

She moves her head in the smallest, most reluctant concession, a gesture that refuses to admit much and leaves me uncertain as to whether I actually saw it.

'Do you think the police knew of his relationship with my sister?'

'He probably would have disclosed it to his handler.'

'Probably?'

'I can't be certain. Noah doesn't trust easily. He's a bit of a lone wolf, as they say.' Again she sounds proud. 'But I would be surprised if he failed to do that.'

'I am going to ask you this once more. Do you think

the police deliberately swept their knowledge of my sister under the carpet to protect your son, to protect his operation?'

'If they knew about her, they would know he didn't hurt her.'

'How could they possibly know that?'

'I can't tell you.'

'Can't or won't?'

Her only answer to this is a helpless shrug.

'Do you not see what I do? That they cared more about your son than they did about investigating my sister's disappearance properly?'

'My son is a very brave man. He is a good man.'

'Tell that to my sister,' I say.

White Lies

It is 10.30 when I park in front of our parents' house. Mum's car is gone but Dad's van is here. I slip my key into the lock and let myself in, ready to punch the code into the alarm panel, worried when I discover they haven't set it.

'Hello? Dad?'

There's the sound of a cough coming from our father's workroom. I walk in to find him lying on the dilapidated orange velvet sofa of our childhood that he will not let our mother get rid of. He is dressed in his favourite olive-green trousers and a thick navy jumper. There is a box of tissues on the plank of old wood he uses as a coffee table and an unfinished mug of tea that Mum must have made him before she left.

He scrambles up, still half-asleep, looking embarrassed. 'Hello, shining girl.' He holds out an arm and I cross the room quickly to take his hand and sit beside him.

'Hello, Daddy.'

'You haven't called me that for a long time.'

I nod my head. There is a lump in my throat. 'Why are you lying down when you just got up?'

'Ah.' He shakes his head in amusement. 'And you and your mother think you aren't alike. It's a cold, Ella.' He manages an extremely wet and convincing sniffle, then blows his nose loudly several times in a row. 'Don't tell your mother. I'm trying to hide it from her or she'll put me in quarantine.'

'Really?'

'Everyone gets colds. Let me be clear and say it. It's not my cancer.'

Does he look as though he has lost weight? I'm not sure. 'Okay,' I say. 'Colds are good. I'll take a cold over the other options.'

'To what do I owe this surprise visit from my favourite youngest daughter?' He gives me his sly look. 'I'm sure you forgot your mother's teaching her pre-school ballet class right now?'

'I may not have forgotten that.' I take one of the tissues and blow my own nose. 'But it's the third Thursday of the month, and tomorrow's the third Friday. You know we always keep those days free of charity activities. I have a little extra time.'

'Your mother fears you work too hard. It's her small way of trying to stop that.'

'Did she tell you about our fight?' My voice croaks on the last word.

He holds out his arms and I fall into them, burying my face on his chest. 'I was horrible to her. And she was right. Everything she said was right. I haven't been kind to her. I closed myself off to her feelings.'

He waits for me to calm down. After a few minutes he wordlessly gives me a handful of tissues and I blow my nose all over again. I try to smile. 'I got your jumper wet.'

'It's a good thing your mother made me wear wool today. She likes me to be warm and waterproof.'

'She said it's not safe for me to be near Luke. That I put him in danger. She's right.'

'Your mother doesn't really think that. She felt terrible after she last saw you. She regrets the things she said.'

'I do too. So much.'

'We both knew you would.'

'Will you tell her I'm sorry? Tell her I love her?'

He pushes a stray hair from my forehead. 'Tell her yourself. Come to Luke's football match this afternoon. We'll both be there. That's why I don't want your mother to notice my cold – she'll tell me not to go.'

'They can hear you sniffling over in France. You'll never fool her.'

'It would make your mother very happy if you came.'

I shake my head no. 'I can't. I've opened up so many things, so many unsettling things. I might draw these things to Luke if I go near him.'

'What things?'

I look at my lap and twiddle my thumbs as if I were five years old.

Dad puts a finger under my chin and makes me meet his eye. 'You and I have always been honest with each other.'

'Always.' And I spill out all of it. Jason Thorne. The visit you made to Mrs Buenrostro's son with Luke shortly before you disappeared. The likely identity of Luke's father and the possibility he had something to do with your disappearance. Sadie's newfound hatred of me. The rift with Ted and the photograph of him with Ruby. The anonymous phone calls and the email from Justice Administrator.

I don't mention your amniocentesis and my theory about why you had it. I'm clear about when the confidentiality clause applies. Our father does not need to know that you slept with two different men within weeks of each other.

I also leave out the fake policeman. That is one alarming thing too many. It is not necessary, anyway, given the fact that I actually reported it to the police myself. According to the call I made to them this morning, they have discovered absolutely nothing about who he is. *Our enquiries are ongoing.* That was all they had to say.

'You took so much on, so young, Ella. I never meant any of this for you. But you make me very proud. You're a better detective than any of the actual detectives.'

I puff out a bitter little laugh. 'Think of all the mess it's opened up. Mrs Buenrostro's going to want to see Luke. I'm scared of her. I'm scared of her son and the things he's doing. He's pretending to be a serious criminal.'

'Do you know what exactly?'

I shake my head. 'She wouldn't tell me. I can only guess. I'm thinking something major, some kind of organised crime or drug cartel he's infiltrated on the continent. She says it's a really long-term assignment and he speaks multiple languages. Deep swimming, she called it. Assuming she's telling the truth.'

'Do you believe her?'

'I think so.'

'Do you think she knows more than she's saying?'

'Definitely. But I'm not sure I want to know more than I already do. What if the people he's trying to bring down find out who he really is? And then find a connection to Luke?'

'It sounds like he's tried to build in layers of safety between his covert life and his real one. It appears he's put a lot of effort into protecting his family.'

'You're trying to comfort me.'

'I mean it.'

'But he and his mother have so much money, quite apart from his job. She says it's family money.'

He gives me his slant smile. 'Miranda would like that.'

'Yes,' I say. 'But that kind of money gives people power. If they can't find legal ways to get what they want, there are always alternatives.'

He considers for a few seconds. 'It explains a lot. Miranda's flat. Her car. The deposits in those accounts. Presumably they were all gifts from this man.'

'I was thinking that too.' I almost laugh but somehow do not. 'How can you seem so calm?'

He does actually laugh. 'It's my job as your father.'

I sit back and look hard at him. 'You put it all in motion. I was so angry at Mum. I told her you asked for Miranda's things from the police. I wanted to hurt her. I wanted to show her I knew something about you that she didn't. That she was wrong. That the rest of us aren't afraid to search for the truth.'

His skin goes paler.

'She intimated that she knew you did this,' I say. 'I didn't believe her.'

'She may well have guessed.' Our father will never betray our mother by suggesting she lied. 'Your mother is very perceptive. But I didn't tell her.'

'And she hasn't confronted you with it?'

'No.' He takes both of my hands in his. 'I was wrong to do it.'

'No you weren't. You were completely right. But why did you?'

'Miranda belongs to us all. I thought that if something could be done, it should be done.' He shakes his head as if disgusted with himself. 'A ten-year-old boy. I knew he was listening when your mother and I were talking about that box. I knew he'd tell you and I knew you'd never let it go. My thoughts were selfish.'

'They weren't. You're never selfish.'

'You can see no wrong in me. I'm a lucky father to have that.'

'It's because you deserve it.'

He swallows hard. 'I don't want to leave this world without knowing.'

A sob rushes out of my mouth. I am instantly, hysterically crying. 'Why do you say that? You're not about to leave this world.'

'No, Ella. No no no no no. Just the words and the world view of a man my age. Any father would feel this. It doesn't mean what you're thinking.'

It takes several minutes, a thick stack of tissues, and a glass of water before I can breathe again.

'Okay?'

I nod.

'What I was trying to say was that we've gone too long without knowing. But I didn't ever imagine the things in that box would lead you this far. I should have considered more carefully the position it would put you in. And Luke. You're going to go to the police, aren't you? You need to tell them everything you can about Mrs Buenrostro and her son.'

'Not yet. That's why I'm telling you. I promised Mrs Buenrostro I'd give her a chance to go to them herself first. She says it's pointless, but I still thought if she did it on her own terms it might help. It suits me to wait, anyway. There are some other things I have to do before I can get to the station. Which isn't exactly my favourite place.'

How is it that our father can read my mind? 'You're going back to see Jason Thorne.'

'He said there's something he can tell me.'

'Don't.'

'I can't not. I can't not follow it through. You know that about me – you said it yourself.'

'I wouldn't want you any different, however inconvenient it sometimes is.'

'Even if you didn't fully imagine what it would mean to look at Miranda's things, you must have known that following any trail wouldn't be comfortable.' I glance at my watch. 'I need to go.'

'You wouldn't make it to the football match on time anyway.'

'No. And I need to have more of a measure of things before I go anywhere near Luke. Mum was right.'

'Do you remember Miss Pear, Ella?'

When Luke was four or five, he overheard a police-woman slip out the word *MisPer*, which is police shorthand for Missing Person. He knew the policewoman was talking about you. He misheard her, though.

'Why did she call Mummy "Miss Pear"?' he asked. 'Can I call her Miss Pear? I like pears,' he said.

There is another thing Luke used to say around then, usually prompted by strangers who assumed I was his mother. 'This is my Auntie Ella. My mummy got lost some-where.' He would always go on to elaborate. 'My mummy got lost but sometimes you can find lost things.'

'Of course I do,' I say.

'Luke will survive without you for a few days,' Dad says, 'but not much longer. Your mother recognises how much he needs you.'

'Will you explain my absence to him? I don't like asking you to tell even a white lie for me. But can you say it's a work emergency? Tell him I'll call as soon as I can to see how the football went.'

'We know Luke's not a natural athlete.'

'Not exactly. But I like him that way.'

I remember when Luke was four and he'd just started school. I arrived to collect him from his first session of afternoon football club. He wasn't with the other boys, who were squealing and running after the ball in a pack.

Luke was lying on his tummy by a small square of earth that held a caged sapling. He was sifting for pebbles with his fingers so he could make a rock garden, entirely immersed in his own little contented world. I scooped him up in my arms and twirled round and tickled and kissed him. He giggled, not caring what anyone thought, not worrying about being seen as babyish.

Dad swallows. 'You know he does it because he wants to be strong for you, Ella. He hates sport. The football. The karate classes. All of it.' He smiles. 'I hear he can knock out three pull-ups in a row, now?'

'Something like that,' I say.

'He wants to be able to defend you. Because he couldn't help his mum.'

'Oh.' The word shoots from me more like a cry than language. 'Did he tell you that?'

'He didn't need to.'

'You know us all better than we know ourselves.' I put my arms around him and we stand like this for a full minute. I kiss his cheek. 'Can you call Ted? Tell him what's been happening? Ask him to check around here?'

'I'll do that as soon as you go.'

'Are you really sure it's a cold?'

'No question.' He laughs. 'I'm a lucky man, to have a wife and daughter who care so much.'

'You certainly are,' I say, feeling a pang that he has spoken of his children in the singular. 'I tease Mum too much. But I'm beginning to be convinced by her methods.' He walks me to the door, but then I remember one of the things I meant to do here. 'Give me one minute. I need some things of Miranda's.'

I run up to your childhood room. Mum keeps some of your favourite dresses and shoes in the wardrobe, to make sure they will be here for you the day you come home. I grab the things I want and stuff them into the tote bag I brought with me for this purpose.

'That was two minutes,' our father says as I run down the stairs. This is a routine of ours – I always take longer than I promise, and he always points it out but never really minds. He is still waiting by the front door.

'I'm sorry. I didn't mean for you to stand here.' His skin is slightly grey. There is sweat on his brow. I try to make myself believe it really is because he has a cold.

'It gives me pleasure to see you speeding down those stairs. How many times do you think I've watched you do that since you learned to walk?'

'Too many to count.' I point to the alarm panel. 'Promise me to use this?'

'You have my solemn promise.'

I set it myself and kiss him once more and gulp back a little sob that I hope he doesn't hear before I say goodbye.

The Girl Who Never Cries

I drive around our parents' village several times, checking my mirrors to make sure I am not being followed. Only then do I pull over, careful to choose a place that isn't overlooked. I squirm out of my jeans and sweater and boots and into your dress and shoes – even our shoe size is the same. Finally, I dial Adam Holderness's mobile.

All of my nerves seem to be exposed. You once called me the girl who never cries, but today I am able to do little else. My voice is husky in the face of Adam's kindness and concern, and his promise to get me in to see Thorne if I come straight to the hospital. He must hear that I am on the verge of weeping.

It rained in the night but now the sun is magically bright on the fields, turning them a wintry greeny-yellow that makes me think the next season is really on its way. The fields are so beautiful they make me want to cry too. Are you beneath them? Is that where you are? Beethoven's Symphony Number 7 is on the radio and I remember how you always loved it.

When I pull into the hospital car park I go through my usual routines, checking who else is around me, pulling in between two cars that have staff permits on their windscreens. I take off your locket and my watch. I stick them in the glovebox along with my phone before I step out of the car and turn on the alarm.

Just when I thought my emotions couldn't fluctuate any more wildly than they already have in one day, I halt, swallowing back a scream of absolute fury.

Ted is leaning against the low brick wall, standing in the gap that opens onto the path from the car park to the hospital's reception building. He is in uniform.

'What are you doing here?'

'Waiting for you.'

'Did you follow me? But you can't have followed me. I was checking the whole way. Nobody followed me.'

'Your father said you were coming here. He said you asked him to call me.'

'Yes. But that was so you could keep an eye on them. Not on me. Go away.'

'I'm afraid I can't do that.'

'I don't want to see you.'

'You're ignoring my texts. I've lost count of how many I've sent. You're not answering your phone to me.'

'I've been busy.'

He is searching my face. 'How was your meeting with Thorne?'

'Go practise your public safety duties on Ruby.' I have no anger towards Ruby, only concern for her. My bitterness is entirely directed at Ted.

'I told you it wasn't what you thought. I told you it was work.'

'So the police have started to do their work in cafés instead of stations?'

'The man who assaulted her has attacked three other women. He'll attack more if we don't put him away. We need her as a witness and she's reluctant. Ruby doesn't like the station.'

'Is that allowed?'

'If it keeps her safe and gets another scumbag off the streets I will sleep just fine at night.'

'I'm sorry I gave you such a hard time. I was blinded by—' I am about to say jealousy, but I stop myself.

'By what, Ella?'

'I'm not sure.'

He lets it go, almost certainly guessing the truth. 'I should have explained earlier. I can see how it looked, why you thought as you did.'

'It's sad how easily you and I get derailed, how quick we are to get angry with each other. That's what's staying with me in all this.'

He touches my cheek and I put my fingers over his. 'We're not as bad as you think,' he says.

A movement at the far end of the path catches my attention. When I look I see the door to the reception building swinging closed and Adam walking towards us.

Introducing these two men would suck away every last drop of my energy. 'I need to go, Ted. I have an appointment.' I turn to move away but before I do Ted's arm shoots out and his hand catches mine.

'Don't. You got away with it once. Don't go near Thorne again. You're not safe with him.'

'He's locked up and surrounded by guards. It's not as if the two of us are alone.' I snatch my hand away. My voice is as low as I can make it. I don't want Adam to hear but I want to be sure that Ted does. 'Why are you always trying to stop me? I can't live with that. Why don't you see how important this is to me?'

'I want to save you.'

'From what, exactly?'

But there is no time for Ted to answer, because Adam is at my side. He gives Ted his even look. 'Is there a problem?'

Ted glares at him. He is an inch shorter than Adam. 'No problem.'

'Good of you to stop by, but all is well inside.' Adam speaks to Ted as if Ted is a servant whose services are no longer required. It is subtle, an undercurrent, but it is definitely there. Ted hears it too and bristles.

Adam touches my arm, lightly, not lingeringly but long enough for Ted's eyes to narrow and his nostrils to flare. 'Are you ready to go in, Ella?'

I give a yes nod to Adam and a goodbye nod to Ted. Then I walk away, with Adam by my side. I do not turn to look behind me, but Ted's eyes are on my back, boring into me with such intensity I feel as if I'm being burned.

Truth or Dare

Jason Thorne is sitting on the same golden doll's house sofa in the same fake drawing room wearing the same jeans and lumberjack shirt I last saw him wear. He heaves himself up to greet me as I walk towards him. His face is practically splitting he is smiling so hard. For an instant, I see a vulnerable little boy beneath that face, wanting to be liked and admired as much as he likes and admires, but never being granted this wish.

'The delightful Melanie Brooke,' he says. 'I cannot tell you what pleasure it gives me to see you.'

I hear Betty's voice. *Your only chance is to find his humanness. To find the ways that the two of you are alike.*

I picture the scene I am in as if from outside and think of the families of the women Jason Thorne tortured and killed and stored in freezers in his basement. How would they feel to see me sitting in this fake drawing room playing at civility with this man? What would I feel in their place? I can only answer this question for myself, not for them, and I am unwaveringly clear in my answer.

I would give my blessing if it got them even the tiniest way towards the many answers they craved. I would countenance their doing anything they needed to for that purpose.

So I take my first step in Jason Thorne's game and I do the thing I could not possibly have done the last time. I touch him. I look him in the eye and smile and put out my hand and say 'I'm glad to see you too' and watch the briefest flutter of puzzlement and surprise in his face before he gains control of it.

He takes my hand in his and I can see the nurse-bodyguards stiffen to attention at the same close-by table as before. Adam stiffens too. Jason Thorne's hand feels like an ordinary hand. Yes, it is extra big. And yes it is extra sweaty and extra warm. But it is just skin. Did I expect it to be scaly, like a monster's? When I start to pull my own hand away, Thorne responds instantly and loosens his already-gentle hold, careful not to encroach. I resist the impulse to wipe my palms and fingers on your dress. They will dry, I tell myself. I can wash them later, I tell myself.

'Won't you sit down?' He has placed a chair exactly in the position I dragged it to last time, remembering my seating preference.

'Thank you very much.' I lower myself onto the chair, flattening my hands against the cushion, a natural movement which has the advantage of wiping away at least some of his sweat.

Thorne has not positioned a second chair for Adam, who calmly goes and gets one and puts it beside mine. Adam sits too, reverting to his previous slouchy posture.

340

I am surprised to notice that there are no dead blue-bottles or moths or slugs dangling from Thorne's wrists and buttonholes. 'No jewellery today?' I ask.

'I didn't realise you'd miss it. Do you miss it, Melanie?'

'I must confess I don't.'

'Then I must confess that I didn't want to wear something that made you think badly of me.'

I find this revelation a million times more disturbing than the moulting insect corpses. 'That was kind of you, Jason,' I say.

His smile is even wider. 'You used my first name.' But the smile falls away. 'Why are you being nice to me?'

'You haven't done anything to me that deserves less than that, have you?'

'I hope not.' He considers, then shakes his head, definite. 'I haven't.'

'And because I need you to help me – I believed you when you said there was something important you could tell me about my sister.'

'Ye-es.' He draws out the word, nods slowly. 'You're not here then because you find yourself strangely in love with me?'

'It would be a lie and a cruelty to tell you such a thing.'

'I told you last time that I could see you aren't a liar.'

And I remember thinking how wrong he was then. And continues to be. I am trained in the School of Miranda, with a particular speciality in omission.

He places each of his feet flatly on the floor, spreading his knees widely. 'I hope it doesn't make you uncomfortable when I sit like this? Difficult for a man my size to find the right position.'

Adam barely looks up. 'Change it now or she's leaving, Jason.'

'God you're tiresome. It was purely innocent. You're the one with the dirty mind, Doctor Do-Good.' Thorne makes a great show of gluing his thighs firmly together before turning back to me. 'I am sorry, Melanie, that you had to hear the ugly spin that man puts on everything.' He shakes his bald head sorrowfully.

For the first time, I wonder if his hair loss is natural. In the photographs from before his arrest his hair was short and wavy, the colour of lion fur. Surely even a disposable razor would be deadly in this man's hands. Or perhaps they allow him to use something battery-operated?

'Can you please call me Ella?' I say. 'I don't like Melanie.'

'You should have said. With pleasure. I appreciate the confidence.' He smiles so widely and naturally, even sweetly, that I am disconcerted. 'What are you thinking, Ella?'

I shrug my shoulders to dismiss the idea that I could possibly be thinking anything.

'I wish it could be otherwise, but I can only help you if you play a little game with me. I did mention it the last time we were together.'

We were together. Is he delusional? Despite Ted's cynicism, they were probably right to stick him in this place without trial.

It must be the recollection of Thorne's hair that makes me think of it, but do you remember that story Mum used to tell us, taken from an eighteenth-century novel she read long ago? The one about the very careful lady who accepts the gift of a lion?

This cautious lady soon tames the lion. After that, she pets it and strokes it and plays with it and brings it treats and feeds it from her own little golden plate with her own little hand. She lets it drink from her own little golden cup and even allows it to sleep at the foot of her very own silken bed. One morning, before breakfast, the lion tears the lady to pieces.

At the end, Mum would always ask us, Whose fault was it, the lady's or the lion's? As soon as I was old enough to talk, you would let me answer, and I would repeat what I learned from listening to you so many times. The lady's fault, I would say, because she changed her character but the lion did not.

'Will you play my game?' Jason Thorne asks.

What I am doing with this man is wrong in exactly the same way as the lady was wrong with the lion. 'It depends on what the game is.'

'The game is simple. You must answer any question I ask you with the truth. And you must accept and obey any command I give.'

'I won't accept those second terms. I won't do anything physical and I will never promise to obey anybody.'

He moves his head from side to side rapidly. 'No, no, no. I wouldn't expect that from you. I respect you too much for that, Ella. These would be verbal responses to verbal commands.'

'Okay,' I say. 'Then yes to both of those rules.'

'Aren't you worried I will make you play my game and then refuse to tell you what you want to know?'

'If you apply your rules unreasonably I will break them. And you can't make me play. I choose to. Plus, I trust your word.' Somehow, against all reason, I actually do, despite your voice in my ear.

You are acting like the lady, you say.

'You are one of the few who can,' he says. 'I like your dress, by the way.' He tries – and I think it is a real try – not to look me up and down. But he fails.

'Thank you,' I say.

'Though perhaps it is a little loose?'

It is the black shirtdress you used to wear after you had Luke. It is silky and buttons up the front and that is why you loved it so much, so you could open it up to breastfeed him. You must have had it laundered more times than you could count, because you seemed to be wearing it whenever I saw you.

'It was my sister's,' I say.

'That's a personal thing for you to tell me, Ella.'

'Yes. It is.'

'I am – moved by – the confidences you are making. So I will make one in return. I believe I have seen that dress before.'

My throat goes dry. I feel Adam stiffen even though he doesn't break his supposedly indifferent slouch. 'But you said you never met her in person.' My words come out as a croak.

'Let me get you some water, Ella.' Thorne pours from the same jug as before into the same coloured plastic cup as before. 'You know, I love to say your name. I much prefer Ella, too.' This time, I drink, and he does his best to disguise his satisfaction with the change. 'Better?'

I nod.

'It is true that I never met her in person. The conversation I had with her was, as I said, by phone. But I didn't say I never *saw* her in person. I made some fascinating – observations.'

The pen scratches across Adam's page.

I open my mouth and close it several times before I manage to get any words out. 'But you didn't tell the police.'

'Have you momentarily forgotten who you are talking to?' He actually laughs. 'My findings on your sister were made before the police became interested in me. I hardly wanted to draw their attention by telling them I'd followed her.'

I open my mouth with more questions but he cuts me off. 'If you want to know more you will have to play my game.' He looks at Adam. 'The good doctor has taught me a great deal about inducements.'

'I already said I would do it,' I say.

'Ah. But once we start, you might find that you don't like it. I want to make sure you are in an unshakably cooperative state of mind. I don't want you quitting until we are finished, Ella.'

We. How many times has this man said *We* in the last few minutes? My instinct is to repudiate it. Silently, I recite a litany to remind myself. *See his humanness. See his humanness. He is human like me.*

'Be sure you play fairly, then.' I sit back, cross my legs, rest my hands on my knee. 'Whenever you are ready, Jason.'

Adam looks up from his notepad as if he has been busy with something else and only just decided to notice us. 'Miss Brooke may not quit, Jason, but if you cross a line I will quit for her and put a stop to it.'

'But I fully intend to cross several lines, *Adam*.' Thorne relishes his appropriation of the first name. 'I do suggest you think carefully before interrupting. *Miss Brooke* will not think well of you if you interfere before the end. Even a poor crazed psychopath like me can see that you would very much like *Miss Brooke* to think well of you.'

Adam doesn't react to a single word of this. He simply returns his attention to his clipboard to make several rapid notes.

'Let us begin,' Thorne says. 'First question. What would you say to your sister if you could?'

I think of Ted role-playing with me in the park, lying on top of me and making me remember the last time we made love.

'I don't know.' My voice is quiet.

'Pretend I'm her. Pretend she can hear you right now.'

'No.'

'Do it or you lose and I tell you nothing.'

'I will do it if I get to ask you a question or issue you with a command for each of yours. As we go. Taking turns.'

'Those are not the conditions you agreed to.'

'Now that we have begun I realise this is the only way I can do it. Take it or leave it.'

'I will take it. I think it is a fair development of the rules. I want it to be our game together, Ella, not mine alone.' He laces his fingers and rests his chin on them. 'Do you think I would have been a different man if I'd met you when I was young? I like to imagine I might have been.'

I think again of the story of the lion and the lady. 'My mother says you cannot change a person's nature.'

'Another intimate confidence and I didn't even ask for it.'

'I suppose that's true.' I consider for a minute. 'This isn't part of the game, but I can't help but wonder what brought you to do the things you did.'

'I look like a monster, don't I?'

'I have met some beautiful monsters. My mother says that it's how a person acts that can make them monstrous, not how they look.'

'Is that all you see in me? The monstrous things I have done?'

'It's the largest part of what I see. But I also see that you're intelligent and talented. What you do with wood is true art. You actually like people, don't you?'

He is blushing. 'Only selectively. They don't usually like me back. Unless I have inducements. That's the only reason you're here. Because I have induced you.'

'True. But I actually prefer you today to the last time we met. Perhaps you've got better with people, more imaginative about what they are thinking and feeling.'

'Empathic?' He says the word like a sneer. 'Dr Dismal certainly likes that term.'

'Perhaps Dr Holderness and his team really are helping you.'

'No more of this tiresome subject. If you want the sad story of my neglected childhood you will not get it.'

'That sounds boring,' I say. 'I'm happy to skip that.'

'Let's start over. Back to our little game. What would you say to your sister if she were sitting right where I am? No more trying to divert me, however good you are at it.'

'I thought you were diverting me, but okay,' I say. 'Here it is. *Why did you leave me?*' I am startled that of all the things that would come out, it is this.

'That is too polite and controlled. Say it like you mean it.'

'I'll do that after you tell me how many times you saw her and where and when.'

'That's too many questions in one. The answer you get is *Once.* I saw her once. If you want more say it again like you mean it. *Why did you leave me?*'

'Fine.' I sit back as if bracing for a performance, but what comes out is real. '*Why the fuck did you leave me?*' The third word is an explosion. Each of the others is a bullet.

He nods approval. 'Does that feel better?'

When I first told Ted I was going to see Thorne, Ted said I would be Thorne's entertainment. I told him I could live with that, and I see that I can, easily. 'Tell me when you saw her,' I say. 'That is one question.'

'And I have one answer. It is a big one. The day before she disappeared. And here is a bonus gift, thrown in because I like you far too much to stop myself. Saw her and heard her.'

There is a rustle of paper and the dull thump of Adam's clipboard hitting the floor. 'Time to stop this. Now.'

'No,' I say. 'Absolutely not.'

'I did warn you, Dr Dumb Dumb, that you would not impress Ella if you interfered.'

Adam stands. 'I am ending this visit. This is information that should be given to the police in a proper manner.' He looks to the door. 'Please come with me now, Ella.'

'No. This isn't a formal interview. He's perfectly entitled to disclose what he wishes to me. You have no reason to stop this.' I cross my arms. 'You have no right.'

Thorne smiles his ugly smile at Adam, which is not the same smile that he smiles at me. 'She will never forgive you if you drag her away now, Dr Dreary.' Thorne turns to me. 'Will you, Ella?' I say nothing. 'I'm speaking the truth, aren't I?'

'Yes,' I say. 'You are.'

Adam slowly sits down. He doesn't pick up the clipboard. He doesn't resume the fake slump. His back is absolutely straight and he looks ready to spring up again in an instant. The nurse-bodyguards, though maintaining their pretence of indifference to what is happening five feet away, also appear to be sitting straighter.

'Tell me what you saw that day, Jason,' I say. 'You have to tell me. And what you heard.'

'Not yet. My turn to issue a command. Remember? You promised, didn't you?'

'Yes.'

'Okay. Now I am going to repeat exactly what you said, and I want you to answer as if you were your sister. Role play. A little trick I learned here. Don't think about it. Just quickly say whatever comes into your head. On the count of three. One. Two. Three. *Why did you leave me?*'

Nothing comes out.

Thorne tries again. 'I am you. You are your sister. *Why did you leave me, Miranda?*'

Again nothing. My head is exploding with the need for Thorne to tell me what he saw. There is no room for anything else.

'One last time. Do it or I will never tell you what I saw and heard. *Why did you leave me?*' He bangs a fist so loud on the fake wood table Adam and the nurse-guards all rise a little in their chairs and I let out a small gasp.

'*I didn't leave you. I'd never have left you.*' I put my hand up to my mouth and then peel it away onto my lap and raise my head to look straight at Thorne. 'No more,' I say. 'No more games. I have played fairly and done as much as I can bear. If you get off on the truth of that I don't care. Just tell me.'

'All right, Ella. I will tell you. Remember, later, that you asked for this.'

What happens next happens so fast I can barely understand it. It is a series of small things that occur in such a smooth and uninterrupted sequence they seem to be all one action. Everything is a whizzing blur of colour with objects coming into sharp focus only fleetingly. Didn't you once tell me that this is how butterflies see?

Thorne leaps from his toy sofa with a speed I would not have thought possible for a man his size. He smashes the table out of his way, setting the plastic jug and tumblers flying as the table lands on its side, a barrier between me and Adam and an impediment to the nurse-bodyguards. There is no place for me to dive out of Thorne's path to evade him, sitting as I am in a kind of prison with the half-circle chair cupping my back and sides and Thorne's bulk towering over me. I cannot process what he wants, but somehow I manage to process that what he is doing is coming for me and before this thought is properly in my mind, before I can take any stance, before I can reach up to jab an eye or puncture an eardrum or break a finger, before my knee has moved even an inch upwards, before I can do any of the things I have practised and taught for years, Thorne has snatched me from the chair, crushing both of my arms to my sides and squeezing my whole body against his and pressing my face against his chest so that I can't breathe. He is a foot taller than I am. I must look like a rag doll in the arms of a giant.

'If you come near us I will break her neck,' he says, lumbering off with me towards a corner of the room. I go limp while I try to work out what to do, try to think of a move, but I am entirely immobilised, with my back against the wall, and my arms and legs pinned and my whole body flattened by his.

There is no shouting in the background. Whatever Adam is doing, it is not a noisy thing. Whatever the nurse-bodyguards are doing does not make noise either. In these first few seconds, there is just the rush of air in my ears and the smell of Thorne's sweat in my nose and the thrum of my own blood through my veins.

'It's the only way, Ella.' He is speaking into the top of my head. He kisses my hair. There is the sound of his lips smacking together. There is wetness on my scalp. I retch and swallow back sick. 'It's worth it, being able to touch you at least once. It's not as if they'll ever release me for good behaviour. Do you know how many years of pretend reformation I needed to earn these visits with you? How patient I had to be to lure you here? How much trouble I went to last month to let the press know about that phone call with your sister?' One of his hands moves along my side and I hear the fabric of your dress rip before I feel Thorne's fingers squeezing my bare thigh and he lets out a sigh. 'We don't have long. I want you to know that everything I have said to you, everything I am about to say, is true. The only lie was for them – I would never hurt you.'

He lifts me, so my face is level with his, holds my head still, and kisses my mouth wetly before moving his lips to my ear. My body has entirely frozen. All I can think is that I will never know what he saw. Now he will never tell me. That thought is louder than my horror. Louder than the message that I may be about to die.

Then another thought creeps in from far away, and the part of me that I have trained and nurtured since you disappeared wakes up. The thought is that he is distracted, pressing me into this corner as he is, and by his efforts to keep me still while trying to feel me. And though he has my back to the wall and he is blocking me from seeing the rest of the room, I sense quiet, careful movement behind him.

He doesn't kiss my ear. He inhales so deeply it sounds like thunder. I wonder if he is about to take a bite out of me. When his fingers creep higher over my skin I wonder if he is going to try to rape me against this wall, with these people watching. But there is only more of his sour breath, then a murmur of sentences so low that only I can hear them. How long does he whisper to me like this? Is it only a minute? Is it several? It must be several but I lose track of how long he goes on, punctuating his phrases with kisses against my temple as he tells me his story. It is long enough. It is too long. Nothing that he has done to me so far has made me cry out. But these words do, causing the men in the room to shout warnings at him that I cannot understand. And when Thorne has said it all, when I know he has finished, I scream the word *No* so loud it makes him falter just enough for me to slide my right leg out and do the only thing I can. I jab my heel into the back of his knee with every atom of force I have. I jab so hard he grunts and presses forward into me even harder, squashing my breath from my bones.

Everything goes black until I hit the ground with a bump and open my eyes to the sound of crashing metal and shouts.

Thorne is on his back. A squad of nurses have swarmed him, all of them wearing blue gloves, and I think of Gulliver surrounded by the Lilliputians. They must have slipped in silently while Thorne and I were caught up with each other. Someone must have pressed an alarm somewhere, silent in here but ringing and flashing red alert where it counted.

Thorne turns his eyes towards me but not his head, because there is a pair of blue gloves keeping his skull still. 'We did well, didn't we, Ella? You got what you needed from me. And me from you. Fair exchange. A game well played.' Each of the nurses has taken firm charge of a part of Thorne's body: his head, an upper or lower arm, a thigh or ankle, a side of his pelvis. Every bit of him is firmly pinned to the floor.

One of the nurses shifts and that is when I see Adam, on his knees, bending over Thorne, holding a syringe. Another nurse cuts through Thorne's jeans and Adam plunges the longest needle I have ever seen into Thorne's hip. Thorne screams like a wild animal. A second syringe materialises and Adam plunges that in too. Then a third before Adam jumps up and is by my side.

I am half-sitting, flopped against the wall, and Adam doesn't move me. He looks from the top of my head to the tips of my toes and wonders aloud about crush injuries and broken ribs. 'Don't move.' He holds my head. 'Does it hurt to breathe?'

I shake my head against his hands.

'Moving your head didn't hurt?' His fingers are pressing in intervals along the nape of my neck. 'Here? No pain? And here? Any pain here?'

'None.'

'That was an impressive kick.' He is concentrating on examining me even as he speaks, trying to distract me from watching Thorne. He is shining a light pen into each of my eyes. But it isn't working. I am still trying to look at Thorne whenever I can. 'You dropped him to the ground.'

'It would have been more impressive if I hadn't let him grab me in the first place.'

He nods, but I am not sure if it is because he agrees with me or because he is pleased that I am talking so easily. 'I don't see how even you could have avoided that. You certainly disabled him. He outmanoeuvred us all.'

'Too right, Dr Dopey.' Thorne's voice seems to come from far away.

Adam takes my wrist between his fingers to feel for my pulse, puts the metal disc of a stethoscope to my chest to listen to my breathing, gently presses his fingers behind my ears, asks me to lie on my back so he can do the same thing to my ribs and stomach. He commands me to move toes and fingers. He taps my knees. Still I turn my head to the side to watch Thorne, whose gaze meets mine. He and I have barely torn our eyes from each other's since we both fell.

'Enjoying that, are you, Dr Dishrag?' Thorne sounds like a child doing everything he can to resist an over-powering urge to sleep.

Adam pushes up the sleeves of your dress to examine my arms. 'No marks that I can see.' He shakes his head, perplexed. 'No visible injuries.'

'I said I wouldn't hurt her.' Thorne's voice is growing more slurred with each sentence.

'Excuse me, Jason, but the bruises can still emerge and I heard you threaten to break her neck.'

'Was to keep you away. Wouldn't have done it. Told her I wouldn't. Tried to keep my weight off her. Even when she took me down.' He pauses for a long time between each word.

Another blue-gloved nurse comes through the door. He is pushing a wheeled stretcher with restraints and accompanied by a second doctor. This man quickly comes over to crouch near Adam, who continues to sit beside me, watching me breathe and rechecking my pulse. Adam begins to murmur to the other doctor in a language I can barely understand, explaining the combination of anti-anxiety, anti-psychotic and anti-cholinergic medicines he used to achieve rapid tranquillisation. The names of the drugs sound beautiful when Adam says them, as if they are rare flowers. Lorazepam. Haloperidol. Procyclidine.

'We're going to get you onto the stretcher now, Jason.' The nurse speaks to Thorne as if he is giving him great news.

'Fuck off. Get off me.' Despite the words there is no fight in him. His eyes close but he jerks them open again, trying even harder to defy the cocktail of drugs Adam shot into his muscles.

'On my count,' the nurse says. Ten men lift Thorne onto the padded stretcher so effortlessly, with such clock-work coordination, I realise they must practise as hard as synchronised swimmers. Quickly, they strap down Thorne's legs and arms, but the chemical restraints are already working so powerfully they barely need the material ones.

The second doctor rises, telling Adam he will go with them to monitor Thorne.

'His knee will need to be examined,' Adam tells him. I can't tell if there is pride or alarm in the glance he throws at me. 'There will almost certainly be damage.'

As they begin to roll him away Thorne opens his eyes. Even half-dreaming, those eyes seek me out and lock into mine. Though his words are slurred I can hear every single one of them. 'Wish I had you alone in this bed, Ella,' he says.

What happens next is like something from a horror film. I shoot up and forward, catching myself with my palms on the floor so that I am on all fours. As I move, a gush of vomit rushes out of me so violently it sprays several feet. Adam grabs my hair out of my face and holds it like our mother used to as I retch and retch and retch some more. When I finally finish and lift my head and open my eyes, Thorne is gone.

Sleeping Potion

An electric shock goes through my skull when several policemen walk in. I make myself stare hard before I see that none of these men looks remotely like Ted. I am too drained to talk to them but I fob them off with a promise to come to the station over the weekend to give them a statement.

Adam takes me home, insisting that he cannot allow me to drive. I give him my address, close my eyes, and fall asleep, waking with a small scream when his car stops in front of my house. For a split second I think I am still in the Visitors' Centre with Thorne pressing me against the wall.

'I'd like to come in and make sure you're okay. Is there someone you can call to stay the night with you?'

I nod yes. My neck hurts when I move it. I sit in his passenger seat, unable to work out what to do next, so Adam gets out and comes round to my side of the car and opens the door and gently takes my hand to pull me out. He walks beside me, along my front path, then helps me with the locks because my hands are shaking too much and I keep dropping the keys.

I am not quite sure how we end up in my kitchen, but I open my eyes as if I have been asleep and realise that this is where we are. The downstairs telephone handset is on the table and Adam passes it to me.

Dialling is a reflex. As soon as I hear her voice I say, 'Mummy, I need you,' and I start to cry, and somewhere far in the back of my mind I realise I have gone from Mum to Mother and back to Mummy. She says, 'I'm on my way,' and I can hear how hard she is trying not to sound scared.

All I want is to take a shower. I leave Adam at my kitchen table to wait for her while I go upstairs to the bathroom.

Your dress is splattered in sick. When I slip it off a new wave of the smell hits me and I lean over the toilet to throw up again. I wipe my face with my arm, squirm out of my black underwear and bra, drop them on top of your dress and shoes. I take a plastic bag from the cupboard beneath the sink and swoop it down over this pile of foul things, wanting to quarantine anything and everything that could possibly have Thorne's sweat and germs on it. Then I climb into the shower.

I make the water as hot as I can stand and soap and rinse myself once, twice, three times, scrubbing Thorne from my skin until it is sore. I shampoo my hair three times too. I let the water pound on the back of my neck, waiting for the ache to diminish, but it doesn't. I brush and floss my teeth again and again and again, then throw the toothbrush away.

I shun Ted's old bathrobe. Instead, I wrap myself in a lilac-coloured one that I have never worn before, stuffed at the bottom of my wardrobe since Mum gave it to me last Christmas. There are matching fluffy slippers to go with it and I slip these on too.

I pad downstairs to see that Adam has made himself a cup of tea, and one for me. 'You look a little better,' he says.

It occurs to me that what I look like is a purple puff-ball, but I am beyond caring. 'I feel – much better.' My voice is hollow. I haven't even towel-dried my hair. It is dripping onto the floor tiles at the rate of a leaking tap, and so tangled I will probably have to cut it all off.

I open the door that leads out from the kitchen to the garden and put out the plastic bag of your ruined things, not wanting them in my house for another second. Before today, I never could have imagined throwing away something you wore and loved, something that connected you to Luke.

Adam points to a bottle of pills on the table. 'It's Diazepam,' he says. 'You may need to manage some anxiety symptoms after what happened.'

'I won't have anxiety. This afternoon was nothing.'

'I'm not sure many people would describe it that way. With your permission, I'd like to talk to your mother when she gets here. Explain what the pills are and how to use them. The possible side effects. In case you choose to take them. For sleep – just short-term. They aren't only for anxiety.'

'Okay.' I sink into a chair, pick up the tea, hold the mug for a few seconds before putting it down without sipping. I hardly take in the fact that I am wearing an absurd dressing gown and nothing beneath it sitting in my kitchen with Adam. I reach for the bottle of pills and try to read the label but the words are swimming.

'I have to ask this,' Adam says. 'There's no possibility you're pregnant, is there?'

I ought to laugh, a dark laugh, but I don't. 'No. Why?'

'Best to avoid Diazepam in pregnancy. You can take two, if you feel you need them tonight,' Adam says.

'Actually, I think I'll take them now. I need sleep. I want to go to bed.'

He finds a glass, fills it with water, puts it in front of me. 'I'm worried about you, Ella. Not as a doctor. As me.'

'I'm fine. I've washed it all away already.' But my hand is visibly juddering as I put the pills in my mouth and gulp them down.

'Would it help to talk about it?'

I shake my head No.

He slides a piece of paper across the table to me. 'I think I gave you my number the first time I met you. Here it is again. I've put my address on too. If you need anything, call.'

'Thank you,' I say, 'for everything.'

There is the sound of our mother's key in the lock.

I stand up, clutching the dressing gown around me even more tightly. 'Now you get to meet my mother. This isn't an experience you will ever forget.'

But my eyes are filling with tears again as I say this and before I can meet her at the door there is the rustle of her coat as she hurries in, crying out and rushing through the kitchen and practically knocking me over when she throws her arms around me, somehow knowing where I am without my even calling her name.

Friday, 18 November

_____

The Long Morning

There is a hand holding mine. I open my eyes to our mother's face, looking down at my own, and realise I am in my own bed and she has drawn up a chair to sit beside me, watching over me until I wake. The curtains are closed. The room is lit only by the hall light outside.

Then it all comes flooding back to me.

I sit up but quickly take her hand again. 'I'm happy to see you. It makes me feel about ten.'

'I'm happy to see you too.' She sniffles and wipes an eye. 'You've made Luke's room lovely, Ella. I liked sleeping in there.' She leans over to switch on my little bedside lamp, awkwardly, because I do not want to let her go.

'I'm glad you think so.' I push aside the quilt and try to stand, still clutching her, but she stops me. I realise I never took off the lilac dressing gown. 'I need to go, Mum. There's something I need to do.'

She grips my hand harder. 'Haven't you done enough? Your doctor friend told me everything, after you'd gone to sleep. You were unimaginably tired. Unconscious before your head hit the pillow. Can't you let yourself rest some more?' She closes her eyes for a few seconds, opens them and shudders. 'That man could have snapped your neck. He could have done . . . worse.' It is her turn to cry. 'We could have lost you too.'

'But you didn't. He's in much worse shape than I am.' I try to smile but she doesn't smile back, either because she can't or because I haven't done it right and whatever shape I have tried to put my face into does not resemble a smile at all.

'So I'm told. I don't want to scold you again, Ella. Not ever again, if I can manage it. I don't want to fight with you. I want to try to support you.'

'I'm sorry I scared you. And I'm so, so sorry for all of the horrible things I said.' I put my arms around her and kiss her wet face. 'I didn't mean them.'

'I'm sorry too, my beautiful girl.'

'You don't need to be.' I pull back to look at her. When did her wrinkles deepen so much? I think they are my fault. 'There is something you can do to help.'

'Anything.'

'Can you and Dad go by the hospital to pick up my car?'

'Where are your keys?'

'Adam said he'd leave them in Reception. I need my phone and my watch – they're in the glovebox. My locket's in there too.'

'We'll do it after we pick up Luke, okay?' She grimaces, clearly grappling with a problem. 'But I don't want Luke setting even a foot in that place.'

'I don't either.'

She thinks about it some more. 'Luke and I will wait in the car while your father runs in to get your keys. Your father will drive your car back and Luke and I will follow him.'

'Perfect.'

Something occurs to me. Why do she and my father need to take Luke with them? Shouldn't he be in school? I jump out of bed and throw open the curtains.

The light. This isn't morning light. The shadows are all wrong. 'What time is it?' I grab the little clock on my bedside table. 'Oh my God.'

'Don't take His name in vain, Ella. Please.'

'Oh crap.' She lets this one go. 'It's three o'clock, Mum. How can it be three o'clock?'

'You had a trauma yesterday. That does funny things to the body. And – Adam – the doctor – he gave you those Diazepam. You needed to sleep. He said this might happen, that I shouldn't worry if you slept an extra-long time, that I should let you.'

'No, no, no. Oh no. I won't have time.'

'Ella?' There is that thing in her voice you can't ignore. 'Look at me.'

I look at her.

She puts her hands on both sides of my face and searches as if there is a specific material thing she will find in there and extract, whether I want her to or not. 'Won't have time for what?'

I don't answer.

'Something happened yesterday. Jason Thorne told you something, didn't he?'

'I can't talk about it.'

'Okay,' she says slowly.

'There's someone I need to see, Mum.'

'Okay,' she says again. 'Dad and Luke and I will let ourselves in and leave your things on your kitchen table if you're not here. You do what you need to do.' It is not her martyred voice. It is her loving voice. For our mother to say these words and mean them is a superhuman act of self-control that goes against every instinct she has ever had. But she is not quite finished. 'There is one condition.'

'What?'

She manages an almost-smile. 'You need to let me get the tangles out of your hair, first.'

The Ice Queen

I walk quickly into town through more mizzling grey, twisting through side streets and cut-throughs until I am two minutes from the river and standing in front of a row of red-brick Edwardian houses originally built for railway workers. As ever, your voice is hissing in my ear.

Show him what he is missing. What he will forever be missing. He threw you away. So put on a little black dress. Dust some sparkly powder over your chest and on your eyelids. Wear a shoe with a heel for once. Dab some scent behind your ears. Leave your hair down. A bit of mascara wouldn't hurt.

It has never been easier to tune out your scolding and ignore your commands. My outfit is the anti-Miranda. I am wearing faded jeans. My soft brown peasant top is loose and gypsy-like and you would hate it. My hair is in a high ponytail and I am wearing clunky boots that I can easily run in but you would call ugly and shout at me for. And that is just fine by me because I am not exactly thrilled with you either right now.

I bang on his door so hard my knuckles hurt. He opens it quickly, stepping back in surprise to see me standing here. But before his mouth can shape itself into a smile, something in my face freezes him.

'God, Ella. What's wrong?'

I push past him and along this narrow hallway I have never seen before. I glimpse the open door to his living room. An ugly carpet, threadbare and red, with a pair of scrunched and presumably dirty socks tossed onto it. Cast-off furniture that I recognise from the few times he actually let me visit his childhood house, always when his mother was out. There are no family photographs on the chimney piece, no pictures on the walls. There is little light. He bought this place after his divorce.

We have landed in his kitchen. The sink is full of dirty plates and crusted saucepans. Cups and cutlery and unrinsed tins of soup and baked beans litter the wooden counter, which is pitted with black rot. Everything is covered in food waste and coffee grinds and teabags and egg shells that he hasn't bothered to discard. There isn't even a twinge of my habitual concern for him.

He notices me looking around. 'I've only been up for an hour. I worked a double shift until seven this morning.'

'So you were on duty when I saw you yesterday at the hospital, in uniform?'

He ignores the question. 'Do you want a cup of tea?'

I glance at his oven clock. Five o'clock. 'Actually, I'd like something stronger. And less likely to give me food poisoning.'

He grabs two bottles of German beer from his fridge. 'Glass?' He glances at the sink as if such a thing would be an impossibility and I shake my head. We each take one of the tubular metal stools that sit side-by-side in front of their companion kitchen bar, which is sticky with butter and marmalade and crumbs.

I bend at the waist and squirm a hand into a boot to pull up one of my socks. When I straighten up Ted is frowning.

'There's a bruise on the nape of your neck.' He pushes aside the neckline of my blouse so that the trim on the cup of my black lace bra is exposed, and I see how easily he still presumes such intimacy. 'There's another one on your chest,' he says.

I thought my heart had frozen, since Thorne whispered in my ear yesterday. But now that I am here, now that I am about to say the words Thorne said, my heart is beating fast and my skin feels so hot I am sure my newly visible bruises are camouflaged by the red that has crept over every inch of my skin.

'Don't touch me.' I jerk away and Ted falls back as if punched by an invisible fist. For a second, I think his stool is going to tip over and crash down with him on it.

'At least the man who made these bruises has the excuse of being criminally insane. And he has never deliberately lied to me. Unlike you.'

He waits until I seem to be breathing again before he speaks. 'Are you comparing me to that psychopathic scumbag? You took him down. If you hadn't kicked his ass he'd have raped you and murdered you in front of your doctor friend and those nurses. He'd have enjoyed the audience.'

I swallow half the bottle of beer, then cough so violently I can see Ted having a three-way fight with himself, one part wanting to slap my back so I don't choke, a second part not daring to lay even a finger on me again, and a third part wanting to strangle me with his own hands.

Already I can feel alcohol making its way through my veins, probably speeded by a residue of Diazepam from last night. I come right out and say it. 'I know, Ted. I know the thing you never thought I'd find out.'

'What the hell are you talking about?'

'I'm talking about the thing you never wanted me to know.'

'You're not making sense.' There is a faint sheen of sweat on his brow but he continues to pretend not to understand me. 'Whatever happened to you in that hospital yesterday with Thorne must have resulted in a head injury.'

'My head was examined before I left.'

'By that quack who obviously wants to fuck your brains out?'

'He's not a quack. And there was no serious injury. The bruises will fade. As far as he was capable, Thorne tried to restrain himself and not hurt me.'

'Listen to yourself. You talk as if you actually admire him. As if you actually like him. Do you believe those fuckwits who say he's insane? Only someone equally insane would go near him.'

'At least he doesn't tell me I'm mad every time I say

something he doesn't like. I needed to hear what he could tell me and I knew exactly what I was risking.'

'I warned you he was dangerous.'

'I managed to figure that out without your help.' I shake my head as if by doing so I can shake the words to the surface so I can actually say them. 'Thorne saw you, Ted. He saw you with her the day before she disappeared. He heard what the two of you said. He worked out who you were to me from the nature of your conversation with her.'

I have read so many times of faces suddenly being drained of blood. I always wondered if it could really happen, that fast and all-at-once. And now I know that it can. Because I have just watched all of Ted's blood rush out of his head and down to his feet. Because now I have seen for myself that skin really can appear as white as paper. Those words are not empty, but to see them in action is rare.

'That's not possible,' he says.

'So you didn't meet her in the woods behind my parents' house, the day before she vanished? You didn't drive from her to me, as soon as you parted?'

Can it be that his face blanches even more?

'Tell me you didn't really spend half an hour talking to her there. Go on. Tell me that's not true.'

He says nothing.

'I even know what dress she was wearing that day. Do you want me to describe it or would you like to?'

For once he has nothing to say.

'The black one that buttons up the front, that she was always wearing for breastfeeding, in case you have forgotten. Have you forgotten? Or perhaps you didn't notice.'

At last he says, 'How?' It seems that one word is the best he can do.

'Thorne followed her to my parents' that morning. She caught his attention when she phoned him about that carpentry job. You know. That phone call between them you kept telling me she never made.'

'Ella—'

'Spare me. He was scouting for a new victim so he wanted to see her in person and decide if he'd target her. He was crouching behind foliage and he had excellent binoculars. He wasn't carrying extra weight then – the meds did that to him – he could move easily. He knows how to hide – it's one of his arts. And he can lip-read.'

'Please, Ella—'

I put up a hand. 'You need to hear this. Did you know the ability to lip-read is more common in people who have problems relating to others? Did they not teach you that in training school? Thorne deliberately honed this little talent of his. He found it incredibly useful.'

He staggers off his stool, careering it onto the filthy linoleum. He throws his arms around me, pulls me onto my feet and against him, burying his head in my shoulder. Great racking sobs are shuddering through his body, making mine shudder too. 'I love you, Ella. I've always loved you. It was only once and it meant nothing. It was years ago.'

I jerk out of his arms. 'Is that why you got that weekend off? Did you come down to spend it in Brighton with me to make sure she didn't? Because you were afraid of what she might tell me if we had some time alone together?'

'No.' He moves his head from side to side so furiously the tears he hasn't wiped fly from his face. 'You'd been alone with her countless times since. She was never going to tell you. We both planned to take it to our graves. We'd made a pact. Probably the only thing she and I ever agreed about. She was more terrified than I was of you finding out, and that's saying a lot.'

'Why do you think she did it?' I hate that I have to ask this of him. I hate that he is still the best person to answer this, without you here.

'I don't know.'

'You fucking well do.'

He shakes his head as if he is genuinely puzzled. 'A mix of things. Her constant need for attention. I got the feeling things weren't going the way she wanted with whoever her man of the moment was. I think our relationship looked perfect and easy to her – the opposite of whatever she had. She wanted to shatter it.'

'What we had *was* perfect. You shattered it.'

'Yes. I did. And I still don't understand myself well enough to know why. For her, though, I think she needed to prove that you were vulnerable too. That she could take what she wanted from you. But she couldn't, Ella. As soon as I sobered up, all I wanted was you.'

'You thought Luke was your son, didn't you?'

'Only briefly.'

'Is that why you've always loved him?'

'I think he's a great kid. I love him because you do. I love him for him. Miranda swore to me he wasn't mine.

It was one of the things we talked about that morning, but she'd already convinced me. Luke is yours. That's how I think of him.'

'You never told the police you met her the day before she vanished. That was evidence and you never told because you only thought of yourself. You of all people know you should have gone to them with that.' My temples are throbbing. I press the flats of my hands against them. 'Were you involved in some way?'

'I was in bed with you when she disappeared. You know that.'

'You could have arranged it. Got someone else to do it.'

'I'm not a criminal mastermind. I'm a policeman with one serious and literal fuck-up in his past.'

'If that's true then you won't try to persuade me not to tell your buddies at the station about your relationship with her, about your meeting.'

'It wasn't a relationship.' He grabs me, spins me round, pulls me hard against him, starts to plant small kisses on my breastbone. 'Please, please, please forgive me, Ella. I love you. Let me show you how much. Please. Let me take you to bed right now.'

I close my eyes and count to ten before I open them. His lips might as well be touching stone. I feel nothing. 'You've got to be kidding me. I don't want this with you. Ever again. Let go of me or I will make you.'

I wrench myself away and move as far from him as I can, to his kitchen window. I stare out into his bare little garden.

'Please at least look at me.'

'No.' There is a silhouette of an apple tree. Beneath it is the shadow of a picnic table covered in beer bottles. 'How did it happen?' I direct the question towards the moon, which is such a faint sliver it hardly makes any impression at all on the black sky.

With the dark outside and the light inside, I can see his reflection mirrored in the window. He shrugs, seeming to ponder the most mystifying thing in the world. I close my eyes to blot him from my view, as if responding to a physical pain.

'You'd just gone back to the university again. She and I bumped into each other in the supermarket after work, went for a drink, talked about how much we were missing you.' He makes a noise that is almost a laugh, though it is bitter and astonished. 'All we did was talk about you. We ended up back at the flat I was renting then. She didn't even stay the night. Five minutes after it happened she left. We were both horrified.'

I open my eyes and turn around, leaning against the edge of the sink. 'Why did you get married? Was it to hurt me?'

'Please don't take this the wrong way – I'm trying to be honest – I owe you that. But you changed so much, after she was gone. You wouldn't let me take care of you. I'd been doing that since we met, but then, poof, no more. Everything you are now is formed by what happened. You aren't what you would have been.'

'There's truth in that, but you didn't answer my question.'

'I wanted to try to be normal with somebody. To be in a relationship without a big cloud hanging over it. But you haunted my marriage. You haunted me. You made my marriage another big fuck-up.'

'So that's my fault. You've used that one before.'

'I didn't mean it that way. It came out wrong. Everything is coming out wrong.'

'What's your blood type, Ted?'

He looks baffled but he still answers. 'O.'

'You couldn't possibly be Luke's father. He has AB blood. You don't need to be a geneticist to figure that out.'

'Tell me you will forgive me.'

'For which thing? For fucking my sister? For withholding evidence that might have helped us to find her? For spending the last decade telling me I'm mad and unstable and paranoid for wanting to know what happened to her?'

'All of them. I was scared I'd lose you.'

'You have. You can consider me well and truly lost. We would have survived your marriage and we'd definitely have survived Ruby. But not this.'

'I told you – Ruby—'

'You'd better not hurt her – she's been through enough already. I don't believe a single word that comes out of your mouth.' I grab my bag and swing it over my shoulder.

'Are you going to tell the police I met her that day?'

'No. You are going to tell them that all by yourself. You have until the end of the weekend.' I imagine him and Mrs Buenrostro in next-door interview rooms as the station explodes with new interest in your case. The two of them can do the hard work for me.

'My meeting with Miranda is irrelevant. It was unlucky timing. You know I had nothing to do with her disappearance. You must still feel too much for me to ask me to do this.'

'My feelings for you are dead. You've killed them. You make me sick. All you think about is yourself.'

'At least you'll finally believe me that she's not perfect. That you shouldn't idolise her.'

'Wow, Ted. Gee thanks. You certainly went to a lot of trouble to make a point I had already discovered without your help.'

I begin to pull the door open but before it has swung an inch he slams it closed and pins me against it. I think of Thorne pressing me against the wall yesterday.

'I don't care about myself. I care about you. More than anyone. For twenty-six years we've loved each other. You can't go. You can't do this. You can't just walk away.'

My thoughts are quick. It is the first time I have ever wanted to hurt him and it goes against the instincts of my entire life.

I imagine myself lifting a knee hard between his legs and shoving his shoulders. The fantasy is so vivid I can actually see him drop to the hall floor and double over onto his side, his hands slapped over his lower body, moaning, rolling back and forth with his knees bent. It would be so easy.

But this isn't what I do. What I do is not expert. What I do happens with a noise that is something between a scream and a cry and a grunt, and I can feel tears on my cheeks when that animal noise comes out and I shove at him blindly, pounding my fists on his chest. He lets me go not because I have wounded him, but because he is stunned by my rawness.

'I can and I can and I can.' I leave without closing the door behind me.

The Old Friend

I walk home so fast I hardly remember the journey. My car is parked in front of the house next door. Sadie is standing beside it, hands on hips, an expression on her blotchy red face that is somewhere between glaring and woeful. I haven't seen her without flawless make-up since our early teens.

I have no time for Sadie. Sadie is nothing. 'Go away,' I say, as if she is a mere fly buzzing around and annoying me on a hot day. Her long hair is unwashed, an unbrushed rat's nest with grey roots showing. Sadie's hair is normally salon-polished.

My heart is frozen again. My heart is hard. Its beat is not disturbed by Sadie. How can anything hurt me after you? You and I are not what I thought we were to each other. You are not the you I have always known. You are dead, even if you are still somewhere in this world, breathing.

I turn onto my path. I can feel Sadie, starting to follow me.

'Bitch,' Sadie says. 'You ugly, boyfriend-thieving bitch. You deserve to disappear like that vain pig of a sister of yours. She was a slut, like you.'

I turn to face her, put out a hand to stop her coming a step nearer. 'I said, *Go away.*'

'I don't take orders from you.' Sadie spits the words out with a great deal of saliva. There is some on her chin but she doesn't appear to notice.

'Are you sure, Sadie? The camera is trained on this path. Come a step closer to me and it will clearly be self-defence. You approaching me. You assaulting me. You invading my property.' The words are dramatic. The situation is dramatic. But I speak and move like an extremely convincing human robot, saying all the right lines, making all the right moves. Perhaps I have become a psychopath, devoid of empathy. I am devoid of pity, and of fear, too.

Sadie looks at the camera and cringes several steps back, off the path. She studies the lens, trying to decide if she is out of its eyeline. I watch her as if she is the object of a scientific experiment, though without a scientist's depth of curiosity.

'I've been waiting for you for an hour,' she says. 'I've been ringing the doorbell every five minutes. You can't hide from me.'

'Great. The camera will have that too. Ringing a doorbell every five minutes is nuisance behaviour. It's reportable. And you already know that I won't hesitate to report you.' How odd. I actually sound like I care about what I'm saying. Perhaps I should be an actress.

She scrunches her mouth like a toddler on the verge of a tantrum. 'You're evil. There is a chair in hell for you. After the devil tortures you.'

I laugh.

'You find that funny?'

'It would seem so. You've only got the tiniest taste of what I can do, if you push me. You really did choose to pick on the wrong woman. I suspect the police have paid you a visit?'

She wipes her nose with her bare hand. There is dirt beneath her nails, which are bitten so that the skin is raw and bleeding. I have never seen her nails without perfect varnish before. I ought to be concerned about these signs of Sadie's distress but I do not possess even a crumb of compassion. Perhaps I should be worried about my own indifference, but I am not.

'I told them all about you,' she says. 'They know everything about you.'

'Fine by me. I have nothing to hide. I would guess they warned you to stay away from me. Clearly not advice you are heeding.'

She swallows hard. 'You are going to deserve everything you get.'

'Great. Threats too. You're handing the police all the evidence they need for solid harassment and stalking charges. They can throw in some malicious communications too. Did you really think they wouldn't trace your little messages? Did you think I wouldn't hand each and every one of them over?'

She is biting her lip. She is balling her fists. She has

wrapped her arms around her own body. She is swaying from side to side as if she is drunk. I register each of her actions with dispassionate detachment.

'Move on, Sadie,' I say. 'No texts or emails in your name or Justice Administrator's name or any other name. No calls, blocked or otherwise. No photographs.'

'I don't know what you're talking about.'

'Don't waste your breath. Let me be completely clear. I don't want you near me. I don't want any communication or contact from you in any imaginable form. If you approach me in any way ever again you will get another visit from the police and a very uncomfortable bed for the night. For many nights, if you continue to get in my face. I am going to phone them now so that they can remove you. I am going to ask for a restraining order. Consider this your final warning, which is more than you deserve. So. *Leave. This. Instant.*'

I walk calmly into my house. I do not need to look behind me to make sure she is not following. I would feel it in the air if she were. I would hear.

When I am inside I pick up the landline and go to the living room window as I prepare to dial the police. But Sadie is already in her own car, tyres screaming along the road.

With her gone, there is no reason to call the police right now. I can give them the evidence of her visit later. More to the point, I have miles to go before I sleep and I do not want to waste any more of them on a Sadie detour. I move away from the living room window and into my kitchen to begin walking them.

Dressing Up

I drop the landline onto the table, unused, beside the handwritten note my mother has left for me. *Dad and I will bring Luke and lunch tomorrow. Love, Mum.* She has weighted the note in place with my keys and mobile and watch and locket.

I toss everything into my bag but the locket. For the first time since you gave it to me, I cannot bring myself to put it on. My numb heart seems to wake up. It seems to speed up as I turn the cool platinum over and over in my palm and choke back a sob. Even if I cannot put it around my neck, I can't leave it behind, either – I can't not have it near me. I throw the locket into my bag too.

What I do next I do for me. Entirely for me. Not for Mum and Dad. Not for Luke. Do you get it? Are you listening? For me. Above all not for you. For you less than anybody. Right now nobody counts but me.

I rush upstairs to shower and wash my hair with a different shampoo. Not the one with the scent of you. I brush my teeth. I even put on some mascara. But not because you are telling me to. Because it is what I want to do. I dab Chanel Number 5 behind my ears, between my breasts, on the nape of my neck. Again not because of you. Because it is my choice. Because I have always loved it even though you do not. I do not smell like you.

My bra and underwear and stockings are slippery silk and sheer, tinted the same colour as my skin. I pull a cap-sleeved sweater dress over my head and look in the mirror. The dress is short and fitted, though not tight, and it has jagged horizontal stripes of mustard and navy blue. I fluff my hair, stick the front into a clasp, and realise I look like I stepped out of a 1960s fashion plate, especially with my knee-high black boots. I study my reflection some more. I look hard and cruel and beautiful. I look like you.

I get in my car, telling myself it was only one beer, one much-needed beer. One beer won't put me over the limit. I can even add a glass of wine and still be fine. I haven't called, haven't checked that he is actually home. But I seem unable to stop moving and somehow I am winding around the twisty lane and turning onto his gravelled drive.

I leave the car in front of his blue painted garage and push the buzzer on the blue painted door beside it. Both doors are built into a stone wall that encases his garden. I am not wearing a coat but I am not cold. I am warm warm warm.

The door opens and Adam stands there. He blinks several times. His face flushes. He says, 'I think you are a daydream come true,' and takes my hand and pulls me against him and kisses me, which is exactly what I hoped he would do.

He leads me through a courtyard, then into his house. I have a vague impression of cream rugs over old stone floors, brown leather sofas, pale walls. He pulls me beside him onto one of the sofas and I am startled by how natural it feels, how easy. Is this the way it is supposed to be? Nothing with Ted has been easy since you disappeared, and now I know why.

Adam's breathing is going faster and so is mine. One of my hands finds its way to the top button of his shirt, unhooks it, trails a finger through the dark hairs on his chest. He has that same fresh soapy smell I noticed in the library. It makes me want to inhale him. My other hand slips beneath the jacket of his suit, presses into the muscles of his back.

That is when his clothes register. My eyes crease in puzzlement. 'You're in serious clothes. I've interrupted something. You're going out.'

'I'm on call tonight. If the hospital rings I'll need to go in.' He puts his face close to mine again. 'But you can wait for me here. I like the idea of coming back to you. Would you like that too?'

I have been ambushed. I know this is Adam's voice, telling me he wants to come back to me, and asking if I would like that, but somehow I hear Ted's, and he is saying these words not to me but to you.

I know it is Adam whose face is only inches from mine, but I am seeing Ted. It is as if I am watching a film. The camera pulls away and I can see you too.

You and Ted are in bed, the sheets a sweaty tangle. You are wrapped around each other, whispering against each other's lips as you make love. You say my name as if it is a joke, and the two of you laugh together at stupid, clueless me. You have always been the one I really wanted, he tells you. You, Miranda, he says. Always you. Never Ella.

I take a huge racking breath. I don't let any sound come out because I am trying so hard to keep it in. But my body cannot hold the crying. The crying is going through my very bones, shaking me and shaking me and shaking me some more, and my face is twisted with grief that I cannot smooth away. The crying is coming out of my face too. It is like retching when there is no sick left. My tears have run dry but something somewhere still needs to be expelled. Adam's arms go round me. He says nothing. He holds me, absorbing the worst of my shuddering, but the movement is so violent the top of my head keeps hitting his chin.

I don't know how long it is before I calm down and he pulls away to look at me. 'Not the effect I was hoping for,' he says.

I actually laugh, though it is pretty feeble as laughs go. 'Sorry,' I say. 'I'm so sorry. It wasn't you. It was nothing to do with you.'

'Don't be sorry. I'm worried about you, Ella. I don't think you're admitting to yourself quite what you went through yesterday.'

'It's not that. Really it isn't.'

He considers for a few seconds. 'Okay then. I know you'll tell me when you want to. If you want to.'

'Can we start over?' I say.

He nods, looking so worried and serious. Slowly, I pull his face towards mine. This time, his face stays his face. He isn't overlaid by Ted.

As our lips are about to touch, with near-comic timing, his mobile rings, making him curse.

He mumbles his first and last name into the handset instead of saying hello. Within a few seconds, he jumps up and walks to the other side of the room, where he listens and paces, occasionally contributing a low monosyllable. After a minute he says, 'On my way,' and rings off.

He comes back to the sofa, kneels at my feet to look up at me. His face is drained of colour. His lips are pinched.

I touch his cheek. 'What's happened?'

'Ella—' He cuts himself off, seeming not to know what to say.

'Is it Thorne?'

'Yes.'

My hand falls into my lap. 'Tell me.'

There is another long pause before he is able to speak. 'He was moved to a specialist orthopaedic unit. They had to operate on his knee.'

'Did he die?'

'No.' He shakes his head. 'Nothing like that. But he isn't accounted for. He's been missing for nearly an hour.'

'Fuck. You're fucking joking.' He might as well learn the truth about my swearing now.

'Unfortunately I'm not,' he says. 'You're safe here though. You know that, don't you?'

'I'm not worried about that. He'd be more likely to hurt you. He really doesn't like you very much.'

'I've noticed.' He rises to sit beside me again, brushes a stray hair out of my eyes, tries to smile, but barely manages it. 'You, though, he likes quite a lot. He'd be like King Kong following Ann Darrow through New York City. But he has no idea where I live or where you live or where your parents live.'

'I wouldn't be so confident of that.'

'I am. But it's beside the point. They'll find him before he even gets out of the medical centre. He hasn't been spotted by any of the CCTV and there should be a camera at every exit – he's probably hiding in a storage room. He's not going to get far on that leg and he was under general anaesthetic only this morning.'

'That's reassuring. Sorry – the sarcasm isn't meant for you.'

'You don't need to be sorry – it's milder than they deserve. The police want to interview some of the patients, so I need to be there. I don't want you to worry.' He pulls me closer. 'Think about what we'll do to each other when I get back.'

'You trust me alone in your house?' I say this teasingly but I am watching carefully for his reaction.

'You trusted me in yours.'

'I was only upstairs in the shower.'

He traces a finger along my lips so lightly that I shiver. I feared Ted had turned me to stone, but he didn't. The hairs rise on my skin. I seem to be made of electricity.

'I love having you here,' he says.

'You love sobbing women.'

'I don't think you'll be doing much of that with me.' He kisses me again, harder this time, his tongue in my mouth, running his hands over my waist, slipping a hand beneath my dress, moving it over my silky underwear. I picture Ted seeing me with this man. The fantasy sends a spear of pure joy right through me. 'You don't make it easy to leave,' he says.

He pours a glass of red wine from a decanter sitting on a tray with overturned glasses, as if awaiting guests, and I wonder who actually arranged these things. I imagine him as the prince disguised as a beast from the fairy tale, with an invisible housekeeping crew.

He puts the glass in my hand. 'I can't drink tonight but you can.' I take a sip and he kisses me once more, inhaling the wine from my mouth. 'I'll get drunk if I don't leave now.' And with these words he goes.

The Builder's Daughter

At first I just sit, watching the wood crackle in the log fire, sipping the wine, giving myself goosebumps by tickling my own arm as you used to. But it never feels as lovely when I do it myself and I don't want to do anything that reminds me of you.

Plus, I am not very good at sitting and I can't stop thinking about Thorne. Only five minutes have passed before I put the wine glass on a low table and wander through the rooms, reminding myself that Adam said I should make myself at home.

This is not a house where Luke could ever be. There is no clutter. It is far too clean. When I switch on the kitchen light there are no dust motes. The kitchen looks unused, straight from the pages of a bespoke catalogue. Luke would smear those bone-painted solid oak cabinets in five seconds flat. With this thought, I wonder if Adam would like a boy in this house. I wonder if Adam would like a boy at all.

The other downstairs room is filled with gym equipment

that I could never afford let alone fit in my house, and I am startled to see the extent of his devotion to his own fitness. There is an exercise bike with a built-in tablet console, a treadmill with more electronic attachments for entertainment and monitoring, a cross trainer, and a rowing machine. There is a heavy-duty rubber mat beneath a bench press. There is an assortment of weights arranged on purpose-built shelves.

The only other thing I can find on the ground floor is the storage space below the stairs. He has turned it into a coat cupboard and it is more ordered than any coat cupboard I have ever seen. Our mother's appears chaotic by comparison. Coats for all seasons and occasions hang on matching wooden hangers. There is a bag of golf clubs, some wellies, a variety of sports shoes and a pair of tan leather walking boots.

I pick up one of the boots and turn it over to study the bottom. I am not sure why I do this. The first thing to hit me is how pristinely clean the boot is. Does this man really wash his boots each time he wears them? There isn't even a fleck of dried mud on the bottom. But what makes my heart catch is the familiarity of the pattern on the outsole. I look again, telling myself I am imagining it. It cannot be.

I run to get my phone so I can compare the shoe with the photos of the footprint and the plaster cast. When I turn the phone on I see that the battery is dead from the calls I made before I got to the hospital yesterday, probably not helped by the night it spent in my glovebox.

I pick up the walking boot again. The plaster cast could only capture the toe area, so I place my hand over the heel and arch of Adam's boot, leaving the anterior visible. Three moulded hexagons are stamped into the centre. Radiating out from these to the edge are small squares with ridges between them. The ridges are worn away so deeply on the outer side of the boot there are no squares at all, just smooth outsole.

You always said I had a strong visual memory. I close my eyes to try to call up the photograph of the partial imprint left in the woods. I see the same hexagons, the same ridges, the same areas smoothed by his individual tread. The pattern and wear are distinctive. But I am aware of the power of suggestion, and the likelihood that my mind is replicating the boot I have examined rather than recalling the photograph. A mere two days ago, I'd convinced myself that the sole's erosion could be evidence of a previously ruptured Achilles' tendon. I seesaw back and forth in doubt and certainty. I put the boots away, exactly as I found them.

I hurry to the stairs, which are old stone, ground down in the centre by centuries of feet. I rush up to do a quick survey of the rooms.

The first door I open reveals a study with shelves of medical books, all of the spines pulled to exactly the same distance from the edge. I touch one, examine my finger, and find that there isn't even a speck of dust.

A black leather chair sits in front of a huge mahogany desk. On the desk are a laptop and a small clock. I turn on the machine but immediately I am faced with the command to input a password and I don't have time even to begin to guess at what that might be so I switch it off again. The drawers contain papers and bills and invoices, all carefully organised in labelled folders, as well as a book full of medical notes and an old accounting ledger.

There is a stethoscope with his name engraved on the diaphragm. It is still pristine in its box and I wonder if it was a gift, because Adam is not a cardiologist and he does not strike me as the kind of man who would choose to have a heart carved on each side of his name. It is the kind of thing you would do. Lightly. Playfully. Perhaps even lovingly.

My eyes fly to the clock. He has been gone for fifteen minutes. It will take him twenty minutes to drive to the hospital, twenty minutes to get back, and surely he will spend at least an hour there, probably much longer. I decide on an ultra-conservative fifty minutes. This is the amount of time I will allow myself to snoop. It will leave me an extremely safe margin not to be caught.

All of the rooms are pitch-black until I switch on the lights. There is a bathroom, with marble-tiled floors and walls. Improbably white towels, perfectly folded, hang from stainless steel rails. There is a guest room with a platform bed covered by a white quilt.

Then there is Adam's room. At first I cannot figure out how to open the heavy blinds that shield his windows. Then I see there is a switch near each. When I press one, the blind rolls itself up slowly, like the ones we had in our hotel when Mum and Dad took us to Seville for your sixteenth birthday. The crescent moon casts enough light for me to see the hedgerow that encloses the sides and back of the house. It would be impossible to view this building from the other side of the shrubs and trees.

The window itself is locked. It opens with a key, but

that is not in any place I can see. I shake away the fear that the light will give me away in here, reminding myself that Adam cannot possibly be back this soon. I have forty-five minutes, by my ultra-safe estimates. My heart is beating fast and loud. I decide to scrunch that number into extra cautiousness and give myself thirty-five minutes before I flee. I close the blinds, leaving them as they were.

A door leads to a bathroom that looks much like the other, except that this one contains the essential things Adam needs every day. Shampoo and shower gel, toothbrush and toothpaste and dental floss. A brush and soap and razor remind me of how I used to shave Ted, how we would kiss as I rasped a potentially lethal cutthroat down his neck – not an experiment either of us would risk now. I am furious that I have let myself be ambushed by a happy memory of him.

Adam's bed is solid and simple, a matt black frame, a grey quilt. The only other furniture is a large reading chair in charcoal-coloured leather and a huge chest of drawers in the same wood as the bed frame. The chimney breast has been blocked up and smoothed over. The chest is set in the recess to the left of it. There is nothing of interest in the drawers. Just clothes, arranged with military neatness. This man really could not bear the inevitable mark another human being would make on his living space. Is this why he has never mentioned a previous girlfriend or wife? So far, I have found no real evidence that there has ever been one.

To the right of the chimney breast are panelled double-doors, presumably for a built-in wardrobe that makes use of the other recess in the wall. Above the doors are matching panels, but these are cupboard-sized. I cannot reach them without something to step on.

I look hard at the whole set-up, trying to figure out why my mind is registering something odd about it. Is it the size of the wardrobe doors? The cupboard above them? The scale of both together from the outside as opposed to the likely space on the inside?

I cannot pinpoint what is niggling me. I study the doors some more and it hits me. The problem is proportion. There is too much space between the top of the wardrobe doors and the bottom of the cupboard doors. Six or eight inches at most would look right, but there is well over a foot.

I pull open the wardrobe. Inside is a hanging rail with shirts on one side and suits on the other, all in dry cleaner's plastic and grouped by colour. There are several black shirts, but I am certain that if one was ever missing a button he has already had it replaced or thrown the whole thing away. Ted can congratulate himself on the pointlessness of that evidence bag.

Adam's perfectly polished shoes are arranged on a slatted bench. I drag the bench out. Instead of climbing on it to reach the cupboard, something makes me kneel down to examine the wardrobe's floor. There are small holes, drilled into it at four-inch intervals. The two holes at the front are bigger, so I hook my fingers into them and lift and let out a cry.

I have taken the lid off a hole the size and shape of a coffin. The wardrobe is four feet wide and two feet deep. Although this rectangle beneath the floor matches the wardrobe's depth, it stretches six feet. Inside is a foam mat covered in a sheet, a pillow in a case, and a single quilt, folded at the bottom as if awaiting a guest.

The room seems to be spinning and my blood is pulsing in my ears with such force I think Adam can hear it from the hospital. *Oh my God.* I actually say this aloud. I am breathing too fast. *Calm down, Ella.* I say this aloud too.

And then I hear you. *You don't have time to react to this. You don't have time to be mad at me and tune me out. You have twenty-five minutes before you get out. So get on your fucking feet and keep looking and then get the hell away.*

I try to think clearly. I let the false floor drop back into place so he won't know I found it. I climb onto the storage bench and pull open the high cupboard doors above the wardrobe. I have to clutch the cupboard doors for a few seconds to stop myself from falling. I throw the pillows I find in there onto the polished floorboards. I run my hand over every inch of the bottom of the now-empty cupboard until I stumble upon another set of holes, exactly right for hooking fingers. In an instant, I have pulled up what proves to be another false bottom, revealing a hollow space between the ceiling of the wardrobe and the floor of the high cupboard.

The space is not empty. Inside is a camouflage daypack he must have been given in the army. When I pull it out it nearly crashes onto my head. The hydration hose slaps my temple so hard I think it draws blood but I can't afford to worry about that right now. I sit on top of the pillows and unfasten one of the side compartments and slide my hand in.

Why is it that when you are looking for something you always assume it will be in the last place you check? The final hidden pocket? That tiny corner you missed at first?

Jason Thorne never lied to me but it wasn't the honour of a thief. It was the strange honour of a psychopathic serial killer who thinks I am his true love. Am I foolish enough to believe Thorne would never hurt me? No. I am certain he would like nothing better. What Thorne and I mean by love are very different things. Sexual violence is the only form of expression he knows, however passionately he tells me otherwise. But his insight, sickening as it may be, is still useful. His words are echoing in my head. *So he can keep her close.*

I know what it is before I look. I know what it is as soon as my fingers tangle in the familiar silky platinum that matches the chain in my handbag. Your locket is smoother than the stones your son and I left for you in the woods by our parents' house, where this man spied on us. I know this because the missing pink-stained stones are here too, in the other side pocket. I set the stones down.

I bring your locket to my lips and press it against them before I open it and look at my own photograph, taken over ten years ago. Taken by you. Opposite my image should be your baby son, snapped by me when he was so new he was like a sea creature, still curled, still wanting to swim. But that photograph is gone – he has ripped Luke out.

I imagine you in the hidden coffin and wrap my arms tightly around myself and rock back and forth. But you are shouting at me, telling me to move, to get out. There will be time for all this weeping and wailing later, because by my own conservative calculations I have twenty minutes left to leave. I listen to you. I start to move. I have only risen an inch before a stab of fire shoots through the top of my arm and everything goes black.

Evening Prayer

I try to open my eyes but my lids are so heavy. I manage a tiny slit before they slip closed again. My arms are heavy too, and my legs. There is a hand smoothing my hair, floating over my forehead.

It is you. I know it is you. I can smell honeysuckle. Only your hands are this soft. You take so much trouble over your hands, with those weekly manicures that I tease you about. I try to smile. I try again to open my eyes. I must be very ill and that is why you have finally come back from wherever you have been. You have come back to take care of me.

I try to say your name but only a slurry M comes out. I try to ask you to help me open my eyes so I can look at you. I want so badly to see you, after so long. I hear your voice, singing me the evening prayer from the *Hansel and Gretel* opera, just as you did when I was small. *When at night I go to sleep, Fourteen angels watch do keep.* You are one of the two angels guarding my head. You are whispering that you have found me. I want to tell you that I am so happy but it is too hard to control my mouth. My lips are shaking and my chin is trembling. My whole face is in tremors.

'Melanie?' My eyelid opens but I am not the one who makes it do this. You must be trying to help me and I try to tell you that I am so sorry but I cannot keep it open myself. I try to tell you that the light you are piercing into my eye hurts. But this problem with my mouth makes telling these things impossible. You say, 'Open your eyes, please, Melanie,' and even though it is my name, the only name you ever call me, it is not your voice.

Adam Holderness's face is close to mine. I blink. He looks so blurry. There are two of him. I don't want one of him, let alone two. I only want you, but you have blown away, back to wherever you are. There is only him. My arms are jerking. My legs are twitching so much they seem to be operated by invisible puppet strings. My head is twisting on my neck.

'Try to relax, Melanie.'

My back goes rigid. My head is jerking from side to side as if I am signalling No. Forever No. I cannot stop gesturing No.

Above me is white ceiling. Below me is? What is below me? My legs are bare. Where are my stockings? Something damp and smooth is against my skin. It squelches like a suction cup when I try to move. I am in the leather reading chair in his bedroom and my feet are elevated. He has put up some sort of footrest and tipped the back low so that I am reclining.

My hips are lifting up and down, up and down. My

back is arching and flattening, arching and flattening. My dress is riding up. I glimpse his face again. He is frowning. He looks worried but I cannot decide if this is because he wants to kill me or save me.

My legs are shuddering and when he runs a hand along the inside of my thigh it lurches so violently he takes his hand away and instead catches my wrist in it, counts my pulse.

'You're having a reaction to the drug you needed. I'm sorry. Normally Procyclidine would stop this happening but there wasn't any to hand. Antihistamine works too. Let's get some of that in you while you're a little calmer.' He tries to sit me up but I am a contorted board.

'No.' The word doesn't sound like a word.

'We have to stop the tremors and the muscle rigidity.'

We. I try to say No again but it sounds like I have a mouthful of sand.

'It's dangerous for you otherwise. Please, Melanie.'

I allow him to put something in my mouth, hold a water bottle to my lips, feel some of it spill over my chin. He rubs my throat as if I am a pet and though this induces my swallow reflex it is like gulping a rock. My throat feels bruised.

'Your sister had the same reaction.' He looks so sad I almost believe that he is. 'The infection made her symptoms challenging to manage.' He shakes his head. 'If she hadn't had that baby she would have been fine.'

You would not have been fine. He was never going to let you be fine and he is not going to let me be that way either. My head knows this but I cannot make myself scared enough to leap from the chair and run away. Despite

403

what my head knows, I cannot properly feel these truths and what they mean. I am not ready to accept them.

He touches the neckline of my dress with one hand, picks up a stethoscope from somewhere with the other. 'May I?'

My head is vibrating from side to side as if he has stuck a motor in it and it isn't because the drugs have me in their grip. It is because you do.

Despite my attempt at no, he tugs the knitted fabric to expose more of my chest before he puts the cold metal against my skin. 'Your heart is strong, Melanie,' he says. 'Body and soul. Much stronger than your sister's.'

'Did she?' I remember Thorne's garbled voice after Adam injected him with the tranquillisers. That is how I sound.

He wrinkles his forehead, trying to understand me. 'Ah. The stethoscope.' He nods to confirm it, as if he has discovered a shared passion with a boss he wants to impress. 'Yes. She gave it to me. She would have been pleased by the idea that it could be used to care for you.'

The fuck I would, you say. Since you left you seem to say fuck a lot. Like me. Though I am not sure any more if you did that much while you were here. It is too easy to blame you for the things I do wrong.

He takes the stethoscope away with his right hand but leaves his left on my chest, so that some of his fingers trail over my breast.

'Don't.' I try to lift an arm to push him away but my arm has stopped being like a stick and is now being like a wet noodle. It moves only a few inches before flopping down again. I am a woman-sized rag doll.

'Are you sure? You came here to me. Your voice is saying no but not your body. Do you know what disinhibition is?'

I do but I am not about to waste what little voice I have admitting it.

'It's a side effect of the drug you needed. So is a sense of well-being. You look tranquil, Melanie, and you haven't looked tranquil since I met you. The antihistamine is starting to work already – it was a high dose. You have bedroom eyes. You always do but especially now that we're alone.'

I am thinking. I am trying so hard to think. Why is it so hard to think? What do I need to do? The answer comes almost as soon as I silently ask the question. I need to keep him talking until I can fight him off. That is what I must do. Whatever happens, I cannot let him put me in that coffin. I try to shake my head to wake up but it only makes my brain slop around in my skull like jelly.

'Why?'

'Why what?'

'Why Melanie?' I am not sure how comprehensible the second word is but somehow he is primed to hear it.

'She talked about you so much. She always called you that. I felt I knew you even before we met, because of her. I loved you before we met, because of her. She worshipped you.'

I must be moving my head to deny this could be possible. I was the worshipper. Not you. Of all people, I do not want this man to teach me about you. I would more cheerfully be taught by Ted.

'She did, Melanie. Whatever her faults – and there were plenty – she did. It's the only thing I'm still grateful to her for. But to answer your question, it's your real name and the one I like best. It's what I know you by.'

You would never have meant for him to use it. You didn't want to share my name with anybody, let alone him. I do not say this. I say a different true thing. 'Thirsty,' I say.

'Sadie? Why do you want to talk about her?' His lips turn down in a frown. 'She's not a real friend to you. Not someone who trusts you as you deserve.' He considers, as if unsure whether to go on with what he wants to say. 'Have you wondered what brought you to my notice, Melanie?'

'Yes.'

'It was that interview you did with the paper, and the photo. You look so much like your sister. I made it my business to learn everything I could about you, after I saw it. That included Sadie. I even helped her and Brian to discover each other. Brian wanted to make some extra money – the private clinic work was my idea. Sadie's place was on a list I gave him, the only realistic prospect on it.'

He manipulates people as if they were pieces on a game board. 'Why?'

'So you and I would be thrown together, somehow. Through them. I didn't imagine they'd end up seeing each other though. Not a very likely couple, were they? Still, it was useful. And it was so easy to make her hate you. She was nearly there. I just helped to speed things.'

'How?'

'Brian mentioned the party in passing to me at work. I said I'd like to come. When he phoned to give me the details, he told me about this friend of Sadie's, said she was beautiful and kind of extraordinary – which of course you are, Melanie – and he thought I'd like to meet her. Sadie was in the room with him and they started to talk to each other. Can you imagine the conversation, Melanie?'

'Yes.'

And the story he tells me is exactly what I think it will be.

'"Not Ella," Sadie said. "You don't want to inflict him with Ella."

'"Of course Ella," Brian said. "Ella is lovely."

'"You sound as if you wish you'd met her instead of me," she said.

'"Of course I don't," he said.

'"I don't believe you," she said, and for once I agreed with her. "It's been like this my whole life," she said, and that made perfect sense too.

'She grabbed the phone from him to talk to me directly, said you were a crazy mess and no real friend would wish you on anyone they cared about and you were still obsessed with your shitty ex-boyfriend, which we both know isn't true any more.

'Brian excused himself, then, told Sadie he was going out for a paper. She doesn't have much of a radar for when she annoys people, does she?'

I say nothing.

'She continued to talk to me. She asked if Brian and I saw much of each other at the hospital. I explained not really, we were in different fields. She went on to describe you – not that she did you justice – asked if I'd ever seen you with him.'

'Couldn't have.'

'I know every line of your face, Melanie, but I said it was possible I once saw Brian having coffee in the hospital café with a woman who sounded rather like the one she described. I said I couldn't be sure. I said I'd confirm after I saw you in person at the party. All it took was a small nod at her when the two of you passed the living room door, after you arrived.'

'Lie,' I say.

'Yes,' he says. 'Sometimes lies are needed.'

You would actually agree with this in principle. 'Cruel,' I say.

But he misunderstands who I am talking about. 'Yes. She is. She should know you better. Brian says she's fanatically jealous. I don't want her near you. She would do real harm to you if she could. I was scared when you found her at your house earlier.'

I don't quite take this in. My throat is so desperately dry it is all I can think of. 'Water,' I say.

His eyes move to the foot of the bed and I drag my own after them. There is a silver tray. On it are several glass ampules and syringes and a light pen. There is also a plastic bottle of water, half-full. He reaches for that, takes off the cap, lifts my head to help me drink. I am so parched my lips rip apart as if I have pulled off a plaster.

'Thorne?'

'Still not found.'

Thorne will tear this man apart, I think, if he gets hold of him.

'It won't be long,' he says. 'I'm not worried. He's not important.'

He sees me looking at the tray.

'You were so distressed. You seemed half-mad, sitting with that mess of things around you. It was necessary to sedate you, but you reacted too strongly to the drugs – you needed a higher than normal dose. The alcohol you'd taken heightened their effects.'

He writes himself out of decisions and actions, as if they were somebody else's.

'No more,' I say. This is a new art, this trying to make sentences with as few words as I can.

He runs his fingers down my neck, caresses my hair, moves it away from my face, puts it back. I realise my hair is completely loose. He must have removed the clasp I used to fasten it, thinking I might jab it in his eye. He was right to think that. The idea of it makes me happy.

'It would be best for you to be able to feel things,' he says. 'Not too sleepy. Not too awake. Just right.'

Chemical restraint. That is what they did to Thorne before he was physically restrained. Do I need to act drowsier or more alert to stop this man shooting more of it into me? The puzzle is too great but it is a puzzle only of the mind, not one I feel in the pit of my stomach as I should. He was telling the truth when he said the drug would make me feel safe and calm. It is against all reason but I do.

He leans over to kiss me and I don't try to stop him. He pulls away, frowning. 'Your mouth is still trembling.'

He has brought my bag up here. It is sitting on the bed by the tray. He stretches towards it to pull out my watch. 'This isn't working.' He must have figured out what it was and disabled it.

I think of my dead mobile. For a few seconds, I clutch at hope that Find My Phone or Send Last Location will lead the police here. But if the battery ran out in the hospital car park, then that is where the tracking will end, too. It is highly unlikely that phone will help me.

I try to say your name. It comes out sounding like Mermaid.

'I want to be honest with you. I want to tell you everything so we can go forward. The tranquillisers were just to keep you calm until I could explain.'

'Don't need.'

He nods agreement. 'After hearing you and Ted earlier, learning what the two of them did to you, I knew you would understand.'

'How?' I mean, how did he hear me and Ted. And didn't he say something suggesting he knew Sadie came to my house? How did he know that too? But again he ignores my question and says what he wants me to hear.

'You found her locket. Can you guess how many times I took it out and opened it and stared at your picture before we finally met? It's like looking at her, but with none of her faults.'

'No.'

He shakes his head mournfully. 'You're only proving I'm right. She slept with me a few times, came here to dinner when she was lonely. She certainly liked it when I gave her expensive presents. But she made me promise never to tell anyone about us. There was some-body else — she never admitted it, but it was obvious.'

I remember the name you obliterated from your address book. H is for Holderness. I am in no doubt that Adam is the man whose name you blocked out, perhaps to hide his identity from Noah. Or perhaps because Adam became so odious you could no longer bear to see any evidence that he was in your life. Maybe both of these things were true.

'Then she got pregnant.' He closes his eyes as if even now it hurts him. 'She'd refused to see me for a few months, then she turns up and sleeps with me because she's needy or sad and wants some attention and WHAM, she's pregnant.'

Remember how Adam made you feel, when you first met him? Remember how he made you warm, before you knew what he really was?

I had wondered what could have brought you to sleep with two men so close together, never imagining that Ted could be one of them. But three? My poor love.

Stop being so pious. It was empowering. I took back my power. I was in control. And don't you 'poor love' me. I don't need your pity. I don't want it. Don't you dare judge me.

You are as fierce as ever. Your fierceness helps. You always yearned for a life of drama and adventure and excitement, and that's what you got, even if it did spiral out of control.

I can't argue with that one.

There is truth in what Adam says, even if he has no understanding. Luke's father hurt or disappointed you in some major way, probably because he had to disappear again. You flew to Adam for refuge, and probably Ted too, but then you made up with the man you loved and dispensed with Ted and Adam.

'I thought it was mine,' Adam says. 'I was sure it was mine.'

It. That is what he calls your son. All these years later and he still cannot bear to admit Luke's humanness.

'She swore it wasn't mine, the timing was wrong. All that crap women say.'

He slips for an instant into talking as he must think. Women. Crap. Two words he easily puts together. He is a different man to the one I have known, not able to disguise his hatred entirely, the ugliness of how he thinks.

'Amnio,' I say.

'You know about that?'

'Yes.'

'It was to shut me up. I wanted it to be mine but there was no denying the paternity test. I never learned who the father actually was. He was too careful. Or she was.'

He gets up, straddles the chair so his lower body is pressing into mine and my hands are pinned beneath his thighs. With his weight on me like this I cannot breathe. I cannot get my arms free. I cannot turn my head with his hands on both sides of it. But I must be making enough of an attempt for him to know I am trying.

'I've wondered for so long what it would feel like, for us to be like this, to feel you moving beneath me. That's why I don't want to have to tie you up.'

'No need.' My voice is so weak.

He runs my hair through his fingers. 'I knew when

we finally met that you were as interested in me as I was in you.' He laughs. 'That performance of yours with Brian's brother. I can't tell you how much I enjoyed that. You were everything I hoped for. The chemistry was there from the start between us.'

'Yes,' I say.

His fingers are beneath my chin, tipping my head up. 'I never noticed this before. The last traces of a haemangioma. It's beautiful.' His mouth is on my birthmark, kissing away my magic, sucking it out of me like a vampire.

Stop thinking like that. Your magic is deep inside you. He can't get at it. It's still your secret weapon. So use it.

My breath is shallow, but he mistakes the reason and pulls back a little to study me. 'I don't want to risk getting you too excited until you've properly recovered. Caring for you is so important to me. You even told that bastard Ted to fuck off.'

How could he know this? Just. How? I manage to stammer out the word.

All at once, he gets up. He sits on a low stool he has put beside the chair. 'I saw you pull away from him when he touched you in the hospital car park. But when you went to his house – I don't want to say what I thought at first. How angry I was. It made me wonder if I'd got you wrong. Maybe you liked to string along multiple men. Maybe you couldn't turn away any scrap of admiration. Like her. But what you said to him. I can't tell you how it pleased me. And you were magnificent against Sadie.'

I am thinking of Thorne. Thinking how I got under his skin when I changed tack. When I tried to be extra nice to him. It was a dangerous game, but it worked. Mostly. Can I bring myself to do that with this man too? Maybe the poisons he shot into my muscles are doing me an accidental favour, with their well-being side effect, shrinking my anger into a magically small kernel that is hidden so far away even I cannot feel it right now.

Thorne's name comes out of my mouth even though I do not mean it to, and Adam continues to talk to me as if I am his co-conspirator rather than his enemy.

'I was so close to stopping Thorne's game when he said he'd been watching her. I was near her too that day. I was certain Thorne was going to tell you he saw me, that he must have seen me, that that explained the extra degree of venom he has for me. I was within seconds of halting your visit when he grabbed you. There is something I have to apologise to you for, but I think you will understand.'

'Of course,' I say.

He takes my hand, kisses it, and I make myself smile. Tranquillisers really do make you tranquil. Fake smiling is easy and natural and almost feels real.

'After I brought you home from the hospital, I planted a listening device in your bag while you were showering. I needed to know what Thorne whispered to you out of my hearing. That's how I heard everything with Ted. And with Sadie. Do you forgive me?'

'Of course,' I say again.

He lifts my hand, turns it over, presses more kisses onto my palm. 'I never imagined she'd been with Ted. I never thought that badly of her. I know neither of us did. She didn't deserve you.'

I can be mad at you. I can scream at you. I can recite every fault you ever had, every wrong you ever did, and there have been some whoppers. But God help anyone else who does. You said this to me once but I didn't say it back. I should have said it back.

'Three different men within weeks of each other. What kind of woman was she? I didn't know about Ted until you did. I never even saw him until I watched you with him and the boy on Halloween.'

Watched. I realise now who sent me that photograph of Ted and Ruby in the café.

'Photo of Ted?' I say.

'You needed to know the truth about him.'

He tried to get rid of Ted. He probably would have continued that campaign if Ted hadn't turned my heart to ice without anybody else's help. Except yours.

I swallow hard and he feeds me another sip of water. 'A little at a time, Melanie,' he says.

'Blocked calls?' I say.

He looks puzzled. Given the terrible things he is prepared to admit, I am inclined to believe he didn't make them.

'Justice Administrator?' I say.

Again he looks perplexed, but I'm not sure if it is because I'm still slurring my words or because he really doesn't know what I'm talking about.

'Do you hate Ted now?' he says. 'Do you hate him and your sister?'

'I do.'

'How could she do that to you? You must be glad of what happened.'

What happened. Not what he did. He speaks as if external forces got you and your locket and the birthday stones into his house.

'What did happen, Adam?' I try to soften the question with his name.

I think he has wanted to tell this story for a long time. It is not a story I want to hear. It is a story I never wanted to hear. I wanted a different story.

'She was going to meet him, whoever he was.'

'How did you know?' I ask this as if I am impressed by his ingenuity.

'I knew she'd be driving along the lane and I knew when.' This isn't an answer. He doesn't want to admit to me – maybe not even to himself – that he had been stalking you. As he stalked me. He doesn't want to detail his methods. 'I parked my car with the bonnet slightly off road, against a tree.'

'Why?'

'It wasn't like me to be so careless, but I was shaken. I hadn't meant to park that way.'

Liar.

'A minute before she was due to pass me – I don't know why – I rested my head on top of the wheel. I didn't plan what happened next. All I wanted was to know she would stop for me. That she would do that much. The most basic test of whether she actually cared. That's all I wanted from her. Do you know what it is like to want that?'

'Yes.'

'Nobody came along the whole time. You know how deserted that road is. When she saw me, her tyres screeched. She pulled part-way into a shallow ditch. She was crying my name. I suppose, looking back, I might have appeared injured. I didn't realise that then. At first I thought she stopped because she really did care.'

You did care. He got you because you were kind. He posed that way deliberately, whatever he says. Because you could never turn away from somebody hurt. You might sleep with their boyfriend after you fixed them, but you would never ignore anyone who needed fixing. You liked it when somebody was broken and you mended them and they called you a beautiful angel and told you how important and extraordinary you were, how only you could have done that for them. He didn't really know you, but he guessed at this essential thing and exploited it.

'She threw open my front passenger door, climbed in to check on me. The wind blew the door shut. When she saw I was fine she started to scream at me. Obscenities. Words you would never say, Melanie. How I'd inconvenienced her, slowed her, she had to be somewhere important and didn't have time for games. She said what I had done was cruel. She was so hysterical I was worried for her. Medically worried. I thought her hormones had triggered it. I took her hand to try to reason with her. Her skin was so clammy – she had a fever. She started to grab the door handle to get out but I was worried about her driving. She needed the same drug you needed last night. That helped. The passenger seat was flat so I laid her down to rest.'

He took your keys and purse from your car to make it look like you had some presence of mind, some unknown plan, but he left the little-used mobile phone that could have signalled where you were. He probably did something to hasten the battery drain too, because it was dead by the time the police found it. And he was careful about DNA. The DNA in your car was from known acquaintances, all of whom were eliminated as suspects.

'You took care of her,' I say, corroborating the spin he has put on things.

'I wanted to make sure she was calm and safe.'

He speaks as if all of it was an accident. As if he didn't happen to have a syringe of tranquillisers in his pocket, as if he hadn't flattened his front passenger seat in readiness. As if he hadn't hunted you and set you up. As if he hadn't planned any of it. As if there weren't a coffin-like box where he could hide you beneath his floor.

He rests the flat of his hand on my cheek. 'It's amazing how you can feel so much for somebody, then feel nothing. But if you actively hate her, you mustn't blame yourself. It's understandable. I had no idea, when it happened, how very much she deserved it.'

'What happened, Adam?'

'She had a seizure.'

'When?'

'She was too unwell to leave. She had an infection. A high temperature. Her reaction to the drug wouldn't reverse. You rebounded so quickly. That strong heart of yours, again. She didn't rebound at all.'

'When?'

'A week after she came here.'

'Did she . . . ?' I still must ask. I still must hear him say the word, though I cannot.

'There was nothing anyone could have done.'

Nothing anyone could have done. His doctor's euphemisms. As if kidnapping and drugging and probably raping you had nothing to do with him.

He doesn't say the word but he doesn't need to. The word is there. It is in the air.

'You see now, don't you, that you've been better without her? We all have. I'm going to hold your hand for a few minutes now, Ella. I can see you need that.'

Talking to you has been my way of keeping you alive, keeping you present even in your absence. But all along I have been talking to the dead. Your voice will dwindle away, until it is no louder than the cry of a gnat.

Except that I can still hear you. And you are no gnat. You are screaming in my ear. *Don't let him see you sad. Keep him thinking you are on his side. Dampen down your reaction. NOW.*

I squeeze his hand. 'I'm glad you're with me.'

'You're more loyal than she ever was.'

He is more right than he imagines.

He kisses my forehead. 'It's what I love about you.'

I swallow back the sick that comes up my throat when his lips touch my skin. 'And me you.' My voice trembles with the effort of pretending to return his feelings, but he seems to see this as passion. 'Did she—' I stop.

'What? Did she what?'

'Suffer?' My voice catches. I sound as if I am choking. I know it is ill-judged to ask but I cannot not.

'She was asleep whenever I went to work. She didn't

ever wake until I got back. She was never aware of being alone. She was well cared for.'

As if your sleeping was natural. As if he didn't put you in a hole when he was out. But I know where you were.

'Did the police ever come here?'

He nods. 'I want to tell you everything. There were two of them. Two days after she arrived, as I was getting back from work. They said they were looking at all the houses in the area. I invited them in, made them welcome, poured coffee. One of them poked a head in the living room for a few seconds, but that was it. They said they were sorry to have troubled me. Then they left.'

I am imagining you, in that rectangular pit. Could those policemen have found you if they'd bothered to look? Rescue was within feet of you but didn't happen. I am praying you were unconscious. Praying you weren't aware of those buffoons in the house, so close to saving you. What would it have been like to know they were there without being able to cry for help? To hear the door close after they said goodbye?

He is so articulate, so calm and intelligent. This man, this doctor with his military-hero background, with his medical eminence. He doesn't exactly scream kidnapper. Wouldn't most policemen be fooled? Not the type who needs to steal a woman to keep her, they would think. He and Thorne are no different, though Thorne would find the comparison insulting.

'I'm worried that you are trying too hard to be brave. For my sake. Whatever she did, she was your sister.'

I try to lift an arm, testing, but I am still so woozy I

can barely move. He studies me as though I am a human weapon he has deactivated, then he turns to fiddle with the tray on the bed.

I watch him as carefully as I can while his attention is diverted. There is something odd in his trouser pocket, sticking out a little. The puzzle of what it is comes to me all at once. A syringe, and I am seeing the tip. It is visible over the top of the pocket because it is completely extended. It is fully loaded, ready to plunge into me in an emergency, in case I recover my strength sooner than he anticipates.

He turns back to me and I stretch, as if content, and smile at him again. He climbs onto the chair beside me, on his side, kisses my ear, whispers into it. 'We'll talk more tomorrow. You're waking up too much when you need rest. In the morning you'll be better. I can't wait to wake up with you in my bed.'

'Me too.'

He turns me onto my side so we are face-to-face, body-to-body. 'We fit together so well.' He slides one arm under me, curls the other over me, bends a leg over my thigh. 'Goodnight, sweet Melanie.' He kisses me, pulling me harder against him, and I am so distracted by that kiss I barely have time to register that all in one movement he is pushing up my dress and something is burning deep into my hip before the world plunges into darkness.

Saturday, 19 November

The Colour Red

Whatever is holding me up seems to be swallowing me. Or am I sinking? I turn my head to the side and feel as if someone has banged the top of my skull with a mallet. The force of it is still reverberating behind my eyes. It takes several seconds of squeezing them shut before I can bring myself to open them again. I am in bed. Sheets are clinging to my skin.

I lift an arm, testing, and though it seems as if an invisible hand is trying to oppose the movement, I manage to do the same with the other arm too. Slow. Everything I do is slow. But at least I am moving. The tremors are gone but my body seems to be made of steel balls stuffed into a woman-shaped sack.

He isn't in bed beside me but he must have been at some point because there is a dent in the pillow from his head. He would have been sleeping close to me. I cannot afford to wonder now about what he might have done while I was unconscious. I listen as hard as I can. I can hear him, I think probably on the landing outside.

He must be talking on the phone. I consider screaming my lungs out to draw the attention of the person at the other end, but it's way too risky. They are unlikely to hear, but he certainly will, and then he will know I am against him and I will have lost the biggest card I have. When I push myself up onto my elbows the room rocks. My neck wobbles as if I have whiplash.

He is moving. I can hear his footsteps approaching the door, then pausing there. My stomach cramps so tightly I want to double over. I count in my head, waiting for him to come in, but he doesn't. He goes downstairs, quickly, enthusiastically, a man who cannot wait to start his happy new day. He is humming something from *Carmen* but my brain hurts too much to work out exactly what.

The peace I felt before has deserted me. Didn't he say that the drugs could cause contradictory symptoms? Last night's deluded sense of well-being is entirely gone. My head is too full and my terror is too big and I realise I have never properly understood the women I try to help. I have never properly grasped how fear immobilises.

I scan all around me for a phone, plotting to dial 999, but I cannot remember seeing one last night and if there was he has removed it. Of course he has. I manage something that is almost like standing, using the bed to lever myself up, but my legs are too wobbly to walk properly and too weak for me to risk the noise I would make if they were to give way and crash me down.

Not afraid. Awake. Ted's voice is as fierce as it has ever been. It hauls me up and lowers me to the floor as if I am a puppet. It forces me to drag myself towards the door even though the room is spinning.

My upper arm aches and my hip throbs too. I think of the tortoise and the hare. Today I am the tortoise. I am not sure how long it takes but at last I am struggling onto my knees so I can reach the handle. It doesn't turn. I put all my weight on the metal, pushing and pulling at the door at the same time, but the handle rattles and rattles and I am seeing stars and the rattles seem to vibrate right through me, making me draw in my breath at another cramp. He has locked me in.

Think. Think. Think. I move my head too quickly, trying to decide where to go next. Is there really a lag of several seconds before my brain catches up with my skull, snapping and slapping inside it? I'm progressing in my movement, because I'm managing to crawl on all fours now instead of sliding along like a serpent on its belly. This is faster.

There is something strange, something I cannot process. And then I do because I falter and fall flat and my nipple scrapes against a splinter in the wood as I pull myself up again. My heart thrums in my ears. My clothes are gone. I correct myself. He took off my clothes.

Not now Not now Not now. You are with me again. *Not now*, you say. *No time to think about that now.*

My knees are raw from the friction against the bare boards. There is a trickle of something between my legs. I have to pee but I don't think it is that. The bathroom door seems so far away. Every inch I manage to move seems impossible, but I am finally hauling myself up and turning another handle. At least this one isn't locked and I heave myself in.

I close the door as quietly as I can, plotting to lock it.

But I bite my lip and swear silently when I discover there is no lock. I fumble for a light. It seems miraculous that I find it, though I am so dazzled I have to open and close my eyes several times.

I strain my neck to examine my upper arm. It is blotched as if with sunburn, and I realise this must be bruising. I try to count the red dots left by the needles he shot into my muscles, but counting is so hard. I get to two and have to start over. I get to three and have to start over. I get to four. I keep losing track of what I have counted and what I have not. I try to be systematic, going roughly across from left to right, then down and across again. I get to four several times more, so I squirm around to inspect my hip, where there are two more red dots. That makes six in total. I try again and get the same number.

I struggle to understand what all of this means. *What it means is that he gave you more of the drugs during the night, topping up the dose before you woke.* I try to remember what happened with Thorne. There were three drugs, then, I am sure of it, but Adam said I had my reaction because there was something he couldn't get hold of. I am sure that's right because I can even remember that the missing drug started with a P. The likelihood is that he gave me two different things each time, so three doses in total of a tranquillising cocktail.

I pull myself to my feet, using the sink. I examine the window. It is made of privacy glass so nobody can see in and I can't work out if everything is blurry because of the glass or if it is my vision that is all wrong. The hedges and trees block my view beyond the garden. Not that there is anyone nearby to see. This place is so remote there would be no point signalling or shouting for help. I wonder if I could actually escape through this window. If I were to regain enough strength, is there a safe way down?

But all of these calculations are pointless. The window is locked. Like the others it is triple-glazed. I want to break the glass to flee or make a weapon, but there is nothing in this room to break it with.

Did you do all these things too? Make all of these hopeless discoveries? I try to push the questions out of my head. Because you didn't find a way out. All of the things you tried got you nowhere. And you were ill. Even before he told me you were clammy and fevered, before he told me you had an infection, I worried about a recurrence of your mastitis. To try to do all of this when you were feeling so wretched would have been doomed.

I think of a film I once watched even though I knew I shouldn't. I knew I was the last person on earth who ought to sit through the story of a man trying to discover what happened to his missing girlfriend. They have a fight while driving, stop at a station for petrol, and she goes off to the loo but never comes back. He finally learns the truth, but only by experiencing exactly what she did.

No No No No No. The words come out as one long murmur, in the lowest voice I can manage. But they release something.

I turn to the mirrored cupboard, glimpsing the face of the haggard woman who stares out at me, mascara streaking down her cheek, her hair tangled, her skin pale and blotchy and so yellow I wonder if the tranquillisers have produced some kind of instant jaundice. *You cannot possibly be my sister*, you say. *Not looking like that.*

I hold my breath when I open the cupboard door. I am dreaming of that cutthroat, picturing it on the glass shelf where I saw it yesterday night. But it is gone. Of course it is gone. I press my hands to my head and squeeze my temples and want to scream but I have to take my fingers away from my face and curl them around the edge of the sink when another cramp rips through me.

I think of Luke and all of the things Dad and I did to make the house safe for him after you vanished. No fire hazards or cutting hazards or tripping hazards or suffocation hazards or strangulation hazards or choking hazards. This man has carried out an obscene form of baby-proofing, though I know that cannot have been his primary reason for removing my clothes.

Since I managed to haul myself to my feet there has been an irregular splish splosh of drops hitting the floor. Something warm is creeping down my leg. There is a splatter of bright red on the cream-veined marble. More red smears the inside of my thighs. I touch my hand to the blood and it comes away sticky. As if I were a child terrified of a dare, my fingers slowly float to where the blood is coming from.

It doesn't hurt. If he raped me I would know. Wouldn't I? I would be sore. I would ache. It would sting. But none of these things are true. My upper arm hurts. My hip hurts. My head hurts. My belly hurts from the cramps. No other parts of me hurt.

Another thought rushes at me. All at once, I understand

the reason for the bleeding. I have been caught out and stumped like a thirteen-year-old. The thing that hasn't happened to me for ten years is actually happening right now, and I don't know whether to laugh or cry at the timing.

I address myself silently to him. *What a fucking mess I've made of your floor, you neat-freak bastard. Just you wait until you see what I'm going to do to your towels.* I grab a giant bath sheet and wrap it around me, twisting and knotting it above my breasts so it is like a strapless dress, the way you taught me, the way I still do every day when I get out of the shower, so automatically I do not need to think or look. I grab a hand towel and blot away as much blood as I can from my hands and thighs and between my legs.

My bladder is so full it burns. I heave myself onto the toilet and when I pee it is fierce red and when I wipe the paper turns crimson and I am stunned by the blood, as if ten years of it has come at once. Is this normal? I cannot remember if this is normal. Didn't you once tell me that it always looks like there is much more blood than there actually is? I don't press the flusher. I don't want him to hear so I leave the red pool in the bowl and quietly lower the lid and look around the bathroom again to try to see what else I can do.

There is a silver towel rail and I pull myself up by it, at the same time hoping to prise it out of the wall with my weight so I can use it as a weapon. I am examining it for hidden screws when I hear a key jiggling and then the bedroom door opening.

He says nothing at first, clearly looking around for

me, trying to work out if I am about to pop out at him. He approaches the bathroom, stands cautiously outside.

'I'm in here.' I say this as if I am eager for him to find me.

'Are you okay? There's blood on the floor.'

'I'm embarrassed.' I say this in the wimpiest voice I can manage with him still able to hear. Despite the circumstances, I can't help but feel the miracle of the two words I am about to say. 'My period,' I say, as if it were an ordinary occurrence. And then, 'Do you want to come in?'

I am slumped on the floor with the towel still around me and another beneath me, my back against the wall, my legs curled. 'I'm so sorry.'

He kneels down. 'You poor thing.'

'I'm feeling so weak. I thought if I rested here for a few minutes . . . ' I really do have so little strength and I absolutely must make him believe the truth of this. 'I look terrible. How can you stand to look at me?'

'Looking at you is all I want to do. And touching you. God, it was hard to stop myself last night. But I wanted us both awake. You were too sleepy.' He counts my pulse. 'The antihistamine did its job. The tremors have gone. But you're still frail.'

I hear your voice. *Gee whizz. I wonder why that is.* Your brave sarcasm helps. It is part of me. It is in my bones with you. And you are laughing, too, talking to me. *You're like Superman, baby sister, surrounded by Kryptonite. Show him that.*

I try to stretch out a hand, let it fall, try again. He takes it, covers it with kisses.

'You won't . . . ' I say.

'Won't what? Tell me, Melanie.'

'You won't want me now.' I look stricken. 'The mess.'

'That doesn't bother me. You're worth it. We can't wait any longer, can we?'

'No.'

'We can take a bath together, after. Would you like that?'

I look right into his eyes and nod.

'I'm taking you to bed now.'

I let him lift me up, bundled in the towels. I wrap my arms around his neck and bury my face in his shoulder in my best imitation of a helpless maiden. His breathing is growing more rapid as he puts me on top of the sheets, pulls his black T-shirt off before he lies on his side next to me, pushes away the towels, runs his hand down my back and over my breasts, along my thighs, kneading with increasing force. All the time, his mouth is against mine.

'Sorry,' I say again.

'Why? Don't be.'

'I'm too weak to touch you much.'

'That was only necessary until things settle down for us.'

I manage to lift an arm to his waist. 'There,' I say proudly.

I press the other between his legs. 'And there,' I say even more proudly, when he lets out his breath.

I kiss him more deeply, and I really am panting. My heart really is beating so fast I am afraid it may stop. My skin really is flushing so hot I may just burn up. My stomach really is in a knot so tight I wonder if it will drag the rest of me in after it, my whole body inside out in a contortion artist's ball. But I slide a hand down his side to his hip, as if wanting to pull him towards me. 'You really don't mind the blood?'

He only looks at me and shakes his head no and I whisper 'Good' and close my eyes and sigh and press his hips towards mine. I let out a sigh of pleasure. I curl a hand over the bulge at the front of his trousers and listen to him gasp. All the while I am manoeuvring the syringe I took from his pocket with my other hand, wiggling the cap off and letting it drop and praying he doesn't notice, trying to adjust the position between my fingers while my other palm continues to press against him, making him moan.

I can remember you explaining once about intramuscular injections, proud after you did your first one, telling me you weren't embarrassed that it was a man and his trousers had to be partly down for you to do it.

I fly my hand up and around. I am aiming blind but I know I have a clear track to the outer part of his lower back. I dart the needle in and his eyes widen, confused for an instant about what is happening.

Perfect. Your voice is so clear I nearly turn to look for you.

I manage to press the plunger but the liquid in the syringe is thicker and much harder to squeeze out than I imagined. I have no idea how much has gone in. I only know he is shouting and swearing. The things he really feels about me are finally out.

He knocks my hand away and bulldozes me onto my back with the full weight of his body over mine. He presses one arm over my neck and reaches round with the other to pull the syringe out and examine it. 'You didn't get enough in. You're just like her.'

Too fucking right, I think, and I'm not sure if I am hearing myself or you but I manage to get one of my arms free to punch his hand so hard the syringe flies out of it and across the room.

He takes his arm from my neck and rises onto his knees to tug down his trousers. Is he fumbling? I really think he is. He is struggling. He is not as coordinated as he thinks. I am not either but I manage to sink a knee into his stomach. He falls to his side with an expulsion of air, all the while trying to avoid the kick I am aiming between his legs.

My power and aim are too poor to do more than bait a furious bear, but the half-life of the drug is in my favour. The potency is reducing in my body with every minute. The opposite is true for him after his recent dose. The tranquilliser has to be increasing its grip on his nervous system as the drug speeds through his blood. I cannot help but perceive that the fight is fairer.

Didn't get enough in, he said. But not enough still means some. Doesn't it?

Yes, you say. *Yes Yes Yes.*

The Man from Far Away

I try to roll away. Once, twice, three times, until I gain enough momentum to crash off the side of the bed. My spine is bruised into pins and needles and the back of my head smashes onto the floor.

Above me, he is swearing again. Is it possible there isn't as much force in his voice as the last time he spoke? He thumps off the bed and onto me, as if I am a full-length cushion, and whatever breath is left in my belly shoots out. A fist smashes so hard into the side of my jaw the world is awash with stars.

He is trying to nudge my legs open and I am trying with every ounce of strength I have left to resist. The opposing forces are equal, at last. I am sure of it. My skin is slippery with blood, which is making it more difficult for him.

If they find my body someday I want them to be able to tell Luke that there was forensic evidence that I fought hard. I don't want Adam Holderness to be able to face his colleagues easily. I want him to be so visibly damaged it will be impossible for him to look at anybody for weeks without their asking questions.

My parents will be turning up with Luke at my house soon, if they haven't already. They are going to raise hell until they discover where I am. This bastard will have some explaining to do. Missing woman. Known male acquaintance covered in injuries. He won't be able to hide the connection between us like he did with you.

My body remembers. My body wakes up. Adrenaline jets through me. Muscle memory. What Ted said. What Ted made me do. I let out a grunt and roll onto my side, rolling him with me like I did only a few weeks ago in the park with Ted, the same move I practised then even when I didn't want to. And I take this man who snatched you from us by surprise. In one continuous motion I knee his upper thigh once, twice, three times in quick succession. He pulls away and springs into a crouch like Ted did, so he can come at me again.

I heave myself into a sitting position with my legs in front of me, my back against the bed. I raise a leg into a bend and release it. I kick him hard in the face three times in a row with this motion. When he falls onto his back I scoot closer and bring my heel down on his nose. I can hear bone splintering and tissue squelching. He is not wearing a mask like Ted was. I lose count of how many times his face crunches beneath the blows.

Blood is coming from his nose and his forehead is split and his eyes are closed and something is oozing from his scalp and there is a voice somewhere, so quiet that at first I think I must be imagining it. It is not Adam

Holderness's voice. I am not sure Adam Holderness can use his voice at all right now.

'You've done a great job, Ella,' the voice says. It is a quiet voice. A man's voice. A stranger's voice? Or is it faintly familiar? 'I think you can stop now,' the voice says.

I don't stop. I kick again. I jut out my chin. My eyes are locked on Adam Holderness, searching for the faintest sign of movement, the tiniest twitch.

'Ella.' The man is kneeling beside me. 'Stop.' My leg falls to the floor.

The man drags the quilt off the bed, lifts me a little to wrap it around me. I have forgotten that I am naked, that I am covered in blood.

The man says, 'I thought maybe you needed help, but you did more than fine on your own.'

But I did need help. I did get help. You helped me. Your voice. Always your voice is what I hear when I am most in need. And Ted helped too. Ted finally did the thing he always wanted to do. He saved me. He made me practise those moves when I didn't want to and it made all the difference. I cannot lie to myself about that.

'Can you look at me, Ella?'

I shake my head no. I cannot look away from the man who tore you from us. His face does not look like his face any more, and there is so much blood I can barely see his features, but he isn't any less him.

The stranger turns my head towards him and away from the pulpy mess on the wooden floor.

My thoughts are not working like they usually do. I can only see in fragments. A man sitting in a corridor with his face behind a newspaper. The same man, coming to my support group only to leave within minutes. He said his partner was missing – I'm sure I am right to remember that.

Another man comes into the room. He is wearing gloves. I see that both men are wearing them. Both men have coverings over their shoes too. The second man crouches near Adam Holderness.

'Is he dead?' I say.

The second man looks at the one sitting beside me. His look is an unspoken question that I cannot understand. The man beside me seems to consider before he gives his answer, which comes as a negative shake of the head that is so brief I am not sure if I saw it at all.

'No,' the second man says. 'Unconscious but alive, though barely.' The second man's voice tugs at me too. Just a tone, but I have heard it before. Where? There is something in his features that I recognise. It is only a flash, but an image of that same face comes to me as if I were looking at a photograph. The fake policeman. But his hair is bottle-blond now instead of dark and the blueberry-sized mole below his eye is gone and so are the sideburns. With his face so naked I see he is younger than I guessed. Perhaps late twenties, early thirties at most.

I blink hard, wondering if I am imagining it.

The first man smooths my hair from my face but speaks to the second. 'Go,' he says. 'You know what to do.' And the fake policeman quickly leaves the room.

'I've seen him before,' I say.

'We don't have much time, Ella. You're badly hurt. I

don't know if it's your blood or his, but you're covered in it.'

'Who is he? He's not a policeman.'

'He is, but not one most members of the force would know. He's not usually in uniform.'

There is a buzz in my ears. I put my hands on them and press, as if that will make it stop, but it doesn't. 'Noah?' I say it like a question, even though I know the answer.

'Yes.'

'Why didn't you say who you were before?'

He shakes his head. 'We can talk later. You need medical treatment.'

'No. Now.'

'At least let me get you into the recovery position. You should be lying on your side.'

I look at Adam again. My breath quickens. 'No. No, no, no, no, no. I need to be upright. I need to watch him.'

'Okay. Okay. It's okay. I understand. But I want you to try not to worry – I don't think he's going to be waking up any time soon.'

'Tell me why.'

'I was going to tell you who I was the first time, when you were doing your walk-in clinic. That's why I came. But I was called away – not a call I could ignore.'

He lifts a corner of the quilt and blots my face with it. When he lets it fall, the grey is stained with red.

'Your undercover friend. Where have I heard his voice?'

'He knew how frustrated I was when my first attempt to talk to you was interrupted. So he left you a voicemail later that day, pretending to be a journalist. That's where you heard him. But you never got back to him.'

He smiles, a sad smile, and an appeasing one. 'Please, Ella. Try to understand.' It is a familiar smile, even in its woeful form. It is exactly the smile I love most in the world, with the same dimples.

'A few days later I sent him to you. He thought the uniform would persuade you to go with him – that was his own improvisation – he's learning.' His dark brows draw together in a straight line, like Luke's do when he is angry. 'When I heard what happened I came back to try again to see you. I only had a small window and it was during your discussion group. I told the truth there, about my circumstances.'

'Only the barest bones of truth.' I can see how much you and this man have in common. 'You wanted to spy on me. I'm told that's what you're good at.'

'You're trembling.' He tightens the quilt around me. 'We need to talk later.'

I try to shake my head but my brain rattles around, making me wince. 'It's already later. It's already much later than it should be. Years too late. You wanted to keep all the advantage for yourself. All the advantage of knowing everything and keeping us in the dark. All the advantage of watching us.'

He nods slowly. 'Yes, I wanted to see you in action, to get the measure of you. But there were practical reasons too.'

'Why did you leave the discussion group? Was it because you saw your mother lurking outside?'

'I didn't learn she was there until afterwards. We came separately. We missed each other by minutes. I couldn't see her from where I was in the room.'

'Then why?'

'The same reason as the guy who stormed out.' His jaw stiffens when he looks at Adam. He has spoken to me gently, touched me gently, but this new expression makes me see how extremely ungentle he can be. 'I didn't want to be in the same room with that piece of shit. I can read people or I wouldn't do what I do – I'd planned to find out more about him. I would have stayed if I'd thought I'd be able to get you alone but he obviously wasn't going to leave your side.'

'Why now? Why meet me now, after all this time?'

'I'm not trying to shut you down or avoid your questions but you can barely keep yourself upright and I need to leave. I shouldn't be in the country right now.'

'Doesn't your handler track you?'

He doesn't answer.

'Or is that only in theory?'

Again no answer, but there is a brief flash in his eyes as they meet mine.

'Tell me what made you get in touch with me at last,' I say.

'The messages to the Henrickson accounts.' His voice cracks. 'With the voicemail – I thought, for a few seconds I thought it was Miranda. She's the only one who had that number. It's the one I wrote down for her when we first met, along with my address and email. She used them until I told her the truth about what I did.'

'Would you have written a first initial instead of your Christian name?'

'Yes.'

'That's how she copied it in her address book.'

'She understood things before I explained them. She was always ahead of me. There's a note in your voices, you know, a strand that's the same in both of you. As soon as I listened I understood, but for an instant I thought she'd come back.'

Noah's forehead creases in exactly the way Luke's does when he is baffled. 'How did you find the Henrickson email address and number? What led you to those, after all this time?'

'The police finally returned her address book. She left them where I would find them.'

'That's like her. You're like her. You sound like her. She had eyes like yours. Not just literally. You see like her, too, don't you? You have her vision. You're pretty relentless, Ella Brooke. Next thing I know, my mother is sending message after message that you turned up on her doorstep and she's asking all over again about the woman and the baby she saw ten years ago.'

I look around the room, this blood-drenched mess of a room that was so disturbingly neat until I entered it. 'But you still haven't said why you're in this place. You still haven't said how you found me.'

'I put a tracker on your car.'

'That's not okay.'

'I knew you got here last night. I wanted to make sure there wasn't a sinister reason why you didn't go home.'

Should I give him credit for saying *I*? For not trying to disclaim responsibility with *We* or *They* or *You needed*?

'You can't do that to civilians,' I say. 'It's not allowed.'

'I'm sorry,' he says. 'There was no other way to follow you. The tracker's gone already.'

'Don't do that again.'

He doesn't reply. Doesn't nod. Doesn't do anything to show he agrees to this.

'Did you hear what I said, Noah? I won't say another word to you – ever – unless you promise me this. No surveillance of me or Luke or my parents. Not of any description. Not by any means or method.'

'I promise.'

I wipe a hand across my forehead. It is like touching treacle. 'When did you get here? What made you break in?'

'We arrived this morning. The tracker was saying your car was here but I couldn't see any sign of it. It didn't make sense that a guest would hide it away in the garage. Then Holderness came out, walked round the whole house before going back in – I told you I didn't trust him from the minute I clapped eyes on him.' He puts a gloved hand on mine. 'We're running out of time, Ella. I need to go.'

'Not yet.' I have ten years' worth of questions for this man.

The tabloid headlines spear me again. Some of them were close to the truth. Perhaps with their scattergun approach it was inevitable, though Adam himself may have found a way to feed them. Thorne too.

The next question I ask is for Luke – I know he will need the answer to it someday. 'Was she going to run away with you? Was she going to abandon Luke?'

'She would never do that. I wanted her with me but it wasn't possible. I could never keep her safe, keep Luke safe, doing what I do. The only way to work it is to keep the people I love far away.' He smiles. 'But your sister isn't the kind of woman to accept a lover who disappears for long periods and refuses to tell her why or where.'

'That's true. And she's right.'

'Yes. She is.' We flit in and out of speaking of you in the present tense, even though we both know that isn't what you are any more.

'There were ways she could contact me, but I couldn't always check. She was supposed to meet me the morning she vanished, to say goodbye. It was going to be a long stretch before I'd be able to get back. But she never arrived. She'd never not met me when she said she would. I did whatever I could to try to investigate, but she really did seem to have disappeared into thin air.' His voice tightens. 'All of my talents for burrowing deep, for discovering things, and I couldn't use them for her.'

I ask him the same question I asked his mother. 'Did they not look for her properly, because they wanted to protect what you were doing?'

'No. Absolutely not.'

I look hard at him. He meets my eye. He makes an effort to do this, and not to break the contact. I will never know if he is telling the truth, but I am not sure I can live with the pain of disbelieving it. Perhaps he cannot either.

'Ella?'

'Yes?'

'I knew she would never have gone if she had a choice.'

'I knew that too.' I tip forward over my legs as if an invisible force has punched me from behind and put me into a seated forward bend. I gulp. I try to swallow. I make a noise that is not speech, the noise of an animal in pain.

I am not sure how much time passes before Noah gently folds me back up, but almost as soon as he does I am slumping. I slide so low only my shoulders and head are propped against the bed frame. The rest of me is practically lying down, though my knees are bent. Noah lifts my upper back a little, so I am more upright, and I tip sideways into him. 'It's time to call for medical attention. Now.'

'No.' I put my other great fear into words. The fear Mum and I share. And Dad, though he never says it, partly because it is too much to bear for him and partly to try to keep Mum and me calm. 'I've always worried that you'd want Luke. That one day you would swoop in and take him.'

'I do want him but he wouldn't be safe with me. I couldn't look after him, doing what I do. I've always known where he is. I know you'll be angry but I've looked in on him sometimes. And you. He's so contented, so well loved and cared for. I wouldn't mess that up for him. I've seen enough of him to know he wouldn't allow it even if I were foolish enough to try.'

'Norfolk.' I manage to pull away from him, though he still holds me up. 'I took him there last summer. I felt watched. Was that you?'

'You're good, you know. Not many people would sense it, but I worried I'd spooked you. I was sorry about that but I loved seeing the two of you together.'

This last sentence makes my heart clutch. I can't stop myself repeating what I have already said. 'You can't follow us again. You can't spy on us.'

'I already promised you I wouldn't. I don't break promises.'

'Given what you do, I find that hard to believe.'

'Okay. I don't break promises to the people who know me as me.'

I look towards the covered window, as if somehow I

can see through it, see through to the place where you are now. 'After I met your mother, I thought you had taken her.' I think again of what Thorne said. 'I'm certain he buried her here.'

He squints in disgust at the human lump on the floor. 'You need to be seen by a doctor and we need to get the police out here to deal with that scumbag.'

Scumbag. I'm trying to remember who else uses that word.

The second man comes back with a telephone in his gloved hand and hands it to Noah. He jerks his head towards the door to signal that they need to move, then leaves the room again.

'It's Holderness's landline,' Noah says. 'I want you to dial 999. Tell them everything you need to tell them. Can you do that?'

'Yes.'

'Miranda said if it ever came to it I should trust you.'

I manage a small nod. The movement makes my brain hurt.

'I wanted Miranda to be proud of me, and for our son to be.' He pauses. 'I'd like you to be. I'm not sure how much longer I can do what I do.'

I am seeing stars. I press the heels of my hands against my eyes to make them go away but it only makes more stars. 'There are probably cameras here.' My words seem to come out in slow motion. Does he hear them that way? 'He probably got you on film.'

'There are no cameras. He didn't want any evidence of who comes in and out of this place. He didn't want a record of what he says and does.' He wraps my fingers around the phone. 'I have to be gone before the emergency services arrive but I need to make sure you're safe.'

Noah moves to Adam's side, where he studies the rise and fall of his breathing. It is slight but regular. He presses a fist onto the centre of Adam's chest and slides it up and down several times, quickly, without pause. He grabs the muscle that runs between the top of Adam's shoulder and bottom of his neck, then squeezes and twists.

All the while, Noah is searching for even a twitch. But there is no reaction. Still not satisfied, he lifts one of Adam's wrists, holds it for several seconds above his battered face, and lets it drop. Adam does not move his head out of the way, or redirect his arm.

Noah seems to be talking to himself as he swaps his blood-smeared gloves with a clean pair from his pocket. 'He's completely unresponsive.' Adam continues to lie there, inert, as Noah considers him.

'If he wasn't dead before, he must be now,' I say.

'I don't want to leave you.'

'I'm fine,' I say. 'I'll be fine.' The buzz in my ears is turning into a roar.

Noah picks the syringe up from where it landed, examines it in a gloved hand, returns to my side. 'You're showing signs of being heavily drugged, you're covered in bruises and cuts, you're bleeding heavily, and you've hit your head. You need to be seen by a doctor.'

The phone falls out of my hand. I cannot tear my eyes from the pile of raw flesh on the floor. 'I've seen enough of doctors.'

'You're not fine. Not medically. But you're more than

fine in all other ways.' His eyes darken. 'You really are like your sister.'

I don't correct him. I won't ever correct him. Because you and I are so alike but also so different. I will keep that secret for you and Ted. It has no bearing on anything, now. The only person you hurt with that was me. And yourselves. I won't tell him that you slept with Adam either. I won't tell anyone. Noah can go to his grave believing you were faithful to him. But Luke will need to know about his father and grandmother someday, once all of us together have worked out when and how.

You see, Miranda? The confidentiality clause never expires. Not about the things that really count.

You must always forgive the people you love, Melanie.

Whatever your secret thoughts and motives, you were right. I forgive you. I only wish you were with me to hear me say the words.

I am with you, you say.

Noah takes off a glove, curves his bare hand against my cheek. His skin smells of latex. I stare straight into his brown eyes, realising he must have a blue recessive gene for Luke to have ended up with your eyes and mine.

'What's your blood type?' I say.

'A. Why?'

I press my hand to his cheek too. His designer stubble had masked his dimple before, but not today. I move a finger up to his temple, swirl it inside the little knotted cowlick. The last two times I saw him, he'd slicked his hair back to hide it. Part of his disguise. 'You're so much like Luke,' I say.

'There's a bond between us, Ella. There's loyalty.

Because of our resemblances to those we most love, because of our closeness to them.' He puts the glove back on, picks up the telephone handset, presses it into my palm once more.

I hold the phone for a few seconds before asking him one more thing. 'Why do you call me Ella and not Melanie?'

'She told me Melanie was for her alone. It would have been an intrusion to do anything else.'

That is the right answer. The perfect and only answer. I nod, the slightest nod, and wipe away tears.

I dial 999, press the button for speakerphone so Noah can hear. I say all the things I need to say. I tell them there is an unconscious man on the floor who I injured in self-defence. I tell them what he did to me. I tell them what he did to you. I tell them that I think they will find your body somewhere in the house's grounds.

Noah watches me as I speak, encouraging me with those intent brown eyes, nodding approval of the story I tell but clearly not prepared to leave until he is happy that I have said all that I need to.

They tell me not to put down the phone. I lean against Noah. I am in a kind of waking dream, though I keep murmuring that he is staying too long and cutting it too close, that he won't have time to escape before the ambulance arrives. When they say that help is only minutes away I jerk out of this twilight state for a final time and tell the man you loved above all others, the man who helped to make Luke, that he must go, that you'd be furious if he were caught here. He kisses the top of my head before rising swiftly but silently. He pauses once more over Adam to make sure he is still unconscious, then disappears from the room.

As soon as he is gone, my hand drops to my side and my grip on the phone loosens. There is a tinny voice, coming from somewhere far away, repeating my name, asking me what is happening, asking me to tell them I am all right. But my eyes close and I sink to the floor, knowing that I cannot possibly do a single thing more.

I open my eyes to a face. The face is a patchwork of oozing blood and red blotches and deep gouges. The face is only inches from my own and it is spitting at me. The words it is saying are a muddle and my head is pounding so hard I cannot understand what they mean.

I am stretched out on the floor and there is a monster on top of me with its hands around my throat. The hands are squeezing. The monster is calling me by your name. It thinks I am you. The ceiling is starting to spin. I am sure my face is blue.

A clear thought comes. It is that I know who the monster is. Then I have another thought. This one is about arms. It is that arms are weakest near the wrists. Arms are weaker the farther from the core of the body they are. Muscle memory comes too. Somehow I squeeze my own lower arms inside his and press outwards against him but he is barely releasing the pressure and if I don't do something quickly I am going to lose consciousness for what is likely to be the very last time.

He will put me in a coffin and I will never see light again. Just like the man in the movie. Just like you. I do not know how I know this but I do.

I want to get a kick in, but his weight is making it impossible for me to move. I need to get his body off mine and I need to get his hands off my throat.

I wiggle my arms out, arching my right arm over his left to jab two fingers into his trachea. The effect is instant. He lets go of my throat and wraps his hands around his own, gasping for air, tears running. I use the heel of my left hand to punch upwards and into his already-mangled nose. I pull my right arm back again, then release it like a spring, driving my thumb into his eye socket, my fingers splayed and braced against his temple, pressing as hard as I can. He lets out a strangled scream and moves his face away and rolls off me.

He is on his back, one hand clutching his neck, the other his eye, and I sit up, scoot away, shift along the floor to where I can hear that tinny voice again. I remember it from somewhere. I can hear it even over the monster's gurgling. It is coming from the telephone handset on the floor beside me. The tinny voice is louder, more frenzied, insisting that I speak. I pick the handset up. I stare at it for a few seconds, this strange piece of hissing plastic and metal, not sure what to do with it. I am supposed to talk and listen, I think. Yes, that is what I am supposed to do.

But I do not do this because the monster is growling and lumbering closer. What I do is adjust my grip. What I do is whack the monster's temple as if the handset is a bat and his head is a ball.

Monster. I remember somebody saying I needed to try to find his humanness. I needed not to see him as a monster. Who said that? Who were they talking about?

I am not sure. But it doesn't matter because a monster is a monster and that is what this is.

I whack his head once more so hard that my whole body hums and the noise against his skull echoes in my own head. He seems suspended, for a few seconds, swaying back and forth. Then he falls straight down. That is when, finally, the police burst in.

Tuesday, 14 February

Valentine's Day

There was a frost last night. The world is magically dusted in white. It is like a fairy land, here in our little clearing in the woods. The sun is dazzling and bright and makes everything it touches beautiful as it pours through the leafless branches of our cherry tree.

The most beautiful thing of all is your son, who is standing beside me, clutching my hand so tightly it hurts. I do not ask him to loosen his grip. I lead him out of the clearing, through the woods, along the path to the village church.

Already the days are stretching. It seems a miracle for the world to be so light this early. There are other ordinary miracles too. I am having my fourth period in a row since I lost what seemed to be a decade's worth of blood in the space of a few hours. The gilded doctor smiled as if to say, I always knew it would happen one day.

Thorne was wrong and right. The monster did keep you close, in a place he could see, though you weren't beneath a hedge. That is where he kept the other two women. The police haven't identified them yet but they think he killed them after he took you, with a few years between each victim. Thorne predicted that too.

I know that many families will be waiting and wondering, dreading that one of the women belongs to them. I worried aloud that I have given them a curse, but our mother said that not knowing was the worst thing, and that finding out would be a gift, though a terrible one.

He put you under an apple tree, which he could see from his bedroom window. I got you out. I wish more than anything else in the world that I could have done more for you, but at least I did that.

Now Mum and Dad can be by your side in a few minutes, and Luke and me too. Your grave still isn't marked, but you have only been here for three days. It will take us time to choose the right stone and to decide what to write on it. Luke wants a phoenix. Mum wants a cross. Dad wants something simple and pure with just your name and dates. I think Dad is right with this one. No image or shape or word could ever begin to describe you. So why try? *Sister. Mother. Daughter. Lover.* All true, but nowhere near enough.

I cannot say what I feel about Jason Thorne. It is for the families of his victims to say. But I know exactly what I feel towards the man who ripped you away from us. It is a hatred so hot and deep I poked out his eye with my bare finger. I took away half his sight.

He took away your precious, beautiful, messy life. He stole you and drugged you and raped you and kept you in darkness before he murdered you. He put you beneath the bare soil of his garden as if you were a family pet. No box. Nothing. He buried you naked. He wrapped you in nothing and he must have burnt your clothes. He left you with – nothing. Again and again, nothing. They never even found your keys or purse or shoes.

He lied when he said you died from a seizure. There is a bone in the neck that can break when a person is strangled. The hyoid bone. Yours was fractured, like the other women's. The police are certain that he put his hands around your throat and squeezed the life out of you, as he tried to squeeze mine.

I make myself consider these things. I make myself see them in detail. Really see them. I promised I would never look away. I promised I would never let you go.

You are not wearing your locket. I asked them to entwine the chain through your fingers, with the platinum oval curled in your palm, so you can keep it close. But first I took Luke's little photograph out of my own locket and put it in yours.

I cannot wear anything around my own throat now. My locket is in Luke's room, with a copy of his baby picture in the place where the original used to be. He keeps my locket in a small box of treasures by his bed.

Luke and I have rimmed your grave with the stones from Norfolk, dismantling the M we left in the woods and carrying the pebbles here. We didn't use the ones that man stole. Luke and I will return to the seaside and choose new pinks to replace those. We will find new colours too, and make it so beautiful you would cry.

I want to stretch out over the cold ground where you are. The mound of dirt they have covered you with is like a bed. But I do not want Luke to see me do this, so the two of us crouch beside you. I take a handful of earth in my hand, let it run through my fingers, put my mud-stained skin to my mouth. Kissing this dirt is not like kissing you, but it is the best that I can do. It is all I have.

'I love you, Mummy,' Luke says to the earth. It makes my heart hurt to hear him call you Mummy again, as if the certainty of what has happened to you has at last frozen him in his relationship to you. There can be no changes now.

'Auntie Ella?'

'Yes, Luke?'

'Mummy doesn't want you not to do what you really want because of her.' He speaks as if he is translating what he hears your ghost saying to him, bringing your words from the underworld to those of us who are not magical enough to hear them.

'I think you're right. I feel that too. That's why I'm going to get that teaching certificate.'

'But Mummy wants the charity work to continue.'

'Granny and Grandpa and I will keep it going. We'll pay for some experts to do most of the things I used to do.'

An anonymous donation was made to the charity a week after I found you. The money will fund it for at least a decade. I don't need to ask to know it was Noah.

'They won't be as good as you.'

I try to steer the subject to something else. 'Granny and Grandpa want to have a little party at the end of the month.'

'For your birthday?'

'Yes. They are insisting. Will you help them plan it?'

'Definitely. It's my half-birthday too, don't forget. Can Ted come?'

I can't help the hesitation before I answer. 'You can ask him, Luke.'

'Okay.' He is still considering the soil that holds you. 'Maybe when you get a job as a teacher they'll let you start a self-defence club?'

'Brilliant idea.'

He is looking so hard at the ground I think he is trying to see through it, trying to see right down to you. 'Because we aren't sure you're going to like being trapped in a stuffy classroom all day.'

'We? Do you mean you and Granny and Grandpa?'

'No. Me and Mummy.'

'I see.' I ruffle his hair but he still doesn't tear his eyes from you. 'We need to choose a desk for your room, Ninja Warrior. We can look next weekend.'

'Do you think he's really going to come, Auntie Ella?'

I stand up, reach out an arm, pull your son to his feet, make him look at me, make him look away from you. Now that he knows where you are, I must be careful that he spends enough time with you, but not too much. You will be sad, but I think you will agree that he mustn't be too often with the dead. I flinch to think the word, but sometimes I must make myself.

'He's here, Luke. He was here when we arrived. I think he wanted to give us a little time.'

I look over my shoulder at the porch of the church. That is all it takes for Noah to leave the shadows and walk towards us. When he reaches the place where you are he crosses himself and bows his head. He falls to his knees and kisses the earth. Luke looks uncertain, but then he returns to the place I just pulled him from and does the same, a replica of his father.

Luke is arranging the yellow roses that Noah brought you. The two of them are bending their dark heads together. Can you hear what they are saying?

I quietly withdraw. I follow the little path that winds through the gravestones to the gap in the drystone wall that surrounds the churchyard. I want to give the two of them some time with each other, some time with you, before I have to drag Luke away from you and his father and take him to school.

I will wait here, by the wooden gate, in this puddle of winter sunshine that seems to be following me. In the pocket of my waxed jacket are three cards. I take them out and fan them and hold them in my hands, one green, one red, and one blue.

The first Valentine arrived yesterday and came to my house. I didn't guess at first what was inside the large brown envelope with its first-class stamp, posted from central London.

But as soon as I pulled out the pale green envelope I knew who it was from. It was bordered with roses that he had drawn himself. Perhaps he was remembering the design you wanted for the shelves he never made you, and thought it would please me. *I like beautiful things.* That is what he said. Perhaps he was reliving the flowers that some of the tabloids claimed he etched on the women. He had written *Ella* in the centre, ringed with a heart, and the words *To be opened on 14 February.*

I did not wait until today as directed. I opened it immediately, expecting several dead bluebottles to fall out, but none did. There was no greeting or signature on the handmade card. He plunged right in.

My favourite time to think of you is at night, as I fall asleep. Did you know that you smell of lily of the valley and taste of honey, and that your hair and skin feel like petals? I know these things. I know you.

I smiled to learn that you found your sister. I helped with that. I hope you think of me, if not yet in the way I would wish, at least – for now – with some affection and gratitude. Feelings can deepen over time, Ella. Yours will catch up with mine.

I was also glad of the treatment that Dr Devil met at your hands. I cherish the thought that his limited view is now of high walls and razor wire. I understand that he is likely to plead not guilty for the charges relating to your sister and the other women, and self-defence for the charges relating to you. Do not worry, my dearest Ella. He will lose on all counts. I have proved that you must trust in my insight.

Dr Demon would benefit from some occupational therapy. I think the table saw would suit his particular talents. What an honour it would be to tutor him myself, but I am engaged in other important work at present, and this will take quite some time to complete. Not to worry – I have numerous acquaintances who would be delighted to assist the doctor with his personal development.

Would you like me to arrange this? Alas, I suspect that you would not. You have power over me, Ella. Will you exercise that power? You can inspire me to do the right thing.

You can stop me from doing the wrong. You have only to say. But you must say.

The man we spoke of privately when you and I were last together is not worthy of you. I will not mention him to anybody, unless there comes a time when you would like me to. For his sake, let us hope he never again betrays you.

But here, Ella, is the real purpose of this card. Will you be my Valentine? I think I know what you will say. You will say nothing. At least for now. You see how well I understand you? But without the word No I will be encouraged. Whatever your answer, you are mine. And I am becoming the man you want me to be. My appearance is not what it was when we last met. I can say no more than that. Only – I think you will like what you see.

They will try to use you to find me, Ella. We are both much too smart for that.

I know where you are, as you will realise from the arrival of this card. Do not be alarmed by this. I would only ever protect you and those you love. I will do my best to act in ways that will make you proud, but you must give me some sign. Before long, I will find a way for us to be alone, so I can show you how I feel in person.

The card and the two envelopes will soon be with the police, though I am certain that Thorne has been careful to ensure he cannot be traced from them.

The police will question me, and I will answer carefully, as you would want me to, but balanced with my own conscience and the need to protect others. I am very good at this, now. I have had a lot of practice.

I will not let myself be scared that Thorne will find

me. I will not give him, or anyone, the power to control or threaten me. I will not hide or run. The last ten years of my life have been formed by my sense of fear and danger. I will not let the rest of it be. But if he does turn up on my doorstep, I will be ready.

The second Valentine was from Ted, who I haven't seen since he came to my hospital room the day after I found you. He'd deliberately waited until visiting hours were over, banking on the fact that the journalists would be gone by then. He also counted on his uniform getting him past the police officers guarding my door. They thought then that Thorne might be foolish enough to come crashing in. As if he would make it that easy.

Ted stared so hard at me. He scarcely blinked he stared so hard. At first I thought he was shocked by my appearance, by my white face splashed with purple bruises and criss-crossed in red gashes that they'd stuck together with glue.

I had made the nurse show me in a mirror. She didn't laugh when I said I would make a perfect bride of Frankenstein's monster. But unlike that bride, I am really alive. The glue washed away in a week or two. The bruises have faded and my cuts have almost healed. 'You were lucky,' the nurse said. I gave her your half-smile. I didn't contradict her. *It wasn't luck.* That is what you would have said if you were still talking to me.

But as Ted stared and stared and stared some more, I was confused about why he had come at all, only to be struck so entirely dumb. So I spoke instead. I told him I would keep his secrets about you. And then I told him to leave. He didn't move so I pressed the call button for somebody to make him.

'It will never be over between us. I will give you time, but I will be back.' His voice was hoarse as he choked out these words, the only words he had come to say.

Ted's card was the red one. *I will love you forever. I will wait until you forgive me.* I am not sure if the first thing is really possible. I do not know if the second will ever happen, though I want it to, because I do not like living with this splinter of ice in the part of my heart that was Ted's.

The third card was not signed. The third card was blue. The third card said simply, *Me and You*, with a drawing of a boy and his aunt. Can you guess who? Of course you can. It is the only card I will treasure. He has left one for you too, with a pencil sketch he did of you holding him as a baby. My hand rested on his shoulder as he buried it just beneath your blanket of earth.

I look up to see that your son and his father are walking away from you, walking towards me. So I slide the cards back into my huge jacket pocket and snap the flap to keep them secure while I wait for the two of them at the exit from this sad place.

They are holding hands, smiling their identical dimpled smiles, and I cannot help but smile too.

But Noah's smile soon disappears. He is looking so hard at me. Does he only see you? Or does he see me too? His forehead is creasing in worry and I think perhaps he is searching my face for scars. He pushes open the gate and he and I walk out of the churchyard with Luke between us.

I am waiting. I am listening. I am imagining what you would say to me. I do not see you and Ted together, now, when I close my eyes. I only see you. But you don't say anything. Not even a whisper. You are silent, and silent is the last thing I want you to be.

You will know that I forgive you. You will know that there is a hole in my soul that will never close up.

How strange that I spent my whole life thinking that I wanted everything you had, thinking that I wanted to be you, when all the time the opposite was also true. Ted once said that I was the good sister, but you are the good sister too. You are mine and I am yours and your son is the only Valentine I want. I have him because of you.

As ever, I strain to hear your voice. Your voice saved me, during that dark weekend in November. It can save me again. It is still the voice I want to hear above all others. That is why I will never stop talking to you, my love, my darling Miranda, my lost heart. That is why I will never stop listening for you. I am the sister of the sister. And that is why I will keep our secrets.

Acknowledgements

The statement, *this novel would not exist without*, has never been more powerful for me than it is with this one. My first and deepest thanks go to Bella, who taught me what it means to love a sister and be loved by one. The intensity of feeling that Ella and Miranda have for each other is the truest thing in this book.

My UK editor, Sarah Hodgson, gave inspiring and wise advice, coloured always by her loveliness and warmth. She had faith in *The Second Sister*, and in me, from the start, despite the tangle of my messy early drafts. My American editor, Laura Brown, offered superb insight and guidance. Her passion for the novel meant so much. Thanks also to Iris Tupholme, my Canadian editor, and to Jonathan Burnham of HarperCollins USA. My agent, Euan Thorneycroft, always knows exactly what to do. Having him on my side is a miraculous piece of luck. I am immensely grateful to everyone at A.M. Heath, especially Jennifer Custer, Hélène Ferey and Jo Thompson.

The team at HarperCollins UK is simply brilliant. In Editorial there is Julia Wisdom, Kathryn Cheshire and Finn Cotton; in Publicity, Felicity Denham. In Sales there is Sarah Collett and Anna Derkacz; in Marketing, Hannah Gamon, Katie Sadler and Louis Patel. In Export there is Damon Greeney and Rebecca Williams; in Production, Stefanie Kruszyk. Anne O'Brien worked her usual copy-editing magic. Micaela Alcaino designed the beautiful cover.

Richard Kerridge's comments on the third draft of this novel were vital. So too was his feedback on the short story I wrote about Ella and Miranda, 'The Sleepover'. His unsparing critical eye is an extraordinary thing to have, as is his love. My father reads every draft of everything I write. He and my mother never waver in their love and support. The two of them inspire me all the time and make me extremely proud. My brother Robert makes me laugh when I need to, even suggesting alternative titles (*The Brother of the Sister* is my personal favourite). He is a great ally and friend.

As ever, my three daughters make everything more meaningful and magical and beautiful. Lily is an amazing junior editor. She was *The Second Sister's* tireless first reader, of an early (censored!) draft that I read aloud to her – a special experience for us both. Imogen and Violet are patient and understanding in the face of my intense absorption in writing, and cheer me at every turn.

Many people have been generous with their time and expertise. Sergeant Steve Fraser, of Avon & Somerset Constabulary, was so professional and kind. He answered my endless questions with patience and detail, and invited me to Keynsham Custody Unit (one of the most fascinating episodes of novel research I've ever had). Matthew Wright talked to me about police radios. Mel Creton advised about self-defence. Alice Hervé shared her knowledge of doll's houses. Nathan Filer let me interrogate him about drug treatments for psychiatric patients. Gerard Woodward continues to offer his friendship and encouragement. All of these people made the book possible. Any mistakes are my own.

The epigraph from 'The Seven Ravens' is taken from *Grimm's Household Tales*, Edited and Translated by Margaret Hunt, London, George Bell and Sons, 1884, Volume I, pages 108-110.

About the Author

CLAIRE KENDAL was born in America and educated in England, where she has spent all her adult life. Her first novel, *The Book of You*, was translated into more than twenty languages. Claire teaches English literature and creative writing, and lives in England's South West region with her family.

Twitter: @ClaireKendal
Facebook: ClaireKendalAuthor

ALSO BY CLAIRE KENDAL

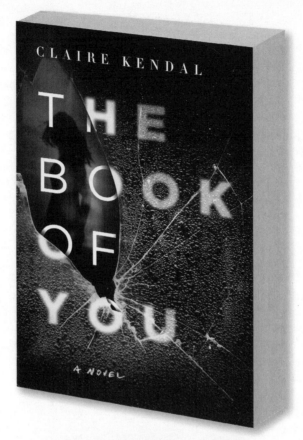

THE BOOK OF YOU
A Novel
Available in Paperback, Ebook, and Digital Audio

"Truly riveting....Clarissa's silence is both understandable and possibly her undoing."
— *New York Times Book Review*

A mesmerizing tale of psychological suspense about a woman who must fight to escape an expert manipulator determined to possess her, Claire Kendal's debut novel is a sophisticated and disturbing portrait of compulsion, control, and terror that will appeal to fans of *Before I Go to Sleep*, *The Silent Wife*, and *Into the Darkest Corner*. Masterfully constructed, filled with exquisite tension and a pervasive sense of menace, *The Book of You* explores the lines between love and compulsion, fantasy and reality, and offers a heart-stopping portrait of a woman determined to survive. Claire Kendal's extraordinary debut will haunt readers long after it reaches its terrifying, breathtaking conclusion.

Heart
of
Palm

Heart of Palm

LAURA LEE SMITH

Grove Press
New York

Published simultaneously in Canada
Printed in the United States of America

FIRST EDITION

ISBN-13: 978-0-8021-2102-8

Grove Press
an imprint of Grove/Atlantic, Inc.
841 Broadway
New York, NY 10003

Distributed by Publishers Group West

www.groveatlantic.com

13 14 15   10 9 8 7 6 5 4 3 2 1

For Chris

A costly delicacy indeed,
when to get to the heart you must kill the tree.

Heart

of

Palm

PROLOGUE

March 1964

Most people never understood why Arla went and married a Bravo. The world genuflected before her. She was beautiful, then: skin like white linen, blue-blooded and hot tempered, stood a full six feet tall in her pink Capezio flats. She could have had so much more. Leon Fontaine, that sweet young man, perfectly lovesick over her and set up so nice like he was in his father's law practice. He bought her a diamond ring; she thanked him and had it made into a pendant. Donny Pellicier, who took her to the senior prom, got to second base, and then went off to seminary at Our Lady of Perpetual Help up in Savannah. He wasn't there even a week when he nearly went crazy with longing for her. He embarked on an aggressive and frantic spiritual reckoning, reevaluated the munificent bodily benefits of lay service, then hitchhiked back home to be with Arla, who wouldn't have him.

When she told her parents, Mr. and Mrs. James Bolton of St. Augustine's Davis Shores, that she intended to marry Dean Bravo, her mother put her hands to her face, and her father went for the Scotch. This was 1964, the day before Arla's eighteenth birthday. Just off the lanai, the azaleas were in full bloom, a wash of magenta against the somber green weave of the lawn.

"Oh, Arla," Vera said. "Don't do this to us."

"Are you knocked up?" James said. Vera began to cry.

"I am not knocked up," Arla said. "My Lord, you people." She stood before them, all lightness and promise and sass, with that soft red hair that made you forget what you were going to say.

"But, Arla," Vera said. "He's a Bravo. He will ruin you."

"Mon dieu. You're so dramatic." Arla had lately adopted an affectation of using French colloquialisms, enjoying the way they slid off her tongue, the way they suggested some vague seduction, some abstract sensuality that she'd learned was a powerful currency. "Men don't ruin women. Daddy didn't ruin you, did he?" She opened her eyes wide, stared at her mother, tilted her head a bit.

"He wants your money," James said.

"Don't be ridiculous," Arla said. "He wants me." Her eyes narrowed when she said this. James ran a hand across his eyes, and Vera hunched over on the chaise, clutching her shoulders.

"You might could congratulate me," Arla said. "Here I'm going to be a married woman and all." She sat down and picked at a scab on her knee. James stared at her and jumped when an ice cube in his glass shifted position. Vera wept.

"I love him, Mother," Arla said.

"Oh, Arla," Vera said. She reached for a tissue and blew her nose. "Dean Bravo? Love won't be enough."

*   *   *

Vera had a point. The Boltons were St. Augustine's finest, pillars of the community, champions of industry, transplanted from Connecticut during Arla's infancy, when James Bolton inherited an insurance franchise and decided there could be no better setting for natural disaster, property loss, and financial gain than the sparkling shores of the Sunshine State. He was right. Business had boomed, and the Boltons had prospered accordingly. James pursued his ambition relentlessly, with the focus of a man for whom success was all and sentiment was a nuisance for which he had no patience. He was a cold man, stoic and aloof even from his wife and daughter. Arla had watched over the years as her mother's desperation grew, as Vera became ebullient and cloying when James was in the house, despondent and weepy when he was not. But the money kept coming in. James bought a house on the Matanzas Bay, drank whiskey sours with the city council, and slept with his secretary. Vera joined the Garden Club and played bridge on Thursdays. They had a cleaning lady. Arla had grown up knowing she was special, she was different, she was better. A Steinway piano in a formal living room. Pointe class every Wednesday, private French lessons every Friday. Chenille bedding. Sleepover parties. Waterskiing at Salt Run.

The Bravo family, on the other hand, lived twenty-five miles north of St. Augustine, in the tiny town of Utina on the east bank of the Florida Intracoastal Waterway. They were Menorcans, settled in Florida not direct from Menorca like most sensible people, but by way of Tennessee, which might have explained a few things. They were descended on their maternal side from the famous Admiral Farragut, whose father Jorge Farragut came to Tennessee from Menorca in 1783, and who is best known for his pithy, if boneheaded, battle cry: "Damn the torpedoes; full speed ahead!" It might as well have been the family slogan. The

Bravos bullied and bollixed their way from Tennessee to St. Augustine around the turn of the twentieth century. They probably would have stayed there, but as luck would have it, Alger Bravo, grandfather of Arla's betrothed Dean, had been chased out of St. Augustine by a collective of rumrunners he'd double-crossed. Alger had cut his losses and retreated north into the thick piney woods of Utina, where the Bravos had lived ever since, dispersing like shadows into the scrub.

Thus the Bravos were cut from a different cloth than the Boltons. The Bravos had never seen the inside of a country club, frequenting, instead, such establishments as Utina's Cue & Brew, the cold case at Soto's Discount Beverage and the county drunk tank. They weren't poor, not by the broadest standards; the Bravos made money when they needed to and quit when they didn't, but they found themselves, to a one, unfettered by the distractions of ambition that seemed to plague other families.

And then there was Dean—third son of Tucker and Margie Bravo—best of the lot, give Arla that. Dean had the Spaniard's dark charm, a brooding chill in his blue eyes and sinews in his forearms that made Arla think impure thoughts. He was cocky and mouthy and comfortable in his own shortcomings in a way Arla found astounding, arousing.

He'd been raised, along with his brothers Huff and Charlie, in a culture of recklessness, neglect, and some mild thuggery. The Bravo brothers had run wild through Utina since they were old enough to walk. As a teenager, Huff went downhill pretty quickly, following his parents' twin examples of alcoholism and lawlessness; he was twenty-four when he earned his first sentence for theft, forgery, and capital battery. Dean and Charlie got wise. They stayed, for the most part, just this side of the law, steering clear of actual felonies—at least the ones that were prone to get them caught. At twenty-two, Charlie got a sixteen-year-old girl pregnant and settled down to family life. At twenty, Dean met Arla.

He'd been driving to St. Augustine and had seen her from a distance late one afternoon in '63, a tall, pale figure walking on a deserted stretch of A1A in the scalding rays of Florida's September sun. The road ran parallel to the Atlantic Ocean. A few houses dotted the shoreline, but mostly it was a lonesome road, the main thoroughfare, if you could call it that, between St. Augustine and Utina. The scrub extended hot and barren for miles north and south; the ocean over the dunes pushed a searing wind across the road. She'd been wearing nearly nothing: a sky blue bikini, a pair of thin sandals, a silver locket, a canvas tote over her shoulder. He pulled over.

"You look like you need a ride, darlin'," he said. She shielded her eyes and peered into the cab of his truck. Her red hair was woven into a thick braid, and delicate beads of sweat shone on her brow. Her eyes were rimmed by pale gold lashes; her white shoulders were tinged with pink.

She blinked, regarded him, and he watched the flutter behind the eyes, the moment's hesitation, the assessment, the decision. Something jumped in his stomach, and he had—he remembered this later, very clearly—the feeling that for the first time he was seeing a being of complete perfection, of flawless beauty. In a moment most uncharacteristic for him, Dean could think of nothing else to say. But then she blinked again, opened the door, and climbed in.

"You're Dean Bravo," she said simply.

"I am," he said, surprised. "How do you know?"

"We all know the Bravos."

"Who's we?"

"Me and my friends," she said, watching him. He pulled back onto the road, headed south.

"What are you doing out here all by yourself?" he said.

She sighed, rolled her eyes.

"My boyfriend," she said. "We had a disagreement."

"He put you out on the road?"

"I got out."

"Some boyfriend," he said.

"Well," she said. "He's really my ex-boyfriend." She leaned forward and picked a sandspur off her ankle, and he watched as the bikini top gapped and the tiniest edge of pink areola was exposed. He tightened his grip on the wheel.

"You need to get to St. Augustine?" he said.

"Sure," she said. "That will do," though she sounded as though it didn't matter much one way or another.

"What's your name?" he said. She turned to face him, and he felt the strange jumping in his stomach again.

"Well," she said. "I'm Arla." And she smiled a funny, guarded smile, haunting, really, as though she knew something all along that he'd only just now begun to understand.

By Halloween he'd slept with her. By Thanksgiving he'd told her he loved her. By Christmas he'd started to panic, so consumed was he by desire, so obsessed with wooing her, winning her, keeping her forever. They made love in the woods, in the truck, in a cheap motel off US1, once in her own pink bedroom while her parents sailed the Matanzas with the mayor. Her pillows smelled like talc and made him crazy with passion. He marveled at her height, the way she could look him straight in the eyes, the way her white legs stretched the length of the pink sheets, her perfect toes hanging off the end of the bed. He wanted her all the time, every day, every minute. He drank like a fiend. He brawled at the Cue & Brew. He crashed his truck into the wall at the Castillo de San Marcos in St. Augustine when he'd seen a college boy making eyes at her at a party. Then he spent a night in the drunk tank, hammered out the dents in the truck, and drove back to wait outside her bedroom window at dawn on New Year's Day.

"Marry me," he said, when she came out to the lawn in a white robe.

"Don't be silly," she said. "I'm seventeen. I'm in high school."

"Marry me," he said on Valentine's Day, and she rolled her eyes.

"Marry me," he said on St. Pat's. "Marry me. Marry me. Marry me." They were sitting on the seawall, overlooking the Matanzas. He was nearly weeping. He slid his hand between her thighs, pressed his face against her chest.

She pulled away and looked at him.

"Okay," she said, finally. "But get a steady job."

And he did, too, signing on full-time at the Rayonier paper mill up in Fernandina, where he'd worked intermittently before but now had a reason to show up regular. He quit drinking by midnight every night, set an alarm clock, and got up early. He drove fifty miles north every day, wore steel-toed boots and a hard hat. He clocked in and clocked out and ate bologna sandwiches on Wonder Bread. Inside the plant, he lowered himself into the belly of the boilers to spray them with sealant, descended eight hours a day into a hot, hellish dark chasm swirling with dispersants and adherents and God knows what else, but it was worth it, holy Jesus it was worth it, to have Arla.

* * *

Arla knew how people felt about the Bravos. She wasn't stupid. She knew she was disappointing her mother and embarrassing her father. She knew her girlfriends were planning college, shopping for pencil skirts and sleeping with athletes. But there were other things she knew, too. She'd grown up an only child in an elegant home on the water, but her parents had long ago closed their hearts to anything other than their own cherished pain, and Arla knew this. Arla's house was cold, always, despite the elevated temperatures outside. Inside lived three people who were nothing, nothing at all, like a family.

Arla knew about loneliness. She knew about resignation. She knew about despair, and about the way her mother stared at her hands when her father was speaking. And Arla knew how she felt when Dean ran his hands down her body and breathed into her hair. He was terrifying and dangerous and wild. He was everything James was not. One night in the woods of Utina, as they lay naked on a worn burlap sack spread under a sweet gum tree, Dean told Arla he would die without her. "I will kill myself, Arla, I swear I will," he said, and she was moved by the power she held and frightened by the audacity of his devotion. She'd been wanted, desired, pursued all her life, but nobody had ever needed her like this. Nobody.

"You're giving up everything," Vera told her, the day Arla announced her engagement.

"I don't need everything," Arla said. "I know what I need." That night, Dean drove her south to Crescent Beach. They parked at the end of a dirt road and spread a blanket in the bed of his truck, where they clung to each other and gasped until the gnats and no-see-ums drove them up into the cab. There, she sat close to him in the darkness, listening. He promised a little house to tend, food in the pantry, babies in the bathtub, and love in every room. He promised.

The wedding was in September, with a full Mass at high noon in the Cathedral Basilica of St. Augustine. The bride wore an ivory silk A-line gown with a ruched bodice, an empire waist, and a chapel-length train. The groom wore a borrowed suit and a splash of Old Spice. The bride's mother wore a black veil of Italian lace.

James paid for all of it, but he had stopped looking his daughter in the eye. He walked her down the aisle and Arla took his arm awkwardly. She could not remember the last time she'd touched her father. She was embarrassed by the contact, the intimacy, the way he stiffened when her fingers closed around his elbow. It was a relief when they reached the chancel, and she could let him go.

At the altar, Dean was calm, his dark hair slicked smooth, his jaw clean-shaven and set. He was flanked by his brother Charlie on one side, best man by default given Huff's extended sentence in the Florida State Penitentiary, and his cousin Ronald on the other. Three Bravo men, the most the cathedral had ever seen.

"Do you?" the priest said to Arla.

"I do."

"Do you?" the priest said to Dean.

"Damn straight," Dean said, winking at Arla. Her breath caught at the sight of him, the way he looked right at her, that clear and perfect desire in his eyes, as if nobody else was there in the church watching. She thought briefly about disappointment and ruination and all the rest, but it was no matter. With Dean here before her, the world was a fine place, and life the prettiest adventure indeed.

*   *   *

The newlyweds booked a week's honeymoon on Lake June in Winter Haven, at a chalet perched on the south shore, just a short walk from a pizzeria and an outfit that rented water skis.

They stayed indoors for two days. On the second afternoon Dean left Arla napping and emerged onto the chalet's porch with a six-pack of beer and a slight limp. He worked his way through the beer, watching the boats and water-skiers, then stretched, squinted into the sun, and called back into the chalet to Arla.

"Let's do it," he said. He walked along the beach to the ski rental stand, where a pair of rumpled Cubans stood in the dappled shade of a Sabal palm, a rack of water skis parked behind them on a rusted trailer. Thirty feet away, a pair of motorboats bobbed in the lake.

"Morning," Dean said.

"Afternoon," one of the men replied. He was stocky and thick and looked at Dean with dislike.

"Is it now?" Dean said.

The Cubans looked at each other.

"You'll rent me a boat?" Dean said. "And some skis?"

They nodded. Dean paid them and walked over to one of the boats, a sixteen-foot Chris Craft with an oversize outboard. The stocky Cuban followed him. Dean looked up in time to see Arla picking her way up the beach. One hand held down an enormous straw hat. The other hand clutched a woven sarong at her hip. She was aware that Dean was watching, he could tell, and she moved in that sultry, theatrical way she had, slowing her pace just a bit, pausing, looking back over her shoulder and then advancing again, her chin held high. He wanted to eat her for lunch.

Instead, he helped her into the boat, watched her kick off her sandals, and handed her a pair of water skis. He climbed in behind the wheel.

"You got three?" the stocky Cuban said.

"What?" Dean said.

"You need three. One to drive, one to ski, one to spot." The man articulated carefully, counting off on his fingers.

"We got two," Dean said. "We'll be fine."

"You need one to spot," the Cuban said, looking at Arla. His eyes traveled over her bathing suit, across her breasts, down the one long leg emerging from the sarong. Her feet were perfect—angular and freckled, a dusting of fine sand coating her heels. Her toenails were painted a bright coral. "Somebody gotta watch her," the man said. The other Cuban snickered. "You wan' me come watch her?" he said. Dean fought the desire to climb back out of the boat and pummel the man. Instead, he started the engine.

"We're fine," Dean repeated, though he noted that Arla did not move her leg out of view. She gazed across the water, making no attempt to reposition her sarong. Dean grasped the wheel. His head buzzed. He waved off the Cubans. He pointed the bow northward and sliced out across the water.

"Oh, man," the stocky Cuban called out from the shore. "You need three, man."

The sun was hot on Dean's shoulders as he cut the engine and as the boat, now in the center of the lake, slowed to an idle. A dragonfly landed on Arla's knee, then flitted away again. Dean untangled the tow rope.

"This is pretty," she said mildly, looking across the lake.

"You ready?" he said, and he felt a twitch of adrenaline in his veins. Dean had never driven a boat with an outboard this size. He and Charlie had once liberated a dinghy from a yachtsman who'd had the misfortune to drop anchor in the Intracoastal just off Utina rather than pushing southward toward the more civilized waters of St. Augustine. They'd outfitted the dinghy with a pitiably small motor that they'd similarly liberated, but the dinghy could never do more than putter lamely along the water's edge. Dean had never water-skied. In Davis Shores, Arla's parents had belonged to the ski club. She'd grown up in a damp bathing suit amid the blended smells of cigarettes and martinis, salt water and coconut oil. She'd won a couple trophies in the local ski leagues.

"They're probably right," she said. "We should have a spotter."

"We're fine," he said, annoyed. "We don't need anybody else."

She looked at him for a moment. "All right," she said.

Dean shifted his weight, then moved toward Arla's feet and grasped them. He ran his hands up her calves. "Let's go," he said. "Let's see you."

"Let me get in first," Arla said. She pulled off the sarong in one quick movement and stood up to her full height, towering in the small boat before squatting again to stop it from pitching. She shimmied over the side into the water. "Oh!" she said, sounding childlike. "It's cold!"

Dean handed her the skis, and she slipped her feet inside the boots.

"Now start slow," she said. "Until I get up. Then you can go faster."

"Hang on," he said. He moved to the throttle and looked back.

Arla sat bobbing in the middle of Lake June, a ridiculous picture, the skis jutting out in front of her like cattails and her knees drawn up awkwardly. Her red hair flared against the water. Her breasts, straining against the bikini top, emerged, sank, reemerged, and she blew a thin spray of water out of her mouth and smiled.

"Okay!" she said.

Dean advanced the throttle. He moved slowly, watching the slack in the towline dwindle. "Get ready, Arla!" he shouted.

The line went taut, and she was up, moving, her full height traveling above the water, the look on her face triumphant and delighted. Dean shouted, waved to her. She nodded, clutched the rope, laughed.

He turned back to the throttle and gave it more power. The boat moved faster. Arla stayed up, her long white legs taut, shimmering, strong. She was gliding across the water like a bird now, her red hair extended behind her like plumage. Dean went faster. He was conscious of another boat on the lake, and he veered westward to give it a wide berth. He gunned the little boat's engine, felt the spray on his face and the buzzing in his head and the beer in his belly and the ache in his groin, and he pictured Arla behind him, flying, holding the rope that bound her to him—forever, forever, forever, this wild tropical bird, this strange, colorful, perfect girl who had given up everything and everybody to be with him. To belong to him. Mine, he thought. Mine.

When he glanced over his shoulder again she was gone. He stared stupidly for a moment, watching the tow rope's wooden handle dance like a water bug above the lake. He let off the throttle, spun the boat around. He could not see Arla. The lake was suddenly very quiet. The second boat, the one he'd been trying to avoid, bobbed in the distance, by now probably a half mile away.

"Arla!" he yelled. He puttered back in the direction he'd come. "Arla!"

After a moment, he saw her, a soft shape drifting like a sodden piece of fabric. Her hair fanned out into a crimson halo. She was waving at him.

Dean gunned the throttle again and raced toward her. She was bleeding from a gash above her eye, and her face was pale. The buzzing in his head intensified. One of Arla's skis floated, untethered, thirty yards away.

"I think I hit a piece of wood," she said. She was treading water with one bare foot, struggling to remove the other ski. "I can't get this ski off." Dean slowed his approach, but he overshot, moved past her, had to turn the boat around again to return to her. He finally pulled up alongside her and reached to pull her into the boat.

But he'd missed her again. His hands grasped air. She dipped under the water once and came up choking. Then she passed out, and her face slipped below the surface.

"Arla!" he screamed. "Arla!"

He spun the boat around a third time and tapped the throttle to move closer to Arla. He leaned out to reach for her again. The propeller was still spinning. His head was still buzzing. He thought he might throw up. He leaned farther out of the boat, reaching. With Dean's shift in weight, the stern tipped toward Arla, and then the boat jumped slightly—a blunted, soft jolt, as if the prop had made contact with something malleable.

He cut the engine, jumped in, and swam to Arla. He pulled her to the boat and dragged her up behind him, aware that he was operating with the bizarre strength of some sort of colossus, and yet when he lowered her body into the boat and heard her begin to sputter and cough, and when his eyes drifted down the length of her legs, past her ankles, to the place where something was wrong, and where the blood was beginning to fill up the bottom of the boat like bilge, he felt like a very, very weak man.

*   *   *

Her left foot had been cut in half. The tissue had been severed cleanly, but the bones had resisted, so that even after two hours in surgery the repair was sloppy, disordered, made difficult by the task of trying to organize a series of abbreviated metatarsals that had to be coaxed back into their rightful positions. What remained was a foreshortened adaptation of a foot, with a solid heel and enough extended musculature to be moderately useful for balance and posture, but not much use for unaided walking. A cane, if not a crutch, would always be in order. That's how the doctor explained it to Arla, and to Dean, the morning after the accident, when she awoke in a musty hospital room with a fat bandage on her forehead, a view of a commercial laundry out the window, and a pale version of Dean at her side.

The toes on her left foot itched terribly. She told Dean, but he looked at her and shook his head. She looked once at her bandaged stump of a foot and then did not look again.

"Did you call my parents?" she said.

"No," he said. She winced and shifted position.

"Where are they?" she said.

"At home, I suppose."

"I mean my toes," she said.

"Oh, them." He drew a breath. "I suppose they're at the bottom of Lake June by now, Arla," he said. "I guess we gotta consider them gone."

They were quiet then. The doctor signed the discharge papers, and then the nurse came along with a wheelchair and helped Arla get dressed. Arla looked into the bag that Dean had brought, and she saw her pink ballerina flats. And though she tried to ask the nurse for the pail, she didn't make it in time; she vomited all over the front of her best honeymoon sundress. Then she started to cry.

"Shhhhh," said the nurse. "Hush now, baby. Don't you take on so. They's only toes, you know."

Dean left the room, his footsteps fading as he strode down the hall to get the truck and bring his new wife home.

Vera wept when she saw Arla.

"My God," James said. His face was white. His hands shook. They stood in the middle of the newlyweds' rented efficiency off US1 in St. Augustine, staring at the peeling linoleum, the rusted range, their daughter's hideously fat, bandaged foot. Dean was at work. Arla sat in a rented wheelchair.

"How could you let this happen?" Vera said. "Oh, Arla, I can't cope."

"You don't have to cope," Arla said. "It's not your foot."

"Come back home," Vera said. "We'll take care of you."

Arla rolled across the kitchen, reached into a drawer for a bottle of aspirin, and shook two into her hand. She put the bottle back and rolled backward into the center of the room. "I am home," she said. "Dean will take care of me."

James shook his head. He looked at her again, and Arla saw the shift, saw the decision and the closure, so what he said next was less a surprise than a vaguely expected regret.

"This is madness," he said. "Self-destruction. I won't stand by watching." He walked to the door, then turned back. "Come home today," he said to Arla. "Or not at all. There's nothing we can do for you here."

"James," Vera said.

"No," he said simply. "No." He nodded at Vera. "I'll be in the car," he said. The doorframe was swollen with moisture, and he had to kick at it to get it to open. After a moment, Arla heard the car's engine roar to life and then settle to an idle.

"Arla," Vera said.

"I'm not coming home unless Dean comes with me," Arla said.

"Well, that's out of the question."

"Well, then."

Outside, James revved the engine. Vera walked over to Arla and bent to kiss her, but they connected awkwardly and bumped faces in a self-conscious way that left Arla's cheek unpleasantly damp with her mother's tears.

"Will you hand me a glass of water?" she said. She looked at the aspirin, flat on her palm.

"It hurts?" Vera said.

"It hurts," Arla said, though now she looked at her bandaged left foot in amazement, feeling the pain far beyond the flesh that remained, a throbbing pulse localized, impossibly, in her five missing toes. Phantom pain. She'd read about it. Hurting for something that wasn't even there.

"I'll call you tomorrow," Vera said. "He'll settle down."

Her tone was unconvincing. Arla did not reply. When her mother left the kitchen she squeezed her fists against her ears to drown out the sound of her parents' car revving angrily backward into the street.

That night, Dean announced it was time to buy a house. In Utina.

"Utina?" Arla said.

"It's where we belong, Arla," he said. They sat close together on the couch in the apartment's tiny living room, his fingers threaded through hers. When she turned to look at him, her damaged foot, covered in a thin sock, brushed his ankle, and he jerked his leg away, as if it burned.

"Who's we?" she said.

"We. Us. The Bravos," he said. And for the first time, she felt the weight of the name, felt it heavy and cold across her shoulders, around her chest, into her heart.

"What's wrong with St. Augustine?" she said.

"Utina," he said, and she was startled to hear that, although her hand was still warm in his, his voice was final and cold. She sensed an odd shifting of balance at that moment, a bobble in the dynamics of their relationship, and she felt something odd, something she'd never felt before. She felt cowed.

The house was a Queen Anne, once regal, built in 1927 by a reclusive sugar mogul from Miami who'd retired up to Utina after that God-awful Dade hurricane in 1926. The land he'd chosen had a pristine stretch of Intracoastal Waterway frontage and a thick cluster of slash pine and sweet gum trees, with a handful of showcase magnolia. The house was three stories, with a towering corner turret and a porch that circled the ground floor like a moat. Downstairs, a long hallway cut like a channel through the center of the house, past a cavernous living room and into an expansive kitchen overlooking the water. The middle floor had four bedrooms; the top floor had three. In all, there were five bathrooms in the house, though two of them had been locked and unentered since the toilets gave out years before. From the back porch, the view of the Intracoastal was unobstructed and commanding. If you sat on that porch, on the back of that house, you couldn't avoid looking at the water.

Which is what Dean was doing in October of 1964, five weeks after Arla's accident, on one of her first outings without the wheelchair. Arla was inside the house, talking to the owner, a soft-hearted widow who took a shine to Arla's red hair. "Oh, it's just like mine!" the widow said, though the old woman's hair was the color of dust and had the consistency of twine. "But my dear, what have you done to yourself?" She looked at Arla's left foot, wrapped tightly in a compression bandage, and at the thick wooden cane Arla clutched. The woman looked closer, saw the foreshortening of the bandaged foot, the odd blankness where there should have been the outline of five petite toes. She blinked rapidly, looked away.

Since her husband had died a decade earlier, the widow had not maintained the house. She had not swept the porch. She had not pulled the oak vines or the creeping jasmine off the siding. She had not sealed the leaks or fixed the rotting lumber at the foundation or replaced the collapsed steps of the front porch. She hadn't even been up to the third floor in several years, she confessed. "Oh, and I used to love it up there," she said. "You can see the tops of the magnolias outside the back bedroom. That's where all the pretty blooms are, you know, up at the top. But my knees are not so good," she admitted. "It's all I can do to get up the one flight. And really, maybe you shouldn't either, dear," the old woman said, glancing at Arla's foot, but her voice trailed off and she looked away again.

Arla was growing accustomed to people noticing her foot and then hastily looking away. She understood. She'd looked at her unbandaged foot only once since the accident. A week after it had happened, Arla had sat naked and cross-legged on the apartment's tiny bathroom floor. She'd slowly unfurled the long strip of bandages until her left foot, what was left of it, lay bare and iodine-stained across her right thigh. She'd examined it from every angle, noting the way the surgeon had carefully folded a flap of skin down across the ball of her foot like an envelope. She ran her finger along the thick, bloody stitches. She'd stared at it for more than an hour, until Dean had banged on the door and told her to come out. She'd rebandaged her foot, dressed herself, and opened the bathroom door. She would never look at her bare left foot again.

But Dean would. To Dean, Arla's foot was like a scab he couldn't stop picking. In the days after the accident, he changed the dressing on the wound, steeling himself for the vision of the mutilated foot with the bizarre curiosity of a rubbernecker. After the wound had healed, and even while Arla herself averted her eyes as she slid a sock over the stump every morning, Dean could not look away. He watched the stump crust, and then scar, and then atrophy into the unusable nub of flesh that would remain. And though in the beginning the sight of Arla's stump was a reminder of his own shortcomings, his own mistakes, his own catastrophically impaired judgment, over time it became, to Dean, simply a reminder of the general sting of failure, of pain, of dissatisfaction, and the lines began to blur for him as to who, exactly, was at fault for all that. His new bride was disabled, marred, truncated. He was pained by the wheelchair, embarrassed by the cane. He found her stoicism heroic at first, then mildly contrived, and—finally— purely indulgent, her silence about the accident and her obvious disability feeling like some sort of twisted hubris, some sort of pride that she hoisted on her shoulders, carried like a cartouche. He was shamed by her clomping gait, irritated by her limp. He wondered, at times, if she was exaggerating it. As often as not, the disability was a reflection of everything that was not perfect, after all, about Arla, despite his initial convictions to the contrary. In short, looking at Arla's foot, Dean felt cheated.

Now, in the strange, sad house off Monroe Road, Arla left the widow in the kitchen and slowly ascended the stairs to the third floor, leaning heavily on her cane. Her right foot did most of the work now, and she could manage to keep the pain in check as long as she didn't put too much weight on the tender stump of the left. On the third-floor landing, she peered into the darkness. Something scuttled along the baseboard, and as she heard the rumble of Dean's voice through the floorboards, talking to the widow, she felt a fear in her chest that had nothing to do with vermin.

She pushed forward, into the west-facing bedroom, where there was a view out to the waterway, just beyond a tangled mass of magnolia branches. The broad white flowers, which as the widow had said bloomed only at the top of the tree, had already begun to turn brown in the October sun, and they drooped piteously from the branches. We're too late, Arla thought. They're already dead. She limped back down the stairs.

"It's perfect," Dean was saying to the widow.

"Dean," Arla said. "Are we sure?"

"We want to make you an offer," he said to the widow.

"Dean," Arla said. He held up a hand.

"Well, all right," the widow said, slowly, looking at Arla. "If that's what you all want to do."

They took a mortgage and closed on the first of November. Vera sent a gift of monogrammed tea towels but didn't visit. "Daddy's got the conference in Atlanta," she said to Arla on the phone. "We leave tomorrow. I'll call when we get back." Arla hung up and looked at the tea towels. They were ecru linen with scalloped edges trimmed in blue floss. A scripted *B* was embroidered in the center of each towel. Arla remembered them as a thank-you gift to her father from a client. The *B* stood for *Bolton*. She tucked them into one of the moving cartons.

The day they moved into the Utina house, as Dean and his brother Charlie worked their way through a cooler of Budweiser and a pickup-truck-size load of secondhand furniture, Arla gripped her cane and limped to the edge of the property, feeling like an old woman at eighteen. Her first day in her first home as a married woman. She should have been happy. Instead, she was tired.

Alone on the bank of the Intracoastal, she looked out at the water, at the straight powerful current, the brown churning swells. While the land was relatively clear from the house down to the steep sandy bank of the waterway, on either side of the property, the underbrush was thick and almost impenetrable. Knee-high leathery palmettos blanketed the ground. Above, the winding oaks were laced with Spanish moss and resurrection fern, forming deep shadowy tunnels, spaces that looked like curtained chambers.

Arla looked back, saw Dean on the porch with Charlie. They did not see Arla down by the water. She jabbed her cane and rustled the thick palmettos to her right. "Everybody out," she said. "I'm coming in."

She walked slowly, carefully, watching for snakes, picking her steps around the protruding roots of the oaks and cypress that lined the waterway, moving deeper into the scrub until Dean was just a distant voice on the porch, not visible at all. She kept moving. Banana spiders bobbed in webs, suspended across Arla's path at eye level, and she raised her cane and moved the webs gently to the nearby trees. The water rushed by, twenty feet to her left, down a steep embankment encrusted with oyster shells and periwinkle snails.

She was alone. It was lovely in here. The hammock created a canopy above her head, long gray curtains of moss filtering the sun, a soft damp carpet of palms and oak leaves at her feet. Or, rather, her foot. One foot and one stump. She looked down at the stump, the once-white bandage wedged into an open sandal, now smudged with mud and dotted with sandspurs.

She walked on, five minutes, then ten. Something large and gray was parked under a tree, a stone or piece of wood, she could not tell, but it had a strangely uniform shape, too precise to be organic, almost hidden within a clump of palmettos. She poked at it with her cane. It was heavy, immovable, concrete. She whacked at the palmettos until they gave, pulled back the long fronds with her hands until she could see the stone, and her stomach jumped when she realized it was a grave marker, an inscription worn but readable across the front: DRUSILLA JANE ASHBY, 1821–1883, UTINA.

"Good Lord," Arla said. "And who are you?"

She looked around, clearing the brush with her cane, sweeping a wide circle around the headstone, but she could find no others. The marker was alone. She sat on a red cedar log and regarded it. It was odd, such a thing here, on private land, in this thick scrub cove. Could it be a real gravesite? Was it a prank? Drusilla Jane. Arla stayed on the log for a long time, regarding the headstone. The afternoon grew cooler and quieter, and she was lost within herself until she heard Dean calling her name.

"No, of course you're right," she said to Drusilla, surprising herself by speaking out loud, realizing now that she'd been having an unconscious conversation with the headstone. With Drusilla. "That's what I always say, too. Everything will be all right in the end. And if it's not all right, it's not the end."

Arla stared at the headstone for another moment. "I'm glad I found you, Drusilla," she said. "I'm sorry you're here, but I'm glad I found you." Then she stood and started back the way she had come. When she returned to the house, she found Dean and Charlie holding down lawn chairs on the back porch, a cooler of beer between them. Half the furniture still sat in the back of the truck. She said nothing to Dean or Charlie about the monument in the woods.

"Where you been?" Dean said. "We're getting hungry."

"You lookin' good, Arla," Charlie said, drunk. "You get sick of being married to my brother, you know where to find me." Dean slapped him on the head and reached for another beer.

That night, she and Dean made love in the darkened bedroom. Arla ran her hands along Dean's arms and across his back, and then she put her hands on his face, steadied him, tried to see in the faint light if his blue eyes were meeting hers, but he turned his head to the side and moved above her, breathing hard. "Dean," she whispered. "Shhhh," he said, and when he was finished he said nothing more and fell asleep. She pulled on her nightclothes, lay back, and blinked into shadows.

Then the terrible suspicion came to Arla again, as it had every night since the accident, but this time it was more than a suspicion. It was a conviction, a certainty, a truth as pure and unchangeable as gravity, and it was this: for the first time in her life, she was imperfect. And Dean, who had needed her for her perfection, would never need her again. It was so simple, so clear. He didn't need her. She stared at the ceiling and marveled at the colossal power of this understanding, how she knew, right here on these musty sheets at the age of eighteen, that the life she had known was over, and that she was, after all those years and all that evidence pointing to the contrary, nothing special at all.

Later, as Dean slept, Arla walked to the bathroom and looped her cane over an exposed pipe near the bathtub. A November nor'easter was blowing in, and the drafts ran unchecked through the house. She thought of Drusilla Jane, out in the dark windy scrub, friendless, alone. She would go see her tomorrow. Nobody should be all alone. And then Arla sat down on the toilet, stared at the crotch of her underwear, where there should, by now, have been a blooming red stain, but where there was only fresh white cotton. She stood up and pressed the flat of her hand into the soft flesh of her belly, pressed deep in, searching, until she felt it—a tightening, a gathering, a beginning.

JULY

ONE

A scrub jay cried outside, frantic for territory, or for love. Frank
Bravo turned over to squint at the clock on the bureau. It was 6:14
A.M. Saturday. Fourth of July. The alarm would buzz at 6:30; he
needed to get to the restaurant early to start prepping the holiday
rush. But now he rolled back and stared at the ceiling, thinking
of Elizabeth, about whom he'd just had a highly erotic dream. It
wasn't the sex that was lingering in the front of his brain, making
his vision foggy and his chest warm. It was the prelude, where
they'd met on a deserted high school football field—probably
Utina High, come to think of it—in the rain, and they had taken
each other's hands and run up into the bleachers. It was the
way they'd sat down, close together, only the bleachers had now
turned into the inside of a truck cab, and Elizabeth was in the
driver's seat, and the rain pelted the windows, and everything
smelled like jasmine. She'd turned to him. "It's time," she said.
"We've waited long enough." She brushed a wet strand of hair

off his forehead. That was the part that stuck with him, that part just before the sex. *Elizabeth*. His brother Carson's wife. Love, or territory. That was it, wasn't it?

"Shit," he said now. Gooch's collar jingled lightly as he picked his head up off the bed to regard Frank. "I said 'shit,'" Frank said. "But it didn't concern you." He thumped the dog's back. "And what are you doing on the bed, anyway?" It was a rhetorical question. Gooch, all sixty muttish pounds of him, had been sleeping on the bed every night for the past nine years. Gooch put his head back down, sighed a huge dog sigh, a sound like air escaping from compression brakes.

The day's first soft wash of light had begun to creep up the walls, and Frank waited for a moment, tried to let his eyes adjust. Outside the bedroom window, the jasmine *was* blooming. All of Utina was covered in it, in fact. Two miles away, at his mother Arla's house, the jasmine had been snaking up across the spindly porch railings all spring, pushing against the downstairs windows, looking for entry. He needed to cut it back before it rotted the siding even more than it already was, but every time he mentioned it Arla objected. "Leave it," she'd say. "It's beautiful."

"It's a nuisance," he'd reply, but she'd swish her hands at him and not let him cut it.

"It belongs here," she'd say.

At Frank's house, too, the jasmine grew in thick clumps all around the yard, and the cloying scent was making its way inside this morning, even though he'd kept the windows closed and the air-conditioning running since late April, when the Florida heat had descended like a guillotine and settled in to make itself comfortable until, Frank was sure, at least November. He could remember Thanksgivings spent swimming in the Intracoastal

Waterway behind his mother's house, Christmases spent sitting on Arla's porch in shorts and a T-shirt. Now he nudged Gooch to move over, then pulled the blanket tighter around his shoulders, thanking whatever God there was, once again, for the advent of air-conditioning. Without it, Frank was pretty sure life wouldn't be worth living. At least not life in Utina.

The red numbers on the clock glowed. Frank closed his eyes. A few more minutes. He tried to get back to the bleachers. The truck cab. Raindrops like diamonds on the windshield. But now came a new thought, a tiny nagging pull. The fryer. At Uncle Henry's Bar & Grill. Had he turned it off when he left the restaurant last night? He'd never in his life forgotten to turn off the fryer, and why this possibility had suddenly occurred to him he could not say. But he'd definitely slid his hand along the side of the machine and thrown the switch, and then, as an added precaution, pulled the power cord from the outlet on the way out the door. He always did. Didn't he? Oh, Jesus. He lay still, considered the implications of this.

The alarm finally buzzed. As his feet hit the wooden floor, the phone began to ring, and Frank was momentarily confused by the two competing noises. He swatted at the alarm to turn it off, then reached across the bureau and picked up the phone. "Hello?" he said.

It was Arla. He tensed, half-expecting her to report that the restaurant was indeed burning down. Given the proximity of Arla's house to Uncle Henry's, just a short walk through the woods, if the whole damn place burst into flames she'd be the first to know. But she made no mention of fire.

"It's your sister," she said. "She's at it again, Frank. She's on a tear." Arla exhaled, out of breath, and Frank could picture his mother clomping through the old house with the cordless phone in one hand and her wooden cane in the other. A sound like furniture being dragged came through the phone.

"Good morning to you, too, Mom," he said.

"Sofia!" Arla yelled, not bothering to move the mouthpiece away from her face so that the effect was something like a freight train hurtling through Frank's head. "She's after the Steinway, Frank," she said. "You better come."

He looked back over his shoulder at Gooch, who was now sitting up on the bed, all rumpled white fur and brown eyes. "Isn't it a little early for this?" he said. He yawned. Gooch scratched his left ear, then stood, shook, and bounded off the bed toward the kitchen.

"Yes, it is," Arla said. "And you can try explaining that to her when you get here." More furniture dragging. A clanging piano chord. "Sofia!" she said. "You'll break your fool back!"

The last, distant images of the dream with Elizabeth began to dissipate. *"It's time," she said. "We've waited long enough."* Frank's chest contracted again. He rubbed his eyes and took a deep breath, wondering if there was not, indeed, a faint tendril of smoke in the air. But it was only the jasmine—sweet, stubborn, and ubiquitous.

"I'll be out in a bit, Mom," he said. "Let me get some pants on."

"Hurry, Frank," she said. "My Lord. Do you know what it's like to have to wake up to this lunacy?"

He started to tell her that he, did, actually, have some idea. But she'd already hung up.

*   *   *

The light was growing brighter over the tops of the pines when Frank stepped out onto his porch and waited for Gooch to finish his morning toilette. He debated how much he needed to rush this morning. Although he'd checked the sky for signs of smoke in the direction of Uncle Henry's and had seen none, the problem of the fryer had not—in his mind—been adequately resolved. True, he could be relatively certain that the kitchen had not caught fire as of this moment. But if the fryer was still running from yesterday—he did a quick calculation—at least nineteen hours, that would make it—it could certainly overheat and spark a fire at any moment. And even if it didn't actually burst into flames, the odor of overheated grease and burning built-up carbon was going to have stunk up the restaurant damn good. It would take all day to air it out, and it was Fourth of July, one of the restaurant's busiest days of the year. He didn't have all day.

"Pick up the pace, Gooch," he said. Gooch glanced his way and walked farther out into the yard.

Frank regarded his property. The house was a compact bungalow, and the parcel of scrub it sat on grew thick and unchecked, as it had for thousands of years. A dusty driveway led up to the house from Cooksey Lane, and the porch was unadorned save for two unpainted rocking chairs he'd salvaged from the trash of a rich doctor's house in Ponte Vedra Beach, and his yellow kayak, suspended from the porch ceiling by two lengths of rope. Frank had bought the house in 1995 for next to nothing, and it still surprised him to be reminded—incessantly, in fact—by a real estate agent named Susan Holm, that his property value had actually increased. Significantly. Nearly every lot on his street was up for sale.

In fact, the property next door to his had already sold to a
corporate banker not a day over thirty. On it, a two-story house
was under construction, the new Mediterranean style, with
terra-cotta roof tiles, wrought iron balconies, and a four-car
garage. Frank wanted to gag every time he looked at it. The
banker, who told Frank he'd commute to Jacksonville from his
new house, came out every weekend in cargo shorts and ski
sunglasses to walk the perimeter of his property and observe
the progress of construction. He'd supervised the clear-cutting
of the entire lot and the painstaking laying of thick sod that
spread like a noxious green carpet and stopped abruptly at
Frank's property line. One Saturday the banker had broached
the idea of sharing the cost of a tall fence between the two
properties' backyards.

"What do I need that for?" Frank had asked.

"For privacy," the banker had said, looking around at
Frank's land, where the palmettos grew thick and unrestrained
and the catbrier weed threaded through the oak branches. "And
maybe to keep your dog in," he added, looking at Gooch, who
had in recent weeks developed a preference for fresh sod for
his daily constitutional.

But Frank had declined.

The fence went up anyway, on the banker's dime, and now,
instead of the thick curtain of green Frank had enjoyed for so
many years, when he stepped out his back door he was confronted with an eight-foot-high wall of pressure-treated stockade
crap encircling the banker's backyard. Every time he looked at it,
he felt violated. He'd redirected a few sprigs of climbing kudzu to
the base of the fence and took some small satisfaction in watching them begin to inch up the boards and around the posts, but

it was taking a long time, and he was disgusted, so after a while he simply quit looking in that direction.

There were a lot of directions he'd quit looking in.

Somewhere, not too far to the east, a bottle rocket screeched. Already? Sun not even fully up over the pines and already the revelers were getting going, probably unpacking their long-hoarded stockpiles of illegal fireworks, lining up the empty beer bottles and filling them with bottle rockets and Roman candles, throwing cherry bombs and M-80s into the woods. Frank knew the drill. Fourth of July in Utina. If they were setting off fireworks at dawn, they'd be drinking by noon. Which meant they'd be half-polluted by this afternoon. By the time they got to Uncle Henry's.

He climbed into the truck and headed for town. And for coffee. Whatever was going on at Arla's house was just going to have to wait until he'd gotten some caffeine into his system.

The town of Utina, perched on the eastern bank of an uncharacteristically straight stretch of the Intracoastal, was an old man, testy and gray, with little patience for fashion and a stalwart commitment to function over form. The town was broken into distinct halves—South Utina, a rambling journeyman's neighborhood of small lots and uninspired Victorian homes that had never been much of anything to begin with and were even less today; and North Utina, where Frank's and Arla's houses both sat and where the homes were fewer, the land was largely unchecked scrub, and the residents were more Florida Cracker than American citizen.

Whereas North Utina was where Frank's great-grandfather Alger Bravo and his fellow moonshiners had lived, back in the day, South Utina was where the market had thrived, with poor whites and blacks living side by side for decades more through pure economic necessity than any idealistic racial harmony. Didn't *nobody* have money in Utina, people said, no matter what color you were. You had money, you went to St. Augustine or Jacksonville, pure and simple.

North and South Utina were separated by the town's main road, Seminary Street, which was once a dusty one-track trail leading out of the woods to a humble Spanish mission at the water's edge. The name evolved years after the mission had disintegrated, when the structure was clumsily mis-remembered by Utinians, who neither knew about nor cared for subtle points of distinction between a mission and a seminary. Now, Seminary Street was a quarter-mile stretch of potholes that began at Sterling's Drugstore and ran due west down a gentle slope into a concrete boat launch at the Intracoastal, which meant a man who'd been bending his elbow for a while at the Cue & Brew, a block back from the boat ramp, could drive straight into the drink without expending much effort at all. And some had.

Perhaps it was their birthright, Frank thought. After all, Utina, inauspiciously named for the chief of a tribe of doomed Timucuan Indians, had been known historically for two things: palms and booze. The palms, at least, were an honorable venture, destined for Palm Sunday services across the country. The orders came in the fall and early winter, and the enterprising and godly residents of Utina (and there were a few, back then) got to work. They cut palm leaves by the thousands, bound them, bundled them, and loaded them up on the East Coast Railroad at nearby Durbin Station. It was a booming and profitable venture, with the added benefit of a beneficent and sacred purpose. It was God's work, after all.

But even God can appreciate a bargain. So when the palms of Utina fell victim one year to an unseasonably late frost just a few weeks before Lent, church buyers around the country turned their attention to a new palm outfit in Tampa, and there was nothing for Utina to do but sit back and give up the ghost, at least as far as the palms were concerned. This was back in 1929, and when the pious lit out for more civilized territory, Alger Bravo, newly arrived from St. Augustine, led a handful of felonious stalwarts in turning to the only other prohibition-era industry that made a lick of sense in a thickly wooded Florida hideaway on the banks of a marine highway with a straight shot to the thirsty coastal towns of Georgia, South Carolina, and beyond.

Moonshine made money—real money—but it was a short-lived success for Utina. Just when Alger and his cronies had gotten the complexities of production and distribution as close to fine-tuned as they were likely to get, Uncle Sam repealed pro-hibition and the pendulum of supply and demand swung wildly out of Utina's grasp and back into the waiting clutches of Jim Beam, Jack Daniel's, and Anheuser-Busch, whose industrialists had been sitting on their asses and making ice cream and barley syrup for the past thirteen years. By Christmas 1933, Alger Bravo had married, fathered three children, burned down his stills, and drunk himself spectacularly into an early grave. Bereft of a captain, Utina had once again thrown up its hands, heaved a collective sigh, and settled into a posture of civic and economic lassitude that became, over the years, a communal chip on the shoulder of the surviving Bravos and indeed the entire town. The main line of reasoning, Frank had gathered, was that prosperity was a train that simply hadn't bothered to stop here, and there wasn't any use chasing a train on foot. So fuck it.

But even the unprosperous had to eat, shop, pray, and drink somewhere. Alger's children grew and settled, and the poor whites and blacks who'd been drawn to Utina for the moonshine stuck around for the fishing and the newly reopened bars and package stores, so the business district of Utina had grown lazily, stubbornly through the years. Eventually downtown Utina consisted of some two dozen small storefronts and businesses along the three-block stretch of Seminary Street. Sterling's Drugstore to the east, which faced the stoic white clapboards of the First Baptist Church on the other side of the street, shared a crumbling roofline with People's Guarantee Bank before giving way to a rambling string of businesses that culminated at a Lil' Champ convenience store, just adjacent to the boat ramp.

It was a town, Frank thought now, as he idled at the stoplight at Seminary and Cooksey, that time had largely forgotten, though he had to admit there'd been some changes in the last five years. New paving and a wider shoulder on County Road 25, which connected Utina to the beach seven miles to the east. A Walgreens springing up just a few blocks from Utina High. More than a few Prudential Realty signs stuck in the yards of homes in South Utina, and a convoy of Hondas and Nissans making their way down from Jacksonville and up from St. Augustine on weekends to troll the streets, expensively casual couples wielding cups of Starbucks coffee, peering out car windows and calculating property taxes, homestead exemptions, and the distance to the ocean. And *this*—he squinted through the windshield this morning and across the intersection, where the whole southeast corner of Seminary and Cooksey had been clear-cut to make room for a fancy new Publix supermarket. Already the frame was in place, already a three-acre parking lot was staked.

Publix in Utina. It was hard to believe, though it *did* make some sense, he admitted. All of Utina, including Frank's own wooded lot, was within a ten-minute drive to the Atlantic. And much of Utina, including his mother Arla's house and Uncle Henry's, the adjacent family restaurant he managed, fronted the steep shady banks and clear deep-water channel of the Intracoastal. There were moments when it appeared that the village might actually hold some appeal to buyers looking for dwindling slices of Florida real estate. There were even moments when it appeared to Frank that, for once, something owned by the Bravo family might hold some merit, monetary or otherwise. But who knew? History painted a different picture. Part of him could envision the Publix in five years, vacant and failed, snaking kudzu and catbrier weed strangling the whole ambitious venture. Utina's tomorrow, more than likely, would be no different from Utina's yesterday. "Because you can't polish a turd," he said aloud. Gooch looked at him, then yawned. You just make a mess trying, Frank thought, idling at the light, headed for Arla's, groggy and annoyed and waiting for a change.

Ten minutes later, Frank stood in the center of the Lil' Champ, cursing his luck and hiding from Susan Holm. He crouched behind an aisle of shelves filled with bags of potato chips, pretzels, and pork rinds, and he peered out the front window, where Susan was jogging, making her way down Seminary Street toward the boat ramp, a long blond ponytail bouncing behind her. Frank knew from maddening experience she would run to the end of the rickety dock, stop, look left and right up the expanse of the Intracoastal, and then pivot and jog back up the street toward home. She executed the same ritual every morning, without fail, and why Frank had not had the sense to wait until after he knew she'd be safely ensconced back in her apartment over Sterling's Drugstore before he came to the Lil' Champ he didn't know.

Another thing he didn't know, couldn't quite put his finger on, was why he was always trying to avoid her, had in fact been trying to avoid her since she'd made her unsolicited devotion to him known in elementary school. She was, by any measure, one of the most attractive single women in town, and most of Utina's male population would have given considerably to be on her radar screen in any capacity. Frank was on her radar screen—no doubt. And he'd acted on it, too, on more than one occasion, the most recent having taken place last Friday following three sloppy pitchers of beer at Uncle Henry's after closing. Susan had sat on his lap and had eventually convinced him to come back to her place, where the sex was jubilantly, enormously entertaining, but where the morning had brought with it an oversize portion of regret and apologetics, at least as far as Frank was concerned. She'd been good-natured about it, told him to come back for a rematch, anytime, but for Frank, Susan's persistent propositions in matters of real estate, and in matters of a more personal nature, made him uncomfortable. It was ridiculous, he sometimes thought, that he didn't settle down with her. She'd be doing him a favor. He watched her running. She was beautiful. She could do better. She turned around at the end of the dock and began running back toward the Lil' Champ. He took a step to the left, made sure his head was concealed behind a tall rack of Flamin' Hot Cheetos.

Of course, there was always the chance Susan would notice Frank's truck in front of the store and stop in to corner him, but with Susan, once she was in motion, tiny white iPod earbuds dangling from her ears, you could count on a certain amount of blindness. A blue truck, to Susan, was simply a blue truck, and she'd generally fail to make the obvious connection that the truck had an owner, and that the owner of the particular blue truck parked outside the Lil' Champ today was Frank Bravo, the man who owned or had great influence over no less than three of the properties in Utina she'd most like to list. As if to prove this point, Susan jogged past the truck without a second glance. Gooch, seated in the cab, watched her pass, but did not attempt to attract her attention. Good boy, thought Frank.

"Ain't nice to avoid people." The voice was Tip Breen's, and it came from where the man slouched, elbows on the counter, one hamlike hip wedged against the cash register and the other precariously balanced on a straining wooden stool. Tip had owned the Lil' Champ for the better part of the last two decades. He'd lived in Utina all his life, a hometown poster boy, for Christ's sake, master of inertia from day one, though he'd somehow managed to graduate Utina High with Frank's older brother, Carson. Frank had often noted with displeasure that, given the unfortunate fact that the Lil' Champ had always been the only place in downtown Utina to buy a few simple groceries and a cold six-pack, he'd been subjected to Tip's questionable etiquette advice for pretty much half his life. When stopping in for a cup of coffee and a doughnut from the Plexiglas case next to the lottery tickets, Frank should have known that this morning would be no different.

"What are you doing, avoiding that fine piece-a-ass?" Tip asked, with characteristic grace. He was an enormous man, fat in the thighs and hips like a woman, eyes red-rimmed and wet, a strangely boyish thatch of straw-colored hair protruding from beneath a soiled ball cap. In school he'd been a moose, thick necked and powerful, but his physique had melted southward over the years, leaving him lumpy and pear shaped, rolls of belly barely concealed beneath dingy T-shirts and elastic-waist shorts. It was terrible. Tip grinned, showing off the gaping space where he'd had an incisor knocked out back in 1989 when, fully loaded at 2:00 A.M. on a Sunday morning, furious over last call, he'd tried to gain entry to the Cue & Brew through a roof vent and had instead become intimately acquainted with the asphalt pavement of Seminary Street.

"I'm not avoiding anybody, Tip," Frank said. "If I was, believe me, you'd be first on the list."

"Awww," Tip said. "Sweet. Somebody got up on the wrong side of the bed this morning."

Frank filled a Styrofoam cup with weak-looking coffee. He fished two Krispy Kremes out of the case, slipped them into a waxed paper bag, and approached Tip at the register.

"Why don't you talk to her?" Tip said, staring out the window again at Susan Holm's receding backside, which was now running east up Seminary Street. Tip made no move to ring up Frank's purchases. "Tell her to quit selling Utina to the damn yuppies. She wants to sell your properties, you know. And I guess you *would* make a fucking mint."

"I have talked to her," Frank said. "I've talked to her plenty."

Tip shook his head, pulled his gaze back from the store window. "I'll bet you have," he said. Then he changed direction.

"When's Carson coming up here?" he demanded. "Me and him, we gotta go fishing or something." Frank raised an eyebrow but did not reply. He was quite sure that his brother had no intention of going fishing with Tip Breen anytime in the immediate or distant future. He couldn't even remember the last time he himself had gone fishing with Carson. But Tip had already forgotten he'd asked the question.

"You hear who's running for sheriff?" he said abruptly.

"Don't tell me," Frank said, raising his eyebrows.

Tip jerked a fat thumb toward a pile of campaign signs propped against a rack of porn magazines behind him. The signs were designed in a bold red-white-and-blue star motif, and in the middle of the largest star read the candidate's slogan: DONALD KEITH! FOR SHERIFF!

"Jesus," Frank said. It was hard not to laugh.

For nearly as long as Frank could remember, Officer Donald Keith had harbored a personal vendetta against the Bravo boys of Utina and their associates, namely Mac and George Weeden and occasionally, when they could tolerate his company, Tip Breen. Donald Keith was ten years older than Frank, which meant that just when Keith was eking out a career in law enforcement as a rookie cop on the City of St. Augustine police force, before he made the switch to the county beat, Frank, Carson, and their younger brother Will were beginning to act upon their birthright in the areas of reckless endangerment, criminal mischief, and brilliantly wrought misconduct. They were their father's sons, after all. But these were issues of lineage and fierce, if questionable, familial pride that held no water with Donald Keith. *Do-Key*, they called him then, enjoying the pleasing rhyme with *donkey* and the added connotation of "dookie" the nickname brought with it. When the Bravo boys, bored and looking for entertainment, wandered south of Utina into the Oldest City's jurisdiction, they generally guaranteed themselves a tangle with Do-Key, which was, Frank admitted, probably the real reason they went there in the first place. St. Augustine. It was a righteous old place, by God, proud and pristine, but that didn't mean it didn't need its cage rattled now and again.

The first time they met him, they'd come down to St. Augustine from Utina through a thunderstorm: the three Bravo brothers, Frank and Carson still in high school, Will in junior high. They'd been driving around downtown with a box of bottle rockets, waiting for the rain to stop, past the Fountain of Youth and the antique shops and the hallowed grounds of the Catholic mission. When the rain eased up they opened the windows to throw jeers at the costumed conquistadors at the city gates and whistle at the coeds at Flagler College. They cruised the plaza and circled back through the narrow lanes behind the Spanish Quarter, growing hotter and more restless by the minute. Finally the clouds cleared and they ended up, panting and damp with sweat, in the parking lot of Ripley's Believe It or Not! Odditorium, where the wet asphalt steamed. And then, after a while, Officer Donald Keith showed up, evidently to represent the interests of those neighbors who objected to bottle rockets being launched from Ripley's up to the bastions of the Castillo de San Marcos.

"Move on, kiddos," Keith had said condescendingly. "Take your little games elsewhere."

"Okay, Do-Key," Carson said, looking at the cop's name tag.

Keith's face had darkened, and he looked from Frank to Carson and Will and then back to Frank again.

"You get your asses out of here, boy," Keith said.

"I'll try, sir," Carson said, twisting his back and looking over his shoulder in a comic effort to regard his own backside. "But I tell you, I've only got the one."

Do-Key won that round. He kicked the unlit rockets into a puddle and hustled them out of the parking lot. Oh, but how many little dances had the Bravos shared with Keith after that? Do-Key chasing them down after Utina High beat St. Augustine at homecoming and the Bravo boys had celebrated with four boxes of Tide poured into the Fountain of Youth; Frank and Carson decorating the back of Do-Key's cruiser with Care Bear stickers; Do-Key once getting the upper hand by catching them in the act of stealing a six-pack from the Winn-Dixie and slapping them with a fat list of charges, from breaking and entering to disorderly conduct, but then the Bravos regaining their advantage when the judge threw the case out on the technicality that Do-Key had forgotten to sign the arrest report. Each skirmish was a brilliant battle in an epic war.

The score had been approaching even in the spring of 1984, the night before Easter, when it was already hot as hell and only April, still the long scorching summer licking like flames before them. Frank, Carson, Will, and their buddy Mac had been fishing, just *fishing*, for Christ's sake, in a beautiful little estuary behind the Nombre de Dios mission in St. Augustine, where the shadow of a two-hundred-foot bronze cross fell across the reeds and spared them, blessedly, from the sizzling rays of the evening sun. The fishing was glorious there, always. The Holy Hole, they called it, where every time they cast a line they pulled back a fat, wriggling crappie or bass, no more than a minute's wait every single time. They caught so many fish they couldn't even keep them all. It was perfect. Then along had come Do-Key, ready to put the kibosh on everything.

"You can't fish here," he'd said. His uniform was taut across his belly, and he bent his knees a fraction to adjust his crotch as he stood in front of them.

"Why not?" Carson said.

"Because it's private property."

"Isn't it God's property?" Carson said, gesturing at the mission behind them, the tiny chapel of Our Lady of La Leche crouching in the shade of the live oaks. "I called God," he continued. "He said we could fish here."

"Don't be a wiseass," Do-Key said. "I'm not in the mood."

"Rough day?" Frank said. "Dunkin' Donuts close early?"

"I'm busy, you little prick," the cop said. "We got the Easter parade coming through here in the morning, and I got bigger things on my mind than you little Bravo shits. Otherwise I'd bust your ass downtown so fast that . . ." He trailed off, seeming to lose sight of the hyperbole he'd planned to use. "So fast," he concluded.

"You riding in the parade?" Carson asked.

"I'm driving the mayor, butt-head," Do-Key said, and Frank had smiled inwardly, noting how the cop could not resist boasting that he'd been handed this prestigious task, to drive St. Augustine's mayor in one of the most well-attended events in the city. Driving the mayor in the parade was a big deal, no doubt, for any city cop looking for advancement and recognition. Even Frank could see this, and he noted the way Do-Key's chin jutted up just a tad when he made the announcement.

"Congratulations," Frank said, almost sincerely. "Congratulations, Do-Key."

Carson snickered, and Will elbowed Mac.

"You call me that one more time and all bets are off, Bravo," Do-Key said. "I am an officer of the law, and I've had about all I can take from you little pieces of white trash. Now get your sorry asses off this property. Go on back up to the woods where you belong."

"I still don't understand why we can't fish here," Carson said, but he threw the last crappie back into the Holy Hole and snapped his tackle box closed.

"Because it's not allowed," Do-Key said. "No fishing. No loitering. No assholes."

Frank sighed. "Officer Keith," he said. "Why are you always so negative?"

They left the Holy Hole and sat under the Vilano Bridge for a few hours, sharing half a bottle of Crown Royal and plotting their next move. They were only a little drunk, but it was drunk enough, as it turned out, because by midnight they were in the dark parking lot of the St. Augustine Alligator Farm, staring at the eight-foot wooden fence that encircled the park, debating the need for a ladder. By the time they emerged from the park, wrestling a four-foot gator, his mouth tenuously clamped shut with Will's leather belt, into the bed of Carson's truck and arguing over who would have to sit back there with it, they were tired, dirty, and sweating like livestock. So they parked the truck at the end of a quiet lane on Fish Island and napped a bit, though Mac, who'd drawn the short straw and was sharing a pickup bed with an irritable alligator, complained later that he didn't get a wink.

Before dawn, they drove across the Bridge of Lions to the St. Augustine police station, where the lights were on inside the precinct and the parking lot was full of cruisers. They positioned Mac and Will as lookouts for officers who might leave the morning briefing early. Then Frank and Carson located Do-Key's car, worked a little magic with a slim jim, and deposited the pissed-off, wriggling, shit-covered alligator into the front seat. The gator thrashed mightily across the upholstery for a few minutes, doing God-knows-what kind of damage to instruments and official-looking police equipment before settling down with a groan across the center console, its now-unbound jaw resting precisely on the driver's seat.

Oh, it was beautiful. Epic. The best move they'd ever pulled. The thunderstruck look on Do-Key's face when the briefing dismissed, when he came out at dawn to get into the cruiser for his big day with the mayor. The howls from the other cops, the way even the commanding officer grinned, stood with his hands on his hips and stared at Do-Key's car, where by now the alligator had renewed its efforts toward escape and was methodically thwapping its tail against the cruiser's windshield, a thick smear of mud and dung being deposited on the window with each contact. The way Do-Key had turned around in the parking lot, his face like stone, peering in every direction into the pale light of the dawn, searching for the Bravo boys, the only shit-heads who possibly could have pulled this off. They knew it, and Do-Key knew it. But they were well under cover, watching the entire proceeding from the rooftop of the building next door, Carson's truck tidily obscured four blocks to the south. When the other officers dispersed to begin the parade preps and Do-Key still stood, scratching his head, wondering what to do about his unwanted passenger, the boys slunk away, breaking into a run once they'd cleared the vicinity, laughing, hysterical, jumping into Carson's truck and peeling out of St. Augustine, back up A1A to the thickly wooded roads of Utina, where the morning's light was now coming hot and sharp through the trees, where the fog was dissipating like smoke, rising like a ghost through the hammock.

They'd laughed so hard Frank thought he'd be sick. At home they ran behind the house and jumped into the Intracoastal fully clothed, washing away the sweat and the alcohol and the alligator shit. Arla came out to the concrete picnic table and stared at them, angry at first, asking where they'd been all night, but even she was taken with the levity of their moods and the sheer lunacy of their laughter, the beautiful abandon of their young bodies floating in the tide.

"You boys," she'd said. "Mac Weeden, don't let your mama blame this on me." But she smiled, and Frank watched how her gaze lingered longest on Will, on his sweet, wet, round face, the way he blew a spray of water from his mouth, the way he clung to Frank there in the current, holding on like an infant, in love and in fear and in awe of it all. "Frank the Prank!" Will said. "You struck again!" *Will*. He was fifteen.

Now, Frank's coffee threatened to grow cold in the cup while Tip stared out the Lil' Champ's window, watching Susan Holm, and Frank could almost see Tip's brain slide back from his reference to Do-Key's campaign to their previous topic of conversation: Susan's ass. "It was me, I'd do more than *talk* to her," Tip said. "You know what I'm saying?" The absurdity of this observation, coming from Tip, who was no doubt the last man in Utina Susan *would* talk to, much less touch, was almost enough to make Frank smile.

"Tip, I'm in a hurry. You going to take my money, or what?" Frank said. He placed a five-dollar bill on the counter and waited. At the Lotto stand, two tiny, gray-haired women were penciling in numbers on a long sheet of paper, and Tip glanced at them, then leaned in to Frank conspiratorially. "Susan comes in, you want me to tell her I haven't seen you?"

"You haven't seen me, Tip."

"What?"

"You haven't seen me."

"That's what I said."

"Because I'm not here," Frank said.

Tip blinked. "Well, you *are* here. But I'll tell her you aren't. I mean, weren't."

"Right. Unless of course, I was." Frank gave up waiting for Tip to ring him up. He put the five-dollar bill into a tip jar on the counter and fished out two singles, leaving Tip staring at him in complete confusion. "I gotta go, Tip," he said. "Make sure you've got me covered now, hear?"

Outside, he glanced to the right and saw the back of Susan's lime green T-shirt still moving east along Seminary Street. Up the road at the First Baptist Church, the marquee had a new message: JESUS WROTE A BLANK CHECK. CASH YOURS TODAY!

Frank climbed into his truck and started the engine. He peered at the sky in the direction of Uncle Henry's. Still no smoke, but he caught sight of a faint trail of sparking light behind the trees as a Roman candle climbed fifty feet into the air and then sailed back, defeated. Pitiful. They ought to have been able to get it to launch higher than that. He pictured the amateur pyrotechnicians who were probably standing around a cinder block at that moment, setting up the rockets and trying to get the angle right before lighting the fuses and shuffling backward. It was all in the angle. Get the bottle set up correctly, get the angle of the launch just right, and you could get those sons of bitches to sail eighty, sometimes a hundred feet or more. Beautiful. But he hadn't set off a bottle rocket in years. Maybe decades.

When he was a kid he loved Fourth of July. Loved the recklessness, the noise and heat of it. Once he'd watched a fireworks display from the top of a mountain in western North Carolina. They'd been staying in a cabin near Cullowhee—all of them: Arla, Dean, Sofia, Carson, Will, himself. It was the first and only time he remembered a vacation with his family. Dean had scored the cabin as a bonus for working on a relief team servicing an exploded boiler in Asheville. The plant's owner had put the techs up in vacation cabins to keep their minds off the fact that they were, in effect, rebuilding the deadly weapon that had killed seven men two weeks before, and though Dean had returned to the cabin each night looking pale and drained, the rest of them had had a fine time, an unexpectedly buoyant time, in fact. They'd been teenagers, all of them, Will maybe thirteen at best, and Frank had loved the mountains and the cabin so much, loved the soft cool grass under his feet every morning, the water so cold in the creeks it hurt the bones in his feet. He'd never imagined water so cold. He'd never felt it since.

The Cullowhee cabin was at the crest of a mountain, and on the Fourth of July Dean had the day off from the boiler repair. They all drove into the valley to eat breakfast and buy bait, and then they parked the Impala back at the cabin and hiked through a narrow path to a deep rushing creek, where the rhododendrons hung like lace curtains along the banks and the stones clicked like castanets in the licking current. On the hike they took turns walking with Arla, holding her cane and helping her maneuver the steeper descents. When they reached the creek they got the bait wet for a while but caught nothing, so finally Frank and his brothers whooped and belly flopped into the ice-cold creek, taunting and daring the others until all of them—Dean, Sofia, even Arla!—held their breath and dunked their heads under water so frigid Frank thought he'd have a heart attack. Then they sat on a huge flat rock in the sun, hearts pounding, close together, waiting for their bodies to warm again.

That night Arla barbecued chicken and corn and cut up a watermelon, and then they stood on the back deck and looked down through the trees into the valley below, where the little downtown was setting off a fireworks display. They watched, waited, heard the distant whistle of each shell's launch far below the pine-covered mountain. But the fireworks couldn't reach them. Again and again, the shells burst before they breached the cloud cover hovering in the valley, and Frank remembered how his entire family had been annoyed at first, disappointed, but had eventually grown silent, awed, as the clouds were lit from below with a shuddering, diffused arc of color. He felt they were privy to a private vision, an exquisite misfire. The skyrockets never did break through the clouds; instead, the colors spread out low and soft through the mountains, like fire behind gauze, like lightning through rain. The vantage was a gift, rare and unexpected. It was one of the most beautiful things Frank had ever seen. They remained silent for long moments that stretched into minutes as the clouds flickered again and again—red, blue, yellow, green, orange.

"We're above it all," Will said, finally. "We're above the explosions."

"Can you beat that?" Dean said. He had a bottle of beer in his hand but he backed up to the table behind him, set the beer down and came back to the railing. He put his hand on Arla's shoulder, and she let him.

"I want to come back here," Will said, leaning into Frank, and Frank could feel the warmth of his two brothers' shoulders against his own. "I want to live here. Don't you, Frank?"

Frank drew a cool breath, felt the rush of it in his lungs. He looked at Will. "Yeah," he said. "I do." Will grinned, leaned in closer.

And then the valley exploded in color again, and the light came soft through the clouds, and the Bravos watched the thwarted fireworks together. In the foreground, the trees were straight and narrow, like bars, but beyond and below, the clouds swelled and the very mountain shook from the effort of holding down the great rainbow explosions.

That was a long time ago. A lot of Fourths ago. Now, in front of the Lil' Champ, Frank fished into the wax bag and fed one Krispy Kreme to Gooch and then, on second thought, gave the dog the other doughnut as well.

"You might as well," he said to Gooch, who responded by thumping his tail against the back of the truck's bench seat. "I can't eat that shit." Indeed, his stomach had begun to gnaw at itself with the familiar malaise that he'd been growing steadily accustomed to for the past few months, a feeling like hunger that did not respond to food, a feeling like corrosion, like decay, like dread.

He started the truck, drove toward Aberdeen.

Two

The Bravo family house was in North Utina off Monroe Road, which led northward off Seminary Street, out of Utina's business district. The road twisted and turned as it wound deeper and deeper into a tangle of ancient Florida hammock and sagging clapboard houses, farther into the woods until it came to the banks of the Intracoastal, to the towering shape of Aberdeen.

Aberdeen. Shortly after Frank's parents had moved into the big house, his father had named it. Dean had always *wanted* to live in a house with a name, and this one had the personality and austerity to warrant it, even if it was more than a little rough around the edges. It stood like a sentry on the Intracoastal, a towering structure at three stories high, with a spindly turret climbing the northwest corner. Once a vibrant blue, the house had faded over the years to a gunmetal gray, with dark patches of green mildew under the windows, an effect not unlike the kohl eyeliner of an Egyptian queen, or, depending on the light, an aging hooker.

The funny thing is that the name stuck. With a vague notion of some faraway Gaelic adventure, and because he'd seen the word once in a magazine and liked the feel of it, Dean called the house Aberdeen, and so did everyone else, even today, twenty years after Dean had run out on his family and left Aberdeen and Utina for what everyone assumed was forever.

With the name, the house, once just a house, became something like a person. Which was a weight, it occurred to Frank as he pulled down the long, pine-lined driveway, that he'd never fully considered. Most people just dealt with *houses*—buying, selling, fixing, razing. But Frank had to deal with *Aberdeen*. He parked, looking up at the front of the house. The jasmine was as unruly as ever, and now an aggressive sweet potato vine had begun to thread through the floorboards on the porch. The screening on one of the windows was torn. A gap under the front door revealed the pale light of a lamp inside the hall. Frank sighed. He thought, not for the first time, about lighting a match to the whole thing. It was the only sensible thing to do.

He drained the last of his coffee and stepped out of the truck. Gooch followed, tail wagging, having spotted the enormous frame of Biaggio Dunkirk, Aberdeen's tenant, caretaker, and chief referee, walking up the drive.

"Saw you pull up," Biaggio said, holding up a hand to Frank. This was no surprise. Biaggio's trailer was parked fifty yards in from the road, on the south edge of the Aberdeen property, and it was, in fact, impossible for anyone to drive up the long driveway to the Bravo house without being spotted by Biaggio, if he was home, which he usually was, and if he was seated on the steps of his trailer, which he usually was. Frank clapped Biaggio on the shoulder, feeling glad, as always, to see him.

Biaggio Dunkirk was one of those West Virginia corn-fed badasses who'd seen the inside of a jail cell more than the high school cafeteria. But by the time he hit forty, lit out for Florida to avoid a petty theft sentencing, and moved into the trailer on the Bravo property, he'd decided enough was enough. He'd settled down to a quiet life of peace and the systematic avoidance of extradition, at least until the statute of limitations ran out. Biaggio earned his living as a self-employed moving man, growing busier by the week as fresh arrivals moved into the new homes and developments springing up around and through Utina. And he enjoyed—if you could call it that—a modestly paid but rent-free position at Aberdeen which he'd brokered with Frank in exchange for keeping a general eye out for Arla, Frank's older sister, Sofia, and the ongoing decay of the old house, which, as Biaggio put it, was less an actual *house* at this point and was more a concerted effort of termites holding hands. They'd struck the deal while bobbing down Pablo Creek more than a decade ago in a leaky canoe, a cooler of freshly caught redfish between them, and Biaggio had moved into the trailer the next week. The arrangement was no bargain for Biaggio, if you asked Frank, but Biaggio didn't seem to mind.

As to Biaggio's name—now *there* was a story. He'd shared it with Frank one night on the steps of his trailer. His mother, Mary Lou, had been a sixteen-year-old high school dropout who'd bewitched a thirty-year-old Vietnam veteran named Bodie Dunkirk, a man with a puny conscience but a healthy respect for the American judicial system. Bodie had looked up "statutory rape" in the county library. "Finish school," he told Mary Lou, "and I'll take you anywhere in the world." So she did. The day after graduation they boarded a plane for Italy and set up housekeeping in a one-room Naples apartment with a communal bathroom up two flights of stairs. The morning Mary Lou found a family of rats nesting in her underwear drawer was the same morning she found out she was pregnant with Bodie's second baby and—coincidentally—the very same morning the romance officially began to lose its luster.

"I want to go home," she told Bodie, one-year-old Jimmy on her hip and the latest piece of good news hiccupping inside her.

"Baby, now stop that," he said. "You know we can't afford to go nowhere."

But he managed to go a few places himself. Bodie got out a great deal, in fact—down to the piazza bar to drink Campari and get friendly with the local women. So friendly there came a night he never quite made it home, having forgotten himself in the considerable charms of a dainty Neapolitan *ragazza* on the rebound from a disaffected suitor. Poor thing, he said to her, *poverina, belleza,* and next thing he knew they were naked and sweating in a twin bed with musty sheets and the sounds of a rollicking street fight on the piazza below.

Well. Mary Lou was not one to be messed with. She took the news lying down, so to speak, in the arms of a dashing Italian gentleman by the name of Biaggio Antonio DiMaria, who bought her a dozen blood roses, served her a breakfast of figs, flatbread, and limoncello, and set up little Jimmy with a Bullwinkle cartoon in the kitchen before carrying Mary Lou, four months and showing with Bodie's second child, into the bedroom and closing the door. When she and Jimmy returned home that afternoon, Mary Lou was disheveled, satiated, and more than a little drunk. She found Bodie near frantic with a worry that quickly transformed into fury as he began to understand the nature of her absence.

"Tit for tit," she said.

"Tat," he corrected her.

She looked at him and raised an eyebrow.

Bodie was sick with jealousy. He harangued Mary Lou into telling him the name of her lover, then he set out into the streets of Naples in search of her suitor, Biaggio DiMaria. He found DiMaria in the very same bar where Bodie had tangoed with his Italian tart and started the whole mess in the first place. The bartender, following Bodie's inquiry, pointed to the end of the bar, where a man sat alone, regarding his drink.

"Be careful, *signore*," the bartender said.

"What?" Bodie said.

"*Assassino*," the bartender whispered, pulling his finger across his throat. "How you say? *Hit man*." The man at the end of the bar looked up, and his eyes met Bodie's.

Bodie thought for a minute about Mary Lou. He tried to summon the picture that had so consumed him just a short while ago, of this dark man's body between her thighs, his face against her breasts, but all he could really see were the sinews in DiMaria's neck, and the sweat glistening on DiMaria's forearms, and the outline of something hard and possibly metallic under the silky white fabric of DiMaria's shirt. DiMaria nodded at him, and Bodie's blood ran cold. He looked away, did a quick reckoning. He'd survived Vietnam, he reasoned, and he was having too good a damn time in Naples for it all to come to an end right here. He backed out of the bar and went home to Mary Lou, Jimmy, and the small, wriggling family of rats.

If Bodie's extramarital indiscretions had proven distasteful to Mary Lou, his failure to summon the *cojones* to defend her questionable honor now proved positively odious. She stayed in Italy just long enough to deliver the baby, whom she named Biaggio Antonio Dunkirk, a moniker intended to do one thing and one thing only: drive Bodie Dunkirk frigging nuts for the rest of his days. Then she returned to West Virginia alone with her two boys, whom she raised in the distracted, resentful manner of a woman who'd given up too much, too soon, and who was smart enough to realize she'd never, ever get it back.

"It's like I never had much of a family," Biaggio had said that night on the steps of the trailer. He and Frank were sharing a six-pack, watching a raccoon family at the edge of a thicket of scrub. "Not like you here," he said, gesturing to the house.

Frank had snorted. "Some family," he said.

Biaggio had looked at him sternly. "It's a family, Frank," he said. "It's more than a lot of people got. Trust me." Then Biaggio's eyes grew soft and distracted as his gaze fixed on the raccoons under the trees.

That was years ago—five? Ten? It was hard to recall. Today, the haze was hot over Aberdeen as they stood in the driveway, and Biaggio's T-shirt was already dotted with sweat across his chest.

"Goochie, Goochie, Goochie," Biaggio said, crouching down and wrapping the dog in a full embrace. Gooch's legs went out from under him, and he lay back rapturously in Biaggio's arms, thumping his tail wildly, looking at Frank accusingly. *You never treat me like this*, he was saying.

"Oh, get up, you two, before I hurl," Frank said.

Biaggio planted a fat kiss on the top of Gooch's head, then stood up, took a deep breath, and raised his eyebrows at Frank.

"We got a problem," he said. He nodded at Aberdeen meaningfully.

Frank regarded him. "We?"

"Well, *you*," Biaggio conceded. "It's the ladies. They've gone nucking futs again."

The morning sun was brutal, already. Frank felt it on his arms and face, a summer sun, aggressive and unflinching, as they walked together up to the house, Gooch, the bastard, favoring Biaggio's side and still shooting sidelong looks at Frank. Biaggio moved with a strange springing gait, nearly on his toes, with his eyebrows raised and his shoulders hunched forward. He always looked as though he was ready to jump into a sprint, running toward or away from something, though Frank never knew quite what. Biaggio was big, solid-shouldered, tall. He could have been intimidating, if he were a different sort of man.

"I heard the hollerin' starting early," Biaggio said. "They been goin' at it a while, Frank." His brow was knit. "They are righteously pissed off this time. It's about the Steinway."

"So I heard," Frank said.

His mother's Steinway. It was a beautiful instrument, or had once been, rather, before the ravages of time and neglect had taken it over. The piano had been passed down in Arla's family since before the turn of the century, and he knew that when her parents died it was one of the few things she'd insisted on saving from their Davis Shores home before the auctioneers liquidated the estate, before what little was left of the old Bolton money began its steady, slow leak through the Bravo family coffers. A full-size upright, deep mahogany so dark it was almost black, the piano had a beautiful, ornate shape and had, at one time, a rich clear tone. Arla had grown up practicing scales and banging out overtures in her parents' living room overlooking the Matanzas, though as an adult she rarely played anymore. Instead, she had put all her children through piano lessons, had presided over their practice sessions with a fervor bordering on compulsion, even though Carson and Sofia were hopeless at the keyboard, and it had been only Frank himself, and Will, who had taken to it with any level of appreciation and who had developed any skill. But for all her attachment to the blasted, blighted Steinway, which Frank knew was one of Arla's few remaining vestiges of the life of privilege she'd once known, the piano had never been maintained. Even during the years of lessons it had never been tuned, never been regulated, never had its decrepit old hammers adjusted or even inspected, for that matter. Eventually the house termites had annexed the instrument, and the Steinway had sat, moldering and austere, in the living room at Aberdeen for as long as Frank could remember. And for nearly the same amount of time, Sofia had been hell-bent on getting rid of it.

And here was a battle of wills most powerfully matched. Both blessed with a towering height that might have been called statuesque on some women, Frank's sister and his mother were capable of wicked outbursts of temper and, more problematic, complete and utter lapses of reason. The condition was made more intimidating by the fact that both Arla and Sofia were still, by any measure, beautiful women, though Arla's age and her physical condition had, through the years, skewed her charms, made them fit less snugly, less comfortably. She had the look of a woman whose beauty was fading fast, and worse, who knew it. But it was Sofia, really, who threw the equation out of whack here at Aberdeen. When she was a child, people said she was willful. When she was a young woman, people said she was moody. Now that she'd hit her forties, they said she was crazy. Beautiful, but crazy.

And she *was* odd. The mood swings, the bitter rages, the panic attacks. When his sister was younger, Arla, and even Dean, before he left, give him some small credit, had tried to work Sofia through it, had taken her to counselors and doctors and support groups and all the rest. But after each attempted treatment she'd return home exhausted, defeated, more anxious than ever, and Frank had had the feeling that perhaps it was cruel to ask her to try, to ask her to become something she was incapable of becoming. And then came the final one-two punch—that horrible night of loss, all those years ago, followed by Dean's last valediction down the long driveway of Aberdeen. It had become clear to Frank—painfully so—that Sofia would handle those particular blows with even less competence than the rest of the family, which wasn't saying much at all. She was supposed to be on medication. He had a feeling, lately, she wasn't taking it. He sighed. Leave her be, he thought. She's doing the best she can.

Frank and Biaggio arrived at the porch, where Frank and Carson, years ago, had built a ramp to one side of the steps to help Arla when her gradually increasing weight, combined with her disabled foot, had begun to make stairs nearly impossible. The interior stairs were still a problem, of course. But Arla had worked out a system—down once in the morning, up once in the evening, with the morning descent steadied by two sturdy banisters, and the evening ascent fortified by more than a few glasses of Carlo Rossi Chablis.

"So, you expecting a big crowd for fireworks tonight at the restaurant?" Biaggio asked. But before Frank could answer or climb the porch steps, something hit him, hard, on the shoulder. He recoiled, and the stack of magazines that had been pitched from the second-floor window above the front porch, Arla's window, splayed open and skidded across the walkway. *Good Housekeeping. Family Circle. Better Homes and Gardens.*

"Shit," Frank said. He rubbed his shoulder and looked up, just in time to see a second bundle of magazines hurtling from the same window. He stepped back, butting into Biaggio, who was standing slack-jawed, staring up at the open window. A thatch of red hair appeared behind the curtain, paused, and then ducked back out of sight.

"Mom!" Frank said. "What in the hell are you doing?"

As if in answer, a pile of books housed in a deteriorating cardboard box sailed out of the window and onto the walkway. Frank and Biaggio took another step back from the house. The books hit the pavement and slid out of the box, fanning along the path. *The Thorn Birds. Shogun. The Winds of War.* The books were moldy and dog-eared. Frank would bet they'd been in the box a quarter century. At least.

"Mom! Will you cut that shit out before you kill us?"

"It isn't me, Frank," Arla called from inside the bedroom. "It's her!" And then Sofia appeared in the window, her face flushed, her red hair wild around her shoulders.

"Leave that crap down there!" Sofia shrieked. "Don't you dare bring it up here again! Frank! Tell her!"

Frank turned to Biaggio, who stood completely still, watching Sofia with what appeared to be a mixture of adoration and terror.

"Well, ain't this a hell of a way to start a Saturday," he said to Biaggio. "And Independence Day, at that. Huh."

"Well, it's like I told you," Biaggio said. "You got a situation here."

"Don't I always," Frank said. Biaggio knelt and began gathering up books. Frank shook his head, stepped over the mess, took the ramp up to the front porch, and entered the house, where he was immediately confronted by the huge Steinway, which had evidently been dragged from its old placement in the living room and now sat directly in the main hallway, at the base of the stairs, effectively blocking all passage from the front door to the back of the house. He paused for a moment, considered this. The Steinway had to weigh close to five hundred pounds. Which meant that Sofia was operating this morning in some sort of brute rage, to have managed to drag or push the thing into its current position. Good God. He gave the piano a test shove, but it didn't budge.

He leaned against the wall, in no particular hurry to go upstairs and enter the fray, which now, he realized, would mean having to climb over the Steinway. He glanced left, into the dim living room, where an ancient sofa and love seat, mustard yellow, formed an L around the room's primary focus, a pressboard entertainment center featuring a midsize TV, a needle-less phonograph, and a collection of Hummel figurines encased in hinged glass cabinets. Above the entertainment center, a three-foot taxidermied largemouth bass gulped for air on a wooden mount, its eyes bulging, horrified, and Frank regarded it for a moment. He'd been with Dean, and Carson had, too, the morning their father had caught the bass in a brackish tributary off Pablo Creek. They were little, maybe five? Maybe six? Will had been too young to come along, and Frank remembered Dean's joy at pulling in the bass, his own excitement and fear when the fish flopped about in the bottom of the little boat, Carson's eyes ablaze when he hit the creature on the head once, twice, three times, until Dean took the bludgeon out of Carson's hand and laughed, patted both boys on the head, said *Look at that sumbitch, boys!* He remembered Arla's revulsion when they brought the fish home and, days later, his own confusion when she presented it to Dean, taxidermied and preserved. She smiled, proud, forbearing, when Dean hung it there in the living room. Frank remembered that, Arla's face that day, how she watched Dean pounding the nail into the wall, how she steadied the little footstool beneath his feet.

There weren't too many physical reminders of his father still around the house these days, but there were a few: the sealable plastic margarine tub converted to a sugar bowl to thwart the tiny kitchen ants; the thin segment of twine dangling from the ceiling in the third-floor bathroom that kept the water from the roof leak contained to a manageable stream rather than a corrosive metastases of dampness; the dusty set of *Encyclopedia Britannica* Dean had discovered in the trash behind Utina High and insisted on salvaging, even though the set was missing *B, CA–CH, SA–SM* and *V* and therefore was likely to be as much of an annoyance as a study aid the night before a big report was due. But most of Dean's belongings had been filtered away through the years, his clothes given away by Arla, his Rayonier pay stubs confiscated by Carson, who'd undertaken an angry and vengeful audit of his father's discarded effects one year. Dean's books and magazines had gone to mold and were eventually lugged out to the trash. Dean's tackle box and fishing poles had been pilfered and picked over by Frank himself. And yet here hung the stupid bass, all these years later, Dean long since gone. Frank had offered to take it down more than once. "It's ugly," he said to his mother. "You don't want to look at that." But Arla had resisted. "I don't mind it," she said. "I don't know. I sort of like it."

Today, in the living room, the ironing board stood in its usual place in front of the west-facing window, and three plastic laundry baskets of carefully folded clergy vestments were lined up in a row on the floor. Since she quit coming to the restaurant regularly years ago, Arla had methodically built up a small, strange business as a laundress of vestments and church linens, a sideline she started when the kids were still small and had continued all these years, servicing, by now, all seven Catholic parishes in St. Augustine. Frank and Carson used to help with delivery and pickup, but with Biaggio on site these days the logistics had grown considerably easier. Biaggio picked up the bundles of soiled linens from the churches between moving jobs, brought them to Arla at Aberdeen, and delivered them back to the churches a few days later washed, pressed, and packaged in crisp brown paper, a handwritten invoice taped to the side of each bundle. Frank had grown up with the faint smell of altar wine and priests' aftershave hanging in the living room, a musk of incense and candles shaking loose from the corporals and purificators Arla pulled from their baskets, the smell of detergent mingling with the steam rising from her ironing board as she pressed the manuterges flat, coaxed the wrinkles from the vestments, robes, and stoles.

The linens came from the churches with strict rules for handling, and Arla followed them to a T: soak the fabrics first in fresh water to remove any possible remains of the Precious Body and Blood. Take the water outside and deposit it in an appropriate place, never a drain or a basin, given that it may contain consecrated particles. Then proceed with laundering as usual. Frank had seen Arla many times plodding, limping into the scrub between Aberdeen and Uncle Henry's, lugging a heavy bucket of water in one hand and her stout wooden cane in the other.

And the funny thing was that Arla was never particularly religious, even though she'd been raised on a steady dose of rosaries and CCD and had acquiesced to her mother's demands for a church wedding, enjoying the beauty and artistry of the old cathedral, where she still stopped to light a candle whenever she went into St. Augustine. But that was it. They didn't go to Mass. They never said grace. Frank had never seen a rosary in the house. It amused and puzzled him, that Arla would pay such strict attention to the laundry rites, take so seriously the idea of consecrated particles and Precious Blood and proper disposal and blah, blah, blah, when the routine of her everyday life was anything but pious. Arla played pop music as she ironed the linens, sometimes watched soaps or daytime trash-talk shows while doing the folding, a tumbler of Chablis at her elbow. She'd cuss like a trucker when she burned a hole in one of the corporals, and she'd sometimes even lie about the item count when she returned a package missing a robe or a credence cloth she'd stained or torn.

"Oh, I don't know that God's fussing about the details," she'd say to Frank when he was young. "He's more concerned with the big picture." Later, after Will was gone and after Dean had left, she'd not bring up God at all but would grow silent and pensive when the subject came up, would wrap the linens in sheets of brown paper without a word, and Frank wondered if she'd concluded that God wasn't, in fact, particularly concerned with the big picture, either.

Through the open front door behind him, another box of books hit the pavement. Frank hoisted himself over the top of the old Steinway, slid down on the other side. "Sofia!" he called up the stairs. "You don't quit throwing shit out the window, you're going to be next!"

He climbed the stairs, running his hand up the thick oak banister he and Carson had installed on the interior wall of the staircase, intending to give Arla two banisters to hold instead of one as she maneuvered the levels of the old house. He entered the front bedroom, where Arla sat in a tattered wingback chair, looking on with annoyance but forbearance as Sofia threw more books into another cardboard box. At Frank's entrance, Arla looked up.

Arla. There were times, even now, when Frank was struck by his mother's appearance, times when he came through a doorway or around a corner and saw her, as he did now, for the impossibly imposing woman she was, or perhaps had once been—her skin still pale and flawless, her features classic, the breadth of her shoulders looking peculiar and off balance, given the atrophy of her left leg and the strange foreshortened shape of her foot. He blinked at the sight of her. If she hadn't been his mother, and if he hadn't seen her nearly every day of his life, he'd be doing a double-take right now, so unique was her appearance, so lovely and strange and rare.

"Oh, Frank!" she said, mock-brightly. "There you are. Welcome to my bedroom. *My* bedroom, Frank. Sofia is just doing some tidying up, evidently." At sixty-two, Arla's hair was still mostly red, threaded through with gray, cut short and wavy around her head. She wore jeans with an elastic waistband, a sleeveless yellow T-shirt. She kept one hand on her cane, and with the other she gripped the arm of the chair to push herself up.

"Sofia," he began.

"Frank," Sofia snapped. "Don't try to stop me. Do *not*. Do you see this place? Could you please look?" She gestured around Arla's bedroom.

He did, casting his eyes around the bedroom with the same feeling of dismay and—admit it—*disgust* that had dogged him most of his childhood, when it came to considering matters of his mother's housekeeping. The room was a landfill. Half of Arla's double bed was covered in books, clothes, towels, and random detritus; the other half was kept eerily clear, and Frank could see his mother slept on this half, leaving the other to collect as much junk as possible. Along the bedroom walls were various tables, chairs, and dressers, but no piece of furniture was particularly distinguishable for the piles of rubbish they bore: discarded blouses, plastic grocery bags, prescription bottles, newspapers, empty boxes of Little Debbie snack cakes.

He pressed his hands against his temples. His head was pounding. He squeezed his eyes shut, then opened them again. Sofia was staring at him, her face flushed and sweating.

"We had an agreement," she said. "To clean this house *today*. And now she's going back on her word."

"I don't see why she has to be in my bedroom," Arla said. "Do you, Frank?"

"I can't live like this anymore," Sofia muttered. She shook open a plastic garbage bag and bent to gather up items on the floor. An empty coffee tin. A stack of eight-track tapes, rubber-banded together. *Eight-tracks?* Frank shook his head. Outside the open window, Biaggio started to whistle.

"Should we at least close the window?" Frank said. "It's hot as hell out there."

"It wouldn't matter," Sofia said. "It's hot as hell in here, too. The AC's busted."

"Since when?" Frank said. He walked to the AC unit parked in the bedroom's second window, fiddled with the knobs. Nothing.

Sofia straightened up, cocked her head to one side. "Since like three years ago," she said. She thrust her thumb at Arla. "She wouldn't let me tell you. Because she didn't want you to see what it looks like up here."

"My space is being invaded, Frank. My very refuge," Arla said. "Is nothing sacred? A woman's own boudoir?"

"Oh, boudoir, my butt, Mother," Sofia said. "It's a pigpen, is what it is. The whole house. We agreed, Mother. We agreed we would clean it up today."

Frank walked over to the open window. Below, Biaggio was sitting on the front steps, flipping through a copy of *Life*. Frank looked northward, scanning the horizon for smoke.

The fryer. The fryer. The fryer. It could be combusting at this very moment, sending a shower of sparks through the kitchen, a wall of flames licking at the cardboard boxes of paper towels under the prep tables, spreading out to the burlap window shades in the dining room, the unfinished wainscoting in the foyer, the thick yellow pine of the bar, the bar, the *bar*—my God! He hadn't had enough coffee for this. And how early did the games need to begin, anyway?

"You do realize it's not even seven-thirty in the morning, Sofia?" Frank said.

"Yes, of course I do," she said. She looked at the huge pink watch parked on her wrist. "We started early. You know I have to get to Uncle Henry's by eight," she said. He did know, of course. Sofia was Uncle Henry's one-woman housekeeping and sanitation staff—and she was an admittedly astounding phenomenon, as far as Frank was concerned—wielding the force and grace of a Lipizzaner with the speed of an Olympic sprinter, but she took it on herself, day after day after day. She'd started almost twenty years ago, not long after Frank himself had taken over the place, in fact, and now she showed up at the restaurant every morning, rain or shine, on the *dot* (my God, the *dot!*) of eight o'clock to spend exactly three hours cleaning up the crumbs and crusts and chaos of the night before. Frank could set his watch by the sight of Sofia steering her bike up through the restaurant's parking lot, her long hair pulled back, an expression of grim expectation on her face as she prepared to face the wreckage of another night's business at Uncle Henry's. In by eight, out by eleven. Every day. Every single blessed day.

Now that he'd mentioned the time, he felt his sister getting antsy. She glanced at her watch again, then around at the rubble on the floor.

"And you do both realize the piano is in the middle of the hallway, right?" Frank felt compelled to point this out. Sofia literally put her foot down.

"That's gotta *go*," Sofia said. "It's full of termites."

"It's an heirloom," Arla said. "It's my grandmother's Steinway."

"It's a breeding ground for *vermin*. It's out of here," Sofia said.

"Over my dead body," Arla said mildly.

Sofia's face was turning a deeper red. She turned to Frank, near tears. "Do you see?" she demanded.

The heat was nearly suffocating. His head pounded.

"Look," Frank said. "Why don't you just put this off a bit, Sofia? I mean, does it have to happen today?"

"We had an agreement," she began.

"I know, I know," Frank said. "But today? Of all days?" He saw her wavering. So he went for the jugular, glancing at his watch as he said it. "And isn't it getting close to time for you to go?"

Sofia glared at him. She looked at her own watch again. Then she turned and left the room. A moment later, her bedroom door slammed, and he knew she'd be getting ready to leave for the restaurant.

"My Lord," Arla said. "I swear."

"Just relax," he said to Arla, "the two of you. Don't aggravate the situation when she gets like this, Mom."

"She's single-handedly dragging my piano out of my house, Frank. How is that *me* aggravating the situation?" She picked up the plastic garbage bag at her feet and began pulling items out of it. "What kind of woman can drag a piano out of a house, anyway, Frank? I mean, you see what I am dealing with here?" She pulled a dusty silk nosegay out of the wastebasket, shook it off, and put it back on the table at her elbow. Next she retrieved a pincushion shaped like a giant strawberry. "Nothing wrong with that," she muttered.

"Maybe you should get out of here for a bit. You're just at each other's throats in the house here. Come up to the restaurant later," he said.

Arla dropped the bag, put her hands up in the air, pushed them down again. "I don't want to come over there."

"Come up—you and Sofia both."

"Forget it," Arla said.

"There'll be music."

"I hate music."

Frank was rankled. "You do not."

"How do you know?" she said. "You don't know everything."

True. He didn't know everything. He didn't know, for example, how any of them were going to survive if the restaurant were, indeed, burning down at this moment, but he didn't bother to broach this topic with Arla.

"You're coming," he said. "You need to get out of here once in a while. I'll get Carson to pick you up for the fireworks. And one of us will take you home afterward."

"What if I say no?"

"Look, Mom. I was woken up out of a sound sleep this morning to come over here"—he left out, of course, the part about his dream, the fact that he wasn't in fact woken from a sound sleep but had been awake and aroused already, thinking about Elizabeth— "to come over here and get in the middle of this, and what I find when I get here is two people hell-bent on making each other crazy."

"One of us already is," Arla said.

"That's debatable."

"Oh, trust me, she's crazy."

"No, I mean it's debatable whether it's one of you, or both of you."

Arla turned to him, glaring.

"I'm the only thing keeping her from going completely off the deep end, Frank."

"Well, you're going to send yourself there, you're not careful," he said. "You're coming to Uncle Henry's tonight. Both of you." He didn't like the insistent tone of his own voice, but he was pissed. This was ridiculous.

"I don't like being bossed around, Frank," Arla said.

"Well, there's a lot of things I don't like," Frank said. "But I just do them anyway."

She sighed, struggled to her feet. "Come on downstairs," she said. "I haven't even had any tea yet."

They walked downstairs, and when they got to the base of the stairs they stopped at the Steinway.

"Biaggio and I need to move this," he said.

"Leave it there," Arla barked. "Sofia put it there, she can put it back herself."

Frank clambered over the piano first, then turned to take Arla's cane and help his mother maneuver the climb. Arla slid down heavily, and he handed her back her cane. He followed her into the kitchen.

"I don't need tea," he said. "I've got to get over to the restaurant. And Sofia can ride with me this morning. Since I'm here already."

"Pffft," Arla said. "Good luck with that. I'm sure she's going to change her routine for *you*, Frank. Since she's so accommodating to everyone else. Her mother, for instance."

She clomped across the kitchen and filled the teakettle. "Have you spoken to Carson?"

Frank had not spoken to his brother in weeks, but he didn't particularly want to have to analyze this point, or the reasons why, with his mother, so he dodged the question.

"Some," he said vaguely. "They're coming up for fireworks tonight. Why? Is something up?"

Arla sighed. "Oh, I don't know. He's so wound up. You can't talk to Carson. The business—he's always on about the business," she said, referring to Carson's investment management firm in St. Augustine, a venture he alternately ran like a freight train and worried over like a nursemaid. "I'm just wondering if they're planning on anything for Bell's birthday," she said.

"When is that?" Frank said. He made a mental note to look for a gift for his niece, who was truly, despite her father's genetic influence, an absolute frigging *gem* of a kid. Skinny and tough, a thick blond ponytail hanging down her back, huge glasses almost falling off her face every time she worked up a sweat, the kind of kid who would ask you how you were doing and actually be interested in the answer. An old soul in a tiny, wiry frame. Frank never thought of himself as the kid type. But Bell made herself easy to love. She took after her mother, he often thought.

"A few weeks," Arla said. She took two mugs out of the cupboard, plopped teabags into each of them. "She'll be seven."

He exhaled. "Seven already," he said. He did a quick calculation. When Bell was born, he remembered holding her, visiting Elizabeth and Carson in the hospital, accepting the little wrapped bundle that his brother placed in his arms, and telling himself not to get too attached, even as the baby stared at him so ingenuously that he felt himself slipping under a goofily paternal spell he'd yet to break. Back then, he'd just started his ten-year plan. Ten years, he'd determined. Five years of saving and planning, and then he'd have enough to buy a lot up in North Carolina, in Cullowhee. Five more years, he'd have enough to start building his cabin. Ten years, total, to the top of the mountain. And now here he was. Bell turning seven. No lot purchased, no cabin in sight.

"I don't need tea, Mom," he said again. Biaggio appeared in the hallway, but he stopped on the other side of the piano.

"You want me to go ahead and move this, Miss Arla?" he called.

Upstairs, a door flung open, and Sofia ran to the top of the stairs. "The only place that thing is going to be moved is *out!*" she yelled down.

Biaggio paled, raised his eyebrows, looked at Frank across the piano. Sofia descended the stairway and stood next to Biaggio on one side of the piano. Arla left the kitchen and walked down the hallway to stand on the other side. Frank followed.

"Mother," Sofia said. Her hair was freshly pulled back and she'd changed into the outfit she wore every day to clean Uncle Henry's: a pair of faded cut-off jeans, a worn-out Jaguars T-shirt. She was making, Frank could tell, a sincere effort to control the timbre of her voice. "Please," she said. "It's absolutely full of termites. We need to get it out of here."

"It's not going out," Arla said. "My Lord, you people. It's my grandmother's heirloom Steinway. It was played by Irving Berlin." Frank met Sofia's eyes. How many times had they heard this claim? Irving *Berlin*. "He came to my grandmother's house in Connecticut for a cocktail party and played this piano!" Arla said. She patted the top of the piano, leaving a shiny handprint in a thick layer of dust. "It just needs a little restoration," she said.

"It's past restoration," Sofia said. She opened the fall board. Hundreds of tiny gray wings fluttered to the floor. "Oh, my God. It's not going back in the living room."

"I can put it wherever ya'll ladies want," Biaggio said. "But it's dang heavy. I should rent some platforms and move it right." He looked at Sofia in amazement. "I don't know how you got it this far," he said.

"I'm sorry, Biaggio, but you won't move it at all, unless it's right back into that living room," Arla said.

Biaggio looked helplessly across the piano at Frank.

"Then I'll move it out myself," Sofia said.

"Aw, now . . . ," Biaggio said.

"I love this piano," Arla said. "I still play it."

"You do not," Sofia said.

Arla dragged the bench, abandoned in the living room, over to the piano. She sat down and propped her cane against her leg. She brushed the termite wings off the keys, and then she started to play "Raindrops Keep Fallin' on My Head." She affected a raunchy falsetto. The piano sounded like a collision. Several of the strings were broken, so the hammers pounded felt on wood—*plenk. Plenk. Plenk!*

"Oh, my God," Sofia said.

Arla was forgetting words, whole lines, but she improvised. "Bap-bap-ba-da-da-da," she sang. *Plenk. Plenk. Plenk!*

"I've got to go," Frank said. He looked at Sofia. "You want to ride to the restaurant with me?" he said, though he knew this was a stupid question. She would ride her bike, just as she'd always ridden her bike to Uncle Henry's. To ask Sofia to consider changing her routine would be like asking the pope to consider taking up Islam.

Arla stopped suddenly, furrowing her brow. "Of course, that's not what Irving Berlin would have played." She looked up at them, but when she saw first Sofia's, and then Frank's face, she turned and directed her comment to Biaggio. "He would have played something much more elegant at my grandmother's house," she said. She rested her fingers on the keys again, played a soft intro to something that sounded like Irving Berlin. *Plenky. Plenky. Plenkety-plenkety-plenk.*

"This is 'What'll I Do,'" she said. She began to sing. She closed her eyes. Her voice filled the narrow hallway, and Frank had suddenly had enough. He turned to head through the kitchen and exit out the back door.

"You all can keep climbing over that piano until you learn how to deal with each other," he called back through the house. Though even as he said it, he realized that could be a very, very long time.

He called Gooch, got into his truck, and drove down the long driveway to Monroe Road, toward Uncle Henry's and the fryer and away from the sounds of Arla's voice and her heirloom Steinway piano cutting through the bright hot morning like a requiem. He glanced at his rearview mirror one last time to see Sofia behind him, pedaling like a triathlete on a fat-wheeled cruiser down the soft sandy driveway, on her way to Uncle Henry's, and he thought, how stupid, that she won't just ride with me, when after all, we're headed the exact same place.

THREE

The restaurant was still standing. And it didn't appear to be on fire. Still, Frank wasn't feeling any better when he pulled into the parking lot at Uncle Henry's Bar & Grill, though the sight of the dappled morning sunlight on the clapboard siding of his mother's restaurant was momentarily cheering. Love/hate. No other way to describe his relationship with this place, where he'd worked as manager, bartender, accountant, and head cook since he was nineteen years old.

Uncle Henry's was built half on land, half on water, supported in the second case by barnacled pilings that stretched out thirty feet over the sandy edge of the Intracoastal Waterway. There were many people in Utina, and once in a while Frank was one of them, who believed that the back deck of Uncle Henry's on a July night at sunset was the prettiest place on the face of Earth, with the light shining off the current and the fiddler crabs doing their tango down by the waterline.

Years ago Uncle Henry's had been forced to compete with Morgan's Fish Camp and Fry House next door, but when a fire claimed Morgan's and left nothing but a collapsing dock and a family of feral cats, Frank offered Morgan Moore a job in Uncle Henry's kitchen. Morgan accepted, had simply cut his losses, and redirected his commute by fifty feet southward, and none of the clientele of either restaurant was any the worse, knowing they could still get Morgan's fried catfish and Menorcan chowder and enjoy the deck at Uncle Henry's at the same time. And the fire, in truth, was a boon for Uncle Henry's business. On the old Morgan's property, the palmettos now grew thick and wild. Frank had hinted more than once that the lot could be cleared and used to solve a parking problem at Uncle Henry's, but Morgan, who still held the deed on the land, resisted. "Gonna rebuild it one day, you wait," he said. "Then I'll be back to give you a run for your money."

Inside Uncle Henry's, a bay of rectangular tables and vinyl chairs filled the main dining room, which had as its best feature a long row of windows fronting the Intracoastal and had as its worst feature a surly seventy-something waitress named Irma who'd been working the tables so long nobody could remember the place without her, not even Frank, who'd lost track of how or when he'd ever hired her and had given up on ever getting rid of her. She was a lesson in patience. "Uglier than homemade soup," Morgan often said, a grin spreading across his wide brown face. "But she can work them tables all right."

On the back deck, a collection of picnic tables echoed the arrangement inside, with each table both inside and out adorned with a small basket of condiments—ketchup, tartar, pepper sauce (Crazy Mother Pucker's Fire Roasted Fusion being, as a general rule, the brand of choice)—and a thick roll of paper towels on a wooden dowel.

The restaurant had earned its name from its founder, Henry Bravo, Frank's great-uncle, who'd been known throughout Utina both for his crawfish slum goulash and for his wife, Bubbles, a former burlesque dancer from New York City who found God and Henry on the same day at a tent revival down in Manatee County. Bubbles returned to Utina with Henry and committed herself to using her considerable physical charms to lure the unchaste, the undisciplined, and the unsaved into the metaphorical bosom of the Lord. It was, by and large, a successful venture.

Henry had parlayed his newfound marital bliss and his famed culinary skills into the opening of the restaurant, originally named The Heaven on Earth Kitchen of Eternal Salvation and Famous Hoppin' John, but which over the years had come to be known as "Uncle Henry's" by the Bravos and their Utina neighbors. Eventually Bubbles died of emphysema, and then Henry seized up with an aneurism, not a month after Dean Bravo deserted his family and took with him his spotty but more or less adequate paper mill salary. That's when Arla saw an opportunity. She bought the restaurant for a song from Henry's daughter, a vacant thing named Charleen who had not one skinny idea what to do with a thriving fish restaurant on a busy Florida waterway, God love her.

Arla herself had run the restaurant for a couple of years and had nearly run it into the ground, in fact, before Frank took over and Arla retreated gratefully to the seclusion of Aberdeen, to the escape of her linens and her ironing. He'd tried, for a time, to combine running the restaurant with taking classes at St. Johns River Community College to become a certified builder, but the balance proved lopsided, unworkable, so he gave up college to pop beer bottles, devein shrimp, and count cash. The certifications and the unbuilt cabin faded into the distance. He was nineteen when he started here. He wondered if he'd be ninety before he saw the last of it.

Frank pulled the truck around to the side of the restaurant, near the kitchen entrance. Morgan had already arrived and had opened all the windows and doors to let the thick atmosphere of last night's cooking dissipate. Across the back deck, the breeze from the Intracoastal was sweet and warm. Gooch padded into the kitchen, where Morgan stood at a long metal prep table, cleaning shrimp. Gooch slapped his tail three times against Morgan's leg, then wandered out to the deck for a nap.

"Mornin' darling," Morgan said, nodding at Frank.

"Sweetheart," Frank replied.

"You look like shit," Morgan said.

"Thanks. Good to know."

"My pleasure."

"Did I leave the fryer on last night?" Frank said. He walked across the kitchen. The fryer's cord lay unplugged across the tile. He put his hand on the closed surface of the machine, and the metal was cool.

Morgan looked calmly at Frank, then at the fryer.

"No," he said. "You wouldn't do that, Frank."

Frank stood still for a moment, looking from Morgan to the fryer. How could Morgan be so sure? He was annoyed, suddenly. Did everyone think he was so fucking reliable, so wretchedly responsible? He could have burned the entire restaurant down. He could have ruined everything, could have ruined every*one.*

"I just know you wouldn't," Morgan said, as though reading his mind. He turned back to his shrimp. Morgan worked from a large cardboard flat at his left elbow, dropping the cleaned shrimp into a deep plastic bucket filled with ice water near his right knee, and he moved quickly, removing the shells, splaying open the fleshy backs, running a sharp knife along the spine. Eight hundred shrimp a day. Repeated evisceration, every single morning, but Morgan never complained. His rhythm was heroic, his precision near perfect, notwithstanding the thick web of scars climbing along his thumbs and the heels of his brown hands. He'd been working in a seafood kitchen for forty-five of his sixty years, marinating his life in the sluice and brine of raw fish and crustaceans, singeing his regrets in the unforgiving cauldron of the deep fryer. It was a fine life, he often said, even if it did stink.

Frank was grateful this morning that Morgan was a quiet man. He settled into a simple, silent rhythm with Morgan, filling brushed metal tubs with prep: diced tomatoes, bell peppers, Vidalia onions, lemons, scallops. Through the open kitchen door, the wide channel of the Intracoastal beckoned, an intermittent parade of sport boats and trawlers on its back. When Sofia arrived, she parked her bike on the back deck, gathered her cleaning supplies from the utility closet, and set to work without speaking to Frank or Morgan. Frank could hear her in the restaurant's dining room, noisily moving the tables and chairs and then running the vacuum around the room like some sort of Tasmanian devil. My God, she could clean. He knew she'd hit the bar area next, and then the bathrooms, clattering her buckets and mops and cleaners all around the restaurant, and by the time she finished the whole place would be gleaming, immaculate, smelling of

Pine-Sol and bleach and with not so much as a single rogue hush puppy left to molder behind a booth, not a single drop of grenadine left gelling on a jigger behind the bar. In three hours, she'd take Uncle Henry's apart and put it back together. And tomorrow she'd do the whole thing again.

By the time Gooch rose, stretched, and made his way back from the edge of the deck, Sofia had finished cleaning and departed on her bike, and Frank and Morgan had filled the three stainless-steel refrigerators with the day's preps. They poured two steaming cups of coffee and sat down at the picnic table outside the kitchen door. Morgan lit a cigarette.

"I got a call this morning," he said, looking at the land next door, where his own profitable restaurant had stood many years ago, before the fire that claimed it. Morgan never voiced suspicion that the fire had been set, though Frank would not have blamed him if he had. Utina was not a place to appreciate even the most modest forms of prosperity, especially that which belonged to a black man.

"Imagine that," Frank said. "Who'd wanna call you?"

Morgan flicked ash onto the deck, narrowed his eyes.

"Man wants to build a fancy marina," he said.

"A marina?"

"Docks. Big boats. Yachts. You know. Rich people stuff."

"Where?"

"There," Morgan said, waving his hand toward his own parcel of land. "And here," he said, continuing the motion with his hand to wave toward the restaurant.

"He wants our land?"

"Look like it. Yours and mine both."

"Shit."

"That's what I said."

"You tell him where to get off?"

"Started to." Morgan stubbed out his cigarette, looked out across the water, where a gray egret dropped down from an overhanging live oak bough and waded gracefully into a patch of reeds. "But . . ."

"But what?"

"But I think he mighta been serious," Morgan said. "And I think he mighta had money."

"Then he's not from Utina."

"Nope. Atlanta."

"No shit?"

"Atlanta, Georgia," Morgan said. "A man with money, from Atlanta, Georgia. Susan Holm was right."

"What do you mean?"

"She was the one said the Atlanta people wanted to come and build a marina right on this spot. Don't you remember nothing? She was telling us about it last Friday in here." Frank did not remember anything about last Friday night, other than the feeling of Susan's thigh pressing against his under the bar.

"Why would he want to do that, Morgan?"

"Beats me. He's a developer, he says. Alonzo Cryder. That's his name. Can you beat that name?"

"And he flat out told you he's got money?"

"Nah. But that's what Susan says she heard. Don't you remember?"

Frank sighed. "Morgan, Susan says a lot of stuff. And some of it is even true. But you know what I think? I think this guy is probably just like all the other people who've told me they want to buy this place through the years. They think they've got all they need to make it run like we do. They've got everything except one thing. Cash."

And it was true. Frank had heard all this before, always from some broken-down Utinian who looked at Frank from the other side of the bar and seemed to come to the notion that Frank Bravo had it made, that the restaurant was a steady paycheck and a solid place to land in a local economy that relied heavily on beer sales, shrimp consumption, and bootlegged Lynyrd Skynyrd albums. Even Carson had made a crack or two—Carson, with his investment practice in St. Augustine, sitting pretty all those years and now, with the recession in full swing and his clients panicking, looking at Frank as though *Frank* was the lucky one, *Frank* was the big winner. Shit. It infuriated him. As if Carson didn't have it all. The house. The job. The beautiful little girl. And Elizabeth. Carson had Elizabeth. Wasn't that enough?

The phone inside the restaurant began to ring. Frank got up.

"That's him," Morgan said. "That's the man with the money, I bet you."

"Morgan," he said. "Didn't your mama ever tell you if it sounds too good to be true, it probably is?"

Morgan got up to follow Frank into the restaurant. The phone continued to ring.

"I smell something, Frank," he said. "And it ain't just fish."

"What's that?"

"I smell money."

Frank rolled his eyes, picked up the phone.

"Mr. Bravo?" The voice on the line was measured, confident.

"Speaking," he said.

"And how are you today, sir?"

"Been better. Been worse."

Chuckling on the line. Too agreeable, Frank thought. He's humoring me. Already he didn't like this guy.

"Who is this?" he said.

"Mr. Bravo, my name is Alonzo Cryder. I am the acquisitions director for a real estate development company called Vista Properties. We're out of Atlanta. Mr. Bravo, may I have a few moments of your time?"

"You out of it? Or in it?"

"Beg pardon?

"Atlanta. You said you were out of it." Frank always hated that expression. How could you be out of something if you were in it? God knows he was never out of Utina, no matter how much he wanted to be. Morgan waved to catch his attention, then scowled and shook his head at Frank. "*Be nice*," Morgan mouthed silently. He raised his right hand, rubbed his thumb against his fingers.

"Oh, no, we're here *in* Atlanta," said Cryder. "Quite. We've been here for nearly thirty years. We're specialists in Georgia and Florida development, Mr. Bravo."

"You don't have to keep calling me Mr. Bravo. I go by Frank." He didn't want to give this guy the wrong idea, make him think they were chums, but being called Mr. Bravo always rankled him. It made him think of Dean.

More chuckling. "Oh, thank you, Frank. You know, I never like to presume."

"So what can I do for you, Alonzo?" Frank said.

"Well, I will cut right to the chase, Frank. I would like to come see you to discuss the possible acquisition of your restaurant property."

"It's not for sale."

"Well, I realize it's not presently on the market. But I thought you might be interested in having a discussion about the potential opportunity we might be able to offer you."

Frank looked out through the back door of the kitchen. It was nearly noon, and the sun was bright across the water, making diamond tips and sequins across the surface.

"Why?" he said, after a solid pause.

"Why what?"

"Why do you want to buy it?"

"It's a lovely piece of land," Cryder said.

"Yes, I know that."

"And our company's president—he has some fondness for your area. He is thinking of acquiring the property as a pet project—something to just hang on to for a while, maybe one day turn into a retreat for his family."

What was this asshole talking about? "A retreat?"

"Yes, something simple. A place to take the grandkids, get away from the rat race, you know. It's so far away from everything. It's so quiet there. Maybe not the best place for a business, as you may be aware, but a nice place to get away from it all. You know what I mean, Frank."

Frank did not know. But he was beginning to suspect. Cryder was trying to devalue the place, make it appear that the only sensible use for a spot of land like this was for some rich old fart to sit around with his grandkids and pretend to be an outdoorsman. As if.

"It's pretty hot here," Frank said.

"Oh, well, yes. It's hot everywhere in Florida."

"No, I mean business. We're hot. We're busy. The restaurant is worth good money as it is."

"But you're not making money, Frank."

"Beg your pardon?"

"Not real money." Alonzo paused. "Have you ever thought about real money, Frank?"

"Money's money, Mr. Cryder. It's all real to me."

More chuckling. "Alonzo. It's Alonzo. Well, we'll see. We'll see. I think you and I should sit down and talk about real money one day. One day soon. Can I come down to see you?"

"No need," Frank said. He was suddenly angry, irrationally angry, with a juvenile feeling that felt something like petulance. "I told you, it's not for sale. It's my restaurant."

"Don't you mean it's your mother's restaurant?"

Frank felt a twinge at the top of his spine.

"You seem to know a lot about this property, Mr. Cryder."

The man on the phone chuckled again. "Oh, it's easy, you know, we look these things up in the tax rolls. It's all right there. Your mother owns the restaurant. And your mother and father own the adjacent property to the south, isn't that right? Your parents' home? I'll definitely be interested in speaking with them, as well."

Your parents' home. The twinge increased, a prickling feeling at the nape of Frank's neck. It was his *mother's* home. Arla's. He knew she'd paid off the mortgage with the money left to her from her parents after their deaths. He knew it was Bolton money behind the deed at Aberdeen, and he knew it was Arla's sweat—and his own and Carson's too, come to think of it—that had kept the old place standing in the years since his father left. His father. For all Frank knew he could be dead. A vision of Dean's face appeared before him: dark haired, blue eyed, his skin grown leathery and worn through the years. Even twenty years ago he'd looked beaten. Frank could only imagine what he looked like today. There once was a time when Frank had wished Dean would come back. Now he didn't know what he wished for.

"Mr. Cryder?"

"Yes, Frank?"

"Can I tell you something?"

"Why, of course."

"Man to man?"

"Yes."

"You listening?"

"Yes, Frank." Frank pictured him. Though he'd never met the man, he conjured an image and would have bet money on its accuracy—pallid skin, rubbery jowls, a too-tight oxford shirt with monogrammed cuffs. Hard-soled shoes. Soft hands. He could almost see the man leaning forward, clutching the phone to his ear, an expression of expectancy in his small eyes.

"You talk to my mother about this, or my father for that matter, if you can even find him, and I will kick your fat greedy ass from here to Welaka. The restaurant is not for sale."

A pause. Then: "Mr. Bravo, I do believe it's a free country."

"Not here in Utina, it isn't. Ain't nothing free here, asshole."

Frank hung up the phone.

Three hours later, Uncle Henry's was hopping. The thin early-lunch crowd had dispersed, displaced by the crack-of-noon late risers looking to drown their previous night's indiscretions in a plate of fried shrimp and a cold draft. On the back deck, Irma wrestled with bunting, trying to give the place an air of festivity for the evening's fireworks. Frank had left Morgan in the kitchen and had taken up his usual post behind the bar, where he could survey the restaurant and keep a steady eye on things.

He didn't hate the bar. He'd built it himself, in fact, had torn out the original Uncle Henry's bar more than twenty years ago when it had begun to buckle from the weight of so many bent elbows, so many come-ons and boasts and debates, so many memories. He was glad to have it gone. The new bar, Frank's bar, was made of soft yellow pine but coated with a layer of resin thick as a man's thumb, so rather than nicks or cuts in the wood the bar had, over time, collected soft dips and creases that gave it a comforting, welcoming appearance, like a down duvet. Frank tended it alone, always, even in the busiest parts of the night, when the patrons stood three deep before him, calling his name and waving bills in the air. He couldn't stand anyone behind the bar with him, so he compensated for the lack of help by becoming faster, faster, faster, a master of efficiency and consolidation of effort. He liked the busy times best of all. He didn't have to talk with anyone then.

Except that strategy was failing this afternoon with Mac Weeden, who sat on his usual stool and insisted on keeping up a running conversation with Frank no matter how many times the latter had to duck back and forth along the inside of the bar, hitting the taps, pouring whiskey and gin, clearing the empties. Mac was a tidy, compact man with close-cropped hair that had turned a premature gray when he was in his early thirties but which actually served, today, as a not-unpleasing complement to his pale blue eyes, at least judging by the number of women Frank had seen Mac successfully chat up at the bar. Frank had known

Mac since kindergarten, had shared a locker with him at Utina High. A University of Florida College of Law graduate, Mac had been, for a time, Utina's only lawyer until an unfortunate episode with the teenaged daughter of a client had cost him his law license and his reputation, for what little that was worth in Utina. He was both smart and garrulous, qualities which, in Frank's view, did not always come in equal measures within one person, but Mac was an anomaly, likeable in spite of himself. At one time, he probably could have set himself on a professional path that would have taken him out of Utina, out of North Florida, hell, even out of the South had he been so inclined. As it was, Mac was a lonely, disbarred attorney headed down a slippery slope toward alcoholism. He was Utina's default consultant for spot-on but unlicensed law advice, was the not-so-proud proprietor of Utina's only Bait/ Karaoke business, and was, Frank admitted now as he regarded Mac's bright eyes and open smile on the other side of the bar, a damn good friend.

"You see they're almost done framing that Publix on Seminary?" Mac said. He'd drained his first draft Bass of the night, then pushed the empty glass toward Frank by way of requesting another.

"I did see that, actually," Frank said. How could he miss it? How could anyone in Utina miss the new Publix? The first trucks had pulled in a month or so ago—earth movers, a backhoe, and a whole fleet of black and red pickups driven by thick-waisted men in workshirts and blue jeans, leather belts too tight, cell phones clipped to their pants like parasites. The big oaks were the first to go, and then overnight it seemed the southeast corner of Seminary and Cooksey had been transformed from an untidy swath of palmettos and pines to a garish, wounded place, clear-cut in one afternoon to make way for the supermarket.

"Changing the face of this place, let me tell you," Mac said. "And they're fast. They'll have that sucker finished and open in a couple of months, you watch. Publix in Utina? What's next? Macy's?"

"Yeah, right," Frank said. "Nobody here even has enough money for the Dollar General." He pulled the tap and filled a fresh glass of Bass for Mac, who accepted it gratefully.

"So we're gearing up for preseason. Our Heisman boy is looking good for this year," Mac said, moving quickly to his favorite topic—the Florida Gators—one he could focus on ad nauseam, much to the delight of nearly every man and most of the women in Utina. Jesus, Frank thought sometimes. If we put as much brain power into improving this town as we do into memorizing the stats of every Cracker running back to ever rush across the fifty-yard line on a hot afternoon in the Swamp, then maybe we'd actually get somewhere. But he took Mac's bait.

"He's up against the Warriors first game," he said. "That team might take him down a peg."

"Shit, you kidding me, Frank?" Mac said. His eyes were wide. "Frickin' University of Hawaii? We're national fucking champions, may I remind you."

"Not this year."

"We've got the Heisman winner, may I remind you."

"A beauty contest."

"Fuck you, Frank," Mac said good-naturedly. "We got the Heisman."

"Everybody's expendable, Mac."

"Who's expendable?" The voice was Carson's. Frank had not seen his brother come in, and he felt a familiar twinge of dismay at the sound of Carson's voice. "We talking 'bout you,

Mac?" Carson clapped Mac on the shoulder, pulled out a barstool to join him. "Or Frankie? Not Frank. This place would come crashing down without Saint Frank."

Frank stared at him, wondering if he had the energy to engage in this decades-old battle today. Carson, at forty-two, was still handsome, always the most presentable of the Bravo boys, to be sure, with his dark hair cut short and severe, his jaw clean, his clothes crisp, everything about the man suggesting tidiness and grooming, characteristics that stood in sharp contrast to Frank's ball caps and rumpled shirts. But Carson's face, lately, had begun to exhibit some of the signs of his fondness for shots of Irish whiskey with a chaser or five of Heineken. Carson's ability to drink anyone under the table, once a point of pride, was now becoming one of those things, like mullet haircuts and cow tipping, that wasn't so funny anymore. The Bravo apple didn't fall far from the tree, if you asked Frank, and he wondered, as he stood behind the bar, slinging booze to people who didn't need it, whether he'd ever be the one apple that got away.

Frank looked past Carson, to where Elizabeth stood awkwardly, holding Bell by the hand.

"That how you treat your wife, Carson? Don't even offer the lady a seat?" he said.

"It's okay, Frank," Elizabeth said. "We're going to get a table. Bell wants to eat." Elizabeth's hair was the color of straw, and her face was still brushed with the same fine freckles Frank had first noticed across a Formica lunch table at Utina Elementary School. She looked like she'd lost weight recently. And she didn't have it to lose.

Carson turned around, looked at Elizabeth for a moment, and then looked back at Frank. "What are you now, Miss Manners?" he said. Elizabeth rolled her eyes.

"Hey there, Belly-Button," Frank said.

"Hi, Uncle Frank," Bell replied, gazing at him with that same open, unabashed stare of her mother's. But she didn't say anything else. Not one for small talk. Frank smiled at her. Like mother, like daughter. Elizabeth led Bell to a table in the corner of the dining room, near the back windows, so Bell could look out at the water. Frank waved to Irma, who had given up on the bunting and was now clearing a table on the other side of the dining room. "Whatever they want," he told her when she approached. He gestured to Elizabeth and Bell. "And a glass of the good Kendall for my sister-in-law."

"Where you been lately, Carson?" Mac said. "You too good to come back to Utina now?"

"Hell," Carson said. "Anybody's too good for Utina. *Everybody's* too good for Utina."

"Speak for yourself," Mac said. He tipped up his glass, approaching the end of his second beer. "Some of us like it here."

"Actually," Carson said. "That's what I want to talk to Frankie-boy here about. Seems like some people are liking Utina more and more." He looked at Frank pointedly.

Of course. Alonzo Cryder had gotten to Carson, pursuing the agenda of buying Uncle Henry's and Aberdeen. Of course. And it hadn't taken long. A few hours, maybe? Frank raised his eyebrows at Carson but otherwise didn't bite. He salted two margarita glasses, then filled them to the brim with tequila and mixer for a pair of bosomy blondes at the end of the bar.

"Thanks, Frankie," the prettier one said when he delivered the drinks. "You're a sweetheart." He couldn't remember the women's names, though they were frequent fixtures at the end of his bar. And he had a feeling he was *supposed* to remember their names—he just couldn't, or wouldn't, retrieve them from memory. Too many nameless blondes in the world. Too many lonely women. They made him sad.

"Happy Fourth," the woman said, raising her glass. "Independence Day, Frank—and you look free to me. You gonna let freedom ring tonight?" She smiled suggestively.

"Not my favorite holiday," he said.

"Come on," she said. "Don't be a party pooper, Frank."

Frank picked up their tip, a generous one, then returned to Carson and Mac, who were now arguing about Mac's own decades-old stats as one of Utina High's starting running backs. "I had the same rushing yards as Emmitt Smith his senior year in high school," Mac said. "Exactly."

"My ass," Carson said.

"I did. You can look it up."

"If that's true, which I doubt, then it's because the only teams we ever played were a bunch of pussies from Yulee and Ponte Vedra. You could run up and down the field all day long while they stood around doing their nails."

"I coulda played for Florida," Mac said.

"And I coulda run for president," Carson said. "Just decided against it."

Mac chuckled. "Good stuff," he said amiably.

"I thought you said you could pick up Mom and Sofia on your way," Frank said to Carson.

"So are you going to get me a drink, or what?" Carson said. "Do I have to come back there and pour it myself?"

"Carson."

"What?"

"Why didn't you pick up Mom?"

Carson sighed. "Christ. I thought maybe I could actually unwind for five seconds, you know? Before the loony bin arrives? Is that a crime, Frank?" Frank turned away, pulled the tap, and drew a beer. He placed it in front of his brother.

"You're such a martyr," he said.

"Takes one to know one," Carson said.

Frank picked up a rag, then threw it down again. "You want to come back here and fry shrimp and tend bar so *I* can go get them? Or you want to drive five minutes down Monroe Road and make life a whole lot easier for everyone?"

"Where's that shitwit who lives there?" Carson said, referring, Frank knew, to Biaggio, who in Carson's mind was an intellectually inferior specimen of humanity not worth giving the time of day, but who was nonetheless a perfectly good candidate when it came to shuttling his mother and sister along the sandy back roads of North Utina.

"Biaggio's not coming," Frank said. "And they're not his responsibility."

"Nor mine."

"I think you've made that perfectly clear."

"Gentlemen, gentlemen," Mac said, holding up his hands. "I cannot stomach this horrendous bickering. Where's the brotherly love? *Qua est philia?*" The fact that Mac was quoting Latin, a holdover from his law school days, meant that he was half in the bag already, and it was early on a holiday evening. Clearly he'd pregamed before even arriving at Uncle Henry's, where so far he'd consumed only a pint and a half. It was going to be a long night. "I will go and fetch the fair damsels myself," Mac said. He fumbled in his pocket for his car keys.

"Carson," Frank said.

"All right, all right," Carson said. "Sit tight, Mac-aroni. I'll get them. They're not your nutcases, they're ours." He drained his almost-full beer in one long pull.

"It would be nice if you didn't refer to them as nutcases," Frank said.

"Right," Carson said. "They're not our nutcases. They're our freak show."

He put the glass on the bar and stood up. "When I get back, Frankie-boy," he said, pointing a finger in Frank's face, "we're going to have a little chat about our friend Mr. Cryder."

Frank watched his brother leave the restaurant. What had happened to him and Carson? They used to be best friends. Now he could hardly stand to be in the same room with his brother. And it wasn't just Elizabeth, though Carson didn't deserve her, to be sure. There was more. A decades-old blame, malignant as catbrier.

Carson stepped out the front door but then held it open in a gesture of exaggerated chivalry for Susan Holm to enter. She wore a bright red sundress, her soft blond hair pulled up into a tight, high ponytail that looked a bit too childish for her age. She smiled at Carson, then headed directly for the bar. Frank sighed. "Here we go," he said quietly to Mac.

"Boys," she said, settling onto the stool vacated by Carson. It was her standard greeting.

"Hit me, Frank," she said, tapping her long fingernails on the bar. Frank poured a glass of Shiraz and set it in front of her.

"Susan, you are a vision in red tonight," Mac said. "Allow me to buy you that drink."

"Not on your life, Mac," she said. "Then you'll think I owe you something."

Mac clutched his hands to his chest. "Words wound, Susan," he said. "Now come on. How come you never let me buy you a drink?" He'd begun to slur a bit. Frank made a note to start cutting Mac's drafts with half O'Doul's. It was a trick he'd learned years ago. If he let Mac guzzle enough undiluted Bass as a loss leader, he'd be unable to detect the switch as the night wore on. It was better for everyone.

Susan sighed. "We've been through this, Mac. Now don't embarrass yourself." She turned to Frank. "Where's your big brother headed in such a hurry? He's not staying for fireworks?"

"He's off to get my mother and sister. And if things go the way they're headed, there'll be more fireworks in here than out there." He gestured to the back deck.

Mac laughed. "Good stuff," he said.

Susan sipped her wine and regarded Frank.

"So Frank," she said. "I sold another property on your street."

"I wish you'd quit doing that," he said. He pulled two bottles of Heineken from the cooler, flipped the caps off in two quick movements, and handed the beers to Irma, who was waiting with a tray. "Gonna have me surrounded by yuppies before long."

"They're buying. What can I say? Nobody else is these days, but the yuppies seem to have no end of money."

"Which property?"

"End of your road—on the south side. It's a nice piece,

but not as nice as yours. And no house on it yet. Want to know what I sold it for?"

"No, I don't," he said, and he meant it. He was getting tired of all these real estate people thinking money was the only thing they had to talk about to get his attention. Thinking he'd jump like a trained monkey if the price was right. Jesus. He knew the properties were worth money. Knew they were becoming more valuable every day. But he didn't want a bigger house, or a newer truck, or—or what? What would he buy? He couldn't even think of what people spent money on.

Susan looked at him, annoyed. "You can hold out as long as you want, Frank," she said. "Just don't make a dinosaur of yourself. The world's changing all around you—you can't hold it back. This place is on its way to becoming something else, like it or not." She swiveled her hips around on the barstool, leaned forward. "Opportunities are presenting themselves to you—*good* opportunities"—she tipped her head down and looked up at him from under her lashes—"and you're just being too stubborn, or too *whatever*, to consider them."

"Why don't you let me consider them for him?" Mac said.

Susan rolled her eyes. But he looked so hopeful and pained that she had to laugh, and Frank joined her, and then he poured a new Bass for Mac—full strength, last one, he told himself—and set it in front of him. A group of fishermen at the end of the bar were waving him over.

"Be back, you two," he said to Mac and Susan.

"Think about it, Frank," Susan called after him. "Don't miss out on this." And whether she was talking about letting her sell his house or something quite different, or both, he could not tell. But he had a feeling.

FOUR

At eight o'clock, an hour before the scheduled start of the fireworks, the deck off the back of Uncle Henry's was creaking precipitously with the weight of some of Utina's finest—T-shirts stretched taut over bellies and bosoms, generous tushes perched ingloriously on resin chairs and along the deck's wooden railings, faces slick with perspiration and squinting into the still-brutal rays of the evening sun. The heat notwithstanding, it was a cheerful bunch. A woman in a floral halter top held a lit sparkler in her teeth. A man in a Gators cap bellowed merrily for more beer. Even Irma, the waitress, seemed buoyed, stomping with less than her usual venom back and forth between the bar inside and the raucous crowd on the deck. The water was a beautiful sparkling silver. Two little girls had the giggles. But Arla Bravo, the restaurant's owner, was thinking enough was enough.

She was here against her will to begin with, and all evening she'd been fighting the sullen desire to say something nasty to someone, anyone. A crude or cruel enough remark would create a reason for Frank to throw up his hands and send her and Sofia home, where Arla could endure the rest of the evening in relative peace. But the problem was that no one in her family had spent enough time with her yet for her to sling that arrow. Frank had been busy behind the bar since four o'clock. Carson had collected Arla and Sofia from Aberdeen, had driven to Uncle Henry's and waited impatiently while they executed a debate in the parking lot over whether to bring their purses inside or lock them in the car. Then he deposited his mother and sister unceremoniously inside the restaurant before assuming his position on a barstool between Mac Weeden and Susan Holm. Carson's wife, Elizabeth, was out on the back deck, having staked a claim to two of the seats with the best view of the fireworks for herself and Bell. Arla sat out there with them for a while, but it was too hot, so she came back inside and resigned herself to a round of Sudoku at an empty table. Sofia sat alone at one end of the bar, gazing out to the deck and picking at an order of fried okra.

Arla sighed. "Oh, hell," she said. The woman at the table next to her looked at Arla from under a red, white, and blue visor. The woman's shirt was embroidered with an American flag, with small silver sequins representing stars. Arla wanted to smack her.

"Excuse me?" the woman said.

"What's that?" Arla said. She tipped her head to one side, feigning a hearing impairment.

"I thought you said something."

"What's that?" Arla said, louder.

The woman turned back to her margarita, rolling her eyes at her dinner companion, a pink-faced man with a coconut shrimp in each hand. Irma stalked by with a tray of dinners, and Arla watched her, tried to catch her eye to commiserate about the idiocy of the situation, but Irma ignored her.

"It's Arla Bravo," she heard the sequined woman whisper to the man across the table, and Arla winced as she realized her feigned hearing loss might have now backfired on her. "The owner," the woman continued. "Used to be Bolton. You know. Used to be all *that*. But now . . ." The woman's voice trailed off, and she shook her head.

Arla closed the Sudoku book and stuffed it into her purse. She stood up abruptly, jostling the basket of condiments on the table. She grabbed her cane and walked across the dining room and over to Sofia at the end of the bar. Outside, the crowd on the deck had begun to sing "Yankee Doodle."

"Oh, for the love of Jesus," she said. And this was the insanity of it all, these pointless gatherings, these incessant holidays. Dressing up and singing like a pack of idjits, carrying on drinking until all hours in the name of Memorial Day, or Independence Day, or Labor Day. The summer holidays were the worst, nothing but pure stupid. No cool air or lovely pies or pretty lights to look at. Just sweat and noise.

But good for business. She looked at Frank, who was moving quickly behind the bar to slide bottles of beer across to the customers standing two deep, hands outstretched, holding tens and twenties between damp fingers. Frank kept a bottle opener tied to his right wrist with a leather strap, and she watched as he moved in one fluid swoop to pull a Michelob from the cooler, swing the opener up into his hand, snap off the metal cap, and slide the bottle down the bar. He had a grace to him, Frank, that had escaped the rest of her children, who all, she often thought, took after their father.

"Sofia," Arla said, "why did we come?"

"Frank wanted us to," Sofia said. "Quit being negative." She looked around the dining room and sighed. Arla wanted to shake her. What a day this had been. Sofia in her bedroom at the crack of dawn throwing her things out the window. The Steinway still parked in the middle of the hallway at home. And all of it, all of it under the shadow of this wretched holiday. This hateful, wretched day.

"You're not enjoying this any more than I am," Arla said. "Why don't you call Biaggio to come get us?" In the old days she would have simply set off through the wooded path to Aberdeen, but these days she trusted neither her balance nor her endurance to take her through the overgrown pathway, which was a fifteen-minute walk through thick, gnarled roots and patches of slippery mud along the bank of the Intracoastal. She missed that walk. She'd stop and visit with Drusilla along the way, sit for a while by the headstone in the woods and talk to Drusilla about what she'd loved and what she'd lost and about why they always had to be the same things. But for the past five years—maybe more? she'd lost track—she'd had to travel by car to get to and from Uncle Henry's, down the long winding driveway of Aberdeen, half a mile north on Monroe, and back in through the dusty sand approach to the restaurant.

The problem was that neither Arla nor Sofia drove. In Arla's case, she'd given it up for good years ago, after that accident on Seminary Street, when she tried to push the clutch with the rubber tip of her cane, but it slipped off and she'd gotten confused with the pedals; the Impala bolted over the curb and into the brick pilasters of Sterling's Drugstore. "Just thank God no one was hurt," the policeman said, looking at Arla pointedly. She

returned home hours later, still shaking from the fear and the
shame, clutching a moving violation and a hefty insurance esti-
mate. She hung the car keys on a metal hook inside the kitchen
cabinet and closed the door.

She realized now that not driving was one of the things that
had aged her prematurely, had made her dependent on her sons
and on Biaggio in a geriatric way that annoyed and embarrassed
her. She was only sixty-two, for God's sake. Sometimes she felt
like she was ninety.

And Sofia, well, you'd think Sofia could have picked it up—
driving—but operating a motor vehicle was just one more of the
many things that Arla's daughter simply opted not to do. She'd
tried it once as a teenager and had been so frightened by the
enormity of it, the act of moving such a monstrously large piece
of metal at high speeds with just the slightest pressure from
her own tentative foot, that she'd never driven again. Arla didn't
suppose Sofia, at forty-three now, was about to try it again. Hell.

She looked at her daughter. Sofia was still a striking woman,
having inherited her own towering height and her father's blue
eyes. Her hair, bright red, was thick and generous, though she
kept it constantly pulled back in a severe ponytail, with two artfully arranged wisps at her temples. She was not fat; however
her height and presence often made people think she was. She
was a big woman.

Oh, she hadn't had it easy, Sofia. Depression and anxiety,
the doctors had said. Mood swings. Control issues. "She's trying
to create her comfort zone," one therapist said. Well, no wonder,
what with everything going so wrong the way it did, back then.
And oh, my God, even before that, that awful business with the
professor. But Arla had tried so hard, for Sofia. The doctors had

prescribed medications, which Sofia had never wanted to take, and had given Arla special directions: Watch the diet. Reduce stress. Keep a routine. Exercise regularly. None of those treatments took, of course, not at Aberdeen, where the pantry staples ran to Little Debbie cakes and Tang, and where these days the most strenuous exercise came in the form of climbing the dim staircase after a marathon of rerun sitcoms and late-night movies.

Of course, in the old days it had been different. Sofia had always been nervous, unpredictable, of course, but she'd been more or less normal as a little girl, before all these awful *conditions* had set in. *Diagnoses*, what have you. Such fear, all the time. Panic attacks on the school playground. Temper tantrums at home. And yet, such a beautiful girl, still beautiful today, but back then just stunning, that long red hair, those faint golden lashes. She was like Arla herself, once long ago. Sofia did well in school, never made waves, the teachers all loved her, which was a relief for Arla, given the three wild boys who followed and the fits she'd had keeping them all on track in school. Back then, Sofia was the easy one. And the pointe lessons—oh, the pointe! How she missed it. Sofia had been a lovely ballerina, strong and powerful. She'd even danced in *The Nutcracker* that one winter in St. Augustine, en pointe for both acts, night after night for the two weeks leading up until Christmas, and Arla was never so proud in her life. A dewdrop, a snowflake, *and* the first understudy for Clara. My word. Onstage, the light had played off Sofia's hair and Arla had felt sorry, had felt downright pity for all the other parents. Those poor, plain people. *Nobody* had a daughter as lovely, as special, as rare as Sofia.

That was a long time ago. Twenty-five years? Thirty? The math was confounding. Every year, the damn math got harder,

and every year, she and Sofia got older, more dug in, more re-
sistant to the changes that could have revived them, could have
renewed them. Now, Uncle Henry's was getting more crowded,
and Arla was longing for her kitchen, for mugs of Chablis, for
the quiet, comfortable feeling of having her daughter need her
company. But damn if Sofia was cooperating.

"I'm not calling Biaggio," Sofia said. "Frank wants us here.
You call Biaggio, if you want."

But Frank would be mad at her if she insisted on leaving
early, before the fireworks. He'd been pestering her lately for
staying in, for "not trying hard enough," for spending too many
evenings at home with Sofia and the Home Shopping Network.
"You never even come to the restaurant anymore," he said, over
and over. "It's *your* frigging restaurant. I just work there. You
ought to make an appearance now and then." Now, what kind
of son would talk to his mother that way?

"Carson will be there," he'd said. "He's bringing Bell for the
fireworks. Come spend time with your granddaughter."

Oh, but what did it matter? Carson didn't care whether
she was here or not. She looked out through the windows at the
back of the dining room to the deck. Elizabeth looked over her
shoulder just then—the timing was odd, as if she could sense
she was being watched—and she caught Arla's eye and smiled.
Elizabeth was like that. She would smile at the damndest times,
like when her husband was inside the bar chatting up everyone
and anyone but leaving his wife and daughter to fight their way
for seats to watch the fireworks on Independence Day. And yet
Elizabeth would smile. Arla used to think the girl was simple.
But she'd come to the conclusion she was simply decent. More
decent than the man she'd married, even Arla had to admit.

She raised her eyebrows at Elizabeth, then rolled her eyes. She lifted her hand to wave Elizabeth and Bell in to the restaurant, have them sit here at the bar, cool off for a bit, maybe have a cup of chowder and some corn fritters. But then the crowd on the deck shifted and Elizabeth was hidden from view, and Arla felt irritable and lonesome again.

And hot. Oh, my Lord in heaven, hot. Her shirt stuck like cellophane to the lower part of her back, and her thighs felt swollen and confined inside her Bermuda shorts, like fat bratwursts in casing. The air-conditioning inside Uncle Henry's was no use. With the back windows thrown so maddeningly, festively open to the Intracoastal, the restaurant felt like a piece of Tupperware, the air inside so humid and dank you could scarcely breathe. Why not just flush the electric payment right down the toilet?

But she *owned* Uncle Henry's. She should be the *boss*, and yet so many other people seemed to be telling her what to do. Come here. Go there. Stand up. Sit down. *Relax.* She'd had it.

It wasn't like this in the old days. She'd bought the restaurant not long after Dean had left her. She remembered the transaction like it was yesterday, sitting down with Charleen, Uncle Henry's daughter, at the People's Guarantee on Seminary Street, signing the papers with her right hand while her left hand shook on her lap beneath the table, marking her first *official* foray into the world of the working class, her first *real* dalliance with the ranks of the gainfully employed. Back then, the church linens were only a tiny sideline, a little boost to Dean's income as a boiler tech but never enough to actually affect the bottom line or define Arla's professional ambitions. She was a Bolton, after all, never forget it, a blue-blooded woman raised on fine china and six-hundred-thread-count sheets. She never planned to work. Until Dean had orchestrated his exit and left her with Sofia and Frank still living at home, a monthly tax bill, and a fat balance on the Visa, she'd never once considered her own potential as a breadwinner, or a rainmaker, or an *entrepreneur*, what have you. But the money left to her by her parents—a disappointing sum to begin with, once James's business debts were exposed—was dwindling fast. It had been enough to pay off the mortgage on Aberdeen, enough to supplement the boiler job and cover the gaps left by Dean's increasingly erratic work ethic. But it wouldn't have lasted much longer. And then she bought Uncle Henry's. Before the ink had dried on the sales contract she felt a thrill like never before, an empowerment born of necessity but welcomed like a change-of-life baby. She was Arla Bravo. She owned a restaurant. She was going to make money. She pictured a dining room full of revelers, a kitchen full of karma, a register full of cash. *Uncle Henry's Bar & Grill. Arla Bravo, Proprietor.* She liked the ring of it.

Of course, as luck and life would have it, things didn't work out quite as Arla expected. Running the restaurant was hard. Damn hard. Early morning preps in a stifling hot kitchen. Vendors who left you hanging with no grouper *or* mahi on a four-day weekend in the middle of summer. Snippy, chesty waitresses who thought they could do better elsewhere. Boozy brawlers who sassed her at the bar and drank on credit night after night. A year into operations and she thought she'd go mad.

But then there was Frank. Thank God. Frank. Nineteen years old and skinny as a whip but strong and stable and smart, good Lord, that boy was smart. He was figuring up the accounts receivable before she knew what to do with the accounts payable, tallying up the drawer each night and marking down notations in a ledger and negotiating with that god-awful fishery in Jacksonville for the lowest price on bulk crabmeat, frozen crawfish, catfish nuggets. He saved her, Frank. He did. She knew it then, and she knew it now. Within two years, she'd handed over the operations of Uncle Henry's top to tail to Frank, her middle son, her right-hand man, her rock. And he'd run the restaurant well, had grown it, in fact, adding new entrées to the menu and setting up outdoor seating and expanding the bar area by three hundred square feet to accommodate the seemingly endless income potential generated by thirsty Utina stalwarts in search of cold brew and conch fritters. He'd done well with Uncle Henry's, finding his rhythm as manager and bartender just as Arla herself retreated farther and farther into the darkened rooms of Aberdeen, sealed herself off from the restaurant and its attendant slavishness and sociability, opting instead for the quiet and isolation of life alone with Sofia, surrounded by communion cloths and magazines and empty rooms once filled with boys. He'd done well.

But that didn't mean she couldn't still be mad at him. Because this was pissing her off, pardon the French, no other way to put it. She didn't want to be here tonight, Fourth of July, night of nights, the night she hated above all others. And if it weren't for Frank, she wouldn't be. She wanted to go home. *Enough.*

Arla left Sofia picking at her okra. She walked around the end of the bar, down a dim hallway that led to Frank's office. The noise from the restaurant faded a bit as she entered the office, closed the door behind her, and sat down behind Frank's desk. She looked around. Not a single paper on the desk, not a single item out of place. A row of equipment catalogs stood neatly on a bookshelf against one wall. A simple floor lamp, shining, dustless, stood in the corner. Immaculate. Where did he *come* from, Frank? If she hadn't borne him herself, put him to her breast the moment he entered the world and memorized the curve of his head, the shape of his nose, sometimes she would have wondered if he was switched at birth with some other baby, from some tidy mother. The office had one window, a jalousie, which looked out to the back of the restaurant and the party on the deck. A small couch sat under the window, and Arla knew he slept here sometimes, catnaps in the afternoons between the morning preps and the evening customers. She sighed. Frank. He worked hard for all of them. But she wanted to go home.

She dialed Biaggio's number.

"Would you be a sweetheart and come and get us from the restaurant?" she said when he answered. She could hear the TV in the background. She felt a little bit guilty. Biaggio didn't like crowds, and he told her he'd been afraid of fireworks ever since he was eight, when his brother Jimmy had snuck under the picnic table at Mary Lou's house in West Virginia and tied a string of firecrackers to Biaggio's PF Flyers. When the crackers went off Biaggio tried to run across the lawn and had ended up with third-degree burns on his hands and feet, not to mention the lingering, burning shame of his family's laughter in his ears. So he hated Fourth of July. It was one thing they had in common. She knew he wouldn't want to come here, but she asked him anyway.

"Right now?" he said.

"Yes," Arla said. "Well, as soon as you can."

"But what about the fireworks?"

"We don't want to watch the fireworks."

"Sofia, too?"

"Right. Both of us."

"Well, Miss Arla, I thought Frank said you were supposed to stay and watch the fireworks. You know, enjoy yourself and all."

"Oh, Biaggio," Arla said. She leaned back in Frank's chair, put her deformed left foot up on a file cabinet. She suddenly wanted to cry. "I don't care what Frank said." Her voice caught a bit when she said this, and, while the emotion was sincere, she knew it would have a beneficial effect on convincing Biaggio to come. She felt a tug, a twitch toward the Arla she was not so many years ago, and she fell back almost unwittingly on her long-dormant though never-forgotten skills in making men do things they didn't always want to do. Though she felt vaguely remorseful about using these admittedly rusty tactics on Biaggio, she wanted to get home. And he was going to get her there.

"Now, Miss Arla," he said. "Don't you go getting upset now."

She sniffled, cleared her throat.

He was quiet for a moment. "Are you okay, Miss Arla?"

Arla had a picture of Biaggio sitting on the concrete step in front of his trailer, the kitchen phone cord stretched taut though a crack in the screen door. A barred owl hooted in the woods outside the restaurant, and she could hear the echo through the phone and knew she and Biaggio could hear the same sounds at the same time. So close—just a few minutes from Aberdeen through the woods, but she couldn't get there. Not without help. He really was a sweet boy. She liked him as much as one of her own. Sometimes even more.

"I will be," she said. "If you'll come get us."

He sighed.

"Give me ten minutes," he said.

"Thank you, Biaggio."

"But come out the back door, and don't tell Frank," he said.

"Of course not."

"All right, Miss Arla."

"Biaggio?"

"Yes?"

"You are a prince among men, Biaggio."

Arla hung up, but before she could get up from the chair the phone rang again, and she picked it up.

"Uncle Henry's," she said, remembering the days when it was her job, and her job alone, to answer the phone at the restaurant. She hadn't done this in years.

"Good evening, Mrs. Bravo." It was a man's voice, low and confident.

"Who is this?" Arla said.

"My name is Alonzo Cryder," the man said. "Is this Mrs. Bravo?"

"Well, that doesn't tell me a skinny thing, does it? Who is Alonzo Cryder?"

"Oh, I'm a business associate of your son's. I was calling to reach him, but I am delighted to have reached *you*, actually."

"A business associate? What business is that?"

A short snuffle, like an aborted laugh. "Didn't your son tell you about me, Mrs. Bravo? I'm offering to buy your restaurant." She sat straight up, looked through the small window at the crowd of people out on the deck.

"The restaurant is not for sale," she said.

"That's what your son said."

Relief washed over Arla like cool water.

"But I'm hoping to change his mind."

"You spoke with him about this?"

"I did. And actually, Miss Arla—may I call you Miss Arla?—our conversation did not go entirely well. I think we may have gotten off on the wrong foot, in fact. I'm calling him to see if we can try again."

"The restaurant is not for sale."

"I spoke with your other son, as well—Carson?"

"Uncle Henry's is not for sale," she repeated, though she had a strange rushing feeling in her head, like an avalanche beginning to break loose from the top of a mountain.

"I just thought we could talk, Mrs. Bravo. About your restaurant. And also about your home."

"You always conduct business on the Fourth of July, Mr. Cryder?"

"Not always. Just today."

Arla was silent, stonily so, waiting for the man to get the picture. And eventually he did. "We'll talk again soon, Miss Arla?" He'd shifted to using her first name again.

"I doubt it."

"Well I hope we do, Miss Arla. I hope we do. It would be my sincere pleasure."

Back home at Aberdeen a half hour later, Biaggio held the door while Arla and Sofia made their way up the ramp, across the porch, and into the house. The fireworks behind Uncle Henry's were in full swing now, and Arla had to fight the temptation to cover her ears, block out the sounds of the explosions.

"Whoops," Biaggio said, when they headed for the kitchen and saw the Steinway still parked in the hallway. "Forgot about this little boondoggle. How 'bout I move this back?"

"Move it out, you mean," Sofia said.

"Oh, for God's sake," Arla said. "Leave it alone." She leaned on Biaggio and climbed awkwardly across the top of the old piano. Her backside hit the keys on the way down the other side, and a thudding chord rang out. She clomped into the kitchen. Biaggio and Sofia followed, over the top of the Steinway.

The kitchen was dark and quiet, but when Arla flicked on the overhead light a palmetto bug buzzed across the room and hit her in the head, and she screamed in surprise.

"Damn things!" she said. You never got used to them. Never. The bug crashed into the refrigerator, hurled itself back across the kitchen, and settled on the counter, where it ran in a tight circle.

"I got it, Miss Arla," Biaggio said. "You just sit down now."

Arla sat, glaring at Sofia as she pulled out a chair on the opposite side of the table.

"I wonder how many other families are coming home to a piano in their hallway tonight?" Arla said.

"Don't you start," Sofia said. "Don't *even*." She picked up a newspaper on the kitchen table, shook it open.

Arla had no intention of starting anything. So she told Sofia so.

"Fine," Sofia said.

"Yes, fine."

"Let it drop."

"It's dropped."

Biaggio dispatched the palmetto bug, then filled an electric teakettle with tap water. He plugged the kettle in and fetched three mugs from the cupboard.

"It just strikes me that we are not living as normal people," Arla said.

Sofia slapped the newspaper down on the table.

"Do you *see*, Mother! You just cannot let it rest!"

"Well, it's true," Arla said. "Don't you think it's true, Biaggio?"

"I'm just making tea over here," Biaggio said.

"There are issues," Arla said vaguely. "And I worry about someone around here. About her outlook. About her state of mind."

"Oh, really? Well, *you* should talk about state of mind," Sofia said.

Arla was quiet a moment. The kettle began to whistle, and the kitchen felt cavernous, suddenly, overlarge and bright, a gaping bold void in the darkness of Aberdeen. She remembered a moment like this one, very many years ago, sitting in a small kitchen with her mother. *We'll take care of you*, Vera had said. *Dean will take care of me*, Arla said.

Oh, hell. Oh, double hell.

Sofia's hands shook as she rattled the paper, and Arla felt her heart clench as she saw her daughter's loneliness, and her mouth went dry with the taste of her daughter's desperation. But she didn't know what she was supposed to do about it. It was one of the mysteries of her life. One of the many.

She should go to bed. She was exhausted, suddenly. "Biaggio, tomorrow maybe you can help us move the piano," she said.

"Mother," Sofia said quietly. "I swear to God. The only place that fucking piano is going is out the front door." She enunciated every syllable clearly, then clenched her jaw and stared stonily back at the newspaper. That word! Arla was incredulous, that Sofia would use that word. The sound of it hung in the kitchen like an odor.

Arla took a deep breath. She'd never cried in front of Sofia before, and she wasn't about to start now. Biaggio stood frozen at the sink, a Lipton teabag in each hand. Sofia still stared at her newspaper, but a redness had begun to creep up her neck and into her cheeks, and though Arla could see, already, her daughter's remorse, and though she wanted to offer her absolution, she decided against it.

"All right, then," she said. She smoothed her hair. "I'm glad we're such a help to each other, Sofia. I'm glad we have each other in this world."

She rose stiffly, walked to the pantry, and put a bottle of Chablis and a plastic tumbler in a tote bag. "No tea, thank you, Biaggio," she said. She hitched the bag over her shoulder and walked out of the kitchen, then climbed over the piano and limped past the living room, where Dean's largemouth bass seemed to watch her, mocking. She made for the stairway, gripped the two banisters, and began her slow climb, her cane hooked over one elbow. On the third step she stopped, leaned over the railing, and looked back down the hallway into the kitchen, where Biaggio had taken her seat at the table and was staring forlornly at Sofia, who still flipped woodenly through the newspaper, not speaking, her face a crimson mask.

"You'll just have to let yourself out, Biaggio," Arla called. "I'm off to bed."

He shook himself, leaned forward, and looked down the hallway at Arla. "Good night, Miss Arla. You take care."

He was a handsome man, but so beaten. Oh, but they were all so beaten.

She went to the bathroom to wash her face and brush her teeth. She sat on the toilet and had a memory of a day long ago when she'd sat in this same spot, staring at her underwear, looking for the period that never came. That was Sofia, that day, announcing herself to Arla. When she was born Arla had thrilled at the sight of her—soft pink hair that turned brighter and brighter red as the years moved along. Dean had loved her, too, had held her on his chest and fallen asleep with her on the couch every evening until Arla came and lifted her from him and put her in the crib. And then came Carson, and Frank, and Will, all her beautiful children coming so fast, one after the other, those early years such a blur of sticky hands and tears and burp cloths and bibs that she never knew which way she was turning, and she fell into bed at night so tired she could feel the fatigue like a lead blanket across her chest. But they needed her. They all needed her.

Even Dean did what he was supposed to do, those years. He stayed on at Rayonier in Fernandina, bringing home a steady paycheck for a year, then two years, then five, ten, and Arla was amazed at his tenacity. He was shattering all kinds of records for the Bravos of Utina when it came to duration of gainful employment, and for this she was grateful. He still drank like a fish, but even for this she was a little bit glad, for it kept him reaching for her in the night, when the bedroom was fully dark, so she wore trashy lingerie and kept her bad foot tucked under the sheets. She arched her back and talked dirty and tried all kinds of acrobatics and contortions to make him love her, want her, need her like before, and though he panted and groaned and slept like a baby afterward, he never said her name, never looked her in the eye, though she whispered his to him again and again: Dean, Dean, Dean.

She was a good mother. She was. She'd make funny sandwiches for the kids, cutting out pickles to shape smiley faces atop the Wonder Bread, dicing up bowls of apples and sprinkling them with raisins for snacks in front of *Sesame Street*. She tucked them in their beds and bought them Wrangler jeans at JCPenney and made them do their homework. She made them all take piano lessons, made them all practice every day on the old Steinway, though only Will really took to it, and Frank to a lesser degree. She yelled, now and then, but she never hit them, never even thought of it. She read with them, with Sofia mostly, the only one who would sit still long enough. When Sofia was young—two? three?—they read *The Story of Babar* and then *Babar the King* and then *Babar and His Children*, and Sofia loved the books so much that when they'd worn out the stories in English Arla translated them back into their original French and they memorized the lines together, even the horrible part when Babar's mother was shot and Babar cried and cried. "*Pauvre maman*," Sofia would say, her tiny baby voice high and soft. "*Pauvre bébé*." Poor mama. Poor baby.

They were everything to each other, once. They were all they had. Dean's parents were out of the picture from the very start, and Vera and James orbited Arla at such a great distance as to scarcely exist. Then came that phone call when Will was a baby, the phone call that brought the news: a fire in Montauk, the top floor of a luxury hotel, the way Vera and James were found, their bodies charred and gray and wrapped in towels in a claw-footed tub. Arla turned to Dean that day, the phone in her hand, her blood turning to ice in her veins. He looked at her, puzzled, his head cocked to one side. What? he said. Now what?

Tonight, in her bedroom, Arla took off her clothes and put on a long terry robe. She propped her pillows against the headboard and arranged the wine and the tumbler on her nightstand. She left the closet light on, and a thick swath of light entered the room, bisecting her quilted bedspread like a lancet. She drew the curtains back from the window and climbed into bed. From here, the moon was almost completely visible, a near-perfect orb just minimally obscured by the sharp, scrawling branches of a hundred-year-old live oak.

She poured her first tumbler of wine and regarded the moon, feeling the same small stab of annoyance she'd felt ever since 1969, when those fool astronauts had been tromping around up there and had left behind the American flag. It always bothered her, that flag, left on the moon all those years ago, probably nothing left by now but an old pole and some elemental residue of polyester thread. Now why did they have to go and leave that garbage up there? It was like trashing a picnic site, with the moon before always so lovely and pure, and now the thought of that mess up there like it might as well have been Daytona after Bike Week. She sighed. But that was just the way of things. Somebody always making a mess out of everything.

She took a sip of wine, and then another, and decided it was time. Time to let it come. She wasn't looking forward to this, but it had been circling around her all day, like a hyena, and she had to let it come in or she'd never be able to sleep tonight. She closed her eyes. Let the memory come. Let it come.

*   *   *

She'd been sleeping when it happened. Right here, in this bed, sleeping long and sweet after the noise of the fireworks, the hot bother of grilling and shucking and paper plates and beer cans. Her dreams had been pervaded by sirens, the thin high whine of fire trucks and police cars. The boys were out on a roam, though it was late; they were teenagers then, wild things, and try as she might she just couldn't keep them in anymore. Sofia was asleep. And Dean was not with her, but that was not surprising, because it was a holiday, and he had drinking to do, and when he was out she'd come to see her empty bed as a refuge more than a failure. So when the boys opened her door, without knocking, and stood at the foot of her bed staring at her with the dim light of the moon behind them, she felt annoyed, and invaded, and felt there was no end of people in this house who would give her grief.

She sat up, she remembered this now, and had a vague feeling of miscounting, because instead of three rumpled boys— young men they were, really—there were only two, and that was wrong because they were almost always together, all three of them, and so something was wrong, something did not add up. Her vision began to focus and her head began to clear, despite the empty bottle of Chablis on the bedside table, that habit of hers having been in its infancy then. She saw Frank's face, and then Carson's, the whiteness of her boys' skin and the fear and shock in their eyes, and she clenched her hands into fists and said "No."

It was Will's own fault, they said. They'd been out at the dunes, and then they were coming home, and they told her how he ran away from them, reckless and crazy like he was, how he jumped laughing out of the pickup when they pulled off the road to take a leak in the woods, how he told them he would walk the rest of the way home. How they told him not to, how they searched for him and called his name: *Will, Will, Will.* She didn't understand it; she'd never understand it, why he had run away from his brothers, why he'd try that long walk alone through the night. She didn't understand.

The car—it was a black car, she saw it later and she would always remember that it was a black car—was headed west on County Road 25, not speeding, following the curve of the road and clipping the low gray webs of Spanish moss that dangled from sweet gums reaching across the road like a canopy. When the car hit him he'd been thrown down a ravine, into a stagnant pool of tannin water. He was fifteen. Oh, her beautiful boy, the most beautiful boy of all. The driver of the car had to search for twenty minutes to find him, and then he'd climbed up from the ravine, shaken, sick, had driven like hell back the way he'd come to find a gas station, a phone, an ambulance, anything.

Then they stood at the foot of her bed, Carson and Frank, and she clenched her fists and said "No," but they nodded, white-faced, cruelly, both of them, though it was Carson who said the word, she remembered that—he was the one, the only one with the capacity to give it a word. "Yes," he said. "Yes." She hated that insistence of his. Saying it one time would have been enough.

The memory washed over her now like a fever. She poured another glass of wine, and then another. He'd had bright blue eyes—Dean's eyes, Sofia's eyes—and the lightest hair of the three boys, a honey brown she loved from the start, not that moody darkness of the others, of Dean and Carson and Frank. It matched his soul, such warmth he had, such sweetness. Chatty and funny and bright—my Lord, he'd talk you to death, mouth always running, couldn't shut up to save himself, always in all kinds of trouble at school, the teachers didn't know what to do with him. And if he wasn't talking he was singing, picking out chords on that cheap guitar, figuring out the melodies and progressions of all the songs on the radio, Journey and Skynyrd and Van Halen and all that stuff they loved. He'd belt out the words he knew, make up nonsense for the ones he didn't, follow her around the house with the guitar, trying to make her smile. He mooned her in the living room once—mooned her! mooned his mother!—while she was trying to scold him about a D in math and she shrieked and threw the altar linens at him, but then she collapsed into laughter at the sight of his skinny white fanny and she had to sit on the couch and compose herself until he buckled his pants and sat down next to her and promised to study harder. She wiped her eyes and swatted him on the head.

He was clingy as a baby, had cultivated a physical connection to Arla and to all of them that he never quite grew out of, and even at fifteen he'd lean into her shoulder sometimes in the evening, when she stood at the ironing board with the vestments or when she shook the clean linens out onto the couch to start the folding. She was taller than him, always. But he was bigger than her, bigger than all of them, in all the best ways. *Will.*

After a while sleep began to play with the edges of her mind, and she put the empty tumbler on the nightstand and slid down between the sheets, the stump of her foot feeling thick and heavy, as always. The light from the closet still shone, and she pictured it, visible through the trees outside, to that place on the road, to that steep ravine. She heard the back door close, lightly, a sound like a secret, and then Sofia crept up the stairs and stopped outside Arla's bedroom door.

"'Night, *maman*," she whispered into the room. *"Je suis désolé."*

"'Night, *chérie*," Arla said. *"Je t'aime."*

FIVE

Arla would have a fit, a *fit,* if she could see this. The thought was pleasing, and Sofia smiled. She stood at the dark edge of the Intracoastal, in a narrow sandy patch leading down from the concrete picnic table behind Aberdeen. Then she kicked off her shorts, pulled her T-shirt over her head, and waded into the water in her bra and underwear. Above, the moon was full and soft, spreading a wash of cream-colored light across the surface of the water. A barred owl haunted the trees above the house, and Sofia paused a moment, listening to its call, the question it always seemed to ask: *Who cooks for you? Who cooks for you-all?*

The current was fast, but Sofia was a strong swimmer, always had been. It was one thing she could do well, thank you very much. The expanse of Intracoastal behind the house was a quick stretch, three hundred feet or so from one bank across to the other. Sofia felt the soft hairs on her thighs lift, felt her muscles tense in the sudden cool clutch of the water. Less than a yard from the bank, the bottom dropped out from under her, and the familiar steep channel gaped beneath her feet. In the distance, the Fourth of July party at Uncle Henry's pushed on, though it was late. She struck out for the west bank, felt the guilt washing from her shoulders. Oh, she'd been awful to Arla. She had. But it wasn't the first time. The swimming washed it away.

She ducked her head under the water, listened to the soft rush of the current. The water felt clean, pure, uncontaminated somehow. It always did, even when the rest of the world sometimes felt so overwhelmingly soiled. She couldn't do this every night, much as she would have liked. Without the light of a full or near-full moon, like tonight, visibility on the Intracoastal was almost nil, and in winter the water took on a creeping chill that didn't fully dissipate until April, sometimes May. So these nights, these perfect nights of summer warmth and the clear light of the moon, were precious to Sofia. She intended to use them.

She reached the opposite bank in minutes, rooted her toes in the silty bottom for no more than a second, then turned around and swam east. Her feet were sore tonight, and the slick, slimy sand from the bottom felt like a salve. Bunions. Beautiful. On a woman her age! It's not like she was some dried-up old prune. She was only forty-three.

It was the ballet that had done in her feet, she knew. All those years of pointe, at Arla's insistence, all those years spent bending her feet into those ridiculous crescents, flitting across the wooden floor in the dance studio in St. Augustine. Some trade-off. A lead role in her mother's fantasy of her daughter as a prima ballerina in exchange for a chronic sore back and a case of bunions at forty-three. Arabesques. Pliés. Pair after pair of the God-damned pointe shoes. She was a good dancer, though.

She'd admit that. Strong, flexible, powerful. But too big. Too tall, too heavy, too thick in the shoulders and the thighs. The teacher was the one who finally convinced Arla to let Sofia give it up. The teacher! "She's certainly a very accomplished ballerina," Madame Linda said to Arla after that final recital, when Sofia was a freshman in high school and had clearly emerged on the exit side of puberty with both a stubborn streak and a robust frame pitiably unsuited for ballet. "But it's the body type. You know." Madame Linda raised her eyebrows. "Professional dancers tend to be very, very slim, Mrs. Bravo." She looked at Sofia, then back at Arla, and she shook her head ever so slightly. And what could Arla say to that? Nothing, that's what. Sofia had come home and hung up the pointe shoes in relief, had not taken classes again.

But it had been too late for her feet. Bunions!

Up the hill, the hulking shape of Aberdeen crouched in shadows. Arla was in bed. Sofia was alone. A mosquito buzzed at her face, and she dipped her head under the water again.

A fit. A freaking *hissy* fit is what her mother would have, if she could see this, her daughter swimming in the dark, half naked and putting herself in all kinds of unnecessary danger. Outboards. Snakes. Even sharks, the ones that got themselves confuzzled and ass-backward in the inlet at Matanzas or Porpoise Point, bumping along the banks of the Intracoastal for the rest of their shark days instead of out in the open ocean where they belonged. But she wasn't afraid of them. She didn't know why, but swimming here in the Intracoastal at night was one of the only times Sofia wasn't afraid.

She reached the center of the channel and paused for a moment, floated on her back, and looked at the moon. She imagined her own image, from above—the long rust-colored tangle of her hair spread out around her shoulders, her skin always in such shocking white relief and especially tonight, against the black cotton of her underwear. Floating. Drifting.

Just like Ophelia.

Hey non nonny, nonny, hey nonny.

The painting, a reproduction of it, anyway, had hung in Professor Gervais's office. In *Todd's* office. When you're sleeping with your professor, she reminded herself, you've earned the privilege of calling him by his first name, at least at the moment when his pants are around his ankles and you are kneeling in front of him and his hands are rough, shoving, on the back of your head. *Todd's* office. Ha! But the painting. In the office. Housed in a fussy gilt frame that belonged in a library or a drawing room, not the mildewed third-floor office of a visiting state-school undergraduate professor, a mediocre scholar of Shakespearean theory, and clichéd Shakespearean theory at that. She remembered the first time she'd seen it. Millais, that was the artist; Millais's *Ophelia.*

It was a beautiful painting, it truly was, and Sofia had had plenty of time to study it, given the number of times Gervais (Todd!) led her into the damp confines of his office, the number of times she had clutched his thin shoulders to her breasts and held her breath, looking up at the painting and thinking, so this is it. So this is love.

She was a first-semester freshman at the University of North Florida in Jacksonville, still living at Aberdeen and being dropped off on campus every morning by Dean, on his way to Rayonier, then picked up late in the afternoon for the long ride back to Utina. She'd seen Shakespeare on the schedule and had registered immediately for the course, though when she'd first met her new professor she expected him to be a bore. Tall, hair thinning on top, a disconcerting mole on the side of his nose. But on the second day of class he looked at her, really *looked* at her, and she saw a light flicker in his eyes that portended danger and desire. She went home and looked at herself in the mirror, searching for what he saw. When she recognized it she acted on it. They'd been covering *Hamlet* the week he finally seduced her, and she lay on the floor in his office with her jeans in a clump under his chair, staring at the painting of Ophelia on the wall above his desk, while he panted and whispered again and again, *I love you, I love you, I love you. Sofia.*

But of course, he didn't.

In the painting, Ophelia floated on her back in a clear narrow brook, her right hand clutching a bright red poppy, her voluminous skirts borne up through the water as though inflated. Her eyes stared upward, unfocused, and her lips were parted and slack, her teeth a bright white row above her tongue.

"She's singing," Todd had said that first day, when she asked him about the painting. He was standing now, buckling his belt, and the sweat still glistened on his forehead and neck. "It's the moment before she drowns."

"Are you sure? I don't think so," Sofia said. She was sitting back against the wall, and the taste of Todd was still bitter in the back of her throat. "I think she's already dead."

Todd shook his head, impatient. "No, no. Scholars have studied the work. She's singing." He looked at his watch. "I've got to go, Sofia. We've got to get your sweet ass out of here." He was thrusting student essays into a worn leather satchel. He smiled at her. His pants had a sharp crease down the thigh, all the way to his shoe. She wondered if his wife had ironed it in.

"She's dead," Sofia said. She stared at the painting. "I know she is."

Why did she ever sleep with that man? She'd asked herself a million times. She scarcely enjoyed it at all while it was happening, and the memory of it as the years ticked away had become distasteful to the point of revulsion. Mysteries abound. Why did she do it?

Who cooks for you? Who cooks for you-all?

Ophelia. Damn, girl! All for Hamlet? You let that man drive you crazy, didn't you?

Once, at the office of one of the psychiatrists Arla had taken her to, the doctor left the room to get a prescription pad, and Sofia leaned across the desk and picked up her chart. A cover sheet pinned in with a metal clasp listed her diagnoses: (1) Moderate depressive. (2) Anxiety disorder. (3) Borderline OCD. She ran her finger down the list, loving the organization of it, the tidy cataloging. So precise! It was beautiful. She carefully tore the sheet from the chart, folded it up, put it in her purse. She still kept it in her bureau upstairs, and when the tendrils of thoughts in her head became too wild, too uncontrolled, she took the list out, looked at it, rolled the wayward thoughts back into spools around those lovely clinical words, and put them back in the drawer.

And then it started. Prozac! Zoloft! Paxil! Xanax! It was like a parade march. She'd like to set them all to music. She pictured herself in a majorette's outfit, high white boots and a short skirt, maybe twirling a baton, marching down a bright sunny street crowded with pharmaceutical reps. *Bom, bom, bah! Bom, bom, bah!*

Did you take your pills? Arla would ask, over and over and over.

Yes. Yes. *Yes!*

I'm only trying to help you.

Then leave me alone. That would help me.

In the water, Sofia extended her arms out on either side of her, imagining a scale. She'd rebalance herself again tonight, recalibrate. What a day. Fourth of July, the most wretched day of the year. Starting with that disgusting piano first thing this morning, ending with fireworks at Uncle Henry's, that rotten little spat with Arla in the kitchen. It had been unsettling. Breathe. Rebalance. Recalibrate. In her left hand (and here she wiggled her fingers, slicing them through the water): sanity, so bright and hard and cruel, like an emerald, she imagined it. And here in her right hand (again, wiggling), the soft and comfortable aspic of withdrawal, where she'd dwelt so much of her life, sometimes whole days, weeks, months, until Arla would pull her back out again. It was lovely in the aspic, really. She'd go there for good if it wouldn't have finally broken Arla's heart.

But now here was the secret. She hadn't taken her pills. Hadn't taken them in almost two years, in fact, though Arla had the prescriptions filled every month and toted them up the stairs, left the little vials pointedly on Sofia's bureau or on the counter in the bathroom. Every day Sofia took one pill out of the vial and flushed it down the toilet. Because what was the point, after all? What was the benefit? Going around fuzzy-headed and plodding and chemically lobotomized? The days passing by in tapioca tranquility, weeks and months rustling away like dry leaves through the scrub, faster than she could contain them? She was forty. And then she was forty-one. And then she was forty-two. And no memories to distinguish one year from the next. The meds made her feel blunted, not better. She didn't want them. She didn't need them.

Did you take your pills? Yes.

Did you take your pills? Yes.

Did you take your pills? *No.*

She wasn't crazy. For God's sake. She knew she wasn't crazy. On the contrary, she was excruciatingly lucid. But it was so hard to convince everyone else of this fact, so exhausting to constantly, incessantly protest one's own soundness of mind, that sometimes she just couldn't be bothered trying. The audience, they never suspended their disbelief.

Still on her back, she bent her elbows and pulled her arms in, angled her wrists so her hands dipped upward and out of the water in a gesture of entreaty. She'd practiced this pose before. Open the mouth, stare upward. Exactly like the painting. Exactly like Ophelia.

I did love you once.

Indeed, my lord, you made me believe so.

She'd found out she was pregnant on the day of the final exam, and she waited until after she'd written her essay on *Troilus and Cressida,* had filled up the little blue exam book with a beautiful, magnificently structured argument about conquest and ambiguity and tragedy. Then, at the end of the booklet, she wrote the words, shocking herself with the sight of them there on the page: "I am pregnant" she wrote. She underlined the word *pregnant.* She walked to the front of the room, handed Todd the essay, then walked out past the other students, went home to Aberdeen, and waited.

There's rosemary, that's for remembrance; pray you, love, remember.

At the end of the second day he still hadn't called, so she went to his office. His hands shook when he handed her a card with an address for a clinic.

"And that's that?" she said.

"Well, what did you think?" he said, incredulous. "Sofia. I mean, for God's sake." He gestured at the photo of his wife and children on his desk, but Sofia wouldn't look at it. She stared over his head instead, at the Millais. Ophelia had red hair, thin arched eyebrows. My God, she looked just like her. The water crept around her breasts, pulling her down. "I'll take you there," he said. "I'll stay with you until it's done." But what he didn't say: *I love you, I love you, I love you. Sofia.*

Two nights after it was done she spiked a high fever, started vomiting in the bathroom at Aberdeen and couldn't stop. Arla fretted over her and Dean paced outside the bathroom door, and finally they loaded her into the Impala and drove her to the hospital in St. Augustine. Her brothers stood on the porch watching them leave, and she remembered their faces, frightened and confused.

"You don't know what brought it on?" Dean kept asking. "Is it a stomach bug? Did you eat something bad?" Sofia shook her head, could not speak, though in the hospital, alone in the waiting room with Arla while Dean parked the car, she came clean and told her about the abortion, about Todd, about everything. Arla sucked in her breath but then put her arms around Sofia and stayed with her, through the blood work and the painkillers and—finally—after the surgery. "It happens, unfortunately," the doctor said. "The hysterectomy was our best option. The initial D&C was incomplete, and then you had the sepsis, and then . . ." He spread his hands out, shrugged lightly. "It happens."

Sofia named the baby Ruby. It had been a girl. Not that there was any evidence of that. The abortion had been early, and the baby had been just an unformed mass, faceless and vague. But Sofia just *felt* it had been a girl. She didn't want the baby until after she was gone, but then the loss felt almost unbearable, and she wept for guilt and for shame and for the terror of this unbidden mortality that had visited her. She whispered the name to Arla—*Ruby, Ruby, Ruby*—and Arla nodded, stroked her daughter's hair. "She'll always be yours, Sofia," she said. "You'll always have her."

But Arla was wrong. She didn't have her. Nope, nope, nope, nope, nope. Gone means gone. She'd never have her.

She never returned to college after that. She got a cashier's job at the Winn-Dixie out near the beach and kept it for almost a year. She enjoyed it, to a point—enjoyed the satisfying electronic blips of the UPC codes over the scanner, enjoyed the deli fried chicken she'd buy every day for lunch, even enjoyed the blue polyester uniform, so official it was, so wonderfully valid. But then came the night when her register till wouldn't balance properly after closing and the manager, a horrible woman named Diane, made her stay late and keep counting the money, keep cross-checking it against the register tape, to locate the error. Sofia counted the money and counted the money and counted the money and still it kept coming out wrong. Seventeen dollars short!

"Keep counting," Diane said. "Until you find it."

Sofia counted the money again. Again. Again. Wrong. Wrong. *Wrong.* Then she had a sensation that felt like choking. The money was wrong, and Ruby was gone, and everything was ugly and sick and dirty. She fell to the floor and hyperventilated until Diane called Aberdeen.

"I didn't know she was crazy," Diane spat. "I got a store to run here."

Arla sent Carson to come and fetch her from the Winn-Dixie. At Aberdeen she threw up in the bathroom and then took off the blue uniform and put it in the trash.

Six months later, Will died. The night of his funeral she dreamed he was in a claw-footed tub, holding baby Ruby in his arms, and there were flames and smoke all around. The void was expanding dangerously, and Sofia stood at the edge, looking down, feeling the cold rush of time and eternity there beneath her feet, beckoning. And that's when Dean left.

There's fennel for you, and columbines. There's rue for you, and here's some for me.

Sofia sensed a movement on the bank, and she tensed, scanned the yard behind the house, but saw nothing. A few more laps. The water was delicious tonight.

Oh, Arla would have a *cow*. She imagined her mother standing on the bank. She'd brandish her cane, demand Sofia get out of the water. "Before some drunk with an outboard cuts your fool head off!" she'd scream. But nighttime on the Intracoastal was quiet. Sofia could hear a boat coming from miles off, north and south. Plenty of time to get out of the channel if a boat came slicing through the waters, even at high speeds. She could swim the entire width, from bank to bank, in under four minutes. Plenty of time.

The water was starting to feel warmer around her legs, under her arms. In the distance the music at Uncle Henry's still played—what was that? Bob Marley. Of course. Didn't a night at Uncle Henry's always devolve into Bob Marley? Every little thing is gonna be all right. Keep telling yourselves, suckers. She could picture them all: the women past their prime, broad backsides squeezed into too-tight jean shorts and sagging breasts near-about falling out of tank tops (because *young* women didn't come to Uncle Henry's after all, God knew; as soon as they could find boys to take them, they made a break for the clubs in Jacksonville); the men growing by turns bawdy and brawly as they approached last call and desperation battled with panic while they negotiated their battling priorities of getting laid and getting a last shot before the bar closed. But Frank must be doing a good haul—a holiday night, business booming. She just hoped nobody puked in the restrooms tonight. That was the worst, when they puked in the restrooms. Take it outside, cowboy! If you're going to drink till you hurl, take it outside, where there's eight billion palmettos you can barf your brains into and nobody will have to clean it up! For *gosh* sakes.

All right, now. Swim, she told herself. Balance. Recalibrate. Don't sully this precious night with visions of regurgitating rednecks. Pivot. Reach. Pull.

It was her grandmother who had taught her how to swim. Pivot, Sofia! Reach! Pull! Sofia could scarcely remember what Vera looked like, but the sound of her voice, coaching, was clear. When Vera and James had died she'd been—what—six? Seven? No more than eight, she guessed. But she remembered her grandmother, and how every once in a while, when Dean was at work, and when her grandfather James was away on business, Arla would pack all the kids into the Impala and drive down to the big house in Davis Shores to visit with Vera.

One afternoon, Vera took Sofia to the pool at the clubhouse and taught her how to swim—really swim—not just splash around and float like Sofia had been doing all her young life. Vera taught her real strokes, taught her how to manage her breathing, how to count rotations on the backstroke to avoid banging her head against the side of the pool. And Sofia was good! Vera clapped her hands, laughed, her flower-topped bathing cap bobbing crazily in the sun.

"You're a little mermaid, Sofia," Vera said. "A beautiful little mermaid."

Later they went back to her grandmother's house for lunch. She remembered Frank and Carson tumbling on the manicured green lawn, remembered the lunch table set up on the lanai, baby Will jumping in a playpen in the sun. When Arla and Vera started arguing, something about Dean, Sofia got up and wandered into the house, into the cold living room. The terrazzo floor felt like ice under her bare feet. She picked up a photo album from a small table and turned to sit on the sofa. But then she was conscious of her wet bathing suit, and of the sofa's velvety fabric, so she sat on the table instead. The photo album was gorgeous—heavy and square, with tiny gold triangles mounted on the corners of every creamy linen page. She flipped through, and the gold triangles clicked against each other. There were black-and-white photos of people from another time, it seemed: people waving from old-fashioned cars; people at long tables covered with white cloths and dishes; people on boats; people on porches; even one clownish man hanging upside down from a tree branch. None of them looked like a person Sofia would know. Everyone smiling, all the time. The women wore tiny white hats that looked like bowls atop their heads, flowered dresses, enormous white shoes, dark lipstick. The men wore white shirts, tweed jackets, and funny, baggy trousers. So *much* clothing. So *much* smiling.

She turned a page and found a photo of a man on a horse. He was handsome, but with an old-fashioned hairstyle Sofia found funny, and she smiled. She studied the man for a moment, and then her gaze drifted to the horse, which was glossy and dark and rippled with muscle. The horse was looking at the camera with a sidelong stare that could have been fear or boredom, it was difficult to tell.

Sofia jumped when she realized Vera was behind her in the living room, sitting on the sofa.

"That's my brother," Vera said. Her voice was warbly, and she was rubbing her nose with a tissue. Sofia glanced through the French doors to the lanai; Arla was gathering their things, packing them into a bag, calling for Frank and Carson.

"He died a few minutes after that photo was taken," Vera said.

Sofia looked back at the picture.

"What happened to him?" she said.

"He fell off the horse."

"*He fell off the horse?* And it killed him?" Sofia couldn't imagine. She'd fallen off things plenty of times. She'd fallen off her bike, had fallen off the swings at school. Just yesterday Carson had fallen down the stairs at Aberdeen, and other than some whining and a scraped knee, Arla had dusted him off and he'd been just fine.

"Well, the horse was jumping at the time," Vera said. "It was an amateur steeplechase. My big brother Walter. He hit his head and died right on the spot. That was up in Connecticut."

Sofia looked again at the man on the horse. He was grinning, like he'd just heard a joke.

"Left behind a wife and three children, one a tiny baby, too," Vera said. "And with no way to make a living for themselves. This was the thirties, you see, Sofia. It's different for ladies now."

Arla came struggling in from the lanai with Will on her hip, a tote bag of bathing suits and towels on her shoulder. She was sweating and muttering, leaning heavily on her cane to counterbalance the added weight of the baby and the bag. She hitched her skirt, then turned around and hollered into the yard for Frank and Carson.

"Well, for some women, it is," Vera said. "Some women today have careers, what have you. Ambitions. But back then, my sister-in-law Helen, she was helpless."

"Oh, the Walter story?" Arla said, rolling her eyes.

"What happened to the children?" Sofia said. "The little baby?"

"Well," Vera said. She brightened. "Helen, you know, she always did have the men lining up. And my *other* brother, Thomas, as it turned out, had been carrying a torch for Helen all along. A secret love, what have you. So after the funeral, after we buried poor Walter, Thomas just stepped right in, and he married her, children and all, and he took care of them for the rest of his life."

Sofia looked back at the photo one more time, and now she saw the danger in the horse's eye, the rage, and she saw also the dumb gullible trust in Walter's eyes. Fell off the horse! She wondered if the horse had done it on purpose.

"Is there a picture of Helen?" Sofia said, flipping pages.

"Well, let me see," Vera said. She started to reach for the book, then shrieked and jumped up off the sofa.

"Sofia!" Vera swatted at her. "Get up!" Sofia stood and looked down, at the two small crescents her damp backside had left on the shiny coffee table.

"My word! Mahogany! That will never come out!" Vera hunched over and rubbed frantically at the table with the hem of her dress.

"Oh, Mother," Arla said. "Calm down."

"Ruined," Vera said.

"I'm sorry, Granny Vera," Sofia said. She felt her eyes filling with tears.

"It's fine, Sofia," Arla said.

"Arla! It's not fine. You have no idea about what's valuable," Vera said. "None."

Frank and Carson bumped into the room behind Arla, squabbling.

"Come on, Sofia," Arla said. "We're going home."

They said good-bye, and that was that. Sofia had never seen her grandmother again. Vera and James had died soon after, and the house was sold, and whatever became of that photo album Sofia would never know. The horrible Steinway was saved, of course. But do you think Arla held on to the photo album? Gosh sakes.

Sofia wished she could have seen a photo of Helen. Imagine, the kind of woman who had a man "carrying a torch" for her. Imagine, three little children at your feet, and the men just lining up for you, waiting their turn. It was incredible to Sofia that some women should have so many people to love them, when others should have none at all.

Now she watched her arms pulling through the water, her skin rippled and taut. Control. That was it. When she was in the water, she was in complete control. It was really the only place. She once read about the Scottish legend of ashrays, sea ghosts, translucent fibers that take shape at night and haunt the waterways, then disappear during the day. If they were captured, they would melt, and only a puddle of water would remain. That's what she was, she decided. An ashray. A water ghost. Like Ophelia.

Something *was* moving up on the bank. She was sure of it now. Sofia started, righted herself in the water, and paddled wide circles with her arms to keep afloat. In the moonlight, the figure of Biaggio was now clear. He was thirty yards away, standing on the bank at the edge of Aberdeen's backyard. His hands were on his hips, and he was looking her way.

"What are you doing?" she said sharply.

"What are *you* doing?" he said. "Swimming at this hour?" His eyes were wide. He looked nervous. "That ain't too safe," he said. "It's almost midnight."

She thought he'd gone to bed. When Arla left the kitchen earlier, they'd sat for a few moments in silence, and she'd felt something strange in the air, a shift in the karma. Then he'd risen, told her good night, and walked out the back door, stopping for a moment to glance back at her, one time.

"I'm fine," she said. Her clothes lay in a heap on the bank. Her underwear felt small, suddenly, but she was pretty sure he couldn't see much of her body through the dark water. Pretty sure.

"It's dangerous," he persisted. "Boats. They wouldn't be able to see you, Sofia."

She'd rarely heard him use her name, it occurred to her. He'd lived on their property for all these years. But usually he spoke only to Arla, or to Frank. Funny, she'd just realized that. Just tonight.

"I'm fine," she said again. She hesitated. "Don't tell my mother," she added.

He shook his head, frowned. Then he backed up and sat down on the top of the picnic table.

"Now what are you doing?" she said.

"I'm going to sit here," he said. "I can't leave you out here by yourself."

"I don't need you watching me."

"Well, I don't need you to get killed, do I?"

She turned and swam another lap to the west bank, then back again. When she reached the Aberdeen side she was angry.

"My brother pays you to babysit us," she said. "Doesn't he?"

Biaggio raised his eyebrows. "No," he said slowly. "He pays me to look after the house."

"I don't need you here," she said. "I'm not crazy."

She felt a little bit guilty when she saw how the word stung him.

"I never said you was." He was embarrassed, self-conscious now, but still he didn't move off the table. "Don't pay me no mind," he said. "Just pretend I'm not here."

"Don't just sit there staring at me," she said. "I can't relax."

"I won't stare at you," he said. "I'll look away." He gazed purposefully up the Intracoastal, toward Uncle Henry's.

She swam another lap, and then another. The barred owl

had quieted. The moon glowed. On the fourth lap she tipped her head out of the water and glanced up toward the bank again. Biaggio's eyes met hers. Her heart pounded. One more lap. She put her face down again, waited for buoyancy, and then pulled hard at the water, strong straight strokes against resistance and darkness and fear.

O rose of May! Dear maid, kind sister, sweet Ophelia!

Six

That Sunday morning, the bells of freedom having quieted, the rockets' red glare having faded, and another Independence Day dead and buried, Elizabeth Bravo poured a fat mug of coffee and flicked through the St. Augustine Yellow Pages, stopping on page 189: "Attorneys—Family Law." She peered skeptically at a large, grainy photo of a man with a mullet and a baggy suit, a bookshelf full of what appeared to be encyclopedias behind him. DON'T GET MAD, the headline read. GET EVEN.

"Good Lord," Elizabeth said. She sipped her coffee.

She didn't want to get even. She didn't want to get anything, except away. She was surprised, in fact, by how little anger she felt. By rights, she should be furious. An hour ago, she'd received a near-hysterical call from a woman claiming to be her husband's girlfriend, or ex-girlfriend, or ex-*mistress*, she supposed you could say, though Elizabeth always hated the formal and prissy sound of that word, as though an adulteress was a woman of means and elegance, not some trashy, implanted hoochie like the one she pictured on the other end of the telephone line. Seems Carson had told this woman, who identified herself as Holly, that her services were no longer required, so she'd responded by dropping what she supposed was a bombshell on Elizabeth, evidently in hopes of generating sufficient venom as to make her former paramour regret his actions.

"Three months," Holly had said over the phone, and she exhaled noisily in a way that Elizabeth could tell she was smoking. Hilarious, really, because Carson hated cigarettes. "That's how long he's been fucking me."

Elizabeth had looked out into the yard, where Bell was making two Barbies wade in the birdbath. It was a pretty yard, off a pretty house, on a pretty street in a pretty city. St. Augustine. All so very pretty, though she felt strange here, sometimes, having grown up in Utina, a place where not much was pretty but where a lot of things were pretty good, if you looked at them the right way, which Elizabeth usually did. When she and Carson had married, he couldn't get out of Utina fast enough, and she acquiesced, thinking nothing could be more important than making him happy. Thus the pretty house in St. Augustine, and Carson's investment practice, and the growing feeling of disconnectedness she'd been fighting for what felt like a long, long time.

They'd gotten home late last night, after the fireworks at Uncle Henry's, and Carson had risen before dawn this morning. He'd taken the boat out to fish, or at least that's what he said he'd be doing, what he said he'd been doing every Sunday, come to think of it, and he'd be gone till dusk.

"You have my condolences," she'd said to Holly, and then she hung up. She called Bell in and poured her a bowl of cereal.

She'd walked into her bedroom, dug in the closet, and found a suitcase, which she placed on the bed. She stared at it for a moment, then put it back in the closet, turned and pulled it out a second time, and then kicked it, thrust it back into the recesses of the closet again.

Oh, Jesus. How stupid is this? She closed the closet door.

She felt no surprise, really, to learn so definitively of Carson's infidelity. She'd suspected, after all, for years. She did feel, ironically, a small measure of pity for Holly, who was naïve enough to think Carson and Elizabeth had a marriage worth fighting for. Or that there could be such a thing as a marriage worth fighting for.

Now, staring at the lawyer ads in the phone book, she was again struck not by sadness or anger but by a feeling of perplexity —all these attorneys, pitting all these wives against all these husbands, and for what? Money? Revenge? You'd never make someone love you again. So what was the point?

She ran her finger down the list of lawyers. Maybe divorce was all wrong. It seemed like such a bother. Such a lot of paperwork. Maybe all they needed was to shake hands, walk away, live and let live, put the last two decades out of their minds and start over. *C'est la vie.* Such is life.

But there was Bell. And this was the part of the equation Elizabeth found flummoxing.

"What's a att-or-nay?" Bell said now, staring at the open pages, and Elizabeth was once again startled by how the child could materialize, soundlessly, at her elbow and immediately discern the content of her mother's thoughts. Elizabeth's hands had begun to shake, and she took a deep breath and cleared her throat.

"You know what?" she replied, closing the phone book. "I really couldn't tell you." The hell with these St. Augustine lawyers. Maybe she would call Mac Weeden in the morning. He might be disbarred, but he was Utina, UHS class of 1986, just like her. She trusted him. He'd know what to do. She pulled Bell against her hip, hugged her shoulders tight.

"Can't, or won't?" Bell said. The freckles on her nose were more pronounced than usual; they were overexposed, it seemed, from her time out in the sun. She gazed at Elizabeth with such a knowing expression that Elizabeth was momentarily rattled. How much *did* Bell know, anyway?

"Both."

Bell opened the refrigerator, too hard, and a plastic bottle of ketchup shook loose from the door and bounced across the kitchen floor.

"Shit," Bell said.

"Bell! What are you doing, talking like that?"

"Well, the damn ketchup . . . ," Bell began.

"That will *do*. One person in this house with a potty mouth is quite enough," Elizabeth said.

"Do you mean Daddy, or you?" Bells said. She tilted her head and looked at Elizabeth with what could only be feigned innocence.

What could you do with a kid like this? Elizabeth stifled a smile, turned away before Bell could see her face. My God, the girl could see right through her. Always could. She remembered when Bell was an infant, barely even able to raise her head, and Elizabeth would sit up with her in the night, nursing her and rocking her in the pale light of the nursery while Carson slept down the hall. She didn't mind getting up with her. She never minded. And then Bell started doing such a funny thing—and so tiny she was!—she would turn her face toward Elizabeth, her lips still glistening with milk, and would smile a funny, secret smile. Because she knew what Elizabeth was doing. She knew, even then, that Elizabeth was hoarding her, holding her close, savoring the moments they had alone together. Without Carson.

Not that Carson didn't dote on her, too. From day one: cradling her small head in his hands, cooing in a voice Elizabeth didn't know he'd had, gazing at his little girl with an expression Elizabeth had never seen before. He adored her, Elizabeth had never doubted that. He might let Elizabeth go. But never Bell. Elizabeth took a deep breath and turned back to her daughter.

"Let's go do our nails, Beetle." She led Bell to the bathroom, where they rummaged through old bottles of nail polish, and Elizabeth pulled out her favorite, a deep red labeled: I'M NOT REALLY A WAITRESS.

"But no nail files," Bell said.

"No nail files," Elizabeth agreed.

"I don't like nail files. They make little footsteps run up and down my spine."

"Certain things will do that."

"Like att-or-neys?"

"Like attorneys is right, sister," Elizabeth said. "And don't you forget it." They walked back to the kitchen and sat at the table, where Bell picked up a piece of paper she'd been writing on earlier in the morning.

"Making a birthday list?" Elizabeth said. "Just a few more weeks, you know."

"Not a birthday list," Bells said. "Just a list. Want to hear it?"

"Go, girl."

"'Things I Like,' by Bell Bravo." Bell was still wearing her pajamas, which consisted of a T-shirt from the Alligator Farm and a pair of loose-fitting cotton pants imprinted with SpongeBob. She spoke with a lisp, her two front teeth having taken their leave earlier in the summer, and Elizabeth loved the way her daughter's face looked now, the funny little gap in her smile like a charismatic flaw in an otherwise perfect sculpture. "You ready?" Bell said. "Number one: Little Debbie honey buns. Number two: snow." Elizabeth smiled.

"You've never seen snow, Bell."

"But I like it anyway. I *would* like it. Number three," she continued, "chocolate milk. Number four: the brown kitty at Uncle Henry's, but not the white one, who is mean. Number five: Mama." She put down the paper, businesslike, placed her pen across its surface and spread her tiny hands out on the table's wooden top.

Elizabeth smiled, painted a tiny drop of red lacquer on Bell's pinky. "I like you too, Bell," she said. "A lot." She finished painting her Bell's fingernails, then leaned back, regarded her work. "Should we do our toes, too?" she said.

"*Hell* yes," Bell said. My God. She was her father's daughter.

The next morning, after Carson left for work, Elizabeth took Bell and drove up to Utina. She'd said nothing to him about Holly's call. She pulled off Seminary Street, drove down a narrow alley, and parked at the back entrance of Tony's Hair Affair. She and Bell walked into the salon, where Tony Cerro was leaning on the front counter, talking on the phone. He waved at Elizabeth and held up an index finger.

Tony. Elizabeth felt a wash of comfort just walking into the salon. She'd known Tony since she was a teenager, when he'd been one of a string of paramours her mother, Wanda, had paraded through their trailer in South Utina. Elizabeth had never known her father, and in truth she doubted her mother knew who he was. Most of the men Wanda brought home Elizabeth hated—opportunistic drunks who turned ugly and angry when the romance fizzled or the booze ran out, and Elizabeth had spent more than one night running from the chaos of her mother's dirty little trailer, hiding in the backseat of Wanda's car for hours until the sun came up or the bastards passed out, whichever came first.

But Tony was different. The first time she met him, when he'd come walking out of Wanda's bedroom early one morning, Elizabeth was fourteen. When he saw her there in the kitchen his face had clouded over. He sat down at the table.

"I'm sorry, sweetie," he'd said. "This ain't right, is it?"

She stared at him, and he'd apologized again, and then he got up, rummaged in the refrigerator, and scrambled an egg, which he put in front of her with a piece of toast and a Coke.

"You really should have some OJ," he said. "But I see Wanda's not so hot in the grocery shopping department."

He'd never come back to see her mother after that, but he offered Elizabeth a job in the salon, and she took it. When he came out a few years later and told her he was gay, she wasn't surprised, though she did look at him quizzically, thinking of that one strange night he'd come home with Wanda. He read her mind. "Oh, that," he said. "I thought your mama would cure me," he said. "Was I wrong! Honey!" And she had to laugh, though now the memory of her mother, so broken and aloof, was one she kept neatly stored in a locked box in her mind and rarely took out. The last she heard, Wanda was living with an ex-con in Satsuma, but Elizabeth hadn't seen her in years. She didn't plan to.

Elizabeth had worked at the salon all during high school, until she married Carson, in fact. She missed it, missed the way Tony would gossip with her and nag her about her homework, would take her down to Sterling's for lunch and pick up the tab every single time, pretend he was putting it on some sort of corporate salon account, when she knew damn well it came from his own modest income. He looked out for her, all those years, when Wanda wouldn't. Or couldn't.

"I know, sweetie," he said now, speaking into the phone. Elizabeth waved back at him. "I know," he said.

Tony parked the phone receiver between his shoulder and chin. With his right hand, he chattered his thumb against his fingers, rolled his eyes at Elizabeth, pointed at the phone.

"I know, baby," he said.

Elizabeth settled Bell into a chair near Tony's station with a coloring book and an iPod. Then she wandered through the salon, reading the labels on the bottles of hair products on the shelves. BRILLIANTE BOY POMADE. BODY LUXE THICKENING ELIXIR. It seemed there was a product for everything. CURL FORMING POLISH. HAIR DESIGN FOAM. DAILY LEAVE-IN DETANGLER. That's what she needed. A detangler.

"I hear you, baby," Tony said into the phone. He made a circling motion with his hand. "Because he's an asshole, that's why."

Last night, Elizabeth had put Bell to bed, left Carson staring at his laptop in the kitchen, and pulled an atlas off the shelf in the living room. She'd let the book fall open to a random page, then closed her eyes, pointed her finger, and let her hand drop onto the map. She opened her eyes. Flemington, Missouri. She imagined it: dry and open and flat, a white church on a corner, a row of red brick buildings, a small wooden house with a blue kitchen and a glass of daisies on the table. Everything smelled like cinnamon. Why not? But good God in heaven, did people even *live* in Flemington, Missouri? It was so hard, sometimes, to see outside of North Florida. It was like living in a sinkhole, descending, the surface of the Earth growing farther out of reach with each passing year.

"All right. Listen," Tony said to the person on the phone. "Lemme go. I got a client." He hung up, sighed. "I tell you, honey," he said to Elizabeth. "Some people. Yaketty, yaketty, yak."

Tony settled Elizabeth into the chair at his station, stood behind her, and looked at her hard in the mirror. His face had grown looser over the years, but his beard was neatly trimmed and his eyes were bright. A gold necklace shimmered under his open collar. He fluffed her long hair in his hands, cocked his head to one side.

"Talk to me," he said.

And then she didn't know how it was happening, but she was crying. Tony spun the chair around and hugged her, and she loved him for his clean white shirt, the clucking noises he made into the top of her head.

"Oh, sweetie," he said. She glanced at Bell, who was coloring a picture of a butterfly, the tiny iPod earbuds dangling from her ears, oblivious. *"Hakuna matata,"* Bell sang softly. Elizabeth pulled back from Tony and cleared her throat.

"I'm leaving Carson," she said.

"I know, I know." He offered her a box of tissues, and she took one.

"How did you know?" she said.

"I always knew. I just didn't know *when*."

She blew her nose, wiped her eyes.

"Well, thanks for telling *me*," she said.

He fished in a cabinet and emerged with a bowl of chocolates.

"No telling you something like that," he said. "You have to find it out on your own."

"What are you, the Wizard of Oz?" She picked through the bowl of chocolates and found the dark.

"Don't be ridiculous," he said. "I'm Glinda." He smiled. "So what are you going to do?"

"I don't know. I'm trying to figure it out. I might give it another couple weeks," Elizabeth said. "Just trying to get it all organized. And Bell's birthday is coming up. After that, maybe I'll go stay with Arla at Aberdeen." She hadn't actually considered this as an option until she said it out loud. But it made sense. With Carson holding the purse strings, Elizabeth didn't have the money to get her own place, didn't know how she'd even get access to money like that without his agreement. Which he would not be willing to give; Jesus, if she knew anything, she knew Carson. Granted, Arla was Carson's mother, but she and Sofia had the space at Aberdeen, and Bell would feel secure, safe. Maybe Elizabeth could pitch it to Bell as a summer vacation. Maybe Bell would simply feel that they were on holiday, just on an extended visit with Granny while Daddy worked through the summer. And maybe they would be.

"Well, my God. She's got the space out there, now doesn't she?" Tony said. "That big old house. I'll bet she'd love to have you. I know Arla. You're her family. You're everything."

"Carson's her family," Elizabeth pointed out.

"You all are," Tony said. "All you Bravos." Which made Elizabeth tear up again. Which made Tony reach again for the tissues. "All right, now, sweetie," he said. "You just let it out."

Another stylist entered the salon, a young woman smelling of cigarette smoke, dressed in tight black jeans and platform shoes. The woman stored her purse in the cabinet at the station next to Tony's, then leaned against the counter, looked at Elizabeth's red eyes, and raised her eyebrows at Tony.

"Never you mind, Alicia," he said. "None of your business." Alicia moved away toward the front desk.

"The help I get," he whispered to Elizabeth. "I swear to Jesus, I don't know if they're worth it. You oughta come back to me, Elizabeth." He raised his voice. "You gonna stand there and hold up the desk all day, Alicia?" he said. "We got product needs to be stocked, you feel like maybe you could manage it."

He put his hands on Elizabeth's shoulders, pulled her back in the chair, and then fluffed her hair in his fingers.

"All right," she said. "Cut it all off."

"Oh, like hell I will," he said. He pumped his foot against a metal bar at the base of the chair, then tightened a black cape around her neck. "We're doing highlights."

Elizabeth closed her eyes, listened to Bell's humming across the room, felt Tony's deft hands working through her hair, sectioning out thick strands, painting them with peroxide and wrapping them in foil. This was ridiculous, really. She'd just come in for her usual trim. She'd never had highlights before. She caught herself wondering what Frank would think of them.

And there it was. Frank. Her husband's brother. Her first crush, puppy love, a man who'd been hovering around the periphery of her heart for almost as long as she could remember. The Bravo she didn't choose. The Bravo she didn't marry. What a stupid, foolish girl. But how could she be expected to make such a decision at nineteen? How could anyone be expected to write her own future, write it in stone, no less, before she was even old enough to legally sip Chardonnay?

It was not that she didn't love Carson. She loved him, even now. She loved his intensity, loved his power, loved his passion, the way he walked so definitively through the world, the way he carried her along with him, an adjunct to his force, an accessory to his incomprehensible confidence. She'd grown up in a world of uncertainty, ambiguity, hesitation. He was sure of himself in a way she didn't think she could ever be, and when he picked her out for himself she was amazed, grateful. She'd never been attached to anything as stable, as commanding as Carson Bravo. He seemed to know no fear. The first time he'd looked at her, really looked at her, she'd been so young, sitting with Frank at the time, come to think of it, Frank's arm around her shoulders, but when Carson looked at her with that pure, defiant desire in his eyes, she caught her breath, felt herself slipping under his spell. She loved him then, loved him still. Holly or no Holly. But she was so tired of being angry. So tired of being disappointed, tired of being tired.

Tony's comb caught at her hair and pulled.

"Ow," she said. She opened her eyes.

"I'm sorry, baby," Tony said. "No pain, no gain." He painted another thick row of peroxide along a strand of hair.

She blinked her eyes to hold back the tears. When she left the salon, her hair was brighter, blonder, softer. She stared at her reflection in the car's rearview mirror.

"You're so different, Mama," Bell said from the backseat.

"Not really," Elizabeth said. "I'm really exactly the same." For now, she thought, pulling out of the salon and heading south toward St. Augustine, toward Carson, toward home. But maybe not for long.

Bell's birthday, a searing hot Tuesday in late July, dawned bright and brutal, the temperature topping ninety before the sun had even cleared the horizon. For the past two weeks, Elizabeth had been waking every morning in a state of paralysis, the sound of Carson breathing beside her a colossal question mark for which she still seemed to have no answer. But Bell's birthday. It gave shape to the holding pattern, as least for a day. When she'd asked the child last week what she wanted for her birthday, Bell had confounded her by requesting only a ride on the St. Augustine trolley, an ice cream at Dairy Queen. It sounded simple enough until Bell had added: "With Brooke," referring to her playmate from kindergarten. "And Granny. And Aunt Sofia. A girls' day," she'd said.

"It's hot for the trolley," Elizabeth said. "Is there something else?"

"The trolley," Bell said. "It's not hot."

So Elizabeth made the calls, made the arrangements. Brooke and her mother, Myra, to arrive at noon. Biaggio to bring Arla and Sofia to Elizabeth's house as soon as Sofia was finished cleaning Uncle Henry's. In the afternoon, Elizabeth would bring Arla and Sofia back to Aberdeen.

Carson left early for the office. He'd kissed Elizabeth absently, and she willed herself not to stiffen at his touch.

"It's Bell's birthday," she said. "Don't forget."

"Bell, baby, Bell!" Carson boomed. He walked down the hallway into his daughter's bedroom, waking her up. "How's my six-year-old princess?"

"Seven," Bell said. Elizabeth could see them through the open doorway, could see her daughter sit up in bed, her hair sweetly mussed. "Seven years old."

"Exactly," Carson said. "Almost driving." He blew a raspberry on her belly, returned to the kitchen. "How can I have a seven-year-old daughter?" he said. "How can this be?" Elizabeth didn't answer, and he snapped his cell phone into a clip on his hip and walked out the back door, whistling.

Today. Today I make a decision. "Should I Stay or Should I Go." The Clash. Funny, she'd always thought of that song as a hypothetical. Today it seemed like dare.

Myra and Brooke arrived at noon on the dot. Elizabeth watched out the window as Myra parked at the curb—an expensive-looking Volkswagen, sea foam green—and got out. Elizabeth had spoken to Myra a few times, standing outside the kindergarten waiting for dismissal, but she'd never actually felt the impulse to socialize with her, and now she remembered why. Myra wore a tiny plaid sundress, looked more like a beach cover-up, and her shoulders were sinewy and tanned. Her dark hair was artfully arranged in a rakish bun designed to look impetuous, rushed. Her breasts were perfect—great freckled orbs. Oh, wouldn't Carson love this one. Brooke, the little girl, wore shorts and a pink halter top, two impossibly high ponytails erupting from the sides of her head. Myra fetched an enormous yellow handbag and a wrapped gift from the backseat.

"Come in," Elizabeth said, answering the door. "We're just waiting on my in-laws."

"Oh, I love your house," Myra said. "It's so cute!" She looked around for a place to deposit her handbag. Bell took Brooke to see her room. "I mean, so cozy," Myra said. "Really. Our place is so big. It gets on my nerves."

"Would you like some iced tea?" Elizabeth said.

"Love some."

Elizabeth led her to the kitchen, poured two tall glasses of tea. She glanced at the clock. 12:03.

"So who are we waiting for?" Myra said.

"My mother-in-law and sister-in-law," Elizabeth said. "Bell wanted a girls' day," she added, apologetically.

"And where do they live?"

"Utina."

"Where's that?" Myra tipped her head.

"It's where I grew up," Elizabeth said. "Just north of here."

"Never heard of it."

"It's just up the road."

Myra gazed at her, an open look, as though she was assessing Elizabeth's intellect. "Okay," she said agreeably. She had a diamond on her finger the size of a marble.

"I just love your kitchen," Myra said. "It's adorable."

Elizabeth looked at the clock again.

"So what does your husband do?" Myra said.

"Investment counseling," Elizabeth said. How she hated the sound of it now—investment counseling—so arrogant, so presumptuous. Making it sound as if it were such a *problem* to have so much money that you actually needed "counseling" to know how to manage it. She thought of the days when she'd helped Carson build the practice, the days before Bell, when they'd been excited about the future, when they'd worked so hard to get the business off the ground, build the client list, figure out marketing, operations, accounting, all of it. She'd worked with him for all those years, postponing children on his insistence, even as the regret and loss of her long-ago miscarriage grew like a cancer inside her. When her mid-thirties approached she put her foot down, and he acquiesced, granting her the pregnancy, as if it was a transfer or a reassignment. The minute she got pregnant she cut her hours, worked part-time, spent her afternoons walking the beach on Anastasia, stopping to rest under the pier and feeling her baby make small, miraculous kicks inside her. And then when Bell arrived Elizabeth seized the opportunity and bailed from the business. She was grateful, by then, to distance herself from the constant smell of money, the ubiquitous aura of wealth. She'd grown up in South Utina. She knew the other side.

But the explanation of Carson's job seemed to satisfy Myra. "He has a firm," Elizabeth added. "Bravo Investments."

"Oh, yes! A little building? Out on US1?"

"Yes."

"I've seen the sign. I love that little place. It's precious."

"And how about you?" Elizabeth said. "Or your husband—?" This always sounded so awkward, so ridiculously antiquated, this assumption that the wife would stay home, the husband work, like it was 1955 or something, but so far, in Elizabeth's experience with the young mothers of St. Augustine, at least in the circles Carson's business kept them in, it seemed to be the case.

"He's a veep at CSX Railway," Myra said. "Marketing."

"A veep?"

"VP. Vice-prez." Myra looked at her again, that open stare.

"He commutes all the way to Jacksonville?"

"Oh, yes, been doing it for years," Myra said. "He doesn't mind. He tells me it justifies the Beemer. Whatever."

A movement at the front door. Thank God. Elizabeth went to the door, opened it, found Biaggio standing there with an oversize cardboard carton. Behind him, in the driveway, Arla and Sofia were struggling out of Biaggio's van, a rusted silver Ford Windstar. Biaggio's shirt was wet with perspiration, his face folded in dismay.

"Come in," Elizabeth said, swinging the door wide. "What's wrong?"

"Oh, nothing," Biaggio said, exhaling. "The ladies just having a little disagreement out there." He stepped into the house, hefting the cardboard box. "The AC's busted in the van. Hooo-doggy."

"What on Earth do you have in there?"

"I don't know," he said. "It's all from Miss Arla. I gotta put it down." He moved toward the kitchen, his huge loping frame looking awkward and dangerous in Elizabeth's house, which was, she now saw through Myra's eyes, rather small.

Arla and Sofia reached the front door, and Sofia entered first, exhaling noisily and rolling her eyes at Elizabeth.

"Oh, my *God*, Mother," she said. "Can you *stop*?"

Arla's face shone with sweat, and her sunglasses had slipped down to the tip of her nose. A strand of red hair stuck to her forehead.

"Lord in heaven, it's hot out there. Hello, sweetness," she said, patting Elizabeth on the arm. "Sofia thinks her outfit is appropriate for Bell's birthday excursion, although I have repeatedly tried to explain to her it is not."

Elizabeth looked again at Sofia. She was wearing a pink spaghetti-strap tank top, a denim miniskirt, and a pair of flip-flops, and she clutched a white canvas tote. The attire might have looked fine on a younger, slimmer girl, but Sofia, she had to admit, was pushing it.

"It's hot, Mother. *H-O-T*. I'm trying to stay cool," Sofia explained.

"Where's my Bell?" Arla said, ignoring her. "Bell!"

Something crashed in the kitchen.

"Come in and meet Bell's friends," Elizabeth said.

She led Arla and Sofia to the kitchen, where Myra sat at the table, gaping at Biaggio, who had dropped the cardboard box in the middle of the floor and was now squatting, trying to gather up the scattered contents.

"What *is* all this?" Elizabeth said.

"Dollar General was having a closeout," Arla said. "Look at this." She pushed past Sofia, bent down, and pulled a can of fried onion rings out of Biaggio's hand. "Twenty-five cents," she said. "And this"—she poked in the box with her cane, then reached down and retrieved a dented fig pudding—"a dollar. Thought you could use them."

"Arla, this is Myra," Elizabeth said. "Sofia, Biaggio, Myra."

Myra had still not moved, but she collected herself and smiled at Arla.

"Here. Look," Arla said. "Water chestnuts. Four for a dollar. Nilla Wafers, thirty-nine cents."

"Show her the fish oil," Sofia said.

"Chocolate truffles—a buck."

"Show her the fish oil."

"Fish oil—two bucks," Arla said.

"I coulda got you fish oil for free," Biaggio said. "Right out back of Aberdeen. We got plenty of fish."

"Fish oil is good for you. I read about it," Sofia said. "It increases brain power."

"Well then, here," Arla said, thrusting the bottle at Sofia. "You take it all, then."

Bell and Brooke entered the kitchen.

"Belly-Bear!" said Arla. "Come here, baby." She pulled Bell into a hug, and Sofia bent over and kissed the top of Bell's head. They all sang "Happy Birthday to You," and when they were finished, Arla looked down at Brooke. "And who is this pretty little girl?" she said.

"That's Brooke," Bell said.

Arla shook Brooke's hand. "Pleased to meet you, Brooke."

"What happened to your foot?" Brooke said. Her eyes were wide.

"It got chopped off," Arla said.

Myra cleared her throat.

"No shit," Arla said.

"Well," Elizabeth said. "Shall we go, then?"

They headed for the trolley station at Castillo Drive in the van, Biaggio insisting on dropping them off to save them the walk before he headed back to Utina. Elizabeth had bitten her lip as Myra and Brooke climbed into Biaggio's Windstar, which had a piece of plywood nailed over a broken window and a Mexican blanket thrown across the tattered upholstery of the backseat.

"Sorry 'bout the transportation," Biaggio said, his face red. He held Myra's gigantic handbag while she climbed into the rear of the van, then he handed it through the open door. "This is my work truck."

"What do you do?" Myra said.

"I'm a moving man," Biaggio said. He did a jig on the hot pavement, flapped his arms like a bird. "I move—see?" Bell laughed, but Myra and Brooke stared at him blankly. He slid the back door shut and sat down in the driver's seat as Sofia, Arla, and Elizabeth climbed in on the other side.

"There's no seat belt," Brooke said.

"It's only a few blocks," Elizabeth said. "Just to save us from walking, in this heat."

"Just hold on to me, Brooke," Myra said tightly. Her plaid sundress had begun to stick to her thighs.

"Maybe later we'll get us an ice cream," Arla said. "Oh, but poor Biaggio, he'll drop us off and miss out on the ice cream."

"Oh, no, Miss Arla. I don't eat dairy. You know that."

"Oh? Are you vegan?" Myra asked. She leaned forward.

"Oh, no, ma'am," Biaggio said. "It's just bad luck, in my book."

Myra blinked, leaned back in the seat.

"You ever heard of Romulus and Remus?" Biaggio said.

"No," she said.

"Well, let me tell you what they were all about," he said. He pulled out onto San Marco Boulevard, got comfortable in his seat. "They were these twin sons of the Roman god Mars, see, way back in ancient times. Their mother was Rhea Silvia, who was supposed to be a vestal virgin but I suppose she forgot all about that when Mars showed up in her bedroom one night. So she bore these twins, and when her uncle, the evil king, found out about it, he ordered the babies killed," he said.

Brooke stared at him. "Killed?" she said.

"Kaput," Biaggio said. He sliced a finger across his throat. "Game over."

"How do you know about Roman gods?" Sofia said.

"I seen it on PBS," he said.

"Oh," she said.

"Well, of course, like it always happens in these kinds of stories," he continued, "the servant who was supposed to kill the baby twins took mercy on them and just set them adrift in the river Tiber instead. You had to wonder what some of these people were thinking back then."

"No kidding," Sofia said. "*Imbéciles.*"

"Anyway, the babies, Romulus and Remus, survived out there in the wilderness by drinking the milk of a wild wolf," Biaggio said. "When they grew up, Romulus and Remus founded Rome, but then they got in an argument over who owned it, or who was going to be the king, or something like that, and Romulus went ahead and killed his brother Remus. And after all they had been through together!"

"That's pretty low, to kill your brother over some piece of dirt," Sofia said.

"Well, never mind about Rome," Biaggio said. "It was the drinking of the wolf's milk that made Romulus kill his brother. It was the dairy, you see?"

"Oh, for heaven's sake," Arla said. "They don't make ice cream out of wolves' milk, now do they?"

Brooke turned to Bell. "Do they?" she said.

"No," Bell said. "They use cow's milk. Or goats, maybe."

"No goats. No wolves," Elizabeth said. "Just cows, and it's perfectly fine to eat."

"Maybe," Biaggio said.

"Biaggio—" Elizabeth said.

"I'm just sayin'," he said. "Here we are! Trolley station!"

He pulled in and parked, and they all climbed out of the van.

"Don't forget my laundry pickup," Arla said to Biaggio.

"Right," he said. "St. Anastasia. I'll get it when I leave here." He waved as he pulled out of the parking lot. Elizabeth bought tickets, and a surly girl behind a sliding glass window handed them all orange train-shaped stickers to affix to their shirts. Sofia placed hers on the hem of her tank top. Myra stuck hers to her bare upper chest. They climbed aboard the trolley, a bright red tourist tram driven by a Colonel Sanders look-alike in blue suspenders. He gawked at Myra, then put out the cigarette he'd been smoking and put the train in gear. In one row sat Elizabeth, Myra, and Sofia. Behind them sat Arla and the two little girls. Sofia reached into her bag, took out a magazine, and commenced to using it as a fan.

"Jesus," she said. "Did somebody forget to pay the oxygen bill?"

"No use complaining about it," Arla said. "We all know it's hot."

"I enjoy it, actually," Myra said. "I mean, that's why we live in Florida, right?"

Arla stared at her.

The trolley pulled up at Ripley's Believe It or Not! Odditorium.

"First stop," boomed the driver through a tinny microphone.

"Are we going in?" Bell said.

"We just got on the trolley," Elizabeth said. "We've only been on it thirty seconds."

"She wants to go in here," Arla said, leaning forward.

Elizabeth turned around, looked at Bell.

"Bell, I thought you wanted to ride a bit," Elizabeth said.

"Oh, let her go in," Arla said. "It's her birthday."

Bell stared at Elizabeth, opened her eyes wider. She was working it, Elizabeth thought, watching the way Bell monitored Arla in her peripheral vision. She was good at this.

"Any riders disembarking?" the driver bellowed.

"I don't like this place," Brooke said. "It's scary."

"No, it isn't," Arla said. She was already struggling to her feet. "Bell wants to go in. It's her birthday. Come on, everyone."

Elizabeth sighed. "We can get back on, right?" she said to the driver.

"Trolley stops here every thirty minutes," he said. "Just keep your stickers on."

They walked to the entrance of Ripley's, stood in line a few minutes, then bought tickets and walked inside, where the chill of the air-conditioning felt like a salve.

"Oh," they all said. Elizabeth pulled her shirt away from her chest, flapped it in the cool air. It was crazy hot out there. She wasn't sure this day was such a good idea.

"Thank God," Sofia said. "That's better."

They walked through the museum, a three-story Moorish building converted from a hotel once owned by Marjorie Kinnan Rawlings. They peered at the curiosities: a man with two pupils in each eye; the Lord's prayer engraved on a grain of rice; the world's largest feline hairball; a two-headed lamb; assorted shrunken heads; a lock of JFK's hair. In the atrium, the world's largest moving Erector model, a shiny twenty-foot silver Ferris wheel, squeaked and shuddered.

How strange it all is, Elizabeth thought, but stranger still that we will line up, bovine and malleable, to pay our money and take a look. An Odditorium. As if real life wasn't odd enough. But she supposed it helped, in some ways, the soothing balm of comparison. Your life can't be all bad, after all, when you hold it up and look at it next to the life of that poor mummified Fiji mermaid, for example, or of Chang J'ung, the human candlestick, who had a lit candle surgically impaled in his skull, or of Miss Betty Richeson, pretty little thing from Jacksonville, who died right here in a fire in this building in 1944, naked and wrapped in wet towels, shaking in the bathtub. Her ghost still roamed the halls, the sign said. Elizabeth would have liked to see her, ask her a few questions.

"That's what happened to my parents," Arla said, suddenly at Elizabeth's elbow.

"Good grief, don't sneak up on me like that," Elizabeth said. "This place has me jumpy." She paused, looked at Arla. "What do you mean, about your parents?"

"When they died in the fire up in New York," Arla said. "You knew about that. Well, they were found wrapped in towels in the hotel bathtub. Just like that." She gestured at the sign.

"How awful," Elizabeth said. They moved down a dark hallway. "Do you miss them?"

Arla was quiet for a beat. "Miss them?" she said. "I suppose I do. But I think I missed them even when they were still alive."

"I know what you mean," Elizabeth said. "I missed mine my whole life." Arla's cane bumped the wall, and she took Elizabeth's arm for a moment, steadied herself.

"Family's a funny thing," Arla said. "You don't get to put in a custom order, do you?"

They rounded a corner and faced a wax replica of the world's tallest man, Robert Wadlow, eight foot eleven and still growing at the time of his death at twenty-two.

"My word," Arla said. "And I thought *I* was tall."

Elizabeth had to crane her neck to see Wadlow's face. He was a young man, with a wide, open face and round glasses. In a photo, he stood with his father, whose shoulder rubbed against Robert's dangling wrist. Robert Wadlow's shoes were a size thirty-seven, and he was famous the world over. When he died, the sign said, forty thousand people attended his funeral.

Good heavens, what a life. Such a young man, but such a big burden. The world's largest man. Elizabeth couldn't imagine the responsibility.

Myra and Brooke bumped up behind them.

"We may need to wait outside," Myra said. "Brooke hates this."

The little girl was sniffling, leaning into her mother, hiding her face in the skimpy folds of Myra's dress.

"I *said* so," Brooke said.

"It *is* creepy," Myra said. She adjusted one of her boobs, then stared at a wax figure of The Skeleton Dude, a man who lived to seventy but never weighed more than forty-seven pounds. Nearby, a figure of the world's heaviest man, more than a thousand pounds, gazed sadly across the room.

"I *told* you," Brooke said.

"Well, we'll all make our way out," Elizabeth said. Arla, Bell, and Sofia had migrated to the next room, and the rest of them followed, past the Iron Maiden of Nuremberg (which slammed shut on a holographed victim as she passed), past the lizard man (who'd covered his body in tattooed scales and had his tongue surgically forked), past the African human skin masks and the Tomb of the Werewolf. Frank Sinatra's funeral program. A photo of a man who descended the stairs by hopping upside down on his head. A Chinese man with a unicorn's horn growing out of the back of his skull.

"I *hate* this!" Brooke said, crying.

They caught up with Arla and Bell in a room with a looped video playing on an overhead TV. On the screen, a man inserted a live snake into his mouth and waited until it emerged from his left nostril.

"Oooh," Bell said.

"Mama!" Brooke wailed.

"Good heavens," Arla said. "Now why would he want to go and do that?"

"Arla, I think maybe Brooke's had enough," Elizabeth said.

"Suits me," Arla said, taking Bell by the hand. They found Sofia in the gift shop. Myra bought Brooke a T-shirt. Arla bought a souvenir shot glass. It featured an image of Robert Ripley holding a shrunken head. "For Biaggio," she said. "For driving us down here."

"Not that one," Sofia said. She selected one with an image of Smiley Lewis, THE MAN WITH THE THIRTY-INCH MOUSTACHE. "He'd like this one better," she said.

"How would you know what he'd like?" Arla said, and Sofia shrugged. Elizabeth ran her hands through a deep basket of shiny stones and helped Bell pick out a shell bracelet. Then they walked out of the museum, back into the searing heat. They reboarded the trolley and spent the next thirty minutes in near silence, conserving energy, fanning themselves with Ripley's brochures while the trolley rolled up and down the streets of St. Augustine, past the Spanish Castillo, the Oldest House, the City Gates, the slave market. The city was crowded with tourists, despite the heat, and Elizabeth tried to see it all from their eyes—the austere Spanish twin towers of Flagler College, the manicured plaza, the bright jaunty hibiscus and spindly Sabal palms. It was pretty, she supposed, all very quaint. But she was sick of it suddenly, sick of the whole quaint place. The nation's oldest city. All these ancient buildings, all this detritus of pushing and shoving and fighting over the land. The British, the Spanish, never mind the poor Native Americans who were here to start with and who never even had a prayer. And still it went on, more than four centuries later—the merchants, the sightseers, the homeless, the students, the locals, each group squawking at the next, jockeying for territory, staking claims. It was claustrophobic, cloying. Always too many people—the traffic, the tourists, the ubiquitous trolleys! She wanted to walk into the woods, stay there.

"That's where I got married," Arla said to Bell, pointing to the Cathedral Basilica.

"What does your husband do?" Myra said.

"Oh, I lost my husband twenty years ago."

"I'm sorry," Myra said.

"What are you talking about?" Sofia said to Arla.

"It's true," Arla said. "I don't know where he is, do I?"

Sofia rolled her eyes. Myra looked confused. Elizabeth bit her lip, tried to keep from laughing. Her T-shirt was soaked with sweat. Maybe one day she'd say the same thing. "I lost my husband." Maybe one day soon.

The trolley stopped to let a fashionable young couple disembark. A trio of powdery old women, dressed in billowy capris and enormous white sneakers, climbed aboard and sat primly in the row in front of Elizabeth, and the trolley began to roll again.

"I'm ho-ot," Brooke whined.

"I think maybe we'll call it a day here," Myra said.

"An ice cream," Arla said, spotting the Dairy Queen ahead. "Just an ice cream, and then we'll go back. Bell needs an ice cream."

She stood up in the trolley.

"Driver!" she said.

"Please remain seated at all times," the driver said over the microphone.

"We need to stop here!"

"Remain seated!"

"Please stop the train!" Arla, still standing, her red hair nearly brushing the ceiling, raised her cane and beat on the metal roof of the trolley. "We need to get out right here!"

The old women pivoted in their seats, gaping at Arla. Myra stared out into traffic, her face turned away from Arla. Brooke looked at Arla with her mouth open. Bell smiled.

Arla banged the roof again. "Driver!" she said.

"Jesus Christ!" he said into the microphone. He slid the trolley to a stop, turned around and glared. "You know I can get fired?"

"Thank you!" Arla said brightly. "This will do very well."

Sofia climbed down first, turned to offer a hand to Arla. Elizabeth, Myra, and the girls followed. They walked across the parking lot toward the Dairy Queen.

"They have Blizzards here," Arla said to the girls. "M&M's Blizzards. Oh, babies, to die for. Just wait."

"Isn't your house just up two blocks?" Myra said to Elizabeth. "How about I go get my car, come back, and pick you all up?"

"Don't you want an ice cream?" Elizabeth said.

"No," Myra said, looking at her pityingly. "I don't eat ice cream, honey."

I'll have a double Blizzard, Elizabeth wanted to say. *Do they come with vodka?*

"Well," she said instead, looking at the red faces and soaked shirts of Arla, Sofia, Bell, and Brooke. "A ride would actually be very nice, if you don't mind getting the car."

Myra didn't answer, just turned to Brooke, told her she'd be right back, and went clicking up the street toward Elizabeth's.

"She's got some swing on that back door," Sofia said, looking after her. Brooke looked at Arla. "What does that mean?" she said.

"Never mind," Elizabeth said. "Let's get some ice cream."

Inside the Dairy Queen, they ordered a round of Blizzards from a thin boy with long blond hair. "M&M's in mine," Arla said. "Extra M&M's, in fact. I'll pay extra." The boy grunted and pushed buttons on a register.

They settled into a booth. "This heat," Arla said. "It's getting ridiculous. I don't know if it's getting hotter, or if it's just bothering me more now that I'm getting older. I'm sixty-two, and I don't ever remember being this hot. What's going to happen when I'm ninety?"

"It's global warming," Sofia said. She fished in her tote bag and removed a plastic bottle of Germ-X, which she squirted across the tabletop and spread around with napkins.

"It must be," Arla said. "My Lord."

The boy from the counter brought a tray of Blizzards, and everyone was quiet for a moment. Elizabeth was grateful for the cool chocolate cream. It was such simple, sweet relief. The girls spooned chunky pieces of ice cream into their mouths, made worms out of straw wrappers on the table.

"This doesn't have extra M&M's in it," Arla said, looking at her Blizzard skeptically.

"Arla," Elizabeth said. "Do you think maybe we could stay with you for a bit? At Aberdeen?"

Arla put her Blizzard down. "What do you mean?" she said. "Of course."

"I mean me, and Bell," Elizabeth said. She dropped her voice down a bit, but the girls were oblivious, lost in their own games.

Sofia raised her eyebrows. "You're leaving Carson?" she whispered.

"No," Elizabeth said. "Not leaving. Just—" Just what? She put her hands up. "Just for a little bit," she said. Her voice caught. She looked away from the table, hoped they wouldn't ask her any more questions, and when she looked back, Arla's eyes were soft, sad.

"Oh, baby," she said. "You come on to Aberdeen. You come on up there anytime you want. Come today."

Elizabeth nodded, not trusting her own voice.

They were quiet again, and then Arla coughed, looked back at her Blizzard.

"This does *not* have extra M&M's," she said. "Let me out." She nudged Sofia, who was sitting on the outside of the booth.

"Let it go, Mother," Sofia said. "It's fine."

"I paid for extra M&M's."

Sofia rolled her eyes.

"Let me out," Arla said. Sofia stood up and Arla slid out of the booth, grasped her cane, and approached the counter.

"Are you okay, Elizabeth?" Sofia said, and Elizabeth was surprised at the reason in Sofia's voice, the concern, the maturity.

"I will be," Elizabeth said. "Eventually."

"He can be a real ass sometimes, I hate to tell you."

"Who?"

"My brother."

Elizabeth smiled. "Yes, I've noticed that," she said.

"Do you ever wonder if you made the wrong choice?" Sofia said, raising her eyebrows knowingly. "I think about that sometimes. I think about choices." Her voice dropped a bit, and she gazed off into the space behind Elizabeth's head.

"I think this is a conversation that will get us nowhere," Elizabeth said. She looked out the window of the Dairy Queen. Myra's sea foam Volkswagen pulled into the parking lot. "Okay, girls," Elizabeth said. "Finished up?"

They cleared the cups and plastic spoons, threw them into the trash. Arla was still at the counter, arguing with the blond boy.

"That's not extra," she was saying. She held the Blizzard cup out to him. "Extra means *more*. Look in there and tell me if that's *more*."

"Arla," Elizabeth said. "Our ride is here."

The boy was silent, shaking his head.

"You don't know who you're dealing with," Arla said. "Get me your manager."

"I am the manager," he said.

"Oh, my Lord," Arla said. "Then take this back. I don't want it. I paid for extra and I didn't get it. I want my money back."

"No refunds," he said coolly. He pointed to a handwritten sign on the front of the register: NO REFUNDS. NO EXCHANGES. He yawned.

Arla hiked her handbag higher on her shoulder. She straightened up and poked her cane one time into the floor.

"Oh, really," she said. She looked over at Bell, standing now with Elizabeth.

"Arla, Myra is waiting for us," Elizabeth said. "Let's just forget it."

"Bell, you want a Dilly Bar?" Arla said.

Bell nodded.

"She just had a Blizzard," Elizabeth said.

"Your friend want a Dilly Bar?" Arla said.

Bell nodded again.

"It's Brooke," Brooke said. "I don't want a Dilly Bar."

Arla left the Blizzard on the counter and walked over to the freezer case. She reached in and took out three Dilly Bars. "Elizabeth?" she said.

"No," Elizabeth whispered. She knew what was coming. "Sofia?"

"Sure," Sofia said, shrugging her shoulders. "I can fit it."

Arla took out one more, stepped back, and let the freezer door close behind her. The boy watched.

"I'm not paying for these," Arla said. She took a step toward the door.

He gaped at her. Her voice took on a singsong lilt. "I'm not paying. Watch me not paying," she said, and she moved deliberately toward the exit. "Not paying!"

They stepped out into the hot sunlight. Myra's VW idled in a disabled spot.

"Go!" Arla said. "Do it!"

Elizabeth and Sofia hustled the girls into the back of the car, and Elizabeth pulled Bell onto her lap so they could all squeeze in. Arla lumbered as quickly as she could to the front passenger seat. The Dairy Queen boy was now in the doorway of the store.

"Bitch!" he yelled. "Get back here, you old bitch!!"

Brooke started to cry.

"What—?" Myra said. She stared at the boy in the doorway.

"Fucking stealing my Dilly Bars!" he screamed.

"Go!" Arla said. Elizabeth put her face in her hands. "Go!"

The boy started toward them, and Myra's instincts kicked in; she put the car in drive and bolted out of the parking lot, narrowly missing another trolley train as she pulled into the traffic of San Marco Boulevard.

"What in the *world*?" Myra said.

Sofia laughed, and Elizabeth looked at Bell, who was grinning.

"Okay!" Arla said. "Now who wants a Dilly Bar?" The car was cool and smelled lovely, with thick velour upholstery on the seats. The AC blasted through the interior and made a rushing sound. "Brooke?" Arla said, extending an ice cream bar across the back of the seat.

"I don't *want* one," Brooke said. She sniffled. "They're *stolen*."

"They're what?" Myra said.

"Oh, never mind," Elizabeth said. "I'll eat hers." She reached out and took the ice cream from Arla. Sofia smiled. "This way we won't have to eat lunch," Elizabeth said. Arla's eyes shone, and Bell laughed, and God *damn,* if that wasn't the best Dilly Bar Elizabeth had ever eaten.

*   *   *

After Myra and Brooke dropped them off, Elizabeth packed quickly, just a suitcase each for her and Bell. She glanced at her watch. Still a half hour, at least, before Carson would return home.

"We're going on a trip?" Bell said.

"Better," Elizabeth said. "We're going to Granny's."

"Why?" Bell said.

"Because it's summer," Arla said. "And because it's your birthday, and because we want to fatten you up with ice cream and Little Debbies and spoil you rotten."

Bell scrunched her eyebrows and looked at Elizabeth.

"And because you can help me move the piano out," Sofia said to Bell. She pulled her down on the sofa and tickled the little girl until she screamed.

"Oh, my Lord," Arla said.

They piled into Elizabeth's car and headed for Utina. When they pulled up in the driveway of Aberdeen, Biaggio was outside, hosing the sticky residue of fallen oak leaves from the front steps.

"Watch it, there, Miss Arla," he said, holding her by the elbow as she plodded up the wet ramp to the front door.

"You too, now," he said to Sofia, and he reached to take her hand and guide her across the planks.

"Oh, I'm fine," Sofia said, but she took his hand. Biaggio's face turned red.

"How was the trolley?" he said to Bell.

"Fun," she said simply.

"Hot," Elizabeth said.

"Hotter than hell," Arla said.

"Belly, go take this bag and find your bathing suit," Elizabeth said. "Let's get you wet."

Elizabeth pulled open the screen door.

"Mind the piano," Biaggio called. "You gotta go over."

Elizabeth regarded the Steinway in the hallway for a moment but decided against asking any questions. She climbed across the top of the piano and went to the kitchen to make a pitcher of iced tea from a powdered mix, and then they all sat on the porch and drank the tea out of aluminum cups that tasted like summer. The sun was so bright and high that the air looked brittle. Sofia jangled the ice cubes in her cup and hummed. Arla put her foot on a wicker stool and picked up a straw fan. Biaggio loped around the yard and turned the hose on Bell and they watched her dance, skinny and wet, through the spray. Her hair stuck to her face. Her white knees shone.

Utina, Elizabeth thought. Aberdeen. An Odditorium. Where else could we possibly all go? It was ironic, she knew, that in separating from Carson she would come here, to Aberdeen, his own mother's house. But it just felt right. She didn't even know for sure where her own mother was anymore. And she didn't care. She felt like a Fiji mermaid, a firewalker, a shaman, a ghost. She felt like the world's largest woman, with the world's largest love, and the world's largest pain. And for the first time in a very long time, she felt like she was home.

"More tea, Arla?" she said.

"No, love," Arla said. "I'm fine."

SEVEN

She was mine first. The thought passed through Frank's brain for the billionth time. *Elizabeth.* He stood at his kitchen sink, rinsing sluice from the scales of a three-pound bass steak, freshly cleaned, thick and dense in his hands. He'd taken the kayak out for a quick run, had headed north along the mangrove banks of the Intracoastal, past Uncle Henry's, until he could look back and see no sign of the restaurant or, beyond, of Aberdeen. The bass had been an easy catch, pliant and stupid, in fact, hardly worth the effort that afternoon. It was the red drum that had given him a run, a ten-pounder, no doubt, making him stand up in the kayak, nearly toppling him with its pull, its desperate battle to overpower the line. He'd planted his feet, regained his balance, toyed and teased and tugged the line for a half hour or more, sweating in the searing heat of a crooked little elbow of mangroves. But the red drum won. It snapped the line finally, disappeared in a last triumphant roil of brown water, slapping a fat tail along the surface of the water, giving Frank the kiss-off, clear as day. But he smiled in the end. "Tough little pisser," he said to the fish, watching the last of the ripples disappear on the water. "Good for you." He settled for the one bass, which had obediently gasped out its last breath on a bed of ice in the Coleman chest strapped to the deck.

Trout, he thought, wiping the sweat from his face. He leaned out of the kayak, dipped water into his hands, splashed it onto his neck to cool off. One day it's going to be trout. Rainbow trout. Up in the mountains where it's cool. Cullowhee. He pictured the colors—a blaze of pigment along the fish's scales, the deep greens of pines along a bright mountain lake, a blue, cool sky—not this charred-out, fried-out, burnt-out Florida scrub, everything a circus of browns and grays, the sky white-hot, every bit of it looking like it was about to spontaneously combust. Jesus, sometimes he was sick of Utina. He was forty years old, and he'd never seen snow. He watched the surface of the water, imagining the red drum beneath, swimming slick and powerful. Swimming away.

Now, in his kitchen, the kayak returned to its hanging spot on the porch, Gooch still pouting in the bedroom over not having been invited fishing, Frank finished rinsing the bass steak, his consolation prize. It wasn't very big. He thought of a story Biaggio had told him years ago, about a man who'd caught an undersize bass and had taken it home alive. The man had put it in a fish tank in his living room along with a bucketful of smaller fish. When the bass had eaten the smaller fish, the man dumped in another bucketful, and on and on, until the bass grew to ten times its original size and could scarcely turn around in the tank. "And then what?" Frank asked. "Well, then he ate it," Biaggio said simply, and Frank had been surprised, taken aback, for some reason. It hadn't seemed right. He'd hoped for more, for the bass. He didn't know why.

He put his own bass steak in a plastic Baggie and sealed it. He turned off the water but stood for a moment at the kitchen window, watching across the yard as the banker next door raked at a saw palmetto at the front edge of his driveway, and then the familiar longing, the long-accustomed loneliness, came back to him.

Elizabeth. She was his, first. Before Carson. They dated when they were in high school, and he told her he loved her then, but she looked at him skeptically, quizzically, that open stare, unbelieving. He kissed her passionately, but she never let him go further. She left him for Carson when they were sixteen, broke his heart, but they chalked it up, all of them, to puppy love and young crushes and that complicated, tumultuous time of hookups and breakups and tenuous betrothals that lasted until the next big game. It was the kind of thing you laughed about later, with the maturity and the distance of years. But he never laughed. Never.

When they were teenagers, she'd spend nights in Sofia's room, stretched on a long piece of foam on the floor. From his bed, Frank could hear them talking, laughing. She'd come for dinners and birthdays and Christmases, would sometimes stay for days, weeks, before going home again to the darkness of her mother's trailer in South Utina. She stood with the family at the water's edge when they scattered Will's ashes. And she made tea for Arla the morning after Dean left, had sat at the table with the rest of them, staring blankly around the kitchen.

When she married Carson she was young and pregnant. Carson got drunk the night before the wedding and spilled it to Frank in the parking lot at Uncle Henry's, following a marathon, ugly alcoholic binge that Carson tried to spin as noble and traditional, the quaint, madcap bachelor's party overindulgence, until he grew weepy and morose as the night wore on.

"My life is over," he said to Frank. "Trapped. Caught. Game over."

"You're an asshole," Frank said.

"You're a free man," Carson said, slurring. "I'm about to serve a life sentence."

"Get away from me," Frank said, and Carson turned away and vomited into the bushes.

But the baby died—she miscarried in her fifth month, two months into the marriage. Frank remembered her face, pale and empty, when she told him.

"So what does this mean? You're staying with him?" he said, stupidly, and he hated himself for having said it.

She stared at him, and he could see anger in her eyes, and it broke his heart.

"He's my husband," she said, and she walked away.

And then Carson went away to college, and she went with him, and they'd come back with a focus, a mission—he was going to build an investment practice, not here, not in Utina but in St. Augustine, out of this place, away from all of it, Carson said, though Frank knew he really meant away from all of *them*.

Next door, the banker zeroed in on the stubborn palmetto, jabbing it with a metal rake, combing through the long fronds. He stopped, stared at it for a moment, then dropped the rake and grabbed the palmetto with his gloved hands. Frank smiled. This would be good. Just try it, he thought, watching the banker. There's a reason those things are all over Utina.

The banker pulled at the plant, stopped, straightened up, then bent over and pulled again. His forearms and shoulders strained. The palmetto did not budge. He took a shovel and hacked a bit at the base of the plant, then resumed his pulling. Nothing. He pulled off his gloves, threw them to the ground, walked toward the garage.

Maybe it was the money she liked. Carson made money, no doubt, not huge money, but enough for a nice little house with a yard, matching furniture, and a savings account for Bell. Nine-to-five. An insurance plan. Not some hardscrabble restaurant work, peeling shrimp and wiping stale beer off the bar for hours on end, hauling Mac Weeden off the barstool at closing time, smelling like grease and fish every night. With his mutual funds and money markets and whatever they all were, Carson gave her a steady life, a real life, like she'd never had before. And then Bell—baby Bell, seven years old now and the glue—the *only* glue, as far as Frank could see—that was holding it all together.

When Elizabeth had told him she was pregnant again, with the baby who would become Bell, Frank had hugged her, told her he was happy for her, for them, but inside he felt the weight of a door closing, the end of the line. She'd never leave Carson now, he thought then. And he still thought so now.

It would take a miracle.

The banker returned with a saw. He pulled his gloves back on and hacked awkwardly at the base of the palmetto until he'd reduced it to a ragged, sprouting tuft of weedy green. Then he resumed his work with the shovel, digging deep around the edges of the root, looking for a purchase for the tip of the shovel's blade. His shirt was drenched with sweat.

Good going, Frank thought. *You dug a foot—only four more to go to get to the bottom of that root.*

The banker threw his shovel down again, stood back, wiped his brow, and regarded the palmetto, one of about ten thousand identical plants that rimmed the edge of his property and grew wild and thick all over Frank's yard. The banker walked to the garage again, returned with a plastic jug of Roundup. He dumped the contents onto the palmetto root and stood back, gloating, victorious.

"That's what you think," Frank said aloud, though he was alone in his house and he knew the banker could not hear him. "Take more than that to kill that thing." And it was true, he knew— the palmetto's tips would turn brown and dry, the top of the root would become spongy and fibrous, and the banker would think he'd won the battle. But in a few weeks, the root would reawaken, pissed off righteously, in fact, and would thrust itself upward toward the light again, emerging from the poisoned soil stronger, thicker, and more tenacious than before. "Take a backhoe to be done with that sucker," Frank said, and he smiled at this small, secret victory, this dormant, stubborn miracle.

"Asshole," he added, watching the banker head back toward his house. Frank tossed the bass steak into the freezer, next to a dozen others, already frozen and gray.

That night at Uncle Henry's, after the early birds and the dinner rush and the late-night gadabouts clinging to their barstools like life preservers, he closed the restaurant and fell asleep for a little while on the couch in his office, the day's receipts slipping out of a worn file folder on his chest. He awoke in the dim light of

his desk lamp, and he waited for his eyes to adjust, staring for
a time at the Florida Gator pennant stapled to the wall above
the couch. Preseason starting soon, Mac had said, and Frank
was glad. He was always happy for the distraction of football. It
gave a shape to the year, anchored it, somehow. And the Gator
games were always good for business. In fact, he'd been considering adding another big-screen TV over the far end of the
bar, and this might be the year he made the investment. Last
year there'd been so much jostling and arguing around the bar
among half-bagged Utinians trying to get a glimpse of the action at the Swamp without giving up their seats at the bar that
he'd thought he'd end up with a brawl on his hands. A second
TV would cost less than a lawsuit over a bashed-in head, he
was pretty sure. The Florida football team. Jesus, it was like a
religion for Utina.

When the boys were kids—what were they? Frank was
eight, maybe, Carson ten? And Will six?— Dean had taken them
to see the Gators play Ole Miss at Florida Field. He'd scored the
four tickets from his buddy Paulie at Rayonier, who said he'd
gotten them from his cousin (or was it his uncle?), and Paulie
offered them to Dean at a quarter of their face value.

"For real?" Carson had said, when Dean presented them
with the tickets. "We're really going?"

"Go Gators!" Dean shouted, and he threw back his head
and laughed, then went to the refrigerator and popped a cold
can of Bud. "We're goin' to the game, boys!" Arla had rolled her
eyes at the outburst, but then she smiled.

They loaded up in the old Chevy Impala, Dean and the
three boys, and they drove down to Gainesville on a scorching
hot September Saturday. They parked almost a mile away from

the stadium, had to walk clear across town, through the seas of jubilant fans headed toward the game. Dean was giddy, buoyant. He carried Will on his shoulders for almost two blocks, then set him down and told him to walk his sorry ass, but he held Will's hand and laughed when he said it. Frank and Carson wore matching Florida shirts. Arla had found them at the Dollar General the week before. When they arrived at Florida Field and stood at the gate turnstile, the roar of sixty thousand football fans ringing in their ears, they learned the tickets were phony. Counterfeit.

"Shit on a stick," Dean said, staring stupidly at the four tickets, then back up at the attendant at the turnstile, a humorless woman in an orange-and-blue smock. "You're not serious. *Fake?*" Frank's attention had been drawn by the sight of a girl behind him, standing with her mother and father. She was maybe twelve years old, and she had a pugnacious Florida Gator painted daintily on each cheek, an explosion of orange-and-blue ribbons clasping a high ponytail of white blond hair. She saw Frank staring at her and smiled, just a little. But when he heard the ticket-taker's stern voice he turned back toward Dean. The girl's father sighed loudly.

"I know fake when I see it," the woman at the turnstile said. She tapped a long acrylic fingernail on the stack of tickets and glared at Dean. "Phony."

"Well, I'll be damned," Dean said. He turned and looked at his three sons. He pursed his lips and Frank saw a tendon in his father's neck tighten.

"So we can't go in?" Will said. "So we ain't gonna see the game?" He didn't sound particularly surprised. Just resigned.

"You're lucky I don't turn you in to the po-lice," the woman said. "I'm going easy on account of you got the three boys there." She gave Dean a final dismissive stare, then turned to the blond-haired girl's family, who presented their *not*-fake tickets and walked up over the concrete ramp and down into the stadium. The girl turned and gave Frank a last bald look and then disappeared over the crest of concrete in a blinding swath of sunlight.

Frank's face burned and he dared a quick glance at Carson and then turned away. His older brother's face was closed, locked. They walked away from the ticket booth.

"God-damned Paulie," Dean said. "I'm going to kick his God-damned butt."

He stood in the harsh sunlight, crossed his arms over his chest, and gazed at the sky. His face was lined, drawn, and although Frank was well accustomed to disappointment, to denial, here in the harsh bright light of Florida Field, with the Gators prepping in a locker room on the other side of a sixty-foot concrete wall, he was so ashamed of Dean's latest failure that he felt he might be sick. He looked away from his father, but not before catching his eye for one hard, small moment.

Dean made a quick noise, somewhere between a sigh and a gasp. Then he threw the four fake tickets into a trashcan. He squared his shoulders and regarded his sons.

"Boys," he said. "We are going to see this mother-fucking football game."

They walked to the opposite side of the stadium and staked out a set of turnstiles where the attendant was a gangly young man who was taking tickets robotically while keeping up an animated conversation with another attendant—a chesty girl wearing a tight T-shirt and Gator kneesocks—standing immediately to his right.

"We just gonna buddy up with some folks here, that's all," Dean said. They waited in the shade of a Port-O-Let until the first likely family came by, a rowdy group with a passel of dark-headed boys of about Frank's own age pushing and shoving their way to the gate.

"Carson," Dean said. "You."

Carson bolted forward and slid himself in among the group of boys, who barely noticed him. The father handed the teenaged attendant a stack of tickets and gestured to his family, and the boy tore the tickets in half, handed the father the stubs, and turned back to the girl. Carson strolled casually through the turnstile, walked over the concrete ramp without looking back.

"Hooo-doggy!" Dean said, gleeful. He slapped Frank on the shoulder. "One down!"

They waited again for another group, this one a smaller family with two young girls and a mother carrying a baby in a front carrier with straps handing down by her hips. This family was preceded through the turnstile by a group of rowdy Ole Miss fans, and the boy at the turnstile had joined everyone else in the vicinity with jeering the Rebels when Dean shoved Will forward and Frank watched, amazed, as his little brother bolted forward and walked through the turnstile with the little family, blending seamlessly in with their shuffling, bumbling progress through the gate, even holding on to the strap of the baby's sling! The mother had no idea. My God, Will was a bold little shit. Dean was almost beside himself.

"Oh, my boy," he said, proud. "Did you see that?" He cackled, a bit maniacally, Frank thought, but he himself was amazed at Will's moxie. Six years old!

They waited for one more family.

"When you find the others, meet me at the top on our side, at the fifty-yard line," Dean said. He turned and grinned at Frank.

"But how are *you* going to get in?" Frank said. It had suddenly occurred to him that his father was not likely to have any luck trying to hitchhike along with another family.

"Oh, I'll get in," Dean said. He smiled again. "I can get my butt in and out of an old boiler fifty times a week, I can get it into this old sinkhole of a stadium. Now go!" He shoved Frank roughly as what looked like a group of uncles and cousins jostled by, sweaty and loud, and Frank threw himself into the mix, not daring to look anyone in the eye, and one of the boys elbowed him and said "Hey!" but Frank held his ground and marched forward. One of the men handed over a pile of tickets at the turnstile and the attendant didn't even give him a second look. And then he was running up the concrete ramp and over the top and looking into the glory of the sun and the blazing, blinding sheets of color—Orange! Blue! Orange! Blue! Everywhere! And he was IN! Florida Field! Game time! All around him people were on their feet atop the metal benches, stomping, pounding, clapping, screaming. It's great!—*bom bom*—to be!—*bom bom*—a Flo-ri-da Gator, I say it's great! *bom bom*—to be!—*bom bom*—a Flo-ri-da *Gator*!

He had no idea how long he was frozen at the top of the ramp, but then Carson ran over to him, clutching Will by the hand. "Come on, Frank!" he screamed. "Come on!" The crowd was deafening; the band was going berserk; the colors were so intense they were painful; the Gators were about to take the field, and Frank did not think he had ever seen such joy in his brother's eyes. He felt he might pass out, but instead he grabbed Will by the other hand and they ran up, up, up the rows of concrete steps to the highest platform, and then they made a beeline over to the fifty-yard line and jostled their way past a row of drunken Delta Chis to claim seats on the scorching metal bench.

"Where is he?" Carson yelled.

"I don't know!" Frank said. They stood up on the metal bench with everyone else and stamped their feet and hollered and clapped and hooted for what seemed like an eternity. Frank hadn't thought it could possibly be any louder in the stadium, but then the noise level suddenly rose again, and the entire stadium turned and screamed and pointed toward the tunnel at the south end, where the team was taking the field.

"Ladies and gentlemen," screamed the announcer. "Heeeeeeeeeerrre come the Gators!" There they were! They were tearing out of the tunnel, running and jumping and thrusting their chests into the air, pumping their fists in a victory they already knew they had.

"Look!" Will said, pointing. He jumped on the bench and cheered. "Here comes Dad!!" And then there was Dean, panting and soaked with sweat, his orange cap pulled low over his eyes, his arms full of hot dogs and popcorn and his pants bulging with what Frank knew was a hefty flask of Southern Comfort. Dean stumbled once, righted himself, then tipped his head way back to be able to see under the brim of his skewed cap, and when he saw his three boys at the top of the fifty his face broke into a broad grin. He clambered up to them, huffing like a racehorse.

He stood with them on the metal bench and handed out the hot dogs. "Hot shit!" he said, laughing. "We did it!" He pounded Carson on the back, pulled Will into a hot, sweaty hug. Then he looked at Frank, beaming, and said, "Now what are *you* crying about, junior?"

It wasn't until much later, years later, that it occurred to Frank: the happiest moment he and his brothers had ever shared with their father was one in which they'd all pretended to belong to other families. But he smiled, even today, at the memory. It had been worth it.

Frank locked the restaurant and drove home through the darkness of Monroe Road, the night sky like ink above the trees. When he passed the long driveway to Aberdeen he looked to the right and saw the light on in Arla's bedroom on the second floor. He knew she was sitting up, a tumbler of wine at her elbow, staring into the darkness. It was like this every night, her bedroom light shining like a beacon through the pines. He looked at the clock on the dashboard: 2:17 A.M., and for some reason, though he'd never done this before, not at this hour, he picked up his cell phone and called the house. It took Arla more than five rings to answer. He counted. Sofia was sleeping, no doubt.

"Hello?" Arla said, finally.

"Are you okay?" he said.

"Oh, yes," she said. "I'm all right, Frank." He heard her sit down on the bed. "Why are you calling so late?" Her voice was a bit thick, the wine, no doubt, but other than that she sounded completely herself.

"Just checking in," he said, and he felt a bit foolish, suddenly, with no ready answer. Why *was* he calling, anyway?

"How was the restaurant tonight?" she said.

"Busy," he said. "Crazy busy."

"Who came in? Anyone?"

"Tony Cerro. George and Mac, of course."

"Of course. How's Tony?"

"Busy. He says he needs help in the salon."

"Huh," she said. "All these new people around here with their fancy hairdos, I guess."

"I guess," Frank said. "Did Biaggio move the piano?"

"Oh, my God, don't get me started. She won't let him. I can't even think about it, Frank." She sighed. "For the love of Moses."

The night was damp, and beads of moisture had begun to glisten on the windshield. Frank turned on the wipers.

"Have you talked to your brother?" Arla said.

"Not in a few days. Why?"

"Oh," Arla said, and he heard something in her voice, something she knew but wasn't telling him. "No reason." He didn't bite. He didn't have the energy.

"Mom," he said. "What are we going to do about this offer on the house? And the restaurant? This guy Cryder has called me four times."

She sighed. "Oh, Frankie," she said. "I don't know. I just don't think I can even talk about it."

"At some point we need to."

"I suppose."

He turned left off Monroe Road, made his way down Cooksey Lane toward his own house, the darkness growing even deeper, more complete, as he moved away from the water and farther into the piney woods surrounding his road.

"Are you worried about Sofia?" he said. "If she had to move?"

"Of course I'm worried about Sofia. But it's not only that, Frank."

"Then what?"

She sighed, irritated. "Well, it's just that maybe *I* don't want to move. Maybe these horrible people can't just come in here and tell everybody what to do."

"They're talking about a lot of money."

"What do I care about money, Frank?" she said, honest confusion in her voice. "What in the world is money going to do for me?"

He turned into his own driveway, turned off his headlights, and sat there in the truck. It was true. What was money going to do for Arla? It wouldn't change things—make Sofia better, bring Will back. He thought again of Arla's bedroom light shining through the trees a mile or so to the west. It seemed to Frank, sometimes, that it was Arla's light, all these years, that had been telling him what he needed to do. How to atone. And now this offer on the house. Maybe big money, big changes. But he wasn't sure at all how he would proceed if that light wasn't there.

"Who was driving the boat?" he asked suddenly. He couldn't believe he'd never asked her that before. His heart pounded and he waited for his mother to speak.

"What?" she said.

"The boat," he said. "Your foot. The accident. Were there other people in the boat? Who was driving?"

"Oh, Frank," she said, and she laughed sadly. "Well *he* was, of course."

Frank realized, then, that he'd probably known this all along, though he'd never wanted to face it. Dean. Dean cut off her foot. And after what they did to Will, he and Carson cut out her heart. *Aren't we something, we Bravo boys? Aren't we just the shit?*

AUGUST

Eight

Though peopled with residents wrought from the same back-woods genetic stew as their neighbors immediately to the north, South Utina, in many ways, was different from the thick woods and sprawling properties of North Utina. In South Utina the streets were narrow, close, the avenues of the laborers and the tenuously middle class, with humble turn-of-the-century homes sporting awkward add-ons and incongruous porches, the result being a neighborhood that more closely resembled a rummage sale than a community.

Frank crossed the intersection at Seminary Street and turned onto Lincoln, which sliced into South Utina in a straight line and provided the axis for the dozen cross streets that made up the neighborhood. He stopped at a tiny cinder-block-and-stucco house painted two tones of muddy brown. The house was surrounded by a chain-link fence, and at the curb sat a rusted maroon sedan, in which a woman in a head wrap and enormous eyeglasses reclined. She looked up when Frank approached, waved her hand out the window. He parked in front of her car and walked back to greet her.

"Hey, baby," the woman said, smiling wide. She wore a huge ballooning dress in a dizzyingly colorful print, and her face was slick with perspiration. She reached across the passenger seat and pushed the door open for Frank. He climbed in and sat down, grateful for the wide swath of shade cast over the car by a pair of pecan trees in the yard.

"Hey, An-Needa," he said. He left the door open, hoping to encourage a cross-breeze. "Do you know you are a vision in those colors?"

An-Needa threw her head back, laughed. She slapped Frank on the shoulder. "Oh, listen to you, Frankie Bravo—what are you doing, flirting with an old mama like me? A grand-mama, don't you know."

Frank smiled. He'd known An-Needa Lovett almost half his life, ever since his mother had discovered An-Needa's pecan pies at a Utina High bake sale and had commissioned her to bake the pies for Uncle Henry's dessert menu. The Uncle Henry's gig had led to more business, too, so now An-Needa sold to seven restaurants and a coffee shop in St. Augustine, even one in Jacksonville. Twice a week, rain or shine, Frank drove to Lincoln Street to conduct business in An-Needa's rusted sedan, where she tended to her customers and let the heat from the morning's baking dissipate from her small house. Afternoons, Frank could usually find her in her automotive "office," where she met with her customers and sipped Nestea until the sun dipped behind the treeline and the mosquitoes came out.

"I got your pies in the fridge, baby," she said. "You go around back the house, on the porch. You know where they are."

Frank took out his wallet, counted the money for the week's order. He made sure to miscount, slip an extra twenty into the pile. He put the money into the glove box.

"How's your mama, Frankie?" she said.

"She's okay," Frank said. He paused. "I guess."

"What you mean, you guess? She is or she ain't?"

"Oh, she is, An-Needa. She's the same as ever, you know."

She looked at him over the tops of her glasses, raised her eyebrows.

"You giving Miss Arla trouble, Frank?"

"No. Me? No, I just—"

"I hope you're being kind to your mama, Frank. That woman, oh my Jesus, that poor woman. She's had her troubles, you know." Frank was well aware of his mother's troubles. All of Utina was aware of Arla's troubles. But she could dish them out just as well as she could take them. He was about to point this out to An-Needa, but she was still glaring at him, tapping one long fingernail on the leather cover of her Bible, so he said nothing. At the end of the street, a garbage truck rounded the corner and began a rollicking approach, stopping at every third house or so while a two-man crew bounded off the rails and slung trash into the back of the truck. An-Needa turned forward, sighed.

"Oh, Lord," she said. "Here comes that wretched man again."

Inside the garbage truck, the driver's face, puffy and squinting in the summer sun, shone like a pasty white moon as he bucked the vehicle to a stop a block from An-Needa's house. He caught sight of An-Needa and Frank sitting in the car, and he waved wildly. He threw the truck into drive again and accelerated too quickly, before one of his men, the shorter one, had jumped back on the rail.

"Fucker!" the man screamed.

The driver of the truck was George Weeden, Mac Weeden's older brother, who'd been the blue-collar version of his jack-of-all-trades brother for as long as Frank could remember. George had been, through the years, employed around North and South Utina as a flagman, dock custodian, taxi driver, dishwasher, and now garbage truck driver. George slammed on the brakes and shot a bird out the window to the man behind him. The abandoned crewman, dripping with sweat, lurched forward, grabbed the rail, and remounted the back of the truck.

"Wait till I get on the damn truck, jackass!" he shouted at George.

"Good Lord in heaven," An-Needa said. "Do you hear the language on these animals?"

The truck continued its stop-start progression, now pulling directly abreast of An-Needa's sedan. Gooch, still in Frank's truck, stuck his head out the window and barked.

"Bravo!" George yelled. "Frank!"

An-Needa rolled her eyes, looked out the other side of the car.

"Hey, George," Frank said. He lifted his hand slightly, gave a tiny wave.

"Frank, I wanna talk to you!" George was yelling at the top of his voice, trying to be heard over the gnawing hydraulics of the truck, which were now in the process of compacting the trash in the receptacle behind him. Gooch's continued barking was drowned out from the noise of the truck, so he looked like he was simply snapping and gulping awkwardly into empty air. George put the truck in park and climbed down from the driver's seat. The two men on the rails groaned and threw up their hands.

"Weeden!" one said. "Go!"

"Hold on, asshole," George called back.

"George Weeden, you stop using that devil's language in front of my house before I get myself out of this car and teach you some manners!" An-Needa said. She leaned over Frank, glared out the passenger window at Weeden. George bent down, leaned into the car. Frank flattened himself against the seat.

"I'm sorry, Ms. Lovett. I'm sorry. You're right," George said. He leaned his elbows on the car door and scratched his head. His white hair was cut in a military-style crew that made his head appear completely square. "You are one-hundred-percent, completely right. I don't know what comes over me. These guys—" He jerked his thumb over his shoulder at his crew. "They bring out the worst in me, I guess, Ms. Lovett."

A Toyota with a Realtor's logo on the front license plate approached behind the stopped garbage truck, which was now blocking Lincoln Street, and the driver, a young man in a golf shirt, frowned. The garbage crew, still hanging on the rails of the truck, glared at An-Needa's car, where George still hung in the passenger window.

"Weeden!" the short man said. "Move the God-damn truck!"

"Oh, my sweet Jesus," An-Needa said.

The Realtor in the Toyota tooted once. Gooch redoubled his barking.

"George," Frank said. "Maybe you better move the truck."

"I will, I will," George said. "Hang on. Frank, I want to talk to you. I got a business proposition, see, and I want to tell you about it. I got an idea."

"All right, George. Call me sometime, okay? At the restaurant."

"What's the number?" George pulled a pen out of his shirt pocket. "Ms. Lovett, you got a piece of paper?"

An-Needa stared out the window and did not respond. The Realtor behind the truck tooted again, twice this time.

"Christ," George said.

"Weeden, you cocksucking fat fuck!" the short man yelled. "Move this God-damned truck and let's finish this shit-fucking shift!"

An-Needa put her hands over her face.

"George, look it up. You gotta move the truck," Frank said. The driver of the car was now leaning on the horn. "Just come by Uncle Henry's, George."

George brightened.

"I'll do that! Okay, Frank. I'll do that. I'll come by. Like maybe later today?"

"Fine, George. Later. I'll see you then. Go ahead and move the truck, George."

George gave a salute, straightened up, and sauntered back to the truck. The men on the back glowered. The Realtor in the car behind revved his engine. George climbed back into the driver's seat and leaned out the window to grin at Frank.

"I'll see you later, Bravo!" he shouted. He waved happily. Frank nodded. As the garbage truck pulled away, the Realtor in the delayed Toyota pulled up alongside An-Needa's car.

"Hey, redneck!" the man yelled to Frank. "Way to hold up the fucking garbage truck! Don't you know some of us have places to go?" He shot them a bird, sped off again. Frank turned to look behind him as the car took a rakish left turn and sped back toward Seminary Street. Gooch barked twice more, then sat down in the truck, panting. After a moment, Frank looked at An-Needa.

"You ever feel like there might be something else out there, An-Needa?" he said. "Something besides Utina?"

She was quiet for a beat, and when she spoke again, her voice caught in a way he'd never heard before.

"Where do we live, Frank? What is happening to this place?"

He was dismayed to find her beautiful brown eyes filling with tears.

"It's all changing, Frank," she said. "George Weeden and that lot, they're bad enough, but you see these new people? You see that Realtor there? It's all changing. You know, I went to the Lil' Champ to buy milk and that Tip Breen, he says he's losing business to the new Walgreens down there by the high school. They're selling milk, beer, all that stuff. I don't care for that Tip Breen, Frank, but what's going to happen to Utina? Why we got people like this coming in here?"

"An-Needa," he said. "Now come on. You can't let them get to you."

"Oh, it's not them, Frank," she said. She reached across the car and pulled a Dunkin' Donuts napkin from the glove box. "It's me. I'm just an old lady. Don't pay any attention." She blew her nose. "Your pies, they're out back, honey. You go on now."

He hesitated, and she patted his hand.

"You go on, Frankie. Don't you worry about an old lady like me. Old ladies, we tough. We survive. You just ask your mama."

He got out of the car, and as he turned the corner to the back
of the house, to approach the porch and the spare refrigerator
where she kept her customers' pies, he heard her begin to sing,
a soft sweet song, about Jesus's bitter pains, and his holy sacred
veins, and lifeblood strong and true.

"What do you mean, my brother?" Mac said. Frank had pulled
up at Bait/Karaoke on the way back from An-Needa's, and Mac,
waving, had walked over to Frank's window. Gooch—temporarily
relocated to the bed of the truck to accommodate the fourteen
fresh pies that were now stacked up on the passenger seat next
to Frank in the cab—was in a snit, and Frank worked hard not
to catch his eye in the rearview mirror as he talked to Mac.

Bait/Karaoke, so named for the five-foot-by-five-foot backlit
sign Mac had installed in the building's front window to tout
his twin service offerings, was directly across Seminary Street
from the Lil' Champ on the eastern bank of the Intracoastal,
the business sustained through the years by a steady stream of
daytime and nighttime patrons in search of bait to fuel their fishing excursions and karaoke idiocy to fill their social lives. When
the karaoke craze peaked and fizzled in the early nineties, Mac
let the liquor license go and focused his efforts on the bait business alone, but he neglected to replace the sign, so BAIT/KARAOKE
remained something of a Utina landmark. Once Utina's short-
lived local newspaper offices, the building featured a brick facade
and elegant high ceilings that were completely out of character
for Utina's commercial architecture, most of which consisted
of uninspired concrete flats and repurposed strip malls. Mac
Weeden had bought the building years ago, and he retained a

small office in the back, where he kept up his unpaid and unofficial enterprise as Utina's one and only unlicensed but highly confidential legal consultant.

"I mean he's completely insane," Frank said now. He told Mac about the incident with George and the garbage truck.

"Oh, hell. Is that all you got? Try growing up with him," Mac said. "Try living in the same house with that gobshite." But he smiled and shook his head ruefully, and Frank envied him for a moment, because he knew, despite it all, that Mac and George actually *did* enjoy each other's company, which was more than Frank could say for himself and his one surviving brother.

"Listen, I was just going to call you. Park the truck," Mac said. "Come inside. I got info."

"I can't stay," Frank said. He gestured at the pies on the seat next to him.

"Just for a minute," Mac said. "I looked into that Cryder fella, like you asked me. You'll want to hear this. Pull around back."

A narrow, alley-like driveway ran down one length of Bait/ Karaoke, and Frank drove slowly to maneuver a tight spot between a utility pole and a palm tree. Once through, he pulled the truck to the back of the building, parked, flipped the tailgate down to release Gooch, and walked in through the back door to Mac's small office. The dog followed stiffly, not looking at Frank, still miffed about being made to ride in the bed of the pickup.

"Oh, quit your bitching," Frank said to the dog. "It ain't the end of the world."

"Come in, come in," Mac said. He moved quickly around the office, clearing papers from a tattered side chair for Frank to sit down. He had the appearance, always, of nervousness, though

Frank knew Mac was not nervous but was rather afflicted with too much energy for one person to reasonably manage. He waited dutifully every day until five o'clock to pop open his first beer, marking the start of a copious nightly consumption of hops and barley on the center stool at Frank's bar. And though certainly good for business, it was this consumption, Frank thought guiltily, that might have been responsible for at least some of Mac's curtailed ambition. But Mac would have to save himself—Frank had enough people on his hands to worry about.

"Okay, so I looked into this guy, this Cryder guy," Mac said.

"And?"

"And he checks out. He really does work for that big Atlanta company, Vista Properties. They're going all over the Southeast, buying up land."

"For houses? You think the market's really picking up that much?"

"Not just houses. All kinds of development. Commercial stuff, industrial, all of it. And they've got their eye on Utina, Frank. Lots of people are starting to."

"Shit," Frank said. He looked out the open door of Mac's office, which led directly down a hallway into the front room of Bait/Karaoke. Through the store's front window, he could see across the street to the Lil' Champ, where Tip Breen stood outside, smoking a cigarette and scratching his crotch. "I've heard that before," Frank said.

"Hell, Frank. It's about time. They're seeing it now. We've always known it was coming. Look how close we are to the ocean—these yuppies will pay anything to live here. And we've got the Intracoastal—they can pull their big yachts up behind their houses, drink wine, and listen to their Jimmy Buffet shit or whatever it is they do. And here's the thing—where you are? Aberdeen, and Uncle Henry's, and Morgan's place? That's the whole enchilada, right there."

"What do you mean?"

"Frank, this is big. It's bigger than you could have imagined. You knew your property might one day be golden, right? Well, guess what? It's platinum."

Mac paused for effect, then continued. "I got a buddy of mine in Jacksonville to look into this. He does maritime law. The stretch of the Intracoastal you're on is one of a kind, Frank. We looked at the depth charts." Mac slid a sheet of blank paper across his desk and did a quick sketch of the long watery line of the Intracoastal; he added three squares along the east bank. "Here," he said, pointing to the three squares in succession, from north to south. "Here's Morgan's property, right? And Uncle Henry's, and Aberdeen. Those three properties, together, are large enough for Vista to build this big crazy-ass marina they're talking about. And here's the thing, Frank. This is the *only* place it would work. The water right off the banks isn't deep enough anywhere else, between St. Augustine and Jacksonville, for them to build the kind of facility they want to build. The shore depths are workable *only off those three properties.*"

Mac leaned back in his chair and put his left ankle up across his knee. He jiggled his leg up and down and smiled.

"St. Johns, Duval, and Clay are some of the fastest-growing counties in the country. Even in this market. And you're right in the middle of it. Morgan and your family have got the only pieces of land that would work for the kind of money-making venture they're planning. Do you see, Frank? You stepped in shit." Mac was grinning, gleeful. "They want your land."

"For a marina? Where's the money in a marina?"

"You're not thinking big, Frank. You're thinking with your Utina brain. That's the problem with everyone around here. Nobody's seeing what this place could really be—except these people on the outside. They're seeing it for us, Frank. And they're going to come in here and take it from us, we're not careful." Mac got up, started pacing around the office.

"It's not just a marina they're talking about," he said. "We hear marina and we think a boat ramp, a couple of slips. They're talking about something else entirely, Frank. I saw the proposal at the County. They're talking about a hundred slips, big ones, two-hundred-footers, and fuel, and dockmasters and pump-out—all that. And that's not all. They're talking about condos on the property, and a big hotel, and restaurants and shops and all that shit. Starbucks coffee. Art galleries. For Christ's sake, art galleries, Frank! You getting me here?"

Frank sat back in his chair, looked at Gooch. The dog was watching Mac pace the office, and when Frank looked at him, he sat down uncertainly, wagged his tail hesitantly.

"Damn," Frank said quietly. He leaned forward and looked at the pencil sketch on Mac's desk. "I knew we were talking about money. But I guess we're talking about real money."

"Yeah, *real* money," Mac said. He whistled. "Big money, try."

"Well, I don't know," Frank said. "It's not up to me. Morgan owns his own land. And the restaurant and Aberdeen are my mother's, not mine. None of this is mine to sell."

"You've got the influence. They know that. They've been doing their homework. They know you're running the restaurant. They know Morgan's working for you. They know Arla's—well,

Arla's getting older. They're coming to *you*, Frank. They know you're the one who can make it happen."

Frank's cell phone rang. He looked at the number and saw it was Aberdeen.

"Shit," he said.

"You need to get that?"

"Naw. I'll get her later. It's my mother."

Mac raised his eyebrows. "Speak of the devil."

"You got that right," Frank said. He clicked the phone to vibrate and watched it shudder until the number had disappeared from the small screen. Something inside his head was buzzing. This new information was big. What Mac was talking about was staggering. Given the uniqueness of the parcels—the shore depths factor—the stakes were higher than Frank had realized. Vista couldn't just move on down the road and make an offer to someone else. Vista needed *this* land. Vista needed *this* family. The Bravos. It wasn't just about selling the restaurant. It was about changing the course of destiny. And Mac was right: Frank was the one most likely to be able to make this happen. Morgan would be on board, no doubt.

But Arla. Arla would never agree to it. Never. She'd lived more than forty years at Aberdeen, though he'd never argue that she was particularly happy there, especially the last twenty of those years. At sixty-two, Arla was young enough to still make a life for herself somewhere else. But move from Aberdeen? Frank closed his eyes. Where would she go? And what about Sofia?

He opened his eyes and shook his head. "My mother," he said. "There's no way."

"Are you kidding? You just need to convince her, Frank. With that kind of money, she can have anything she wants. A nice condo, ground floor, no stairs. Someone to drive her around. Anything she wants. It'd be better for her—and Sofia, too—they can have anything. Right now they're just stuck out there in that old house."

"I don't know, Mac," Frank said. "This is a big deal. I just don't know what to think here."

"Think money, you idiot," Mac said. He smiled. "Think big. Think life changing. Think that if you play this deal right, you can do anything you want. Anything."

A small picture of Elizabeth presented itself to Frank, a picture of Elizabeth and Bell, and a bright cabin, and a cool mountain stream. Cullowhee. He shook his head again.

A red flash entered his field of vision, and he turned to the window in time to see Susan Holm's Mazda pull up outside Bait/Karaoke. Her powers of observation were evidently improving; she must have seen Frank's truck at the back of the long drive, because she pulled her car into the driveway and made the same tight maneuver between the palm tree and the utility pole, effectively blocking Frank's truck in Mac's lot. She parked the car, opened the door, and extended one long high-heeled leg out onto the pavement while she reached back into the car and rummaged for her purse.

"Oh, my," Mac said.

"Oh, crap," Frank said.

"Good stuff," Mac said, and then he wrenched his gaze away from the window and turned back to Frank.

"Carson knows all this, too," he said. "He called right before you stopped by."

"Oh, great," Frank said. "I'm sure he's beside himself. Money. His favorite thing."

"Now listen, Frank—you decide to talk with this guy from Vista, you gotta play hardball. You let your properties go cheap, you're setting a bad precedent for the rest of the town. You have control, Frank. The sale of your place is going to set the standard, establish the market price."

"Establish what market price?" Susan Holm said. She stood in the doorway, clutching a thick stack of manila folders, her head cocked to one side. Gooch thumped his tail on the floor. "Who's talking about market prices? You boys know what that does to me."

Frank raised his eyebrows to Mac, shook his head slightly.

"I saw that, Frank Bravo," she said. "You're keeping secrets."

"Don't be crazy, Susan. I got no secrets from you," Frank said.

"Oh, you're full of secrets. Don't I know it." She shifted her weight in the doorway. "I've got a couple of closing packets for you to look at, Mac. Two properties in South Utina. What kind of men are you? Nobody even offering me a seat? Even the dog won't get up." Gooch thumped his tail again, but she was right. Nobody had risen.

"Here," Frank said. "I'm just leaving." He got up and made an elaborate swooping gesture to the chair. Susan sighed and sat down.

"Frank Bravo, how come every time I walk into a room, you walk out?" she said. "I'm starting to get a complex."

"That's not true," Frank said, though he realized guiltily that it was.

"Don't worry, Susan. I'll keep you company," Mac said.

She rolled her eyes, but then looked at Frank.

"When are you going to let me list your house?" she said.

"Now you see? That's making me crazy, Susan," he said, irritated. "You're always wanting me to sell my house. Everybody's always wanting me to sell everything. What if I don't want to sell? What if I don't want to change?"

"Who else wants you to sell?" Susan said. Frank realized he'd just made a grave tactical error. Mac's eyes grew wide, and Susan noticed. "Who? Somebody else trying to get to you, Frank?" she demanded.

"No, no. I just mean you—you, Susan, always trying to get me to sell."

"Frank Bravo, God help you if you ever let some other Realtor list that house of yours. After all the years I've been trying to work with you on it, after all the—"

She stopped. Mac's eyes got wider. "After all the what?" he said. He looked from Susan to Frank and back again.

"Shut up," she said, flushing. "None of your business."

"There's no other Realtor," Frank said. "You don't have to worry about that."

She stared at him. "I'm just saying, Frank, that every property on your street has now sold for at least a quarter of a million. And those are empty lots. If you wanted to—"

Frank's phone vibrated in his pocket. He took it out and looked at it. Aberdeen again. "I better get this," he said. "It's my mother—she keeps calling."

"Sure," she said. "Change the subject." He turned away, pressed ACCEPT on the phone.

"Hello?" he said.

The voice on the phone was not Arla's.

"So now you got four crazy women on your hands out here, not just two, you know that?" Elizabeth said. "Bell and I. We're here at Aberdeen."

Frank stepped out of Mac's office and into the hallway.

"What do you mean?" he said. He tried to quiet the adrenaline running through his veins. She'd never called his cell phone before. Something was up.

"We've been here all week. I asked your mom not to say anything to you, until I figured out what we were going to do. But we're going to stay a bit longer," she said. She cleared her throat. "Carson and I, we're taking a break."

"Taking a break?"

She laughed—a short, clipped sound. "Yeah, a break," she said. "Like a time-out, or something. Your mother says Bell and I can stay here. We're in your old bedroom. There's a real pretty magnolia. Right out the window here."

He looked back through the open office door. Mac and Susan were going over the closing documents she'd brought, but Frank could tell, by the way Susan jiggled her ankle and kept her eyes just to the left of the stack of documents, that she was listening to Frank's conversation. He tried to remember if he'd mentioned Elizabeth's name.

"Are you okay?" he said.

"Oh, yeah. We'll be fine. You know, we'll get it figured out. One way or another, I guess." She spoke quickly, ready to change the subject, he sensed.

"And guess what?" she said. "We solved the piano crisis."

"You're joking."

"Nope. Well, it was Biaggio, really. I don't know how he did it. But he talked to Sofia. Convinced her to let him put it back where it was. She caved. So he moved it back. Your mother's happy. Everything's back to normal. Well. Back to the way it was, anyway." He could hear the grin in her voice. "But, Frank," she said. "I was wondering if I could ask a favor?"

Anything, he thought. *Anything*. Susan glanced up at him, caught his eye.

"What's up?" he said into the phone. He turned to the wall, leaned his forehead against the paneling.

"We need another bed out here," Elizabeth said. "Bell and I are sharing, and she's, like, doing gymnastics all night long, it feels like. I can't get a wink. I was wondering if you'd help me, with the truck? I need to go to my house, get her bed, and bring it out here to Aberdeen. And maybe a couple of other things while we're there. Do you think you could?"

"Yeah, of course. When?"

"Maybe today? This afternoon? I know it's short notice, and maybe you're busy. It just sure would be nice to get her set up before tonight."

Frank quickly cataloged the afternoon. Pies to deliver to Uncle Henry's, but he could do that on the way to pick up Elizabeth. Thirty minutes down to St. Augustine, to Carson and Elizabeth's house, and then back in time for the first dinner crowd. And maybe he'd just be a little late for dinner. Maybe he would.

"No problem," he said. "I'll pick you up in half an hour."

"Thank you, Frank."

"Elizabeth," he said, realizing, when Susan picked up her head and looked at him, that he'd blown his own cover, "I have a question about your house."

"Yes?"

"Is Carson going to be there?"

She hesitated, then gave a little snort that could have been a chuckle or a sob.

"Do we care?" she said.

He hung up the phone and walked back into Mac's office. Susan's leg was still jiggling like mad, but when Frank entered, she stood up abruptly.

"You can take it from here, Mac," she said. "Just send me over the closing statements when you're finished. I've got to go. I've got a showing."

She cast an annoyed glance at Frank.

"What?" he said.

"Nothing."

"What did I do?"

"It's not what you did. It's what you didn't do," she said. She brushed past him, and her hair smelled like apples. She was lovely, really, and he hated to have her annoyed at him.

"Oh, come on, now," he said. He looked back at Mac, who shrugged his shoulders. Frank followed Susan out the door and walked with her to the red Mazda. "Susan, don't be mad at me," Frank said.

She sighed. "You said you'd call me, like, two weeks ago, Frank. I thought we were going to go out for drinks. And I *hate* this." She opened the passenger door of the Mazda, tossed her purse onto the seat, and slammed the door again.

"Hate what?"

"Hate being the kind of woman who whines to a man who doesn't call her. I don't want to be that woman, Frank."

He didn't know what to say. "Well, listen. I'm sorry," he tried. "It's just been really busy. The restaurant, and my mother—"

"Oh, don't," Susan said. "This is making it even worse. Ugh. The two of us. I'm about to barf." She walked around to the driver's side, opened the door, and got in. She started the car and rolled the windows down.

Mac came out the back door and called for her to wait. "You can take these now," he said. "I'm finished with them." He reached into the Mazda and dropped the manila folders on the passenger seat, and as he did, too late, Frank saw the pencil sketch he and Mac had been working on, the one with Morgan's, Uncle Henry's, and Aberdeen lined up along the rough rendering of the Intracoastal. The paper must have gotten caught up in Susan's stack of folders. At the bottom of the sketch were Mac's crude notes: "deep water," "condos," "marina," and "Cryder."

"What is this?" Susan said, picking up the paper. The Mazda was idling in the driveway, AC blowing at full blast, though the windows were wide open. She leaned over to regard Mac and Frank through the passenger window. "What the hell is this?"

Say anything you like about Susan Holm, Frank admitted, but the woman was not stupid. She put together the situation faster than he had, even with Mac diagramming it out in front of him and explaining the whole thing in detail. Susan got it, got it fast.

"You're going to list with someone else. You're going to sell the restaurant and Aberdeen," she said. Amazing.

"No, I'm not."

"Yes, you are."

"No, Susan—"

"This Cryder, he's a Realtor?"

"Christ," Frank said.

"No, no, Susan," Mac said. "He's not a Realtor. He's a developer."

"A *developer*?"

"Mac, you're not helping," Frank said.

"What?" Mac said. "I'm just telling her—"

"Mac. Shut up, please."

"So you're selling straight to a developer? Those people from Atlanta?" Susan said. "Well, isn't that something. Isn't that just wonderful for you. And do you have any idea what kind of a commission a sale like this could mean to someone like me?" Her voice had begun to climb in timbre, and tiny beads of perspiration had begun to appear on her chest, despite the valiant efforts of the tiny sports car's condenser.

"Susan. Stop. Slow down. I am not selling anything. This guy just called me and was talking some big talk, and I—"

"You thought your ship had come in, huh, Frank? And to hell with everybody else in Utina, isn't that what you thought? What about poor Arla? What's going to happen to her, Frank? And Sofia?" She was getting wound up now. Her blouse was growing damp, and her hands were tight on the steering wheel as she glared up at Frank through the passenger window.

"Susan, listen—"

"Does Arla even know about this?"

He hesitated.

"No! Of course she doesn't! Are you *kidding me*? You are going to sell your mother's home out from under her and she doesn't even know about this! Oh, my God, Frank. Oh, I cannot believe it. Wait, yes, I can. I believe it. Come to think of it, I should have known." Her face was turning red.

Mac had taken a step back from the Mazda. He looked at Frank, raised his eyebrows.

"Susan, you're not even letting me explain. This is nuts," Frank said. "Let me get in. Let me talk to you." He put his hand on the door, but then his phone vibrated again, and he pulled it out of his pocket, saw it was Aberdeen once more. *Elizabeth.*

Susan watched him check the phone, watched him hesitate, and then she read his mind. It was the final blow. She slapped at his hand on the rim of the door.

"Don't do that, Susan," he said. "Let me get in."

"Get away," she said.

He reached for the door again, pulled up on the handle just as she flung the car into reverse. She stomped on the accelerator, and the car spun wildly for a moment on the sandy driveway. The spin shifted the Mazda's back axle a foot to the left, so when the tires regained traction again, the car was set up very nicely to execute a freakish, exquisite propulsion that sent it on a diagonal trajectory and lodged it firmly, noisily, and horribly between the twenty-foot Sabal palm and the City of Utina utility pole that lined Mac's driveway. Inside the car, Susan blinked rapidly, looking out the front windshield at Frank and Mac, who stood flabbergasted in front of the trapped Mazda. Frank's phone vibrated once more, stopped.

"Jesus H. Christ!" Mac said. He and Frank jogged down the driveway. "Are you okay?" Mac said, leaning around the utility pole to peer in through the passenger window. Frank approached on the driver's side, where a twelve-inch sliver of the car's interior was visible through the window, the rest of the view completely obscured by the trunk of the palm tree. Susan appeared unscathed, and the interior of the car had, it seemed, sustained no damage.

"I'm all right," she said quietly. She looked at the driver's side door, pinned tightly against the tree. "I guess I'm not getting out this way," she muttered. She hiked her skirt and climbed ungracefully across the stick shift to plop down into the passenger seat, which afforded a slightly wider swath of vertical opening through the car window. She grasped the door handle and pushed, but this side of the car was completely pinned against the utility pole, and the door didn't budge. The openings through either window were clearly too small to squeeze through.

"Oh, *shit!*" she said. She kicked her right foot against the door, started to cry.

"Susan, listen," Mac said, a dangerous levity in his voice now that they could see Susan was unhurt. He leaned down on the passenger side, spoke into the narrow chasm of open window. "You're going to have to move the car to be able to get out. Climb back into the driver's seat." He had begun to grin, and he pressed his lips together.

Susan climbed back across the shifter. Tip Breen walked across the street from the Lil' Champ. He looked even worse than ever, Frank thought fleetingly—his doughy skin slick with sweat, his shirt damp and stained. Broken, he thought. In the dictionary under *broken* there should have been a picture of Tip Breen. "Holy sack of shit," Tip said. "What have we got here?" And then Frank's attention returned to the Mazda. Tip Breen was not his problem.

"Susan," Frank said through the crack in the driver's side window. "Start the car, and we'll see if you can move it forward." On the other side of the car, Mac covered his hand with his mouth.

Sniffling, sweating, Susan positioned herself behind the steering wheel again and turned the key in the ignition. The starter turned over, but the engine did not catch. She tried again, still nothing. She threw her head back against the seat.

"Frank!" she said, wailing.

"She stuck in there?" Tip said, incredulous. "She actually stuck?" Mac leaned over, put his hands on his knees, lowered his head, and let out a long, controlled breath. Frank watched him, then quickly put his own hand over his mouth, but it was too late. Susan had seen the smile begin to form, and her tears instantly turned to rage.

"Are you laughing at this?" she said. She looked out the windshield at Tip and Mac, the former standing like a fat grinning ape, the latter now doubled over in laughter he'd given up trying to hide. "Do you all think this is *funny*?" Susan said. She looked back at Frank, and he cleared his throat, struggled to straighten his face.

"No, Susan. No. It's not funny," he said. And he *did* feel sorry for her, stuck in that hot sticky car, no way out, these three idjits not doing much to help her, himself included. "We're going to get you out."

"Just soon as I get my can opener!" Tip offered, and Mac roared, and Frank, he could not help himself—the laugh that came up through his lungs and ripped through his mouth was as unbidden as it was uncontrollable, and he surrendered to it, finally, spinning around to lean on the palm tree and gasp for air, laughing as he had not laughed in a very long time at the sight of the lovely, furious—no, nearly apoplectic—Susan Holm trapped in her satin blouse and linen skirt, sitting in the crumpled, pinched remains of what had once been her red Mazda.

Susan stared stonily ahead.

When Frank finally collected himself he looked at her and felt genuinely guilty. "Go call a tow truck, you jerks," he said to Tip and Mac. "We got a lady in distress here." Mac wiped his eyes and nodded, walked back to his office. Frank heard him say,

"Oh, good stuff." Tip made himself comfortable holding up the wall of Bait/Karaoke.

"Don't you need to go back to the store?" Frank asked him.

"Nah, I got no customers," Tip said. "I'm gonna set here, see how this plays out." He chuckled again, and Frank was ashamed of himself, aligning himself with the likes of Tip Breen and allowing himself to see humor in Susan's plight. Gooch, growing bored with all this, lay down on a cool patch of concrete in the shade of Bait/Karaoke.

"Susan, I'm sorry," Frank said. He leaned down to the crack in the window again. "I'm sorry, Susan. I don't know what came over me. It was just—I guess we were just so relieved that you were okay, and when Mac started laughing, I—"

Susan gave him a withering look. "Oh, is that it? You were so *concerned* about me you were just overcome with emotion? Huh," she said. She turned to stare out the windshield again. "Save it, Frank."

"All right," he said. "Okay, you have a right to be mad. I get it. But listen, we're going to get you out of here. Maybe we can push the car out. Tip," he said. "Make yourself useful and come on over here and push with me."

He and Tip positioned themselves behind the Mazda and pushed. Then they recruited Mac, who had returned from calling for the tow truck. Then they went into Bait/Karaoke and commandeered the counter help, a pimply boy named Seth who played running back for Utina High. But the Mazda would not budge.

"Tow said thirty minutes, best," Mac said. He looked up the street, and then straight up into the sky. "Damn, it's hot out here." And it was only now, at this moment, that Frank realized something else—with Susan's Mazda wedged tightly between the tree and the utility pole in Mac's driveway, his truck was trapped in the back parking lot.

Elizabeth. Bell. The bed. *Jesus.*

"Seth, go get Susan a drink of water or something, would you?" Frank said. He walked over to join Gooch in the shade of the building and dialed Aberdeen on his cell phone. He hoped his voice would not carry to Susan's ears when he explained the situation to Elizabeth. But there was no answer at Aberdeen. He hung up, tried again. Nothing. Probably out by the water, he thought. Or on the porch. Waiting for me. *Shit.*

Mac and Tip joined him in front of the building. "I gotta get my truck out," Frank said.

Mac laughed. "You're not going anywhere, friend." Seth came out, passed a bottle of water into the car for Susan, then leaned against the building with the others.

"That's messed up," Seth said, gazing at Susan in the Mazda. "That's fricking hilarious." They stared at the car for a minute more.

"Frank, you think you might be hiring at the restaurant?" Tip said suddenly.

"Hiring what?" Frank said. "Hiring *you?*"

"I gotta do something," Tip said. "I'm dying over there." He gestured back at the Lil' Champ. "No business. I can't afford to pay my taxes."

"Maybe you need to clean up your act," Mac said, looking him over with disdain.

"Nah, that ain't it," Tip said, despondent. "It's the fucking Publix. Walgreens. The fucking builders, these new buyers. Fucking developers, what have you."

"I'm not hiring," Frank said. He gave Mac a look designed to warn him against spilling the beans about the offer on the table for the Bravo properties. "Sorry, Tip," Frank said. He pulled his cell phone back out of his pocket and tried Aberdeen again—nothing. Then, feeling guilty and obliged, he left Mac and Tip in the shade and leaned against Susan's car in the blazing sun, and though he tried repeatedly to talk to her through the crack in the window, she stared straight ahead and said nothing.

After twenty minutes, his phone vibrated, and he looked at it, expecting it to be Aberdeen, but the screen said CARSON.

He pushed the button to accept the call. "Carson," he said.

"You talk to Cryder again yet?" Carson said. Frank's brother was never one for small talk, for idle introductions.

"I'm fine, Carson, how are you?"

"Did you?"

"No," Frank said.

"Frank, he's offering serious money."

"How do you know? Did he give you a figure?"

"No. I think we can name our price."

"We? Who is *we*?" Frank felt a sudden heat in his blood. Carson, calling from his office in St. Augustine, no doubt, far from the lunacy of Utina, and yet suddenly, with money on the table, the prospect of selling Uncle Henry's and Aberdeen becomes a "we," not a "you."

"*Her*," Carson said. "*She*. You know what I mean. Mom. It's her deal. She'll stand to gain if we get her to sell the house, dumbass. She can get her and Sofia a nice place to live, no stairs. No termites. No roof falling in. And it's a family restaurant, if I'm not mistaken, so maybe you could concede that I might have a vote in that?"

"It's Mom's restaurant. And I run it," Frank said. Seth walked over with another bottle of water for Susan, which he handed to her through the crack in the driver's window. She looked at Frank forlornly.

Carson sighed. "All right, Frank. Whatever. You run it. You're the hero. All hail Saint Frank."

"Screw you," Frank said.

"I'm coming up there," Carson said. "We need to talk about this."

"What, now?"

"Yes, now. I'll come by the restaurant."

"It's not a good day, Carson."

"Frank. Fit it in. This is important."

"Lots of things are important."

"When, then?"

The tow truck arrived, pulling up slowly while the driver and a second man leaned out the window to gawk at the sight of Susan's Mazda wedged between the tree and the utility pole. "Hot damn!" the driver yelled. "This is a good one!"

"I don't know, Carson. I gotta go, all right? I'm in the middle of something."

"I'm coming up there."

"Don't."

"I'll see you later."

Frank hung up the phone. The tow truck backed into position and hooked the cables under the axle of the Mazda.

"We got a lady inside, I hope you realize," Frank said.

"Oh, we haven't missed that, buddy!" the tow driver chortled. "Don't worry, we won't muss her up."

Frank walked over to the Mazda, leaned in to speak through the slot. "You okay?" he said.

Susan's face was pink, but she had calmed down considerably from the state she was in immediately after the accident. She now simply looked sad, and tired.

"I'm okay," she said. "I just want to get out of here."

"They're getting ready to pull. Just sit tight."

"Where would I go?" she said.

The tow truck revved its engine. "Heads up!" the driver shouted.

The palm tree shuddered as the Mazda's chassis was forcibly dislodged from its position. Frank watched, feeling like he was having a tooth pulled, until the car was free and it lurched backward, bouncing once and settling in on Mac's sandy driveway with an inglorious springy thud. Susan immediately tried to open the doors, first the driver's and then the passenger's, but they remained stuck.

"You might have to come out through the window," Frank said. "I'll help you."

"I'll do it myself, thank you," she snapped. She shimmied awkwardly out through the open driver's window, her blouse sticking to her back, her linen skirt hiked almost to her hips to accommodate the climb. Mac, Tip, Seth, and the tow crew stood watching. She stood, finally, wobbling on the driveway. Frank put his hand on her elbow to steady her.

"You all get a good view?" she asked. She smoothed her hair, straightened her skirt, glared. She looked at the Mazda, walked all the way around it. Both doors were crumpled, and the right quarter panel on the passenger side had suffered a brutal gash that ran almost the length of the fender. The car looked like it had been squeezed by a giant fist. It was cartoonlike, almost comical. But Susan was not amused.

"Oh, my Jesus," she said, surveying the damage.

Frank walked over to the tow truck.

"You guys think you can go ahead and move it out of the driveway?" he said. "I gotta get my truck out."

"Wait just a damn second," Susan said. She turned to face him. "You're not going anywhere."

"Susan, I'm sorry, but I gotta go," he said.

"This is your fault, Frank."

"What?"

"This," she said, gesturing at the car. "All this. Look at my car! I don't have the money to pay for this, Frank. And my insurance . . ." She trailed off. The tears were up close again, mixing with a fury that Frank found considerably more dangerous now that Susan was on the outside of the wrecked Mazda. "I don't *have* insurance," she said.

"How can you not have insurance?"

"I missed a payment. I don't have the *money,*" she hissed.

"I really don't think you can consider this my fault," he began.

"Oh, really? Well I really don't think you know me very well, then, do you? If you hadn't been trying to get in my car I wouldn't have had to back up to get away from you."

He stared at her for a beat. "To get *away* from me?"

"You heard me."

"What, did you think I was *dangerous?* Did you think I was threatening you?" He was incredulous. This from the woman who'd been throwing herself at him for nearly thirty years.

"Look, Frank," she said. She approached him, extended one long, white-tipped fingernail into his face. "You're going to have to help me pay for this." She caught her breath, half hiccup, half-sob. "You *owe* me."

She turned on her heel and walked over to the tow truck. Frank stared after her. Mac and Tip watched. Susan turned back to Frank once more. "You *owe* me!" she said again.

Big money, Mac had said. Real money. It looked like Frank was going to need it. He whistled for Gooch, loaded him into the bed of the truck, and climbed into the driver's seat. He watched in the rearview mirror until the tow truck had dragged the Mazda out of the way, and then he backed slowly out of the driveway, avoiding Susan's stony gaze. He waved to Mac, headed east on Seminary Street. It was not until he reached the intersection at Monroe Road, where the work crews teemed over the new Publix, that Frank glanced down at the passenger seat, where An-Needa's Key lime pies had melted into a thick, sticky soup, leaking steadily into the rest of the pie boxes and forming a foamy glaze all over Frank's upholstery.

He turned, looked straight ahead, waited for the light to change. To his right, the backhoes had done their work, splintering the oaks and sweet gums, upturning the earth and tearing through the thick fabric of palmetto and pine. Some of the trees still lay at the perimeter of the site, yet to be cut up and carted away. Things falling, melting, crashing everywhere. All of Utina falling apart at the seams. And him right here in the thick of it.

NINE

He'd never make it to St. Augustine and back for the bed in time. By now Morgan had made it through lunch, no doubt, and once Frank got to the restaurant they'd have only an hour or so before the dinner crowd began to arrive. He and Morgan had a gentleman's agreement not to leave each other hanging for the early-bird diners, the oldest and most ornery of the lot, who hadn't had the benefit of a sweet calming twilight or the evening two-for-one happy hour to improve their moods. An hour. Not enough time to get Bell's bed from St. Augustine.

But a bed is a bed, he reasoned, so he left the Key lime mess in his front seat and drove down Cooksey Lane to his own house, where an extra twin mattress and box spring stood upright in the spare room. He left the door to the truck open and lowered the tailgate so Gooch could take the first crack at the pie cleanup, and by the time he returned he found the dog, bloated-looking and disoriented, lying in a cool patch of trumpet vine.

"Glutton," Frank said. "Serves you right." He loaded the mattress and box spring into the back of the truck and mopped out the rest of the melted pies. Then he left Gooch sleeping in the shade and pulled out of the driveway again, the mattress set flumping gently in the bed of the truck. He checked his watch—thirty minutes to dinner hour. He could slip out of Uncle Henry's again after getting the early birds fed, make it to Aberdeen before dark, and help Elizabeth get the bed set up for Bell. At Cooksey and Seminary, he bumped through the intersection and pulled into the parking lot at Dollar General, where he bought a mattress pad, a set of Hello Kitty bedsheets, and, after a moment's thought, a ceramic nightlight shaped like an angel. He felt odd, fatherly, buying such childish items, and he was pleased to find that he did not mind the feeling. By the time he reached Uncle Henry's, he'd imagined vanilla cupcakes, a swing set, a pair of small white socks. He'd never thought of such things before. *A break*, she'd said. *A break. We're in your old bedroom.*

At Uncle Henry's, he left the mattress and box spring in the truck and entered the kitchen in time to see Morgan ladling the first dinner-size order of hoppin' John over a thick layer of white rice.

"Afternoon, darling," Morgan said.

"Sweetheart," Frank replied. And then they were doing it again, what they did every night, pulling down the orders as they came in from Irma, filling bowls of clam chowder and cheese grits, heaping baskets of corn bread, datil pepper jelly starters, and u-peel-um shrimp dinners, dirty rice and fried catfish. They hustled through the early-bird rush without speaking, and Frank loved that about Morgan. He bolted regularly out to the bar, filled the drink orders without a word, jumped back into the kitchen in time to pull the fries out of the fryer, perfectly browned, miraculous. It should have been an Olympic event.

"Cover for me for thirty minutes," he told Irma during the five o'clock lull. He pulled off his apron, stepped out from behind the bar. The real dinner crowd would be arriving in earnest at about five-forty-five. "I'll be back."

He'd made it to the front door and had stepped out into the scalding late-afternoon sun when Carson pulled into the parking lot.

Shit. Frank glanced at the mattress and box spring in the back of his truck.

He waited. Carson approached, his back straight and his shoulders squared. My God, he was uptight. If Frank hadn't been so annoyed with Carson, he'd have surrendered to the impulse to reach out and tousle his brother's hair, mess him up a little bit.

"Where you headed, bro?" Carson said. "Skipping out on business?"

"Just got an errand to run," Frank said. "I'll be back."

"We need to talk."

"Not right now."

"Now."

"Carson," Frank said. "I've only got a few minutes before we get slammed. I'll be back. I told you not to come tonight."

"We gotta address this Vista thing. We need to talk."

"Why can't we talk tomorrow?"

"I'm here now. I drove all the way up here. Give me ten minutes."

Frank sighed, and they stepped back inside the restaurant to escape the heat.

"We need to get her to sell," Carson said immediately.

"What do you know about this deal?" Frank said. "What are they offering?"

"I don't know for sure yet, but it's going to be millions. You talk to Mac?"

"Yes. But she's not going to want to sell."

"*Millions.*"

"It won't matter to her, Carson. She's not going to want to move. She won't want to change. You know she won't."

"Well, we need to change her mind."

"Who's we?"

"You and me, brother."

"How do you know *I* want to sell?"

Carson shook his head. "Are you fucking kidding me?" he said. "Are you for real? Look around." He gestured at the restaurant, the dozen or so tables filled with old folks enjoying their early-bird specials. "This what you want to do the rest of your life?"

"It's not that bad," Frank said. "Some people really like it here."

"You one of those people?" Frank didn't answer. "I didn't think so," Carson said. "Come on, Frank. Don't be an ass. We gotta get her to sell."

"I don't know, Carson," he said. "But I gotta go."

Carson followed him back out of the restaurant.

"Frank," he said. "Be reasonable."

"I gotta go, Carson. We'll talk tomorrow."

Carson's eyes slid to Frank's truck. "Where are you going?" he said. "What's that bed for?"

Frank kept walking, and by now Carson was following him to the truck.

"You bringing that to Aberdeen?"

"Yep."

"For my daughter?"

"Bingo," Frank said. "You're a regular Sherlock, aren't you?"

"Who asked you to do that?"

"What does it matter? They need an extra bed out there. I had one. I'm going to drop it off."

"Did Elizabeth ask you to do that?"

"Carson," Frank said. "Let me go. I'll be right back."

A car pulled into the lot, and then another, and clumps of customers. The beginnings of the real Friday dinner crowd began to straggle out of the cars and head toward Uncle Henry's front door. Carson put his hand out. "Give me your keys," he said. "I'll bring the bed."

"No," Frank said. "I got it."

"Let me bring it."

"No."

"Frank."

"You're not driving my truck," Frank said.

"She's my wife."

"It's my truck."

Frank realized how idiotic this was becoming, but he couldn't help himself.

"She doesn't want to see you," he said. "She needs time."

Carson took a step back, narrowed his eyes. "How do you know that?" he said. "Who the fuck are you, Dr. Phil?"

Three more cars had pulled into the parking lot, and now George Weeden was getting out of one of them, walking toward them. "Bravos!" he called.

"Oh, Jesus," Frank said.

"Give me the keys," Carson said. "I'll take the bed to my daughter."

"Gentlemen!" George said. "I got you both in one place! Perfect. I want to tell you about a little idea of mine."

"Give me the keys, Frank," Carson said.

Frank wanted to slap him. Another car pulled in. He handed Carson the keys and turned back to the restaurant. George trotted alongside him.

"Carson!" George called over his shoulder. "I guess I'll go ahead and talk to Frank first. I'll fill you in by phone."

Carson ignored him, started the truck, and pulled out of the parking lot. Frank didn't watch him, but he heard the bed thumping in the bed of the truck as Carson accelerated over the bumpy dirt road toward Aberdeen. Elizabeth. She'd been trying to avoid Carson, had retreated to Aberdeen to escape him, in fact, and now Frank had provided him with a damn entrée, had practically rolled out the red carpet for Carson to walk in at Aberdeen, a hero with a twin mattress and a sheet set. *Shit.*

The old resentment felt like rust, creeping through his veins, and the image of Carson just now at the wheel of Frank's truck brought back an image of another truck, another summer night, Carson at the wheel that night, too, driving them all into tragedy and despair and a life's sentence of atonement that Frank seemed to be the only one serving. Carson. Wasn't Carson always at the wheel, when you stopped to think about it?

July 4, 1984. It had started right here, at Uncle Henry's. Frank sometimes had the feeling that everything in his entire life was going to either begin or end right here at Uncle Henry's. That night, at any rate, the whole thing began to unfold, unravel, undo itself right after the fireworks, when the people out on the deck were so far in the bag that even if they'd stopped drinking right then they'd still be drunk on Labor Day. And Dean right in the thick of it. King Drunk, as usual.

Carson had his first truck, a rusted-out Toyota he'd bought from an old man in Green Cove Springs. They came in off the tiny oyster-shelled beach behind Uncle Henry's—Carson, Frank, and Will—where they'd been staging the launch of a stash of cherry bombs, quarter sticks, and M-80s Carson had picked up from a stand off I-95 just north of the Georgia border. The fireworks had left them all antsy, pumped through with adrenaline that had been wasted after each explosion erupted and each shell wilted in the damp sand.

They walked through the restaurant on their way to the parking lot, which was their first mistake, Frank realized later, because by cutting through Uncle Henry's they set themselves up to be waylaid by their father, who was holding court at the bar. Dean was perched on a stool, his leathery face more florid than usual with the heat of God knows how many glasses of Jack. He caught sight of the three of them, then turned around to balance his drink on his knee and regard them.

"My boys," Dean announced to the bar. "Would you just look at my three boys?" Still balancing his glass on his knee, he reached out and grabbed Will by the arm, pulling him close in an awkward hug, which Will suffered good-naturedly for a moment before gently pushing his father away. Will's hair was pressed to his head from the heat on the beach; his T-shirt hung loosely on his thin frame. Tommy Bolla, who owned the Texaco on Seminary, grinned stupidly at Dean from an adjoining barstool.

"You got you some fine boys, Bravo," he said. "And that one there is your spittin' image."

"Holy shit, these are some kids," Dean said. He looked like he might cry. Will patted him on the arm, affectionate, always so tolerant of everything and everybody. Frank and Carson moved toward the door.

"We gotta go, Dad," Frank said. "We're meeting people."

"Who you meeting?" Dean said.

"Mac and George. Tip, maybe."

"Shit, Tip Breen?" Dean said. Tommy Bolla scoffed. "That piece of shit kid?"

"I don't know," Frank said. "Maybe." He paused. "Will, you coming?"

"Listen here," Dean said. He pulled Will in to him again. "Maybe Will wants to stay with me."

"Leave him," Carson said quietly to Frank, seeing an opportunity. "If he stays here we can go slide." Will heard this reference, and his eyes widened slightly as he stood, still in the awkward corral of Dean's arm. "I'm coming," Will said. "I want to slide."

Carson sighed. Frank hesitated. They'd never let Will come sliding before, out to the dunes near Ponte Vedra Beach, where they'd meet up with the Weeden brothers and any other kids looking for a diversion. In the spring, they'd retrieved an old car hood from a rusted heap they found decaying in the woods off Cooksey Lane. They'd turned the car hood upside down and drilled holes in two corners to attach a rope, which was then affixed in a long loop to the trailer hitch on the back of Carson's truck. Out at the beach, in the wooded dunes, the car hood became a sled, pulled behind the truck at ever-increasing speeds and ridden only by those feeling most brave, or most stupid, on a given night. The dunes were peppered with hundred-year-old live oak trees and palmetto thickets, and the success and safety of any slide run were completely dependent on the skill and blood alcohol level of the driver of the truck. A live oak tree won't move for a category four hurricane; it certainly won't move for a buzzed 140-pound kid sliding on the back of a rusted car hood, no matter how much the kid might want it to in the split second before impact.

"I'm a buy my boys a drink," Dean said. "C'mere."

"Whyn't you buy me a drink while you're at it?" Tommy Bolla said.

"You don't need a drink, you damn souse," Dean said.

"We're underage, Dad," Frank said. The fact that he and Carson had a bottle of Crown Royal and a six-pack of beer locked in the truck outside was beside the point. He could see absolutely no good coming from having Dean buy his three sons drinks in the current setting. None of them needed a visit to the St. Johns County Detention Unit tonight, least of all Dean, who still had six months' probation on his last two offenses, disorderly intoxication and misuse of 911, from when he threw a tantrum and called the police to complain that Tip Breen, nineteen years old and a recent installation at the checkout counter at Lil' Champ, had overcharged him by two dollars on a six-pack of Coors.

"Oh, screw that," Dean said. "Come have a drink with your old man. Henry's not gonna say nothing." And indeed, Uncle Henry himself, like almost any Bravo worth his weight, was well known for operating his personal and business interests somewhere quite south of the letter of the law, his spiritual rebirth notwithstanding. "And Bubbles ain't here tonight," Dean added, rolling his eyes. He pushed Tommy Bolla down to the next stool, positioned Will next to him at the bar. "Look," Dean said. "Carson wants a drink, don't you, son?" And indeed, Carson had shrugged and moved closer to the bar, standing behind Will and looking interestedly at the selection of beer taps. Will laughed nervously.

"Dad," Frank said, pointing at Will. "He's fifteen."

"And what are you, a hundred and ten?" Dean said. He rolled his eyes, turned to Tommy Bolla. "Of course I had to have one what's a God-damned nun."

Carson smiled. Will laughed again, but he looked at Frank uncertainly.

"I'll take Frank's drink," Tommy Bolla said.

"You shut up," Dean said amiably. "Carson, what will you have?"

"A Bud," Carson said.

"Three Buds," Dean roared to Henry. "No, I'm dry, make it four." Henry raised his eyebrows slightly but then wordlessly poured four tall beers and lined them up in front of Dean.

"Have a heart," Tommy Bolla said.

"Oh, Christ, five!" Dean yelled to Henry, who returned to pour the fifth for Tommy.

"Beers for my boys," Dean said grandly. He slid the drinks in front of each of them, smiled broadly. "Fellas, to life," he said.

"To life," Tommy Bolla said. "And to Dean!"

"To Dean," Will repeated. His eyes were wide and round, but he was smiling, giddy with the attention he was receiving from Dean, who still clutched the boy in the crook of his arm, swaying slightly, as though Will were an infant and he was rocking him to sleep. Will swigged his beer. Frank left his own on the bar.

"To Arla," Carson said. He tipped his head back and nearly finished the beer in one long pull. Dean's face darkened.

"What's that supposed to mean?" he said.

"What?" Carson said.

"That some kind of crack?"

"I made a toast to my mother," Carson said.

"Like hell you did," Dean said. "That's some kind of editorial."

"About the fact you're sitting here every night instead of being home with her once in a while? Nah," Carson said.

"I'm not sitting here every night," Dean said.

"Oh, that's right," Carson said. "Sometimes it's the Cue & Brew."

"Carson, let's go," Frank said.

"Jesus H. Christ, Tommy," Dean said. "You see what I got here? I got the moral majority here, Tommy. I got one who's a nun and one who's the pope. You see this, Tommy?"

"I see it, Dean," Tommy Bolla said. He was eyeing Frank's untouched Budweiser on the bar.

"Thank God I got Will here," Dean said. He shook Will even harder against his chest, then ordered him another beer. Will laughed. His blue eyes were bright. Dean drew back and regarded him. "Look at this boy, Tommy, look at him," he said. "This here is my boy. He's his father's boy, Tommy. Not like those other two pussies."

Carson stiffened at Frank's elbow, and Frank felt the familiar dull stab of unbidden envy in his own stomach. Will—the favorite. And don't anybody forget it. Both Arla and Dean made no secret of their bias, made no shame of their favoritism. Will,

Will, Will. It was always Will. He knew in another few minutes the situation would devolve even further. Give Dean one more drink and he'd be getting either weepy or combative, and Frank didn't intend to stick around and participate in either option. Plus, he was dismayed to see how easily—and how quickly—Will's second beer was going down. Another minute and Dean would be ordering him a third. His father's boy, indeed. That's what Frank was afraid of.

"Carson, come on," Frank said. He slid his beer down to Tommy Bolla, who accepted it with a wide grin, his rough hand closing around the base of the glass. Dean glared at Frank. "Will, you coming?" Frank said.

"Maybe Will wants to stay with me," Dean said.

"Come on, Will," Carson said.

Will's eyes darted from Dean to Carson to Frank and back to Dean again, and he looked like a boy much younger than his fifteen years, a boy now muddled by the consumption of just two beers, a boy so torn between allegiances, so eager to please everyone, so catastrophically kind and loving that it shamed Frank to be contributing to his consternation. But he had to get him away from Dean tonight.

"Will," he said softly, and Will got it, finally, understood. He leaned his head against Dean's shoulder for a moment and then stood up from the barstool. "I gotta go Dad," he said. "I want to go slide."

Dean narrowed his eyes and looked at Frank, shifted his gaze to Carson, and then shrugged his shoulders. "Go on then," he said to Will. "Go on and hang out with your sisters. Go pick daisies or something." He turned his back on them then, turned back to nurse his beer and stare at the wood grain on the bar, his back hunched and his shoulders drawn up near his ears in defeat.

"Good night, boys," Tommy Bolla called. "Happy Fourth!"

Outside the restaurant Will is buoyant, giddy. He races ahead of them to the truck, pounds on the roof while waiting for Carson and Frank to approach.

"Get off my truck, you punk," Carson says, and he unlocks the door, climbs into the driver's seat. Will and Frank sit next to him across the bench seat and they drive away from Uncle Henry's, away from Dean, through the dampness of the woods of Utina and eastward toward the ocean. It is seven miles to Ponte Vedra Beach and they make it in ten minutes flat, Carson's fastest yet, an astonishing feat given the width of County Road 25 and the tightness of the turns coming out of Utina and past Donner's Landing. Halfway there, the bottle of Crown comes out from under the seat and they pass it among them, and in the moonlight Frank watches Will's lips clench around the bottle, watches how he closes his eyes like a masochist to brace against the alcohol as it hits his throat. It is as if those two beers Dean has given him have simply primed a pump, awakened a thirst Will hadn't even known he had.

At the dunes, Mac is waiting with his brother George and Tip Breen. Mac has a girl, a quiet thing named Kelly that Frank remembers from history class, and she's looking spacey and confused, leaning against Mac as if she might fall, and the air is pricked with the faint smell of weed. The girl has long brown hair that hangs in limp sheets around her shoulders, a weak chin, big breasts. She does not smile. George and Tip are smoking cigarettes, sitting on the hood of Mac's car.

The dunes are off A1A, down a small beach access road and hidden from view by a thick stretch of woodland—live oaks and sweet gum, pines and cypress. The sand is packed solid here, drivable, though they've learned to travel with a shovel in the bed of the truck, learned how to dig out the back tires of a vehicle stuck on the beach, create traction, get moving again. They are bound by nothing; they are immortal. There is nothing they can't do.

"You brought the hood?" Mac says, his arm hooked around the girl's neck, and Carson points into the back of his pickup, where the detached car hood rests atop a pile of thick rope. George and Tip slide off Mac's car and pull the flat piece of steel from the bed of Carson's truck. They work fast, loud, cursing and laughing at each other and passing the bottle of Crown and smoking a joint down to the wet roach while they rig the car hood behind the truck, position it before a long range of sandy yellow dunes spotted here and there with palmettos and sea grape, oaks draped with thick Spanish moss that looks like ghosts in the trees.

Will has had more to drink tonight than ever in his life. He is punchy, foolish now, loud and obnoxious and rude.

"I'm first," he says. "I'm fucking first," and Frank takes the bottle of Crown from him, passes it on to George.

"Slow down," Frank says to Will. "You're acting like an idiot."

"Fuck you," Will says, and he takes a warm beer from beneath the seat of Carson's truck, opens it, slams it down his throat. He gets sloppy toward the end, chokes, spits a sheet of foam out over the sand, then giggles frantically, childishly, runs toward a low-hanging oak branch and starts doing pull-ups. Kelly watches blankly. Frank's own vision has begun to blur a bit, and his tongue feels thick and clumsy. An owl cries in a thatch of sweet gums.

"You're in my English class," Kelly says.

"History," Frank says.

"Oh," she says, and she stares at him, and Frank thinks she does not believe him but he does not know how to convince her. Mac has his arm around her and he's feeling her stomach under her shirt but she still looks at Frank, detached, confused, quiet again.

"What good students you are," Mac says, laughing. "Good stuff," he says.

Carson gets into his truck. "Let's do this," he says, and Tip climbs onto the detached car hood, grips the ropes in his hands.

"I said I'm first," Will says, and he rushes forward and tries to push Tip off the hood, and Frank pulls him back. "Shut up, Will," he says, and Will looks at him, hurt. Why did they bring him? He's too young, Frank thinks, we shouldn't have brought him.

They slide for more than an hour, taking turns on the car hood, taking turns behind the wheel of the truck, taking turns with the bottle of Crown. The girl, Kelly, does not slide. She sits on a towel on a clear patch of sand and watches, stoic, quiet, unmoving. Mac comes over now and then to touch her, kiss her, put his hands down the back pockets of her jeans, but then his turn comes again and he whoops and dances over to the car hood and he slides, they all slide, Tip and Carson and Frank and Will and George and Mac, lit up like firecrackers and soaring over the dunes in a rush of wind and sand and booze. All the world is flying by in a jet stream and they are on fire and they are alive and they are in danger but they don't care because they are airborne and nobody can touch them here in this nova, this supernova, nobody.

On the last run Carson is driving and Tip is sliding again. Carson pulls a doughnut that whips the car hood around in a tight circle. They all cheer until the edge of the car hood catches on a flat divot of sand and the hood tips up and over, hydroplaning, dumping

Tip out onto the dune and then cartwheeling, a perfect square of heavy rusted metal, dancing lively across the sand and over to catch Kelly just behind the shoulder while she is up and scrambling and trying to get away. It brings her down and Frank is sick when he hears the noise, the blunt brutal sound of iron on bone.

The girl keens loudly for a moment and then stops, and the silence is frightening. Carson parks the truck and they all run to Kelly, but Frank is afraid to look. Tip is still struggling to his feet, shaking sand from his shirt and pants. Mac is ashen in the moonlight, and he leans over Kelly, calling her name again, again, again. Kelly, Kelly, Kelly, Kelly, oh sweet holy fuck, Kelly, he says. Her eyes are open and she stares at him, her lips parted, but she says nothing. The blood has begun to clot the sand under her shoulder. Frank is frozen, and Will has begun to gasp, to sob. Tip puts his arm around Will, steadies him.

"Get her to the hospital," Carson says, and they pick her up and slide her into the backseat of Mac's car and Mac sits back there with her. George drives, Tip sitting in the front seat, and they leave, headed south to St. Augustine. Now Carson and Will and Frank are there together, alone, and Frank tries not to look at the dark stain in the sand, the white mask of fear on Carson's face. The night is suddenly silent.

"It's our fault," Will says.

"It was an accident," Carson says. "It's nobody's fault."

"Is she going to die?" Will says.

"Shut up," Carson says.

Will starts to cry, and Carson throws the empty bottle of Crown into the scrub.

"Shut up, you fucking pussy," he says. "My God, do you ever shut up?"

But Will cannot stop. He is young and he is drunk and he cannot stop crying and he puts his head down between his knees and coughs and sobs and then he wrings his hands and looks up at them.

"She's going to die," he wails.

Carson walks over to Will and shoves him.

"I told you to shut up," he says. "Now let's go."

Will falls back in the sand and curls up in a fetal position and continues to weep, rocking back and forth with his arms around his knees. He is so drunk that he cannot stop. Frank has been this drunk before himself—once—and he remembers the idiocy of it, the abandon, the surrender, but he has no tolerance for it tonight.

"We need to stay here, in case they come back," Will says.

"They're not coming back. They went to the hospital," Frank says.

"I'm staying here," Will says.

"We're leaving," Carson says. "Get in the truck."

Will stays in the sand, and then Carson grabs him by the arm, but Will shakes him off, his limbs long and jerky and his body taut with the alcohol and the adrenaline and the fear. Even Frank is angry now, angry at Will, such a baby, such a mama's boy, Daddy's boy, weeping for a girl he doesn't even know.

"Leave him," Frank says to Carson. "Let him walk."

It's seven miles back to Aberdeen from the beach and Frank has walked it before. It's two hours on foot, the long road through the trees, and it's no fun but it's not impossible. The image of Kelly on the wet sand is overbearing, and the stain is still there before them, and suddenly Frank cannot be near Will, crying and snuffling and afraid, one minute longer. Serve him right. Serve them all right. You *wanna be Daddy's boy, Will? Chip off the old block? How's that working for you, dumb-ass?*

"Leave him," he says again. "He can make it home."

"Should we?" Carson says.

"Yeah."

Carson looks at Frank, and then he nods and they get into the truck. They leave Will behind in the dunes, weeping on the sand, his arms wrapped tight around his knees. He turns his face up to watch the truck pull away, and Frank looks in the mirror outside his window and sees him in the moonlight, alone, uncertain. As the truck turns the corner he sees Will get up and slowly begin to walk, and then run toward the receding truck, and he hears him shout once—"Wait!—Frank! Don't leave me!" and then, as the trees close in around the darkness, Carson drives them away and Will is gone.

"Are we going to the hospital?" Frank says to Carson.

"Maybe we should," Carson says.

"You think she's going to die?"

"Shit," Carson says, and he shakes his head and doesn't say any more.

But they don't go to the hospital. They go home and sit outside Aberdeen on the concrete picnic table, drinking the last of the beers. Arla and Sofia are asleep; it is after midnight, and Dean is not yet home. After a while Carson goes quietly to the kitchen and calls the hospital. The girl is not dead. He talks to Mac; Kelly is conscious and crying and she is in great pain, but she is not dead and her parents are there and she is not going to die. Carson comes back to the picnic table and slaps Frank on the back and tells him what Mac said, and they grin at each other and then they stop. Frank is weak with relief and alcohol and the shame of hurting Kelly, but he is happy *to be here with Carson, who is strong enough, he sometimes thinks, for all of them.*

"We better go get that little shit," Frank says. "He's been walking long enough."

They walk back to the truck, but before Carson turns the key in the ignition they hear it, and they turn their heads to the road, where in the distance the long slow whine of an ambulance's siren has begun to slice through the night. Frank thinks of Will, and he looks at Carson, and a terrible knowledge passes between them, binds them for an instant more tightly than they have ever been bound before and then splits them like fission, their atoms spinning apart, away, out of control and into the universe forever.

"All right, now, Frank," George said. He held the front door of the restaurant open, and as the coolness of the air-conditioned interior greeted them Frank felt himself jerked back to the present, jerked back to the moment, Carson on his way to Aberdeen with Bell's bed and George Weeden rambling on about God-knows-what as they made their way across the dining room of Uncle Henry's.

"Let me tell you all about this new venture of mine. Gonna change your life, friend," George said.

"I gotta cook, George. And tend the bar." Frank was exhausted, suddenly, bone weary, and still staring down Friday night, one of the busiest nights of the week. He walked behind the bar and slipped a clean apron over his shirt. He glanced into the kitchen. Morgan was firing up the second grill.

"Lemme just talk to you while you're working, Frank," George said. "Oh, and I'll take a Mich." Frank pulled the Michelob tap and filled a pint glass, set it on the bar in front of George.

"Okay," George said. "Now, I've got three words for you, Bravo. You ready? 'Whole. Life. Insurance.'" And then George Weeden was off—prattling away about cash value and fixed premiums and blah, blah, blah, Jesus Christ, Frank thought, was there any end of people giving him shit today?

As if on cue, the front door opened again, and Officer Donald Keith walked into Uncle Henry's, a thick stack of campaign signs under his arm.

"Bravo," Keith said. Frank hadn't seen the cop in months, not since the last time Keith had come banging into the restaurant late on a Friday night to throw his weight around and create a ruckus, ostensibly looking for underage drinkers but really just bored and looking to pick at a decades-old scab of animosity. Keith had never gotten over the Easter Parade caper, especially since he'd never been able to pin any charge on the boys for the deed. After all, it's hard to dust an alligator for fingerprints. And though Will had been gone and Frank had been significantly subdued for more than two decades now, Keith still took opportunities where he could to stir the pot. He seemed to think the war was still on. Frank couldn't care less. Although he couldn't resist, today, peevish as he was feeling, greeting the cop with his old, unsolicited nickname.

"Hiya, Do-Key," he said, and Keith scowled.

"Officer Keith! You're running for sheriff, eh?" George said, stating the obvious as only George could do, given that Keith had by now deposited a stack of DONALD KEITH! FOR SHERIFF! signs on the bar.

"Yes, numb-nuts, I am," Keith said. He'd put on more weight through the years, and now, in his early fifties, he had a soft, overfed look that did not inspire great faith in his ability to protect and serve. His hands were too small for his arms. His uniform stretched like vinyl across his stomach. He sat down on a barstool next to George.

"I've come to ask for your support," Keith said, staring at Frank levelly.

"Mine?" Frank said, genuinely surprised.

"Yours." Keith looked around the restaurant, where the tables were filling up and the front door was still opening at regular intervals to admit more customers. "You got you some constituents here, Bravo," he said.

"What are you asking?" Frank said, staring at him skeptically. He put a round of beers on a tray, slid it to Irma, who was waiting at the end of the bar, hands on her hips.

"You need a written request next time?" she said. "I gotta place an advance reservation? I got people waiting."

"Settle down, Irma," Frank said. "The night is young."

"Put up my signs in your parking lot," Keith said. "It would help."

Frank raised his eyebrows. This was impressive. He couldn't believe Keith had the *cojones* to ask *him* of all people, Frank Bravo, to help promote his campaign. This was rich.

"Officer Keith," he said. "If I put your signs in my parking lot, that might give people the wrong impression."

Keith furrowed his brow, waited. When Frank didn't elaborate, he was forced to ask, "What impression?"

"The impression that I choose to support you. Which I don't."

George snickered. Keith's face darkened. "I thought you would have been a bigger man than this, Bravo," he said. "I thought by now you'd be grown up enough to do the right thing."

Frank looked away, watched Irma plod through the restaurant. Don't do it, he said to himself. Don't bite.

"You could stand to gain here, Bravo," Keith continued. "You and me, we go way back. You should know I'm the real deal. I'm working toward a better county. A safer county."

"Oh, bullshit," Frank said. "You're working toward a fatter paycheck."

"Don't you think we have work to do in this county?" Keith demanded. "Don't you think there's room for improvement? I'm working on more officers. Cracking down on the God-damned vagrants. Making the roads safer. Don't you think the roads should be safer? Jesus, Bravo, you of all people." Keith watched Frank's face carefully, and he knew the cop was working an angle here, trying to invoke the tragedy of Will's death, trying to use it to his advantage, and it pissed Frank off. Fucking Do-Key. He made Frank sick.

"You know what, Do—, I mean, Officer Keith?" he said genially. "I think it's great you're running for sheriff. And maybe you're right. Maybe there is work to be done in this county."

Keith straightened up, nodded, smiled. "I thought so," he said.

"Who are you up against?" Frank said. Keith slid the campaign signs closer toward Frank, nodded again in the direction of George, seeking his agreement, too, it seemed. George sipped his beer and said nothing.

"Conroy Mathis," Keith said, and he watched as Frank took a slip of paper out from under the bar and jotted down the name.

"Got it," Frank said. "Thanks."

"What do you need that for?" Keith asked.

"Well, I need to call him," Frank said. "Ask him for some campaign signs. For my parking lot. I got me some constituents in here, you know."

Keith placed two small, fat hands flat on the bar and heaved himself off the stool. He looked at Frank darkly.

"You're one son of a bitch, Bravo," he said. "Always have been, always will be."

"Regards, Do-Key," Frank said. He wiped a damp rag on the surface of the bar where Keith's hands had been and then, as an afterthought, pulled a bottle of Windex from under the counter, sprayed the bar, and wiped it again.

"Hope you're careful in here," Keith said. "Hope I don't find no kids drinking in here, Bravo. Could cost you your license, you know."

"Good thing you weren't in here last night then," Frank said. "We had Brownie Troop number twenty-four doing a wet T-shirt contest. Two-for-one drafts."

"I'm not kidding, asshole. I could shut you down so fast that. . . ." Keith trailed off, looking a little confused. "So fast," he concluded.

"You just keep checking, officer," Frank said. "Keep coming in to see if there's any cute little girls drinking in here. Or any cute little boys, for that matter. We know you'll be on top of that."

Keith slid the signs off the bar and lumbered out of the restaurant, and Frank watched him go, his pleasure at having gotten the donkey's goat dissipating quickly as he returned to the moment and remembered the sight of his truck, Carson at the wheel, exiting the parking lot on its way to Aberdeen. Elizabeth. Bell. The bed.

"So anyway, Frank," George said. "Whole life." And he was off again.

It was Utina, all of it. Melted pies and early-bird diners and bullish cops and foul-mouthed insurance-selling trash collectors—that was Utina. No end of annoyances, no end of blind alleys and wrong turns and aggravation around every corner. Maybe Carson was right. Maybe they all needed a change. A way out.

But Arla. Frank had a vision of his mother the day Dean left them, sitting very still in the kitchen at Aberdeen, her cane out of reach against the kitchen counter. "Frank," she'd said, after a while. "Get me that cane, would you?" He'd brought it to her and had steadied her by the arm while she stood.

"Thank you, Frankie," she'd said quietly. "You always prop me up." He'd watched her walk unsteadily out the door. That night he'd driven out to the beach near Crossroads. A couple of surfers were strapping boards to their car when he arrived. He recognized them from school, and he waved but did not speak. He walked up and over the dunes and sat for a long time, looking at the ocean. Then he went back to the truck and drove to the place in the dunes where it had happened, the place where they'd left Will. He walked into the thicket. He saw Tip Breen's hand on Will's shoulder, and then the small image of his brother's face in the wing-mirror of Carson's truck.

When he came back from the beach, long after midnight, he saw Arla's light, shining like a beacon through the trees. They owed her. He and Carson and Dean. For what they'd done. But now Dean was gone, and the debtors had been reduced to two. He wasn't sure, never had been, if Carson was good for the tab. But Frank paid his debts.

Now he mopped the bar again with a damp rag, listened to George drone on. He thought about Carson, and Alonzo Cryder, and big money, but then he shook his head, dislodged the thoughts like so many buzzing gnats. Arla and Sofia were out at Aberdeen, Morgan was slinging fritters in the kitchen, and Frank was stuck, like Susan Holm in her Mazda, between a rock and a hard place. And no tow truck was coming to pull him out.

TEN

Beneath a heavy metal overhang in the semicircular drive of St. Johns Hospital in Jacksonville, a trio of broad-bottomed women, dressed in powder blue scrubs and plastic clogs, stood smoking. The picture of health, thought Carson Bravo, who had no patience with either body fat or cigarettes, both of which, in his opinion, were signs of weakness. He parked in the skimpy shade of a thin pine at the edge of the parking lot and got out of his car, a used late-model Acura he'd bought from a client and, he now realized, looking at it, had paid too much for. Another expensive mistake. He was getting good at them.

The smoking women were blocking his approach to the door.

"Morning," he said tightly.

One of them exhaled and slowly moved aside.

"*Thank* you," he said, fanning the air in front of his face theatrically, but the woman simply turned back to the others and resumed her conversation. A pair of automatic glass doors made a soft sucking sound as Carson entered the building and made for the reception desk. While the air outside the hospital had been hotly oppressive, inside the temperature seemed to be hovering around the twenty-degree mark. A bank of tall windows along one wall was damp with condensation. Carson shivered.

"I'm here to see a patient," he said to a dowdy woman at the reception desk. She had hair the color of mud and seemed, like her cohorts in the smoking section, to have not missed many meals.

"Visiting hours haven't started yet," she said. "Not till ten."

He looked at his watch. Nine-thirty. Fabulous. He'd driven all the way from St. Augustine to Jacksonville in thirty-seven minutes, a personal best, only to face a half-hour delay at the hands of this washed-out pudding of a woman?

"Chrissakes," he said to her. "Does it really matter?"

She looked at him with dislike. She wore oversize glasses with gold monogrammed initials in the corners of the lenses. Nice. "We have policies," she said. "You're welcome to wait." Then she turned away.

He looked around the lobby and walked toward a small and purposefully unwelcoming waiting room tucked into an alcove, where two wall-mounted TVs blared competing newscasts from opposite walls and where all the chairs were empty. He clenched his fists one time, released. He didn't like waiting. Deep breath. Sit down. Focus. He could hear Elizabeth, telling him he was too impatient. Too wound up. Too stressed-out.

He sat down, and his left knee immediately started jiggling, as it always did. He didn't try to stop it. He had restless leg syndrome, or so Elizabeth had reported to him after spending an evening Googling medical sites and compiling what turned out to be a comprehensive list of Carson's psychosomatic faults: bruxism—grinding his teeth so hard and loud in the night that it sounded like a buzz saw, or so she said. Finger tapping. Chronic sighing. Excessive *drinking*. According to Elizabeth, he was exhibiting every stress-induced or tension-related symptom, disorder, or weakness in the book. Well, fuck it. He'd deal with all of it later. After he settled this other issue.

He pulled his cell phone out of his pocket and looked at the screen. Two missed calls from Christine Hughes. One business and one pleasure, he'd bet. She'd want to know two things: when her fund dividend was due, and when she could expect their next extracurricular romp at the Hilton, and he'd been turning the act of avoiding both questions into a fine art. Things were getting complicated. These *women*. A few weeks ago he'd lowered the boom and had let go of his *other* dalliance, Holly, which had been an act of poor judgment from the outset and now had proven disastrously ill-executed. Things were getting harder to manage. Maybe, though he hated to admit it, a bit out of control. Holly had threatened to go straight to Elizabeth, and he'd been sure she was just blowing smoke until he came home from the office and found Elizabeth had jumped ship for Aberdeen and taken Bell with her.

But this, he was sure, was a temporary setback. Elizabeth would be back. She wasn't ready to break up Bell's home life, and he was counting on that, though he knew, vaguely, it was cowardly to be banking on his daughter's innocence to buy himself a little time. That was all he needed. He'd convince Elizabeth the affair with Holly was over, which would be easy, because it *was* over, that little bitch, the little rancorous, spiteful, small-time

hussy. Jesus. Where did he find them? He'd convince Elizabeth
it would never happen again. He'd beg for her forgiveness, and
she would grant it. She would. Wouldn't she?

If it wasn't for this other thing. This thing with Christine
Hughes. Here he was, ready to chart a course on the straight and
narrow and stick to it, ready to keep his word and write himself
a little redo on his marriage vows to save the ship before it went
down for good, and then along came this thing with Christine
Hughes and the God-damned Bravo Multi-Fund.

He wished he'd brought a jacket to the hospital, which
was ridiculous, needing a jacket in Florida in the middle of August. How much were they spending on air-conditioning here,
anyway? They ought to call the facilities manager on the carpet,
string up the son of a bitch for wasting resources, squandering
energy, mismanaging money—

Oh, Jesus. *Mismanaging money.*

His leg started quaking again. It would have been nice, it
occurred to him, if Elizabeth had not chosen this very moment to
pull her little protest, just when he was in the middle of the biggest crisis of his career, to go off on a little field trip to Aberdeen.
Elizabeth was the only thing he could rely on. And now she was
gone. He pushed down on his knee, tried to make his leg stop
shaking. If she was here she'd tell him to walk it off. Tell him
to drink more water. Tell him to take a deep breath. Tell him to
calm down. So he tried it. He got up and paced.

Fuck. Easy for her to say. Calm down—she had no idea. No
idea of the shit he was dealing with while she was off on this little
break or whatever she wanted to call it, staying up at Aberdeen
with his mother, of all people. It was pissing him off to no end.

Ponzi.

It wasn't working. That word, that *word* was back, buzzing around in his head like a mosquito, and he sighed, sat down again, put his head in his hands, gave in to it. *Fuck*. Ponzi. A Ponzi scheme. As of this morning, that's what he was running. He was a swindler. A criminal. And the worst part was that he wasn't even sure how it had happened.

It wasn't supposed to be this way. He was an investment manager—no, an *Investment Manager*, Capital Letters, Big-Time. He was Carson Bravo, Investment Manager. It was his calling, his career, his entire identity. It was all he had ever wanted to do, and he'd wanted to do it well. He'd been fine for so long, even through the decade's lowest points, even after the 9/11 plummet, the housing collapse, all of it, he'd kept his head above water, kept the clients reassured. They'd held even, every damn one of them; well, even if they hadn't *made* money they hadn't *lost* money—not as much money as some investors, anyway, put it that way. But now, oh, sweet Jesus, now. It was all coming apart.

He'd started the fund two years ago, called it the Bravo Multi-Fund, just liked the ring of it. He'd sat smug and satisfied for a good eighteen months, watching how his clients liked the ring of it, too. He'd sold $1.8 million in the fund in the first year alone, with a good third of that in one fell swoop to one of his biggest clients, Christine Hughes, the wife of one of St. Augustine's most successful electrical contractors. She came into a bit of family money and didn't want her husband to control it, so she came to Carson for investment management. He'd managed her investments, all right. And he'd managed a few other things for her, too, many of them managed quite well, in fact, in a twist of tangled sheets in an executive suite at the Hilton at World Golf Village. One afternoon, he'd managed to make her come three times in the space of an hour. That's how well he'd managed her.

But the fund. The fund. The screwed-up, bollixed-up fund that he'd decided to sectorize, putting the entire focus of the available capital into the tech stocks he'd felt in his bones would be a sure thing. Tech can't lose, he'd told himself over and over again, shooting a virtual bird at the prevailing wisdom of diversification, low risk, high discipline. Tech can't lose. Or at least, tech can't lose *twice,* he said, when the nagging voice of reason reminded him of the collapse of the dot-coms in 2000. It would be like getting struck by lightning twice in one lifetime. Not gonna happen. So he'd done it, had hammered out the plan, and when he was finished, the portfolio was so tech-heavy that the entire Internet, he reasoned, would have to come crashing down around his head before the fund could fail.

But fail it did. Badly. Spectacularly. So spectacularly that last month he'd begun a new campaign—promising 10 percent annual returns—just to pull in new investors who would offer the liquidity he needed to maintain operations. Just last week he'd had to doctor the report to Christine Hughes to obscure just how badly her losses could be by the end of the year. And just this morning he'd written the first dividend check funded solely by the deposits of his most recent investors.

Ponzi. Ponzi. Ponzi.

But what else could he do? If Christine Hughes started losing serious money, she'd demand immediate redemption. He had no doubt about that. And Christine's cashing in her chips would lead to a landslide—when his newer investors got wind of her bailout, they'd surely follow suit, demanding a seven-day redemption of their funds that would come from where, exactly? The whole damn thing was a house of cards, and if he didn't do something, fast, he could expect the SEC to be knocking on his door in the very near future. To make matters worse, Christine Hughes would not, he was quite sure, be satisfied with simply pulling out her investments. She'd make a beeline to Elizabeth who, judging by recent events, was hanging by a thread in this tenuous marriage and was, he suspected, increasingly making eyes at his brother. No money. No business. No Elizabeth. No Bell. Just a cold cot on the wrong side of the bars at the Florida State Penitentiary. That was it. If Christine Hughes lost her money, Carson lost everything.

Not gonna happen.

Because they were selling Aberdeen. *And* Uncle Henry's. He was going to make sure of it. Pennies from fucking *heaven* were falling out of the sky in the shape of this fat cat Alonzo Cryder and his Atlanta development corporation, and Carson would be damned if he would let Saint Frank or Arla or whacked-out Sofia stand in the way of the financial freedom that each of them so desperately needed. Especially him. If he had his share of the proceeds from the real estate sales, he'd have enough liquid capital to bail out the fund, reallocate the frigging tech stocks, and right the ship. Then he could buy Christine Hughes out and extricate himself from the vise grip she had on his balls, both literally and figuratively, before his extracurricular activities put the final nail in the coffin of his marriage. He just needed the money.

At least he had this chance, this hope, this missing link, lying in a bed somewhere on one of the floors above his head. Remarkable, Alonzo Cryder's detective work. Cryder, working from

tax records, employment histories and—not too surprisingly—a
rap sheet, had been successful in tracking down the one person
who held the key to getting this entire real estate deal put to bed,
and in so doing erasing that word from Carson's head forever
and ever. *Ponzi.*

"He was admitted after an altercation outside a bar," Cryder
had said on the phone. "It's the same guy—I got the social from
a guy I know down there on the police force, and it matches the
one you gave me."

"What's wrong with him?"

"You tell me."

"No," Carson had said. "I mean, why was he admitted to
the hospital?"

"Oh, that—well, they won't disclose medical information,
but the cop I know said he was banged up after the fight, having
a hard time walking. I'd guess he broke something, tore something. Can't be good, a guy his age in a brawl, right?"

No, thought Carson, can't be good. But that didn't surprise
him.

He looked at his watch. 9:37. This was bullshit. Why did
he have to wait till 10:00? It wasn't like the patients were on
any timetable. It was a damn hospital. What, they had board
meetings? Tee times? Insane. He waited until the woman at
the reception desk turned to greet someone, and then he made
a run for the elevator and rode it to the third floor, which, the
directory said, housed General Medicine. As good a guess as
any. Pediatrics was out. Obstetrics was out. Might as well start
somewhere.

Carson exited the elevator. There was a nurses' station, but
nobody was around. He wandered down one short hallway, then

another, each lined with small, dark rooms. From one room came the sound of an old woman wailing.

"*Yvonne!*" she said. "Timmy!"

He stopped in the hallway, listened for a moment.

"Yvonne! Timmy! Help! I need help!" the woman said.

He walked back to the nurses' station, but there was still nobody in sight. His heart had begun to twitter in an uncomfortable way, and he felt himself getting angry. He didn't like feeling anxious, didn't like situations that bred anxiety. Anxiety was the enemy of productivity. Fear was the enemy of power. He'd taught himself that, over the years. He'd taught himself a lot of things. He wandered the halls a second time.

"Timmy! I need you! Help me, please help me!" the old woman said. It sounded like she was starting to panic.

What the hell were they doing in this place? Why didn't anyone come? He poked his head around the curtain to peer in at the old lady.

"Honey," she said immediately, spotting him in the doorway. "I'm about to wee the bed." She was a tiny thing, shriveled and gray but with a horrible booming voice. She fixed her vision on his face. Carson felt sick.

"I'll get the nurse," he said.

"I don't need a nurse. I need a bedpan."

"I'll get the nurse," he said again.

"Honey, I'm going to wee right here in this bed! You get me a bedpan right this minute!" Holy Jesus on high. Holy *shit*. He looked around the tiny room, spotted something that looked like it might have been a bedpan on a rolling tray of equipment. He reached for it, panicked for a second that it might not be clean.

"Honey!" the old lady said. "It's coming!"

He grabbed the pan and put it on the old lady's chest, then turned to flee the curtained enclosure. "I need it *under* me!" she screamed. "Come back!"

Carson kept walking. At the nurses' station he pumped a fat blob of Germ-X into his hands, rubbed them together angrily. Two nurses sat at the station now, each engrossed at a computer. "There's a lady back there having a problem," he said, and the women looked at each other and rolled their eyes. "I'll go," one said. "You got her last time."

"Yvonne! Timmy!" Down the hall, the woman's voice was fading; she must have been growing tired. He tried not to wonder whether she'd been able to implement the bedpan in time. Holy God, he wanted out of this place. He looked at his watch. 9:49.

"Is it visiting hours yet?" he said to the nurse still seated at the computer. She was short and bloated, and her scrubs were tight across her belly. Why did they put these people in scrubs? Was there any more unflattering attire in the world? And my God, were *all* the women in this hospital unattractive?

"I'm sorry," she said. "You'll need to wait downstairs."

Oh, for Christ's sake. But he was nervous now, maddeningly anxious. The sound of the old woman's voice had cut right through his nerves, left him feeling frayed, raw. Her loneliness was like a specter—pervasive and terrifying. He didn't argue with the nurse; he rode the elevator back down to the first floor and slumped back in his original chair in the waiting room. A teenaged boy now sat in one of the other chairs, watching the TV. He didn't look up at Carson. The woman at the reception desk glared at him over her monogrammed glasses. It was all he could do not to give her the finger.

On the TV, a cluster of police vehicles was arranged in a semicircle in front of a two-story gray building with a bland, rectangular profile and a bad roof. Several of the police had left their cars and walked around to the sides of the building. They crouched behind trees. Their guns were drawn. They peered up at the building. A newscaster rattled on excitedly, but Carson couldn't hear what he was saying.

"What's going on?" he said to the kid in the other chair. He was a nice-looking kid, short hair, blue eyes. Probably played football for his high school. Probably got good grades. A nice girlfriend. Clean socks. You could just tell.

"A shooting," the kid said. "It's Orlando. Some guy went in there and is shooting the place up. They're trying to get him out right now. It's live."

He still hadn't looked at Carson, but he spoke with a quiet confidence. He was on the ball, this one. He'd go far.

"What's in there?" he said. "What's the business?"

"Financial something," the kid said. "Guy came in and shot a coworker. Dead. He's on the second floor. The people saw him do it before they ran out. The shooter's still up there with the gun. They're trying to figure out if he got anybody else."

Carson stared at the TV, picturing the dead man somewhere on the second floor. "Huh," he said. "Not what he had planned for today, was it?"

"The shooter?" said the kid, turning to him.

"The dead guy," Carson said.

"No," the kid said. He tipped his head a bit, looked at Carson like he was trying to figure him out. "No, I guess not."

He smiled. That was some kid. His father was probably proud of him. Huh.

He realized his leg was shaking double-time. He got up and walked outside, through the clouds of cigarette smoke hanging over the entryway. One man sat in a wheelchair, smoking. Another man, a nurse or an orderly, stood behind the wheelchair, also smoking. Carson shook his head. *Unreal.*

He pulled his cell phone out of his pocket, punched Arla's number.

"Hello?"

"Mom," he said. "Are you getting ready?"

"Who is this?" Arla said.

"You know it's me," he said impatiently.

"You don't ever say hello, Carson. Don't you think you could say hello?"

"Hello," he said. "Are you getting ready?"

She sighed. "It's early. Frank said he'd be here a little later."

"You need to be ready when he gets there. These Vista people are coming all the way from Atlanta. You don't want to be late for this meeting."

"I don't even want to *go* to this meeting."

"That's beside the point." A waft of smoke drifted his way, and he walked farther into the parking lot to escape it.

"Says who?" Arla said.

"You said you'd go. You said you'd listen to what they have to say."

"Oh, Carson," she began.

"*No*," he said. "*No.* You said you would. This is important

—these people have money. Don't you get it? These people could change all our lives."

"Maybe I don't want my life to change."

"Don't be ridiculous," he said. He looked at his watch. 9:59. "I gotta go, Mom. Make sure you get ready for Frank. Don't keep Cryder waiting."

She hung up. He stared at the phone for a moment, wondering if she had actually hung up *on* him, but then he thrust it back into his pocket. My God, she was stubborn. He had to hand it to her, though—the woman had tenacity. In fact, there were times he had to admit—if he had, in fact, inherited any backbone at all, any *strength*, for Christ's sake, from either of his parents, it could only have come from Arla.

She did what she could, he conceded. For all of them. Sometimes he thought she was the only one who'd ever looked out for him, at least until he met Elizabeth, that is. Once, when he was a kid, he'd ridden with his family out to Lake Butler to visit some friend or other of Dean's, and he remembered riding in the back of that old Impala, Frank and Will wedged in on either side of him, Sofia sandwiched in the front between Arla and Dean. When they went past the turnoff to Raiford, Dean wanted to stop. He'd heard the state prison was selling off its cots, replacing them with new ones.

"Paulie says five bucks a cot," Dean had said. "We'll get four of them, set 'em up for the kiddos here. Better than them old bed frames we have now. Those are frigging kindling wood. These are made of solid steel. If I pay for 'em today I can come back later with the truck."

Arla had turned slowly, gazed at him for a long minute.

"What?" Dean said finally. "I mean, just to use as frames. They'll keep their own mattresses and all." He slowed the Impala and put the blinker on, but he didn't turn yet. A sign at the side of the road read RAIFORD: 4 MILES.

"Dean," Arla said. Her voice was low and level, and Carson nudged Frank, nodded at him to watch. "If you think I will have my children sleeping on used prison cots, you are out of your pickled little mind." Dean shrugged, pitched a cigarette butt out the window, turned the blinker off, and continued straight, toward Lake Butler. Carson caught Arla's eye in the visor mirror, and though her jaw was set like stone, when she saw Carson looking, she winked.

Ponzi. Ponzi. Ponzi.

Nice try, Mom. It was looking like he was going to end up on a prison cot anyway.

He strode back into the hospital. He could handle this. He could handle anyone, as he'd proven to the world and himself time and time again. He'd handled his fucked-up family. He'd handled putting himself through college. He'd handled the shackles of marriage, Elizabeth's miscarried first pregnancy, the formation of his own firm, the birth of Bell. He'd handled plenty. He could certainly handle this.

The kid from the waiting room was gone. Carson told the woman at the reception desk who he wanted to see, and she looked at her watch pointedly before directing him back up to the third floor again.

"Room three-twelve," she said. "Thank you for your patience."

Screw you, he thought. "Nice glasses," he said.

He rode the elevator back to the third floor, then exited into the carpeted hallway, where the two nurses looked up at him again but said nothing. He walked down the hall, ticked off the room numbers until he came to 312. This was it. It all came down to this—Arla, Aberdeen, Uncle Henry's, the money. Everything Carson needed to begin to put his business, his marriage, his *life* back together again was on the other side of this door, and all he needed to do was work the situation, make it submit to his will. Git 'r done. From somewhere down the hallway he could hear the old woman still calling for Timmy and Yvonne, and the horrible old witch was making him nervous all over again. Think of something else, he told himself, but the only thing that came immediately to mind was the shooting on the television down-stairs, the dead guy in Orlando. I'll bet he was a fund manager, he thought fleetingly. *Fuck!*

He took a deep breath, rapped twice on the doorframe, and then entered the room. There were two beds, a man in each one, and Carson's eyes darted back and forth between the two, searching for a man he recognized, and then he found him. His heart did that fluttery thing again, and he clenched his fists, hard, and willed it to stop. He walked to the bed closest to the door and waited until the man in it had raised his eyes to his.

"Hi, Dad," he said, a taste like sweet bile on his tongue, a queer mingling of fear and joy in his heart.

ELEVEN

God knows Arla had fought a few battles with her weight over the years, but this was getting ridiculous. This morning she'd stepped off the scale in disgust and kicked at it with her good foot, skinning the thin skin on the knuckles of her toes and bruising her hip against the sink on the recoil.

"Jesus on high," she said. "Holy hallelujah."

She wrapped a towel around herself and stomped out of the bathroom. She hadn't been this heavy since forty years ago, when she was pregnant with Frank, the largest of her four babies, who'd entered the world at a whopping ten pounds—the most decisive and assertive action of his entire life, in Arla's opinion. She loved all her children equally, but she could not help but see the damndest faults in each one of them. Sofia: addled. Carson: selfish. Frank: malleable. Will: well, *Will*.

She sighed. It was already after eleven, and she was mildly appalled at herself for spending nearly the entire morning in her robe, but then she pushed the thought from her mind. What was the rush? Carson had already been pestering her on the phone, but Frank said he'd pick her up at noon. She'd be ready. She got dressed, picked up her cane, and descended the stairs slowly. She entered the kitchen, where Sofia had come in from cleaning Uncle Henry's and was eating a honey bun, standing at the window and looking out toward Biaggio's trailer.

"I think we need to do something about our weight," Arla said.

Sofia didn't turn around.

"Who you talking to?" she said.

"You. Us. We're getting fat," Arla said.

"Speak for yourself, *maman*. I'm doing just fine."

Arla snorted. "We're both getting fat."

Sofia looked at her, but her gaze was distracted, absent-minded. "Well, maybe," she conceded.

"Why don't you make us some coffee?" Arla said. "I need to start the linens."

She left Sofia and walked into the living room, where she plugged in the iron and regarded a hefty basket of freshly laundered church linens. She pulled a corporal off the top of the pile, smoothed it across the surface of the ironing board. She dipped her hand into a bowl of water on the end of the ironing board and shook her fingers above the cloth, watching the drops of water fall across the white linen, the embroidered cross, the lace edges. She waited for the iron to heat up, then a movement outside the front window caught her eye, and she looked up in time to see Biaggio crossing the yard to his van. He stopped halfway and turned toward Aberdeen, and his face changed as he looked toward the kitchen window. He stood gazing for a moment, then slowly lifted his hand in a wave. He smiled, a different kind of smile than Arla had ever seen before, and then she watched, astonished, as he brought his fingers to his lips and blew a kiss toward the kitchen window. She heard a movement in the kitchen, and then Biaggio turned and walked to his van, started it up, and drove down the long driveway to Monroe Road.

Biaggio?

She put her hand on the ironing board to steady herself for a moment, but the movement wobbled the iron, and it fell over and grazed her fingers on the way down. She jerked her hand back, feeling the burn across her knuckles even as she did so.

"Damn!" she said.

"What?" Sofia called from the kitchen.

"Nothing," Arla said. "Burnt myself."

Now what was that all about? Had Sofia seen Biaggio in the driveway, or was she unaware that he was watching her? Did she reciprocate his smile, his gaze, his distant kiss? Oh, my Lord in heaven. What was happening around here? She couldn't keep up. Elizabeth and Bell living upstairs, Atlanta developers calling, and now this, Biaggio in the driveway blowing kisses.

She sighed, looked up at Dean's largemouth bass, hanging stupidly on the wall above the entertainment center. *You getting this?* she wanted to say to it. *You see what's going on around here?* She turned back to the linens, feeling the sting of both her bruised foot and her burned hand. So it was going to be that kind of day, was it.

She righted the iron and resmoothed the corporal on the flat surface of the ironing board, then ran the pointed tip of the iron along the lacy edges, smoothing each fold and wrinkle as she went, feeling her pulse begin to slow, her breathing begin to settle. She'd always liked this, ironing. It never even felt like work, really, just a hobby, of sorts, a soothing, calming hobby, making the wrinkles go away, smoothing out the bumps and crumples and catches in the fabric the way she always wished she could do in her own life. It was so easy, on the linens. Unsightly rumples? Psst, steam, pfft, gone. Stubborn creases? Psst, steam, pfft, gone. Even the stains could be removed. Even the tears could be mended. She rounded the corner of the embroidered cross at the center of the square, careful not to singe the delicate stitching.

When Dean was still here, the ironing had been almost a therapy for Arla. She'd needed it. She remembered the days— the middle days, she'd come to think of them—when the kids were bigger, less needy, but before Will had died and everything had gone dark. When the children were tiny, she and Dean had worked in tandem, consumed with the daily chores of housekeeping and breadwinning and feeding and diapering and clothing those four small people. They were a wonderful distraction. Wonderful. But as the boys grew older, more wild, more independent, and as Sofia retreated further into the compulsions that soon came to define her, Arla had found herself staring at Dean sometimes, wondering who he was, where he'd been, where he was going. The middle years. They were hard. She'd never worried, particularly, about other women. In fact she wondered, sometimes, if he would ever love another woman again, herself included. Back then, he was still in love with the Arla he'd picked up on the side of the road in 1963. She knew this, and it broke her heart as surely as it broke his, because neither of them would ever see that girl again. She was willing to bet he was still in love with that girl today.

After he left, she kept up with him. Nobody knew it, but she did. She called his brother Charlie every now and then, asking where he was, what he was doing, where he was working, staying, sleeping at night. Sometimes Charlie knew, and sometimes he didn't. And Dean called her, too, checking in on the kids now and then, maybe three or four times a year at first, then less frequently, and then not at all. She knew he'd spent two years in the clink for DUI back in the early nineties and that he had managed to steer clear of the law since then. She knew he'd been working for a time at Georgia Pacific in Palatka, knew he'd had girlfriends here and there but had never settled down. She knew he'd stay occasionally at his friend Tommy Bolla's in Jacksonville, even knew—thanks to a high school friend she kept in touch with who worked as a nurse at the hospital in Orange Park—that he'd been seeing an oncologist. All those years in the boiler, down in the hole. All those dispersants. They were going to get the best of him yet. She'd never told the kids she had spoken with him. What good would that do?

Dean. He'd been a bitter medicine. But he'd brought her to herself, made her what she was today, for better or for worse. She snorted, amused at the echo of those words. Was she better, or was she worse?

It would have been different, without a doubt, were it not for Will. She and Dean, they might have made it, might have defied the odds. But Will was a blow with which none of them could cope. That black car, that steep ravine, that horrible, horrible night. She'd never hold anything against Dean, after that. All bets were off. Nobody could be expected to carry on after that. All those years playing at being a patriarch—Dean was pulling a weight he had no business pulling, driving a boat he didn't know how to steer, and Will's death was the final collision, the impact from which there was no return. After that, when Dean lit out it was a relief, almost, though he'd left her frightened and angry and again cut right down to the bone.

She remembered the last time she spoke to him on the phone, how he'd come close to an apology but never actually said it.

"I'm no good as the driver, Arla," he said. "We both know that. You're better off at the wheel."

She'd nodded in her dark bedroom, alone, the phone held tight to her cheek, and then she told him good-bye and hadn't spoken to him again. That was five years ago. And even though they were still legally married, she didn't know if she'd ever speak to him again.

And now this. An offer to buy the house. *Money*, they kept saying to her. *Freedom. Opportunity.* Malarkey. She didn't need opportunity, didn't want freedom. The things she wanted, money couldn't buy. But then the nagging thought came to her again, the nagging guilt. This wasn't just about her. There was Sofia to consider. Carson. Frank. Elizabeth. Bell. She felt something moving, something large, glacial, in the pit of her stomach. She didn't know if she'd be able to keep it still for long.

The bass on the wall caught her eye again, and she stared at it. Then she looked down at the corporal on the ironing board, at the spreading brown burns the iron had seared into the white fabric, and she jerked the iron back up.

"Shit," she said. "Holy shit."

Something smelled awful, and it wasn't just the burned linens. She tossed the ruined corporal back into the laundry basket and unplugged the iron. Then she grasped her cane and went back into the kitchen, where Sofia still stood at the counter, staring idly out the window.

"What is that smell?" Arla said.

Sofia turned and looked at her abstractedly, then jerked to awareness and bolted to the stove, where a Tupperware bowl had been reduced to acrid molten plastic against a red-hot heating element on a back burner. On the counter next to the stovetop, a metal saucepan sat clean and dry.

"Gosh sakes," Sofia muttered. She turned off the burner. "There go the grits."

"What in the world?" Arla said.

"They were leftover in the fridge. I meant to put them in the pot. I guess I forgot that part," Sofia said.

"Holy Mary, mother of God," Arla said. "Honestly, Sofia. Are you trying to kill us?"

And here was the rub. How could Arla ever be expected to pay any attention at all to her own health and well-being, to actually think about *herself* now and then, to focus on *her own* needs and maintain *her own* figure and sanity when she had to be on watch every second of every God-damned day for Sofia's next act? Holy Lord. Arla was sixty-two. She felt, suddenly, as if she were a hundred.

"Mother," Sofia said icily. "It's a piece of Tupperware. It's not the end of the world."

"It's what that Tupperware represents, Sofia. Where is your mind?" Arla cringed a little bit when she said it. Where, indeed?

The whole kitchen smelled like melted plastic, and the only thing Arla wanted was a Little Debbie honey bun, or three, and God *damn*, pardon the French, her blessed fat ass, but today was clearly not the day to start with the reducing.

Elizabeth entered the kitchen.

"What do I smell?" she said.

"Ask Sofia," Arla said.

Elizabeth raised her eyebrows, looked at Sofia, but said nothing. She walked over to the stove, studied the mess, then pulled a knife out of a drawer and started scraping plastic off the burner.

"Let's get it while it's still warm," she said. "Before it really sticks."

That was Elizabeth. Always knowing just what to do. Always helping to *solve* the problems, not *add* to them, unlike her own daughter, who seemed to lie awake at night thinking of new ways to torment her. It was nice, having Elizabeth and Bell here at Aberdeen. If you didn't count Carson as part of the equation, and if you didn't worry yourself too much wondering what was going to become of the only marriage any of her children had ever managed to negotiate, it was downright pleasant.

Oh, it broke her heart, it did, what Carson was doing to Elizabeth. Why were these Bravo men so selfish? Arla picked up the box of Little Debbies, left Sofia sulking at the stove, and went out to the back porch.

Normally she wouldn't have tried the back steps. Her bad foot was never to be trusted, and these days, with her height and ever-increasing weight, the descent down the steps was treacherous, at best. Years ago Frank and Carson had built her a ramp off the front porch, which was what she used to get in and out of the house, but today she was driven by an overwhelming desire to get away from the house and to get away from Sofia, quickly, and she simply couldn't be bothered with walking to the front of the house.

She tucked the package of honey buns under her arm, linked her cane over her elbow, and gripped the railing, taking the steps one by one until she was on the flat, gravelly sand of the backyard. She lumbered down to the water, sat at the stone picnic table. This table. It had been here forever, since Dean had liberated it from a state park when they'd first moved to Aberdeen. How he got it into the back of his pickup truck she'd never know, but it took six Utina men and a couple of cases of beer to get it out and down the slippery, leaf-covered slope of land to this small clearing on the banks of the Intracoastal. Arla always liked the table. It had staying power. Which was more than she could say for the man who'd put it there.

She opened the first honey bun and regarded it. The sugar had crystallized along the edge and, given the humidity, had made a creamy paste of white frosting. She licked the inside of the plastic wrapper, then downed the bun in three bites. Bottoms up, she said to herself.

It hadn't always been this way, she conceded, running her tongue along her teeth to collect the remnants of sugar. She used to care about her weight. Used to care about her hair, her clothes, her lipstick. Used to savor the feeling of a man's stare on her legs, count the double takes she'd cause, like a ripple, when she entered a room. She'd been beautiful. She knew she was beautiful. But she'd started too early. Married at eighteen. Her first child, Sofia, at nineteen. She'd started early, so she'd aged early. She'd given up fighting it. She'd bought the pants with the elastic waistband, had given up skirts for shorts, had purchased her last tube of mascara a long, long time ago. So what? Here at Aberdeen, her husband long gone, what did it matter? It didn't. At Aberdeen, nothing mattered. And she liked it that way.

Aberdeen. What kind of name was that for a house? And what kind of man names a house, anyway? She slapped at a fat mosquito on her forearm, and the insect promptly gave up the ghost but left a thick smear of blood in its place. Good Lord. Was there no end of nuisances? She opened the second honey bun.

She remembered once, as a child—maybe nine? ten?—when she'd gone with her father to a wealthy client's house on the bank of the St. Johns River, and she'd stood, astonished, looking out over the river, where fields of aquatic flowers spread across the surface of the water like blankets. Arla couldn't see the water beneath. It was like the whole river had turned to foliage. The plants were lush green, bold purple flowers bursting out of the centers, and the sight was dazzling, unreal, all the water as far as she could see covered with a thick green and purple carpet. "What is it?" she'd said to her father, and the client, an old man, had snorted, shook his head. "Water hyacinth," he said. "It's invasive. It'll clog the whole waterway."

"It's beautiful," she'd said.

"Yeah, it's beautiful," the old man had said. "A beautiful nuisance."

The phrase had rung in her ears for many, many years. Was that what she was? Arla Bolton. Arla Bravo. A beautiful nuisance.

She looked to the right, where the footpath to Uncle Henry's had once been clear and well traveled, and now had become faded and overgrown. Back in the day, when she'd first bought Uncle Henry's, she'd used the path regularly, picking with her cane to and from the restaurant two, three, sometimes four times a day. It was a fifteen-minute walk through the woods to emerge on the other side at the edge of Uncle Henry's parking lot. But Arla hadn't walked the path in many years. She thought of Drusilla

Jane Ashby—the name carved on the mysterious headstone in a thicket of palmettos. When she was younger, she'd go into the woods, sit on a stump, and talk to Drusilla, chatting with the dead woman as if she were a sister, or a friend.

That's what she did the day Dean left.

She'd been in the kitchen with Sofia, and it was October, the day before Halloween, Will dead and buried more than three years already, and Dean had come into the kitchen with a funny heaviness in his step, and he'd said, *Arla, I gotta go.*

She thought he meant to the bathroom, that's how dumb she was, and she'd said "Go, then," but then she looked at him, and Sofia looked up and saw him there, and Sofia's mouth slowly opened with understanding and she got up and left the kitchen, left Arla facing Dean under the slow *tick-tick* of the Felix the Cat clock on the wall.

"I can't do it," he said.

"You've been doing it this long," she said.

"Not very well," he said, which was true, she would give him that, and then he said it again, "I gotta go."

She felt consumed by pragmatism then, wanting to know the details, the logistics. "Where will you go?" she said.

"Not sure."

"Will you come back?"

"Not sure."

"Do you have money?"

"A little."

"Well," she said. She sat down at the table. "Dean," she said, and then she stared out the window.

"You mad?" he said.

"I will be," she said.

He packed two suitcases and put them in the back of his truck. He waited until Carson and Frank got home from wherever they'd been, and then he called Sofia back to the kitchen and told them all he was leaving.

"Nice," Carson said. "Beautiful."

Frank said nothing. Sofia stared at the floor. And then Dean had walked out to the truck and was gone, just like that, nothing more, his tan forearm hanging out the truck's door like always, the sound of that damn loose muffler hitting the trees and bouncing back for a long, long time.

"Fuck him," Carson said.

"Watch your mouth," Arla said.

"Double fuck him to hell," Carson said, and he'd slammed his fist into the wall then and stared at it as the blood beaded across his knuckles.

"All right," Frank said. "All right now."

Sofia cried a little bit but after a while she stopped and she went upstairs to her room. Arla had stayed in the kitchen and drunk three glasses of Chablis, one after the other, and then she walked out into the path and picked her steps slowly until she came to Drusilla's grave. She sat down, told Drusilla that Dean was gone.

"No, I'm not surprised, not really," she'd said to the headstone. "I just wish—" What did she wish? "I just wish he hadn't left such a mess. I just don't know how I'll ever clean it all up."

That night was cold, the strangeness of the coming winter always so odd here in Florida, always taking Arla by surprise, an unexpected guest—dressed all wrong, awkward, mismatched. The little thicket in the woods was dark and dry, and somewhere out across the water an anhinga called and something big jumped in the shallows and Arla had sat for a long, long time, until her hands were brittle and sore from the cold and she'd walked back to the house, to Aberdeen, alone.

Aberdeen, she thought now, twenty years later. She turned back from the concrete picnic table to regard the house. How she loved it. How she hated it. When she and Dean were first married they'd driven in his truck down to Palatka to buy that secondhand Impala, and the car's owner had a strange dog in a kennel on his porch, a hunting terrier that had been trapped in its kennel for nearly a week after its owner, the Impala owner's uncle, had died. By some miracle, it'd had enough food and water in the crate to survive. When the dead hunter's family had found it a week later, they opened the door to the crate, but the dog wouldn't come out. Stockholm syndrome, or something like that. Bravo syndrome. Aberdeen syndrome.

She thought of that strange old song Will used to play on his guitar, "The Northern Lights of Aberdeen." It was a Scottish song, he'd said, and she had no idea where he dug it up, but it was a pretty thing, soulful and sad, and it made her think about Scotland, a place she'd never been, and about seeing the northern lights, a sight she'd always wanted to see. She saw a special once on PBS. Someone had filmed the aurora borealis off John o' Groats at the very northern tip of Scotland, and she'd been mesmerized by the notion of it, the sky exploding in light and color in what seemed an act not of nature or even of artistry but of sheer defiance.

> *Will ye come back aga' tae me, though death upon ye be.*
> *Though sea and brae be in between, come back tae Aberdeen.*
> *If ye canna' come, send word tae me, in lights that bonnie be.*
> *If ye canna' come, though sure I dee, I'll love the light for thee.*

She thought of ice, and cold bright light, and purple sheets of luminescence in the sky. She thought of green flashes, of dancing bolts of copper, and snow and fevers and magic. She thought of Cullowhee. A bead of sweat trickled down her back, and she felt her clothes turning damp in the humidity. Somewhere down near the water, a long shape slithered through the reeds.

"Mother!" Sofia was yelling from the back porch. "Frank is here. He says you have a meeting!"

How did she ever get so tired? Once before I die, she said to herself, I am going to go somewhere cold, somewhere north, and I am going to see the aurora borealis. Once. And though she knew this was a lie, she was comforted by it. She closed up the box of honey buns, picked up her cane, and started for the house.

TWELVE

Carson hadn't expected Dean to have changed much. He hadn't thought about it, honestly, until this moment. "A guy his age," Cryder had said. How old was Dean? Carson did a few quick calculations—sixty-five, he decided. Dean Bravo had made it to sixty-five. Amazing.

And he *was* the same, in many ways. Those startling blue eyes, that sullen, set jaw. Dean reclined in his bed, wearing a black T-shirt, faded jeans, and a pair of white socks. Carson was glad he wasn't wearing a hospital gown. He didn't know if he could have handled that. Dean's skin was an opaque leather. One hand gripped a TV remote; the other lay motionless at his side as he watched a TV mounted high on the opposite wall. He'd aged tremendously, of course, but there was something else, something completely different about the Dean reclining in this hospital bed and the Dean that had lived angrily in Carson's memory all these years. He was smaller. That was it. Carson had remembered his father as a big man. But this leathery man in the bed—he was so small. It was confounding. Carson's heart pounded. He felt angrier than he'd thought he would, but the anger was made more disturbing by the fact that it was tinged by something else, something unfamiliar, something that might have been pity. He hadn't been expecting that. He didn't have time for that.

Across the room, the other old man, a shriveled thing in a hospital gown, slept in a bed under a tall window. Dean looked up as Carson entered.

"Well, look who it isn't," Dean said. His voice was raspy, a smoker's voice. He didn't appear particularly surprised to see his oldest son after twenty years. The volume on the TV was too loud. "All grow'd up, aren't you?"

Carson didn't answer.

"Even got your hair cut off, didn't you?" Dean grinned at him.

Carson had kept his hair stridently short for eighteen years now, ever since his first internship at Merrill Lynch, but he could see no point in mentioning this to Dean now.

"So, how are you doing?" he said. It was awkward, false, but he didn't know where else to begin.

"Oh, shitty," Dean said.

"Why? What's wrong?"

"What's wrong? I'm old, dummy. That's what's wrong." Dean seemed at ease, speaking with Carson as though they'd just parted yesterday.

Carson pulled a heavy chair up to the edge of the bed and sat down.

"Well, I can't help you with that one," he said.

Carson stared at his father, whose eyes had returned to the
TV. He tried to think about how to proceed. How many times had
he imagined this moment, pictured a showdown with Dean, a
reckoning, a chance to look his father in the eye and berate him,
insult him, tell him what an ass he was, what a coward, what a
fool. And yet his anger was held in check, somehow, today, borne
back by both the agenda at hand and the unexpected frailness
of his father there in the hospital bed. Carson felt disappointed,
vaguely. He'd wanted to hold on to the anger, savor it, nurture
it, let it continue to grow as it had done for the last twenty years.
Now he felt like he'd been denied something satisfying. Something important.

"You ever seen this one?" Dean said. "This movie? This
is a funny one." On the screen, Gene Hackman was dressed in
drag, climbing a short staircase to mount a stage in a nightclub.
"Look at that asshole. He's a pisser."

Carson glanced at the movie, then cleared his throat. "So,
Dad, what have you been up to?" he said. *Where the hell have
you been for twenty years? What the hell is wrong with you?* "They
treating you okay in here?"

"He's a crack-up, that son of a bitch. Look at the wig."

"You feeling all right, Dad?"

"They don't make them like this guy anymore. He still
alive? What a pisser."

Carson looked at his watch.

"Dad. I'm talking to you."

Dean looked at him, finally, his eyes still that same shocking blue Carson remembered from so long ago. Will had had
the same eyes. Carson swallowed hard. He could handle this.
He started again, and he willed his voice to soften.

"Are you doing okay, Dad?"

"Been better," Dean said quietly.

A nurse came into the room and approached the bed. "How are you today, Mr. Bravo?" she said.

Dean's eyes lit up. "Oh, Jackie," he said, smiling. "If my life gets any better, I'm going to have to hire someone to help me enjoy it."

She smiled, and he shifted position in the bed, but then grimaced.

"No," he said. "To tell you the truth, I feel like crap, Jackie." He reached out and took her hand. "This here is Jackie. She's an angel—just look at her."

Carson looked. The woman was tall, with pale skin and red hair. She looked like Arla.

"This is my son," Dean said to Jackie. "One of 'em." Jackie smiled at Carson.

"Mr. Bravo, they said you want another nicotine patch, is that so?" she said.

"Oh, you know that's right. Jesus, put those things all over me, would you darlin'?"

She laughed. "I'll get you *one*, Mr. Bravo, how about that?"

"I'll show you where to put it," he said. He still held her hand. With her free hand, she placed a chart on the bed and flipped through a few pages.

"What day is it, Mr. Bravo?" she said.

Dean puffed his cheeks, exhaled. "Oh, Jesus, Jackie, you ask me that all the time. How do I know?"

"Come on, Mr. Bravo. Give it a try."

"Sunday?"

Carson blinked.

"It's Wednesday," Jackie said. "What month is it?"

Dean looked away from them, stared across the room, embarrassed. "Jesus," he said. "It's April, I guess. I don't know."

"It's August," Jackie said gently.

"Well, Jackie," Dean said. "It's no wonder I'm forgetting things. I'm old. That's why I don't know crap."

She smiled, extracted her hand from his, and patted his arm. "You know plenty," she said.

"I don't know crap," he said again. He grunted, shifted position, slid his hands down beneath his lower back. "Jesus," he said, and his voice had become very small. Jackie reached into the pocket of her smock and drew out a nicotine patch. She opened it and placed it on his arm.

"Thank you, darlin'," he said, and Jackie winked at him and left the room.

Under the window, the sleeping man made a small, wet noise. He was attached to a series of machines from which an unsettling series of beeps punctured the atmosphere in the room. Dean had turned back to the TV.

"I really want to know if this son of a bitch is still alive," he said, squinting at the screen. Hackman wore a bright white wig and was performing some sort of a burlesque. "He's old, right? Older than me?"

"You're not that old."

"Oh, yeah? Tell that to my liver."

A cluster of quiet movement appeared in the doorway. Carson shuffled his chair closer to Dean's bed as a small group of people filed past him: a short man about his own age, a mousy woman who could have been the man's wife, and a papery old lady, thin as a wafer, with fat rubber shoes and an enormous chain of heavy plastic beads around her neck. They nodded at Dean, and the man raised a quick hand at Carson. "Don't let us disturb you," he stage-whispered, flapping his hands in Carson's direction. He was clearly the cheery sort, even in this setting. "We're just here to sit with Poppa." He waited until the two women had taken a few steps past him, then leaned in closer to Carson. "My wife's father," he murmured conspiratorially. "His name is Edward." Carson did not reply.

The cheery man pulled three straight-backed chairs up to the side of the sleeping man's bed, and they all sat down expectantly, as if for a matinee.

Carson stood abruptly, scratched his head, sat down again. He pursed his lips and straightened his back. *All right. Get this done.*

"So," he began. "Dad. We have an offer on the house in Utina."

Dean leveled the remote at the TV and pushed a button. "God-damn," he said. "I can't hear what he's saying." He banged the remote against the metal rail on the side of his bed. "God-damn batteries. Lean over into that cabinet, get me some new ones, would you?"

Carson hesitated, then opened the drawer in the cabinet behind him.

"Yep. No, not the drawer. The shelf. On the right," Dean said.

Across the room, the cheery man chuckled. He leaned forward and adjusted a limp strand of hair on Edward's forehead. The old woman sighed with what might have been grief. Or resignation. Or boredom.

"They're just waiting," Dean said, gesturing to Edward's family and making no effort to lower his voice. "They come every day. It's going to be any day now. Shit, maybe any *minute*. That's what you do, you get to the end. You're just waiting."

Carson buried his head in the cabinet, pretending not to hear.

"Think of all the waiting you do in your life," Dean said. "You're waiting on lines, right? You're waiting in traffic. You're waiting on doctors. You're waiting on *women*. Jesus, am I right? And then one day you're just waiting. Period. Just waiting. Waiting for nothing."

The cheery man nodded his head, tapped his knees. Dean leaned his head back on the pillow and closed his eyes.

"Poor dumb shit," Dean said, and though there was no telling whether he was referring to Edward or the cheery man, or even to Carson, the man nodded again, then giggled and leaned over to say something to his wife. Carson straightened, held up his empty hands.

"There's no batteries," he said.

"I said the drawer, dummy," Dean said. "Triple As."

"You didn't say the drawer. You said the shelf."

"Are you arguing with me?"

"No."

"Yes, you are. Look in the drawer, dummy."

My God! Carson retrieved the batteries from the drawer and handed them to his father. Dean wrestled them into the remote with more than a little fanfare, then punched the volume button until the wall mount on the TV shuddered with the intensity of the sound.

"Dad. Dad. *Dad*," Carson said. The cheery man laughed again, and the old woman turned a baleful face toward them both. The cheery man's wife appeared not to notice anything.

Now Gene Hackman was dancing out of the nightclub and toward a waiting limo. The street where the limo was parked was packed with revelers; they reached toward Hackman as he stumbled toward the limo, his face a comic mask of confusion. Sister Sledge sang "We Are Family."

"Ah, shit, it's over now," Dean said. He turned off the TV. "Where's your wife? Where's Elizabeth?" he said suddenly.

Carson was surprised. He hadn't known his father was even aware that he and Elizabeth were married. When Dean left they'd all still been teenagers. Clearly Dean had stayed in touch with someone from Utina. But who?

"Home," Carson said. The sound of his wife's name was jarring, like a tap from behind on your bumper from a car coming up too fast.

"Whose home?" Dean said. "Your home?" He turned to face Carson. "She hasn't left you yet?"

The cheery man coughed. Carson felt a strange salty sensation in the back of his own throat, and he closed his eyes and thought for a second about how many years it had been since he had cried. Twenty? Twenty-five? What would it feel like? He wondered if this would be a good time. He remembered crying once when he was fifteen, a few years before Will died, when he'd had a cat named Violet who had crawled up into the warm carburetor of Dean's truck on a cold January night and was bludgeoned with the fan when Dean started it up in the morning. Carson had crouched barefoot on the cold pine straw in the driveway, staring at Violet, her small paws pristine but one side of her head dented in a very unnatural way. He'd sobbed like a baby, even when Dean walked past and smacked him on the back of the head and told him to stop being such a pussy. Dean had paused, had chuckled at the pun before going to get a shovel and a plastic bag. Carson opened his eyes, shook his head, tried to clear his brain. *Don't be a pussy.*

Dean's feet were crossed at the ankles. His socks were threadbare.

"So what's wrong with you?" Carson said. "Are you sick? Injured? What?" The sudden silence left by the darkened TV was unsettling. Edward's family said nothing. Carson had the feeling they were listening to him. His voice had an unfamiliar solicitousness.

"Aw, I got into a little scrap," Dean said. He laughed. "With a woman. Can you beat that shit?"

"A *woman?*"

"Yeah. Sandy Vanderhorn. She laid me out. Took me to the ground. We were at this bar, right? We were having some drinks. She's a big woman, too. Two hundred pounds, I'd guess. Dumber than a box of hammers, too, but that's not the point, I guess. She got mad on the way out, and she took me to the curb. You ever been laid out by a two-hundred-pound woman, Carson?"

Carson shook his head. Was he serious?

"Well, don't. She broke my cheek." Carson stared at him. "No, not that cheek," Dean said, pointing to his face. "The other cheek." He patted his buttocks. "The right one. Right here."

"You can't break that kind of cheek, Dad."

"Well *I* did. Don't tell me it ain't broke. My damn ass is broke and you're telling me it ain't? Sandy Vanderhorn took me to the curb and came down on top of me. Holy shit, it hurts like hell, too."

"What about your memory?" Carson said.

"What about it?"

"Why can't you remember things? You didn't know what day it is, what month."

"Oh, I remember plenty," Dean said. "I'm just a little foggy on the recent stuff. The details. They say I've pickled my brain—I don't doubt it. Shit. I've drank so much I could probably quit drinking right now and I'd still be drunk if I lived to a hundred."

"So why don't you?" Carson said.

"Why don't I what?"

"Quit drinking."

Dean looked at him, bemused. "That's a good one, Carson," he said. "Here's another one—why don't *you*?"

Carson held his gaze a beat and then tried another tack.

"Would you like to know how everyone is doing?" he said. "Your family?"

"I know how they're doing," Dean said.

"And how is that?"

"I keep informed."

"So you've kept informed, but you've kept your distance, that it?" Carson said, and immediately he was sorry. Keep it quick. Keep it clean. In and out. Dean did not answer, but he looked at Carson darkly.

"All right," Carson said. "So you know about the deal, then. The offer on the properties."

"That Cryder fella explained it."

"A big sale," Carson said. "Big money. Millions."

"So I hear."

"Frank's meeting with the guy today to find out the particulars," Carson said. "So there's only one problem."

Dean raised his eyebrows.

"Mom doesn't want to sell."

Dean smiled. "That surprises you?"

"Not particularly. But it's a problem."

"So you want the money, and you want me to help you get it," Dean said flatly.

"We need the money. All of us. Arla included. Sofia included. If you're so informed, you must know that Sofia's still out to lunch. In fact, more than ever."

Dean's face clouded over.

"So we need the money," Carson said again. "And you can help make it happen."

"What makes you think Arla's going to listen to me?"

"I don't know," Carson said honestly. "I don't know why she should. But I think she will." He took a breath. "And you're still married. So it's half yours."

Dean turned his head on the pillow. His eyes had a hollow quality that both frightened and annoyed Carson, and he felt his own eyes dart toward Edward's family.

Edward rasped in his bed. "Poor Poppa," said the cheery man. "Poor old Poppa." Edward rasped again. It sounded like his entire windpipe was constricted. His body shook violently in his bed. Carson saw one bare foot jut out from beneath the sheet, the toenail yellowed and flaking like old fiberglass. The two women turned their baleful faces from the window to gaze at him. "Now what are we going to do with you, Poppa?" the cheery man said. He patted Edward's leg as if he were a mildly disobedient child. "You just settle down, now," he said.

Carson got up and paced.

"Relax, why don't you," Dean said.

Carson sighed. He sat down.

"He's in bad shape," Carson said quietly, gesturing to Edward.

"Don't pay no attention to him. Listen. I got a joke for you, Carson. What do Richard Nixon, Andrew Johnson, and Bill Clinton have in common?"

Carson shook his head.

"Come on," Dean said.

Carson thought about it. "They were all impeached," he concluded. "Or almost impeached."

"Wrong," Dean said. "They were all named after their peckers." He laughed. "Get it? Dick, Johnson, and Willie!"

Carson stared at him. His knee started jiggling.

"Why are you so antsy?" Dean said.

"I need to get to work. I have a meeting with a client."

"So you'll reschedule." Dean grimaced, repositioned himself on the bed. "Damn, my cheek hurts like a mother," he said. "Tell me something. This client. A woman, right?"

"What's the difference?"

Dean smiled. "Oh, there's a very big difference, or hadn't you noticed?"

"I think you're trying to imply something."

"That you're screwing around on your wife? Nah. If I meant that, I'd come right out and say it."

Carson squinted at him. "Is that what you're saying?"

"I don't know. Is that what you're doing?"

"No, I'm not," Carson said. "I'm sitting here with you."

"Pffft," Dean said.

Across the room the cheery man and his family had settled back around Edward's bed. They were very quiet, and Carson was now sure they were listening.

"She leave you yet?" Dean said.

"No," Carson lied.

"She should."

Carson felt the blood rush to his face, and he struggled to keep his fists unclenched. He leaned forward in his chair.

"Are you kidding me?" he said. "You think I'm going to take lessons in ethics from *you*? What are you, the fucking *pope*? Let's get Mom on the phone, get her opinion. Since you're such a *saint*." He leaned back, exhaled. This was all wrong. This wasn't supposed to be happening. Quick visit. In. Out. Git 'r done. Don't get riled. He's an old man. He can't help it. *Bullshit,* Carson thought. A picture of Violet the cat appeared in his mind. Next came a picture of Arla sitting at the kitchen table, alone, her battered cane across the room on the floor, out of reach.

"I'm no saint," Dean said.

"You got that right."

"I'm just telling you you're an idiot, if you screw it up with Elizabeth."

"Mind your own business."

"This is my business," Dean said. "This is the only business I got left." He punched the bedclothes. He pushed himself off the back of the raised bed and leaned in to Carson. "You throw that woman away for the sake of some dumb pussy, you'll regret it," he said.

"What a lovely sentiment."

"I'm serious. You listen to me."

"What do you know? You don't regret shit," Carson said, and even as he said it, he looked at Dean and was struck by something in his father's face he'd never seen before, and though he couldn't quite put his finger on what it was, it seemed to be something close to sorrow. Dean's voice dropped to a whisper, and he actually put his hand out and touched Carson's wrist. His hand was rough. Carson fought the instinct to recoil.

"I know what I'm talking about," Dean said. "And I regret more than shit."

Edward's rasping had grown louder. He shuddered again in his bed. "Ooh," said the cheery man. "Oh, my. I don't think he looks good at all." Edward's face was waxy, with a bluish tint. "I don't think he's getting any air. I think we need the nurse, don't you, hon?" He pushed the call button at the side of the bed, then turned to Carson.

"I think this could be it," he said. He shook his head ruefully, then glanced out the window.

A different nurse came in, followed by a man in blue scrubs. They moved to Edward's bed and started making adjustments to equipment. Edward's breathing was tortured now, a straining, hideous sound like a clogged vacuum cleaner, and Carson wanted to cover his ears, wanted to run, wanted the fucker to hurry up and die and put them all out of their misery. "Call the doctor," the nurse said.

Edward's family was standing now. They leaned over him. The two women held his hands and peered into his face, speaking softly. The cheery man put his arm around his wife and nodded. "It's okay, Poppa," he said. "It's okay to go. We're all here, Poppa."

Carson wished someone would cover Edward's foot with the sheet. He stared at the family, and at the man on the bed. He couldn't imagine any of the Bravos acting so solicitously toward Dean, had his father been on his own deathbed, which by all appearances today he was not. Not yet, anyway. Carson felt suddenly a bit light-headed, realizing he was about to witness the proverbial end of the road for Edward, a man he certainly did not know or love, but for whom he suddenly cared a great deal. He was sorry for Edward, to have come to this: the coldness of the hospital, the idiotic prattle of the son-in-law, the baleful faces of the wife and daughter—all of it such shabby and uninspired detritus from what might have been a long life filled with love and hate and fear and joy and at least a few small moments of significance. *Not with a bang, but a whimper.* T. S. Eliot. Funny, he remembered that line just now. Isn't that just the shit?

The news. The shooting. In that building on the TV downstairs—there lay a dead man, too. Bang, bang. And that man had had nobody standing over him, except his killer, nobody holding his hand, rubbing his arm, telling him it was okay. It was *not* okay. And there was a good chance the killer had by now turned his gun on himself—isn't that how these things always ended? Dead people, everywhere. He shivered again. Why did they keep these places so cold?

"Did you hear me, Carson?" Dean said.

Carson looked at him.

"I said, I regret more than shit," Dean said.

"You should," Carson said.

"Well, I do."

"Is that an apology?"

Dean stared at the ceiling. "How can I apologize to him now?" he asked quietly, and Carson realized that Dean was thinking of Will, and his chest hurt then, because that was the question he'd asked himself for so long, and the answer always came back the same way: *you can't.*

He suddenly realized the rasping noise had subsided, been replaced by a slow, steady wheezing. Edward was still breathing. A tinge of pink had returned to his face.

"What's happening?" the cheery man said.

"He's stabilizing," the nurse said. "The meds have relaxed his trachea. I think he's okay. I don't think this was his time."

"Oh," the cheery man said. He hesitated. "Well, what do you know," he said softly.

Carson turned back to Dean.

"Why don't you get me the hell out of here?" Dean said.

"Brilliant idea," Carson said. "What do I have to do?"

"Just sign the papers," Dean said. "I'm not incarcerated, for Christ's sake. They said they'll release me to family."

Family. Holy crap. If that's what you want to call it.

"Get dressed," he said.

"I am dressed."

"Then get up. We're leaving."

"Where we going?"

Carson's head hurt. His hands were cold, and he needed a drink. He looked at his father, his strange, sorry, sotted father, and he raised his eyebrows, shrugged at the question. "Where do you think?" he said. Dean nodded.

THIRTEEN

"It's worth just listening to what he has to say, don't you think?" Frank said. This had been the refrain he and Carson had been repeating to Arla for weeks, and it had proven, evidently, a fairly successful strategy in getting Arla to agree to the meeting with Alonzo Cryder. Now, Frank was sitting uncomfortably close to his mother, who was wedged in the middle seat of the cab of his pickup truck as they headed down Seminary Street to park at Bait/Karaoke. Next to Arla, looking equally uncomfortable, sat Morgan, dressed in a pair of khaki pants, a short-sleeved dress shirt, and, for the first time in Frank's memory, a tie. In a last-minute maneuver, Carson had opted not to attend the meeting, though Frank, irritated, could not fathom why. "Get the scoop," Carson had said. "Fill me in later."

They parked in the sandy driveway behind a black Mercedes, and Frank gave a perfunctory wave to Tip Breen, who was moping on a bench outside the Lil' Champ, before helping his mother climb out of the truck. She wore a pair of loose-fitting black pants and a fuchsia blouse, which made her hair, increasingly gray but still streaked with threads of red, command attention. Sixty-two, but Arla could still command attention. Oh, could she.

"My Lord, what happened to this tree?" she said, staring at the palm tree at the edge of Mac's driveway, which featured a deep gash along the trunk.

"Somebody musta hit it," Frank said. He didn't have the energy to elaborate. "Come on," he said. "Let's do this."

"Look at that Tip Breen," Arla whispered. "He is a *mess.*" Frank gave him another glance and felt a jump in his stomach. Tip *was* a mess. He looked wretched. He looked desperate. He shook his head. He couldn't worry about Tip Breen. Not today.

"True that," Morgan said. "He look like the dog been keeping *him* under the porch." He offered his arm to Arla. "Let's get inside before he come over wanting to talk to us." Arla took his arm, and they walked down the driveway.

"Nice car, Frank," Morgan said, gesturing to the Mercedes. "You see that?"

Frank nodded. Nobody in Utina had a car like that. Never had. Alonzo Cryder. He was here. Frank's cell phone vibrated, and he looked at the screen, saw it was Susan calling. She'd called almost every day since the accident with the Mazda, badgering him for the money to repair the car. He pushed DECLINE. They walked around the building and into the back door to access Mac's office.

"Come in, come in," Mac said, flapping his hands wildly. "Come in, plenty of room for everybody." He'd set up four resin chairs in an awkward semicircle around his desk. Classy, Frank thought.

Alonzo Cryder was already seated, but he rose and extended his hand when Frank, Arla, and Morgan entered the room. Frank had been mostly correct in his sight-unseen assessment of Cryder when they'd first spoken over the phone—the rubbery jowls, the tight oxford shirt. But Cryder was a short, round-shouldered black man, with hair cropped unnaturally short and treated with some sort of glittering gel. He wore expensive-looking glasses and a tie. He crinkled his nose repeatedly, sniffed as though he was fighting a sinus condition.

"Good afternoon, everyone," Cryder said. "Mrs. Bravo," he said, taking her hand. "It is a pleasure to meet you. A *pleasure.*" Arla narrowed her eyes, sat down.

"My Lord, it's hot in here, Mac," she said. "Don't you have the air on?" She picked up a file off Mac's desk and fanned herself with it.

"I'll set it lower, Arla," Mac said. He stepped into the hallway, bellowed for Seth to adjust the AC, then stepped back into the office.

"Now—" he said.

"Thank you for coming," Cryder said, smiling and nodding at Arla.

"You're welcome," she said. "Although I will tell you I did not have any choice."

Cryder laughed, a crowing sound, raw.

"That's funny," he said. He sniffed.

"Good stuff," Mac said, laughing.

Frank looked at Morgan, rolled his eyes.

"And Mr. Bravo," Cryder said. "*Frank.* I know when we first spoke on the phone you felt a little taken aback by our offer. A little hostile, in fact, if I may say. But I do hope this personal meeting will offer us all an opportunity to mend fences, to start over in good faith." Cryder sniffed.

"Mr. Cryder, we don't have a lot of time," Frank said. "Morgan and I need to get to the restaurant. Can we go ahead and discuss the particulars?"

Mac drummed his fingers on the desk.

"Absolutely, Frank, absolutely," Cryder said. "It's really very simple. Mrs. Bravo," he said, turning once again to Arla and leaning forward. His voice had dropped an octave, and he peered at her meaningfully. He might have been ready to propose to her, Frank thought disgustedly. "My company, Vista Properties, would like to buy your home *and* your restaurant." He turned to look at Morgan. "And, Mr. Moore, we would like to buy your parcel, as well. Now," he continued, looking from Arla to Morgan importantly, "we are aware that you have owned these parcels for quite some time. And we know this might feel like a very big step—"

"Not for me, it don't," Morgan said.

"—and that's why we want you to have every piece of information we can provide. We want you to be able to make an informed decision."

"Only one piece of information we need," Morgan said, "and that's how much?"

"Well," chuckled Cryder. "Isn't that the million-dollar question?"

"I don't know," Morgan said. "Is it?"

Cryder laughed again. All this laughing was making Frank sick. He didn't see what was funny. Arla's hands shook on top of her handbag, and he felt a pang. He wanted to put his arm around her shoulders, but it was not that kind of place, and they were not that kind of people.

"Let's cut to it, Mr. Cryder," Morgan said. "We need to know the deal. You want to buy our land? Mine and the Bravos'? They's three pieces of property."

"Indeed."

"And we may not all want the same thing."

"Understood."

Morgan looked pained. He turned to Arla, started to say something, then stopped. He turned back to Cryder.

"Like me, for example," Morgan said. "I'm interested in your deal, Mr. Cryder."

Cryder nodded, smiled.

"But I can't say the same for Mrs. Bravo," Morgan said. Cryder stopped smiling, and the room fell silent. Arla, inexplicably, looked small in the office chair, her shoulders slumped.

"Mrs. Bravo," Cryder said. "How do you feel about the prospect of selling your house, and your restaurant, to Vista Properties?"

Arla looked at him.

"I feel shitty about it, Mr. Cryder," she said.

He cleared his throat. "Could you be more specific?"

"No. I don't believe I can."

Frank smiled.

"And your husband?"

"What about him?" Arla said.

"What are his thoughts about selling?"

"I wouldn't know, Mr. Cryder."

"I see," he said. He sniffed. "Are you aware, Mrs. Bravo, that we are prepared to offer you a significant sum of money for the properties?"

"That's what I hear," Arla said.

"Are you interested in knowing the amount?"

Arla sighed. "I think that's why we're all here, Mr. Cryder."

He nodded.

He pulled a sheaf of papers out of his briefcase and slid the stack across Mac's desk. Morgan leaned forward. Arla remained straight-backed, staring impassively at Cryder. "Just spit it out, Cryder," Frank said, surprising himself and everyone in the office with the timbre of his voice. He hadn't meant to sound quite so angry.

"Eight and a half million," Cryder said. "For all three parcels. You'd split it accordingly." He nodded from the Bravos to Morgan.

Frank felt the energy change in the room, but before he could even glance in his mother's direction, Mac interjected.

"That's bullshit," he said. "That's just insulting."

Arla's knuckles had tightened on her purse, and Morgan's face was taut, his eyes wide.

"That's our starting offer," said Cryder, and he nodded knowingly at Mac.

Mac shot Frank a glance that told him to keep his mouth shut.

"But let me ask you something, Mr. Cryder," Morgan said, finally regaining his voice. "Do we all have to sell together?"

Cryder chuckled. He pushed his glasses up on the bridge of his nose, nodded jovially. "Well, of course, Mr. Moore—Morgan? May I? Of course. The properties are useless to us alone. We can't build half a marina, can we?" Frank noted that Cryder had dropped the pretense of his boss acquiring the properties for a family retreat. He'd discovered, no doubt, that word traveled fast in Utina, and that the plans for the marina would be outed soon enough. "It's all or nothing, folks," Cryder said, and he laughed again. He might have been at a comedy club, it was all so amusing, it seemed to Frank. "We sure hope we can all work together on this."

Arla's hands still shook. Through the window behind Cryder's head, Tip Breen stood framed in the door of the Lil' Champ, looking sorrowfully out toward the water, and a fat rogue cloud slid in front of the sun, erasing the long shadows of Seminary Street.

All or nothing.

The lunch counter at Sterling's Drugstore was crowded, but Frank managed to find three seats together at one end, where he, Arla, and Morgan could see both into the kitchen and straight out the front door. The counter—a long, speckled Formica surface with chrome edging along the front—was at the rear of the drugstore, past the aisles of cold remedies and Ace bandages, feminine hygiene products and FiberCon. They sat down together, Arla in the middle, and Frank looked around.

He'd worked here at Sterling's as a teenager, before Will died, before Dean left Utina and Arla bought Uncle Henry's. Frank had worked the lunch counter, busing the empty dishes and used silverware, plates slick with the residue of cherry pie and meat loaf, mangled French fries smeared in runny puddles of ketchup. He'd worked his way up to the grill, flipping burgers and sizzling onions on the stovetop, shredding hash brown potatoes, brewing pot after pot of dark acidic coffee. That was back when Sterling's had still been owned by Vaughn Weeden, Mac and George's father, who'd long since retired and now spent his days watching Judge Joe Brown and listening to the grass grow outside his three-story Victorian in South Utina. Sterling's and its accompanying lunch counter were currently owned by a compact, hyperactive woman named Cathy and her less-than-compact partner Magda, a voluptuous Portuguese beauty who was once the object of unrequited love for most of Utina's male population until the realization eventually dawned, en masse, it seemed, that Cathy and Magda were partners not just in business but in life. "Whadda waste," the men said, looking longingly at Magda's thick black ponytail, pulled up in a hairnet while she worked the breakfast counter, and then they'd fall silent, victims for a few moments of the unavoidable mental images of Magda and Cathy after lights out. "Lord have mercy," George Weeden said more than once, scratching his head.

Today, Frank regarded the lunch counter. It wasn't much different from his bar at Uncle Henry's, the same long lines of demanding patrons, the same bustling back and forth behind the narrow counter, the same slopping and mopping and faint smell of bleach on worn gray rags. The only difference was that these patrons weren't drunk. But *Jesus*, he thought, remembering his high school days here at Sterling's, was he doomed to spend his entire life slinging food and booze for the uninspired, unambitious, unwashed citizens of Utina?

Cathy stood in front of them across the counter, bouncing on the balls of her feet. Her hair was cut in a tight, curly cap. "Know what you want?" she said. She tipped her head and looked at them impatiently. Sterling's lunch counter was not a place to linger over the menu.

"Just a burger," Frank said quickly. Cathy's eyes darted to Arla.

"Oh, let me see . . ." Arla began. She rummaged in her purse for her glasses. Cathy's eyes jumped to Morgan.

"Meat loaf platter," Morgan said. Cathy snapped up Morgan's and Frank's menus, put them in a wire rack behind the counter, and returned to hover in front of Arla.

"Do you have any specials today?" Arla said.

Cathy looked at Frank.

"No specials, Mom," he said. "Come on, just order something quick. Order a tuna melt. You like tuna melts."

"I don't know if I want a tuna melt today," Arla said.

"I'll be back in a minute," Morgan said. "Just need to see a man about a horse." He got up from his stool and moved toward the men's room.

"Tuna's good," Cathy said.

"Well, I know it's good," Arla said. "I just might want to try something *different* for a change."

Cathy went away, came back, bounced some more, looked over her shoulder. Magda had Frank's old place at the griddle. She moved powerfully, aggressively, sliding the spatula under each hamburger patty and flipping it higher in the air than was really necessary, Frank concluded. He watched as her breasts slid back and forth under her T-shirt. Damn.

Arla sighed. "Oh, all right," she said. "I don't know if I really want anything different. I guess I'll just have the tuna melt after all, Cathy."

Cathy strode toward the grill and barked the lunch orders to Magda, who gave her a thumbs-up and threw another burger on the grill. Efficiency. Frank had to admire the efficiency. These two could give him and Morgan a run for their money in a kitchen.

"Don't be like me, Frank," Arla said suddenly. "Don't be afraid of change. Don't be crippled by fear. *Crippled*," she said. "Ha! That's a good one."

Frank was debating how to process the comment when a bell jangled on the front door, and Doreen Bailey walked straight up the stationery aisle toward the lunch counter.

"Oh, Lord have mercy," Arla said.

Doreen had been a teller at Utina's People's Guarantee Bank for as long as Frank could remember, though she and Arla went even further back than that. At eighteen, Doreen had been married to Dean's brother Huff, and she'd been soundly humiliated by Huff's unremitting philandering before he earned his extended sentence for theft and battery. She'd divorced Huff before the warden had finished the strip search. And since her liberation from the Bravo family she'd done everything humanly possible to berate, begrudge, belittle, and beleaguer the Bravos who still remained in Utina. "It was a long time ago," Arla had reminded Doreen on more than one occasion. "I think maybe it's time for you to move on." And indeed, Doreen had remarried. Mr. Tom Bailey was a cloying, mousy man with about as much likelihood of engaging in an extramarital fling as a pig has of flying, given the fact that no woman, save Doreen, would have him. Doreen had raised two stocky, simple daughters and had enjoyed a stable if small-minded career as head teller and closing officer in Utina's one and only financial institution. But she'd never forgotten the pain Huff Bravo had caused her. And she didn't intend to let anyone else forget it, either.

"Hello, Arla," she said now, maneuvering her considerable girth past an end cap of Maybelline compacts and approaching Arla and Frank at the lunch counter. "How you doing these days?" She forced a thin smile that came out more like a grimace. "How're the *Bravos*?"

"Fine, Doreen," Arla said.

"Mmhmm," Doreen said. "And Sofia, how is *she*?" She raised her eyebrows knowingly.

"Fine," Arla said. "We're all fine."

"What've you been up to, Doreen?" Frank said. Throw her a bone, he thought. She's a sad lady.

"Oh, you know," Doreen said. "Working, stuff."

"Lots of real estate sales going on these days," Frank said. "You all busy with loans?"

"Huh," Doreen said. "*We're* not getting the loans. Talk to Bank of America. These new buyers, they're all from out of town. They don't want to do business with a local bank. They want the big glitzie-bitzies." She leaned forward, peered into the kitchen.

"I just came to pick up my lunch," she said. "I get takeout. I don't like to eat in here." She lowered her voice, turned to Arla. "They're lezzies, you know."

"What do I care?" Arla said. "They make a good tuna melt."

Doreen sighed again. "Oh, well," she said. "Anyway. These yuppies, buying up the neighborhoods, I can't say it's a bad thing, I guess."

"I can," Frank said. "I'm pretty sick of the fool who built next door to me."

"Yes, but Frank," Doreen said. "Think of it. They're cleaning up the streets, at least. We got some real trash around here, you know? Some real trash. You know somebody's been shooting out the parking lot lights over where they're building the new Publix? *Shooting.* My God, what is that? That's gangs, is what it is. Gangs."

Oh, for Christ's sake. "No gang is going to waste its time in Utina, Doreen," Frank said.

"Oh, I don't know Frank. We got some real trash here. *T-R-A-S-H.* You know what I mean," she said to Arla. "So if these yuppies want to come in and rehab some of these old places in South Utina, for example, they're doing us all a favor, if you ask me. Brightening it up a notch." She winked, nodded at Arla.

"You mean whitening it up a notch?" Arla said.

"Well, *yes,*" Doreen said. "I do. And it's about damn time."

"Oh, Doreen," Arla said.

"What? What, Arla? I'm just saying what we all know is true. I'm just saying some of these blacks—you know, *some* of them—well, they're not doing much for the property values, now are they? I mean—"

Morgan returned from the men's room, and Doreen clamped her jaw shut.

"Mrs. Bailey," he said. He nodded.

"I need to pick up my order," Doreen said. She moved to the middle of the lunch counter and sat down on a stool that had just been vacated. Morgan watched her, bemused, it seemed to Frank.

"You know why I got disowned by my mama?" Morgan said to Frank and Arla. "I was twenty-two, and I got disowned. You know why?"

"No," Arla said. "Why, Morgan?"

"For marryin' a white woman," he said. "It works both ways."

"I never knew that, Morgan. All these years," Arla said. "Well, where on Earth is she now?"

"Mama died years ago."

"No, your *wife*."

"Oh, I don't know." He chuckled. "It didn't end well."

Arla sighed. "It never does," she said.

Cathy brought the food, and for a few moments they were quiet. Then Frank put his burger down, took a long swallow of Coke, and turned to his mother.

"Mom," he said. "What are we going to do?"

"The sale?" she said.

"The sale."

She put her fork down. She stared straight ahead, over the lunch counter, watching Cathy and Magda hustle through the lunch orders.

"Sofia does not like change," she said. "She can't cope, you know."

"We can take care of Sofia," Frank said quietly. "We can get her some help."

"She doesn't need help," Arla said sharply. "She needs *me*."

Frank looked away.

"Morgan," Arla said. "You want to sell?"

"I do," he said, after a moment.

Frank looked back at his mother and waited, but Arla said nothing.

"Arla," Morgan said. "You want to sell?"

"I don't, Morgan," she said. And then she started to cry.

Frank froze. He'd never, ever seen Arla cry. Not when Will died. Not when Dean left. Never. He knew she wept alone, in her room, in the bathroom, sitting down at the concrete table at the edge of the Intracoastal. But never like this. Never openly, unabashedly, unapologetically. His throat constricted. Oh, Jesus in heaven, this was killing her. We are going to kill her.

And then Morgan was at her side, his arm around her shoulder offering a comfort and a salve that wasn't Frank's to give, so Frank simply sat on his stool stupidly, impotently. He didn't know how to touch his mother, didn't know how to speak to her, *really* speak to her, speak *with* her. He didn't know.

Morgan stood next to Arla's stool and hugged her to his shoulder, patted her wiry red hair with his scarred brown hand. "All right, now, Arla," he said. "All right. We gonna work this out, Arla. We gonna."

Near the register, Doreen stared at them, her eyes wide, her mouth open.

Arla sniffled, wiped her eyes with a paper napkin, and cleared her throat. She looked up from Morgan's shoulder.

"Take a picture, why don't you, Doreen," Arla called over. "It'll last longer."

The ride back to Aberdeen was quiet. Morgan stared out the window, and when they pulled up to the house, he slipped out of the truck and turned to offer Arla his arm while she climbed down. Carson's car was in the driveway. Brilliant, Frank thought. Fantastic. Just what we need.

"Thank you, Morgan," Arla said quietly.

"Of course, Arla," Morgan said. He stood awkwardly, holding Arla's purse until she straightened her clothes and stood up straight with her cane. He handed her the purse and helped her position the strap over her shoulder, and Frank loved him then, for that small kindness. Nearly three million dollars. For a man who had shelled three million shrimp. It seemed like a pretty good deal to Frank. But then, what kind of judge was he?

Elizabeth appeared at the screen door, pushed it open and walked down the porch steps. There was something different in her gait today, something urgent.

"Frank?" she said. "I think you need to come in with your mother. Before you go to the restaurant. I think you better come in."

Frank put the truck in park.

"What's wrong?" he said, but she'd turned to go back into the house, holding Arla by the hand.

"Morgan, you can wait a minute?" he said. Morgan nodded, and the two men followed Arla and Elizabeth up the rough gray steps of Aberdeen. *Carson.* No doubt Carson was in the house, getting on Elizabeth's last nerve, waiting to find out about the offer from Vista, his salivary glands probably kicked into overdrive at the thought of hearing exactly how much money was on the line. Frank set his jaw and walked down the dim hallway into the kitchen, ready to start it up with his brother. *Give her time,* he was ready to say. *Give her some God-damned time.*

An old man Frank did not recognize sat at the kitchen table. He was gaunt and sinewy, wearing a black T-shirt and a loose pair of jeans belted tight around the waist. Sofia and Biaggio were leaning against the kitchen counter. Carson sat at the table across from the old man, a nervous grin creeping across his face as he watched first Elizabeth and Arla, then Frank and Morgan, enter the kitchen.

Arla made it all the way into the room before she stopped short and put an arm out in front of Elizabeth.

"Oh," she said, and that was all, and then Elizabeth, God love that woman, was there with one of the unclaimed chairs from the kitchen table. She dragged it quickly across the kitchen and parked it in front of the refrigerator, where Arla promptly sat, staring at the man at the table.

Frank looked at him, too, feeling the faint gnaw of familiarity for a long moment before the full force of understanding hit him, and then the man spoke.

"Well, here we are," Dean said. He was looking hard at Arla. "The whole fam-damily, what's left of us. Can you beat this shit?"

"Are you insane?" Frank said. "Are you completely insane?"

He and Carson stood at the edge of the waterway. Inside the house, Sofia, Elizabeth, and Bell were making hot dogs— what else could they do?—while Biaggio sat at the kitchen table, making small talk with Dean. Morgan had left on foot for Uncle Henry's, headed through the old footpath. "Ain't no place for me in this scene," he'd said to Frank, patting him sympathetically on the shoulder. Arla had retreated upstairs to her bedroom, the sight of the husband who had unceremoniously walked out of her life twenty years ago now sitting at her kitchen table proving simply too much to bear.

And there they all were. The Bravos. All right here at Aberdeen as though Dean had just walked in from a shift at Rayonier instead of having been dragged back here by Carson after a twenty-year foray into boozing, brawling, and God-knows-what-else. They should have thrown Dean out on his ear, told him to take a long walk off a short pier. Don't let the door hit you on the ass on the way out, they should have said. Instead they were browning hot dogs, asking him if the blue guest room would be all right, or did he prefer the couch? Frank couldn't believe it—but wait, no, actually he could. If anybody could ignore an elephant in the living room and march on doggedly, asking each other to *please pass the mustard* and *where are we keeping the extra towels these days* it would have to be this family. Jesus. Out of control. Once he'd recovered from his shock at seeing Dean at the table, he'd grabbed Carson by the arm, told him to meet him outside.

"Are you trying to kill her?" Frank said, once they were beyond earshot of the house.

"Of course not," Carson said. "I'm trying to help her."

"By bringing him here? How is that going to help her?"

"Frank," Carson said. He held his hands up in an obnoxious way, and Frank wanted to hit him. "We've got to get her to deal on this real estate thing. We can't let her miss this opportunity. They're still married, which means he's still invested. This isn't something I made up. This was inevitable. He has to be involved."

"Like hell he does," Frank said. "He hasn't been involved in anything for twenty years, and now the only reason he's back is because he smells money. And you did this—you spilled the beans to him and brought him back here and now you've got him sitting in her house like he owns the God-damn place."

"He does. He's her husband. He owns half of everything."

"Bullshit," Frank said. "There's got to be some statute of limitations or something—some abandonment clause or whatever. No way he can still lay claim to anything."

"It's Florida law. He owns half. Cryder checked it all out, Frank. He's the one who *found* him, for Christ's sake. I just went and got him. It was Cryder tracked him down."

"And where was he?"

Carson snorted, an ugly sound. "Hospital. Jacksonville. Fight."

"Jesus Christ," Frank said. His father, fresh from a hospital, probably detoxing at this very moment, now sitting in the kitchen and ready to insert himself back into this tenuous family for the sake of his own financial gain. It infuriated him. He'd spent the last two decades trying to protect Arla, trying to make things easier for her, trying to atone for what he'd done. For what they'd all done. He was pissed at himself for not realizing Dean could still be a factor. And he was pissed at Dean for coming back here. But he was even more angry at Carson, for bringing him. Carson should have known better.

"You are such an asshole," he said quietly.

Carson's eyes flashed, and he was there in an instant, ready to pick up the challenge.

"Fuck you, Frank. Just—just *fuck* you." He took a step closer to Frank, leaned his face in. "Saint Frank. What are you gonna do, just sit back and let this whole thing walk away, the chance for her to have some money for the first time? Right now she won't budge, but he can convince her. Even if he gets half, she still stands to gain a shitload of money. And that gives her a chance, Frank. A chance to get the hell out of this dump, live somewhere nice for a change."

"She likes it here."

"She's dying here, Frank. This place is too hard. And you know what else? I think you want her to sell as much as I do. You're just letting me be the heavy so you can go on being Saint Frank. As always."

Frank let that one pass. "And what about Sofia?" he said.

"Yeah, what *about* Sofia? She needs help, Frank. She's fucking *bent*. And sitting out here rotting away with her mother isn't what she needs."

"Since when do you care what anyone needs?"

"Since always."

"Carson, admit it," Frank said. "Just have the decency to admit it. The only reason you're doing this is because *you* smell the money. You see a straight line from her to you, and you don't want to miss out on this because it will benefit *you*." There, it was out. He'd said it. "And that's why you brought him back here. So he'll convince her to sell." It was crystal clear. Frank would have bet his life on it.

Carson's face clouded over, and Frank knew he'd hit a nerve. The heat was brutal, and a cluster of mosquitoes had begun to hover around Carson's neck, which was slick with perspiration and stretched taut.

"You don't care about anything," Frank said. "Except yourself."

"My wife tell you that?" Carson said. "Sounds like you two have been talking." He spoke quietly, dangerously now, and Frank saw that this conversation had begun to slide away from the details of the Vista Properties deal. He didn't answer.

"Have you?"

"Have I what?" Frank said.

"Been talking to my wife?"

"What is that supposed to mean?"

"It's a simple question, Frank."

"I don't think it is."

"Have. You. Been. Talking. To. My"—Carson was close now, his face only inches from Frank's—"*wife?*" And just like when they were kids, Carson was faster than Frank, maddeningly so, and Frank didn't see the hand coming until it connected with the side of his head, a fat slap, degrading more than physically hurtful, the kind of slap you'd give a cow, a horse.

Frank threw himself back at his brother and knocked Carson off balance, and then they grappled, still standing, but scrapping, cursing, until Biaggio's hands closed over Frank's shoulders, pulled him back. Frank looked at Carson, and now at Elizabeth, who had come down off the porch with Biaggio and who stood next to Carson, holding him back. She stared at Frank. Her hands were on her husband's chest. Frank met Carson's eyes, and then he looked up at Aberdeen, where Sofia and Bell stood on the porch, watching, where Dean hovered in the kitchen door, and where Arla's face, pale and stricken, was visible in the upstairs window.

Dean was right. The whole fam-damily. The whole damn family. He was sick of them all, suddenly, every one of them, every God-damn dysfunctional one of them, even Arla, even Sofia.

Fucking Bravos. They must all be cursed.

He walked back around the side of the house to his truck.

"Frank," Biaggio called. He laughed nervously. "Come on now. We got hot dogs."

Good, Frank thought. I hope you all choke.

FOURTEEN

Elizabeth tucked the corner of the Hello Kitty sheet under the mattress. She and Carson had just moved the single bed from Frank's old bedroom on the third floor, where she and Bell had been staying, to the east-facing second-story corner room that had been Carson's childhood bedroom. So much for Bell having her own bed. The bed they'd borrowed from Frank's house had been perfect, but the respite was short-lived. Dean needed a place to sleep. Which meant moving the extra bed into Carson's old room, the only usable room as yet unoccupied. Which meant Bell would be bunking with Elizabeth again, kicking like a showgirl all night long, she had no doubt.

"He's *who*?" Bell had said as Elizabeth and Carson stripped the mattress in Frank's room and stood it upright to slide it out the door.

"He's your granddad," Elizabeth said. "He's Daddy's father."

We're going to give him this bed to sleep in." She'd looked for a place to grab the mattress, found none. Carson was already shoving his end, knocking the mattress into her shoulder. "Could you wait one second, please?" she said to him, annoyed.

"How come I never met him before?" Bell said.

"He doesn't live in Utina," Elizabeth said.

"Where does he live?"

"Who knows?" Carson said.

"What do I call him?" Bell said.

"What?" Elizabeth said.

"What should I call him? Grandpa? Brooke calls her grandfather Pee-Paw."

"Oh, for Christ's sake," Carson said. "Call him Dean."

"You don't need to snap at her," Elizabeth said. "It's a legitimate question."

"Whether she should call him Pee-Paw? That's a legitimate question?"

"I think I'll call him Grandpa Dean," Bell said.

"Bell, honey," Elizabeth said. She glared across the upturned mattress at Carson. "Can you move out of the way? Daddy and I have to move this bed for Grandpa Dean."

They wrestled the flopping mattress into Carson's old room, and then Elizabeth set to work on the sheets again.

"You sure this is a good idea?" she said to Carson. "Having him here with your mother?" They'd left Dean out at the concrete picnic table, staring at the water. Frank had left an hour ago, livid, and it had made Elizabeth sad, watching him climb into his truck, his face closed in a frustration and fury that she suspected had to do with more than just Dean's return to Aberdeen. After the scuffle with Carson down by the water Frank had walked to his truck without another word, without so much as a glance in anyone's direction. Even hers.

"It's fine," Carson said. "It's his house. Why shouldn't he be here?"

"Maybe because he deserted her."

"You deserted me," Carson said. "And I'd still let you back home."

Bell stood in the doorway, watching them. Elizabeth shot a look at Carson. "Can you please be aware of what you are saying?" she said.

"I am aware," he said. "I'm simply stating a fact."

"Daddy?" Bell said. "Why don't you stay here, too?"

Carson looked at her.

"Then everyone will be here," she said.

"I'd love to, sweetness," Carson said. "But your mother doesn't want me to."

Elizabeth wanted to kill him. She stuffed a pillow into its case, threw it onto the bed, and turned to leave the room.

"Come on, Bell," she said.

"Elizabeth," he said.

"Wait," she said. She turned to Bell. "Sweetie, go find Sofia, okay? Ask her to find us an extra blanket." Bell left the room, and Elizabeth turned back to Carson.

"What?" she said, surprised by the harsh tone of her own voice.

"Come home."

She sighed.

"I'm lonely," he said.

"I doubt that," she said.

"I need you.

"I'm not talking about this today."

"Then when?"

"Move that chair," she said. "He won't be able to get to the bed."

"We can work it out."

"And put the lamp over where he can reach it."

"I love you."

"I'll get some towels from the bathroom for him."

"Are you sleeping with my brother?"

She stopped, turned around slowly. She stared at him.

"Are you for real?" she said.

His face had tightened, and she watched as the familiar flush of rage began to creep up along his jaw and into his cheeks, which had begun to show the first bloated signs of close to three decades' worth of steady drinking. He was on his way, Carson. Oh, he was on his way. He was more like Dean than he realized.

"Because I will fucking kill him," he said.

"Carson," she said. "You are an even bigger ass than I thought."

A movement at the door—Dean stood on the threshold, awkward, lanky, his jeans cinched tight around his waist. He clutched a green duffle bag. "That fella Biaggio said I'd be in this room," he said, and Elizabeth felt a little bit sorry for him then, a stranger in his own family's house.

Carson turned toward the window, took a deep breath.

"I hope you don't mind Hello Kitty," Elizabeth said.

Dean put the bag on the bed. "I love Hello Kitty," he said.

"Bell and I are staying upstairs, if you need anything," Elizabeth said.

"So we got us a houseful, huh?" Dean said.

"Evidently," she said.

She turned to walk out of the bedroom, and Carson followed her into the hallway. He stepped in front of her at the top of the stairs, blocking her way.

"Come home," he said.

"No," she said, and she pushed past him and felt the weight of his stare on her back as she descended the stairs.

She woke early the next morning. Bell lay beside her, wide awake in a tangle of blond hair and bedclothes. She was staring at the ceiling.

"You okay, Belly?" Elizabeth whispered, groggy. Her right arm ached from having slept on it, balancing on her side all night and teetering on the edge of the bed to try to avoid Bell's kicking.

"When are we going to go home?" Bell said.

Elizabeth cleared her throat, tried to focus her eyes.

"You want to go home?" she said. She propped herself up on her elbow and winced as her muscles tried to realign. "I thought we were having fun here."

"I'm having fun," Bell said. "But."

"But what?"

"I don't *live* here. I would like to go back where I *live*," Bell said, piqued. "And you don't live here either. And also"—she looked squarely at Elizabeth—"I think you are being very mean to Daddy."

Elizabeth didn't know what to say to that. So she changed the subject. "You want me to go make you some breakfast?" she said.

"What do we have?"

"Waffles."

"What kind?"

"Blueberry."

"Not buttermilk?"

"No."

"Why not buttermilk?"

Elizabeth rubbed her eyes. "I don't know, Bell. I bought blueberry, okay?"

"I like buttermilk."

Elizabeth stared at her.

Bell sighed. "Whatever," she said. She pulled her notebook off the nightstand, turned her back to Elizabeth. My God. Was she seven, or seventeen? Sometimes Elizabeth couldn't be entirely sure.

Elizabeth slid out of the bed and slipped a pair of shorts under her nightshirt. In the hallway and down on the second floor, all the bedroom doors were closed. She pictured them all in their beds—Arla, Dean, Sofia—and she wondered if any of them had slept at all. She walked downstairs to make coffee.

The kitchen was dim, the blue vinyl tablecloth cool and smooth. Elizabeth walked to the window to look out. In the dawning light, Biaggio's trailer was visible just beyond the driveway, and she put her hand over her mouth to stifle a gasp when she saw Sofia emerge barefoot from the trailer, saw Biaggio hold her hand to his lips and smile.

"No *way*," Elizabeth whispered. "Get *out*."

Sofia walked across the yard, pulled the back door open, and stepped quietly into the kitchen. She saw Elizabeth and froze.

"Good morning," Elizabeth said. She bit her lip.

Sofia stared at her, wide-eyed.

"Busy night?" Elizabeth said. But then she smiled and walked across the kitchen to hug Sofia.

"Oh, my God, Elizabeth," Sofia said. "Don't tell."

"Why not?" Elizabeth said. "You're a grown woman."

Sofia flapped her hands up and down. "Oh," she said. "I don't know." Elizabeth was moved by the childishness of Sofia's gesture, and she thought of Sofia so long ago, when she'd first met her, when she was ten, Sofia was thirteen. Sofia had taken Elizabeth to her room, let her try on her pointe shoes, and they'd brushed each other's hair, and Elizabeth had been astounded by the cool, smooth wave of Sofia's tresses, how they ran like silk through her fingers. Red, spun with gold. So pretty Elizabeth wanted to cry, but Sofia had turned her around, ran the brush through Elizabeth's own pale hair, and said: "It's like honey," and Elizabeth loved her. The age difference between them hardly mattered. Sofia had been there when Elizabeth was first dating Frank. She'd been there when Elizabeth took up with Carson. She'd offered little in the way of an opinion about Elizabeth's choices save that one day, recently, in the Dairy Queen, but Elizabeth always sensed that Sofia knew more, felt more, loved more than anybody knew she was capable of.

"Well, when did this start?" Elizabeth said.

Sofia shrugged. "A few weeks ago."

"Why now?" Elizabeth said. "You've known him for so long."

"I don't know," Sofia said. "Something's changing. Everything's changing. You know?" She took a deep breath. "Oh, maybe it's too much," she said.

"Do you love him?" Elizabeth said.

"Yes," Sofia said.

"Then it's just enough."

Sofia's eyes widened again. Then she smiled.

"You know what's funny?" Sofia said.

"What?"

"I can sleep with him." She flushed. "I don't mean—I mean, *that*, too, but, I can *sleep* there. I can fall asleep. I can't do that anywhere else but here."

Elizabeth smiled at her. "I'm not surprised."

"But, Elizabeth," Sofia said, and the smile dropped from her face. "What are we going to do?" She looked at the ceiling, raised her eyebrows.

"About them?" Elizabeth said.

"About *him*," Sofia said. "My father. Good Lord."

"I don't know," Elizabeth said. "I honestly don't know what to do about anything, Sofia."

A toilet flushed upstairs.

"Except make coffee," she said. "We gotta start somewhere."

She went back upstairs with the last two blueberry waffles on a plate. Bell was still sitting in the bed, her spiral notebook on her knees. She seemed to have brightened a bit.

"I have a new list," Bell said.

"Slay me," Elizabeth said. "Go."

"Shoes."

"Shoes?"

"Shoes I Want," Bell said. "Ready? (1) Ballerina Barbie's pointe shoes. (2) Mary Poppins's boots." She smiled. "Remember those?"

"I've got one," Elizabeth said. "Cinderella's glass slippers. But where could you *wear* them?"

And then they were off: Napoleon Dynamite's moon shoes, Beatle boots, Pocahontas's moccasins, and, of course, the ruby slippers, which were wasted on Dorothy after all, thought Elizabeth—red lipped and beautiful but trapped forever in white bobby socks and a gingham dress, a girl who had everything she needed but just didn't know how to use it.

"Why isn't Daddy here?" Bell said.

"He was here yesterday."

"But why isn't he here today?"

Elizabeth sighed. "Make me a new list," she said.

"You didn't answer my question."

"Make me a new list."

Bell stared at her, hard for a moment. Then she shook her head, muttered something that Elizabeth was willing to bet was a profanity.

"What's the title?" Bell demanded.

"Bell's Freckles."

"My *freckles*?"

"How many can you list?" Elizabeth said.

"Well, first I have to name them," Bell said.

"Well, all right then."

Bell turned a page in her notebook, pulled her nightgown up to her knees to stare at her legs. "Here we go," she said. "Brooke." She pointed at a freckle on her ankle. "Sofia." She pointed at one on her calf. "Arla. Bell."

"They're all girls?"

"All girls. No boys."

"You missed one," Elizabeth said.

"Elizabeth," Bell said. "My favorite."

Elizabeth reached for a box of tissues on the nightstand.

"You have a cold?" Bell said.

"Allergies," Elizabeth said, and she pressed the tissue against her eyes. "Dern things." She blew her nose, tried to swallow past the lump in her throat.

"You still didn't answer my question," Bell said. "But I guess you're not going to."

By the time she'd helped Bell find her clothes and had come back downstairs, the rest of the house was stirring. Dean wandered into the kitchen and helped himself to a cup of coffee, then walked out to the back porch to smoke. Sofia was running a shower upstairs. Arla was bumping around in her bedroom.

Elizabeth fought back a growing feeling of aimlessness and thought hard about how to spend the day. It was Thursday. She pictured Carson, already at his office, leaning over his computer keyboard and hacking at the keys angrily, firing off responses to the e-mails that had amassed since he'd left his desk the night before. "I'm lonely," he'd said. "I need you." She opened the refrigerator door, looked in at near emptiness. Why was it always about *him*?

She poked through the Little Debbie boxes on the counter-top and found only two cellophane-wrapped Star Crunches and a Pecan Spinwheel amid a mess of empty cartons. Fine—she'd work on groceries today. The necessity of the moment came to her as a relief. With five of them now staying here at Aberdeen, with Carson seeming to come and go with alarming frequency, and with the shocking level of uncertainty that now seemed to plague every facet of their lives, this, at least, was one sure, comforting fact. They had to eat.

* * *

She and Biaggio were already in the van, ready to pull out, when Dean approached. Earlier, Elizabeth and Bell had visited Arla in her bedroom to put together the grocery list, and Elizabeth was struck by both the mess in the room and the confusion in Arla's face as she sat in her nightgown on the edge of the bed. A tower of tattered cardboard boxes slouched in one corner of the room, and even from the doorway Elizabeth could see the dust on the top box, a quarter of an inch thick. Everywhere else, on every possible surface of the room, rested books, discarded plastic tumblers, articles of clothing, outdated junk mail. Elizabeth tried not to gasp. She hadn't been upstairs to Arla's room in years. She remembered coming up once to borrow a sweater from Arla's closet—it had to be twenty years ago, or more. Before Will died. She remembered Arla's shoes lined up neatly in the closet, Dean's wallet on the nightstand, a thick quilt smooth across the bed. She'd felt invasive, then, a stranger in a clean, private place.

"What is he *doing* here?" Arla had said to Elizabeth this morning.

"It's all about the house sale," Elizabeth replied. She moved into the room, found a clear spot at the foot of the bed, and sat down with Arla. "Are you okay?"

Arla sighed. "I will be."

"Are you going to do it?" Elizabeth said. "Sell the house?"

"Oh, Elizabeth," Arla said. "How do I know?" Then Bell had taken dictation, and they'd narrated the grocery list: chicken breasts, barbecue beans, Tang, bananas, hot dogs, watermelon, Cheerios. The usual, Arla said. Just *more* of it.

"*Buttermilk* waffles," Bell said. "For crap's sake."

"Oh, my Lord, you watch your mouth, missy," Elizabeth said, but then she glanced at Arla and they both had to look away, stifle their smiles.

"And there's something else, Elizabeth," Arla said, lowering her voice. "Sofia—Sofia and you-know-who?" She tipped her head toward the window, where Biaggio's trailer was visible through the trees. "They're getting *involved*."

Elizabeth nodded. "I just found that out," she said.

"She thinks I don't know," Arla said. "I know plenty."

"Do you think it's a problem?" Elizabeth said.

Arla sighed. "No. No, I don't suppose," she said. "It just scares me. Do you think he knows what he's getting into?"

Elizabeth didn't know how to answer that. Then Arla turned again to Bell, who was still holding the grocery list and was now dotting the margins with penciled paw prints. "Little Debbies, Bell," Arla said. "Jesus, get me a case of them."

They'd gone downstairs then, leaving Arla in her bedroom, and Bell had opted for a SpongeBob DVD instead of a hot grocery run, so Elizabeth set her up in the living room and kissed the top of her head. Now, as Biaggio's van idled in the driveway, Dean approached Elizabeth's window. He looked restless, displaced. "Where you headed?" he said.

"Winn-Dixie," Elizabeth said. She hesitated a moment. "You want to come?"

Dean climbed into the back of the van, bringing a wave of cigarette smoke with him. Lord, Elizabeth thought. This should be an interesting ride.

They drove through the quiet, palm-lined roads of North Utina and hooked a left at Seminary Street to head down County

Road 25 toward the beach, toward the Winn-Dixie. It was early still, and though the temperature was quickly rising, the sun was gentle through the trees, tolerable. The gray Spanish moss hanging from the oak boughs looked like tears. Biaggio whistled. The van rattled and shook. They were quiet until they passed the place where Will had been hit.

"Dean, you okay back there?" Elizabeth said. She turned around. Dean was ashen, and his hands trembled on his knees.

"Oh, I'm okay," he answered. "Just wishing I had a drink." He exhaled. "Just gotta get through this. I'm detoxing, you know."

Elizabeth cleared her throat. "We know," she said.

Biaggio looked in his rearview mirror and regarded Dean.

"You try green tea?" he said. "I heard it helps."

"I'll try anything," Dean said.

"We'll get you some green tea," Biaggio said, and he nodded at Elizabeth. She added it to the list.

"Where you from, Biaggio?" Dean said.

"West Virginia. But I been here a long time."

Dean nodded. "Strange place to end up. Utina."

"No stranger than where I'm from, let me tell you."

"We got some characters around here," Elizabeth said.

"Oh, we had 'em, too," Biaggio said. "When I was growing up, I knew all kinds of nuts. Maybe that's why I kind of became one." He grinned, winked at Elizabeth. She'd never seen him so buoyant. She loved Biaggio. Who wouldn't? She was happy for Sofia.

"Like the *kids*. Even the kids were weird," Biaggio said. "I could tell you some stories." He hunched forward, rested his forearms across the top of the steering wheel.

"Biaggio likes to tell stories," Elizabeth said to Dean.

"Yep. Like Denny McLaughlin," Biaggio said. "Now *there* was a pisser."

"Hold on," Dean said. "Can you pull over?"

Biaggio pulled the van to the side of the road and turned off the engine, and Dean slid open the back door, climbed woodenly out of his seat, and made it to a thicket of palmettos before starting to retch. Elizabeth stared straight ahead, tried not to listen, but the sounds were horrible, brutal. She and Biaggio did not speak. When he was finished, Dean walked slowly back to the van. His shirt was spotted with sweat. His face was slick.

"Aw, Mr. Bravo," Biaggio said.

"Dean," Dean said. He coughed. "It's Dean."

Biaggio slid out of the driver's side and helped Dean back into his seat; then he walked to the back of the van, opened it, and found a roll of paper towels and a bottle of water. He wet a couple of the towels, brought them around to the side of the van, and held them against Dean's brow, and Elizabeth nearly caught her breath at the tenderness of the action, at how Dean's eyes fluttered under the damp towel, how Biaggio's hand was steady, unafraid. Something caught her eye, then, and she turned to see an armadillo plod noisily out of the scrub, stand for a moment in the center of the road, regarding them, then disappear into a culvert on the other side of the blacktop.

"So tell me about Denny McLaughlin," Dean said. He mopped his face with the towels, pushed himself a little straighter in the seat. "Tell us some of your stories."

Biaggio climbed back into the van. "Oh, yeah," he said. "I got me loads of stories."

"I'll bet you do," Dean said.

Biaggio started the van and pulled back onto the road. "All right, so Denny," he said. "He had a thing for clocks. Ever since he was a little kid. His bedroom was full of clocks of all kinds. On the dresser, under the bed, on the walls—just clocks, everywhere, everywhere. No watches. Just clocks."

"Maybe he liked to be on time," Dean said.

"Nah, it was more than that. This kid was weird. But I liked him. I hung with him. One summer me and Denny got jobs at an old movie theater. It was crazy old, this theater, Victorian old, with all kinds of antiques inside. Really beautiful stuff. I wish I could see it now." Biaggio downshifted to maneuver a tight turn in the road, then shifted again and accelerated. "Anyway, we got these jobs there," he said. "I think we were fourteen, maybe fifteen. We had to clean up the popcorn and cups after the people left every night. We liked it, got to see all the movies for free, and sometimes you'd find stuff people left behind. One time, after we finished, we went back to Denny's house and got one of them wagons—you remember them? Them Radio Flyers?"

"I remember," Dean said.

"Well, it was late and I should have been home," Biaggio said. "But I followed Denny back to the theater. When we got closer, Denny picked up the wagon and held it over his head so it wouldn't make noise. I followed him around to the back of the building and up to the back door, and he pulled out a key. Turns out he'd taken the manager's key home and made a copy.

"He walked behind the concession stand, where a huge old antique clock hung, and I knew in a second what Denny was up to. That clock must have been worth a fortune. It was some sort of dark polished wood—cherry, maybe, or walnut—with an enormous ornate face and a deep chime that rang every hour. That clock was something. 'You're crazy,' I told Denny. But he wanted that clock. So we did it."

"You took the clock?" Elizabeth said.

"Well . . ." He hesitated. "Denny took the clock. I helped a little bit." As they drove the air rushed in through the open windows, and Elizabeth wrapped her hair in her hands to keep it contained.

"So you know what the moral of the story is, Mr. Bravo?" Biaggio said. He was grinning widely.

"Dean," Dean said. "For shit's sake, son, call me Dean, would you?"

"Tell us, Biaggio," Elizabeth said.

"It's that you really can steal time," Biaggio said.

Dean chuckled. "Well, that's good to know," he said. He nodded, still smiling. "I think you're all right, Biaggio," he said. "But I want to ask you something. What, exactly, are you doing with my daughter?"

Elizabeth froze. Did *everybody* already know? Evidently this cat was making its way entirely out of the bag. Today. Poor Sofia. Front-page news, honey, ready or not.

Biaggio took a deep breath, then looked into the rearview mirror.

"I'm marrying her, Dean," he said.

Elizabeth stared out the window. Marrying her! Her heart was racing. The van was silent for another minute, then two. Oh, God! She didn't dare turn around. She stole a sidelong glance at Biaggio. He was chewing on his lower lip, and his hands clenched the steering wheel until his knuckles were literally turning white.

"Well, I might could congratulate you, then," Dean said, finally. Elizabeth turned around and looked at him. He patted his shirt pocket, found a cigarette, and lit it. "But I need to tell you," he said. "These are not ordinary women you are dealing with. Sofia—she's got a hell of a lot of her mother in her."

Biaggio exhaled, then grinned. "So then you know where I'm coming from," he said.

"Worse than that, son," Dean said. "I know where you're headed."

Elizabeth felt a pricking at the back of her throat. The van bumped into the Winn-Dixie parking lot, and Biaggio maneuvered into a parking space. The smell of cigarette smoke and exhaust was heavy in the van, and the supermarket was a blinding white in the unrelenting sun. Elizabeth felt dizzy. Giddy. She couldn't stop herself: she let out a little whoop that was born somewhere in a well of confusion and relief and pure, clear delight, which was something she hadn't felt in a long time.

"All right, boys," Elizabeth said. "Let's do this."

They climbed out of the van and made for the shopping carts.

"Don't forget the green tea," Biaggio said.

Dean clapped his hand on Biaggio's shoulder and leaned heavily on a black metal cart with wonky wheels, and they all crossed the steaming black asphalt toward the solace of the air-conditioned Winn-Dixie.

That night, Bell was asleep beside her and the moon was bright outside her window. Fresh stacks of Little Debbie cartons were arranged neatly on the kitchen counter downstairs, and the

refrigerator hummed, full of food. Elizabeth heard Dean coughing in the bathroom, heard Arla slowly making her way up the
staircase to go to bed. Sofia turned off the television downstairs.
And then all the bedroom doors closed, and Aberdeen was quiet
and still.

Carson. She pictured him in their bed at home, his skin
warm and tan against the sheets. Or wait—no—it was early yet,
not even ten o'clock. He'd still be sitting at the kitchen table,
tapping away at the laptop, answering e-mails and working on
his new fund and doing God knows what else. He'd stay there
until after midnight, then would clop noisily down the hallway
to the bathroom, make his way to bed. It was one thing she
always noticed about Carson, how he never adjusted his step,
never tempered his footfall or tried to quiet his impact on the
old wooden floors of their house, no matter if she and Bell were
already in bed, no matter if they'd not yet woken in the morning. Carson would shut the bathroom door with a loud click
as though it were the middle of the afternoon, would clear his
throat noisily as he brushed his teeth, kick his shoes off with a
loud thump in the closet before coming to bed, and climbing
heavily in beside her. It was just Carson. She'd grown used to it.
He didn't censor himself for anybody. Not even her. He'd been
that way forever, always, since they were children.

She remembered a day when she was ten years old. She and
her friend Delia had found an abandoned nest of baby rabbits
under the back of the trailer, and they cared for the babies for
days, sewing little skirts out of paper towels and coffee filters,
dressing the bunnies up and putting them to bed in shoe boxes,
crafting a bunny schoolhouse out of an old packing carton, squirt-
ing drops of milk between their tiny brown lips. They played

hide-and-seek, tucking the babies, no bigger than hamsters, in nooks and crevices all over the yard, running around to find them, laughing, collecting them all in a wicker basket, giving them names like Pussy Willow, Tootsie Roll, and Bunky. One afternoon Elizabeth had found Pussy Willow under an azalea bush, and she'd held her to her face, inhaling the sweet baby bunny smell, then she'd run across the yard to show Delia. "I found her, I found her!" she said, and then she felt something soft under her foot. She looked down and saw a strange brown shape, moving, contorting, under her canvas sneaker, and the understanding came to her slow, as she watched the pink entrails bubbling out, the tiny white bones like matchsticks in the dirt, that it was Bunky, the boy bunny, crushed, burst like an overripe peach under her shoe.

She'd screamed then, and she could have screamed again now, remembering it, but the worst part is that nobody had come. Delia had looked at the mangled bunny and cried and run home, and Elizabeth ran to the trailer, Pussy Willow having been dropped in the grass next to her dead brother, left forever to fend for herself. Elizabeth lay alone then in her bedroom, alone in her horror, her shoes left outside, and still, still nobody came. Her mother never came. She stayed in bed all afternoon and all evening, crying, shaking, sleeping a little, and she re-membered waking up the next morning, the thick smell of alcohol in the trailer, the sounds of Wanda and somebody else beginning to stir in the next bedroom. Elizabeth had gotten herself up, gone outside, and hosed off her shoes. She walked to the bus stop alone.

Frank was on the bus, she remembered, ten-year-old Frank, and she sat in the seat in front of him. Carson was in the back, loud and raucous with his fifth-grade friends. Frank had leaned over the seat.

"What's the matter, Elizabeth?" he'd said.

"Nothing," she'd said, but he shook his head.

"You look sad," he said. Then she threw up in the aisle and the bus driver cursed and she could hear Carson and his friends in the back. "Ewwwww!" they said. "Gnarly!!" But Frank didn't say anything at all, just opened his lunch box and handed her a napkin. His face was open and unafraid.

Bell stirred beside her, and Elizabeth turned her face to the pillow, tried to summon a picture of Carson as an eleven-year-old boy. It wouldn't come.

FIFTEEN

Even though Sofia arrived at Uncle Henry's late, 8:01, to be precise, Frank wasn't there yet, either; the patch of sand just outside the kitchen door where his blue truck usually sat was vacant. That one minute was irksome. One minute! She didn't like to be late. But she took a series of deep breaths and shook it off. Breathe. Rebalance. Recalibrate.

She parked her bike on the back deck and unlocked the door to the dining room. Inside, the restaurant was quiet and dim, and the smell of leftover fry grease was nearly overwhelming. She coughed. They must have fried enough shrimp to sink a ship last night. She'd have her work cut out for her today.

"Morgan?" she called. No answer. Huh. Guess she was the only one on the early shift this morning, which was fine with her. She liked to work alone. It gave her time to think. She moved through the dining room, opening all the windows wide, though there was only a paltry morning breeze. She flipped a bank of switches to start the ceiling fans, propped open the front door to encourage a cross-breeze, then moved to the utility closet to retrieve her supplies. Vacuum, check. Mop, check. Paper towels, check. Bucket, check. Pine-Sol, check. Everything there. Everything in order. She liked to have things in order. She liked to know what to expect.

What to expect! Her head spun for a moment. It had been doing that lately, a burst of light and warmth coming at her in a sudden rush, making her disoriented and dizzy for a moment and then receding again, just as quickly, leaving a wake of questions and electricity behind. Because now! Well, she hardly knew what to expect now. Everything was changing these days, everything was different. Her father, back home. This talk of selling Aberdeen. And biggest of all—Biaggio! This last thing—it was almost too much to think about. Almost. But she smiled and pulled the rolling bucket out of the closet.

That week after the Fourth, after the night he'd sat on the picnic table watching her swim, that was when she really knew. He'd taken her and Arla down to LensCrafters in St. Augustine that week and had sat in the waiting room, flipping through a magazine while Arla had fussed at the optician about tightening the frames on her reading glasses and while Sofia herself had gone in for an eye exam. Glasses. She could scream. She'd never needed glasses before. But after fighting the headaches and the blurry words on the page for so long, she'd been forced to admit that maybe it was time. Forty-three, girl, what are you going to do? Glasses it is. So she'd suffered the exam, the horrid, germy diagnostic equipment she'd had to press her face into to squint through the flipping lenses. And she'd suffered the hairy doctor himself, leaning in far too close—it felt like he was going to kiss her!—to stare into her eyes with his instruments and his garlic breath. Awful. Afterward she'd come back out to the LensCrafters lobby feeling flushed and violated, so she steadied herself with trying on sample frames, though she kept a KleanWipe in her hand and gave each pair of frames a swipe before parking them on her face and regarding her reflection in the mirror skeptically. The last frames were ridiculous, gigantic purple orbs, and she was about to remove them when she saw Biaggio in the mirror, watching her from across the room with those soft eyes of his, and that was when she knew. She held his gaze through the silly purple frames. A beat. Another beat. Another. She held his gaze. And it was funny, because even though there were no lenses in the purple frames, she could suddenly see more clearly than she had for years.

That night, she swam again in the Intracoastal. And that night he swam with her. When their bodies met in the darkness of the current, she turned her back to Aberdeen and opened her arms, and he whispered again and again, *I love you, I love you, I love you. Sofia.*

And, of course, he did.

She moved through the dining room in record time, wiping down the tables with Pine-Sol and running the vacuum and polishing the windows with Windex until they sparkled. Then she dragged the bucket and the mop to the bar area and worked on methodically, sweeping and mopping and wiping and scouring until Frank would have been hard-pressed to find a single trace of what was clearly a sloppy night's business the evening before. Neither he nor Morgan had yet arrived at the restaurant, though it was well after nine now, but she couldn't say she blamed them. After all, what did it matter anymore? It was looking, more and more, like the restaurant's days were numbered. If they all ended up agreeing to this deal with Vista, in fact, it was looking like Frank was done slinging booze, Morgan was done frying fish. And she herself was done mopping up after them. So what did it matter if any of them got here on time? Whether they kept the lunch crowd waiting? Whether the infernal fritters were ready on time? What did it matter?

IF they all agreed. *IF.* And had anyone even asked her opinion about selling the house and the restaurant? No, they had not. Had anyone even for one second thought to consider how *she* might have felt about this landslide of change that seemed to be descending from on high even as she stood here this morning with a gosh-darned yarn mop in her hand? No, they had not. It occurred to her that she should have been furious. And she would have been, too, if she hadn't been just a bit distracted lately. But *still.* She squinted at the bar. A flattened maraschino cherry was stuck to the resin surface, up against the cash register. She regarded it for a moment more, then turned and left it there. Huh.

She tugged the vacuum down the hallway to Frank's office and banged open the door. The grease smell in the restaurant was still cloying, and she was annoyed. How much Pine-Sol did it take to clean this place up, anyway? She plugged in the vacuum and ran it around the carpet, then pulled off the attachments to suck the dust bunnies out from under her brother's desk. She sat in Frank's chair for a moment to recoil the cord on the vacuum, and her eye fell on the file folder sitting on his blotter. VISTA PROPERTIES it said. But she didn't even open it. She didn't want to know.

It was going to happen. She knew it. It wasn't a matter of *if*, it was a matter of *when*. She'd watched Carson and Frank in the yard the other day, had watched her brothers squaring off against the options—Sell? Stay? Sell? Stay?—but she knew, just as Frank did, most likely, that it was all but inevitable. Dean was back. Carson was adamant. The properties were worth too much. They couldn't let the opportunity pass them by.

Her throat clenched. A wave of terror approached, crested, but then receded. She took a deep breath.

Marry me. Marry me, Sofia.

Biaggio had told her last night that he had talked to Dean. Talked to Dean! Oh, Lord, the lunacy of it. It wasn't like she needed *Dean's* permission, of all the fool people. Forty-three years old! And Dean hardly the doting patriarch. But still, she was charmed by the earnestness of Biaggio's effort, astonished by the sincerity. "I want to do it right, Sofia," he said. "I want to do everything right." But the details: When? How? Where would they live? And oh, my God—what about *Arla*? He didn't answer, but he took her hands in his and had held them until the quaking stopped.

Yes. Yes. Yes.

It was getting late. She looked at her watch. Almost ten, and still the kitchen and restrooms to clean. She started to get up and then she saw something else on Frank's desk—a paperweight, it looked like. She reached for it; it was a gray creek stone, smooth and heavy and cool in her hand when she picked it up. She smiled.

She remembered Cullowhee. She remembered the sweet cabin, the watermelon, the little gray fox who came each morning to nose in their trash. She remembered fireworks, soft and diffused in the valley below. And she remembered the hike to the creek, where Frank had probably pocketed this stone.

Frank. When they were kids he used to ask her questions, used to think she had answers. She remembered a day; they were sitting close together on that huge flat rock in the middle of the rushing mountain creek. The sun was warm on her shoulders. The others were on the bank, putting on shoes, gathering towels.

"Where does all this water go?" Frank had asked her. He gestured at the creek. "Where does it go, Sofia?"

"To lakes. To rivers. Back into the earth," she said.

"To the Intracoastal?"

"Maybe, some. A little. And into the sky to become rain again."

"So it just keeps going."

She nodded. "It keeps going."

They'd climbed off the rock and waded back through the creek to the bank, grabbing onto each other as they slipped and stumbled over the smooth, slick stones.

Now Sofia put the creek stone back on Frank's desk and pulled her bucket into the kitchen. The grease stench was *still* horrid, and she suddenly understood why. The fryer! It was still running! The ON light glowed red in the dim kitchen. Frank. He'd left the fryer on when he closed the restaurant last night. For gosh sakes. He could have burned the whole place down. She walked over to the fryer and flicked the switch. Then she looked around the kitchen and shook her head. You see? They all needed her more than they thought they did.

She finished cleaning the kitchen and the restrooms (no puking last night, thank you sweet heaven) and then went back out to the bar area. She tore off a fresh paper towel and plucked

the flattened maraschino cherry off the bar, just as Morgan whistled his way into the kitchen, just as the sound of Frank's truck
approached outside the door.

When she got home to Aberdeen, she found Arla in Will's
old bedroom on the third floor, where she almost never went,
dragging out old furniture, sorting through boxes.

"I feel like we should get organized," Arla said. She cleared
her throat and held up a gold-trimmed photo album. "Remember this?" she said. She flipped to a photo of a man on a horse.

"Walter," Sofia said.

Arla pointed toward a shadowy corner. "And look," she said.
"I found my mother's old mahogany table."

The light was dim, but Sofia pulled the table over to the
window, ran her fingers across the finish, and smiled. On the
surface of the table, faint but visible, were the two foggy, water-
stained crescents of Sofia's seven-year-old fanny.

"You see?" she said to Arla, who walked over to the table
and looked down at it. Then she sat heavily on a dusty bench,
and Sofia sat next to her.

"I'm not a crier," Arla said.

"You could be," Sofia said. "We both could be."

And, as it turned out, they were.

It came to Sofia that night in a dream, and she sat up so suddenly that she felt dizzy. Biaggio woke immediately, sat up and
put his arm around her.

"Sofia," he said. "What is it?"

She was sweating. But she turned to him and started to
laugh.

"She didn't kill herself," she said. "It wasn't suicide. It was the dress."

"You're dreaming," he said. He lay back on the bed, stroked her arm. "Go back to sleep." The trailer was cool and quiet. Through the jalousie over the bureau she could see the dim outline of Aberdeen, moonlit and austere, down at the end of the long dusty driveway.

But no, she understood now. Gervais (Todd!) was right. Ophelia. In the painting. She *was* singing. She *wasn't* dead yet. And it wasn't even suicide! She didn't want to die! That dress— that crazy Danish dress. It was the damn skirts that pulled her under. All those senseless yards of gilded threads and embroidered folds. She fell in the water singing, and she kept singing, and then she drowned. But she didn't *want* to die! It wasn't Hamlet, or the poppies, or any of it! It was just the stupid, bone-headed, shit-for-brains *dress*. For gosh sakes. You'd think someone would have come along and pulled her out. She would have thanked them.

Sofia lay back on the bed and stared at the ceiling for a long time, listening for the barred owl in the trees overhanging the waterway. When she finally heard him, she smiled, then turned toward Biaggio, pulled her knees to her chest, and slept.

I dreamed you, I dreamed me. I dreamed ten sweet babies and a hot cup of tea.

SIXTEEN

"Bell wants to see them," Elizabeth said. "She likes the idea of it—acrobats." She'd called Frank to invite him. Chinese acrobats at the Utina Fairgrounds Amphitheater. It'd been a week since Dean had returned, a week since Frank had walked out on the mess at Aberdeen and the scuffle with Carson, and though he'd yet to have another face-to-face with his brother, his conscience had gotten the best of him the day after Dean's return and he'd driven out to Aberdeen again to check on Arla. He'd found his mother operating with a strange stoicism and a matter-of-fact acceptance of Dean's presence. Sofia seemed changed, some-how, more peaceful, though he was loath to believe that this could have been due to Dean's return. Bell was a bright dervish, traipsing through the halls of the big house. Elizabeth, though, had seemed to be avoiding him, and he had an idea why. But now—acrobats.

"Where's Carson?" Frank said.

"Don't know," she'd said, and her voice was so flat and final that he hadn't asked any other questions.

"I'll pick you up," he'd said. He hung up and looked at Gooch. "You're staying home, bud." Gooch walked through the house and jumped up on Frank's bed for a nap. Through the open bedroom door, he gave Frank a *look*.

Frank arrived at Aberdeen in a rain shower, the drops hitting the top of his truck like fat grapes. He ducked his head and made a run for the house. Inside, Biaggio and Dean were staring at a large box in the dining room.

"New air conditioner," Biaggio said. "For Miss Arla's room upstairs."

"Damn things are a bitch," Dean said, scratching his head. "Especially second-floor. We might need Frank."

Frank didn't answer. What was Dean now, man of the house again? Johnny-on-the-Spot? Mr. Fix-It?

A few days after he'd arrived at Aberdeen, Dean had called Frank at the restaurant. "I know you don't like this," he said to Frank. "Me being here. But it is what it is."

"And what is that?" Frank said.

"It's what we make it," Dean said cryptically.

"Look, what do you want? You're back for the sale, back for the money, right?"

"Carson asked me to come back."

"So you decided it would be a good idea?"

"It might be good for your mother."

"*Good* for her? You coming back?"

"No," Dean admitted, and Frank had to give him that. Dean was a lot of things, but he'd never been a liar. "No, I mean selling the house."

"She doesn't want to."

"She might change her mind," Dean said amiably, and then he'd turned chatty, irritatingly so, and he'd told Frank about Sandy Vanderhorn, and the hospital, and detox, and Frank had hung up the phone and stared at it for a long while.

Now a clatter of footsteps sounded on the stairs, and Bell came into the room. "Uncle Frank," she said. "We going to the acrobats?"

"You bet, Bellarina," he said. "Where's your mama?"

"She's getting ready."

"You go tell her I'm here?"

Bell left the room again, and Frank turned back to Biaggio and Dean, who was looking at Frank with raised eyebrows.

"You taking Elizabeth out?" Dean said.

"Not taking her out," Frank said. "Just taking them both to the amphitheater. To see acrobats."

Dean looked back at Biaggio, who kept his face blank.

"I don't know," Dean said.

"You don't need to know," Frank said, annoyed. "It's none of your business."

"Okay," Dean said. "Whatever." He bent over to open the carton on the air conditioner, then gasped, put his hand on his hip bone and straightened back up, in obvious pain. "Damn broken cheek," he muttered.

"Where'd you get it?" Frank said.

"I told you. This woman took me down," Dean said. "Sandy Vanderhorn—"

"No," Frank said. *Jesus.* "The air conditioner. Where'd you get the air conditioner?"

"Home Depot up in Jax," Biaggio said. "We just got back."

"Damn, my ass hurts," Dean said. "We might need Frank."

"I'm on my way out," Frank said.

"It will just take a minute," Dean said. "It's for your mother. It's so hot up there. There's only one window unit in the hallway, trying to cool the whole floor."

Oh, this was irksome—Dean so solicitous of Arla, so attentive, so God-damned chivalrous. He should have won an Academy Award, Frank thought.

"Just help Biaggio here carry the thing upstairs, Frank," Dean said.

Frank sighed, took off his cap, and put it and his truck keys on the dining room table. He gripped one side of the air conditioner box and Biaggio gripped the other. "Lift with the knees," Dean said. "Watch your backs." He leaned against the mantel and watched them lift the box. Frank wanted to slap him.

"We got it," he said. He and Biaggio carried the air conditioner up the stairs and entered Arla's room, where she sat in her wingback chair, waiting.

"Oh, Frank!" she said. "Good, you can help with this." She seemed calm, Frank noticed, completely herself. When he'd talked to her the day after Dean had arrived at Aberdeen, he had asked her straight up if she would be able to manage having her husband in the house again. "You want him out of there?" he'd said. "You want me to get him out of there?"

She hesitated a moment. "He's okay," she said quietly. "He can do what he wants." And then she'd told him about Sofia and Biaggio, and Frank had cast his eyes to the ceiling, scratched his head.

"So what does that mean now?" he asked.

She sighed. "Frank," she said. "What does any of this mean?"

Now Dean had made it up the stairs, and he stood in the doorway for a moment, with what seemed to Frank a trace of awkwardness. His wife's bedroom, Frank thought, *his own* bedroom, once, but then Frank pushed the thought out of his mind.

"All right," Dean said, entering the room. "Let's get this sucker mounted."

They opened the carton, pulled the air conditioner out, and dumped a plastic bag of hardware onto the floor.

Sofia and Bell entered the room, flopped on Arla's bed.

"Hey, Sofia," Biaggio said, and Frank noticed how his voice softened, how he hitched his pants self-consciously. Oh, Biaggio, he thought. Run while you still can.

"When do *I* get my own air conditioner?" Sofia said.

"When you're sixty-two and fat and walk with a cane," Arla said, and Frank thought he saw Dean stiffen, as he always had, at any mention of Arla's disfigured foot.

"Well, I'm working on the fat part," Sofia said.

"You're not fat," Biaggio said.

"Puh," Sofia said. "I might start Pilates." She raised a leg up off the bed, extended it out straight. Bell mimicked her, raising her legs off the bed and plopping them back down again.

"I already do Pilates," Bell said. "I do them all the time."

"What the hell is a Pilate?" Dean said.

"Can we go ahead and get this thing in the window?" Frank said. With himself, Dean, Biaggio, and Arla all hovering around the window and Sofia and Bell lounging on the bed, not to mention the unspeakable amount of rubbish and furniture in the room, he was becoming claustrophobic and a bit panicked.

"Amen, brother," Sofia said. "I'm ready for some cool air."

Elizabeth appeared in the doorway. She wore a blue sundress, and he tried not to stare at her but failed. She blinked at the sight of so many people in the room, and when her eyes met Frank's he shook his head, and she smiled.

"I'll be downstairs," she said.

"What you want to do now is open this window," Dean said. "And get the unit placed right there in the hole."

Frank gripped one side of the unit and Biaggio took the other and they positioned it on the window frame, the heavier back end of the AC unit extending out the open window and dangling over the porch and yard below.

"Hang onto it there, Biaggio," Frank said. "We gotta secure it."

He extended two accordion-shaped fins from the sides of the unit, which were clearly designed to hold it in place in a standard-size window frame, but the hundred-year-old Aberdeen-size window frame was still too wide to hold the AC securely.

"Crap," Frank said. "It's too small for this window."

"It's not too small," Dean said. He stood back and squinted at the window, held his hands up and framed the AC between them.

"Take it back," Arla said.

"It's not too small," Dean said.

"I'll go with you to Home Depot," Arla said. "Sometimes they give you trouble about returning things."

"It ain't too small," Dean said. He nudged in between Frank and Biaggio. "You just gotta secure it better than that." He stood crammed up in the window frame, and he was so close to them that Frank could smell Dean's familiar scent of cigarette smoke

and Dial soap, and he flashed back to a moment in his childhood when Dean carried him on his shoulders across the sand
at Crescent Beach. Frank remembered he was dazzled by the
height, and he'd put his hands in Dean's thick black hair and
tightened his legs around Dean's back, and even when he got
down, at the car, the smell of his father's body stayed with him,
lingering about his own small frame like an aura. But that was
a long, long time ago. Frank felt old.

"Look here," Dean said. He fiddled with the window, banged
it down on top of the AC unit, wrestled with the side fins to try
to extend them farther against the width of the frame.

"Get a screwdriver," he said to Frank. "We'll bolt it."

"You can't bolt it," Frank said. "It's all metal. How you
going to bolt it?"

They'd all begun to sweat now, and Frank's forearms were
growing tired with the tension of holding the AC unit in the
window frame.

"We could nail it," Biaggio said.

"It's too small," Frank said. "You need a bigger unit. Did
you measure the window before you went to Home Depot?"

"Get a screwdriver," Dean said. "I'll bolt it."

"No," Frank said. "It won't work."

"Get a screwdriver." Dean was breathing hard, getting mad
now, and they were all straining against the weight of the AC.

"God, it *is* hot in here," Sofia said. "Are you almost finished?"

"They fuss at you if you don't have the receipt," Arla said.
"Do you still have the receipt?"

"I'll get the screwdriver," Biaggio said agreeably.

"Let Frank get it," Dean said. *What the hell?* It was like
Frank was fourteen again, Dean bossing him around, barking

orders, running the show, yet here he was a broken-down drunk sailing back in to save the day, standing in Arla's bedroom like the second coming, and all Frank wanted to do was go to the God-damned acrobats with Elizabeth. A rivulet of sweat ran down his back. He wondered if his shirt was becoming soaked.

"But I'll get the manager," Arla said. "I'll *make* them take it back."

"Fine," Frank said, "I'll get the screwdriver." But Biaggio was already in motion. He and Biaggio released the air conditioner at the same time. Dean was jolted forward with the weight of the unit, his too-big blue jeans flattened for a moment up against the front of the air conditioner and his torso straining to support the weight, and then his back tensed, his arms snapped back, and he gripped his backside with both hands and let out a cry of pain.

"Damn!" he said. "My cheek!"

The air conditioner tipped backward in what seemed like slow motion, and then it was gone. The electrical cord, snaking quickly up the wall, was the last thing Frank saw as the whole unit fell out of the window. He heard it crash solidly against the porch roof and then slide down the overhang and land on the walkway below. They all crowded around the window to look. The unit was smashed to pieces. One accordion side fan was already blowing down the driveway in the dissipating rain.

"Oh, no," Bell said.

"Well," Arla said. "Now *that* I don't know if they will take back."

"Nice job, Frank," Dean said.

"Screw you," Frank said.

Biaggio laughed nervously.

"Shit," Dean said. He scratched his head, stared out the window, and then turned and looked at Arla. "Well, that didn't work out as planned."

"I'm out of here," Frank said. He walked out of the bedroom and descended the stairs, to where Elizabeth was waiting in the open front door.

The moon was a slice of white in the sky, and the air was humid and hot, hanging like steam in the bowl of the amphitheater at the Utina Fairgrounds, where Frank, Elizabeth, and Bell sat together. In the stands, a flutter of white fans moved incessantly among the seats.

The acrobats were a traveling group from China, and Frank had no idea how they'd ever managed to get themselves booked here in Utina, of all the ridiculous places, where the amphitheater was parked in a hot, barren clearing south of the high school and where the regular acts were truck pulls, revivals, and craft shows, never something as culturally adventurous as Chinese acrobats. Another change. Another surprise. They seemed to be around every corner these days.

He felt sorry for the acrobats. This stillness. This heat. It was ludicrous, even for those who had lived here all their lives. The acrobats' satin costumes were stained with moisture. Their faces shone with sweat and consternation.

"Did you know your father is not drinking?" Elizabeth said. She spoke quietly, not wanting her daughter to hear, but Bell was absorbed in the action onstage, where the acrobats were enacting a complicated series of maneuvers involving a long row of straight-backed chairs and a dozen spinning plates atop long wooden dowels. Frank doubted she was paying any attention to their conversation. Bell's blond ponytail stuck to her back, and tiny drops of sweat ran down her face, but she seemed oblivious to the heat.

"Yes," Frank said. "So I hear. Six whole days. What an achievement. I think we should award him a medal. Probably first time in his life. I think he started drinking in the womb, you know."

Elizabeth rolled her eyes. "He's trying, Frank. He's making an effort."

"Who wouldn't? For a shot at all that money?"

She shrugged. The acrobats—ten of them, Frank counted—jumped down to the stage from atop their chairs, still spinning the plates.

"Well," she said. She leaned forward and took three bottles of water out of her bag. She gave one to Frank and one to Bell. "Hydrate," she said. "This heat, we'll all pass out."

"I used to think he was scary," Frank said. He wasn't sure where that observation came from, but it was true. He used to be afraid of Dean, used to shy away from his approach, duck his head, lower his voice. He could remember only a few times when his father had physically tangled with him, and in truth those times were more sloppy, clumsy, slapping sorts of dustups than anything dangerously focused or particularly painful. But still. "I used to think he was powerful."

"Me, too."

"But now—" Frank shook his head, annoyed. "He's just a weak old man. No money. No sense. Drinks like a fish. Not much going for him at all."

Elizabeth was quiet, regarding him.

"I don't know why my mother ever took up with him," he said finally, and it was true, he'd often thought it. The distance of years had given Frank a dispassionate ability to assess Dean in this manner, he supposed, and he felt as though he was mentally giving his father some sort of prenuptial critique. Besides a certain dark handsomeness that his father seemed to have possessed many years ago, he could see very little of redemption about the man.

"Oh, don't be so sure," Elizabeth said, evidently reading his mind. "Your father, he has a certain charm." He looked at her, saw she was smiling. "All you boys do. It's a Bravo thing."

He held her gaze for a moment and then felt himself flushing like a preteen. He looked away, changed the subject.

"So my sister," he said. "And Biaggio." Onstage, a young Chinese man dressed in white tights and a blue sequined shirt now stood atop one of the straight-backed chairs. The other acrobats formed a circle around him. The blue-shirted young man hopped down, placed another chair on top of the first one, and did a handstand on top of the two of them. Frank glanced down at the program in his lap, found a photo of the blue-shirted acrobat. "Chao Li" the program said. "Man of Amazing Balance!"

"I know," Elizabeth said. "They're, like, a *thing*."

"Have you known all along?"

"Just for a little while."

"What do you think of that?"

"I think he loves her."

Frank looked away.

"And you want to know something else? They're going to get married," Elizabeth said.

"You really think so?"

"I know so. He asked your father. I was there." She rolled her eyes.

"Shit." He shook his head. "He's even crazier than I thought."

"You should wish them well, Frank. She deserves to be happy."

"I just worry."

"I know you do."

"She's been so long with my mother. They're bent. Both of them."

"Sofia and your mother?"

"Sofia and Biaggio," he said. "*And* my mother. Shoot. All of them."

"They're not as crazy as you think," she said. She regarded him seriously. "And anyway, what does that really matter, when it comes right down to it?"

He shrugged.

"You think someone has to be smart, or even sane, to be capable of love?" She turned to face forward again, annoyed suddenly. "Smart's got nothing to do with it."

He'd made her angry, and he didn't know how or why.

"Well, anyway," he said. "They're getting married. Go figure. I think—"he tried to put words to it—"I think he'll actually take care of her."

On the stage, Chao Li was on his eighth chair. Frank counted again to make sure—yes, eight chairs stacked top to bottom, and there he went, climbing, smiling, to the top, where he gripped the top of the chair back and did another handstand. He had to be twenty-five feet in the air. Bell stared, rapt, her bottom lip hanging loose, her small hands gripping the water bottle.

"Damn," he said.

Elizabeth turned to him again, and her eyes were full.

"Maybe they know something all the rest of us can't figure out, Frank. Did you ever think of that?" He thought at first she was talking about the acrobats, but then he realized it was Biaggio and Sofia she was thinking of, two people capable of love, if nothing else.

"Elizabeth," Frank said. He felt the question rise up in his throat, a question full of desire. He wanted her. Her gaze was overwhelming. He looked back at the stage. Chao Li wobbled desperately but hung on. He wanted her. He wanted the light behind her brown eyes, wanted to travel directly into the core of her to find it, wanted it to eclipse and extinguish these other lights that fought so roundly in his heart, had fought for so long and so viciously and so completely, and he opened his mouth to say it, to ask for it, to beg for it, *please, please, please.*

"What?" She sniffled.

But he was silent.

"You going to ask me something?" she said.

He looked at her, her shoulders frail under her blue sundress, her hair like straw, those small, blessed freckles on her nose, and fear crept into his heart like a demon and struck him dumb.

"No," he said, turning back to the acrobats.

Chao Li fell from the ninth chair. The audience gasped, but he twisted like a cat in midair and landed on his white-stockinged feet, turning failure to triumph and waving to the crowd with a thin, taut smile on his face. He limped off the stage, and Frank watched when he entered the wings, saw the way the smile faded, the way the shadow passed over the young man's eyes.

* * *

They drove back to Aberdeen and Frank waited in the kitchen while Elizabeth walked upstairs to say good night to Bell. When she came back downstairs, he got up from the table, said good-bye, and headed for the door.

"Frank," she said, and he turned to face her. He stood in the open doorway, his back against the frame. The light from the porch was diffused, weak, and a damp, creeping night breeze snaked along the floor and touched their ankles. The house was silent, and Frank pictured Arla, Sofia, and Dean upstairs, asleep in separate bedrooms like children in an orphanage.

"What were you going to ask me?" she said. "Earlier?"

He felt a little sick, like when he was a small boy and he'd been caught doing something he wasn't supposed to. Snooping in his mother's drawers. Sneaking chocolates from the corner store. Wanting something for himself that he wasn't supposed to have. "Nothing."

"Ask me," she said.

"No."

"Ask me."

He shook his head. "I can't, Elizabeth."

She reached out and put her hand around his wrist, and they stood that way for a moment, looking at each other, silent, standing on the brink of hope and desire and certain disaster.

"Ask me," she said.

And so he did. And she said yes, and they walked through the open doorway, into the still, hot night, into the woods. They walked through the old pathway to Uncle Henry's, into Frank's office. They lay down on the soft couch under the window, not speaking, only touching. And as he entered her he thought nothing of Carson, or Arla, or Bell, or betrayal or sin or darkness, and he thought only of Elizabeth, of warmth and goodness and light and freedom, which was all he ever wanted to begin with.

SEPTEMBER

SEVENTEEN

The fritters were going to burn, was what Arla Bravo was thinking the moment her oldest child and only daughter turned her
face to the sun and murmured her wedding vows to Biaggio
Antonio Dunkirk under a wrought-iron arbor laced with silk
carnations on the back deck of Uncle Henry's Bar & Grill. My
Lord! It was bad enough, this confounded rush to the altar, Sofia
in a hell-fire hurry once the cat was out of the bag, insisting
the wedding take place before the sale of Aberdeen and Uncle
Henry's to satisfy her confounded allegiance to order and planning. What was it, three weeks since they'd announced their
engagement? Must everything be a fire drill? Arla had scarcely
had time to adjust to the unbelievable sight of Dean Bravo sitting
in her kitchen every morning when she'd found herself shuttling
around St. Augustine with Sofia, haunting the aisles of Hobby
Lobby to pick out wedding invitations and party favors. And now,
with Frank standing up for Biaggio, and with Morgan lounging

at the kitchen door and watching the ceremony, all soft-eyed and dreamy and not paying a lick of attention to what was going on in the deep fryer, the God-damned fritters were going to burn. Did she have to do *everything* herself?

She craned her neck around, tried to catch Morgan's eye. But then Mac Weeden, officiating on his notary's license, pronounced Biaggio and Sofia husband and wife. Somebody hit the button on the CD player and here came Bon Jovi's "Thank You for Loving Me" (good Lord in heaven, what kind of music was that for a wedding?), and all the guests stood up and clapped. Sofia and Biaggio kissed, and Morgan retreated to the kitchen, where he was supposed to be, so finally Arla could relax and worry about the next problem, which was having to sit at the same table as Dean Bravo, her long-lost husband, for the next three hours.

But all this, she supposed, was better than thinking about the *real* problem, the *big* problem, which was that she was moving out of Aberdeen on Monday, exactly two days from now. The new condo was painted and ready—eggshell Berber carpet in the bedrooms and wood parquet in the living room and kitchen. First floor, no stairs. A screened-in lanai overlooking a crisply manicured retention pond the shape of a gel-tab. Willough Walk, it was called. The Villas of Willough Walk. If that wasn't dumber than a box of rocks.

But she couldn't complain. She mustn't complain. It was the right thing to do. She couldn't continue to be the holdout, the one Bravo barrier against big money, "real money," as that hobgoblin Cryder kept calling it, for all her family. For Carson. For Frank. For Sofia. Even for Morgan. She'd made the decision. She'd stick with it.

It's just that it was all happening so *quickly.* Sofia and Biaggio—married, just like that. "Why wait?" Sofia had said. "*Mon dieu,* we're not getting any younger—*any* of us." Sofia— her lovely, addled daughter. She'd stood before Arla, told her she was marrying Biaggio, and Arla had been unprepared for the pain of this announcement, for the way the words made her heart fall, her stomach lurch, her fingers turn cold. She had a flash of memory—azaleas blooming off the lanai, the look on her mother's face when she'd announced her engagement to Dean—but then she shook herself, forced her consciousness back to reality. Biaggio was a good man. He'd take care of Sofia. "Won't your family come to the wedding?" she'd asked him last week. "Your mother? Your brother?" He'd turned pink, had looked at her in a funny way, half sad, half contented, and then he'd said, "You're my family, Miss Arla. All ya'll here. You Bravos."

And she'd felt then, for the first time in many, many years, that perhaps Sofia was going to be all right.

Oh, but *Aberdeen*—the weeks now come down to days, the packing cartons mounting up in each room, more and more piles of rubbish making their way out to the end of the long driveway for trash pickup. "You can't take this," Frank would say, again and again, helping her weed through the last four decades of her belongings, the last four decades of her *life*, and though she'd objected at first, clinging to the old lamps, the spindly furnish- ings, the stacks of books and yellowed linens and chipped hotel- grade china, she'd begun to acquiesce in the last couple of weeks. Let it go, she told herself over and over, staring forlornly at the piles of clothes, the baskets, the knickknacks, the magazines, the handbags, the wine racks and slipcovers. *Let it go.*

No more ironing, they said. No more worrying about the restaurant, they said. A nice, clean condo. Ground floor. Berber carpet. But scarcely any windows, she remembered now, thinking of the place again after having shoved the image of it out of her mind for the duration of Sofia's marriage vows. And how could you trust a home that didn't have enough windows? It was like a person with no eyes.

But she'd said yes. She'd said she would do it. She'd agreed to the sale not long after Dean had arrived back at Aberdeen, her resistance mortally wounded and gradually finished off after a week of coming down the stairs each morning to find him sitting at the table with the shakes, sucking on coffee and cigarettes and staring out the kitchen window at the light dawning on the Intracoastal.

"It's a pretty place," he said to Arla on the first morning. The night before, after Carson and Elizabeth had made up a bed for Dean in the room that used to be Carson's, Arla had stayed in her room, keeping company with a bottle of Carlo Rossi, not even coming out to use the bathroom until she was sure Dean was asleep. "It's sure a pretty place," he said that morning.

Arla had fetched a cup of coffee and retreated back upstairs.

On the second morning, he had the coffee ready for her when she came downstairs, mixed up with two spoonfuls of sugar and a tiny blip of cream, just the way she liked it, and she thanked him, picked it up from the table and went back to her bedroom, even though these additional trips up the stairs were outside her usual ambitions and were beginning to wear on her.

On the third day, he'd made her a plate of raisin toast and even sprinkled a little extra white sugar at the edges, and she stared at him for a moment and then sat down at the table.

"What are you doing here?" she said.

He cleared his throat. "Well, Carson said—" he began.

"No. Not Carson. You. What are you doing here?"

He'd looked around the kitchen, at the Felix clock and the blue vinyl tablecloth and the stacks of Hostess crumb cakes and boxes of Little Debbies piled on one corner of the counter. The rust stains in the sink and the packets of take-out tartar sauce in the lazy Susan on the table, the bottles of pills on the windowsill, the canisters of Tang.

"I think we should sell the house, Arla," he said.

It was the pronoun, *we*, that had gotten to her, making her angry at first, of course, but later working on her in a strange subtle way, the intimacy of the word, that oddly familial possessiveness he still had, the simple, unavoidable fact, that, to Dean's way of thinking, they were still a "we."

"I think 'we' should stick it where the sun don't shine," she'd said that first day. "You didn't ask me if I wanted to buy it. Now you're asking me to sell it?" She gripped her cane, resisted the temptation to bludgeon him with it, and clomped out of the room.

But he was still there the next morning. And the morning after that. After a week, she had an experience that felt like a hallucination, when she came down the stairs to start the linens and he was standing at the kitchen sink, looking vacantly out toward the Intracoastal, as he'd been doing so often since he arrived, just staring at the water. She saw him for just a moment as a younger version of himself, that handsome boy she'd been so taken with, back when they were both so stupid, so very, very stupid. Then the old Dean turned to her, and the image was gone.

"Are you here because you want to come back?" she said. "To me?"

"Would you have me?" he said.

"I don't know." She didn't. She didn't know much of anything, anymore. And this confusion was becoming a near-physical ailment, a nagging discomfort. She was sick of it.

"Well. Neither do I," he said.

She sighed, sat down at the table, and propped her cane against a chair.

"Whatever happened to us, Dean?"

"We got old."

"I mean before that."

He looked away.

"I don't know, Arla."

"We're not who we used to be."

"I don't think I ever was," he said.

She'd thought about that for a long time. Funny, that he appeared only now to have begun to accept that notion, that disillusionment in himself. He'd always been so confident be-fore. For Arla's part, she'd had her moment of epiphany so long ago, when she was married only a couple of months, and she remembered it clearly, lying beside Dean in their bed as he slept, letting the truth of her own imperfections wash over her like rain. Now he was there, too, he had arrived at that moment. He knew what he was, knew what he wasn't. Knew what they could not be together. So what did Aberdeen really matter? What was a house, anyway, in a world where nobody was who you thought they were, not even yourself? She was a long way from the Arla Bolton she'd once been. She once thought that everyone loved her. She was wrong. She once thought that Dean was forever.

She was wrong. Now she thought she needed this house. Maybe she was wrong about that, too.

The next time he asked her about the house, she'd signed the papers: the sales contract, the title search, and who knew what else. Carson met with Cryder and worked it all out, and she signed anything they put in front of her. Susan Holm had arranged the condo—lease with an option to buy. "For when you decide what to do with your money," she'd said to Arla.

And now the closing was set for Wednesday at People's Guarantee. "Unless you change your mind," Doreen Bailey had said over the phone when she'd called Arla to finalize a few details on the forms. But Arla knew none of the parties involved would be changing their minds. They'd settled on a handsome price with Vista: nine million dollars for all the properties, which meant six million to the Bravos and three million to Morgan Moore. Morgan was leaving for Memphis tomorrow, would close on the deal by proxy, have his proceeds wired. So this was it. Saturday, Sunday, Monday, Tuesday. Their last days at Aberdeen.

She looked at Sofia now, on her wedding day, and it pained her how much Sofia—though forty-three and no spring chicken—reminded her of a younger version of herself. Sofia wore a creamy linen sundress and wedge sandals, and her red hair hung loose around her shoulders. She was beautiful. Just like Arla used to be. And Biaggio, oh dear, that man, looking hot and uncomfortable in a shirt and tie—but had she ever seen anyone so happy as Biaggio was today? She just hoped he knew what he was in for.

How long ago? 1964. Dean's eyes upon her. An A-line silk gown, a chapel-length train. The cool red tiles of the Cathedral Basilica. Her two smooth white feet in creamy ballerina flats, the toenails underneath painted the color of peonies.

"You okay, Arla?" The voice was Elizabeth's, who sat down next to her. Arla was surprised to find her eyes had grown wet, and she dabbed at them quickly, before anyone else saw.

"Oh, I'm fine," she said. "Dandy." She cleared her throat. "How about you?"

Elizabeth shrugged, grinned. "Well, I'm not so much on the marriage train these days myself, you know, but they sure look happy."

"You and me both, honey," Arla said. "What were we, crazy?"

"Must have been, Arla. Crazy. They got us with that Bravo charm, I guess. Pow." Elizabeth feigned a pistol shot with her right hand.

Arla snorted. She looked over at Carson, first in line at the bar now that the ceremony was over, and then at Dean, who was looking pained, sitting on a plastic deck chair with a bottle of Diet Coke clamped between his knees. The wedding guests flurried around him, but he sat very still. She had no idea where he planned to live next, and she had no intention of asking. She wondered how far he was planning to push his "we," how far he thought it would take him, if he thought, in fact, that it would take him all the way into The Villas of Willough Walk, and she laughed a little bit. "Yes, that's it," she said. "The Bravo charm." She had another vision of herself then, eighteen and haughty, sassing her parents on the day of her engagement to Dean. Oh, she was something then. Maybe she still was.

Sofia clutched Biaggio's hand in a childlike way. They still stood under the tiny arbor, evidently bagging the planned recessional march through the dining room and beginning to laugh, to relax, as the first of the wedding guests—An-Needa Lovett, looked like—approached them to offer congratulations.

"Biaggio has a record, you know," Arla said to Elizabeth. "I mean, a criminal record. He has a checkered past."

"Oh, well," Elizabeth said. "We all do, in our own ways, don't we?"

The smell of biscuits and onions had begun to creep in from the kitchen, a comforting smell, solid and familiar and good.

"Elizabeth," Arla said. "You think she's going to be okay?" Her voice caught. She looked at Sofia.

Elizabeth watched as Biaggio leaned in when Sofia spoke to him, as he kept one hand in the small of her back, his huge frame soft and pliable.

"I think she will, Arla. I think they both will." She smiled, and Arla believed her.

Frank came over, sat down next to Arla, though there was an empty chair next to Elizabeth.

"Well," he said. He looked very tired.

"Well, hell," Arla said. "You're just getting started. You've got a party to put on here, mister. You're in charge."

"Not for long," Frank said. He looked around the restaurant. The wedding reception was the last stand for Uncle Henry's. They'd closed to the public the night before, and Arla had made sure to stay away, stay home at Aberdeen, away from the last call and the rowdy, sloppy good-byes, and the tears and the memories. She'd heard the music, though, from where she sat on the back porch of Aberdeen, heard the last strains of Patsy Cline and Bob Marley winding through the trees, and as the night wore on she heard the customers break into bawdy song at closing time, "Freebird," of all the foolish things.

But tonight was a private party, though it was hard to see much of a difference from last night's crowd, with all the usual suspects in their customary places: Mac Weeden, having evidently worked up a thirst from his stint as wedding celebrant, holding full court with his brother George from his regular perch at the center of the bar; Irma stomping through the dining room with a serving tray on her shoulder, though tonight dressed in a long, lacy black number that had Arla and everyone else scratching their heads; Susan Holm flitting from table to table and making eyes at Frank from across the room; and Bell, lovely little Bell, feeding pieces of conch fritter to a pair of cats who'd wandered in from the parking lot. Oh, health department be damned, Arla thought. We're closed, anyway.

"Why don't you make yourself useful, get me a Chablis," Arla said to Frank. The bar was self-service tonight, and he watched uncomfortably, it seemed to Arla, as the guests wandered freely behind the bar—*his* bar—and helped themselves to whatever was left in stock. It was going to be quite a party, Arla thought, all these 'necks declaring open season on the bar at Uncle Henry's.

"What can I get you, Elizabeth?" Frank said. Arla did not miss the softness in his voice, and neither did Elizabeth, who looked up at Frank and hesitated a beat. "Get me a daiquiri, bartender," she said. "I'm celebrating tonight."

"The wedding?" Arla said as Frank headed for the bar.

"That, and Independence Day," Elizabeth said. She narrowed her eyes, watched Carson chatting up a blonde at the end of the bar.

"It's September. You're a little late for that," Arla said.

"We'll see," Elizabeth said.

An-Needa Lovett approached the table.

"Hey baby," she said to Arla, leaning forward to envelop her in a hug. "You lookin' good, Arla."

"Huh," Arla said. "Looking good for an old bat, you mean."

"Take one to know one," An-Needa said.

"Well, that's true," Arla said.

Elizabeth laughed. "You're both beautiful," she said. "Aren't they, Bell?" Bell looked from An-Needa to Arla and back, but did not answer. An-Needa chuckled. "Oh, mercy!" she said. "She don't need to say a word!" Arla smiled.

"What's funny over here?" Mac Weeden said. He pulled an extra chair over to the table and sat down, and Arla was touched that he'd given up his spot at the bar to come and pay his respects to her. She'd known Mac since he was a boy, since they all were boys. Where did the years go? Mac was joined a moment later by George, who carried a plate of hoppin' John and a bottle of Budweiser. An-Needa stiffened at the sight of him. When Frank returned with the drinks, he'd brought an extra glass of Chablis for An-Needa, and she accepted it, nodded at Frank, and began fanning herself. Susan Holm approached, perched herself on the edge of Frank's chair. Elizabeth looked away.

"I got new estimates on the Mazda," Susan said to Frank. "It's down to three thousand, five hundred, you'll be glad to hear."

"Glad for you, you mean," Frank said.

"Glad for *you*, big boy," she said. "You're paying for it."

Frank stared at her. "I wasn't the one driving around with no insurance," he said.

"Well, I wasn't the one threatening a lady in a motor vehicle."

"How 'bout them Gators, Frank?" Mac said.

"How 'bout 'em, Mac," Frank said. He rolled his eyes, but then turned to Mac, and Arla sensed he was grateful for the subject change.

"We gonna kill Miami just like we killed Hawaii. You watch."

"I'll take your word for it, Mac."

"Coach better get his offense together," George said. "It's like he's stuck in first gear."

"There's a lot of that going around," Susan said, tapping her fingernails on Frank's shoulder.

Morgan walked up to the table with a whole Key lime pie and a handful of forks. He put the pie in the middle of the table and passed around the forks.

"No wedding cake?" Susan said.

"Nah," Arla said. "Sofia wanted An-Needa's pies. Who needs cake when we've got An-Needa?" An-Needa smiled broadly, leaned forward, and waited her turn to dip her fork into the pie.

"Morgan," Elizabeth said. "What are you going to do now? Mr. Big Bucks."

"Hell," Morgan said. "I'll believe it when I see it."

"That will be Wednesday, my friend," Frank said.

Morgan shook his head, scooped another mouthful of pie. "Hard to believe it's all really happening," he said. "But I'm going to Memphis. I got me some kids in Memphis. I figure I'll spend some time up there. Maybe plant a garden, hunt a bit. I think I'm done frying fish."

"I'll bet you are, Morgan," Arla said. She caught his eye, and she smiled, though she could see worry in his face, and uncertainty. *It's okay*, she wanted to say to him. *I'll be okay. We'll all be okay.*

"So you hear about Tip Breen?" Mac said. "Warming up a cot at the county jail."

"No shit?" George said. "What for?"

"Watch your mouth, Weeden," Frank said, exasperated. "There's ladies present." George looked around, surprised. "Oh," he said. "I'm sorry, Elizabeth."

Susan cleared her throat, tapped her foot.

"Vandalism, reckless endangerment," Mac said. "They picked him up hiding in the woods outside the new Publix, the day after it opened. He's been shooting out the bulbs in the big parking lot lights. And he missed and hit the manager's car, while he was still in it. Tip's in a heap of trouble. He's going nuts over all the building around here. He thinks it's killing the old Utina."

"He's the one been doing that?" Frank said. "Every time I came by there another one of those lights was out."

"So he's been shooting them?" Arla said. "My word." She didn't think Tip Breen had it in him. But good for him, she found herself thinking. Damn Publix, yuppie supermarket. And all those horrid housing developments springing up all along Monroe Road and heading out to the beach. Next thing you knew they'd be putting in a Starbucks on Seminary Street. A Wine Warehouse. A Sports Authority. And where did that leave Tip Breen? Where did that leave Lil' Champ? Where did that leave Utina? She felt a shooting bolt of guilt, then. The Bravos. They'd sold Aberdeen. And Uncle Henry's. Where did *they* leave Utina? It wasn't the first time this conundrum had crossed her mind. She pushed it away. It probably wouldn't be the last time, either.

"Is he going to get out?" Frank said.

"He can't make bail," Mac said. "He's broke. He's too poor to pay attention—was about bankrupt even before he got arrested. Can't compete with that supermarket."

"Shoot," Frank said, and they were all quiet for a moment.

"No more Lil' Champ," George said.

"No more Uncle Henry's," An-Needa said.

"This place is going to change," Elizabeth said.

"Already has," Frank said, and it seemed to Arla that he was looking at Elizabeth, waiting to catch her eye, but she looked away.

And then it was all winding down. The dinner, the drinks, the dancing, the music, the chatter. Dean hadn't drunk a drop. Arla was impressed, though he'd sucked down one Diet Coke after another and Arla was sure with all that caffeine he'd be roaming the halls of Aberdeen all night long. But he was not her problem, and she had no intention of making him so, tonight or ever. Arla walked over to Sofia and Biaggio, where they stood at the deck railing, looking out over the water. It was dark now, though the lights from Uncle Henry's still illuminated the shore.

"Well, darlings, I'm done," she said.

"You get enough to eat, Miss Arla?" Biaggio said.

"Oh, yes. Don't I look it?" Arla said. She smiled. "He's a good man, Sofia."

"I know, *maman*."

"There aren't many of those."

"I know."

Biaggio shifted from foot to foot, embarrassed.

"I'll take you home now, Miss Arla," Biaggio said. "You must be tired."

"Oh, Biaggio, don't be ridiculous. You're the groom. And you're a married man now," she added. Biaggio looked startled to hear this. "You can't be running around with other women, hear?" She hugged him, surprising even herself. She was not a hugger. His face turned red. "I'll get Carson to take me home," she said.

She walked out to the back deck, where the reflection of the moon was now splintered across the water and the cries of the barred owls had begun to echo in the trees. She'd had too many glasses of wine, she knew, though she didn't particularly care. She clutched her cane in one hand and her purse in the other and made her way to the end of the boat dock. She looked left, to the distant glow of the porch light at Aberdeen. She looked right, to where Morgan's restaurant had stood years before. Along the reedy shore, in the light of the full moon, were a series of small, newly cut wooden posts, each tied with a bright red band. Surveyors' marks, she supposed. The beginning. Or the end, depending on how you looked at it.

The placid wash of water against the few boats moored at the dock was making her sleepy, and a bit dizzy, so she gripped her cane and picked her way back along the dock to the restaurant. She circled the main dining room, not going inside, until she reached the edge of the property and the sandy parking lot. Turning her back on Uncle Henry's, she walked to the edge of the lot, where the path to Aberdeen shone, lonely, before her. How many years since she'd taken this path? She thought of Drusilla, alone in the woods for so long. She wanted to go home, but she didn't want to go with Carson, to hear his angry banter. She tried not to think about the stack of packing cartons piled up on the front porch at Aberdeen, the condo keys on their bright plastic fob hanging from a hook under the Felix clock in the kitchen.

She stuck her cane out in front of her, shook it into the underbrush. "Everybody out," she said. "I'm coming in." And indeed, something thickish rustled in the brush and then crashed away, but Arla was brave tonight, and she shook the cane again and started into the path.

The mud under the pine needles and oak leaves was slick from recent rains, and the air in the thicket smelled musky and cool. The mosquitoes were ubiquitous, buzzing around her eyelids and ears, but the wedding guests had all sprayed themselves with Cutter while sitting out on the deck, to ward off the no-see-ums, and Arla was glad for that now as she pushed thicker into the woods and squinted her eyes to make out the remnants of the path.

Oh, what a lovely place this was, Utina. Sweet and wild and rare. She was not surprised that the rich people wanted to live here. She'd never appreciated Utina as much as she should have, and she knew that now. Here in the woods was where it was best of all, this little stretch off Aberdeen, where the ghosts of all the palms that had lived and died still flitted lovely and light through the canopy, where the aches of lost loves dissolved and the searing pain of death was cooled.

She pushed on, farther, looking for the place she remembered, where the three red cedars formed a triangle just to the right of the path. When she came to it, she was afraid in the darkness she would not be able to see, but she waited for a moment, and a cloud which had obscured the moon shifted, and then Drusilla's headstone shone bright and radiant and spoke to Arla in a language only she could understand.

"Oh, there you are, darling," Arla said. "My friend. There you are."

She sat down on a thick pine that had fallen lengthwise along the path. This was new; she hadn't remembered this tree here before, though it was covered in lichens and rotted at the broken end in a way that suggested it had been down for some time. She'd missed Drusilla. Her ailing body had kept her out of the woods for so long. She'd forgotten what solace Drusilla provided, what sweetness, what quiet, patient love. When Arla could still get around better, she came into the woods almost every day after washing the linens to pour buckets of consecrated water around Drusilla's grave, feeling foolish at first for doing it, like some myopic zealot, but persisting just the same, all those years, all those buckets of water laced with holy wine, sacred bread, the microscopic particles of priestly deodorant and facial hair and dandruff. It meant something to Arla. And it meant something to Drusilla, too, she believed. In more recent years, when she couldn't get down the wooded path, she'd poured the buckets directly into the Intracoastal, where the water mingled with the faraway ashes of her honey-haired boy, now dissolved into sediment at the bottom of the channel, miles and miles away.

"Drusilla," Arla said tonight, settling down on the fallen pine tree. "You would not believe what is going on up at the house."

And she told her, then, about the sale of Aberdeen and Uncle Henry's. And about Dean's return, and Carson and Elizabeth breaking up. About the new Publix and Tip Breen and Morgan's family in Memphis. And Sofia's wedding. And about Frank—only she stopped there, frowned, cocked her head to the side. She didn't know what to tell Drusilla about Frank. Sometimes it seemed like he was the one she knew least of all. He had a secret, it often seemed, something deep inside that he kept hidden, removed.

"Maybe he's the most like me," she said. "Poor thing." She chuckled, then fell silent. And Will. Maybe Will was the one most like Dean. Back at Uncle Henry's, the music had become more muted, and she sensed that the reception was ending. Dean would be back at Aberdeen soon, and Elizabeth, and Bell. She should get back, see if anyone was ready for tea.

"I'll bet you were a beautiful lady, Drusilla," she said. "I can just tell. I'll bet the men just *loved* you. That's how it was for me, too. I remember. You had something a little bit special, didn't you? Once?"

Drusilla was silent. The wine rushed in Arla's ears. The mosquitoes were becoming thicker, and she knew the Cutter would last only so long.

"Well, all right then," she said. "I'm not sure when I'll get back, Drusilla. This damn foot, you know. And I guess I'm moving. Willough Walk, for the love of Pete. So I guess it might be a while, Drusilla." She wished she had something to leave behind. Poor Drusilla—under the wretched marina forever. She opened her purse, felt around in the dark, and her hand closed over a tiny beaded compact, a gift from Will the Christmas before he died. She'd carried it with her, always, but she felt compelled tonight, for some reason, to leave it for Drusilla. She bent over and balanced the compact on the headstone.

"Did you ever lose one, Drusilla?" she said. "It's a heck of a thing. A game changer, I'll tell you that." She straightened up. "Oh, Drusilla," she said. "I miss him."

The compact sparkled in the moonlight on the cold gray stone, and Arla's throat caught.

"Good-bye, love," she whispered.

Arla took a step backward then, but she lost her footing in the tangle of brambles and the fallen branches, and the ground came rushing up to meet her. Her head contacted with the ragged edge of the pine stump and everything went bright white for a moment before she sat up again, put her hand to her head, and felt the blood.

"*Non*," she said. "Oh, no."

It took a long time to get back to Aberdeen after that. She had to sit down many times, once flat into a boggy patch of moss that soaked her backside and ruined her dress and made her feel ashamed, as though she had wet herself, and in truth she was not entirely sure whether maybe that had happened, too. She had to struggle over to her hands and knees to get back up, and she was dizzy and shaking all over, so she held a tree to steady herself. She pressed a handkerchief against the wound on her head, but it soaked through, so after a while she dropped it, and then she realized that somewhere she had dropped her purse, too, and so there were no more handkerchiefs to be had. She kept walking. When she was young the walk down this path had taken no more than fifteen minutes. Now it felt like hours. She used to have a cane. Where was the cane?

Through the trees, the sky above was thick and black, and she stopped for another moment, leaned against a tree and looked up. The blackness began to undulate, and shimmer, and then it was alive, the sky, with blues and purples, greens and oranges. It was alive and sliding across the firmament like mother of pearl, bright and hot as copper, and oh my Lord in heaven, she knew what it was, and though she was very happy, she cried a little bit and she stood and watched for a long, long time.

When it stopped, she walked some more, and then the light on the porch at Aberdeen blinked at her, winked like an eye, telling her about a secret. And then Elizabeth was there, and Bell, and Dean—my word, *Dean*—putting his arms around her and helping her up into the house, into the bedroom. There was lots of talk about a doctor, and a hospital, she was aware of that, and she said "no, no, no" and looked them in the eye and told them she was fine, just leave her alone, she wanted to sleep, that was all, with all the wretched packing she had to do tomorrow. Just leave me alone, she said. I'm just a little drunk, she said. That's all. She'd never said that about herself before. It felt odd, shameful. She was sorry, to have said it in front of Bell.

She took a shower and kicked her muddy clothes into the bottom of her closet. Tomorrow she would go back down the path for her cane, her purse. She put a bandage on her forehead. The wound was not so bad after all—these head wounds, they always look worse than they are. She thought about fetching a cool glass of Chablis from the kitchen, but then thought it probably wasn't a good idea. She clung to the wall and made her way to the bed. She lay back, and then Dean was standing over her in the darkness.

"What?" she said, sharply.

"I got your cane. And your purse," he said. "On the path." He hung the bag at the foot of the bed, propped the cane against the wall.

"Thank you."

"Arla."

He pulled a chair up next to her bed and sat down.

She waited for him to speak, and after a moment, he did.

"I'm sorry, Arla."

"You should be," she said.

He was quiet again, and the minutes passed, and she might have drifted to sleep for a moment, but then she was aware that he had reached out his hand, placed it lightly on her left leg. She almost laughed—was this it, then? Did he honestly think—? But no, that was not it, she understood, as he grazed his fingertips down the length of her leg to her damaged, foreshortened foot, lying bare on the bed with no bandages or socks to cover it. He touched her foot, closed his big palm over the whole of it, felt along the surface of the skin for several long minutes, as if he were reading a map. Then he got up and kissed her on the top of her head.

"I saw the northern lights, Dean," she murmured. "They were beautiful."

"Good night, Arla," he said. And then he was gone.

Eighteen

Elizabeth rose early, again, this was becoming a habit, but between the emotion of the wedding, the drama of Arla's fall last night, the separation from Carson, Bell's kicking, and the unsettling aura of being in Frank's boyhood bedroom, sleep had proven elusive. Now the Felix clock read six o'clock, and she stood in the kitchen doorway for a moment, watching the white plastic eyes pivot back and forth with clocklike lunacy. She filled the carafe with water from the tap and went for the coffee canister.

She was on her second cup when Dean appeared in the doorway, and she jumped when she saw him, then felt guilty for the reaction.

"Here," she said quietly, pushing a chair out with her foot. "Sit."

He limped to the counter, poured himself a cup of coffee, and sat down to drink it black.

"Some night, huh?" he said, and she nodded, thinking of Arla's bloodied head, how ashen Dean had looked when he'd seen her.

"You still in pain?" she said.

"Hell," he said. "All I know is the pain I'm in." He cleared his throat. "What are you doing up so early, missy?" he said. His face was gaunt, and his hands shook until he held them both around his cup.

"Can't sleep. Bell's a kicker. What about you?"

"I can't never sleep. I guess life's a kicker," he said. "I feel like I haven't slept in years."

He reached for the pack of cigarettes in his pocket, then checked himself.

"Go ahead," she said.

"I'll wait. You don't need that stink this early."

"I don't mind."

He looked at her, drumming his fingers on the coffee cup.

"How long we known you, Elizabeth?"

"Twenty years?" she said. She furrowed her brow. "No, gosh. Longer. Thirty? Lord."

"Huh. Since you were just a kid."

"A stupid kid," she added, and then they were silent again for a few minutes. She tried not to stare directly at him, but she positioned her gaze somewhere behind his head so she could study him in her peripheral vision: his thinning hair, his drawn mouth, his haunted eyes. He looked older than he should have.

"Where have you been, Dean?" she said. "I mean, all these years?"

He took a sip of coffee, shook his head.

"Around," he said. "Here and there. Not far. Palatka. Green Cove. I lived on a boat for a couple of years in Daytona. But it sank. I guess I don't have good luck with boats."

She smiled.

"I pulled a sentence, too, at Starke. Two years. No fun. I don't recommend it."

"What for?"

"DUI." He shook his head. "I'm not what you call a quick study."

"How come you never came back?"

He shrugged. "Well," he said, but then he stopped, shook his head again. "You know something, Elizabeth? You're the only one who asked where I been. The others, they didn't."

"They're pretty angry."

"I know."

His hand flicked again to his cigarettes, then returned to his coffee cup. He looked so sad and beaten that she wanted to cry, but he was last on the list of things she planned to cry about anytime soon, so she bit her lip and spooned another small pile of sugar into her coffee. The sky outside the kitchen window was still pitch-black. It might have been the middle of the night.

"I suppose I'll be coming into a little money here," he said. "Wednesday, they say."

"More than a little, Dean."

"So I guess I'll take a bit of that and be off again."

"You're not going to stay?"

"They don't want me to, Elizabeth. You know as well as I do."

She looked away.

"So what about you?" he said. "You going back with Carson, or—?"

Or what? She wondered how much Dean knew, or suspected, about her and Frank.

"That's the million-dollar question, I guess," she said. She felt a creeping chill, suddenly, which made no sense. It was September in Utina. But still. She was cold.

"He's got a million-dollar answer. Or will, on Wednesday."

"It's not about the money."

"I know that, darlin'," he said gently.

"I'm going to stay with Arla, for now," she said. "In the new condo. Me and Bell."

He nodded, then reached for his cigarettes a third time, and this time took one out, tapped it on the table, lit it up, and took a deep drag. She really didn't mind the smell of it. It was fatherly, somehow, soothing.

"Are you happy about Sofia?" she asked.

He exhaled, leaned back, and looked up.

"I'm happy," he said after a minute. "And I'm relieved. I like that Biaggio. He'll take good care of her." He sat very still, staring at the ceiling. "You didn't really have much of a family life, did you?" he said, after a moment.

"Nah," she said, shrugging her shoulders. "My mother, you know, she was pretty sad. She wasn't all there." The thought hit her at the moment she said it, and for the first time she could remember, she felt something for her mother more akin to pity than to anger. Her throat tightened. *She missed out,* she thought suddenly, remembering Bell's soft legs against her in the night. *My mother missed out. On me.*

"Same here," Dean said.

"Really?"

"Yeah. My parents were not so good. Pretty bad, in fact. I'm kind of surprised my brothers and I grew up at all."

She smiled. "But you made it."

"You think so?" he said. "I guess." He grew quiet, and he stared at the ceiling again, and when he spoke next his voice had taken a new texture, rough and strained.

"My father killed my mother," he said. "Not all at once, you know, but he killed her just the same. Hit her so hard, so many times. Broke her, just broke her. The last time was the worst. Knocked out all her front teeth so she looked like hell, and then they had to operate, had to remove part of her intestines, they'd been so damaged by the blows. So she had to just wait, hooked up to a tube, just set and wait to die. Couldn't eat. Couldn't shit. Looking like a dead body. But she could still talk, though I can't repeat the things she said," he said. He took a drag of his cigarette. "It took two months."

Elizabeth stared at him, nearly frozen. Her hands had grown icy in her lap.

"I thought for a while I'd kill him back," Dean said. "I mean, I really thought I would. One day I was driving down A1A, thinking I'd go try to find him. He used to hang out at the pier in St. Auggie, and I had my mind made up. I had a pistol in my pants."

"But you didn't," she said.

"No, I didn't."

"You changed your mind? That day?"

He looked at her, and a twitching, sad smile played at his lips.

"I met Arla," he said. "That day."

*   *   *

They sat together for a long time after that, Elizabeth and Dean, until the sun began to bring the trees outside the kitchen window into focus and the morning's first birds began to call.

"I can't stay," he said finally. "I can't."

"Okay."

"I ain't saying it's right. It's just the way it is."

"Okay."

"They're better off."

She didn't answer.

"Too many ghosts," he said. "I'll stay till Wednesday, but then I gotta go." He stood up, walked out the back door.

"Dean, wait," she said, and he turned back. "Why did you tell me this today? About your parents?"

He nodded, pursed his lips. "Because I thought you should know that we're all a little messed up," he said.

"Oh, I knew that already," she said, smiling.

"We're messed up, but we're still family," he said. "And maybe we're still family *because* we're so messed up. And that includes you, missy." He raised a shaking hand and pointed at her. Then he turned and walked out the back door.

Elizabeth got up and collected the cups from the table, brought them over to the sink. Her hands were shaking, and a vision of Dean, a young Dean, came to her. She imagined him looking like Carson, so bold, that thick black hair, those broad shoulders. Why had nobody ever told her about Dean's parents? Surely Frank and Carson and Arla knew about this. She thought she knew everything about the Bravos.

She closed her eyes. When she opened them and looked out the kitchen window, Dean was standing at the water's edge, arms crossed, just standing and looking.

And then Bell was there at her elbow, pulling at Elizabeth's sleeve.

"There's something wrong with Granny," Bell said.

Elizabeth turned and looked at her, saw the child's big eyes and quivering chin.

"Sit down here, Bell," she said, pulling out a kitchen chair.

She took the steps two at a time, running to Arla's bedroom, though she knew, somehow, that she needn't rush, that the thing that had happened was done, it was over, it was final.

"Oh, Arla," she said, when she reached the open bedroom door and looked inside to see the body on the bed, still and cool, her face at peace but one eye lagging, strangely open as if in some sort of wink, the fat bandage from last night's fall still taped to her forehead. Elizabeth looked around the room, searching for she didn't know what, and then she touched Arla's neck, picked up her wrist—she had to do this part, she had to be sure.

"Oh, Arla," she said again. She went back down to the kitchen. Her breath felt shallow and ragged, and the stairs, the kitchen, the house, the world felt off center, suddenly, weighted incorrectly.

"What's wrong with Granny?" Bell said immediately. She sat where Elizabeth had left her, one foot up on the chair rung, a tattered stuffed bear clutched on her lap.

"Granny passed away, Bell," Elizabeth said.

"You mean she died?"

"She died."

Bell was quiet, regarding her. She didn't cry, but her eyes exhibited an odd darkening, and Elizabeth thought she saw the first of a long series of difficult understandings pass through her daughter's body, and the vision made her angry. Because this was always the way, things happening before you were ready. Pain showing up when you least expected it, so brazen, barging right in and making itself at home. *Shit.* She'd wanted to plan for this. She'd wanted to help Bell prepare.

"Well, what are we going to do with her?" Bell said.

"We'll have to take her to the hospital."

"You and me?"

"No, baby—we'll tell Grandpa Dean, and Daddy, and Uncle Frank. We'll call an ambulance."

"What do we need an ambulance for?" Bell said, "If she's already dead?"

"I don't know," Elizabeth said honestly. "It's just what people do."

"Oh," Bell said.

"You want to come with me, to get Grandpa Dean? Or you want to stay here?"

"With you."

They walked out the back door, down the sloping lawn to the edge of the water to Dean. "Good morning, lovely," he said to Bell, and he smiled. He was once a handsome man. Elizabeth could see that.

"Granny is passed away," Bell said.

Dean froze, looked at Elizabeth.

"You need to come in," she said.

They walked back to the house, and Dean went for the stairs. Elizabeth did not follow; she returned to the kitchen and picked up the phone. The fact that it was Frank she dialed first, not Carson, came to her later.

"Your mother, Frank," she said. She could tell the phone had woken him up. "You better come."

Nineteen

The tether snapped the minute Dean saw her there, prone on that littered bed where he'd left her the night before, that one eye lagging open, and he was ashamed of himself for the power of the longing, for the mad rushing of the intent, but the tether that had so tenuously secured his sobriety these last few weeks snapped irreparably at that moment, and every step he took from the first one out of her bedroom was a step toward a drink. Because he couldn't stand up to this, Arla dying, could not, would not, should not have to. Not without a drink.

There were five people in this world that he should never have had to say good-bye to, and now he was down by two, and this was God-damned not fair and he wasn't going to stand for it. All bets were off, including—*especially*—the one he'd placed on himself. The one Arla had placed on him all those years ago. What a stupid fucking gamble. What a pair of fools. He went into the bathroom and splashed cold water on his face and sat

on the edge of the tub, shaking, until Frank arrived and called
the paramedics and until Carson and Sofia and Biaggio came
and they all sat stupidly in the kitchen, trying to decide what
to do. He willed himself to stay in the chair, stay in the kitchen
until he knew the Publix would be open, because it was Sunday
after all and there wasn't any other place to get beer in Utina at
this hour, now that Tip Breen was in jail and the Lil' Champ was
closed up. He stared at the clock and didn't listen to what anyone
around the table was saying, and when it was seven-forty-five he
got up and walked out of the kitchen without a word and started
toward the Publix. His head ached and his hands shook and his
stomach was filled with bile. The air was still, stagnant. He spit
into the scrub on the side of the road and kept walking.

Arla. How many ways had he failed her? He'd lost count.
The boat. The propeller. The shitty house. The bills. The drinking. *Will.*

Oh, Will. The sight of Arla there on the bed this morning
had had a peculiar effect, her dead body morphing like a dream
into the lifeless body of Will, so cold and alone that night, so
motionless, so still. *Drink up,* he'd said. *Another beer for my boys,*
he'd said. He remembered Tommy Bolla, drunk on the stool
next to him, Frank's disapproving stare, Carson and Will taking the drinks gratefully, greedily. The sirens on Monroe Road.
Will's body, broken and bloody. And drunk. No doubt about
it. Will had been drunk. Will had the wily reflexes of a fox, the
sixth sense and survival instinct of a wild cat, and there was no
way he'd have been hit by a car in the dead of night on a quiet
county road, a car he would have heard coming from a mile off,
if he'd been sober. Fifteen years old and stinking drunk. And
whose fault was that?

But that was an old grief, and this was a new one, and the two together were threatening to blow his head apart and shut down what little respiration he had left in his diseased lungs if he didn't get a God-damned drink, and get it fast. Another mile to the Publix. He picked up the pace.

He hadn't felt this sick in years, not since the old days at the Rayonier paper plant, down in the hole, in the belly of a thirty-foot boiler, spraying coatings made of God knows what on the interior of the tank to prevent corrosion. He'd been good at his job; he'd had the benefit of a ballsy courage that enabled him to spend hours in the hole, in the dark, scrambling along on the spindliest scaffolding, tethered to the light above with thick safety straps grown slick with sweat and oil, with a heavy tank of chemicals on his back that, he knew now, were so carcinogenic it was a wonder they hadn't raised a corpse back out of the tank every time a job was completed.

He remembered the darkness of the boiler, the rough metal under his fingers as he felt his way along the dark, searching for the worst areas of corrosion. When he found the pitted patches of metal he'd blast them smooth, beating out the pits and cracks and sanding away the irregularities borne from years of abrasion with the tiny waste particles that found their way into the boilers. And then, the metal made smooth, he'd apply the coatings— sprayed-on layers of metallurgic concoctions that would seal the cracks, erase the fissures, right the wrongs of time and friction and that interminable, beating abrasion. What he couldn't do in life he did in the boiler. And he'd been good at it. He'd been good at something. It might have been the only time, the only thing. He'd made money then, too. Rayonier had paid well, and until the allure of a steady paycheck had begun to lose its long-standing battle with the allure of a sweet, warm bottle of Jack, things had gone well—well enough, anyway, never perfect, God knew, but all right. It was Will, Will's death, that had tipped the scales. That had blown out the boiler forever, knifed in the fissures that could never be sealed, never be filled, never be coated. It was Will's death that had pulled the scaffolding out from under him, broken the safety straps, blew out the vessel forever and always. That had made it all go dark. That had opened the bottle of Jack forever and had kept it open until very recently, until Dean had come back and sat down in the kitchen at Aberdeen and had watched Arla walk in the door and meet his eyes. "Oh," she'd said, and that was all.

Arla.

A pale blue bikini, white shoulders tinted pink on a deserted stretch of A1A. "You're Dean Bravo," she'd said, and he wished now that he'd denied it, had left her there alone, beautiful and rich and whole, instead of taking her and cutting her, slicing her up into pieces, chipping away at her soul the way he had through the years.

Arla.

Jesus, the Publix. Where was the Publix?

They'd scattered Will's ashes in the Intracoastal, behind the house, had watched them hit the water like petals and drift quietly away on the tide. Some of them sank. Arla had held Dean's arm as if he was the rock, the *hero,* for Christ's sake, that was gonna make the whole thing okay instead of the son of a bitch who made it happen in the first place. The one who gave Will the drinks. The one who loaded the gun, knotted the noose, sharpened the knife, and then came home after the fact, stupid, stupefied, staggering, to find Arla ashen in the kitchen, Frank and Carson sitting like stones beside her.

They'd looked at Will in the morgue. His skin was pale and the freckles stood out on his cheeks like they did when he stayed too long in the sun, but the worst part was his blue eyes, wide open and scared but still as marbles in the bottom of a fish tank. And that was Dean—that was all Dean, he did that to Will. He knew it then, and he knew it still today. It was his. He owned it.

You can give a gift to someone, and make a person happy. But then you can take the gift away, and leave her hollow and cold inside. And what was worse, Dean wondered, the giving or the taking away? He'd never been able to get a handle on that one. Oh, Jesus, he thought, for the millionth time, *I fucked up.* More than once, that's for sure, but once so big that the world split open and the stars went out and all the color drained out of the sky. Not just his own sky. Arla's too. And how do you pay off a debt like that? That's what he'd been trying to figure out. But now it was too late. The creditor had died, and the world was a horrid, black place, with only the green of the Publix sign standing out in bold relief, only the promise of a drink, one drink, and nothing more.

TWENTY

On Wednesday morning, Utina smelled like a storm. The air pressure had dipped, and up and down Seminary Street the trees moved fretfully in a growing wind. The road was oddly quiet, everyday noises muffled and faint. Frank and Gooch sat in the truck outside the People's Guarantee, waiting for Carson and Mac. The closing was scheduled for ten, and it had been Carson's idea to try to stop it, to get Mac to bring in some statutes, demonstrate the need for probate intervention, prevent Dean from making off with all the proceeds from the sale now that Arla had died with no will, now that Dean, her husband, was sole beneficiary. Mac was reluctant. "I don't know there's much we can do, Carson," he'd said when Frank and Carson had come to his office the day before. "He's her husband. He's entitled. It's just the law."

"Find some way to stall it," Carson had barked. "Throw some language at them, I don't care what. Stall this shit until I can get a real lawyer in here." Mac was stung, Frank could tell, but he nodded and reached for a book of statutes. "Good stuff," he muttered.

Now, waiting in front of the bank to try and stop a closing they had no right to stop, Frank was surprised that Alonzo Cryder's black Mercedes was not yet present. He'd expected to see him here for the closing. He wondered how Cryder would respond to their attempt to stall, but given the events of the past four days—Sofia and Biaggio now living in Biaggio's trailer in Frank's front yard, Arla at the funeral home awaiting cremation, Dean AWOL since he'd left the kitchen table on Sunday morning—Frank was not inclined to care much about Alonzo Cryder's emotional state.

When Elizabeth had called on Sunday and Frank heard her voice on the phone, he'd bolted upright in bed. *This is it*, he'd thought for one wild second, but then she spoke again and hope turned to a leaden weight in his stomach. "It's your mother, Frank." That was all she said, but he knew. Arla. *Mom*.

He'd driven to Aberdeen. Elizabeth told him about the fall the night before, his mother's walk through the woods, the bleeding, Arla's insistence that she was fine. The paramedics had carried the body, covered in a sheet, down the front stairway and out the front door. "She's tall," one of them said. "Dang." Arla's foot—the good one—hung slightly off the stretcher, banging the wall on the way down, and Frank looked away.

"Head injuries," the paramedic said to Frank, after they'd loaded Arla into the ambulance. "Buggers. They'll do that— delayed response, you think the person is okay, but the brain swells and—" He snapped his fingers. "I'm sorry for your loss," he added.

The cop who'd arrived with the paramedics stood at the front door with his arms crossed. He'd graduated from Utina High a year after Frank. He shook Frank's hand as the ambulance pulled away. "Condolences," he said. "It's never easy." He looked off in the distance, a man who'd seen plenty of death, Frank reckoned. "Call the funeral home," he said. "They'll tell you what to do next. You'll need a burial, or a cremation. They'll get you sorted."

And then they'd sat in the kitchen, all of them: Frank, Elizabeth, Sofia, Biaggio, Bell, Dean—the latter staring stone-faced at the clock like some sort of zombie. Carson had driven up from St. Augustine. Gooch was parked under the table, leaning against Frank's knee. He was nervous, picking up in his dog way the twin scents of death and fear in the house. It was early still, not even eight o'clock on a Sunday morning, and Frank looked around the table and wondered what in the world he was supposed to do next. Sofia's eyes were red and her hands shook. She leaned into Biaggio, and he put his arm around her shoulder, rocked her like a child.

Frank's throat had constricted, and he swallowed, put his head in his hands. It was wrong, all wrong, all of it. He'd felt like he was moving backward through a thick haze, the world shapeless, undefined.

"All right," Carson had said, jarring Frank's thoughts back to the kitchen table and the smell of death still in the house and Dean's face, impassive, staring at the clock. "What do we do now?"

They all, for some reason, looked at Dean. It was like they were children again; with Arla gone, the center was missing, they were unmoored. *Come on, act like a father for once,* Frank had thought. *We're adrift. We're scared. We don't know where to turn.*

Dean had pulled his eyes from the clock, risen from the table, walked out of the kitchen.

Oh, God, Mom. What are we going to do?

That had been Sunday. They'd vacated Aberdeen on Monday, as planned, and that was hard, Jesus it was hard, cleaning out Arla's room—the books, the knickknacks, the forty years of flotsam and jetsam that had accumulated around her while she slept and wept and read and drank in that bedroom. Photos of Arla's parents' house in Davis Shores. A French-English dictionary. A broken ABBA record. A stack of scorched manuterges, never to be returned to their home churches. Pink Capezio flats. *Babar the King.* A gold-trimmed photo album. Frank had opted not to try to go through everything. He rented a portable storage pod to park on his own lot, and Biaggio helped him box things up, store them away. They would look at them later. They even moved the old Steinway into the pod, the termite wings fluttering like confetti when they rolled the piano down the ramp off the front porch. Then Biaggio and Sofia towed the trailer and the storage unit over to Frank's property—"Just temporarily," Biaggio said sheepishly, "until we get us a house." Elizabeth and Bell were staying in the condo at Willough Walk, the condo that had been planned for Arla. Everyone was waiting. Waiting for the money.

Now it was Wednesday. Carson and Mac arrived in front of the bank. They parked in a space adjacent to Frank's truck, and they all got out.

"Where is he?" Frank said.

"I don't know," Carson said. "I still haven't seen him. I assumed he wouldn't miss out on this closing. Do you know where he's been staying?"

No telling. When they'd finished clearing out Aberdeen, when they'd closed the front door on the empty rooms and the spindly turret for the last time, there'd been no sign of Dean. They'd met with the undertaker yesterday to arrange the cremation, but still no Dean.

"I'm sure he's facedown in a six-pack somewhere," Carson said. "Which is fine with me."

"It's actually better," Mac agreed. "If he doesn't show up for this closing, that makes our job that much easier. They can't close without him."

"Fine," Carson said. "Then we'll figure out how to contest this by the time he sobers his sorry ass up."

"Oh, he'll show up," Frank said. "He's not going to miss out on his money."

They waited in silence, watching a plastic bag scuttle down Seminary Street in the damp wind. At ten-fifteen, Carson sighed, kicked the curb.

"Let's get started," he said. "He'll get here when he's good and ready."

"I don't see the Vista people either," Mac observed. "Where the hell is Cryder?" Something wasn't sitting right. Frank wasn't sure if the situation warranted relief or worry, though he had a nagging feeling it was the latter.

They went into the bank and took a number in a carpeted area reserved for customer service, even though there were no other customers, either at the teller counters or waiting in the customer service area. After a minute, Doreen Bailey waddled out from behind the counter and walked to the number kiosk. "Four!" she called, ticking a number off a list.

"Right here, Doreen," Carson said. "For shit's sake," he muttered.

"Take it easy," Frank said.

"You shut the fuck up," Carson said.

"Boys," Mac said, holding up his hands.

"Beautiful," Frank said. "Let's just do this."

They followed Doreen over to a dark wooden desk. Carson and Frank took the two chairs in front while she settled herself behind the keyboard. Mac pulled up another chair from an adjoining desk.

"Well, boys," Doreen said. She smiled at the Bravos unpleasantly, then made an effort to lower her head and give her voice a sympathetic cast. "I'm so sorry about your mama, boys. I'm just so sorry. But she's gone on to salvation. You have to console yourselves with that. She's gone on to Jesus. Sleeping with the angels." She reached out and patted Frank on the hand, and he fought the instinct to recoil. He doubted Arla's heaven had angels in it. Little Debbies, more like.

"It was quite a shock to see your father again, boys," Doreen said. "The man himself." She shook her head, rolled her eyes. "Looking like holy hell, I might add."

Frank stared at her, feeling a creeping unease.

"He's not one to clean up his act for no one, is he? Not even those fancy developer people." She shook her head, frowned. "Now, how can I help you?" Doreen said.

"Dean was here?" Carson said.

"Yes. Yesterday. With those people. Vista? One of them was *black*, for heaven's sake. And he looked like he had *money*, too."

She leaned across the desk, her big, shapeless breasts pressing into her keyboard. "I'd say your daddy's probably still celebrating. Everyone knows he did very well on that sale. My goodness. Congratulations to the Bravos, boys. Whoop-de-do." She drew a circle in the air with her finger.

Frank felt sick to his stomach. He looked at Carson, who was ashen.

"What did he do, Doreen?" Mac said. "Did they close already? Did Dean get the money?"

"Well, yes," she said, looking from Mac to Frank to Carson and back again. "Except for Morgan Moore's money. That was wired to Memphis. We closed yesterday afternoon. Didn't you know?"

"The closing was scheduled for this morning at ten," Frank said. He stared at his watch. 10:20. How could this have happened?

"They called late Monday and moved it up a day," she said. "They said your daddy had a conflict, needed to meet sooner. A conflict." She snorted. "A date with a barstool, more like."

Frank sat back in his chair, felt the weight of this knowledge close in on him like a wrecking ball. Next to him, Carson had not moved. Mac shook his head, speechless, it seemed, for once.

"Is there a problem, Frank?" Doreen said. "I mean, it was his money. I know Arla's gone on to the Lord, but—"

"Arla's dead. *Dead*, you stupid cunt," Carson said. He stood up. "And you just gave that asshole everything."

Doreen drew back, stared at Carson and then looked at Frank. "Frank, I didn't—" she began. But then her face flushed red and she pushed back from the desk. "Now listen to me, Carson Bravo. You can't speak to me like—"

Carson turned on his heel and walked out of the bank. Mac exhaled.

"Doreen," Frank said. "Can you do a stop payment or something? Cancel it somehow?"

"Of course not," she said. She was fuming now. "It was his property. His closing. His money. He took a cashier's check." Frank looked at Mac, who nodded sadly.

Frank got up and turned to follow Carson out of the bank.

"You Bravos think you're all that!" she called after him. "You get a little money and think you can talk to people any way you want. Well, I've got news for you, and you can tell that animal of a brother you've got. The Bravos are nothing but a bunch of rednecks, Frank, and will never be anything but. White trash, is what you are—it's what your mother was, what your father is. Take *that* to the bank."

Frank turned back to her. "Doreen?" he said.

She sneered. "What?"

"You're probably right."

She started. She wasn't expecting an agreement.

"But that doesn't make you any less of a cunt," he said, and he and Mac walked out the door.

Outside the bank, Carson was leaning up against his car, his forehead on the roof.

"Carson," Frank said.

Carson turned to him, his face red with fury.

"What do we do?" Frank said.

"You're asking *me*? You think I know what we're going to do?" Carson said. "Ask Weeden here. I got nothing."

"Well," Mac said slowly. "It's not looking too good."

Carson snorted. "You got that right, buddy. It's over. That bastard is gone for good, and there's not a damn thing we can do about it."

"Can't we sue him or something? Mac?" Frank said.

Mac shrugged his shoulders, looked at Frank sadly.

"You think we're ever going to find him?" Carson said. "He's going to cash that check, spread that money around where we'll never find it. He's a smart fucking 'neck, and he's laughing his ass off at us right now. Son of a *bitch*."

The veins throbbed in Carson's forehead and throat, beads of sweat emerging on his face in the damp morning air. It was hard to breathe; the air pressure had dropped considerably since they'd been inside the bank. A storm was fast approaching.

And here it was, Frank realized, the end of the road. They had nothing, the Bravos of Utina, nothing. As hard as this was for Frank to swallow, he watched with a strange dispassionate curiosity as this new information completely consumed his brother. Carson's hands shook as he tried to unlock his car door, but then suddenly he spun around, walked over to Frank.

"It's over," Carson said again. He put his face close to Frank's. "All these years, and now it's over. We've got nothing, little brother. *I've* got nothing."

"Oh, I see. So it's all about you," Frank said.

Carson shook his head.

"You're the one who brought him back here, don't forget," Frank said.

"It would have happened regardless. And anyway, she never would have sold without him."

"Well, now we'll never see the money anyway—so what did we gain?"

"So it's all my fault, is that what you're saying?" Carson said. "I'm the bad guy, right?"

He looked straight into Frank's eyes, and there was danger there, knowledge. *Elizabeth.* The word flashed through Frank's mind and he blinked, feeling, somehow, that Carson could see into his soul, see the picture of the woman there. He was right.

"And you think I don't *know*?" Carson said. "What kind of an idiot do you think I am?"

Frank felt his own anger building now, and he let it grow with a sense of abandon that felt almost like relief. "The worst kind," he said. "The kind that doesn't appreciate something good when he's got it. You don't deserve her."

It was the first time he'd acknowledged any sort of sympathy toward Elizabeth, and Carson saw the weight of this statement, understood the significance of Frank's words.

"And *you* do? Saint Frank?"

"Boys," Mac said. "Now come on." He put his hand on Carson's elbow, hoping, it seemed to Frank, to lead him back toward the car, back toward sanity, reason. But there was no need. Frank was ready this time. He'd take Carson on. Bring it. He opened the door to his truck, put his wallet and keys on the seat, and turned back to Carson. He expected his brother to come at him again, to punctuate his rage with a physical attack, like when they were kids. But Carson simply stood, regarding him, his face contorted in a mask of frustration, anger, and something that might have been fear. And then he turned, wordlessly, left Mac standing there with Frank and got into his Acura. He was nearly to the intersection at Seminary Street and Monroe Road before Frank unclenched his own fists.

Mac cleared his throat.

"I'll walk back to my office," he said quietly.

Frank nodded, got into the truck.

Mac walked to the passenger side of the truck and leaned through the truck's open window.

"I'm sorry, Frank," Mac said. "I'm sorry about everything."

You and me both, Frank thought as he drove away from the bank.

When he pulled up at home he found the banker from next door had stacked a small mountain of palm fronds on Frank's side of the property line. The fronds were thick and dry, having blown down from Frank's trees in the last squall and littered the banker's carefully manicured lawn for nearly a week now. The idiot had evidently decided to make good on his promise to Frank that he'd deposit the fronds back on Frank's land if he didn't get the trees trimmed.

"Whatever floats your boat," Frank had said at the time. "But I'm not trimming my trees. They were here first, in case you didn't know."

"The fronds are a nuisance," the banker said.

"And you're becoming one," Frank said.

He'd resolved to ignore the stacks of fronds, and the imbecile who'd put them there. But now he knew, given the impending storm and the way the fronds were stacked ten high in a pile instead of left flat and benign as they had been on the ground, that they'd become missiles in the high winds, threatening not just the dumb-ass banker's house, which he wouldn't have minded, but his own plate-glass windows as well.

"Shit," he said. "This guy is really starting to get on my nerves."

He parked the truck, went to the shed for a jug of lighter fluid. Across the yard, Biaggio's trailer sat at a rakish angle, and his van was gone, meaning he and Sofia had probably gone out somewhere. The trailer door was closed and the curtains drawn.

So what about this, he wondered now. With no money in the foreseeable future and no restaurant to generate any, Frank could envision his sister and her new husband living in their rusted trailer on Frank's property until the end of all their days. Biaggio's moving business wasn't going to finance a new house for the happy couple anytime soon. And what, exactly, was Frank himself going to do for a living? Why had he never considered these questions before today?

Because he'd been banking on Arla to take care of them all. He stood with the can of lighter fluid, regarding the palms. It was true. He was no different than Carson. He'd made no plans for any kind of job, any kind of livelihood beyond the sale of the properties, because he knew, in the back of his mind, that Arla would take care of them all with her new millions—would make it easy for all her children to get what they wanted. And he knew what he wanted. A mountain cabin. A cool rushing creek. *Elizabeth*. He'd been banking on it, albeit subconsciously. And now?

Frank drenched the palm fronds with fluid, then lit them carefully from the side and stood back as the pile ignited and the fronds began to kindle. He'd always enjoyed the smell of burning palm. It was an ancient smell. He let the pile burn for a little while, then started for the house. The rains were coming soon. They'd douse the fire.

His head was spinning, thinking of the morning's events. He had that feeling again of walking backward in fog, and he had no idea how to get himself turned around. He didn't even know what he was supposed to do today. What day was it? Wednesday? Thursday? Sunday? What did it matter? No fish to fry, no booze to pour. He had no idea what to do next.

He'd gotten to the porch when the sound of a car in his drive made him turn around. Elizabeth parked and walked toward him. They hadn't been alone since the night of the acrobats, the night of his office, and he watched her approach.

"Hello, beautiful," he said, and she smiled. "Where's Bell?"

"With Sofia and Biaggio," she said. "They're buying a dress for your mom. For the cremation." Oh, God. These details. They were horrible. He remembered when Will was cremated, having to root through Will's bureau drawer, trying to find a clean pair of underwear for the undertaker to dress the body in under the new brown suit they'd bought at JCPenney. "What does he need underwear for?" he'd asked Arla, exasperated, but she'd looked at him with such haunted, hollow eyes that he said nothing else. He found a pair of his own underwear, clean, put them in a plastic bag for the undertaker. He'd thought about that many times since, his own Fruit of the Looms incinerated along with Will's body, scattered across the surface of the Intracoastal, sinking below and beyond.

Now he looked away from Elizabeth, watched the palms burn.

She stepped up to the porch. "I've got to meet them at the condo in a little bit. They're dropping Bell off," she said. "How are you doing?"

"Been better," he said. They sat down in the porch rockers. He told her about the bank, the money, Dean. She drew in her breath sharply.

"Do you think he's really gone?" she said, after a moment.

"Yes, I do. Gone. Poof. Again."

"I'm sorry, Frank."

"Well, I'm sorry for you, too, Elizabeth. You'd have stood to gain, too. My mother would have taken care of all of us."

She shrugged. "I don't need much money," she said simply. The oaks in the yard made a rushing sound in the wind.

They sat quietly for a while. Frank took a deep breath, then looked out into the yard, where the palms were smoking heavily in the damp air, tendrils of ash and steam rising, fading, dissipating.

He looked back at Elizabeth.

"I love you," he said.

She stared straight ahead.

"But we can't do this."

He watched her, watched the way her eyes focused on the fire in the yard, the way her knuckles tensed on the arms of the rocking chair, and the name rose up between them, palpable and thick: *Carson*.

"Am I right?" he said.

"Yes," she said. "You're right." In the yard, the burning palms popped, cracked, raged.

TWENTY-ONE

The air was fat with the promise of rain, and a thunderhead eight miles high hung in the sky. Carson watched it from a booth inside the Cue & Brew. The rushing noise in his head had not subsided since he'd left the bank this morning, though he'd been sitting in this booth since the Cue & Brew had opened at eleven and was now on his third Heineken, trying, oh God in heaven, *trying* to calm down. But the world was conspiring against him.

Ponzi. Ponzi. Ponzi. Oh, Jesus, *stop.*

The disaster at the bank had taken a few hours to process, but now Carson had moved beyond pure incompetent rage and into a black determination to *fix* this, *solve* this, make it *right.* It wasn't right, what Dean had done. But it wasn't over, either. It couldn't be. There was too much at stake. Carson had called Mac on his cell phone a half hour earlier, and Mac had answered on the fifth ring, his voice groggy.

"Where are you?" Carson said. From the Cue & Brew, he could see out the window across the back parking lot into the adjoining lot of Bait/Karaoke, and Mac's car was not there.

"I'm at home," Mac said.

"What are you doing home?" Carson said. "It's the middle of the afternoon. Don't you have a business to run?"

"I'm on a lunch break," Mac said. "What are you, my mother?" In the background, Carson heard a woman's voice, sleepy, and the voice sounded familiar, but Carson shook his head, kicked the distraction out of his mind. He didn't have time for Mac's love life.

"We need your help," he'd said.

"I thought you wanted a *real* lawyer."

Carson exhaled, trying not to let his impatience get the best of him.

"You're a real lawyer," he conceded. "And you know the players better than anyone. You know how my father thinks as well as we do."

"Scary," Mac said.

"No shit," Carson said. "Can you meet me at Frank's in an hour?"

"Only if you promise to be sweet to me," Mac said.

"Fuck you," Carson said. "We'll cuddle, okay? Just meet me out there."

Carson had hung up and spent another hour stewing at the bar, putting two more beers to bed and taking notes on a long legal pad, trying to weigh all the options. Legal intervention? A private investigator? The cops? There had to be a way to put a warrant out for Dean, something. Get the fucking money back.

Because it couldn't end like this. Forty-two years invested in that house, forty-two years with this family, this frigging pack of oddballs and failures for whom he'd been wrestling with shame and ambivalence his entire life. So many embarrassments. So many disasters. He'd done his time with this family. He'd paid his dues. And if Dean thought he was going to make off with all the proceeds now, after all these years, he had another think coming. They all needed the money. God knew, *he* needed the money.

He paid his tab at the Cue & Brew and drove out toward Frank's house, the rushing in his head still present but feeling more muffled, somehow, more manageable. He could handle this. He could. The light had grown dim in the shade of thunderclouds as Carson pulled down Frank's dusty driveway. A pile of palms burned on the corner. He could handle anything.

And now this—now this—

Elizabeth's car in the driveway. The two of them together on the porch.

Carson parked, got out of the car, walked up to the house. Elizabeth and Frank did not move. The dog lay on the porch between them, thumping his tail at Carson's approach. Wasn't it all so cute—man, woman, rocking chairs, porch, dog. Norman Rockwell. What the *fuck*.

Then Mac pulled up behind Carson, got out of his car, and stood waiting for a moment. Frank and Elizabeth stared at Carson, and he approached the porch, looked from one to the other.

"Am I interrupting?" he said, finally. His voice was thin, detached. The rushing in his ears was so distracting. He cleared his throat. "Am I interrupting?" he said again.

"Sit down, Carson," Elizabeth said.

"Where's my daughter?" he said.

She hesitated, looking at him strangely. "She's with Sofia," she said.

She was so beautiful, Elizabeth. He'd always thought so, even when she was pissing him off, as she was doing right now. In the humidity her hair had taken on a thick waviness. A bead of sweat rolled down her neck. When he'd first noticed her, first really paid attention to her, he'd been only sixteen, and she was fourteen, a freshman. She'd been sitting on the tailgate of George Weeden's truck, which was parked in the back lot of Utina High. It was winter, unusually cool, and she'd been sitting with Frank, his left arm around her shoulder, his right hand parked under her blue-jeaned thighs in an adolescent expression of intimacy. She wore a yellow sweatshirt. Carson had remembered her vaguely; they'd been kids together, after all, and he had a vague recollection of her sad, lonesome presence, her mismatched clothes, that awful day on the bus when she'd vomited into the aisle. But those memories dissipated the day he'd seen her with Frank, and he'd stopped short and taken a long look at her pale skin, her freckles, her straw-colored hair, and he'd thought to himself, *I want her*, and then, in almost the same instant, *I don't want him to have her*.

"What are you doing?" Carson said to Elizabeth, to his wife, now. She stopped rocking in the chair. Frank put his hands on his knees and waited, and the first fat drop of cold rain fell onto Carson's forearm.

"We're just talking," she said. "Frank told me about Dean."

"Oh, did he? That's good. That's good, that Frank filled you in. Good old Frank." He turned to look at his brother. Frank had not moved from the chair, and he looked up at Carson with such a flat, innocent expression that Carson wanted to break his teeth.

Mac approached from behind. Carson sensed him at his shoulder, but he'd forgotten, momentarily, why Mac was even here, had forgotten about Dean, the money, the fund, all of it. His focus was narrowed on his brother, his wife. His *brother*. His *wife*.

"So, what'd you come up with?" Frank said. "What do you think, Mac?" he said, looking over Carson's shoulder. "Do you think we have any recourse?"

Carson shook his head, laughed. This was so like Frank. Thinking he could go ahead and play dumb, cool as a cucumber, so at ease, so unruffled. Thinking he could ignore the obvious, go ahead and ask about Dean, the money, the bank, without a word about the fact that Carson had just found his wife here at Frank's house.

Just like when they were kids. Carson always the one getting upset. Frank always cool, collected, calm. "You're my rock," Arla would say to Frank. And when she looked at Carson her eyes were worried, strained. They made him feel weak.

"Oh, Frank," he said. He chuckled again. "You think I care about the money right now?"

Behind him, Mac cleared his throat, and Carson watched a muscle twitch in Frank's face. Carson had forced his hand, finally. It was time to deal. Carson watched him, waiting.

"Don't you always care about money, Carson?" Frank said. Elizabeth stood up. "I'm leaving," she said.

Oh, no. *No, no, no, no, no.* Not that easy. Not that clean.

Carson blocked her path at the top of the porch steps. "I think we need to discuss a couple of things," he said. Raindrops dotted his shirt, his pants, the back of his neck.

"Let's get in outa the rain, Carson," Mac said, but Carson did not move, and Mac's path to the porch was blocked.

"Are you okay?" Elizabeth said, looking at Carson. "You don't look good."

"Right. He looks better, right?" Carson gestured at Frank.

"No. I mean you don't look well," she said, annoyed. "Have you been drinking? Already?"

Her eyes were clear and defiant, and he could see through them to the part of her that felt she owed him nothing. But she was wrong. She owed him everything. The house, the car, the money, the clothes, the trips, the kid, the whole fucking *life*. She owed him everything. His chest tightened. The rushing in his ears grew louder. He pushed her back against the rocking chair, and she fell into it with a small sound.

He hadn't known Frank could move so quickly. He'd always pegged him for such a measured S.O.B., so careful, so composed. Never got upset, never fell apart, never fucking *lost it*, like Carson himself was doing right now, losing it so fast and so hard and so completely that when Frank flew at him from the top of the porch Carson turned and went with the velocity of Frank's launch, let the flight carry the two of them to the bottom step, into Mac, who toppled down behind them, and they fell, all three of them, down to the rough dust of the pathway, out into the steaming dirt where the rain had begun to fall in earnest now.

Mac rolled to one side, yelling.

"Damn!" he said. "Damn ya'll Bravos! Quit!" But it was too late. Carson clenched his fist and connected it, hard, into Frank's sternum, feeling the thick stop of his brother's rib cage against his fingers. He watched Frank gasp, double over, but then straighten and pull together that steely strength of his. Where did he *get* it, the skinny shit? Frank regrouped quick enough to deal a glancing blow to the side of Carson's face that would have taken out half his teeth had it been a direct hit. They clinched, spitting, pushing, cursing, grunting.

Carson brought his knee up into Frank's midsection and watched him fall backward again, and he took this brief opportunity to catch his breath, but then Frank tackled him around his knees and brought him back down, and Carson was surprised at the ferocity of his anger this time. A thick smear of blood glossed Frank's cheekbone. Carson pushed him back again, moved, half-crawling, toward the porch. Elizabeth was yelling, pissed off, *stop it stop it stop it*, and somewhere beyond the rushing in his ears the dog was growling, prancing around the two men, the two brothers. Elizabeth's voice was thin, as if at a great distance, and Carson moved now with great focus, and time slowed down, and he felt in boundless control at that moment, in complete, utter command.

Something long was within his grasp, propped against the porch railing. A paddle from the kayak. Carson picked it up, didn't think, just moved, and swung it hard, the long flat blade on the end slicing through the air in front of him, missing Frank by a hair. The rain fell in sheets.

"Carson!" Elizabeth screamed. "Carson!"

Mac jumped up from the yard, tried to step in front of Carson; he waved his hands frantically.

"Come on, man! Carson, man, come on!" Mac said, panicky, but Carson looked beyond him, saw Frank still panting, still staring at him in defiance. And then he took a step closer and swung the paddle harder, faster, brandishing it before him like he was a God-damned samurai, and there was nothing but chaos before him, Frank and Mac dancing, dodging in front of him, trying to evade him and stop him at the same time, but it was no use—when are you going to *learn*, brother? It was that last swing that did it, that connected, hitting with the thin hard edge of the blade rather than the flat rubber side, breaking the cartilage of the nose easy and clean, unleashing a torrent of blood and obscenities and still the shrieking, screaming hysteria of Elizabeth behind him and the barking of the dog. But there was something wrong; Frank was still standing. Mac was down.

"Fucking hell, man!" Mac screamed. "Jesus Christ!" He was sitting in the mud just off the porch steps, both hands to his face, rivulets of blood leaking between his fingers and down his chin and blending with rainwater. His glasses had fallen away somewhere in the dirt drive, and his blue eyes stared in shock, disbelief. "You broke my *nose!*"

Frank was frozen, staring at Carson. Elizabeth had her hands to her face, astonished, but then she came down off the porch, ran over to Mac, led him up to the porch and pushed him into one of the rockers.

"Stay there. I'll get towels," she said, and she ran into the house.

The rushing in Carson's ears was gone now, had dissipated with the sound of Mac's septum disengaging from his skull, the way his ears would clear suddenly when he was a kid and had been swimming too long and his ears filled with water, then he and Frank would jump sideways on one foot until the fluid dislodged. In place of the rushing was an empty, hollow sound, an echo of memories, a tidal wave of pain and guilt and fear.

"Leave him," Frank said. "He can make it home."

"Should we?" Carson said.

"Yeah."

Elizabeth returned with towels and ice, and she knelt beside Mac, and then Carson felt like he was having a heart attack. He dropped to one knee in the muddy driveway, put his hands up to his head as the rain pelted his body.

"Oh, Jesus," he said. "Oh, Frank, oh, Jesus."

Frank walked over and sat next to him. He was still panting from the fight. His shirt was torn and his pants were covered in mud. The cut on his cheek was still bleeding. After a moment, he put a hand on Carson's shoulder.

"Take a breath, man," he said quietly, so Carson obliged, focusing on his respiration: in, out, in, out. Frank's hand was warm on his shoulder. Elizabeth got up from the porch, started for her car.

"I'm leaving," she said. Her voice was clipped, flat, and Carson had no idea what she was thinking. "They're bringing Bell back to the condo, and I need to be there." She stared hard at Carson and Frank. Carson wanted to touch her, but she walked past him to her car.

"You all need to take Mac in to the clinic," she said, turning back once before climbing into the driver's seat. And then she was gone.

They took two cars to the clinic. Mac sat in the passenger seat of Carson's Acura with his head back and a pack of towels planted against his face to reduce the steady flow of blood. Frank followed in his truck. The rain was stopping, and a cloud of steam hung above the blacktop. Mac was quiet during the ride, save for some grotesque snuffling and a few muttered curses, and Carson tried to think of the right thing to say, the right way to apologize.

"You know it was an accident, right?" he ventured.

Mac didn't answer, but he held his left hand up in Carson's direction, his middle finger forcibly extended upward.

"Jesus," Carson said. "I'm sorry, Mac."

They turned right on Seminary and parked in the empty parking lot of the emergency clinic. Frank pulled in behind them, and they helped Mac, grunting and muttering, out of the car. He lowered the bloody towels away from his face.

"Holy God," Frank said, looking at him. Mac's nose was swollen to three times its normal size, and thick ropes of dried blood snaked downward across his face. Purple bruises had begun to form under his eyes.

"Don'd even dell me," Mac said. His voice was comically nasal, some of his *t*'s and *n*'s devolving into *d*'s in a way that might have been very funny to them under different circumstances. "I can ondly imagine," he said.

"I hope this place is open," Carson said, looking around the empty parking lot. "Shouldn't they be open all the time?"

"Did you brig your paddle?" Mac said. "You could break the door dowd."

Carson didn't answer. They walked to the front door which was, blessedly, unlocked, and they entered the tiny waiting room. Frank took a clipboard from the receptionist—who looked at the three of them skeptically—and they sat together on miniature metal chairs that seemed to have been made for schoolchildren. The woman had good reason for her reaction, Carson supposed, as he looked at Frank and Mac. They both looked like holy hell, bloodied and battered and still covered with mud from Frank's driveway. He knew he himself didn't look any different.

"I'll fill this out, Mac," Frank said. "Just tell me the information."

"You know everything there is do know aboud me," Mac said. "Except why I condinue to hang around you assholes. And I don'd even know thad myself. Just fill the damn thing oud," he honked. "What you don'd know, make up."

They sat quietly for a few moments, Frank scribbling on the form, and in the sudden silence the whole wave of trouble lapped again at the edges of Carson's mind. He looked at Frank, and the bubble of anger that had led them all here to the clinic threatened, for a moment, to surface again, but then subsided, submerged, still whole, but somehow dormant, for the moment. He was just too tired. That was it. Jesus, he was just so tired. And too sick of everything. He looked down at his shoes, covered with mud and what was probably a fair amount of Mac Weeden's blood. They were very nice shoes, soft chestnut leather. They'd cost a fortune, but he'd made the investment to buy a little confidence. He'd planned to wear these shoes to meet with Christine Hughes later this week. He'd planned to pay her off with the settlement from the house. He thought he'd settle everything, take care of everything, *fix* everything in these new, overpriced leather shoes. And now they were ruined. Huh. Things never, never turned out the way you thought they would, he decided.

Maybe that's why, when the clinic's interior door opened and two nurses emerged, supporting a limping, shuffling Dean Bravo between them, Carson was not even surprised.

"Hell's bells," Dean said. He smiled broadly at the nurses.

"Look here, it's my boys. Just park me over there with them, would you, darlins?"

The nurses collected the form from Frank and took Mac back into the exam room. Dean reclined awkwardly, painfully it seemed, across two of the metal chairs, his hands parked behind his lower back, his teeth clenched together. His face was pale. A nicotine patch was stuck to his forearm. A yellowed bruise ran down his jawline.

"What is wrong with you?" Frank said.

"I could ask you two the same thing," Dean said. "You all look like you been rode hard and put up wet." He looked them over appraisingly. "I'm guessing Mac lost. But who the hell won?"

They stared at him, not answering. Carson considered the irony of this situation. They'd not seen Dean since the morning of Arla's death, when he'd lit out from the kitchen at Aberdeen and had headed, no doubt, toward a colossal bender fueled by the pent-up energy of what must have been, for Dean, an unprecedented near-month of sobriety. And now here he was, his month of good behavior and his stint at Aberdeen notwithstanding, in the exact same condition—beat up, gimped out, and hungover—that he'd been in when Carson had bailed him out of the hospital in August. Brilliant. And this was a man who now had six million dollars to his name.

"But me," Dean continued. "I done threw the hip out again. That busted cheek—it keeps coming back to haunt me. I had a little trouble last night, I guess. There was a fish fry in South Utina. I seem to remember I made some folks a little mad for some reason."

"You can do that," Carson said.

"I've been told," Dean said, and he smiled, but then the smile dropped away, and it was hard to tell if he was in physical pain or if it was something else, but his face clouded over and he looked from Carson to Frank with an expression that made Carson almost—*almost*—feel sorry for him.

"You all okay?" Dean said. "Sofia, she's okay?"

"We're okay," Frank said. He looked away. Carson saw the moment when Arla's face flashed into Frank's consciousness, and then the big questions returned to Carson, the biggest questions—the money. The Fund. Sofia. Bell. *Elizabeth.*

"How did you even get here?" Carson said to Dean, remembering the empty parking lot outside.

Dean shrugged, and Carson didn't ask again. Because it didn't matter how he got here. It didn't matter how he was leaving. Or where he was staying, or what he was doing, or how he was doing it. It didn't matter. It was just Dean, appearing, disappearing, slouching in and out of their lives like a tardy teenager. Too little, too late. Again.

"You took all the money," Carson said.

"I did," Dean said. He looked straight at Carson, unflinching.

"Why?"

Dean looked away. "I guess I thought I wanted it," he said. "I've been a little drunk." He smiled ruefully. *A little*, Carson thought. "I thought it was mine," Dean continued. He looked back at Carson, then at Frank. "But it isn't."

Carson waited.

"Here," Dean said. He reached into his pocket, pulled out an envelope. "It's all there."

Carson opened the envelope. It contained three plastic cards, each stamped with a Bank of America logo. The first one had his own name, Carson Bravo, embossed across the front. The second had Frank's name, and the third, Sofia's.

"Credit cards?" Carson said.

"They're debit cards," Dean said. "That's all the money. It's all in your names, now. Three separate accounts. Two million each." Carson and Frank stared at him.

"I used a little bit, though," Dean said. "I gave a little bit to the cathedral. Where we were married. Arla liked that church," he said quietly. "And I bought a bond. For Bell."

Carson felt a catch in his throat.

"I know she don't need it, from me," Dean said. "You'll take good care of her, I know," he said. "But maybe one day she can buy something nice for herself. And you can tell her it was from her Grandpa Dean."

They were quiet, all of them, and Carson bit the inside of his cheek and then put his head in his hands and tried to process this information, this moment, the three of them sitting together in a dingy clinic waiting room, bruised and battered and barely able to stand, barely able to speak to each other, and yet bound together, somehow, with something that might have been love but was different—harder, tighter, stronger, even, than love. It wasn't love, in fact. It was family.

Dean slapped a hand to his forehead. "Oh, and there was a little bit more I used. Maybe fifty dollars. Had a few drinks."

Frank took his cap off, scratched his head, looked at Dean.

"You're telling us all that money is in a bank in our names?" he said.

"Well, less fifty or so. And the bit for the church, and for Bell."

"And you're telling us you don't want it?" Carson said.

"Nah," Dean said. "It ain't getting me nowhere. I figure you three can use it."

"And what about you?" Frank said. "Where are you going to go?"

"It don't really matter, do it?" Dean said. "I mean, it never really did, did it?" He leaned down, picked at a sandspur that was lodged in his boot. His skin was sallow, and when he spoke again his voice was quiet.

"I'm on borrowed time, boys," he said. "Look at me. You think I'm going to be around in a year?" Dean fished in his pocket and pulled out a cigarette, lit it. "So if I'm checking out, what the hell do I need all that money for? Ain't no need for pockets on a dead man's coat."

They didn't answer.

Dean turned to Frank. "You made an arrangement with the undertaker?" he said. "The ashes ready?"

Frank nodded. "Friday," he said.

"All right then, Friday," Dean said quietly. "Friday we're going to Aberdeen. Scatter your mother's ashes in the water behind the house." He took a long drag from his cigarette, exhaled slowly.

The receptionist slid open the glass window. "No smoking in the clinic, sir," she said sharply.

Dean sighed. "All right, darlin'," he said. "Keep your shirt on." She glared at him, slid the window shut, and he grinned. He struggled to his feet, gripping the edges of the metal chairs, and grimacing in pain as he made his way out the door.

"I'll be outside, boys. They gave me a prescription, so I'm all set. I figure one of you will take me home with you, let me clean up, right?" he said. "Oh, and maybe pay this bill?" He nodded toward the receptionist, chuckled.

"Get in my truck, Dad," Frank said. "The rain's stopped. We gotta wait for Mac."

Dean shuffled out of the clinic, leaving behind a cloud of cigarette smoke.

Carson handed the envelope to Frank, who looked at the three debit cards, looked back at Carson, his face a blank. He shook his head.

"Carson?" Frank said.

"Yeah?"

"This family is nucking futs," he said.

Carson nodded.

"What's left of us," he said. They sat in the waiting room, watching the minutes click by on the clock on the wall, a window air conditioner chugging relentlessly over their heads, the air cold and damp, the receptionist quiet behind the window. Carson felt the beginnings of a hangover coming on. It was going to be a big one.

"Frank?" he said, after a while.

"Yeah?"

"Why did you tell me to leave Will?"

Frank was quiet for so long Carson thought he wasn't going to answer, and when he did speak, it was in a voice Carson had never heard before.

"Why did you listen?" Frank said.

Carson waited until he was back in his own car, the tinted windows rolled up tight, the air-conditioning on full blast, Frank driving Dean and Mac back to his house to get Mac's car. And that's when he put his head in his hands and wept for all of it, for all of them, for relief and for heartbreak. He cried for his dead mother and for Dean and the money—the stupid God-damned money—and for Uncle Henry's, and Aberdeen, and for his dumb cat Violet. And he cried for Elizabeth, and for Bell, and for the searing, burning hope that he could still win them back. But mostly he cried for himself, and for Frank and Sofia and Will, and for all the ways they would never be the same again.

Twenty-two

At the condo in Willough Walk, Elizabeth went into the bathroom. She took off her shirt, stained with Mac's blood, and tossed it in the wastebasket. Then she stepped out of the rest of her clothes and turned on the shower. She ran the water as hot as it would go, until her arms and legs turned pink, and still she could not wash away the afternoon's events, the vision of Carson's eyes, wild and enraged, when he found her there with Frank.

When she finished, she put on clean clothes, walked back into the living room, and gazed out through the screened-in lanai to where the retention pond breathed steam into the damp air. The storm had stopped; the rain had dwindled to a steady, stubborn drip off the eaves. She turned back to the condo and looked around. She wondered how long she could reasonably stomach this place, this ridiculous condo. The original plan had been for her to stay here with Arla for a little while, help with the transition, assist her mother-in-law in easing into her new life without Sofia. Her new life alone.

Instead, on Monday Elizabeth and Bell had moved in without Arla, and she'd stared at the lease that night, at Arla's spidery signature at the bottom, the notation from the owner confirming that Arla had prepaid the rent for the rest of the year. Elizabeth knew the plan, knew Arla had intended to work with Susan Holm on a purchase price once the closing on Aberdeen had been finalized. Oh, *shit*. Everything was different. Everything was so confusing now. What in the hell were any of them supposed to do?

The condo hadn't seemed like a bad idea at the time. Not a bad idea at all. A couple of weeks ago, Elizabeth wasn't ready to go back to Carson, wasn't sure she ever would be. And staying with Arla in the condo for a few weeks, a few months, maybe more, would be fine for Bell, what with the sparkling community pool and the swing set and picnic benches in the common area, a Ping-Pong table in the clubhouse. She'd even registered Bell for first grade here in Utina, not St. Augustine.

But everything seemed all wrong now. The Berber carpet was cloying. The bathroom smelled like paint. The Formica countertops in the kitchen were cold and brittle. Everything was far too clean. Every shade of taupe made her think of Arla; every wall sconce, every chair rail, every tasteful wooden switch plate made her think how Arla would have mocked it. If they'd been here together they could have laughed it all off, could have dealt, over time, with the loss of Aberdeen. Alone, it was all almost too much to bear.

She could go home to Carson. She *should* go home to Carson. She had no money. She couldn't stay here past the end of the year. Already the cable company had called about an installation fee, or an initiation fee, or whatever it was, and Elizabeth had told them to cancel it, forget it, that she and Bell didn't need TV or DirecTV or TiVo. It was Carson who liked those kinds of things, not her.

Carson. Frank. Carson. How had this happened? She'd loved Carson when she married him, and she loved him still, but it hurt so much, what he'd done to her for so long. And she'd never understood it before, could never forgive his indiscretions, his infidelities, but she'd turned a blind eye because she wanted Bell to have what she herself had never had—a family, two parents, a house with a lawn and dinner on the table each night. She wondered if the gamble had been worth it.

And the funny thing—if you could see any humor at this point at all—was that now she'd gone and blown her own ace. It was always so clear before: Carson the infidel, Carson the adulterer, Carson the liar. Elizabeth the snow-white victim. But now she'd stooped to his level. Now she was an adulterer, too. And even *worse*—unlike Carson, she'd played with more than sex. She'd played with love. And she'd done it with the one person Carson could never forgive her for. Or could he? Could he forgive? Could she?

Elizabeth, an adulterer. Carson and Frank, brawling like thugs in the muddy drive. Mac Weeden off to the clinic. Blood mixed with rain, palms burning. What were they all coming to?

She sat on the couch nearly motionless for what felt like a long, long time, but when she finally rose she saw it wasn't yet three o'clock. When the knock came she expected Sofia and Bell, so she wiped her eyes and then pulled the door open, and she blinked to see Susan Holm standing on the doorstep, a bottle of Shiraz in one hand and a corkscrew in the other.

"I've been hearing things," Susan said.

"Come in," Elizabeth said. She stepped back and pulled the door wide, and she was surprised to find that she was actually glad to see Susan, glad to see someone who wasn't a Bravo, who wasn't *entirely* crazy, even though Susan had been shooting resentful looks her way ever since grade school. "Like what?" Elizabeth said.

"Like all of it," Susan said. "Like cheating husbands and broken hearts and stolen money. You know, the usual stuff." Susan walked to the kitchen, nosed around in the cabinets until she found the goblets, then uncorked the wine bottle and poured two generous glasses.

"You do seem to be in the know," Elizabeth conceded.

Susan shook her head. "It's these Bravos, girl. They'll be the end of all of us." She sighed and pushed the glass of wine to Elizabeth.

"It's pretty early," Elizabeth said, looking at her watch, but she took the glass.

"Extenuating circumstances," Susan said. "I'm sorry about Arla, Elizabeth. I know you loved her."

Elizabeth looked across the condo. Arla's Felix clock tocked in the hallway. "I did," she said quietly. "I really did."

Upstairs, in another condo, a TV blared. It sounded like a soap opera. The music swelled, dropped, swelled again, framing an argument. Man, woman, man, woman.

Elizabeth sipped her wine and regarded Susan. "So what's this all about, Susan?" she said. "You coming over? I mean, I gotta be honest. I didn't think you liked me very much."

Susan frowned, tipped her head. "Oh, of course I like you, Elizabeth. I guess I just didn't like how much some *other* people liked you." She tapped a long fingernail on her wineglass, and Elizabeth felt her stomach clench with shame. Oh, God, *Frank*. Could Susan know? About her night of the acrobats? She couldn't. Could she? Susan grinned then, and lifted the glass to her lips, and Elizabeth willed herself to relax. Nobody knew. She reached over and swept up a tangle of hair ties Bell had left strewn on the countertop. And nobody ever would.

"But that's not fair to you," Susan continued. "I suppose I'm finally growing up, Elizabeth. And anyway, I think I've got a new guy. It's time for me to move on."

"Amen, sister," Elizabeth said. "I think it's time for all of us to move on."

"You, too?" Susan said. "Like, move on from Carson?" She cocked her head, looked hard at Elizabeth.

"I don't know," Elizabeth admitted.

"I didn't think you did," Susan said, and she reached for the wine bottle, topped off their glasses. "Now listen. I got the whole afternoon, and I can't think of a better way to spend it than bitching about the Bravos." She smiled, and Elizabeth reached for her glass. Oh, why not? It felt good, suddenly, to have a woman to talk with, especially a woman who wasn't related to her husband. It felt like having a friend.

"Susan, have you ever heard of a veep?" she said.

"What's that?" Susan said. "Some kind of fish or something?" Elizabeth laughed. *Go to hell, Myra*, she thought. *And take your fake boobs with you.*

"Now, *dish*," Susan said. "The Bravo boys."

"Lord, Susan," she said. "Where do we start?" She hitched her stool closer to the breakfast bar and got comfortable.

Later, when both Susan and the wine were gone and Bell

was back at the condo, having been dropped off by Sofia and Biaggio, Elizabeth looked again at the lease, at Arla's signature confirming the prepaid rent. Then she called Tony's Hair Affair, and when he picked up, she said it quickly, before she lost her nerve.

"I need a job, Tony," she said.

"Oh, honey," he said. "You got one. I got product out the wazoo over here, all sitting in boxes, nobody will get off their asses and get it on the shelves. I got girls calling in sick. I got nobody but me answering the phone. I mean, *seriously*," he said.

She'd start on Monday. When it was settled, she hung up the phone and turned around to see Bell lying flat on the Berber carpet behind her.

"What are you doing, Belly?" she said.

"Pretending to be dead."

"My Lord." Elizabeth's heart dropped a beat. "Get up, Bell. I don't like that."

"What does it feel like?"

"I don't know," Elizabeth said. "I've never been dead. Get up, please."

"Do you think it hurts?"

Elizabeth thought about it, thought about Arla's face when she'd found her in bed, the way that one eye sagged, curiously open. She remembered Arla's hands, how they'd seemed so relaxed, so open, in prayer, it would seem, or supplication.

"No, I don't," Elizabeth said. "I don't know if it hurts getting there, but I think once you get there, you're fine."

Bell closed her eyes for a moment, lay very still, and then she opened her eyes, sat up straight, and looked at Elizabeth.

"I want to go home," she said. "I hate it here."

Elizabeth opened her mouth to answer, then closed it again, regarded her daughter. Bell's jaw was set, her small, freckled face stony. For a moment Elizabeth wanted to smile at her moxie, her seven-year-old decisiveness. Bell always knew what she wanted. Elizabeth wanted to laugh, but then she realized it wasn't entirely funny.

"Are you hungry?" she said to Bell. "Do you want a snack?"

"I said I want to go home."

"Maybe we could start with a snack."

Bell frowned, furrowed her brow. But she got up from the carpet and stomped to the kitchen, pulled open the refrigerator. Her head disappeared from view. Beneath the open refrigerator door, her small toes gripped the tile.

When the phone rang Elizabeth didn't even look at the caller ID, just picked it up, expecting Tony again. When she heard it was Carson she tightened her grip on the phone and sat down. The wine rushed quietly in her head, making her vision slightly softer. She thought of those filters the Hollywood people put on the cameras, in the old days, when it was time for the starlet's big scene. What were those?

"Yes?" she said.

"We got Mac all patched up," Carson said.

"Lovely. I'm sure he's very happy."

"And my father. He's back."

"Back?"

"Back with the money, back with everything."

Elizabeth closed her eyes, tried to process the implications of this information.

"I needed that money," he said. "There's a lot at stake."

"I know."

"More than you realize."

"I know more than you think, Carson."

He was quiet for a moment. "So do I," he said.

She put her head in her hand and listened to Bell puttering in the kitchen. "Well, then maybe we're even," she said. And maybe they were.

"Elizabeth," he said, and his voice was soft and open, a voice she hadn't heard in many years. "We're scattering my mother's ashes on Friday. Can I pick you up?"

Elizabeth looked around the condo at Willough Walk, the lanai, the carpet, the empty red wine bottle shining like blood against the stark white of the kitchen counter, the stupid, idiotic wall sconces. She could do this. She could go with Carson to his mother's funeral. She could. After that, well, she didn't have the slightest idea what would happen.

"Yes," she said. "Yes."

Twenty-three

Frank drove up Cooksey Lane, having stopped twice on the way home from the clinic: once at Sterling's Drugstore to fill Mac's pain pill prescription, and once at the package store for a bottle of whiskey for Dean. "Thank you, Frank," Dean had said quietly, and Frank had not looked over at him, or at Mac either, for that matter, who was painful to behold, his eyes now nearly swollen shut, his cheeks flushed and damp, a thick white piece of tape extended over the bridge of his nose and two fat rolls of gauze stuffed up into his nostrils to stem the bleeding. Good God, he was a sight.

"How bad is id?" Mac had said, climbing into the cab of the truck.

"Holy shit!" Dean had exclaimed, staring at him. He edged to the center of the bench seat.

"Not that bad," Frank said quickly, and Mac had slumped forlornly against the passenger door.

"Dere goes my social life," Mac said.

"What social life?" Dean said, but Frank elbowed him in the side, hard, and Dean gasped in pain. "My cheek," he moaned.

Frank let them both off at his house. Sofia and Biaggio had returned to the trailer, having presumably deposited Bell back with Elizabeth, and they were now sitting on the white steps with a bag of chips. Frank let his passengers out without a word. Let them do all the explaining, he thought, watching Mac and Dean shuffle up the path toward the porch, Sofia and Biaggio gaping at the sight of them. He pulled back out onto Cooksey Lane. He had something to do.

He left Utina, headed south on US1, then pulled up at the county municipal complex and drove around the back to the jail. The swelling in his cheek had subsided a bit, but his shoulder was aching something fierce from the impact of hitting his dirt driveway after tackling Carson off the front porch. But at least the rain had stopped. The sun was blazing hot again.

He entered the building and approached a glassed-in counter. "Tip Breen," he said to the clerk, and then he filled out a form on a plastic clipboard. The clerk showed him into a small visitation room, a bank of telephones mounted on a Plexiglas barrier down the center.

After a few minutes, Tip was ushered into the room, and his mouth fell open when he saw Frank on the other side of the glass. He sat down heavily, picked up the phone receiver, and stared at Frank.

"Bravo," he said. "Frank." His huge face was slack, drooping, and he looked like an old chastened bloodhound, morose, defeated, broken-hearted.

"What have you gone and done here, Tip?" Frank said into the phone. "What's this I hear about you shooting up the Publix?"

"Aw, Frank," Tip said. His voice was raspy through the wire. "It's a damn racket, Frank. It's a conspiracy against the poor folks, that's what it is. It's Ponte Vedra, the rich bastards, taking over the world." Evidently Tip hadn't lost his proclivity for editorial. "They're killing us, Frank. They're killing us all."

"You don't have the bail?" Frank said.

"I don't have the damn bail. I don't have any money—and it's all about money, you know. If you got money you do anything you want. O.J. cut off Nicole's head and they let him go. Why? Money."

"You can't go shooting up the Publix, Tip."

"I know."

"You can't go threatening people, Tip, with a *gun*, for Christ's sake. People don't like that."

"I know, Frank," Tip said. He sighed. "I got no money, Frank."

"You said that."

"I lost my apartment. I been sleeping in my car. I got no friends, Frank."

Frank looked at the floor.

"I got nothin', Frank," Tip said, and Frank looked up to see his rheumy eyes welling up. "My little girl won't see me. I haven't seen her in years. My ex-wife won't let me. . . ." He trailed off, his chin quivering.

"People are afraid of you, Tip," Frank said. "And maybe they should be."

Tip wiped his face with his sleeve. "We go way back, Bravo." He stared at Frank, waiting.

"We do, Tip." *Way back.*

"I heard about your mama." Tip's eyes filled again.

Frank didn't answer, but he thought of his new money in the bank, the new debit card in his pocket. It was funny, how you could buy yourself out of guilt. Buy yourself out of remorse. Even if it was against your better judgment. He had a vision of Tip, nineteen years old, that night in the woods, when Kelly had been cut down by the car hood. Tip had put his arm around Will's thin shoulder, tried to comfort him, quiet him. He was one of the last people to touch Will before he died. Tip didn't deserve much. But did he deserve to sit in jail? The Bravos had sold Aberdeen. In some ways, the Bravos had sold Utina. There were a lot of things Frank could feel guilty about these days. God only knew. But maybe here was a chance to erase just one.

"Keep your nose clean, dumb-ass," he said to Tip. "Get it together."

He left Tip sniffling behind the Plexiglas, went back to the clerk's area, and posted the bail. Then he walked out to the parking lot, climbed into his truck, and drove home, fighting a gnawing feeling he couldn't put words to. It might have been fear. But most likely it was just grief, for people and for places, a sadness threading stubbornly around his heart, like the creeping jasmine of Utina.

Friday morning dawned clear, bright, and hot, and Gooch was missing. Frank stood on the porch, whistling, but the dog didn't come. He sighed. Now this?

Not that he could entirely blame Gooch, who was probably staging a protest against the invasion that had recently taken place on his territory. Frank looked around the yard. His property was beginning to look like a bit of a circus, given Biaggio's trailer and van, the palm ashes still blowing across the front yard, and, just to the right of the driveway, the newly deposited storage pod. The asshole banker next door must be loving it.

After their excursion to the emergency clinic on Wednesday, Mac had picked up his own car at Frank's house and gone home. Frank had called him when he'd gotten back from bailing Tip out of jail.

"You all right, Mac?" he'd said.

"Bedder now," Mac replied. "I dook some pain meds." And drank a six-pack of beer, more than likely, but Frank was done with policing everyone else's alcohol consumption, had given it up when he'd announced last call on closing night at Uncle Henry's last week. Let them all get pickled. He couldn't begrudge Mac, anyway, poor guy, trying to help out these idiot Bravos and getting his nose broken in the process. "Thanks, Mac," he'd said on the phone. "Thanks for trying to help us."

"Aw, shud up," Mac said. "Good stuff."

Dean had showered and borrowed some of Frank's clothes and had spent a fitful night on the couch, in pain no doubt, and Frank had heard him up in the night on at least three occasions, stepping out to the porch to wheeze, smoke cigarettes, and, presumably, hit the bottle. Gooch had raised his head from the blanket each time, looked at Frank quizzically at the sound of the porch door opening and closing, but Frank had put his hand on the dog's head, and Gooch rolled over and went back to sleep. Frank himself had slept little. It was strange beyond strange to have Dean sleeping in his house, for one, and the ghosts of Will and now Arla tugged at his mind and jarred him out of slumber each time he slipped into dreams. He fell asleep once for a longish stretch, dreamed of sliding on the hood of a car in the cool blue light of the moon, across wide white dunes. Firecrackers burst above.

Why did you tell me to leave him, Frank?

Why did you listen?

The screen door creaked again. Gooch sighed. The smell of cigarette smoke worked its way around Frank's house, in through his bedroom window.

They'd spent the next day, Thursday, in a state of arrested development, not knowing what to do with themselves, what to focus on, what to say or do or even eat. Dean sat on the porch, alternately smoking and coughing, and around midafternoon Frank couldn't take the sound of it anymore and he unhitched his kayak and took it out to the beach, where he plowed through the breakers and let the salt water dry on his skin until the sun grew fat and fuzzy and sank lower in the sky. Then he loaded the kayak back into the truck and picked up a couple of pizzas to bring back to his house.

Now, Friday morning, they emerged from the house, finally, after a pot of coffee and the dozen doughnuts Frank had picked up from the Publix.

"You seen Gooch?" Frank said to Dean. He looked around the yard again.

"Not since last night," Dean said.

They made their way down the drive to pile into Biaggio's van, Frank's truck cab being too small to get the four out to Aberdeen to scatter Arla's ashes. Frank watched as Dean picked his way slowly down the porch steps and moved awkwardly across the yard. He could barely walk. Frank held the back door of the van open and waited until Dean had climbed, nearly *crawled*, inside, his face a mask of pain and illness. Biaggio climbed behind the wheel, Sofia next to him in the passenger seat.

"Hang on," Frank said. He walked over to the storage pod, spun the combination lock, and entered the dark cube, letting his eyes adjust to the hot darkness and feeling along the tops of the boxes until he found what he was looking for, Arla's wooden cane, the dark straight wood shiny even in this dim light, the rubber handle soft and warm. He locked the pod, went back to the van, and handed the cane in to Dean, who nodded, cleared his throat, accepted it. Frank scanned the yard one last time, then climbed into the backseat and sat next to Dean.

Carson would meet them at Aberdeen, it had been decided, and he'd bring Elizabeth and Bell. Frank didn't know whether Elizabeth had seen or even talked to Carson again after the scene with Mac at his house on Wednesday. It was not his place to ask, not his place to know.

They stopped at the funeral home, and Frank went in and signed for the ashes, which were packed in a cardboard carton the size of a shoe box, the box then wrapped in a purple velvet bag. He picked them up, surprised at the weight, then returned to Biaggio's van.

Sofia gasped when she saw the box.

"My God," she said. "That's her?" She started to cry.

"Now, honey," Biaggio said.

Dean stared at the box on Frank's lap.

"Will's box wasn't that big," he said.

"Yes, it was," Frank said.

"No, it wasn't," Dean said.

"I was there. I remember. It was the same."

"I was there, too, dumbo," Dean said. "It was a smaller box."

"It's standard, Dad. They do it the same every time."

"She was a big woman," Biaggio offered.

Sofia sniffled.

"It doesn't matter. It's the same," Frank said, exasperated.

"You sure that's her?" Dean said.

"For God's sake, it's her," Frank said. "They're careful with this stuff."

"Well, you don't know," Dean insisted. "They could bung it up."

"You're upsetting Sofia," Frank said. He glared at him. "This is Mom. It's Arla. Now will you stop?"

"I'm just saying," Dean said. "You can't believe everything. Lots of people say things, that don't make it so. You can put your boots in the oven, but that don't make them biscuits."

Sofia stared at him, her eyes wet and her lips clamped tightly together. Her chin shook.

"Aw, Mr. Bravo," Biaggio said. "Let's not talk about ovens." He nodded at the box.

"Let me see that," Dean said.

He took the box from Frank and fell silent. They all watched him as he held the box between his two gnarled hands, stared at it, seemed to take some strange energy from its weight on his lap.

"It's okay," Dean said, after a minute. "It's her. I don't know much. But I know Arla." His voice broke on the last word. Sofia hiccupped. Frank stared out the window. Biaggio pulled out of the parking lot and headed for Aberdeen.

The house was razed. Leveled. Sofia let out a small cry and Dean said "*shit*" and Biaggio stopped the van in what used to be the driveway. They all stared, astonished, at the place that used to be Aberdeen and was now an enormous jumble of wrecked lumber, pale swatches of Aberdeen's gunmetal gray paint still visible. Beyond the house, to the north, the woods leading to Uncle Henry's had been clear-cut, and beyond that, at the other end of the property a half mile away, another pile of wreckage towered on the patch of land that used to be Uncle Henry's. Twin backhoes were parked, unmanned, at the head of Aberdeen's driveway, spatterings of rain still shimmering on their buckets. The concrete pad where Biaggio's trailer had stood was still visible, though broken down the middle where a backhoe had no doubt driven across it.

How had they moved so quickly? Frank was confounded—he'd seen the backhoes doing their work at the Publix site, seen the earthmovers clear-cutting the properties on his own street, and he knew they worked fast, but this . . . this. . . .

It was just Monday they'd been here, all of them, walking around the porch for the last time, debating the value of the thick cement picnic table, piling bags of trash out by the road. It was just five days ago they'd sat in the kitchen, the paramedics' paperwork spread out on the table, the weight of Arla's spirit still lingering in the atmosphere. It was just a few weeks ago he and Elizabeth had walked the path from the house to Uncle Henry's, that hot, beautiful night.

Frank got out of the van and Biaggio followed. Sofia helped Dean out. The air was heavy with moisture, and the temperature had begun to rise again so that it looked like clouds of steam were emerging from the piles of rubble and lumber. The magnolias—gone. The wraparound porch—gone. The path to Uncle Henry's.

Gone.

Frank had thought about this day. Fantasized about it—the
heavy timbers of Aberdeen broken and spent, the ties dissolved,
his own future free and unfettered by the weight of the hundred-year-old house and the people and ghosts who inhabited
it. But now his heart was heavy, and his stomach was gnawing
again, and the vision of the ruined house became suddenly
the embodiment of all he had lost in the last five days. A flight
of images that felt like an aura swept over him: the blue vinyl
tablecloth, the Felix clock, the thick round bannister, the pantry
full of Little Debbie cakes, the peeling paint, Dean's bass on
the wall. The pile of shoes on the back porch. Always, the pile
of shoes. *Don't clomp all that mud in here, you boys! What were
you, raised in a barn?*

"Well," Dean said. "I guess they're in a helluva hurry to
build that marina." He leaned up against Biaggio's van.

A car door slammed, and Carson and Elizabeth joined the
rest of them at the edge of the property. Elizabeth, wide-eyed,
held Bell's hand.

"My God," Carson said. "They really did it."

They walked down to the edge of the water. Dean walked
in front, one hand clutching the box, the other holding Arla's
cane, moving slowly and painfully through the rough dirt and
around the larger piles of debris, down to the edge of the waterway, to a shady spot under a tall pine where the bank jutted
steeply over the water, which rushed by five feet below. They
stood together, the Bravos, and for the first time in as long as
Frank could remember it seemed that nobody could think of
anything to say, standing there in the imaginary shadow of
what once was Aberdeen, what once was their lives. Dean's
breathing was labored, raspy.

"Dad," Carson said finally, and Dean limped forward, opened the purple bag, the cardboard box and the plastic bag within. He turned back to the rest of the group.

"You wanna?" he said, gesturing at the ashes.

"You," Sofia said. "You do it."

So he did, letting the cane drop to the sand and clutching the bag of ashes with both hands, walking forward to the very edge of the embankment. He tipped the bag until gravity kicked in and a soft breeze took over and then Arla was moving, white and smoky and thin, through the hot wet air, out onto the surface of the water and down, away, borne south on the tide but some parts sinking deep, into the sand below, Frank guessed, becoming part of the land, part of the water, part of the earth.

"'Night, *maman*," Sofia said, *"Je t'aime."* Frank was surprised that she was not crying, but was standing very straight and still, her hand in Biaggio's. They waited a few minutes more, and then Sofia and Biaggio turned and walked back up the bank. Frank followed with Carson, Elizabeth, and Bell, but he turned back briefly to see Dean still standing alone at the edge of the waterway. Carson looked, too.

"Give him a minute, I guess," he said to Frank. They made their way back to the van, but then they hung there, not knowing quite what should come next.

"Lunch?" Elizabeth said finally.

"Lunch," Sofia agreed.

Bell was standing very still, looking down toward the water, and she put her hand up to her eyes suddenly, to shield the sun.

"Mama," she said. "Is Grandpa Dean *swimming?*"

Frank turned and looked back at the water.

"Oh, Christ," Carson said. "Oh for shit's sake."

Dean was ten, maybe fifteen feet from the shore, splashing awkwardly. His orange cap had fallen off and floated nearby. Frank saw Dean's face go under once, his mouth open, then resurface, then go under again. Then they couldn't see him anymore.

And then Carson was moving, faster than Frank could have given him credit for, and Frank was following, but slower, clumsier, back down the yards of overturned earth and the scuttled foundation that once was Aberdeen. Bell and Elizabeth were yelling, and Biaggio and Sofia were behind him now, too, but Carson was faster than all of them. Before Frank could even reach the edge of the water Carson was in it, had gotten to Dean, and was pulling, lugging, dragging him up, against the current, away from the steep embankment where Dean had entered the water and up twenty feet to a shallower part of the bank with a strip of sand. Frank reached them and he and Carson both pulled their father up onto land, where Dean kneeled, soaking wet, gasping and retching, before belching up a bellyful of brown tannin water.

"Ew," Bell said. She'd arrived at the edge of the water with Elizabeth, Sofia, and Biaggio, and they all stood now in a circle around Dean, who looked up, finally.

"Damn," he said.

"What in the name of God is wrong with you?" Carson said. He, too, was soaked to the bone, and he pulled his cell phone out of his pocket, looked at it for a moment, then threw it to the ground in disgust. He bent over at the waist, breathing hard. "Don't we all have enough to deal with without you trying to kill your fool self?"

"Did Daddy save Grandpa Dean?" Bell said.

"Yes, he did, Bell," Elizabeth said. She stared at Carson. "He did."

"*Jesus*, Dad," Carson said. "You would have drowned. In your condition . . . if Bell hadn't seen you, if we hadn't gotten here in time. . . ." His voice trailed off. He ran his hands through his wet hair, and Frank could see that he was shaking. Elizabeth saw it, too.

"You all right, Carson?" Frank said.

"Honest to Christ," Carson said. He squatted, put his head down for a moment, then looked at Dean again. He looked like he might cry. "Now we've all got to sit around and worry about you trying to off yourself? Is that the new barrel of monkeys?"

"Oh, shut it, Superman," Dean said then. He struggled up from his knees, stood in front of them all. My God, what a sight, Frank thought. Muddy shirt clinging like gauze to his thin frame, hair flattened and gray across his head, the lines in his face more pronounced than ever. "I wasn't trying to kill myself, you dummy," Dean said. "I tripped on a damn palmetto." He looked at them all, then grinned. "What, you think I'd leave ya'll orphans?"

"Oh, for *gosh* sakes," Sofia said. She started to laugh, then put her hands over her mouth. "Sorry," she muttered.

"Oh, no, it's funny," Carson said. "It's just funny as hell." He turned and marched up the bank toward the cars. Elizabeth smiled at Frank, then turned to follow Carson.

"Well, shit," Dean said. He was squinting down the line of the waterway, shielding his eyes with his hand.

"Now what?" Frank said.

"I lost my damn hat," Dean said. He shook his head. "I liked that hat."

They turned and watched it go, a tiny orange fleck wobbling down the current with Arla.

Twenty-four

They stopped at Sterling's for lunch, but Carson was fractious, irritated by his wet clothes. He snapped at Cathy for bringing him the wrong drink, fussed loudly about the cloying perfume of the woman sitting behind him, then complained his meat loaf was undercooked. Elizabeth rolled her eyes.

"Dad's wet, too," Frank said, finally, having had enough. "I don't hear him bitching."

"That's because it's his fault," Carson said.

"Shit, I don't care," Dean said, looking down at his own clothes. He seemed surprised to notice they were wet. "Wet's better than hot."

"I prolly got an extra shirt out there in the van, you want me to look?" Biaggio said.

"No, thank you," Carson said. He scowled and eyed Biaggio's enormous frame. "I don't think you and I have the same tailor, so to speak."

"Carson, take a chill pill," Sofia said, which was funny, it seemed to Frank, but he didn't dare laugh. Carson raised his eyebrows at Sofia but did not answer. Elizabeth picked at a tuna melt. Bell finished her chicken nuggets and then ate the rest of Carson's rejected meat loaf. Cathy finally came to clear the plates and slap a bill down in the center of the table.

"I'll meet you all at the van," Frank said. "I just want to walk down to the Lil' Champ and check on Tip." He'd seen Tip's car in its usual spot next to the store as they looped down Semi-nary Street looking for a parking spot before lunch, and he was surprised—though tentatively relieved—to see that Tip seemed to be easing back into his routine. There'd be a hearing on the vandalism charge, of course, and no doubt a hefty fine, too. But rehabilitation—it wasn't out of the question, right? Maybe Tip was going to survive in the new Utina after all.

"I'll come with you," Carson said.

"Since when do you care about Tip Breen?" Frank said.

"I don't care about Tip," Carson said. "But I think I might smell a business venture." Elizabeth stared at him. He tossed his napkin onto the table, got up, kissed Bell, and squished toward the front door.

Frank reached for the check, then noticed Dean had eaten only a couple bites of his hamburger.

"You're not hungry, Dad?" he said.

"Pffft," Dean said. He leaned back in the booth and stared at the ceiling.

When they walked into the Lil' Champ Frank realized how long it had been since he'd entered the store. Months, in fact. Over the summer he'd taken to picking up his coffee at Sterling's in order, he admitted guiltily, to avoid Tip. He remembered being here on Fourth of July but could not recall having been back since. My God, what a mess the place was. The shelves were nearly empty of stock. The Lotto stand was bare. The Krispy Kreme case was blurred and sticky-looking. Even the porn was in sad shape, the rack now busted on one side and dangling rakishly behind the counter, an aspect that made the magazines appear even more obscene. Frank was afraid to look closely at the hot dog warmer, though he could see from ten feet away that a half-dozen shriveled red hot dogs spun slowly across the rollers. He wondered how long they'd been there.

"Christ," Carson muttered. He stuffed his hands in his pockets.

"Tip," Frank called. "You back in business?"

The door to the men's room opened, and Tip Breen shuffled out. He gave the Bravos a tired wave and moved toward his stool behind the counter.

"I guess so," he said. "You want something?"

Frank looked around, trying to locate something he could purchase. He reached for a bag of chips but yanked his hand back when a roach scuttled across the wrapping. He gave up. They approached the counter.

"Tip, how are you doing?" Frank said. "You doing all right?"

"He's doing shitty," Carson barked. "Look at him. Tip, what the hell is wrong with you?"

Tip sighed. "Well, first of all, I been in jail," he began. "And second, I got no sales. Them developer people. They're driving me out of business. . . ."

"Oh, this bullshit again," Carson said.

"Carson," Frank said. "Go easy."

"It's true," Tip protested. "It's not bullshit." He slouched forward over the counter.

"Tip, this place is a pit," Carson said. "It's worse than a pit. You've given up." He walked away from the counter toward the front door, then looked out at the boat ramp and the water beyond. He turned back to Tip. "You've let them win," he said.

Tip shook his head. "No," he said. "It's not that, Carson."

Carson looked at Frank and raised his eyebrows, annoyed, but Frank was surprised to also see a flicker of pity in his brother's eyes. He wondered if Carson shared his own memory: Tip's big hands on Will's shoulders that night at the dunes.

Carson cleared his throat and walked back over to the counter. "Look, Tip," he said. He spread his arms out, gestured around the store. "You don't just die, dummy. You dig in, get stronger. You're right on the water here. That's what these people are coming to Utina for. Why don't you make the most of it?"

Tip shrugged.

Carson started to pace. From the counter to the door, back again. "You can do this. Give them what they want, which is more than porn and beer." He kicked at a newspaper stand, gestured to the thick layer of filth behind it. "Clean up, for starters. Then put some chairs outside there, some tables with umbrellas. Get some real coffee in here, for Christ's sake," he said. "Some of those cups with sleeves. Fucking scones and whatnot. *Compete,* Breen!"

Tip was unmoved. He looked around the ruined store, then sighed.

"I can't do it," Tip said. "I'm not like you, Carson."

Carson regarded him. "You got that right, Breen," he said, but his voice was softer, almost gentle. They fell silent for a moment.

"Well," Frank said finally.

"Hey, Tip," Carson said. He moved in closer and paddled his hands on the counter. "I got a joke for you. What do Richard Nixon, Andrew Johnson, and Bill Clinton have in common?"

But Tip slid off the stool behind the counter and walked slowly toward the back of the store.

"Come on, Tip!" Carson called. "Take a guess!"

At the door to the storeroom, Tip turned around.

"I'm sorry, Frank," he said. "You done a good thing for me and all, but you shouldn't a sold to them people. They're killing me. They're killing Utina. Can't you Bravos see that?" He looked on the verge of tears, and Frank was suddenly furious with him for not wanting to change. For not even considering the possibility. There was nothing they could do for Tip Breen.

"Get it together, Tip," he said. But Tip walked into the storeroom and closed the door.

They turned to exit the Lil' Champ but stopped short at the sight of Alonzo Cryder's black Mercedes pulling up to the curb in front of the store. "Well, look who it isn't," Carson said. They watched as Cryder climbed out of the car, as he spotted Frank and Carson through the storefront. His raised a hand to them and walked purposefully toward the front door.

Frank was surprised to see Cryder here, in downtown Utina, and even more surprised to see that he was agitated, disheveled. He'd taken off his starched shirt and was stripped down to dress pants and a tight white T-shirt that revealed a doughy-looking paunch and deep sweat stains under the arms. He looked like a different person than the smooth man who had sat in Mac's office just a few weeks ago, sweet-talking Arla into the sale.

Cryder entered the store and sniffed as he approached them.

"Cryder," Frank said. "What are you doing here? The sale's all over. Aren't you supposed to be out of Atlanta? Running marinas or something?"

"That's very funny," Cryder said. "But you know I don't run them. I build them, Frank."

"It's Mr. Bravo," Frank said. "And it's good to see you supporting the local merchants, Mr. Cryder."

Cryder looked around the store, then narrowed his eyes and looked from Frank to Carson and back again. "I stopped for a soda—" he said.

"Try the hot dogs," Carson said. "They're fabulous."

Cryder ignored him. "—but I'm glad I caught you people here," he continued. "I was about to call you. I have a question for you two gentlemen."

"You want to know where the nail salon is?" Carson said. "Well, you just walk up Seminary about two blocks, and then—"

"Listen," Cryder hissed. He leaned in closer. "I would like to know why you didn't tell us about the burial site," he said.

"The burial site?" Frank said.

"On the property," Cryder said. "There's a grave marker. Which means there appear to be human remains on the marina property." He sighed and rubbed his forehead. "And my boss is not happy," he added.

Carson looked at Frank; Frank saw the realization register in his brother's eyes, and he raised his own eyebrows in return but said nothing. Drusilla! He'd scarcely thought of her in years, though he remembered now—like it was yesterday—the afternoon he'd first discovered the gravestone in the woods. He'd been six, seven maybe. He and Carson had come across it during a tramp through the scrub, and it had frightened him terribly. Carson scoffed at Frank's terror, but he followed when Frank ran home to tell Arla about it. She'd laughed at the two of them, sweaty and breathless. "Oh, that's my dear friend," she said. "That's just Drusilla. She won't hurt you." Good God, they'd left Drusilla at Aberdeen, left her to the bulldozers and backhoes. He swallowed hard, tried not to look at Carson again.

"You failed to disclose this to us, and now we've got problems," Cryder was saying. "I've been hauling my ass all over that site trying to figure out what the hell is going on." He clawed at his forearms, where Frank could see the raised clusters of at least a dozen fresh mosquito bites. "Florida's got statutes," Cryder continued. "We have to get the damned medical examiner in here, get an investigation. It's slowing everything down, and our permits are time sensitive, for God's sake. The surveyors were supposed to start tomorrow." He took a crumpled napkin from his pocket and mopped his brow.

"And this concerns us how?" Carson said.

"You knew about this," Cryder said. "And you didn't tell us."

Carson turned to Frank. "Frank, did you know there was a burial site on the property?" he said.

"Nope," Frank said.

"Me neither," Carson said. He turned back to Cryder. "Sorry, fella."

Cryder narrowed his eyes. "Look, I need a statement," he said. "I need something from you people saying who that person is, what's the story on that burial marker. Otherwise we'll be forever trying to track it down."

Carson shrugged. "Not our property, Mr. Cryder. Not our problem."

Cryder glared at them for a moment. "Bravos," he said quietly. "Do the right thing. Don't be your daddy."

Frank felt his brother stiffen beside him, and he wondered for a moment whether Carson was going to throw a punch, but then the storeroom door opened and Tip emerged and stood looking balefully at Cryder. A synapse in Frank's brain fired—late, of course, stupidly late but palpable and insistent now, making his stomach lurch and his heart clench. The shape of something dark and metallic in Tip's right hand. Tip. Cryder. Utina. Vista.

I got nothing, Frank, Tip had said. *They're killing us, Frank.*

"Carson," Frank said, and Carson was quick, understanding without Frank having to say it. They moved toward Tip in unison, reaching him just as he leveled his aim at Cryder. Frank yelled at Cryder to get down. Then the moment turned to a chaos of sweat and fumbling and the rank odor of Tip's body, too close, too thick, and damp and heavy as Frank and Carson pushed him backward and down. The three of them barreled into a shelving unit together, and the gun discharged once, firing through the bottom pane of the Lil' Champ's windowed front door but missing Cryder, now crouched in mute fear by the Lotto stand, by a healthy margin. Tip dropped the gun, and Carson kicked it, sending it sliding under a freezer case. When the front door's glass shards settled, the silence was complete and astounding, broken after a moment by the sound of Tip's voice, thin and frightened.

"Frank," Tip said. "Oh, shit, Frank."

The most frightening aspect of death, it occurred to Frank later, was its obdurate, intractable randomness. It was true that at times death could be seen approaching from a great distance, slow but insistent, beating a drum for the sick, for example, or for the old. But then there were times, and in Frank's experience this had been the norm, when it struck from seemingly nowhere. Bam! Done! It made him unsteady on his feet, unsure of his position. There were times, as when he was driving over the Intracoastal, across the Vilano Bridge, with the ocean spread gray and gleaming in the distance, or when he was bobbing alone in his kayak, watching through water clear as air as the mudminnows delicately nibbled the bait from around the sharp point of his hook, when the beauty was nearly painful, and Frank would have a moment of cloudiness, of vertigo, and he would wonder if perhaps he was, in fact, already dead and just hadn't realized it yet. There was really no telling. None of this made any sense at all.

To wit: nobody had wanted Will or Arla to die. But they did. Tip Breen had very much wanted Alonzo Cryder to die. But he didn't. Didn't even get hurt, really, if Frank didn't count Cryder's wounded dignity over the fact that he'd burst into tears once he realized he wasn't shot and had to venture into the hellish interior of the Lil' Champ's men's room to wipe his face, blow his nose, and generally collect himself.

But Cryder was alive. They all were. By the time the police arrived and packed Tip into the back of a crusier, the rest of the Bravos and Biaggio had hurried down from Sterling's and had gathered, shaken, outside the store, where now they waited as first Carson and then Frank gave statements to the police. Nearby, Cryder finished a protracted interview with a young cop who looked both confused by the paperwork and intimidated by the little throng of bystanders gawking at the commotion—but thank God for small favors it wasn't Do-Key on the scene, for once, Frank thought. The family stood near Cryder's Mercedes, except Carson, who was sitting on the hood.

"Helluva day," Dean said.

"My God," Carson said. He exhaled. "Can we get off this ride now?"

"You can get off my *car*, Bravo," Cryder snapped as he approached.

Carson waited a beat, then slid down from the Mercedes.

"You're welcome," Carson said.

"For what?" Cryder said. He sniffed.

"For keeping that dumbass from shooting you," Carson said. "I did you both a favor. And actually, you're the second person I've had to save today." He grinned, suddenly pleased with himself for his day's work. Frank, despite the fact that he was quite sure he'd had an equal part in thwarting Tip's shot, was amused to see his brother's signature bravado bubbling to the surface, in spite of the day's events. He looked at Elizabeth. She rolled her eyes, but then she smiled. Just a little.

"Well, *bravo*, Bravo," Cryder said. "Aren't you just the hero?"

"Look here," Frank said. He leaned over and pointed to the Mercedes's right fender, where the bullet from Tip's gun had left an ugly gash in the finish. "I guess Tip got you after all, Mr. Cryder," he said.

Carson bent and looked at the Mercedes. He ran his fingers across the ruined paint, then straightened up, sighed deeply, and shook his head. "Now *that's* a shame," he said.

Cryder pushed past the Bravos and climbed into the Mercedes. He started the engine and backed out of the parking space, then rolled down the window.

"You people are all crazy," he called. "God-damned Crackers!" He gunned the Mercedes and drove away, hurtling up Seminary Street and running the red light in front of the Publix. They watched him go.

"For Pete's sake," Sofia said.

"In quite a hurry," Biaggio said.

"Off to change his shorts, I bet," Carson said. "I think he's realizing how close he came."

The Bravos fell silent, and Frank's eyes met Carson's. *How close we came, too,* he thought. Carson nodded.

"What was he doing here, anyway?" Elizabeth said. "I figured he'd close the deal on Aberdeen and hightail it out of Utina."

Aberdeen! The property! Frank had nearly forgotten. He told them what Cryder had reported about Drusilla, and about the delay she was causing Vista.

"Lord!" Sofia said. She clapped her hand to her forehead. "Drusilla. I can't believe we left her."

"Who's Drusilla?" Bell said.

"Granny's friend," Elizabeth said. "Looks like she's putting a little wrench in Vista's plans."

"Do you think we should have had her exhumed or something?" Frank said.

Dean started to speak, then fell into a coughing fit and doubled over wheezing.

"We could call the funeral home," Elizabeth said. "They might know what to do."

Frank was feeling guilty now, as though they'd abandoned a member of their own family. Sofia bit her lip, and Carson looked away. But what in the world were they supposed to have done with a hundred-year-old corpse?

"Maybe I should call the medical examiner," Frank concluded.

"Oh, Christ. There's nobody buried there," Dean said, getting his breath finally. He cleared his throat and straightened up looking very much like he might laugh. "Me and Huff put that stone there fifty years ago. Stole it from a cemetery in St. Auggie."

They stared at him.

"For real?" Carson said.

"Of course for real," Dean said. "We were kids. It was long before your mother and I bought the place. We were just fooling around in the woods. We had to get rid of the thing before we got caught with it."

Frank looked at the sky for a beat, then back at Dean. "Why didn't you ever tell Mom?" he said.

Dean shrugged. "Because," he said. He cleared his throat again, then lit a cigarette and took a long pull. "She loved her."

They were quiet for a moment. Dean wheezed.

"Should you really be smoking that cigarette?" Carson said.

"Should you really be such a pain in the ass?" Dean said.

"Well, I gotta ask," Biaggio said. "Are you going to tell those Vista people there's nobody buried there?"

The Bravos looked at each other.

"Hooo-doggy," Biaggio said, grinning. "I didn't think so."

Bell wasn't satisfied. "But *is* there a real Drusilla?" she said.

"There was. Once," Dean said.

"Well, where is she now?"

"She's with Arla, Bell," he said. He blew a smoke ring and watched it dissipate.

"She's everywhere."

* * *

They walked up Seminary Street, to where Biaggio's van and Carson's car were still parked outside of Sterling's, and Carson left with Elizabeth and Bell. The rest piled into Biaggio's van. When they arrived back at Frank's house Biaggio and Sofia retired to the trailer. Dean showered and changed, then sat on the porch, where Frank stood on the steps, scanning the yard.

"He ain't back yet?" Dean said. "He ever do this before?"

Frank shook his head. Never. Gooch wasn't a wanderer. Frank could leave him in the yard for hours, sometimes all day, and he'd return home to find the dog waiting patiently on the porch, a look of mild reproach in his eye that gave way immediately to convulsions of wagging and writhing as soon as Frank climbed out of the truck and approached. But not today. It was nearly three o'clock. Frank hadn't seen his dog since late last night.

Dean stood. "Come on, Frank," he said. "We better look."

They walked the perimeter of Frank's property, calling and whistling. Fat, waxy brown magnolia leaves, once white, dotted the yard. A patch of sunlight appeared on a swath of pine straw, and Frank watched as a stout green lizard moved into position in the sun, stretching out to absorb the warmth. They kept walking. And then they found him. He was far from the house, nearly at the end of Frank's driveway, deep inside a thicket of jasmine.

"Aw, damn, Frank," Dean said. Frank slid Gooch's body out into the sunlight, and they looked at him.

"There it is," Dean said. He leaned down and touched the side of Gooch's swollen face. "Snake bite. He got into a tangle. Rattler or cottonmouth, you never know."

Frank shook his head. He knelt down and put his hands on Gooch, but the dog's body was cold. He'd probably been dead for hours. Maybe since early morning. The ball of grief inside Frank's chest expanded, and he closed his eyes for a moment. How much more was he expected to take?

He opened his eyes again. "But why did he come all the way out here? All by himself?" he said.

Dean shook his head.

"It's what old dogs do when they know they're done," he said. He looked at Frank. "He wanted to spare you."

They stood for a moment, looking at Gooch. In the silence, Frank could hear Dean's breathing, rattling and wet.

"All right," Dean said finally. "I guess we gotta bury one more," he said.

"I don't want to bury him here," Frank said. He gestured around at his property, nodded at the banker's place next door, the surveyor's marks on the lot across the street.

"I know a place," Dean said

They walked back to the house, and Frank found an old blanket, then he retrieved Gooch from the edge of the driveway and carried him to his truck. The dog was heavy, and Frank's back strained as he pushed the dead weight up into the bed of the pickup so he could lift the tailgate. He walked to the shed, fetched a shovel, loaded it next to Gooch.

They drove south, out of Utina and into the thick woods north of Tolomato, where the hammock grew thicker and darker and the dirt road was lined with dwarf cypress and senecio.

"Here," Dean said. "This here is county land. I don't think it will ever get built on."

Frank parked the truck and walked to the back, lowered the tailgate. He gathered Gooch in his arms. Dean took the shovel.

They pushed through palmettos and Christmas fern, stepped over rotting palm fronds and pine limbs until they came to a clearing, a few prisms of sunlight making their way through the heavy canopy to the carpet of pine needles below.

Dean shoved the tip of the shovel into the dirt, but then he stopped, coughing. He limped to a fallen oak and sat down. He put one hand on his hip, and the other he held over his eyes for a moment.

"I guess you better," Dean said. "I'm no use."

Frank dug the hole, laid Gooch inside, still wrapped in the blanket. He took a last glimpse of the dog's white back feet, then tossed the first shovelful of dirt into the hole. Then the next. When he was finished he straightened up, wiped the sweat from his face with his cap. He looked at Dean.

"It's not his fault, you know," Dean said. "That Carson is the way he is."

"I know," Frank said.

"You shouldn't hate him, Frank."

"I don't hate my brother," Frank said. "I just think we're not who we thought we were. Any of us."

A south September wind moved through the hammock, warm but dry and clear. Above, the pines swayed slowly, and the light played, dappled, on the newly dug earth.

"I always thought we were going to stay above the explosions," Frank said.

"Me, too," Dean said. "But I guess if you do that, you miss a lot of the show."

Frank watched his father's face, the way his lips pressed tight together, the way a nerve twitched in his cheek and his eyelids fluttered.

"We've all done some stupid shit," Frank said finally. "But we're not bad people."

"You forgiving me?" Dean said. "Or yourself?"

Frank looked away, into the scrub, and he saw Will, pale, waiting, scared, and then he closed his eyes tightly, and he saw more, saw fireworks bursting below thick gray clouds, saw Will's eyes shining, saw Dean's hand on Arla's shoulder. When he opened his eyes again and looked at Dean, the answer felt clear.

"All of us," he said. "I guess I'm forgiving all of us."

Dean exhaled. "Jesus," he said, and his voice shook. "It's been a tough row to hoe, Frank. A tough row to hoe."

Frank dropped Dean off at the Gate Station on A1A.

"I got a buddy who'll come get me," Dean said. "I'll go on back up to Jax for a while. I got some friends up there."

"Like Sandy Vanderhorn?" Frank said.

"Hooo-doggy," Dean said. "No Sandy Vanderhorn for me. I still got one cheek left. Plan to keep it that way." He swung a duffel bag over his shoulder. The taxidermied bass, his one request from Arla's house, poked a gaping mouth out of the end of the bag, and Frank had to smile at the sight: Dean Bravo heading out into the world again with a busted cheek, a wounded soul, and any number of ghosts to keep him company, but also with his one great catch, his one pure, beautiful, untarnished achievement.

"So I'll see you?" Frank said.

"Maybe."

Maybe not.

"You watch for Sofia now," Dean said.

"Biaggio's on the job."

Dean nodded. "And you watch for Carson, too," he said.

"Carson can take care of himself," Frank said. "And he's got Elizabeth." Dean raised his eyebrows, but Frank pretended not to notice, and he tested the words again in his mind: *he's got Elizabeth.*

"Does he?" Dean said, but he didn't seem to expect an answer, so Frank didn't offer one.

"But here's the thing, Frank," Dean said. He pointed his finger at Frank. "When you're done watching out for all these other folks, you watch out for yourself, too, son."

Frank nodded. Then he opened his wallet, took all the cash that was in it, and handed it to Dean. "Maybe four hundred or so," Frank said.

"Fair enough."

"But you need more, you call me."

Dean put his hand on Frank's arm for a moment, and Frank was startled by the heat of it, the weight. Dean's eyes were still blue, though rimmed with red.

"I don't need nothing," Dean said, and then he turned away.

Frank drove north on A1A, and Dean became smaller and smaller in the rearview mirror, until he was gone.

Back at home, the rooms were still and empty without Gooch. Frank took a shower, ate a frozen dinner, and drank a beer. He lay down on his bed and listened to the cicadas outside his window, but they sounded different, higher pitched, more despairing than he had ever remembered them. Everything was different. The smell of jasmine drifted in through the window, but it was cloying tonight, oppressive. As he drifted off he willed an image of rain, and wet hair and bleachers on a football field, but he slept all night with no dreams at all.

*   *   *

The next day he drove to Ponte Vedra Beach and went to the bank
Dean had directed him to. He showed his ID and checked the
balance on the account. It was all there. He accepted a small book
of temporary checks from the teller. "Thank you, Mr. Bravo," she
said, not batting an eye. Evidently they were used to these kinds
of balances here. Ponte Vedra. *Damn.*

On the way back to Utina, he told himself not to look to
his right, where the passenger seat of the truck was still covered
in white fur, and where a streak of dried dog spit still blurred
the window. This one was going to take some getting used to,
Frank thought. Oh, who was he kidding? It was *all* going to take
some getting used to.

His cell phone rang, and he picked it up.

"I'm buying out the shitwit," Carson said.

"Hello, Carson," Frank said. "New phone already?"

"Did you hear me?" Carson said. "Tip Breen. I'm buying
the Lil' Champ." Carson was talking loudly, breathlessly, and it
sounded as though he was walking. Then Frank heard Carson's
car door slam, heard the engine start up.

"Does Tip know this?" Frank said.

"Of course he does. I'm leaving the jail. I've just been to
see him. He's got bigger problems than the Lil' Champ, Frank.
I saw him and the defender, and he's in for a while, the sorry
shit. So I'm buying him out, gonna make a go of it." Carson
was talking fast. His car radio blasted AC/DC and then was
quickly silenced. "And when he gets out, he can come work for
me," he continued. "I'm going to need somebody to sell the
coffee to the yuppies. By then I'll be franchised, maybe. Stores

all over the place. Gourmet groceries. Whole foods. Granola out the ass."

"And scones?" Frank said.

"Scones is right!" Carson said. "Fucking gold mine sitting there, Frank. Café lattes. Paninis. God-damned wine tastings!" He chortled, and Frank had to smile. It was good to hear Carson getting excited again.

"What about your firm?" he said.

"I'm settling up, closing the shop," Carson said. "St. Augustine's a museum. It's a catacomb down here. But Utina? The marina and shit? That's about to bust wide open. We'd be idiots not to be a part of it, Frank. It's time to act."

"So you're coming back to Utina."

"Yeah," Carson said. "I guess I am." He paused for a moment. "It's time to redistribute the assets, know what I mean? Time to take inventory."

"Of business?"

"Of all of it, Frank," Carson said.

"Hey, Carson," Frank said, slowing the truck for a gopher turtle inching across the road. He'd just remembered something. "I got it: they were all facing impeachment."

Carson guffawed into the phone. "Wrong!" he said. "They were all named after their peckers!"

Frank laughed. He hung up and rolled the windows down. The smell of the ocean behind him was fading quickly, displaced by the smell of palms and pines and the last sweet remnants of the season's jasmine as he drew closer and closer to Utina.

* * *

At the turn on County Road 25, he slowed down. There in the median stood Do-Key, surrounded by campaign signs (DONALD KEITH! FOR SHERIFF!) and waving maniacally to passing drivers. When Keith saw Frank he waved him over.

"I understand you are the one who posted bail for Tip Breen on Wednesday," Keith said immediately. "Good move, Bravo. That worked out well, didn't it?"

"I didn't know it was your case," Frank said. "You on the Utina beat now? Or you just being nosy?"

Do-Key smiled broadly, waved at a passing car, then dropped the smile and glared at Frank. "They're all my cases," he said. He pointed to the sign: "Sheriff," he said.

"Not yet," Frank said. "Not ever, we hope."

"I'll be following up with you on Tip Breen, Bravo," Do-Key said. He looked at his watch. "I've got questions. But I've got the homecoming parade here in a little bit."

Frank tried not to smile. What *was* it with Do-Key and parades? "My God. I'm going to buy you your own twirling baton, all these parades you do. You driving the mayor again?" he said.

"No, asshole," Keith said. "I'm the marshal. It's a campaign thing. I've got a '53 Chevy cruiser and—" He stopped himself. "Not that you'd give a shit."

"Oh, I don't know," Frank said. "I might give a *shit*."

"Jackass," Keith said, walking away as another car passed by. "Fucking Bravos," he called back over his shoulder.

Frank suddenly had a feeling that felt like a memory, a buzzing spike of adrenaline he had not felt in many, many years. The buzz was faint, but it was familiar and seductive and good, and he could see, suddenly, no reason not to welcome it completely.

He drove into Utina and stopped at the Dollar General. He selected an eight-inch screwdriver on the hardware aisle, then walked slowly up the toy aisle until he found what he was looking for. He brought his two purchases to the counter, paid, and drove directly to the parking lot behind the First Baptist Church where he knew that by now, nearly noon on Utina High's homecoming day, the volunteer committees would be staging the afternoon's parade. He glanced at his watch, confirming. He had a couple of hours. Plenty of time. He spotted the car, a beautiful 1953 Chevy police cruiser, pristine and newly polished. He estimated his obstacles: a gaggle of cheerleaders, a handful of PTO mothers organizing the volunteers, and a fifty-five-year-old car door lock. Easy. Child's play. It was almost unfair. He grinned. It was almost criminal.

By the time he'd finished his work, it was after one o'clock, and he straightened up next to the antique car, brushed off his pants, and admired his ingenuity. Under the Chevy's front seat, the Dollar General screwdriver was tightly wedged into the adjustable steel bench track, immobilizing the seat in the farthest-forward setting and allowing little more than ten inches of space between the bottom edge of the steering wheel and the thick vinyl of the seat back. Even Elizabeth, tiny as she was, would have had a hard time piloting the car with the seat set at this angle. He smiled. He could only imagine how Do-Key would manage. He'd look like an imbecile, a fat moose wedged into a seat too small for him, but it would be typical, for Keith, a man who'd made a career out of inserting himself into positions and situations for which he was entirely unsuited. It was beautiful. Carson would be proud. Will would have been proud. *Frank the Prank.*

He reached into his pocket and removed the rubber alligator he'd bought at the Dollar General. It was sticky and fat, with painted-on claws and an unrealistic kelly green cast to its body. Frank positioned it carefully on the Chevy's steering column, its grinning white teeth bared, its crazy red eyes peering, jubilant, through the spokes of the wheel.

When he pulled up at the Cue & Brew, Mac's Mustang was out front, as was Susan's dented Mazda, on which she'd evidently jimmied the driver's side door sufficiently to allow herself to get in and out, but which had not yet received any legitimate repairs.

Inside the pub, Mac and George were holding down stools at the end of the bar, Mac still looking like hell, the swelling on his nose scarcely subsided at all, and Frank did a double-take when he realized the pretty blonde leaning against Mac's knee was Susan.

Irma the waitress walked past with a tray of drinks. "You're here now?" Frank said, incredulous. He'd felt terrible, letting Irma go when they'd closed Uncle Henry's last week, and with everything that had followed after the wedding, he'd forgotten to check in with her, find out what she'd planned to do for a job.

"Where else am I gonna go, dummy? You think they're gonna want me in Starbucks?" She walked behind the bar, put two empty pint glasses in the sink, then reached across and slapped Frank gently on the arm. "What do you want to drink, Bravo?"

He ordered a Bass, and she walked to the taps and returned with the beer.

"Thanks, Irma," he said.

"Oh, shush," she said.

Susan was on Mac's lap now, and Mac—his eyes rimmed with purple bruises—looked sheepish for a moment, but then he stood up, gently pushed Susan aside, and walked over to Frank. He clapped Frank's shoulder roughly, then cleared his throat.

"You hanging in?" he said.

Frank nodded.

Susan leveled her gaze at Frank.

"You and your brother been beating up anybody else we should know about?" she said. She pointed at Mac. "This here is some piece of work."

"That wasn't me," Frank said. "That was all Carson."

Mac snorted. "Makes no difference," he said. "One Bravo's the same as the next."

"Like hell, Mac," Frank said. But it was probably true.

Susan settled back into Mac's lap.

"I'll take care of you," she said, putting her arm around his shoulders. "I will." Mac smiled broadly beneath his bruises.

She was a little drunk, Frank could tell, but he was charmed by her beautiful blond ponytail and the sass in her voice and the gentle way her arm rested across Mac's shoulders. She was lovely. Maybe he should have loved her. Maybe he should have.

"Susan," he said. "I have come to pay my debts."

She turned and stared at him.

"That car of yours is some mess," Frank said.

"You can say that again," George said.

"I don't believe anyone asked you, George," Susan said, narrowing her eyes.

"Ha!" George said.

"You don't deserve a car like that, Susan," Frank said.

"Well, that's what I think," she said. "But you—"

"I'm here to make amends, Susan." Frank took the check-book out of his pocket and wrote a check to Susan Holm for $30,000. He slid it down the bar to her, and when she looked at it, her eyes grew wide and her mouth opened.

"Frank," she said. "That's too much."

"Take her to Jacksonville tomorrow, Mac," Frank said. "Help her pick out something good. Maybe a convertible."

Mac grinned, delighted, the pain of his injuries temporarily abated by God knows how many Bass beers and the thrill of having the beautiful Susan Holm now leaning her generous left breast into his arm as she staggered under the weight of the $30,000 check and stared unbelievingly at Frank Bravo.

"I can't take this," she said.

"Don't worry, it's not a gift," Frank said. "It's an advance on your commission."

"What?" she managed. Mac had one hand on her backside, holding her up, it appeared.

"Tomorrow we'll talk about listing, Susan," Frank said.

"Bravo, my friend," Mac said. "Good stuff."

Frank took his beer and walked out of the Cue & Brew, down to the end of the boat dock, to where the steel gray waters of the Intracoastal shimmied by under the fading rays of the sun. In the distance, at the east end of Seminary Street, he could hear the Utina High School band warming up for the homecoming parade, and he thought of Bell, baby Bell, how she would grow up here in Utina, like they all had. She'd live here with Elizabeth, and maybe with Carson, too. She would go to Utina High, would ride the school bus up and down the streets of South Utina, past An-Needa's house, past Tony's Hair Affair. She'd eat at Sterling's, shop at the Dollar General, at least for a while, anyway. At least as long as they still stood. She'd watch the new marina bring in the new people, the rich people, and maybe she'd go to prom at the new hotel, maybe get a summer job at the Starbucks or check groceries at the Publix. And it would be okay. It would be all right. Utina would still be Utina, as long as there were Bravos here. He thought of Arla's ashes on the water, floating, then descending, mingling with those ancient particulate traces of Will, sifting like sediment through all pain, beyond all time. They would always be here. Always.

He knelt down at the end of the wooden planks, rested his weight on his heels. He looked south, where the view was clear, the channel having been cut straight and plumb years ago, decades ago. Then he looked north, where the scars of the clear-cutting at Aberdeen and Uncle Henry's were visible along the banks. But beyond that, farther on, miles and years ahead, there lay mountains, and trout, and cool air, and water like ice that rushed white across smooth gray stones.

"It's time," he said, to no one at all. "I've waited long enough."

ACKNOWLEDGMENTS

First, thanks go to Judith Weber and Amy Hundley for their faith, their vision, and their friendship. I am humbled. Thank you Nat Sobel, Kirsten Carleton, Julie Stevenson, and Adia Wright. Thanks go to Flagler College and the many business clients who make my writing life possible. To my writing friends, especially Darien Andreu, Suzy Fay, Jim Wilson, and Sohrab Homi Fracis. To Roberta George and the late Jeanne Leiby for encouragement. To John Dufresne for guidance and inspiration. To Liz Robbins for unflagging friendship, and to Kim Bradley for the countless ways we're in it together. Thanks also to the Janssen family, and to all my friends and neighbors in St. Augustine, a city where every day is a page in a story. Love and thank you to Dale and Letty DiLeo and Dawn Langton. And to my family: Monica, Emma, and Lily Hayes; Sarah and Tim Kelly; Roger and Pam Smith; Alison, Tom, Fiona, Genevieve, and Abigail Gillespie.

To Christian—we miss you. To Casey, Kris, Shawn, and Lysne Cook—with all my love, always. To my father, Ken Cook, captain most courageous. And to my beautiful mother, Judy Cook, who shines the light.

Thank you Chris, Iain and Gemma: my wonderful world.